IRIN

A THRILLER

JOSEPH VAN NYDECK

Copyright © 2021 by Joseph Van Nydeck

All rights reserved.

This book is a work of fiction. Names, characters, businesses, organizations, events, and incidents either are the product of the author's imagination or are used fictiously. Any resemblance to actual persons, living or dead, events, or locales is entirely coincidental.

No part of this book may be reproduced in any form or by any electronic or mechanical means, including information storage and retrieval systems, without written permission from the author, except for the use of brief quotations in a book review.

www.josephvannydeck.com

ISBN-13: 978-1-940808-02-4

❀ Created with Vellum

For my son…

Attack him where he is unprepared, appear where you are not expected.

— SUN TZU

In the **Books of Enoch**, between the 2nd-1st century BC, the *fallen angels*, described as the disobedient sires of the Nephilim were known in the ancient Aramaic tongue as — the *IRIN*.

PROLOGUE

GULF OF FINLAND

There's an answer to every question. Sometimes it's simple, and sometimes it's not.

From the moment the assassin's mother had been killed in front of her, the question had always been —*why*?

The thirty-three-year-old assassin moved like a leopard seal through the frigid waters wrapped in sleek deep-sea diving gear, armed with the most advanced weapons in the Company's arsenal, and fast approaching her destination, everything was a *GO*.

Riding the swells onto the rocky beachhead, the assassin timed her exit to coincide with the searchlights, emerged from the freezing waters, and hurried up the embankment. She stared up at the star Sirius as it fell toward the horizon and knew that time was running out.

Everything about the mission had been researched down to the tiniest detail and had played out as expected, until an unexpected visit from a European Parliamentarian increased the naval patrols in the area, delaying her insertion. Calculating the number of thermal signatures relayed back from the reconnaissance drone, she reset her estimates and adjusted her angle of attack. With a biting arctic wind renewing a sense of urgency, the assassin shut off her uplink and moved into position.

Cresting the inner wall, she recoiled in pain as an out-of-sync searchlight seared both retinae, peeling her vice-like grip on the crumbling stoned wall in a sharp reflexive gesture, extorting a loud grunt. *Sonuvabitch*! It was never going to be easy.

Moving into a blind spot, the aquatic intruder changed out of her wetsuit, pulled her pistol from an ankle holster, and stuffed the scuba gear under a nearby hedge. Timing was everything. With the faint chatter of guards in the distance, she switched on her night vision and transformed into a more comfortable —hunter-killer mode. *Focus*.

Assassins worked alone. Despite the overwatch drone and a designated satellite feed, friendlies were thousands of miles away even if it was a sanctioned hit, but it wasn't and nobody was on ready alert to swoop in for an assist. As the night lengthened, the assassin cleared one obstacle after the other until she'd scaled the final stoned terrace, and taken up a position by a colossal marbled pillar, pausing while she ran through the approach in her head one last time, because once she'd penetrated the residence all bets were off. *Only fifty more yards*. Pivoting onto one knee, she watched as the sweeping lights passed by one last time. *Here we go... WHIRR!*

The assassin collapsed into a squatted position as the piercing alarm blared across the courtyard, filling the manicured gardens, and screeching beyond the perimeter fencing. *What the fuck?* Keeping her kneeled position she checked her drone feed. Scores of thermal images burst into the compound surrounding the marbled statue.

"*Prover'te terrasu, prover'te sady, prover'te vnešnie steny*," a deep baritone voice echoed in Russian as the intruder flinched from the stampeding footfalls as the gunmen neared, passed, and disappeared into the darkness. *Ten, eleven, twelve...*

"*Ničego, kapitan*," a voice responded.

The assassin lay coiled like a waiting viper, ready to attack, dissecting every syllable of the Cyrillic language. "*Ničego, kapitan*," another responded. *Nothing*.

And so, the parade continued, guard after guard, searching every inch of the perimeter. They looked for any sign of a security breach but passed over the hidden intruder nestled at the base of the elaborate garden centerpiece. Everything remained a *GO* but on an accelerated timeline. With the veil of darkness fading, navigating undetected proved a challenge, but not impossible. With the star Sirius on her right flank and melted into the surroundings, she'd successfully shadowed the guards up to the main house.

For the assassin, infiltrating the compound of a world-renown criminal wasn't a problem, but doing so alone was insane, nevertheless, she was committed to her endeavor. Minutes ticked by as the assassin watched the henchman file back into the main house, biding her time, waiting for the opportunity, watching as they scurried inside seeking warmth until a weak pull on the door by the last man provided her invitation. *SPASIVA, my careless friend.*

For millennia, a small clique of bloodlines had controlled the wealth of the world through their vast land holdings, and managing control of the global monetary systems, rising, and falling, but always re-emerging in a new and more integrated iteration. This iteration was no different. Within only a few centuries a thriving undercurrent had once again torn the reinvigorated social fabric into a thousand pieces heralding its inevitable decline.

Driving the demise was a global organization headquartered in St. Petersburg, Russia, that was run by a powerful man that'd proven his ferociousness time and again on multiple continents, but it was only through a twist of fate that he'd crossed paths with the assassin, and landed himself in her crosshairs, an encounter she'd never forgotten. Despite the progression of time and change in circumstance, the assassin relived the scene as if it was yesterday, her motivation to act had never been more clear.

Time to die. Slipping through the opened doorway, shrouded by the guards' lack of awareness as they yammered amongst themselves while storing their coats and rifles in their respective lockers, oblivious to the danger passing them by through the unsecured door and up the back staircase. *Where are you hiding mister big stuff?*

Despite the months of planning, there'd been no accurate way to ensure the target's exact location inside the house, but improvisation was her specialty.

Following her instincts the intruder navigated the labyrinth to the front of the house, creeping along the darkened corridors heeding the murmuring voices in the distance, and keeping in the shadows. But after a few minutes, everything fell silent, she stopped, flattened herself against the wall as a broad-shouldered man burst through a nearby door, then disappeared in haste down the front staircase, leaving the door ajar. *What's wrong with these people?* She crept toward the door, pivoting, and snapping a quick look through the hinges. *I wonder what's going on in here.* Without a shred of intel about the room, she dropped the pistol to her side and moved through inviting double doors.

Turning through the doorway, a glowing fireplace crackled on the far side of the room surrounded by three tufted leather chairs and walls of books. The dossier on the Russian kingpin had said he was more than just a street thug. *A library,* she thought. *So, he is a man of letters.* Moving her hands across several books until they'd found an open tattered book, she paused a long moment as she read several scribbled passages and references to a renown bloodline: *Romanov.*

A chill ran down her spine as she realized something didn't add up.

Looking up from the book with her newfound knowledge, the assassin inventoried every book laid out across the table, noting each one was related to genealogical or biographical histories. Why was the man who ran the most powerful mafia family in the world worried about his ancestry? The confused spy paused a long moment. *He's already on top. What's he got left to prove?* Entranced by the drama unfolding in the opened pages, the next revelation marked a turning point. *What the hell's going on?* Staring up from the pages was another Russian surname, but one that hit *too* close to home —Andreevna. *That's my mother's name.* But more concerning than finding her mother's maiden name in a book opened on a mafia leader's table was the level of importance he'd assigned it with several red circles highlighting the finding.

A new chorus of voices echoing along the corridor broke the assassin from her trance, pushing her to react. The book fell shut in her hands as she exited a door opposite her entry point to the library. First, it was the unexpected arrival of a European Parliamentarian, now she risked being discovered before she'd completed her mission. Everything that she'd planned was unraveling as she froze on her mother's name. Why was the gangster studying the Andreevna clan history? There was only one way to find out, but it meant delaying a promise. She melted into the surroundings as the approaching voices grew louder.

"Čto obnaružila vaša komanda?"

As she peered through the gap between the door hinges, the assassin watched as the brooding guard replied to his boss's question, "Is another false alarm."

A devious smile stretched across the assassin's face as she basked in their distress over the repeated false alarms, nothing was sweeter than knowing her hack had successfully thrown the gangsters for a loop. With the night slipping away it was time to act.

Moving from behind the servant's entrance door, the assassin stepped into the room leveling her pistol at the two men who stood in front of the crackling fire across the room, dumbfounded at their predicament.

A tall hulking man dressed in a silk shirt and dark pants stepped toward the intruder, unafraid, and demanded. *"Kto ty, čert voz'mi, takoj?"* realizing the intruder wasn't Russian, he repeated his demand in English, "Who the hell are you?"

The assassin raised a finger to her mouth, "Shhhhh."

From the Duma in Moscow to the Capitol Building in Washington D. C., she knew the gangster's reach and wasn't impressed. The weakness of her government made her hate him even more. A bitter taste erupted in her mouth as the moment had finally arrived. Navigating the room while keeping the targets in her sights the assassin secured the main doors and walked toward the men.

The man stepped up to the table. "What do you want?"

A patient assassin repositioned into the shadows, outside the line-of-sight to anyone bursting through the main door while keeping a clear path out through the servant's entrance, replied, "I saw you on the bridge that day, Igor Petrushenkov."

Petrushenkov smiled. "So, you know who I am, and you have broken into my home. This is brave."

"This was nothing. Your encryption is a joke, and your guards are drunken buffoons. A five-year-old could've outsmarted your protocols," the assassin snapped.

Over the last few centuries, the control of Russian society had been stripped from the dynastic families, and incompetent politicians, until it fell into the hands of men like Igor Petrushenkov, head of the *Akhemenov Bratva*. The glaring difference between the new regime and the old regime was a technological one, Petrushenkov and his men were programmers and hackers, which amused the assassin because their security protocols sucked.

"So, CIA sent you to kill me or buy me off?"

A coolness washed over the assassin as she stopped within arm's length of Petrushenkov, pointing the pistol dead between his eyes. "I came here to kill you."

"Kill me, then," Petrushenkov demanded.

Pressing the pistol against the gangster's forehead, the assassin twister her hips exerting her power forward while looking at his underling, then whispered, *"BANG"*.

Petrushenkov smiled broadly, "Hmmm...why are you *really* here?"

Dropping her pistol to her side, the young woman backed away from the Russian strong man. "You tried to recruit me, but failed to understand my price, so I'm here to explain my terms and give you another shot."

Petrushenkov rubbed his stubbled face, pondering the intentions of the mysterious intruder. "Bridge. Recruit...It's you."

"*Da*, it's me" the assassin replied.

1

PENANG, MALAYSIA

Chloe Campbell thrust her arm across the Ambassador as a wall of spray hit the front windshield of the SUV like a direct blast from a water cannon. Recovering in time to see the receding taillights of a tour bus disappearing into the strengthening typhoon ahead, she was still off balance when the armor-plated beast hit a stretch of standing water the size of a small lake. Water exploded around the vehicle, blinding the driver, and eliciting a stream of vulgarities from the retiring CIA agent. The SUV fishtailed once as Chloe's hand stabbed out blindly for a handhold to steady herself.

"Sorry about that, ma'am," a young Marine Lance Corporal shouted from the driver's seat. "But it looks like we're heading into an absolute shit-storm."

Chloe snorted a chuckle and righted herself. "More than you could know soldier, but if we miss this meeting, it's my ass, and I like my ass the way it is, don't you Corporal?" She caught his glance in the rearview mirror, watching as the young Marine shifted in his seat.

"Err...yes ma'am?" he stuttered.

Enjoying the moment, Chloe flashed a devilish grin at the State

Department Personal Protective Detail Officer riding shotgun, but a dismissive Scott Anderson bounced her focus back on the driver as she placed a reassuring hand on his shoulder, "Relax Marine, just get us back on schedule."

"How are we on time?" Her patron interrupted from the back seat.

Perfect. The Southeast Asian specialist left the Lance Corporal and Captain Anderson to their tasks, and turned a smiling face toward a familiar VIP, Ambassador John Dekker, Sr. "Well, the good news... is that the typhoon has cleared the freeway of traffic, but the bad news... is that there's more debris than we'd expected, which has slowed us down a bit. That said, we're still only about fifteen minutes behind schedule, sir," she replied, avoiding the cold pair of eyes she knew condemned her off-the-cuff lie from the front passenger's seat —*grumpy old jarhead*— she thought to herself.

Ambassador Dekker stared at Chloe a long moment, digested the information, and then replied. "Perhaps we should've flown after all?"

Chloe released her death grip on the front seat, holstered her sidearm, and settled back in next to the Ambassador. *Keep it together, Chloe.* Despite her years of training, Chloe had broken the first rule of VIP escort protocol —*Don't spook the passenger.* A single misstep that she needed to correct. She studied the Ambassador's face, one that she'd seen a thousand times while visiting his Washington office, and one she'd never betrayed. "That would've been a trick, given that all flights in the region were grounded due to the typhoon," she replied with a glowing smile.

Ambassador Dekker chuckled, then leaned into the front cab, placing an unexpected hand on her thigh as he engaged the Marine captain. "Any chance we can make up the lost time?"

Chloe caught her breath with clenched teeth as she watched Anderson pause, throw up an "OK" with his fingers, then continue his surveillance of the spewing darkness. A deafening pounding echoed through her head as her elevated heart rate waited for the Ambassador's response, but with a slight tilt of his head, and pause, she felt his hand come off her thigh as he retreated into his seat just as the Suburban pitched sideways and railed across a cluster of potholes scattered along the remote freeway. *PHEW! That could've gone another way,* she thought to herself.

With the Ambassador buried in his reports, Chloe righted herself and nestled in for the long road ahead, escaping into her thoughts. It'd been a while since she'd been able to relax, and prematurely drawing her sidearm hadn't lessened her anxiety, but the metronomic cadence of the typhoon spurned deluge now engulfing the convoy sang to her road weary mind like the ancient Siren's call to the sea dogs of old. She snapped her holster closed with her left hand, angled her still reddened cheeks toward the window, and attempted to hide her embarrassment. *What the hell were you thinking letting them corner you into this sideshow?*

Hours earlier, Chloe and the Ambassador both had been cruising in relative safety, if not outright comfort aboard the USS John C. Stennis, the flagship of the American Carrier Strike Group taking part in a major biennially naval exercise called RIMPAC. It was an odd duty station for a newly appointed diplomat, (much less his soon to be daughter-in-law), but the Ambassador had been invited to oversee operations during the naval exercise due to his previous involvement with the compartmentalized Special Access Program — Archangel. Part military research program under the Defense Advanced Research Projects Agency (DARPA), and part collaboration with industry, it had begun life under the Ambassador's direction at CIA and had grown to include some of America's best minds in cybersecurity and advanced artificial intelligence (AI) initiatives. The program's revolutionary achievements in quantum-resistant cryptography had sparked an evolution in the US CyberCommand's infrastructure and security protocols, while at the same time improving the quantum entanglement calculations instrumental in the operation of the Pentagon's expanded X-37B space plane squadron. Now, more than a decade after its inception, Archangel's fledgling AI —IRI—was getting its sea-legs. While it would only be seeing limited play, this year's RIMPAC celebrated the first time the

AI was being deployed alongside live forces. It was a small win for the project, but big enough that the public affairs wonks assigned to the interagency task force surrounding the project decided to make a dog-and-pony show of it. With funding dollars and jobs on the line, rolling out the red carpet to a VIP like Ambassador Dekker, a diplomat, ex-spook, and former head of the Dekker banking empire, just made sense.

Or at least made sense to someone. What made less sense, Chloe reflected as the Suburban hurtled through the successive layers of the menacing rain, was why she'd pushed to get this assignment, let alone agreed to a last-minute detour. Was it out of loyalty to Johnny? Was it her inherent need to push the company's agenda? Or was it simply a couple of bad calls?

"Who else are you going to send, sir?"

"You're a month from retirement, not to mention your wedding. Don't you want to wind all this down and get ready for the next chapter of your life?"

"I've finished the transition with Chambers. And now, I'm just punching a friggin' clock, sir."

It had taken a fair amount of prodding, wheedling, and mild threats, but in the end, Chloe was reassigned to the RIMPAC detail, which aimed to fulfill her contract requirements and her exiting process. So, less than 36 hours later, she'd joined the elder Dekker on a series of long, noisy flights aboard military aircraft that had taken her from the heart of Virginia to the middle of the Pacific.

What followed had been confusing. At first, she'd thought that when the Ambassador was informed about her assignment, they'd spend time discussing the wedding, the Council, and other family matters during the extended flights.

I should've known better.

Another shudder reverberated down the Suburban as it pushed through the mythical storm causing her to prairie-dog up momentarily before falling back into her thoughts and the closing ceremony aboard the USS Stennis, remembering that when Ambassador Dekker wasn't glad-handing interagency reps and talking up IRI's exceptional performance with various defense contractors, he'd peppered her with random geopolitical questions. From the state of the Malaysian economy to its various political factions and their positions on current affairs, everything that was squarely in her wheelhouse, and she'd expected to answer on the "unexpected" base trips, but after the closing ceremony, something had distracted him. Within a short time, she felt an unspoken narrative forming beneath his distinct line of questioning, *something sensitive and urgent.*

"Does Malaysia still set the tone for the ASEAN bloc?" he'd asked.

She'd paused a long moment. It was happening. She brushed the ambassador's jacket, checked over his shoulder for prying eyes, and whispered in his ear. *"It's an economic alliance. They generally fall in line behind the Malaysians, but this trade deal isn't about just trade, it's about regional security, and that's where the alliance wobbles."*

"The White House has redeployed our entire Asian diplomatic corps to corral the regional votes, no matter the cost. What are the odds of a splintered ASEAN vote?"

After a momentary pause, she'd stepped forward into the ambassador's space and straightened his tie. *"You need more intel, but for that, you're gonna have to meet with the new department head at Langley when we get back stateside, I'm retired."*

From the moment she'd begun to wind down her decade long career at CIA, it was like Pandora's box had spilled open directly onto the Southeast Asian desk, and anything that could go wrong, did. It started with the growing uncertainty of support for the United States and its policies in Thailand and quickly spread throughout other ASEAN nations, which now threatened the President's signature trade agreement. And if that hadn't been complicated enough, an abrupt abdication of the Malaysian throne, by a reluctant king added another theatrical twist, adding credence to the adage stranger-than-fiction. The move cast shade against all the progress of the American diplomats. Although the king of the nine-state constitutional monarchy sat outside the Malaysian political system, the five-year rotation of the crown amongst its member states kept the politician's fluid in their commitments and ready to embrace the incoming wishes of the various royal families that retained most of the land and wealth of the sprawling Southeast Asian nation. She'd remembered how the incoming call from Langley had surprised her, but not Ambassador Dekker.

"Sorry to interrupt your celebration Mr. Ambassador, but we've been directed to contact you by the White House. There's a situation in Malaysia. An on-the-ground asset has informed us that a consensus is building around opposing the Pacific Trade Agreement in the Dewan Negara, the Southeast Asian nation's upper house of parliament. Tell Chloe this came from Striker, she'll understand."

Chloe flashed a thumbs-up about Striker and brushed her hair back as she leaned against the Ambassador, trying to get closer to the earpiece and the gist of the situation. And although she knew Striker's information was infallible, nothing had prepared her for what happened next.

"We need to get someone on the ground and walk these guys back, ASAP," the Ambassador replied. Chloe felt a sharp pain rip through her stomach as she realized this hadn't been his first conversation around this "developing" situation.

"You know where I stand on this Ambassador. I agree that the trade agreement is important, but State can send the deputy director in KL to handle this. We've put too many resources into IRI's development to leave the decision to the bureaucrats," the director replied.

"Without the Malaysian vote and its influence with the other nations, the trade agreement is dead in the water."

She'd tried to intervene. "Sir, it's not your responsibility."

"IRI's a lock, but the trade agreement is on a knife's edge, and if we don't get down there to sort it out, it could mean the difference of controlling the shipping lanes in the South China Sea or operating solely under the United Nation's freedom of navigation tenets."

"Okay then. Striker has arranged a meeting later tonight in Penang if you can make it?" the director replied. Chloe distanced herself from the ambassador. *This was the plan all along, IRI was just his cover. When had he become so deceptive?*

The next thing she knew she was aboard a CH-53 Sea Stallion

cutting through unexpected weather on its way to the nearest airfield where a C-17 Globemaster III refueled for their trip to the Royal Airbase in Kuala Lumpur, Malaysia. Her only solace was the confirmation that two CIA special operators from the Special Activities Division, and old buddies with Johnny, would join them once they'd touched down in Malaysia.

Chloe barely caught herself against the passenger's headrest as the young Lance Corporal jerked the SUV to the left jarring her out of her reverie, she looked up in time to see the dark outline of two jeeps as they blasted by her vehicle. Another wave of water rolled off the windows as the Marine brought the diplomatic suburban back under control.

"Someone's in a hurry," Anderson growled as he white knuckled the overhead handholds. "Give these idiots some breathing room, Lance Corporal."

Chloe watched as Anderson surveyed his charges before shifting his attention forward again. She felt the Suburban slow a little as the driver worked to create a safe interval between the Ambassador's vehicle and the unknown newcomers. The taillights of the two vehicles were just barely visible through the blinding spray, and Chloe felt a vague sense of unease begin to prod her, as if she'd forgotten something important, but couldn't put her finger on it. She felt herself move to the edge of the seat, her smoke gray eyes probing the rippling veil of rain and road spray. Unable to see more than the dim red glow of the two pairs of taillights in front of them, and unable to quantify the unsettled feeling it gave her, Chloe leaned in toward Anderson.

"Captain?" She began, then stopped short at the agent's his raised hand. A tingling sensation ran down her spine as she felt the hair on her neck stand up watching the captain grab one of the diplomatic vehicle's short-range radios. *What's he doing?*

"Red 4-2 this is Red 6," Captain Anderson said.

Static carried over the handset for a moment before a reply came through, barely audible over the sounds of big tires at speed, rain, and static.

"Go for 6."

"4-2, take lead and keep an eye on these two assholes in front of us," Anderson said. He waited for an acknowledgement before putting a hand on the young driver's shoulder. "Get ready to put on the brakes so Sergeant Johnson can take lead." The Lance Corporal nodded, and Anderson hung poised over the center dashboard, the handset gripped tight. He seemed to be silently counting to himself before stopping and glancing back at Chloe and the ambassador. "Sir, ma'am, heads up. We're gonna let our trail vehicle take lead, might get a little bumpy." Turning away from them, he keyed the mic again. "4-2, go, go, go."

Chloe felt her seatbelt dig in as the driver fed the Suburban its brakes, the taillights ahead of them immediately fading to almost nothing as their vehicle lost ground to the vehicles ahead of it. The sound of the large V-8 at full acceleration battled with the dull roar of wind and rain as the trail in their small convoy sped by the ambassador's vehicle, its own taillights bright and reassuring as it settled into its place ahead of them. The entire maneuver had taken seconds and Chloe watched as Anderson fist-bumped the driver's shoulder and congratulated the young man on a well-executed maneuver. He turned back to his passengers.

"In weather like this, I would normally keep the ambassador's vehicle in the lead, so we have better visibility," he explained. "But I'd rather have us in trail if there will be traffic in front of us." He shrugged a little as if embarrassed when Ambassador favored him with a raised eyebrow. "Sorry sir, I'm a little paranoid. I blame it on two tours in Iraq."

Chloe nodded as flashbacks of her time in the field confirmed his action and motivation. Some years back she'd received operations training in several areas including defensive driving techniques. Several of the scenarios they would run through had included protecting a VIP while traversing an urban area. It had been a lot of fun, racing around a simulated cityscape in battered rent-a-cars, practicing convoy techniques, fast-stops, fast-starts, and other James Bond style vehicular bad ass. For protective details, she knew that to some extent; you used plain old uncertainty to protect the VIP. After all, it was tough for the bad guys to target a specific vehicle, if they didn't know which one their target was riding in.

"*The problem,*" her instructor had told them as he rode along in the VIP vehicle. "*Is that you can never underestimate an enemy that's willing to take out your entire convoy to get the job done,*" he'd said. That had been the instant before he would trigger the ambush, destroying both lead and trail vehicles with simulated IEDs.

Still, Chloe felt better with the reassuring bulk of the other embassy Suburban forging through the weather ahead of them. She couldn't say why, but it'd unnerved her when the two cars overtook them.

First the explosive water, now the passing cars. I AM paranoid. A little traffic on a main thoroughfare during a typhoon evacuation normalized the situation. *Probably just a couple of locals tired of eating road spray from the big American SUVs.* It made sense and Chloe knew they shouldn't worry her. But somehow, when something hit the Ambassador's Suburban from behind and sent the SUV into a massive fishtail, she wasn't the least bit surprised.

The Lance Corporal overcorrected, although small it was quick and sharp, but proved enough to send the Suburban slewing back and forth down the rain-soaked freeway, nauseating if nothing else. Chloe spotted the small black jeep, barely visible through the spray and the storm as it tried to overtake the Ambassador's SUV but swerved off and ripped back as the big Chevy slid over the midline. A lot began to happen even before she'd fully recovered from the first hit. She heard the radio in Anderson's hand erupt with garbled voices as brake lights from the lead SUV flared like twin supernovas in the gray wash of the ferocious storm. She braced herself with the handhold but failed to keep the Ambassador in his seat as his casual attitude while reviewing his papers sent him lurching forward against the seat and then bouncing off the protective glass.

"Ambassador, you, okay?" Anderson said as he ripped his seatbelt away and turned toward the injured VIP. And although, he saw blood cascading down the AMBOs forehead while intermittently slurring his words, he knew that the CIA liaison had him contained as he refocused on the incoming threat.

"What the hell's going on?" Ambassador Dekker finally blurted.

Chloe smiled as she ripped a piece of cloth from the bottom of her shirt and pressed it against the ambassador's head. "Nothing we can't handle, sir." As she finished strapping in the ambassador and dressing his wound, Anderson's thunderous voice exploded through the cabin.

"Break left!"

Tires shrieked as the driver threw the Suburban out of the way of an uprooted tree strewn across the freeway. Flung like a rag doll, Chloe hit the door igniting every single nerve ending in her cheek as she planted against the bulletproof glass. Radio traffic spiked as the convoy simultaneously updated the fluid situation. Through the chatter Chloe discerned Sergeant Johnson from the lead vehicle as he rattled off an update.

"We put one into the ditch, still got the first vehicle trying to slow us down. Heads up, the offramp to the Penang Bridge is coming up in thirty-seconds."

Chloe braced her arms on the seat in front of her and held onto the Ambassador as the driver whipped the heavy plated SUV through a series of rapid-fire lane changes trying to keep the trailing jeep from overtaking them again. She glanced over at the wounded diplomat wiping the blood from his eyes with the sleeve of his suit jacket and holding the torn cloth against his head. Despite being a little shaken up he was reasserting his focus to the convoy and the chatter booming over the radio.

"Who are these guys?"

Chloe flashed a quick smirk. It could be anyone. There wasn't enough data to make a determination who had the gall to attack a sitting diplomat from a friendly country during peacetime. "Unclear, sir," she responded.

"Is it the Chinese?" Dekker questioned the vehicle at large.

Chloe paused a moment. Then turned toward the ambassador. "No sir, I don't think so. If we'd pissed the Chinese off, they'd build another trash island or start calling in our debt. No way they'd come after you specifically, or like this. It's not their MO."

Ambassador Dekker coughed and cleared his throat. "What if I'm not the target? Could China be trying to get Malaysia kicked off the Trade Agreement?"

Chloe's arms tensed as her grip on the front seat stretched her sore tendons with the Suburban making another sudden lane change. "I love conspiratorial thinking, but again, I don't think so. From my understanding, the current agreement, doesn't contain any military provisions that'd pull Malaysia into our broader containment agenda. No basing agreements or cooperative efforts that we don't already have, just opportunities for trade and China has their own specialized methods for outmaneuvering us from that angle, sir, think Vietnam subsidiaries."

Despite the percussion of road noise and storm, the Ambassador's next question was quieter, and meant for Chloe alone as he pressed the bloodied cloth against his head and leaned over toward her. "What about the Council?"

Chloe leaned away from the ambassador, both shocked, but taking in his proposal at the same time, twisting her arms around the headrest and turning inward for perspective as she digested the possibility that another one of the member families of the Council of Thirteen had initiated an attack. *An attack on a patriarch of the Thirteen families had never happened.* Despite the constant rivalry with the Eastern European families, the Group of Four and Group of Nine had never entered an openly combative posture. And with the Ambassador's son, her fiancée, now managing the Dekker family's global interests, an attack on the elder Dekker made no sense. *Could something have changed?* Although not a member of the Council herself, Chloe's family oversaw the Council's South American Zone activities, and her father believed in confiding its business in both his daughters, his heir apparent as well as Chloe. She blanched at the thought and turned back toward the ambassador. "Impossible."

BASEL, SWITZERLAND

Johnny Dekker felt the retrofitted passenger train decelerate as he took one last wistful look at the distant snow-capped mountains disappearing one-by-one behind the rising cityscape of Basel, Switzerland. *Finally.* After the seven-hour hop across the Atlantic, followed by a memorable London Black Cab experience, and the unexpected necessity of the SBB sleeper train, he welcomed the journey's end.

Despite sitting at the heart of Europe, nestled between feudal empires, the Swiss cantons had escaped the continent's chaotic and bloodied past. Whether by accident or design it'd proven to be the ideal post-war location for the reorganization of the global banking infrastructure. A network that understood Statecraft and endeavored on behalf of its member states toward an expansive global agenda, while at the same time sitting outside of any and all of their respective jurisdictions, artfully crafting rules and regulations inside its storied walls. From the moment Director Brown had informed Johnny on his re-assignment within the Clandestine Services, he knew it meant the one thing he'd hated the most about leaving the Special Activities Division, a suit and tie, something, to-date, he'd only endured for the Dekker Banking Group's annual board meeting.

Johnny stared out the window as the train navigated its way through the waking city past historic churches and medieval architecture. *Where's all the action?* The unfolding scene echoed a late 17th Century Europe with only sprinkles of modernity splashed across its surface, but a refined look into its inner workings proved it was much more than that. More than any other nation, Switzerland fostered opportunities for those who understood networks and hierarchies. Affluent families and governments from around the world, both new and old, flocked to the various supranational organizations headquartered within its boundaries over time remaking the Swiss image of neutrality into an indispensable deal making hub.

As a young man, Johnny had accompanied his father on his

annual business trips to Geneva and Zurich. However, rather than spending time roaming the parks and lakes like most young men of his age, he stayed by his father's side and learned the family business. And like the Swiss, he learned the importance of networks, diligence, fraternity, obedience, perseverance, and loyalty. Now, as he balanced his unexpected path within the agency and his ultimate responsibility at the Dekker Banking Group, the familiar images brought those lessons, under his father, home. And although this trip wasn't about the family business or the Council of Thirteen initiatives, his destination and the work within its committees was of great importance to the continued networking of the global banking system and the United States.

From the watchful eyes of the Young Committee, established after the First World War and designed specifically to manage the complicated task of war reparations on Germany, it not only outlived the financial sovereignty of its constituents and two world wars, but had become the Mecca of the financial world governors and their minions. Johnny stretched out his arm across his private cabin toward a large pile of clothes heaped upon the seat.

"Uncle Rupert, we're here."

After a moment, a deep voice echoed through the cabin almost in mid-conversation. "What did I tell you?"

The young deputy cut a grin from ear to ear as he turned away from the window, beaming with intrigue of the historic city. "It's magnificent."

"Remember, we're here on state business, so keep our familiarity to a minimum. We don't want to emphasize our families' relationship. Subtlety, please?"

The shift in tone reminded Johnny of a scolding by his principal in elementary school as he retreated from the window with a boyish smile. "Yes, of course, Mr. Chairman," Johnny corrected himself. "It won't happen again."

"Well, not until you finally make my niece an honest woman, at least," the elder banker said with a laugh as Johnny felt his heavy hand clamp down on his shoulder.

Johnny snorted a laugh, then turned back toward the window. *Yes, the wedding? How could I forget?*

PENANG BRIDGE, MALAYSIA

"Big turn coming!" Captain Anderson barked.

With less than a second to react, Chloe braced with the Ambassador against the passenger seat as the SUV cut hard to the right. The tires protested the angle and Chloe felt the armored sport utility wallow dangerously as the Lance Corporal pitched the offramp onto the Penang Bridge at speeds even her wannabe motorhead fiancée would question. The pursuing headlights fell back precipitously as its mere mortal driver braked hard unwilling to tempt a pursuit into the afterlife. The diplomatic Suburban seemed to hang poised somewhere between fiery crash into the winding guardrail and catastrophic spinout when suddenly the driver cut the wheel hard left, bringing the military-grade beast back into a semblance of a straight line. Chloe heard the big V-8 roar back to life as signposts listing the distance to the bridge and various toll amounts flashed alongside her window.

"What the fuck was that?" She screamed in a rhetorical rage ripping her sidearm from its holster. In the fraction of a second, she caught her breath, a quick upward glance revealed the blinking lights of the superstructure as it rose like a mountain in the cloud and storm choked horizon. *The bridge, we're here.* She knew the young Marine had robbed fate of a valuable prize with his maneuver and was glad, but as the bridge narrowed the chase vehicles began to catch up and bump into the convoy one by one prodding for a reaction as they searched for their American prey.

Chloe paused a long moment then popped forward looking over Captain Anderson's shoulder at the road ahead. A cascade of sparks spewed from the lead vehicle as Sergeant Johnson jammed the assailant into and over the guardrail sending them spiraling into the bay below.

"Hoorah," Anderson erupted.

Then, a brief thought blinked into Chloe's mind as she nodded at Anderson and watched the lead vehicle swerve back onto their forward path. *It's a setup. It's gotta be a setup. How could they know we'd be here?* "Captain..." she yelled but was drowned out by the road noise and a spike in radio chatter. Her mind raced with plausible scenarios as the unexpected attack awakened her training. Somehow, she knew the chase was a ruse and they'd fallen for it like a prey flushed through a narrow canyon, something was waiting on the other end. Just as she reached over the seat to get Anderson's attention a flashing light on his sat phone drew him further away as he plugged one ear with his finger and the phone against the other.

"Anderson. Roger that, two vehicles. There was a third, but 4-2 put him to the wall."

Chloe paused a moment, waiting for Anderson to turn around, but a growing sense of doom gripped her mind as she turned back to the Ambassador, a barrage of heavy weapons fire ripped through the convoy. Sledgehammers pounded the back of the Suburban. Bullets that shouldn't have been able to penetrate the hardened exterior of the diplomatic grade SUV cratered the armor and sent shattered glass spraying through the interior. Chloe lurched forward putting the AMBO to the floor as another barrage of bullets shredded the plush leather seats screaming past her like raging banshees and forcing the Suburban into an uncontrolled wobble. "Drive, drive, drive," she screamed at the Lance Corporal

A strange sensation fell over the bride-to-be as she pressed her body down over the Ambassador, the veracity of the attack awakening the protective instincts as she pivoted into a defensive position. Pressing her hand down as she turned, she felt an all too familiar texture, something that was the reason she'd taken the desk job at Langley in the first place. Following her arm down to the floor her eyes confirmed, it was blood, lots of blood. She ran her hands over her torso searching for a wound, *nothing*. WTF? A frog caught in her throat as she looked down at Dekker lying motionless on the floor, blood gushing out of his head and neck. Her emotions took over. In a fit of primal rage, she emptied her sidearm through the rear of the vehicle, then pulled her leg out from under the slumping body as the bullet riddled SUV skidded back and forth across the median.

"AMBO down!" Chloe jammed her sidearm in its holster and burrowed under the seat into the weapons hold, retrieving the 50-caliber showstopper and unleashing an entire extended clip into the unknown assailants. Within a few seconds, the swerving unsteadiness of the vehicle brought out the inner spook demon that lived inside all agency operators.

"Anderson, get this shit under control."

"BRACE, BRACE..." Anderson screamed as he leaned over the center armrest taking the wheel from the wounded Lance Corporal. "You're okay Mikey, you're okay. Just keep your foot on the gas and keep us going brother, I'll keep us straight."

Anderson squirmed into the driver's seat holding the wheel straight with one hand and pulling his wounded buddy onto the center armrest with the other. After he'd dropped him in the seat another flurry of ricocheting bullets cut through the canopy as he jerked the wheel and sent the Suburban hurtling back across the median into the guardrail. With the road ahead obscured from the rain and lead SUV he spared a desperate look into the back seat.

"You okay, ma'am?"

"Where are those goddamn Predator drones? I told Langley we needed air support. Where's our fucking overwatch?" Chloe screamed.

Anderson refocused on the road but pleaded for her condition. "Ms. Campbell, ARE YOU HIT?"

Chloe hovered above the Ambassador with her back to Anderson, oblivious to his inquisition, and unloaded the 50-caliber recoil rifle into the closest fucking set of headlights with deadly precision. "Two down. GET US SOME FUCKING COVER!" She ripped off her shirt and wrapped the ambassador's head as Anderson dodged the sporadic fire of the remaining jeep.

Within moments the secondary diplomatic Suburban pulled behind the ambassador checking the rear assault. Muzzle flashes blossomed out of the storm behind them as the secondary and assailant exchanged gunfire in the torrential downpour. Sergeant Johnson's voice crackled over the radio as Anderson pressed on the Lance Corporal's chest wound and steered the bullet-riddled hunk of metal with his knees.

"Guns up again, sir." Without warning, intermittent static and distinct rapid fire of the Marine issued M4s interrupted the transmission "POP, POP, POP" exploding through the transmitter like the enemy Guns of Navarone.

Anderson dropped the bloodied cloth on the Lance Corporal and grabbed the wheel with both hands as headlights darted in and out of the rear-view mirror. Another series of muzzle flashes and muffled automatic fire confirmed the rear was still at risk. An explosion, which was felt as much as heard, followed the faint rumble of the automatic weapon.

Chloe prairie dogged up from the back having stabilized the Ambassador. Sparing a quick glance she saw 4-2 lurch sideways, smoke and debris streaming from the left rear quarter panel of the SUV.

"Goddamn it, they shot the run-flat out," her eyes met Anderson in the rear-view mirror as the tension peaked another level. Then, out of nowhere, another jeep appeared alongside the chase vehicle and closed in on the Ambassador's Suburban like pack hunters closing in on a wounded prey. Anderson pumped the accelerator, but nothing happened. It was already on the floor.

"It's a trap," Chloe yelled at the captain.

With the end of the bridge in sight, but their flank exposed as Red 4-2 lurched to a smoking halt Anderson needed a plan. He needed to safeguard the wounded Ambassador but leave no man behind. "Hold on," Anderson shouted back. He grabbed his M4 from Mikey's lap and slammed on the brakes sliding to a stop. Then, the tortuous sound of grinding metal echoed in Chloe's ears as Anderson threw the Suburban into a high-speed reverse toward the sputtering security vehicle. With his free hand Anderson keyed the radio. "Johnson - get sideways in the road, lay down suppressive fire and get ready to cross load casualties into our vehicle."

Chloe sat Ambassador Dekker upright as he drifted in and out of consciousness, put his hand on his bandages, and pressed his hand down. "I'll be right back." She grabbed three more rifle clips from the weapons hold, looked at Anderson and nodded.

"CLEAR A PATH!" he shouted.

"Hoorah, cap'n," she screamed. Her fighting spirit alive and resonating through every ounce of her being, fueled by the adrenaline and ancient warrior bloodline that coursed through her tiny body as her Suburban headed straight into the oncoming vehicles. Whether it was her Viking family genes kicking in or the deafening recoil of the 50-caliber rifle she unleashed, everything fell silent. A sharpened mental focus broke through the fiery explosions blossoming like a Fourth of July celebration around her streaming down a canvass of rain and darkness as she paused her assault. *Wait for it. Wait for it.*

Then, with less than 20 yards between her and their attackers Chloe fired three controlled bursts at the approaching engine blocks creating a hole as both vehicles spun away from the center line. Chloe eyeballed the jeep on her right as they zipped past 4-2 on near the midpoint of the bridge. She climbed over the Ambassador, hopped out the vehicle, and began laying down cover fire.

"Let's go Marines," she screamed as she stood defiant raining down havoc on their decommissioned attackers scattered across the bridge in flaming wreckage.

The bullet riddled doors of the security convoy SUV flew open as Sergeant Johnson and the agency operators tumbled out. Another marine was being half dragged by Johnson when she waved through the smoke toward the remaining vehicle.

"Fire in the hole," one of the agency men yelled as he released a couple of farewell grenades into their crashed-out ride as a matter of habit, then pushed up with an assist on the wounded marine.

Chloe ducked behind their ride as the explosion pulled in the varied hues of red and orange from the flaming debris. As the last man was squeezed inside, she jumped onto the running boards alongside one of the paramilitary boys and pounded the roof as Anderson gunned the Suburban forward into the waning deluge. *Smoke that.*

With the smoldering wreckage in the rear-view mirror, Chloe paused a moment, reached through the opened window reassuring Ambassador Dekker, and even affording a slight grin as their eyes met. "We're here."

A sudden jolt pulled her attention back to the road and a lone slender figure with flowing hip-length hair holding something all too familiar, her relief fell away as the figure hefted an RPG-7 to its shoulder - and fired.

She didn't even scream. The missile arced toward the struggling Suburban, its contrail visible in the actinic light of the rocket propelled grenade's launch. The warhead crossed the distance from one breath to the other, striking the Suburban's grill. At the moment of impact, the grim half-light of the storm was banished. Chloe felt heat on her hands, there was an overwhelming sense of pressure, followed by a distant pain, and then there was nothing at all.

2

SWITZERLAND

Johnny Dekker was no stranger to beauty, but the awe and majesty of the Swiss Alps never disappointed. As a Navy SEAL and special activities operator for the CIA, he had the dubious opportunity to "tour" the scorched desert of the Middle East and the dense tropical maze of violence and poverty found in much of the African continent. In fact, both locations had been on a twisted sort of replay for him and his teams for much of the last eight years. And, despite the unexpected disruption to his planned exit from the agency alongside his fiancée, the change in scenery that came with his "Semi-retirement" from the harder side of clandestine operations was proving to be a nice, albeit uneventful, change of pace.

This is amazing. I need to bring Chloe here in the Spring.

"You're seeing the touch of the divine in nature, Johnny. It's something that man cannot reproduce, and it's something you should always try to protect," his father had told him during a late season trip to Montana years earlier. No matter where he found himself, Johnny tried to find those divine moments. He'd seen it from a sniper's hide at 7,000 feet in Eastern Afghanistan, and as the sun broke over the frost-covered moonscape of the Hindu Kush. Even glimpsed rare moments of it as

young boys played soccer on an uneven pitch somewhere in the Ivory Coast, black thunder clouds promising rain and red dirt roads filled with mud. He'd also seen it in Chloe's smile.

With the air brakes howling, Johnny emerged from his reverie as the conductor coddled the train to a gentle stop. He gathered the rest of his luggage and poked his snoring companion, the Chairman of the Federal Reserve Board, who had nestled himself into a comfortable position atop Johnny's overcoat. He breathed a long sigh, then with another nudge, wrangled his Burberry from under the sleeping giant's body and turned toward the door. A searing light cut through the window as Johnny stretched his luggage over his head to shade his eyes. The midday sun cast long shadows through the double-paned glass making giants of lines of commuters standing in perfect, ordered, rows preparing to board the train for its onward journey. He nudged the chairman, again.

"Sir, we're here," he repeated as he watched the gentle giant brush the dust off his coat and sit upright.

With a blink and a yawn Chairman Rupert Meyer stretched his arms toward Johnny and stood facing him with a furrowed brow. "Right, shall we?"

Johnny hung outside the door as his boss bumped around the cabin gathering his bits and bobs giving him another chance to retreat into his own thoughts. A slight grin crossed his face as he replayed the sight of one of the most powerful men in the world sharing a sleeping car with his newly appointed deputy. He knew that the chairman didn't see him as a deputy, after all, their familial seats on the Council of Thirteen had informed their relationship since his birth, so why should it matter? Still, Johnny felt he deserved his privacy. As he twisted his toes inside his newly handcrafted *Berluttis*, tapping them ever so gently against the stairs, a sense of urgency swept over him until he felt a gentle heavy hand grip his right shoulder.

"I know what you're thinking. Why the blasted train?"

Johnny paused a long moment. "It had crossed my mind."

Meyer pulled on his jacket and reached toward the handrail as he wobbled past Johnny and into the hallway. "Through all my years of travel, I've found that feeling the rail under the train soothed me allowing me a restful sleep, something that one needs before one of these longwinded forums. I've never been able to sleep on planes as you saw when we hopped across the Atlantic, terribly annoying."

As the chairman of the Federal Reserve Board, Meyer had been on a non-stop annual tour around America's financial institutions when he got the call from Director Mark Brown about Johnny Dekker's re-assignment to the de facto central bank of the United States. When the call came Meyer wasn't the least bit surprised given all the recent disruptions in the global banking systems and Johnny's intimate knowledge of those disruptive technologies, where it'd helped carry his family's private banking empire into the twenty-first century.

"Shall we?" Johnny pointed toward the stairs.

"I'm right behind you young man."

The two men maneuvered with their bags down the narrow-paneled corridor and filed off the hissing passenger car. The air was crisp. Across the platform, a hurried, but organized, exchange of passengers resembled the precision of a massive clockwork mechanism, executing a preordained methodology. From every corner of the platform, swarms of school children bustled past them in uniformed lines as the two Americans measured the length of the platform.

"Ah, I think I see our minder," Meyer said and nodded his head toward a very tall, broad-shouldered man standing near the crowded passenger drop off and pick up area. The man stood at least a head above Johnny, but thick, and bespectacled like most other middle-aged men in the country, dressed in a worsted wool suit and wearing a proper hat holding a placard that read: MEYER/DEKKER.

Johnny, in one top-to-bottom glance, sized the man up without breaking his practiced smile. "Yes, the placard," Johnny said. He'd expected something more low key. Johnny wasn't one for advertising his arrival and with the added responsibility of protecting the chairman it ran counter to his purpose. He cleared his throat as the two men moved down the platform toward their waiting liaison.

While Basel wasn't exactly downtown Kabul, someone as important as the FED chairman normally came equipped with a full security detail when traveling abroad on official State business. Not to mention the normal assortment of aides, flunkies, and functionaries, but this was no ordinary trip, nor was it as dull and simple as official United States business. This bank committee was special, and it had special rules. And the bank of banks' rules allowed for only one accompanying deputy at their monthly general meetings. Johnny knew that his off-cycle appointment as the chairman's deputy in attendance to the Bank for International Settlements was replaying a blueprint from the legend Allen Dulles and had the potential for another intelligence windfall if things went according to plan. Johnny felt the warm moist air of a whisper on his neck as the chairman leaned toward him.

"His name is Fredrik. He's an Oxford educated scholar who speaks the Queen's English but has an unfortunate surname."

Johnny raised an eyebrow as they shuffled along the platform. "Really?"

Chairman Meyer cut a side-eye at Johnny. "Don't even think about it. I know you've a sharp wit, but please try to keep it in check while you're here."

The stage was set. And like the actors in a Shakespearean play, the men entered the scene stage left led by Johnny playing the key role of the American banker McKittrick, a spy who'd infiltrated the Swiss banking elite during the Second World War and managed to not only win over the other BIS representatives, but the chairmanship of the bank for the duration of the war, all the while chumming with Schroder from the Deutsche Bank and reporting back key information to Allied Command. But, despite their similar roles, Johnny had a more complex and tutored background prior to his mission. Further, with his family's banking contacts and his own sharp intellect, he was tailored made for this mission. And with his appointment as deputy, he'd now received his own set of identification and documents, issued by the BIS, that gave him unfettered access to more than two hundred countries, a claim that no other nation could boast, save the Vatican. As such, it'd been drilled into him from the start at the importance of this meeting. Johnny held his smile and held close to the chairman as they approached their contact.

"Chairman Meyer, welcome to back," the man's baritone voice flowed mellow with a charming accent, like a character out of a Rodger's and Hammerstein film.

"Fredrik, it's good of you to meet us here. How are you?"

Fredrik blanched. "All is well. How was your trip?"

"Slept through the whole thing, as usual, it was glorious," Meyer said and gestured toward Johnny with a swollen right digit. "Fredrik, may I introduce my new deputy from the Commonwealth of Virginia, John Dekker, Jr."

Fredrik smiled and stretched out his hand toward Johnny. "I'm pleased to make your acquaintance, Mr. Dekker. My name is Fredrik Fuchs."

Johnny fought back the idiot grin that struggled to surface on his face as he shook the gentle giant's hand. "It's my pleasure, Mr. Fuchs," he managed, feeling the burning glare from Meyer burning a hole in the back of his neck.

"I knew your father," Fuchs continued, nonplussed. "He was a great thought leader at the bank, we've missed his insight and pragmatism."

"Yes, a hard act to follow for sure. Nevertheless, I shall try."

"Wonderful! Now then, gentlemen, would you please follow me? I have a car waiting for us to transport us to the meeting." Fuchs motioned toward the station exit across the width of the platform.

Johnny let a scowling Meyer step by him and fell in behind his mentor as they followed the towering Swiss national through the arrival hall. The warm midday sun shone down through the magnificent windows above the atrium coaxing Johnny to remove his Burberry and unbutton his suit jacket. He heard the boarding calls booming across the loudspeaker in multiple languages as they passed through the crowds capped off by a train whistle in the background nothing short of a quaint Hollywood movie set. Although careful to keep one eye on the chairman Johnny cast about the terminal taking in the authenticity of the scene.

"Mr. Dekker, is this your first time in Switzerland?"

Johnny stretched a smile. He knew he'd been caught playing tourist. "No, but it's my first time in Basel. Your city is quite the eye opener, and it's nice to be outside again after our modern-day odyssey."

He saw Fuchs turn back toward the men with a suspicious grin. "If you'd like to stretch your legs, we can have your luggage brought directly to your rooms at headquarters? The bank is only a short walk from here."

Johnny shot a curious look at the chairman. Then patted his mentor on the back as he received the nod of approval. "Perhaps a short walk is just the ticket," he said to their Swiss host.

Content in their decision, Johnny helped Mr. Fuchs load the luggage into a dark gray BMW sedan, pausing a few moments as Mr. Fuchs instructed the driver. Once the car had pulled away, Johnny followed the expansive gesture of their host as he led the two Americans forward into a picturesque cityscape not unlike any path imagined by the great French painter Claude Monet.

While Fuchs led them north, Johnny turned and pointed out the building opposite the Bahnhof entrance, an indistinct old brick building that had seen better days, but still drew the eyes with his faded rustic allure. Without missing a beat Johnny began to fire off questions at Fredrik.

"Isn't that the old bank headquarters?"

Johnny felt the giant slow to a halt. "Indeed, you've a keen eye Mr. Dekker. You've done your homework, as they say in America." The men stopped and walked back a few steps toward the almost invisible alleyway that snaked between two nondescript buildings sitting directly across from the train station's arrival hall. Johnny ran his hand along the crumbling wall as cracked bits fell to the ground. A crooked smile stretched across his face like he'd found the entrance to a treasure trove.

"Hidden in plain sight you might say."

"It served its purpose Mr. Dekker," Fuchs replied.

Johnny breathed a sigh. He wanted to pursue the statement of purpose, but again felt the burning stare of the chairman boring a hole in his head and relented to the moment. "Indeed," he responded.

"As you're most certainly aware Mr. Dekker the establishment of the BIS was a low-key affair. Its purpose was to create a vehicle and monitoring system for the German reparation payments post the First World War, and as such there was no need for anything more than a quiet and comfortable space for the representatives to set about their task," Fuchs concluded.

Johnny nodded along with their host's explanation as he kept the chairman in his peripheral view. Despite his desire to delve into the metamorphosis of the BIS during the Second World War as the German Reichsbank International branch that, for the most part, circumvented Allied banking restrictions under the direction of Herr Schroder, he smiled. "Complicated times. How many member nations are there now?" he inquired following their host north.

"We're happy to report that the membership has grown from the original eight during this building's golden age to now a sixty-nation strong membership with some others that attend select functions as observers."

Johnny snorted a laugh. "Globalization through affiliation? Remarkable," he said as the three men crested the small hill and came into view of the modern fourteen-story headquarters sparkling in the distance unlike anything else in the city.

The current Bank for International Settlements building was the exact opposite of its original building, and some would say purpose, today, it stood out. The bronze and silver terraced structure dominated the local skyline, especially given the fact that few buildings rose above five stories.

"*Voila mon amis,*" Fuchs said.

It fell short of the gravitas of the Federal Reserve Building in Washington, but what it lacked in gravitas it made up for in brilliance, something quite unexpected, and mysterious. Johnny took in the spectacle a moment before noticing Fredrik motioning toward the steps that led up the steps into the foyer of the bank.

As Johnny and the chairman followed their jovial long-legged friend up the endless steps toward the entrance, a buzzing in his pocket pulled him away from another random fact about the city that his mentor was sharing with him. When he pulled his cellphone from his pocket and saw the number on the screen, he excused himself and stood at the top of the stairs craning his neck 360 degrees, scanning his surroundings, as he took the call.

"Dekker."

"This is overwatch, go secure, please," the autonomous voice said.

Johnny blanched and thumbed his phone screen and then tapped a small black icon labeled 'CRYPT'. "Secure - go."

Three quick bleeps, followed by someone coming online.

"Johnny, it's Mike Chambers."

Johnny sighed. Chambers was one of his assigned handlers from his early days at CIA, but he'd not spoken to him in years. He was also not one of the officers read into this compartmentalized program as far was he was aware, which made Johnny suspicious. "Mike? It's been a while, what's up buddy?"

A short silence followed. "It's bad news brother, but I thought you needed to know. I'm breaking protocol by telling you this, but we go way back, and I wanted to give you a heads up. We think the ambassador's been in an incident."

Johnny scratched his forehead as he stood under the midday sun in front of the contemporary steel structure of the BIS. "Oh shit. Which ambassador?"

The line went silent. "Your father, Johnny. He's gone dark in Malaysia."

Johnny paused a long moment then turned toward the building entrance and motioned the two men hovering at the door to go ahead without him. Then, he turned his back to the bank and prodded for details. "When did the IRI dog-and-pony show get moved to Malaysia?"

"I can't get into specifics, but the State Department lost contact with him a few hours ago. And I thought you should know," Chambers replied.

Tuning out Chambers voice Johnny felt a sharp pain hit him in his gut as he reacted to the insufficient and alarming information, "Lost contact? What the fuck does that mean, Mike?"

Chambers cleared his throat. "During the last radio check his security detail made with the embassy in Kuala Lumpur they mentioned something about an attack on the freeway outside Penang. We're working the on-the-ground assets to find out what's going down, but the weather is all kinds of fucked up."

"Fucked up like monsoon winds and rain fucked up or insurmountable haze from the corporate brush fires blanketing the peninsula in Indonesia fucked up?"

"I'm afraid it's a bit more severe, an actual typhoon and it's expected to make landfall at your father's planned rendezvous. On top of that, the government has grounded all air traffic until it dissipates."

Johnny felt his heart pounding in his throat. This was the last thing he needed, and he was literally on the other side of the planet with no feasible options. "What kind of overwatch do they have? Predators or Naval?"

"Grounded."

Confused, Johnny stopped pacing and switched the phone to his left hand. "If you need people, there are at least three guys I know in Coronado right now that can help get this sorted without any questions."

Chambers interrupted. "No locals on this one. The director thinks there's something bigger at play. The trade agreement is pretty big, and there are plenty of people that aren't willing to go along with the proposed terms."

"What else?"

Johnny sensed the hesitation in the reply before Mike continued.

"It's a Malaysian asset that pulled your father from the IRI ceremony and set up the meeting in Penang in the first place, so we're keeping this in the family. Look, we're blowing up the phones in Kuala Lumpur right now trying to find out what's going on. We've got Keyhole satellites moving into position to lens the area, not to mention the U.S.S. Stennis has moved closer to Penang as the typhoon edges closer to landfall, but it's slow going."

A pop echoed down the phone line as Johnny expressed his dissatisfaction with the response twisting the plastic molded cellphone in his hand. "How long?"

"The storm's winding itself down, but it's still unclear. Perhaps in about another hour or two we should have more intel," Chambers said.

Johnny brushed the side of his face with a sweating palm trying to hold his composure underneath a chorus of eyes staring down at him from the lobby and populated surround. "Why are you calling me and not the director?"

A loud crashing sound in the background solicited a string of vulgarities from several indistinct voices as Chambers cupped his hand over the phone, then replied. "I've taken over the ASEAN desk from Chloe, which brings me to my last point."

"There's more?"

Chambers cleared his throat again. "Chloe went with him."

Within a millisecond Johnny felt his entire body start to shake like a Falcon 9 rocket tugging at its constraints atop an aging Cape Canaveral launchpad. A wave of anger scorched through his veins as the oxygen depleted cells turned his entire face bright red, he felt an eruption building but then an inner voice gently pulled him back to center. "She's retiring at the end of the month, and she's already transitioned her portfolio to you. What was the reasoning behind Penang?"

An awkward silence echoed between the satellites as Johnny felt blood coursing through his veins and his patience wearing thin at Chamber's blatant reluctance to give him one single satisfying answer. He needed more information. With a dozen pair of eyes watching his every move he knew his time was short, but without the most basic information any attempt to assist his father and fiancée was dead on arrival. "Chambers?"

Chambers stuttered. "The director, in consultation with your *father*, approved her attendance as an ASEAN subject matter expert, with field experience, and she agreed."

Johnny snorted a laugh. "How convenient…"

Chambers interjected before Johnny finished his sentence. "Not to mention the fact that she not only agreed, but she also volunteered, brother."

A descending midday sun blinded Johnny as he climbed a few more steps, then stopped and again turned away from the building one last time to avoid any lip readers and an attempt at privacy. "This isn't a random call. You sent my fiancée and an aging ambassador into an unknown situation, into the ring of fire where they prey on Americans for sport." He felt the tendrils of a headache starting to flicker out and wrap themselves around his eyes. He fought through the panicky urge to simply bolt from where he stood, poised at the entrance of the BIS where he'd already started to turn heads with the lengthy phone call. He could be back at the train station and to the airport in a flash. He could be on a connector from Basel-Mulhouse-Freiburg airport to Zurich or Paris in less than half an hour. He was already parsing lists in his head, his contacts clandestine, business, and personal were in or near Malaysia. Places to pick up a satellite phone, weapons, and ground transportation. He was trying to work out the best way to get to Penang when Chamber's voice finally broke through.

"…Are you listening to me? You gotta focus, man."

The voice was right. He shook off the planning fugue, composed himself, and refocused. "Mike, thanks for your call. You can tell the director I'm on point and I'm looking forward to your update on their status." A quick sigh later he'd pocketed his phone and trotted up the steps toward the chairman where he was waiting patiently with a smile. Johnny returned the smile, patted him on the shoulder, and led the chairman toward the lobby entrance.

But after a couple of steps, Meyer's paternal voice halted his forward progression while a forceful arm pulled him to the side. "What's going on?"

Johnny paused, lifted his head to the sky, then back to his mentor. For reasons he couldn't understand, Meyer had always been able to see through his smoke screens, so he didn't bother. "Find me an exit strategy."

The near instantaneous response and deliberate tone from his mentor told him he wasn't going anywhere. "If the plan is to present you as my deputy representing the United States Federal Reserve, and you're to be effective in that role, there's no exit strategy without you first completing your entrance and introductions. Whatever it is… will have to wait."

Johnny cast his eyes about the entrance, threw his right arm around the chairman and gapped a wide smile, then leaned toward Meyer, narrowing the chances of any lip reading lookie-loos floating around. "There's been an attack."

Confused, Meyer pulled his head back as if he'd smelled something putrid and rotten welling up between the two men. "And the agency needs you to deal with it?"

A sense of calm swept over Johnny as he cracked his knuckles and leered past Meyer into a scattered group of bankers winding their way into the institution's foyer. "Once again, my father's failed to heed my advice, but this time he's also dragged my fiancée along with him, Chloe and dad are in trouble, sir. So, you understand… I need to deal with it."

Meyer breathed out gesturing toward the door. "Your father is one of my closest and dearest friends, and there's nothing I wouldn't do for him. That said, he's also one of the most capable men I know. Whatever it is, I'm sure he's got it under control, Johnny."

A brooding Johnny closed the space between himself and the chairman. "You don't get it. Yes, this meeting is important and could impact our intelligence mission in Europe for decades to come, but this is my family, and family comes first."

Meyer pivoted on his back foot and led Johnny by one arm as he smiled toward the BIS entrance. "As you said, family comes first, and it's the exact reason the Council of Thirteen had you accept the Agency's assignment in the first place, despite your early retirement. Only you understand why this BIS committee appointment is crucial in the grander scheme of things..." Meyer paused a moment and then raised his hand toward the edge of his mouth as he took in a deep breath of fresh air and finished his sentence "...we cannot allow any one state or its intelligence community control over the inevitable deployment of a global blockchain technology, and the following neural networks."

Something about his words grabbed Johnny's attention. "Agreed, but..."

Meyer interjected before the young banker could finish his sentence trying to settle the matter and get them inside and preempt any negative chatter about their arrival. "I'm certain that your father's taking care of business and if he knew what you were thinking, he'd tell you to stay on point."

Johnny scowled back at the remark. "A hard day for my father's having to walk the entire back nine at Pinehurst, Rupert. Not dealing with terrorists and kidnappers, he's not that man...not anymore. I need to get to KL."

Meyer put his hand on his protege's shoulder. "We can't all be the hammer Johnny, but your dad still has a trick or two up his sleeve. Don't count him out, not yet."

Aside from the usual security protocols that were in place, Johnny was certain that his fiancée wouldn't have allowed the mission to go forward without extra assurance, not his girl. A slight grin crossed his face as he nodded along to the Meyer's diatribe about the situation. "I'm sure you're right."

"At the end of the day, this is probably a scare tactic someone in Malaysia is expecting will have an impact on the trade agreement. After all it's not exactly the most popular piece of legislation moving through the Asian community at the moment. There are plenty of parties that'd love to see our foothold in Asia fall flat on its face," Meyer said.

Johnny raised an eyebrow. "That seems a bit simplistic."

Meyer shrugged. "Nothing is ever what it seems, I'm afraid. I'm not sure what transpired that Director Brown thought it was necessary to put your family in this situation, but it must've been necessary given his attendance at RIMPAC was a request from the White House." The two men spoke in whispered tones as they approached the entrance now some ten minutes after their arrival. "My guess is that someone is playing for a bigger hand beyond that trade agreement and are using your father's presence in Asia to give it more punch. Frankly, I'm concerned about what it means for us."

BASEL, SWITZERLAND

Johnny lost in the labyrinth of the seasoned wordsmith tilted his head. "How?"

Meyer tightened his hold on his deputy as they passed through the lobby doors. "Think about where you are." Johnny followed the chairman's left-hand waving in the air signaling the importance of their surroundings. "The decentralization of the global financial system is not something either the Council or the BIS can ignore. Once the last U.S. Administration launched their cyber-attack and lost control of their crypto tools to hackers in the now infamous breach, it was open season on the global order." Johnny felt his blood pumping harder through his veins as he listened to his mentor lay it out. "The director pulled you from the mud and put you in the front office to leverage your unique skillset and social standing within this global fraternity of financiers to deal with the coming threat. The *Vollgeld* Initiative is the first step to the consolidation of financial authority, they're designed to cut out the commercial interests. Then consolidate the expanded club of monetary authority and keep the world from nosediving into financial anarchy."

It wasn't a secret that someone had made the American Intelligence community look like fools when their cryptography toolkits were sold on the open web, but Johnny knew there was more to it. "The Russians?"

"We can't be certain," the chairman said. "But if our intelligence is correct then this meeting may be the single most important meeting of our lives."

Johnny paused a long moment as they stepped away from the entrance inside the BIS marbled lobby. "The best I can promise is get through the introductions, but then I've got to get on top of the Malaysian situation."

Meyer dropped his hand and looked Johnny in the eye. "With the rapid adoption of cryptocurrencies, and the impending flood of artificial intelligence initiatives permeating from every corner of cyberspace jumping on and off at various Internet nodes around the world, we're exposed, and opened to rogue actors as well as enemy nation states. And when I say we, I mean the entire planet. The entire financial network is at risk, daily. That's why you're here. We need you here to focus on this agenda. Figure out what the others are conspiring, because I guarantee you the responsible hackers are in that room. Let the agency deal with your family. The Council and our country needs you right here doing what you do best."

Johnny cleared his throat as the two men stepped forward into a group of bankers milling around the elevator. From the moment Johnny and the chairman had entered the lobby, countless pairs of eyes had followed their every move. The level of curiosity was palpable. He knew that he'd raised questions upon his appointment, but he had a job to do, and nothing was going to get in his way. As they neared the elevator, he heard his name cross the lips of several prominent bankers as they spoke in hushed tones. Johnny remembered the one truth of international banking. *Whomever controls the money supply, controls the world.* "I'll stay as long as I can sir," Johnny said as they entered the elevator.

"That's all I ask," the chairman replied. "There are over sixty central bank governors and deputies that are looking for ways to rein in or control the technology behind the decentralized ledgers that'll inevitably going to run the world."

"The power structure must not be disrupted," Johnny interjected with a devilish grin as the doors closed on the elevator a low hum whisked them to the top floor.

Meyer cut an eye at his protege. "The Basel Accords are about order, Johnny. As the world becomes a global village it's tantamount that a global body manage an otherwise selfish and individualistic universe that would create more division than community."

Johnny snorted a laugh. He'd read the intelligence file on the initiative and knew that his mission here was to stop the Russian delegation's influence at the conference, but he'd never imagined that the chairman was so clued into the impact of the disruptive blockchain technologies running rampant across global currency markets. With the Russian success in Estonia through their third-party proxies, they stood front and center at providing the blockchain technology along with its artificial intelligence monitoring that had caught the eye of the Economic Consultative Committee attention. "A New World Order," Johnny said.

A double ding from the elevator control board announced the arrival at their floor as the two men exchanged serious looks, neither willing to back down. "Order being the key word, Johnny."

Johnny flashed a smile as the two bankers stepped out of the elevator to a joyous cheer of their fellow members. With the family concern pushed to the back of his mind, Johnny raked the room with his eyes. As he catalogued the possible threat areas and then cleared them, he felt his overall sense of tension and angst settle down. Of course, that's when he saw —the Chinese spy.

3

BETHESDA, MARYLAND

Somewhere in the darkness a phone was ringing. Jack Sorenson woke long enough to acknowledge the sound, recognize that it was his phone, and not his girlfriend's, before rolling over and going back to sleep. He'd considered, for a moment, getting up and answering the call, but decided that no good would come of it. So instead, he burrowed into his pillow, and eventually, the ringing stopped.

Good.

Moments later, the tale-tell beep of someone leaving him a voice-mail echoed sadly through the house. Jack groaned. He lay in bed, half in and half out of sleep, contemplating whether or not to get up and check the message.

No good will come of that either, Jacky-boy. You're not on call, and you've put in almost 80 hours at the Fort this week. YOU deserve to lie in this big fucking bed next to your half-naked girlfriend. You deserve to sleep-in until at least 09:30 and have mind-blowing morning sex before scarfing down some waffles and watching college football all day. You stay in this bed you silly bastard, do not check that message.

Jack stayed in the bed, and for a long moment the house was

serene. Outside there was a strong nor'easter blowing up, gusts of wind making his Georgetown condo creak ever so slightly. He put his hand out blindly and it came to rest on a very warm, very bare hip. *Yup. That settled it — staying in bed.*

The phone rang again. A smooth slender leg struck his shin.

"That's your phone," Isabella murmured sleepily, and shifted in the bed next to him. Before Jack could respond, she pressed a pair of impossibly cold feet into the pit of his stomach.

Jack flashed open his eyes at the surprise. He stifled a curse and twisted away from the probing blocks of ice. He staggered up and out of the bed, fully awake and annoyed. He glared down at Isabella Dekker's still form and for about half a second; he loathed her, every satin skinned, keenly intelligent inch of her. Grumbling in annoyance he listened to the phone go quiet, followed a few seconds later by the forlorn "beep" of another message being left on his voicemail.

Well, since I'm up…

Clad in boxers he staggered out of his bedroom, grabbing a robe off the hook on the door and pulling it on as he padded out into the hall and down the creaking wooden stairs. He took longer than he'd expected to find where the invasive demon lay, but after he removed a coat and set aside something frilly and delicate, that was not his, he located the beeping menace. Thumbing it alive, he scrolled down through the missed calls. He frowned, both were the same Maryland number, and that could only mean one thing, work. Before he could get to his voicemail, the phone rang again, startling him, and eliciting a string of inaudible curses.

"Sorenson," he barked into the receiver.

"Jack? It's Walter."

Sorenson's heart dropped. The voice lashed out through the dark and eviscerated any chance of cursing down the caller and salvaging his weekend.

"Director Moore, what can I do for you here at," he glanced at his watch, "Three AM?"

"I can't get into details on the phone, but we've a situation developing in Malaysia that we could use your help with this morning."

Jack cleared his throat. "Sir, I'm an intercept monkey, not an ASEAN specialist."

Moore exploded. "I know what you are but leave it to your folks to stumble across unencrypted chatter that crosses a couple of our active operations. Both of which are of particular interest to you."

Well, that's fucking cryptic.

"Two, sir?"

Moore sighed into the phone. "It's a family affair, a father and son thing." Silence hung on the phone as the director paused a moment waiting for his head of cryptanalysis to reply. "The point is I need you down here an hour ago, got it?"

Sorenson blanched. It was way too early in the morning, and he had had way too much wine with dinner, as evidenced by the strewn pairs of clothing, to be playing word games with his boss. Drawing a complete blank, he tried to think of the active missions he'd been read into. Before he could admit to the director, he still couldn't understand what he was talking about, the director threw him one last bone. It was a big one.

"Isabella's uncle has gone dark. We've lost communications and location. I need you at your desk as soon as possible."

Holy shit. He was talking about Ambassador Dekker. He was missing. What does that even mean? Where was his security? Was he abducted? What does it have to do with his son, Johnny?

Jack had known Johnny Dekker for years, they'd grown up together, gone to the naval academy together and even survived *Hell Week* during their SEAL training together. He was like a brother, albeit one that was annoying as hell with his passion for flying, but they were as close as any two friends could be without being related. But unlike Johnny, who'd been a collegiate superman, Jack's body hadn't held up to the rigors of field work. After one too many training injuries, and a nice dose of shrapnel in equatorial Africa, he'd left the SEALs and returned stateside to take up intelligence work at Fort Meade inside the National Security Agency's global headquarters.

"Jack...Are you still with me?" the director's voice boomed through the earpiece.

What the hell had they gotten themselves into? Jack slowed his mind. "I'm ten minutes out," he replied. A plethora of scenarios raced through his mind as he tried to grab a granola bar of his counter and end his call, knowing this was only the beginning of the conversation.

"I've got you and the team set up in SCIF 17," Moore replied and followed up with an awkward request. "Don't say anything to Isabella, not yet. We can't have you distracted dealing with her and then this turning out to be nothing but faulty communication gear."

Sorenson pulled a face like he was a ten-year old caught with his hand in the cookie jar. He'd never been good about keeping things from Izzy. "This is work, sir."

"I'll see you at 17," Moore said as the line went silent.

Jack sat down on the arm of his couch and let everything he'd just learnt sink in. He held a private moment of sorrow for his now lost weekend plans and then stood up and started back upstairs to grab clothes and his overnight bag. He pulled up short when he noticed Izzy standing on the landing of the stairs leading up to the bedroom. She was wide awake, clad only in one of his old sweatshirts, her dark honey-brown curls pulled into an unruly ponytail.

"Three am?" she said.

"Work."

Isabella sighed and leaned against the wall. "What aren't you supposed to tell me?"

FORT MEADE, MARYLAND

Jack powered his Shelby GT500 down the Patuxent Freeway, its big 5.5-liter engine roaring out its familiar melody in a tighter-than-usual pattern of notes as he navigated the pre-dawn traffic.

Getting out of the house after three in the morning without an explanation to Izzy hadn't been easy. Short of outright lying to her, he'd managed to beg off explaining exactly why he was going back to work at 0-dark-30 on a Saturday morning. He'd convinced her to go back to bed and promised to tell her everything just as soon as he got back, which he hoped would be soon, but knew deep down that was nothing but wishful thinking.

Slowing just long enough to make the offramp to Fort Meade, Jack brought the rumbling aluminum-engined beast into the military checkpoint far too quickly, spooking the tinned-hat Military Police on duty. *Fuck.* He ignored their glares, and probably lost a few minutes while the on-duty sergeant took his sweet time to verify his ID. Cleared to enter, he made his way through the maze that was the NSA campus to his designated parking spot. Jack glanced at his watch as he made his way toward the building, it wasn't quite 04:00 hours, but it was close. Almost as if on queue, his phone rang. He answered it quickly, half hoping it might be Moore calling to tell him it'd been a false alarm and to just "go home."

"I'm entering the Westend door now, sir."

Isabella spit fire. "Oh my God Jack, it's Uncle John."

Jack jerked his head around. "Honey, what're you talking about?"

"He's been attacked."

"Where are you getting this?"

Isabella deadpanned. "Johnny."

Jack quickened his pace, panting as he crossed the parking lot. "Izzy…"

"Is this why Walter called you in? I can't believe you didn't tell me about this, oh my God, Jack."

Sorenson swore to himself, as his quickened pace turned into a jog. In true Dekker form, Isabella had transitioned from awe-struck horror to pissed-off in record time. If she followed her normal pattern, there would be yelling, quickly followed by threats, which would then likely escalate into violence. Jack shivered a little. He feared for all those expensive and breakable things delicately placed around his townhouse, alone and helpless, with his furious girlfriend.

To counter her anger, Jack immediately adopted a gentle, placating tone he'd used successfully on angry teenagers and very junior officers. "Honey, I don't know what's going on. I swear to you. The director just told me I needed to come in and that it was important."

Okay, that was a tiny little lie.

"You tell Walter there's going to be hell to pay if he's deliberately keeping me out of the loop on this."

"Okay honey, I'll let him know. But I'm heading into a checkpoint, gotta go."

Isabella chuckled in disgust. "Find out what the hell's going on, please."

"I gotta go." Jack slipped the phone into his pocket mid-stride and jammed open the double-doors, then stopped, caught his breathe, and tried to regain some semblance of composure. After a moment, he pushed through the second set of doors, and snapped to attention at the sight of Director Walter Moore lingering behind the Westend security checkpoint, waiting. In his mid-sixties, he was still an imposing man, well over six feet tall and as lean as a whip. With his perpetual scowl and a long aquiline nose, he looked like a very martial version of a college professor. Even now, with the clock on the wall hovering right around 0400, the director of the NSA looked sharp, and focused.

"Jack, Thanks for getting here so quickly."

"Don't thank me sir, but the cat's outta the bag as grandma used to say."

Moore cut an eye at the half-dressed cryptanalyst trying to slow his mind enough to catch the meaning of the reference. Then raised an eyebrow as he watched Jack clear the checkpoint and stuff his keys back in his pocket. "You mean Isabella?"

"If you weren't ready for her to know you shouldn't have told Johnny."

Moore nudged his head, herding Jack toward the elevator. "Well, it wasn't us, but I'm sure Langley felt the need to keep him up to speed, especially given the sensitivity of his current mission in Basel."

"What about the ambassador? What do we know?"

"He was at RIMPAC when Langley received intel that a Malaysian political faction was set to disrupt and vote down the trade agreement."

"And Brown thought it was a good idea to send a walking talking encyclopedia of our AI program into an unknown situation with minimal support?"

Moore clenched his teeth. "So, you're aware of the implications for this year's RIMPAC exercise?"

"I read the report."

"I don't think this attack was about the trade agreement, or at least not its primary goal, the expected disruption is a bonus."

Jack blushed in confusion. "You're saying you have no clue?"

"I need you to break down the intercepts your team snatched from the air and deal us back into the game. Can you do that?"

Jack loosed a long sigh. "That's why you pay me the big bucks."

As a result of recent cyber threats and increased espionage against the United States, a formal set of enhanced security measures had been rolled out at the beginning of the year with armed marines stationed at every building entrance, which included a string of security measures inside as well. When the Jack and the director reached the designated SCIF they handed over their cell phones to the guards and slipped their tickets into their pockets then proceeded through another metal detector. Until at last walking into the newly appointed command center. Jack's somber mood sunk as he saw an unexpected face on the other side of the door.

"Ah, good, reinforcements," Moore said as he stepped inside.

"*Hoorah*," Jack said under his breath.

"With a little help from these Virginia farm boys, I think we'll be able to make short work of this and get back to our weekend plans. Am I right?" Moore paused a moment as he watched the unspoken uneasiness between the two teams. "Jack, you know Director Brown."

"Of course, good morning, sir." Jack reached out his hand to welcome CIA Director Mark Brown. Then followed up with the infamous aspiring director, but still toiling through the confines of section chief, Mike Chambers.

Moore cleared his throat. "Now that we're all acquainted, let's get down to business." He gathered them around the conference table and began to speak as Jack looked beyond the directors at his team in the background, the geek squad hard at work beyond agency politics, and far removed from the Langley visitors focused on the task at hand, just as he'd ordered.

Director Brown coaxed Jack back into the conversation. "Jack, Mike is one of our field operatives that I think you'll find very helpful in the hours to come, anything you need from us he can get for you."

"Good, I need a list on all the projects that Johnny and the ambassador were working on..." A deep raspy voice cut him off mid-sentence.

"I understand you and Johnny worked together?" Chambers said.

Jack looked at Director Moore, then Brown, before turning into the question from the section chief. "Worse than that, I grew up with the guy. He's the really annoying, overachieving brother I never wanted." Silence dropped across the table as the two men waited for the other's move.

"So, it goes without saying that you know the ambassador pretty well then?"

Jack nodded.

Chambers dropped his head a little and leaned in with a sympathetic voice. "Damned, sorry brother."

Jack pierced the sympathetic veil with a direct question. "Does Johnny know?"

A professional liar by trade Chambers still felt uncomfortable with the directness of the question, especially in front of the directors, which put him off his approach as he shifted in his seat then answered dryly. "Yes"

Jack watched as his questions prompted Moore and Brown to excuse themselves and leave him and Chambers to get further *acquainted*. From Izzy's call he knew that Langley had briefed Johnny on the situation, but to what degree, and what did Johnny have to offer in return was uncertain. "So, you know more than you've told me?" Jack continued.

Chambers shot a piercing gaze at Jack. "What ruffled your buddy's feathers wasn't the fact that the ambassador had gone dark, but that his fiancée was along for the ride."

Jack blanched. A wave of confusion swept over him as he unconsciously grabbed the spook by the arm. "Chloe? What about Chloe?"

Chambers looked down at his arm, then at Jack as he removed Jack's hand. "I thought you'd been briefed. We sent Chloe along as liaison to the RIMPAC event, since it was a legacy agency project, and she was the subject matter expert on hand when the call came through about the Penang meeting."

Something was off, Jack saw through the agency speak. He wanted answers, but before he could respond his bosses voice pulled his attention toward the geek squad and their cluster of monitors.

"The weather around Penang has dissipated, the typhoon's made landfall and is winding itself out, which has given us a live feed from our Predator drones currently over the scene." Moore motioned Jack toward an array of monitors streaming the live feed, a hushed gasp swept over Jack like a tsunami as the geek squad watched the devastation coming through the feed. Jack stepped closer. "Our BDA people say a rocket attack took out one vehicle, but we believe the wreckage on the bridge is the ambassador's Suburban. Under the orders of the Secretary of the Navy, the USS Stennis has re-entered the Malacca Strait, and is coordinating with the embassy to scramble local assets to the scene. But the trail of destruction left by this once in a hundred-year storm, the infrastructure has been compromised. Suffice it to say it'll be some time before they can reach the site. This is what we're dealing. You know what to do. Get it done."

"Fuck me."

Moore snapped his fingers and pointed to Jack. "This is your team lead - Jack Sorenson. He'll handle all interdepartmental coordination and strategy. You need anything you talk to him."

Jack pulled himself from the monitors long enough to nod at the director's acknowledgment then bid them all get back to their stations and work the data, all of it, especially the signal intercepts. He pulled Moore out of earshot by the elbow. "Since when do we gift wrap high-value targets for our enemies?"

Walter Moore looked down at his analyst, a mentee since the naval academy, and one of the most effective tools in his arsenal of talent. "Since POTUS and the ambassador decided that they knew better than their intelligence chiefs."

Jack paused a long moment. "Anything else I should know?"

Moore patted him on the back. "You've got less than three hours to get our guys out of there before the local police turn the scene into an international incident."

Jack smirked and turned back to the live feed.

4

GEORGETOWN, MALAYSIA

A high-pitched whirring from under the hood warned Kit Lee that his 4.4L M TwinPower Valvetronic engine was redlining, but instead of easing off the accelerator, he pressed his Gucci loafers to the floor and whipped the vibrating chassis onto the Penang Bridge; he was late, maybe too late. If there was ever a meeting, he couldn't afford to be late for it was this one, but the storm didn't care about his agenda, or the importance of his meeting never mind its geopolitical implications. This meeting, a meeting he'd scrambled to arrange, was the most important ask by the Company since their initial cooperation in the jungles of Thailand twenty years ago and it was coming apart at the seams.

What the hell?

A shock hit his chest like a bolt of lightning. Involuntary reactions triggered across his body as the explosion of red and orange hues rippled out into the stormy sky ahead of him. Dumbfounded a sudden numbness swept over his hands as Kit tightened his left grip on the steering wheel and downshifted with his right, providing the taxed engine momentary relief, but only momentarily as inner rage welled up and he straightened out his approach.

From the time he'd joined the Malaysian Army, his interpersonal and negotiating skills had managed to impress his superiors, and everyone else he'd come into contact with, propelling his career toward the Directorate of Intelligence. The increased exposure to internal and external agencies gave him insight and contacts he'd never thought possible, while pulling him deeper into a brotherhood he'd never known existed. Before long, his achievements had landed him in a special liaison unit coordinating military incursions into various locations across the Asia Pacific region. In a short period of time, Kit became the Company's go-to man in Southeast Asia, a former military consultant, Malaysian Intelligence Officer, and personal friend to the retiring agent Chloe Campbell. Together, they'd infiltrated and dismantled dozens of threats snaking their way through the region. So, when this off-the-books meeting between a splintering faction of Malaysian lawmakers and a sitting U.S. Ambassador landed in his lap, he'd made sure that Chloe was in the loop, deep in the loop, whether she liked it or not he needed her one last time; it was that important.

As his mind drifted back to the present moment, he felt a blistering heat followed by a wave of blinding light slam his triple-coated Obsidian custom paint job, regressing its finish to a matte black. Without warning his fully dilated pupils were scorched with the piercing light of a thousand suns as he wrestled with the torque of 550-horses wildly pulling him toward an unknown destination across the steel and cement superstructure. A pain shot through his cerebral cortex as he white-knuckled the steering wheel back under control and forced his eyes adjust to the blinding light. When he blinked back into reality, he saw a stream of flaming wreckage stretched across the fabled bridge as his Bimmer zig-zagged its way through the devastation. Confusion gripped his mind. A series of terrible images bounced off his retinas, his mind refusing the admittance of the facts, something that he'd been conditioned to do during his special forces training those many years ago, but nothing could've prepared him for the searing physical pain that brought his BMW to a screeching halt, yards from his destination.

What the fuck?

He took a quick breath allowing the smoky air to inflate his lungs, then took another while his heart raced with emotion, an unfamiliar pain set in, something he'd not felt since his mother had passed away. Fire and chaos shimmered across his glassy eyes as he slammed the car into park, pulled his Glock 23 from under the dash, and exited the vehicle. He wasn't more than ten minutes late, but from what had unfolded in front of him, proved to be the most devastating ten minutes he'd seen since he'd left the army.

With the nearest wreckage on his right, Kit maneuvered to the opposite side of the bridge for a better angle of approach. His ears pricked up to the sound of a fading car horn wailing into the vacant approaching morning hours, an uncensored and unanswered call for help. Kit had pulled to a gut-wrenching stop, just short of the rendezvous; a cafe on the edge of Georgetown where he was meeting the politicians, the Ambassador, and his old friend, Chloe Campbell.

What the fuck? Please God Chloe, don't be in this mess.

Kit felt his palms clam up as he moved forward. *Don't be in this mess.* And although his primary concern was the American convoy, a fleeting thought of the Malaysian politicians stabbed at his assessment adding another wrinkle that he wasn't prepared to deal with, let alone explain should they be assailed by local authorities, he peeked his head from behind his Bimmer and through the smoking debris reading the make and model of the nearest sport utility vehicle.

Chevrolet, Suburban. Fuck.

He approached the first burning pile of mangled wreckage weapon drawn and ready for anything. Somebody had betrayed him, but he'd told nobody about the meeting or the location aside from the Americans and the local politicians attending the meeting, which now seemed like an ill-conceived plan. *Stupid, bastards. They've no idea what they've unleashed.* As he moved toward the smoldering Suburban, a string of scenarios played out in his head, none of them ending well as he knew Langley would now question everything he said and did, nothing short of a full and complete rescue, as well as the apprehension of the attackers would keep his head off the chopping block. He knew what he had to do, pistol close and squatting down, he approached the first vehicle with measured caution.

An unbearable heat wafted over him sucking the moisture from every pore in his body as he paused a moment, then yelled into the wreckage. "Anybody in there?" He blinked away the sweat rolling down his brow as the ensuing silence shattered his eardrums. Another pivot and he'd cleared another bullet riddled chassis and moved with cautious haste towards the failing horn and growing agonized screams. One after the other, he cleared the piles of wreckage until he'd arrived at the end of the bridge. Kit panted through the smoked filled air maintaining vigilance as he waited for the other shoe to drop, cautious but resolute until the residual rain from the spun-out typhoon subsided, he moved forward. He knew that the multiple explosions, evacuated city or not, had drawn the attention of the police and they'd arrive at any moment, he needed to clean the scene.

Keeping his crouched position, he pressed his fingers against his ceramic Austrian pistol as he scoped out his final path toward the far side of the bridge, the last Suburban, and in spitting distance of the cafe. By the time he'd crossed the road leading off the bridge, he'd counted five smoldering vehicles, three conscious, but disoriented marines, and a couple of severely injured men in black jumpers, the rest were dead or on fire. *Ugh!* A horrific smell of burning flesh swept through the twisted metal as he moved on the last Suburban. Then he saw him, a half-charred Marine pulling a suited body from the shredded SUV, *Ambassador*. The sprawling flames and unbearable heat bit and clawed at him as Kit ran toward the fire.

"Ambassador Dekker?"

Kit grabbed the exhausted Marine by the neck and shoulder adding extra manpower as they pulled the suited limp body free of the demolished American vehicle.

"Mr. Ambassador? Are you all, right? Can you move? I'm Striker," Kit spewed at the disoriented diplomat.

Kit Lee, codenamed Striker, had been a Company asset for more than a dozen years, he was a known quantity within the Administration and friend of his soon to be daughter-in-law, of course the Ambassador knew him although they had never met.

Ambassador Dekker clinched his left fist then looked up. "Striker?"

Kit nodded. "Any idea who hit you?"

A wisp of smoke swept across the ambassador's face as he stared at the man hovering over him with a look of disbelief, then coughed out a confusing question that left Kit stunned. "Where's Chloe?"

Kit caught the ambassador by his elbow as he struggled to his feet, dazed, and confused, but reanimating himself back to reality and the situation as he waved off the security detail as they stumbled into view weapons drawn. "I thought she was with you?"

"She was standing on the runners right before the explosion," the Ambassador replied.

Kit grabbed his left hand trying to stop the shaking. "We can't stay here."

Ambassador Dekker stood upright and stepped into the Malaysian's space, less than an inch from his face, and seething with anger. "Well, you arranged this meeting. Where should we go to next, Mr. Lee?"

Kit blanched. Through the surrounding chaos, he heard the Marines radio in their position, and acknowledge a response, probably confirmation of a quick response team en route, he thought to himself as the stared blankly at the Ambassador. "The storm's cleared and the police are on the way, we need to get you off this bridge."

"Negative. We got this. And we're not leaving until I find Chloe."

Kit clenched his teeth, resisting the urge to shake the Ambassador to the gravity of the situation if they were there when the police arrived, but refrained as his inner voice called him away. "Copy that, sir. But I need to check the cafe. I need…"

Ambassador Dekker raised his hand. "Do what you gotta do, but don't go disappearing on me. We need to know how the fuck this happened. You understand me, Mr. Lee?"

That was his cue, but before he turned toward the rendezvous, he added one last thing. "I'd never do anything to endanger Chloe. If she'd spoken to you about me then you should already know that." And with that Kit turned away from the Americans and disappeared through the burning debris toward the cafe.

As Kit scrambled across the road toward the cafe, he thought about Chloe and the Ambassador and what it meant, why they'd been ambushed, who'd don't it, and where they'd gotten their information. Getting Langley, and Chloe, to agree to meet the Malaysian opposition party was the crowning achievement of his career, the culmination of years of cultivating influence across the entire political spectrum and with the Americans. And now, after all his work, and all of his planning, what did he have to show for it? Nothing, but death and destruction.

A defining crack of thunder like the sound of Thor's hammer against the sky pulled his attention back toward the bridge, within moments an ensemble of repetitive hammers announced the arrival of the USS Stennis' Search and Rescue Team as it encircled and landed near the Ambassador. *Not much time left*. Kit ducked in the doorway of the dimly lit cafe and navigated the shattered glass coating the tired and faded tiled floor. It was the perfect meeting place for the Americans and the Malaysians, owned by an old family friend and off the radar of any intelligence units working the country, and stubborn enough to disregard the evacuation orders during the historical storm. The crushing shards of glass under his feet slowed his pace, but within a moment he found what he was looking for. The two parliamentary legislators standing pale-faced behind the counter next to the shopkeeper's daughter, Anja Singh. He rushed toward the confused and frightened men. "Bro, you all right? Are either of you hurt?"

"What the hell, bro?"

Kit saw the men had superficial cuts from the flying glass, but otherwise looked healthy enough to leave. He corralled the men and pushed them through the cafe entrance ushering them into their car without explanation. He stretched his arm toward the windshield and pointed out their exit down a lower access road to another parallel bridge further up the island. "You guys need to go, now!"

"Kit, what the hell happened?" The pair said in unison.

"Some other time, now get outta here, bro!"

Kit closed the car door and watched them disappear into the breaking dawn peaking over the horizon and illuminating the full carnage of the assault. The melodic dance of the chopper squadron grew louder as the circling gunships secured the area. *Fuck, me.* He jumped through the splintered doors, rushed back inside the cafe, but a nonchalant look from Anja caught him off guard. He paused a long moment then took her by the arm and led her toward the rear exit.

"Anja, I don't have time to explain all of this to you. I barley understand it myself, but you need to trust me," Kit said.

The shopkeeper's niece, a close Lee family friend, shook her head in understanding, but stared into Kit's confused eyes. She'd just returned from studying abroad to help her aging uncle's business. Her features were Asian, and something else, Slavic cheekbones, Russian maybe, Kit had never asked or been too involved in their family interactions, but yes that's what it was, Russian. He remembered her uncle telling him about how his brother had married a beautiful Russian woman years ago, but he'd never met her or their child. She was close to his age entering his early thirties, very attractive, and strangely calm.

"Don't worry," she said.

Something about her tone unnerved him. Kit's mind was running in overdrive as he tried to fit all the pieces together and clear the scene before the local authorities arrived and dragged everyone in for questioning, or worse splashed it across the six o'clock news. He urged the young woman to hurry as she stuffed some things in a large black canvas bag. "I'm sorry to drag you into this, but we've got to go...now; forget all that stuff," he said.

Anja snorted a laugh. "You've done exactly what any fixer would do, and you've brought him right to me, *SPASIBO!*"

Kit blanched as he felt a cold steel pierce his skin, followed by an awful hollow burn that ran all the way up his arm and into his chest. He jerked his eyes wide in horror as the realization that he couldn't move, couldn't breathe, couldn't even blink his eyes set in. The stunning brunette said nothing as she laid his head down on the glass covered floor. He watched as her eyes fixated on his like she was trying to memorize every feature of the shock and horror that she could find. As his head fell limp and flopped to the side, he saw the hypodermic needle buried in his arm, the white knuckled grip of his murderer, and her delicate polished thumb holding down the plunger. Panic seized his mind as he summoned every ounce of strength. "Who are…"

Anja smiled. "Don't worry Striker, you won't be alone for long. Nighty night, handsome." She dropped his head to the floor, stepped over his limp body, and walked toward the cafe entrance.

5

BASEL, SWITZERLAND

The spy grinned at Johnny. *What the hell?* the American thought to himself as he pivoted left and right avoiding a steady stream of Savile Row-tailored bankers that broke his line of sight on the unexpected intruder. *Where'd you go, buddy?* Johnny scanned the crush of round jovial faces clogging the bank's fourteenth floor lobby, while edging around Chairman Meyer and his cohort, trying to get a bead on the elusive Chinese intelligence officer that had sprung out of the crowd like a Jack-in-the-box against a canvas of dulled grey automatons, then blinked out of sight. Johnny knew this wasn't a coincidence, nothing involving the Chinese Ministry of State Security was by accident; it was a game and Johnny was losing. *Damn it.* Johnny fought the annoyed grimace off his face as he turned toward the forceful tug on his arm, and the smiling face of his mentor and waded into the crowd of well-wishers eager to meet the American central banker and his new young companion.

Johnny seethed. He'd followed Meyer's lead and pushed down the raw, gut-twisting anxiety he felt after learning that his fiancée and father had gone dark in Malaysia, despite the continuous knot in his stomach. He'd smiled at the dizzying array of sharp-eyed and exquisitely dressed professionals with their cuff links and stick pins throughout his parade across the bank's private restaurant. He'd exchanged polite greetings; he'd shook every proffered hand, he'd nodded, he'd played the game and danced the dance, everything that was expected of him, but nothing he did had calmed his mind that still raced toward disaster. It wasn't until Chairman Meyer and his newly acquired entourage drifted into a large and luxurious conference room that Johnny broke away from the pack, determined to find a quiet moment and settle his mind.

"You look like you could use a drink," a dry, but familiar, voice offered.

Johnny snorted a laugh, pulled his hands from his pocket, and looked up from the railing. A half-smile crossed his face as his eyes confirmed the voice of the elusive Chinese spy, Li Junxiong. "Man, I thought they said this was an exclusive conference?" Johnny fired back. "Who let you in?"

"Let?" Li paused and clasped a vein-popping handshake with Johnny as he finished his thought. "Perhaps my American friend forgets that the People's Republic of China has become more to offer than just an exploited workforce lined up for Western corporations to mint returns." He paused a moment. "Plus, I heard the Hors d'Oeuvres were splendid so, *voila*." He released his grip and slapped Johnny on the back as they stepped onto the balcony.

A military man by trade, Johnny doubted Li knew much about fractional banking, credit default swaps, or the Ins and Outs of the incestuous politics of these raggedy old European financiers. Nevertheless, he surmised it was the Colonel's grasp of the disruptive blockchain and encryption technologies that landed him the deputy governor gig at the People's Bank of China (PBOC), and nothing to do with the growing relationship of the two men. He looked his friend in the eye. "The world will never be the same."

Li laughed. "It's why we're both here, isn't it?"

Johnny chuckled under his breath. "That reminds me, I've got something for you on the chance I ran into you here." He reached into his suit pocket and pulled out a Statue of Liberty fountain pen and handed to his blushing companion. "Perhaps for when you're writing your report to Beijing later tonight."

After a quick inspection of the gift, Li replied. "And what kind of friend would I be if I didn't have something for you as well buddy." Within a flash he'd retrieved a copy of Chairman Mao's Little Red Book out of thin air and placed it in the palm of the American's hand. "The author has a famous saying that is one of my all-time favorites. It reads: Political power grows out of the barrel of a gun." Li paused as he watched Johnny's face turn red. "Perhaps in your reading you will find something that you like as well."

"Perhaps, we'll both focus on the technological threat zeroing in on the global financial infrastructure, and together make sure that any unwanted or rogue disruptions don't incinerate the planet," Johnny replied as he tucked his gift inside his inner jacket pocket.

"Agreed." Li pulled a cigarette from a small crumpled yellow packet and stabbed it in his mouth, exhaling a strong plume of smoke within a matter of milliseconds as he led Johnny away from the crooning bankers inside. "I'm sure you've heard that the Russians are working on a new decentralized ledger, one that they alone control. The Estonia X-Road experiment was just the tip of the iceberg. They've got their proxies working from Silicon Valley to Singapore taking stakes in anything and everything that has even a whiff of cryptocurrency viability."

Johnny smiled. "I've missed you, buddy."

He watched as Li took another drag from his cigarette and then hit him head on with the question he knew was coming. "What do you know about the *Vollgeld Initiative*?"

As a sitting member on the Council of Thirteen, the American spy knew more than he cared to acknowledge to the Chinese operative, regardless of their friendship. But playing dumb wasn't the solution either, so he turned toward his friend and offered what he thought sufficient. "It's something about bringing the power of money creation back to the central banks by cutting out multinational corporations and commercial banks." Johnny paused studying Li who'd nodded along with perked-up ears, but Johnny knew his sharpened intellect wasn't satisfied with his simplistic assessment.

Li turned toward Johnny. "That's it? A simple reassertion of state power."

Johnny shrugged his shoulders as he motioned for another drink to the bartender. "What? A large data grabs. Not everything's an info scraping exercise."

"We've intercepted some SIGINT between a Russian advocate and an anonymous third party that point toward a break-through in their Artificial Intelligence program."

Johnny blanched. *Coincidence?* He felt his throat tighten and his mouth go dry as he pivoted on his left heel and leaned in toward Li. "What's that?"

"There's only one way to control a globally Quantum Resistant Blockchain based cryptocurrency," Li said.

"A Human Level Intelligent AI," Johnny finished Li's sentence.

Li blew a stuttered plume of smoke over the balcony as he studied his American friend. "What have you heard?"

Everything clicked. Johnny ran his tongue along the inside of his mouth brushing against his clenched teeth pushing down his emotion as he smiled back at his friend. "A truly strong AI is still years out, if even achievable in our lifetime."

As the two intelligence operatives danced their usual dance sharing, but holding back, relaxed, but probing for more information, the room continued to fill with immaculately dressed whispering bankers. Johnny saw more back slapping and glad handing than he'd ever seen during his time at the Davos conferences, which reinforced everything that Li had been talking about, deals were getting done, and it was time for Johnny to make his own.

"So, the United States isn't testing a strong AI in the Pacific?" Li persisted.

Johnny paused a long moment, his mind sorting through the new strings of possibilities around the attack in Malaysia, then turned to his friend and clinked glasses. "Aren't we all busy in the Pacific?" He watched as his Chinese counterpart loosened his tie, then sipped his wine. He continued. "If the Russians gain support on the committee, we're headed down a rabbit hole that neither your government or mine will recover from fully intact; a world of cyberwar and zero-day vulnerabilities even Philip K. Dick never dared to dream."

"Agreed."

Johnny laid his hand on his friend's shoulder. "They have no idea what they're up against," Johnny replied.

He watched Li snub out his cigarette and point his long-manicured finger toward a small bar in the corner of the plush private restaurant, away from the endless stream of rambunctious bankers. Johnny felt his split focus had not gone unnoticed, and he needed to address the elephant in the room. He rubbed his fingers together and rapped them on the mahogany bar as the two men sat down inside the cozy private alcove, away from the bustling herd.

"What's going on?" Li asked.

"I'm pissed." Johnny gave the room an irritated glare. Meyer was holding court over in a corner, no doubt discussing the difficulties of the cryptocurrencies, policy debates and the impact of decentralization, and the security of the global financial infrastructure. He seemed safe enough surrounded as he was by men and women that wanted to curry favor with the American central banker, a lifelong senior member of the BIS committee.

"Whatever it is, we can sort the Russians, Johnny," Li replied.

Johnny blanched. Then sipped his Manhattan, and finally caught his friend up on the troubling news out of Malaysia. When Johnny finished, Li gave a silent whistle of appreciation to the gravity of the situation. "You probably shouldn't be telling me this," he said.

Johnny shrugged. "Either you hear it from me, or you find out from the Internet. What does it matter at this point? The news cycle will catch hold of this, eventually. I'm honestly kinda surprised it hasn't already."

"What are you gonna do?"

He shrugged again, placed his empty cocktail glass on the counter, and asked the bartender for something with a little more kick than his typical Manhattan, a *Caol Ila* 25-year-old, a nice peaty single-malt whisky. After a quick sip and a pleasing smile on his face, he turned to Li. "Not much I can do at the moment. I gotta let the powers that be handle it."

Li considered his words. "That doesn't sound like you," he said, a troubled look flashing across his sharp features so fast that Johnny almost missed it.

"What?"

Li shook his head. "I know how your mind works... This wasn't us."

"Us?"

"The People's Republic had nothing to do with this business in Malaysia."

Johnny raised an eyebrow. "Are you sure?"

A subtle popping sound filled the air around the two men as Li stretched his neck from side-to-side then took a step closer to Johnny. "Despite the advice from the military hawks in our party and our external security associates around the world, we haven't interfered with your precious Pacific Trade Pact, which, by the way every school kid knows is aimed at hemming us in and keeping us away from the international shipping lanes. Or it's true purpose."

"What's that?" Johnny asked.

Li looked Johnny in the eye. "You're creating a buffer zone to head off our leader's Belt and Road Initiative, a simple modern-day Silk Route that would inspire and transact billions in mutual trade benefits for all those who wish to partake in global trade. Even with all that, we did not do this. This attack was not orchestrated by my Party." Li downed his drink and adjusted his *Ermenegildo Zegna* striped tie, waiting for his friend's retort. "Your people are worried about the Pacific Trade Agreement floundering that you can't see the forest for the trees. It's that simple," he said in an unwavering voice.

Johnny slammed his whisky tumbler on the mahogany bar and twisted his face at his excited partner. "Maybe you're right. Or perhaps it's because your government insists on unilaterally extending its maritime borders by lining up every available land reclamation barge in the country and dispatching it to the South

China Sea along every atoll and reef in the region, despite the World Court's ruling."

Li turned beet red reflecting the sour look swept across his face. "Your nation spends an exorbitant amount of tax dollars on its military for a *'peaceful and God fearing'* nation."

Johnny gave a toothy grin. "We have 1.4 billion good reasons."

"How can a nation of industrious and community-focused people threaten the *all-powerful* United States of America? We don't spend half your annual budget."

"Tell that to your defense industry. Didn't the PLA navy just launch the Liaoning Aircraft Carrier? With another already going through its sea trials. And hasn't it already carried out several missions north of the Philippine Islands?"

Li snorted a laugh as the two men had stood up from their barstools and now stood face to face in the dimly lit bar as the bartender hurried in to refill their crystal tumblers. Johnny scoffed as he watched Li crack a smile. "Well, it sounds like our countries have much to discuss, but let's leave it to the stuffed shirted diplomats and focus on our agreed mutual Russian threat," Li said.

The two friends lapsed into a companionable silence for a few moments as they reseated themselves, watching the adjacent conference room fill with all manner of eccentric bankers and aides from all over the world. Johnny quickly noticed that the meeting included not only bankers, but an odd combination of technology representatives. *Wasn't this supposed to be an exclusive central banker meeting?* He watched as Li turned stone faced, but knew he was mulling the same question in his head as he sipped on his drink.

"Tech geeks and bean counters," Johnny said dryly.

Li finished his drink and placed the glass on the mahogany countertop. Then interrupted the short silence. "Don't forget aristocrats and spies."

Johnny rolled his eyes at his friends' obvious assessment. From the far corner of the room another entourage made its way into the throng of bankers like sharks through a school of lesser fish. Where most in the crowd exuded an unapologetic air of wealth and entitlement about them, the new arrivals were blunt featured, and hard eyed. Their suits, while expensive and masterfully tailored, hugged frames that appeared more comfortable in a weight room or combat fatigues. Broad Slavic faces and cheekbones sharp enough to cut like razors predominated.

"Ah, the Russians are finally here," Li said mildly as he motioned to the bartender for another drink.

Johnny sighed. Another wrinkle in his day had presented itself as the newcomers quartered up the room. He felt the hair on the back of his neck stand up a little as the fighter in him recognized other professionals at work. *Tradecraft.* "So, where are their bankers and geeks?"

"Oh, they have one all right," Li replied.

"Do I know him?" Johnny asked.

"Yes, you know him. He's a finance specialist and investment advisor for a number of global firms through his family's own private bank."

Johnny cut his eye at Li as he pushed back from bar. Following the gaze of his cryptic Chinese friend his eyes returned to the cluster of Slavic cheekbones and overdeveloped pectorals, a single figure emerged from the clot of Russians that twisted his face into recognition. The man was tall, whipcord lean with a cold masculine beauty that shared more in common with very expensive surgical tools that genetic coding, he was the epitome of enhanced. If his companions were sharks, then this man was a contagion, a sightless, odorless, killer with no remorse. "Derek Hamilton-Smith." Johnny spat the name like a medieval curse. "I don't have time for this arrogant son-of-a-bitch right now."

Li set his tumbler down. "Too bad brother, it looks like you're in his sights," Li finished as Johnny felt his hand land on his shoulder.

Johnny worked a neutral mask onto his face with an almost invisible effort of will, nothing he hadn't done a dozen times today for the last thirty years. Not a patient man by nature, he'd only barely held onto his temper and his bearing after learning of the attack on his father and fiancée. But running into his family's archrival and ever dissenting voice of the Council of Thirteen, here on neutral ground, was pushing him to wits end. *Calm yourself.*

He watched as the heir-apparent navigated the delirious crowd in the conference room like a sleek meandering eel searching out its prey. A tingling sensation ran down his spine as his temperature began to rise thinking of all the times the insensitive and arrogance of the bank raiding Belgian had derailed compromise on the Council, he couldn't let that arrogance prevail here, not if he was to stop the Russians from securing a foothold in the Consultative Economic Committee, and that meant action.

"Junxiong, I'm afraid I'm about to upset the tranquility of this space."

Li quirked an eyebrow. "Far be it from me to interject into others affairs, but it's not worth it brother. There's too much at stake today." As soon as the last words exited his mouth, a loud distinctive voice invaded the small bar area.

"Johnny Dekker, as I live and breathe. I must say I'm more than a little surprised to see you here. Shouldn't you be in Washington spreading lies to your Congress or off playing in the mud somewhere?" The Belgian's English accent wreaked of aristocracy and privilege, something he flaunted at every opportunity.

"Hello, Derek."

Derek's grin widened a little and only a faint hardness around his eyes betrayed the depths of the man's intense focus, and his obvious dislike of the head of the Dekker Banking Family. "And who's this you're conspiring with today?" He peaked around the American and pulled a dramatic head jerk. "Ah, if it isn't Commander Li Junxiong of the People's Republic of China. Oh, Do tell, gentlemen. What government are we plotting against today?"

Johnny placed his hand on Li's shoulder, restraining him from ripping the insolent Belgian banker apart, as he moved forward with fire in his eyes, and an eloquent smile on his face, fighting every urge in his body to follow the commander's first instinct, but instead delivering a short indistinctive rebuttal. *"Du bist einen..."* he stopped short.

"What would your father think of you toasting with Communists, Johnny?"

Johnny pivoted and shrugged. "He, like myself is a diplomatic liaison, here by request of our respective governments. Or didn't you get the memo before stealing some poor bureaucrat's invitation? My guess is that the Americans and Europeans would be more interested in your traveling companions. They're lovely Derek, where'd you find them? Chechnya? They certainly clean up well for rented thugs."

As the men around him bristled at the accusation, Derek flashed an exquisite grin. "Johnny with your aptitude in technology you can't mean to tell me that you don't recognize who I'm traveling with?" Derek gestured grandly off toward a burly blond bearded bear of a man with a ghost off-white blond hair cut into a military styled flat top. "I would like you to meet Dr. Igor Petrushenkov, Hamilton Smith Group's (HSG) latest hire. He's here as my cyber security advisor." The smirking Belgian then gestured to the man on his left, a brooding thug with a rough, gray-shot beard and a build like a defensive back for the Dallas Cowboys. "And this, is Pavel Grigorovich, he's…" and here Derek made a gentle muse of consideration, as if he didn't quite know how to sum up the hulking man's qualifications. He brightened after a moment. "He's a project manager in our encryption and cryptocurrency initiative."

Johnny raised an eyebrow. "I'm impressed, I didn't know you could get *Spetznas* in those flavors."

Li Junxiong chuckled under his breath, but Derek's insouciant smile never faltered, a testament to his thick skin and disdain for anything but the sound of his voice. He waved an admonishing finger at the American and his companion.

"Mock all you want, Johnny, but I think you'll end the day quite surprised by just how important my partner's contribution to these talks will be on them. Now, I've no doubt you spent all weekend on researching the blockchain proposals and understand the impact to the decentralization of our global financial institutions, so I won't bore you with the details. Just know this, the world is moving away from your American scheme of the Petro Dollar, and the future lies in *my* pocket. My partners have already rolled out a successful blockchain cluster in several European nations as well as made our technology a household name across the world, all backed and developed by proprietary HSG technologies, good luck Johnny boy."

Johnny gave the smug Belgian a considering look, but nothing more. "I'm sure your father is proud."

Derek's carefree facade slipped, just for an instant, something most people wouldn't have noticed, but Johnny had been needling Derek Hamilton-Smith since they were boys, and he recognized the subtle tightening of the lines around the man's mouth and eyes. He was angry. *Good.*

"My father no longer manages the day-today operations at HSG," Derek said icily. "That honor has now passed to me, as you well know."

"Sorry, I've a hard time keeping up with the inner workings of the Hamilton-Smiths, too much YouTube, you know."

Derek rolled his eyes theatrically and gave Dekker a withering look. "Have it your way, Johnny. Enjoy the conference and let me know if you need me to explain any of the technical bits to you. I'm always glad to help a *colleague*." He gestured his entourage and turned away from Johnny and Li. "Gentlemen."

Johnny gave Derek a dismissive nod of farewell and turned back to Li when a trilling noise erupted from within the Belgian banker's suit. Derek paused his departure, fished his phone out and studied the screen for a long moment. Johnny saw his lifelong adversary's eyes widen in surprise.

"Shit, Johnny, you should see this."

Johnny looked for a trap, or a jibe, but the look of surprise on Derek's face was genuine. He bit back an acerbic response and simply stared at Hamilton-Smith in question.

Derek turned and stepped in close to Johnny, angling his smartphone so the American could read the text scrolling across the OLED tinted screen.

"This just came across the AP wire. What's your father doing in Malaysia, hey?"

Johnny's eyes locked on the smart phone. It was poor quality video of a gutted and burned-out SUV sitting in the middle of a bridge. A headline centered over what could only be body bags read: "Firefight in Penang, No Survivors."

The blood ran out of Johnny's face and without a word he turned and walked away from the bar, Derek, and Li bolting out of the conference room and toward the elevator bank.

6

ROYAL AIR BASE, KUALA LUMPUR

Scott Anderson watched his crooked silhouette stretch enormous across the busy tarmac as it fled the radiance of the midday sun. A sun that had done little at warming his cold bones or brighten his demoralized mood. Nothing could stop his mind from pontificating the *What Ifs*. He shook his head as he paced the length and width of the converted hangar. *You're a disgrace soldier.* He jabbed his bloodcaked hand into his pocket and pulled out a faded *Zippo* lighter, which, like himself, was his prized possession and a relic of the past. Perhaps that's where he should've stayed and things wouldn't have ended up as they had, and his men would still be alive. He knew a debriefing was in his immediate future and time was not on his side as he strained through the medication to get the details of the attack straight in his mind. *Who the hell hit us? Why did they hit us?* A gust of wind blew out his struggling flame. He cupped his hands and dipped his head low enabling the following flint strike to catch spark and ignite his crumpled and bent sad looking death stick. As the embers caught hold, he took a long drag, then exhaled a stuttered stream of smoke. He watched it dissipate into the air around him forgetting the reason he was in a makeshift hospital in Southeast

Asia. *What would the director think of your filthy habit?* He loosed a short audible chuckle.

Scott was living in the past. Although smoking wasn't allowed, he didn't care as he took another drag scorched paper bled the length of the cigarette and extinguished against his gnarled hands. This wasn't the twentieth century anymore, command wanted their operatives lean and mean, and that meant everything outside of high intensity fitness and carnivore diets was banned. He was a dinosaur, and he knew it. They called him *Grandpa; Pops; and the old man*. When he'd been a marine, a thousand years ago, that was par for the course and had always set him off, but lately it'd bothered him less. After twenty years in the Corps, with more than a third of it spent chaining together combat tours in Iraq and Afghanistan, the appellations not only fit, but he figured he'd earned them. He'd realized he'd seen some serious shit in his time. Still, nothing in his long career, first as an enlisted 0311 Infantryman in the Corps, to his time running security and covert ops in the CIA and State Department had prepared him for how fast this mission had gone south. A tremble echoed along his neurological pathways from his brain, down his shoulder and arms to his hand before he finally steadied and relit his cigarette, when an ear-piercing shriek erupted behind him. He pocketed his *Zippo* and forced a smile.

"Captain Anderson," the voice echoed off the metallic maze of hangars surrounding his location inside the Malaysian Royal Airbase.

With a cigarette frozen in his hand, and a slight breeze catching his ears, he turned into the verbal disruption. About fifty feet away a slender blond-haired medic scurried toward him from inside the hangar. "What?"

"You shouldn't be out of bed. You need your rest."

Proving his outdated sensibility, he replied. "I'm feeling fine, darling."

"Now," she ordered as she reached out securing his right arm and angling him to lean against her as she escorted the battered soldier back inside.

Anderson offered no resistance as he hung his head and balanced himself on Nurse Ratchet's shoulder. He snubbed the nub of his cigarette in the palm of his hand as they trekked back into the makeshift emergency room where he, the Ambassador, and what remained of his detail had been deposited by the Search and Rescue team from the USS Stennis.

"Thanks corporal, How's the Ambassador? When are they getting us out of here? And when can I talk to my men?"

The medic blanched as she turned him around and sat him on his bed. "I'll be back in an hour."

Anderson forced a smile across his face and nodded, nothing was as it should've happened, and he knew that Washington wasn't going to be happy with his performance. *Shit.* He punched the two pillows on his bed, flung his legs up from the floor, and leaned back grimacing with pain as he listened to the symphony of sounds echoing off the metallic hangar all around him.

Scott licked his lips. He needed to think. He needed to recall every element of the attack and wasn't going to do it lying in a hospital bed, not to mention, while he was still jonesing for a cigarette. He twirled his lighter in his hands. From the moment the medic had departed he'd begun counting the seconds until the coast was clear, he checked his watch and after enough time had passed, he untethered himself from the hospital bed. A quick scramble across the floor and he was back in the open air, ready to tar up his lungs just a little bit more, but more importantly he could think about what to report to Langley. After a couple more cigarettes, he made his way back inside to see if talking to the staff or team could help fill in the gaps and blanks in his memory. He lingered around the nurse's station and tried to find out where they'd taken the Ambassador and what condition he was in, but all he was told was that he was still in critical condition and couldn't have any visitors.

Inside an hour, with no further details on the Ambassador, his hand wandered down the familiar path to his pockets seeking solace in his crumbled pack of Pall Malls. *Nothing I can do about any of it now.* He sighed. He was alive, which meant something, but without the status of his men, the Ambassador or Campbell, he could only give a partial picture to the coming Inquisition. He needed more details, something that might point to who'd orchestrated the attack, and why they'd left the job half-done. He paused a long moment then caught a glimpse of a group of medics exiting another cordoned-off area in the far corner of the hangar, covered in blood, he cracked a smile like he'd solved a riddle. *What's over here?*

"Excuse me Captain," a voice interrupted.

Anderson blanched. "Have you taken your meds?"

"About twenty minutes ago," he replied.

Keep the conversation going before they corral you back into your bed. "Are those my men?" Captain Anderson asked leaving the nurses station on his rear right flank as he meandered toward the cordoned-off area, until he heard an enormous clatter behind him and a voice calling him away from that area.

"Your men are over here, captain."

Anderson paused a long moment, stopped, and turned back toward the eager nurse pointing vehemently in the opposite direction of the Ambassador. For the moment, he obliged and followed the direction toward his men, although small, the hangar had proven an inescapable labyrinth. "Can I see them?"

"They've been out of surgery for a while, but they took a lot of shrapnel, it's not a pleasant sight. And they need their rest." She opened the curtain and led Anderson inside, but instead of greeting his banged up, but ready soldiers, he opened the curtain to a battered and bloody detail all passed out from the trauma and surgeries.

From a distance, Anderson heard the arrival of another aircraft, of course it was an airport, and it was common, but this had a very distinct sound, the sound of an American engineering, their flight had arrived. "What about the woman with the Ambassador? Can I see her as well?"

"What woman?"

Anderson's heart stopped. He pivoted toward the medic. "Campbell, Chloe Campbell, she was traveling with the ambassador. Is she all right?"

"I'm sorry, captain, but you, the Ambassador, and these three men were the only ones the rescue team brought in." The medic flipped through some pages on her clipboard then offered it to Anderson. "Here's a list of who they brought in and their injuries as of an hour ago."

Anderson took the list and ran his finger along each row, nothing about Campbell or any female for that matter. "Could she have been on another chopper?"

"That's the complete list Captain, the choppers have already returned to the Strike Group." She paused a moment then touched Anderson on his shoulder. "Why don't you get some rest and I'll let you know of any changes with your men and the Ambassador?"

Time for that smoke. "Thank you Corporal, I'll do that." He watched her return to her nurse's station and then pulled another death stick from his pocket and lit up as he once again stepped through the hangar door.

A thick haze crept across the Malacca Strait as he fingered the stunted cigarette taking intermittent drags as he fought his subconscious for answers, answers to questions he knew Langley needed, without which they couldn't do their job and bring those bastards to justice. He closed his eyes and slowed his breathing, exhaling a long-winded plume of smoke. The tobacco was stale and tasted awful, but then they always tasted awful, but it gave his hands something to do while his mind raced for answers. Smoking wasn't *verboten* in the Corps, but it was frowned upon, particularly in the officer ranks. They expected Devil Dog leaders to be lean, mean, killers with a warrior-monk's attitude toward the body, and an athlete's discipline when it came to nutrition and healthy habits, and that excluded the little pleasures of smoke-filled lungs. The smoking was a relic of his time as a young Lance Corporal, a habit learned during the dull hours of guard duty and the interminable and often mind-numbing tours aboard troop ships. Still, healthy, or not he figured that if a point-blank hit from an RPG wasn't enough to take him out, then cancer at least would have to wait its freaking turn. Scott took another pull but noticed the return of the tremble in his hands. He cursed his luck and flicked the cigarette away. It was at that moment he remembered aircraft surrounded him, and more than half dozen "NO SMOKING" signs in at least three different languages. He watched in grim fascination as the cigarette spiraled away, bleeding red-orange sparks across the tarmac. A part of him hoped that one of those sparks found a stray pool of AV-gas and cooked off. It would be, he decided, a fitting end to a terrible day. *Come on Scotty, it's not the first time someone almost punched your clock, but maybe it needs to be the last.*

"Captain Anderson?"

Anderson raised brow turned toward his head and acknowledged a tiny, very attractive Malay Military Policewoman standing in front of him. "I wasn't smoking," he said with guilt scribbled across his face like a five-year-old boy caught with his hand in the cookie jar.

"Sir, you've wandered out of the designated area, and the medics have been looking for you everywhere. You're needed back at Hangar Seventeen. Please follow me." Without further explanation, the Malayan MP, who could not have been over five feet tall in her jaunty dark-blue beret, turned and led Anderson back down the flight line. After a few minutes, they stepped through a door marked "Personnel" into the military hangar, he'd shrewdly abandoned a short while earlier.

Anderson ducked his head as he stepped through the metallic facade. A FAST team had choppered in from the USS John C. Stennis and delivered with them every piece of medical *whizbangery* imaginable. There was a wall of portable surgical areas marked off inside, he started see more clearly as the drugs he taken began to slow his anxiety. "This looks like my stop," he said with a grin.

The tiny MP stopped in her tracks and gestured to a panting young medic holding a satellite phone. He hadn't planned on straying from the hangar, but between his failing memory and the medications, not to mention the light headedness from the cigarettes, he'd managed almost a kilometer distance away from the facility. "Thank you, sir."

Scott Anderson exchanged a quick look with the MP as she smiled and disappeared through the hangar entrance. Then he took the sat phone from the medic willing his hand through its persistent shaking. "Anderson," he growled.

"Captain Scott Anderson?" the female voice sounded as if she was calling from one of Space Force's newly established forward bases on the lunar surface.

"I'm not interested, honey."

A quick digital tone echoed through the line and confirmed his suspicion. "Please confirm your DOD identification number."

Anderson shoved his crusted bruised hand into his pocket and fished out his identification and relayed it to the caller. Memory was the first thing he noticed failing, and now his reaction speed was past its peak. After a moment of silence, the phone crackled back to life. He imagined some bespectacled analyst in Washington looking through his personnel records on a computer screen, verifying his information.

"Please hold for the director."

Ah shit, not State. Anderson cleared his throat and straightened his spine as he prepped for the onslaught of questions for which he had no answers.

"Scott, this is Director Brown with Jack Sorenson, he's leading the investigation and response team. We're glad you made it. What's your status?"

Anderson frowned and stuffed his cigarettes back into his pant pocket. "My people got blown to shit, sir. Other than that, I was doing some reconnaissance on area R&R spots when you rang." A short pause followed as Anderson wiped his sleeve across his face. "Do you know who hit us sir?" He continued with a more humbled tone.

Jack Sorenson redirected the conversation. "The SAR team said there was a Malaysian national with you when they arrived. Was it Striker? Where is he?"

Anderson exhaled a moment as his bandaged body leaned against the outer hangar wall. He felt it. A deep wrenching pain welling up inside him again, deep inside his gut. It'd been a few hours since he'd taken his medication and the pain signaled its fading effect. It started low and sporadic, but as the conversation continued and intensified, the throbbing grew unbearable and pulled his focus to another place, somewhere in his subconscious where he could level out and mange a reply. "Rocket attack, sir." Anderson wrung his hands together allowing the friction of his battle-scarred hands to scrape off the dried blood and grime that the medic had failed to wash off, avoiding further details of the attack. The details weren't pretty, and he wanted to forget. He thought about his ranch and his wife on the porch feeding the dog.

Jack drew a question mark on a piece of paper as the director shrugged his shoulders at the Captain Anderson's answer in the echoing silence. "Yes, you were hit by rocket attack. It's on the international news, but that's about it, nothing about the dead or wounded. Is there anything you can tell us about Striker?"

Anderson paused a long moment. "We were attacked along the freeway, and it spilled over onto the bridge, we were within spitting distance of the rendezvous."

"Who fired the rocket?" Jack blurted.

Another long silence hung over the line as intermittent pops from the satellite signal danced across the connection like a faceless devil on an empty stage when the captain finally responded. "They were waiting for us."

"Who was waiting for you?"

"The rocket hit us head on, sir. Whoever it was knew exactly where and when we were coming. They were waiting. They were waiting in front of the cafe."

Jack leaned down toward the speakerphone. "Was it the Striker?"

"They were holding an RPG."

Jack blanched. "Was it Striker?"

Jack felt the director tapping him on the shoulder and motioning multiple hand signs getting him to back down. Then, Jack changed tactics and continued. "How's the Ambassador?"

"AMBO's alive, but he's got a collapsed lung, concussion, and he looks like he's been worked over by the defensive line of the New England Patriots, but he'll make it. The squid doc tells me that as long as there isn't any secondary infection, he should be fine for transport."

"And your Marines?"

"We left the embassy with a six-man team. They're still fishing some of them out of the strait. One of them will be in a burn ward for a good year - if he lives. The other two should make it, just burns, bandage, and a couple of breaks. The agency's two roughnecks also made it through and are with me. They appear to be fine but aren't in a talking mood. It looks like besides some smoke inhalation and minor scrapes they're good to go and are up and about. Thanks for asking."

Jack sighed. "Goddamnit, Anderson, I'm sorry."

Another awkward silence hung on the line. Anderson felt nauseous, and his head began to swim. He scrubbed a hand across his face and back through what remained of his short-cropped hair. "Sorry, but I think my meds are wearing off."

Another pause in dialogue as Jack muted the line and exchanged a quick opinion with the director as they worried about divulging too much over the encrypted but still vulnerable signal, but after a moment it was decided, and Jack hit the button again. "Scott, what about Chloe? What's her condition?"

Anderson paused a moment as the throbbing turned to pounding and he grimaced while clutching the sat phone, trying to give an accurate account, but unable to recall anything other than a blast ricocheting in his mind. "You mean the CIA chic?"

A smile shot across Director Brown's face as he turned toward Jack before answering the captain. "Not exactly the way I'd describe her, but yes, the CIA chic."

From the moment he'd awoken on the hospital gurney, he'd thought about the devastation and fate of the young aide to the

Ambassador, as well as the rest of his charges, he'd failed. He'd not known her long, and only by reputation for the most part, but he recognized her bravery and tried to form the words to describe her demise, but the link between his mouth and brain began to short circuit. He realized it was the head injury. The result of his skull getting bounced around inside the Suburban like a ping-pong ball. His gray matter was as bruised and tired as the rest of his body, and it seemed to have finally decided that short-term memory recall was simply a bridge too far. "What was that?"

"Chloe Campbell, the CIA liaison traveling with the Ambassador, where is she?" Jack screamed down the speakerphone overcome with anxiety and losing patience with the security team captain.

A moment passed, then another, and Anderson heard the director's repeated inquiry of his ASEAN operative. He pinched the side of his nose and tried to regain his focus as the dead air numbed his sense of reality, he fell into a surreal state of mind. After a long moment, he shook his head as he gazed over the medical hangar cluttered with blood-spattered gurneys telling of a previous rush to save the wounded, but nothing of their inquiry. "I don't think.... I don't think..."

"Did she make it?" Director Brown and Jack implored simultaneously.

Anderson ran his arm across his seeping wound and answered. "She's dead."

Jack calmed himself and spoke again. "Are you positive?"

"Neither my Marines nor the SAR team could find her before we bugged out, sir," Anderson replied taking a quick breath as the chaotic scenes of the exfiltration played back in his head. "The RPG strike took us high on the passenger side, right around the engine block as she was riding the driver's sidestep holding on through the window, clearing a path of resistance. But her grip didn't hold after the impact."

A fire welled up inside the presiding cryptanalyst that he'd not felt since his last forward deployment in the SEALS alongside Chloe's fiancée Johnny. "She was outside the vehicle?"

"No, not at first, but the small weapons fire had injured our driver, and the AMBO was bleeding from his head and chest, we were taking heavy fire. I moved into the driver's seat, and she stabilized the AMBO, grabbed the SHOWSTOPPER, and exited the vehicle to lay down suppressing fire as we limped toward the island side of the bridge. She got my people out of a tight spot with her quick thinking." Anderson pressed his free hand against his head wound as he paused a moment. "She saved us."

Jack pursed his lips. "Did you recover her body?"

"Not that I've seen. You need to check with the Search and Rescue team to be for certain, my head is leaking and feeling nauseous. I might be wrong about everything." Anderson tightened the bandage on his head then sat down on the hangar floor and put his head between his legs, all while pressing the phone to his ear.

Director Brown spoke again. "We're getting you and the team out of there ASAP, so listen up. A C-17 Globemaster III has been diverted from Ali Al Salem and is headed your way if it's not already there. You're being evacuated to Ramstein Air Base. The FAST team that's working on your people will accompany you and hand off to the trauma teams in Landstuhl, got me? Hang in there, captain."

"Thank you, sir" Anderson replied through his increasing brain fog. Snapping the phone shut he lifted his head toward the hangar door. *Jesus I could use a cigarette.* Ignoring the warning signs and the patrolling MPs, Anderson fished another cigarette out of his pant pocket and stuck it in his mouth. The stickiness of the pack informed his diminishing state, he needed a medic, but how to get their attention. He took another drag. Captive to impossible gravity and a spinning room, Anderson felt himself wobble until his head hit the floor and the red and orange sparks bounced across the hangar floor like a Fourth of July fireworks at the State Fair when he was a child.

7

BETHESDA, MARYLAND

Isabella Dekker was complicated. As an unapologetic micromanager she thrived on order, yet she could rarely order her personal life. She was also detail oriented, and impatient, holding others to rigorous personal and professional standards. Yet despite all of this, she'd fallen in love with a man she recognized had all the emotional maturity of a houseplant. In her career, she was known as a consummate planner, yet with all her personal and professional acumen, she'd failed to execute a simple romantic weekend with her boyfriend-cum-houseplant without a business disaster getting in the way.

But if she was complicated, it was because her life was complicated. She was thirty-five and the senior managing partner for Dekker Banking Group, and her family was — complicated.

People my age are raising kids, paying a second mortgage, and looking forward to a Pats game on Sunday. Me? I'm juggling a family full of spies and international bankers.

In truth though, all the activity in her life was a salve of sorts. Being impatient, she was often (And easily) bored. Activity, emergencies even, had a soporific effect on Isabella. Unlike most people, stress made her happy.

So, here she was, it was a stormy Saturday morning, and everything was in shambles. Her weekend with Jack had been sent careening off the tracks thanks to the news of the attack on her uncle and best friend. But where a lesser woman might have spent the rest of her morning wrapped in a bathrobe, wringing her hands, and glued to the telephone, Isabella - Izzy to her close friends and family - was made of sterner stuff. She knew there would be fallout associated with the attack on her uncle's diplomatic convoy. While the senior Dekker was no longer the acting head of the company, he remained a central figure in its operations, despite both her and her cousin Johnny's encouragement to relax and spend more time golfing. An attack on him would be an attack not only on the United States, but an attack on the Dekker Group. That meant she needed to be ready for whatever the market, or the press, or her investors would throw at her.

So, while she worked out the potential repercussions and subsequent courses of action in her head, she felt the uncomfortable twinges of a building anxiety growing in her belly. She was worried, not only for her business, but for her uncle and Chloe. Chloe was Izzy's best and closest friend. Another complicated woman, Chloe Campbell was the daughter of an allied family on the Council of Thirteen, and another woman of gravitas.

Izzy had been thrilled when she found out that the Dekker family heir, Johnny Dekker, (also a houseplant), was going to marry her best friend. She was excited that another complicated and spectacularly capable woman would join her at DBG upon her retirement from the Central Intelligence Agency, and that her houseplant cousin would have such a fine and obviously superior partner to guide the Dekker family into the future. Plus, Chloe would help add a little estrogen into the testosterone polluted Dekker bloodline - something they desperately needed.

She frowned at her melancholy mood. Family was inordinately important to her, they gave her balance, purpose, and joy. That something might have happened to them, made her angry - and impatient.

"Damn it, I'm useless just sitting here," she growled at the walls and snatched up her phone.

What she could really use, was a SITREP. She, like most of the Dekker clan had spent her formative years serving within the American Intelligence apparatus, the *other* family business. Though Izzy's tenure had been far shorter than most of the men in her clan, she relied on the interconnecting web of resources she could reach out to when she needed information as much as any other. Still, she had contacts in other parts of the government and throughout the business world that could always clue her in. She began to wake people, and once they realized why she was calling, all of them wanted to help. But good intentions aside, none of them had anything to offer as far as useful intelligence on the situation.

"Kirk, it's Isabella Dekker. What do you know about this Malaysian business?"

A quick silence raised her eyebrow. Then the voice replied. "I know that Director Brown told me to tell you to let *him* handle it if you called me."

Izzy snorted a laugh. "Really, it's like that?"

"Sorry Izzy, but he signs my checks." The deputy director hung up as Isabella thumbed the phone shut and whipped it at the sofa.

With most of her telephonic reconnaissance coming up dry, she tried getting in touch with, Johnny. But that too went nowhere. The Dekker heir was purportedly in Europe with his new boss, the FED chairman, hobnobbing with blockchain geeks and central bankers. And given his status within the CIA she knew he'd be hard to get in touch with. So, with Johnny unreachable, unless he wanted to reach her, and Jack swallowed up by the NSA, she found herself cut off, frustrated, and more than a little scared.

Unable to abide by inaction, she killed forty minutes on Jack's sleek Perception Rower and blew through a six-mile workout in a near personal record time. She wiped her brow with her sleeve, panting like a wolf on the hunt. With no word from Jack forthcoming, and nothing new from any other sources, she decided enough was enough. It was time to go home and get to work.

She grabbed a shower and stole the last pair of low-carb protein shakes from Jack's fridge. She powered one down as she gathered her things from the happy wreckage of their evening of Italian food and old movies and saved the other for the trip into Manhattan. With a last look at the disorganized heart of Jack's townhouse, she locked the door and headed for her car. As she made her way down to the underground parking garage, she brought her phone out and thumbed her way to Jack's number. The call went straight to voice-mail - again, but what did she expect, he was in a secure room beneath Fort Meade.

"Jack, it's me. I need to get back to New York. Call me when you can. I love you."

Moments later she was in her BMW X6M and headed north on the I-95. It was over three hours to Manhattan on a good day, and the weather had been absolute crap overnight. Still, driving gave her something to do and the torquey pull of the BMW SUV's turbo-charged engine soothed the part of her that required constant forward motion. Better yet, the ridiculously posh SUV had blue tooth and built-in WIFI hotspots to it was for all intents and purposes a moving office, which she liked. She scrolled through her list of contacts again on the built-in display and phoned her assistant in Manhattan. The phone rang three times and was picked up by a very groggy sounding Ian Blake.

"Ma'am?"

After a short sigh she blasted him. "Three rings Blake?"

Ian's voice betrayed nothing, but Izzy knew he was irritated with her.

"My apologies, Ms. Dekker, I thought you were on a no-contact personal time this weekend?"

Isabella snorted. "It was a beautiful dream. Listen, you need to get caught up. John Dekker, the Ambassador, was attacked in Malaysia. No, wait, don't interrupt, let me get this out. We have no details yet, and no independent confirmation of anything. We'll move forward as if this is all true, do you understand me?"

"Yes, ma'am," he replied, the mild buss of annoyance that had been hinting around the edges of his voice gone, replaced by shock and disbelief. "What's first?"

Weaving her way through a string of slow-moving cars, Isabella took a moment to collect her thoughts. This would take some time she realized, and she needed the flexibility to be away from the office if the worst really had occurred. *She frowned at the thought. Better to plan for the worst and be over prepared than the other way round.*

"First things first, I'm going to need you in the office ASAP. Regardless of how this shakes out, we're going to take a hit when the markets open. So, we need to be prepared to do damage control. Call in the department heads, start with the Capital Markets team and go from there. Nothing less than a deep-dive into our recent Asian deals and our partners."

"Princeling deep?"

A number of global investment banks had been fined by the U.S. financial regulators a few years earlier after hiring practices were found to have violated accepted protocol and blurred some self-regulatory lines to win favor in the emerging Chinese Capital Markets, the people targeted were known as "Princelings", they were the sons and daughters of well-connected businessmen and Communist Party members, who'd been educated overseas and understood both sides of the trade. Isabella thought about it for a moment. "Absolutely," she replied.

Her first thoughts after learning of the attack was it might be related to the Pacific Trade Agreement. It wasn't as popular as the media portrayed, especially as it excluded China, which itself probably wasn't the best trade decision. But what if it wasn't? What if this was closer to home? A direct response to something the Dekker Group had done. Isabella felt the synaptic explosions of possibilities firing across her neural network as she pressed down on the accelerator and started working her way through the slow-moving traffic like a quicksilver drop along the car studded ribbon of I-95. This new line of thinking suddenly erupted into a kaleidoscope of possibilities, the most concerning being the involvement of another family from the Council. While the Thirteen families were normally good at avoiding unintended entanglements, her father had confessed to her that they did occur from time to time.

What would a family involvement mean? What would the optics mean for the global committee? Stop it. Don't go down that rabbit hole, not yet.

She split the difference. "Go back three years," she told Ian as she swerved around another clueless commuter. "We also need to dig into all of our ASEAN specific deals. Look for anything out of the ordinary."

"So, everything then?"

Isabella powered over her assistant's snarky remark like a freight train. "Who we backed, what we backed, who benefited, who didn't, who might still hold a grudge, tell them to be thorough, nothing escapes scrutiny, nothing." She paused a moment and smiled in her rearview mirror. "Tell them I'm on a warpath, so when I say thorough, I mean *uber* fucking thorough, you got me?"

Ian snorted with mild amusement. "Yes, ma'am, what kind of deadline should I give them?"

"YESTERDAY."

Ian sighed, still shaking off the sleep in his brain. "Can you narrow that down for me a little bit, boss?"

Isabella glanced at the digital clock on the Bimmer's HUD. It was 0600, and she was holding a steady 85MPH. With clear roads and a reasonable weather forecast she would be in Manhattan in a few hours. "I'll be in Midtown around lunchtime, so they'll need to have me a preliminary review by 1400 hours, that's 2PM for the uninitiated."

"Understood. Feels like a working lunch ma'am, correct?"

"Sharp as a tack, even on a Saturday."

"Thai or Sushi?"

"Surprise me," she replied, and clicked off. The light rain was getting heavier with dropping temperatures, blue-black clouds building to the East bringing with them the promise of more bad weather, perhaps that nor'easter the news rambled on about. Isabella growled in irritation and pushed the German engineered machine even harder.

BASEL, SWITZERLAND

Johnny had pushed past the outer-lobby door when his cell phone rang, something told him that it was urgent. He stabbed his hand into his breast pocket and fished it out. A quick glance at the display revealed another unfamiliar Virginia area code number. Desperate to know what had happened to Chloe with his selfish father, he knew was his newly acquired handler calling to update him on the attack. But as his thumb hovered over the "answer" button, a cold tentacle of fear started to wrap itself around his heart. Was he ready to hear that the impossible had happened? Was he ready to learn that his father had led his fiancée to her death despite his urging against her tagging along on his RIMPAC celebration? Was he ready to hate his father for eternity?

Quit stalling. This gains you nothing. He started to answer the call when the doors of the BIS sprang open, and an elderly voice called down to him.

"Johnny, wait."

Looking up from his phone, Johnny saw Chairman Meyer hurrying as fast as his eighty-year-old legs could carry him down the steps toward him.

"Don't answer that," Meyer said calmly. "Unless you want to get stuck here with me."

Johnny's mouth fell open. Surprised, he lowered his phone and let it ring itself into his voicemail. "Where do you think I'm going?"

Meyer's eyebrow peeked over his black-framed glasses at Johnny. "My best guess? The first flight you can get out of here. After that, it depends."

"On what?"

"On whether your father and Chloe are alive."

Dekker pulled a face. "I thought you said we couldn't stumble here. That you needed me to head off these aggressive Russian tactics." He motioned vaguely back toward the glimmering bronze tinted Tower of Basel rising like a Babylonian masterpiece behind them. "Stability, trade agreements, blockchain, and all that jazz."

Meyer snorted a retort. "I'm afraid it's too late for that. Your Belgian friend had the staff put the breaking news on the monitors in the conference room. So, everyone here knows about the attack, the damage is done, you have to go."

Johnny spat an inaudible curse. Glancing up toward the one-way reflective glass of the BIS entrance he could imagined the group of truffle stuffing bankers clustered around the windows staring down at him, waiting to see what he did next. "Wonderful." He gave Meyer a considering look. "How did you get out of that mess without drawing a crowd?"

"Your friend, Li, good man, ran some interference, but I'm afraid that's fallen by the wayside now as well."

Johnny couldn't help but smile at the thought of Li Junxiong, commander of the Second Bureau of the Third Department of the PLA Unit 61398 making idle gossip with those round-bellied automatons. *You find true friends in the strangest places.* "Perfect."

"Listen, Johnny, you need to be careful. Someone's just taken a cheap, but serious shot at the United States, and they've put your family in their cross-hairs while doing it."

Dekker immediately thought back to his conversation with Hamilton-Smith and his collection of militant-looking technical advisors. The families had their intrigues, but outright confrontation and bloodshed was more than just frowned upon and rarely, if ever, occurred. As much as he wanted to blame Derek Hamilton-Smith for the coordination of the attack, something inside him told him it didn't fit.

His phone started ringing again. Johnny checked the number; it was another Virginia area code. "I'll have to take this, eventually."

Meyer put his hand on Johnny's shoulder. "Do what you need to do. I'll handle this. And don't worry about your spot on the committee, I've still got some pull around here, and it'll be waiting for you when you get back."

Johnny blanched. "I'm supposed to be your deputy and make things happen for you, not the other way around Uncle."

Meyer scoffed. "I've been dealing with these gentlemen for decades and no sudden influence of a brown-nosing Belgian pre-Madonna or Russian clique is going to change that behind these walls." He motioned toward the building. "Not to mention, I think your friend, Li will back my play and should make for a great conversationalist when I get back upstairs." The FED chairman gave Johnny an affectionate squeeze on the shoulder then turned up the stairs.

Alone, Johnny stared at his phone for a long moment as his feet began to navigate toward the Basel *Bahnhof*. *You can do this.* He stabbed the "Answer" button.

"Dekker..."

"Holy shit, Johnny, why haven't you been answering your phone?"

"Jack?"

A sigh of relief echoed across the line. "Who else? I'm here with Matt Chambers and Director Brown. We've got word about your father... he's alive, Johnny, he's all right."

For all his angst that he'd held inside about his father, a feeling of relief swept over him, but before he could even process it, the next words out of his mouth brought him to the edge of the precipice. "What about Chloe?"

The follow-on pause from the other end of the phone was so slight that most wouldn't have picked up on it, but to Johnny, the silenced yawned as wide and impassable as the thirteenth century ocean that separated the childhood friends.

"We're not sure."

The exasperated sound that Johnny made next was strangled into a hiss. "What does that mean, Jack?" "You guys put her into the same car as that arrogant self-centered old man, hell bent on staying in the game long past his expiration date, and then, you put them into an unknown situation with no prep or backup. And now you're not sure what happened to Chloe?"

Jack lowered his head. "It means we don't know." He paused a moment then continued to explain to his friend. "We're still piecing together what happened form a couple of bystanders and the security team survivors."

"Survivors?" The word fell from Johnny's lips like molten lead. This time the pause was poignant and long.

"Yeah, survivors, it was bad, Johnny. Several Marines are dead."

"Jesus, Jack."

"That's the job, they all knew it. That doesn't mean that she's dead too, Johnny," Jack cautioned. "The tropical storm did a number on the whole region last night. And the Search and Rescue teams only had time for a quick search of the area before they had to exfil the Ambassador. They couldn't find her body, she might..."

Johnny snorted. "...be alive? Find her, Jack."

"I'm on it, you've got my word." A brief uneasy pause cut short, by Jack most important piece of information. "Now, how fast can you get to Germany?"

UPPER EAST SIDE, MANHATTAN

The Manhattan skyline loomed gray and flat, almost indistinguishable from the pane of glass that separated Isabella Dekker's corner office on the 32nd floor overlooking Central Park from the spitting rain outside.

While business never truly stopped in Manhattan, it was mostly quiet in the offices of the Dekker Banking Group. True to their small-town Texas roots, the Dekkers didn't believe in working on weekends, and did their best to send most of their U.S.-based employees' home, though some worked remote regardless.

For Izzy, the quiet floor was a poor salve for the anxiety she felt. Since arriving at her office she'd been on a tear, calling up years of documents on her system, and spinning off more than a half-dozen database queries. Ian, bless him, had arrived a full hour before she had and delivered most of the data she'd requested on the phone. At the moment, he stood outside her door, talking animatedly, but quietly on his cell phone. He was apparently having a hard time chasing down all the players the boss wanted present in her 1400 meeting. He'd met her at the door to her office, a folder in hand, and a hot cup of coffee in the other.

"This is the Lee deal, and the abstracts from the last years' worth of South Asian work we've been involved in as a firm."

She snatched up the coffee and bee-lined to her desk with Ian in her wake. "I could've sworn I wanted three years' worth of the ASEAN files, didn't I, Oh, and why are the systems so damned slow?"

"Your requests are on the way ma'am. We'll have the rest of them ready for you by the time you've cracked the cover on this one."

"My EXCO meeting?"

"Almost there, ma'am. I've spoken with all of them except Vicky Chan, who's on maternity leave."

Isabella frowned. "She can conference in over Symphony."

Ian flinched and threw a quizzical look at his boss. "No ma'am, she went into labor a couple of hours ago."

"Didn't you tell me she wasn't due for another month?"

Ian shrugged. "Yes, ma'am I did, last month."

Before Isabella could respond, Ian pointed toward her array of flat screen monitors on her desk. "Query complete."

And like that - he'd gotten her back on track. Isabella glanced at the query results and frowned. "Ian?"

"Ma'am?"

"What's wrong with the network?"

"It's upgrade weekend, remember? The reason you took the no intrusion getaway weekend."

Isabella blinked dumbly.

"The geek squad needed this weekend to swap out new servers in our data warehouse and trading systems. You approved it last month." Ian patted her gently on the shoulder.

Izzy grinned in spite of herself and took a quick sip of her coffee to hide the smile. She watched through hooded eyes as her assistant moved about her office gathering reports and tidying the small explosions of clutter that always followed in her wake. She'd always felt particularly lucky that the young Texan was as capable as he was. After all, she'd hired Ian in a fit of spite after a run-in with one of Jack's more impressive ex-girlfriends. At the time, she'd been more interested in Ian's rugged good looks than his professional acumen. Luckily, he'd turned out to be far better at his job than even she expected. Still, as pretty as Ian was, it was his completely unflappable nature that made him so valuable to her. No matter how frantic and high-strung, Isabella might get, Ian remained as calm as a West Texas heatwave. Jack hadn't been happy when he met the young man, but over time, and after meeting Ian's equally attractive boyfriend, he'd warmed to her new assistant, and things had gotten better all around.

For a while, she'd buried herself in the abstracts. Most of the information was high level, but it gave her an opportunity to reacquaint herself with the deals long forgotten, as well as those that had simply never risen to her notice. Names and places scrolled through her mind, some of them not meaning anything, others brought memories of her time in their Taipei office screaming back. A far too brief, and extremely enjoyable period she still looked back on with genuine pleasure. There was a part of her that could've enjoyed bouncing around the Pacific Rim, honing her language skills, and exploring the countryside's of the ancient cultures that laid the foundations for our modern civilization. But between family expectations, as well as her own fierce sense of competition, the exotic names and places had to remain as fond memories and wishful daydreams.

After an unproductive hour, she set the abstracts aside and looked glumly down at her empty coffee mug. She tipped the lid on the coffee service that Ian had brought in for her before disappearing to coordinate the afternoon meeting. *Empty.*

Just like these abstracts. Nothing is standing out as an issue. Maybe I need to broaden the scope, or maybe there's nothing to be found? What about the sovereign wealth funds? She tapped her fingernail on the stack of reports. *It might be worth looking into.* Rising competition in the regional capital markets scene spurned by the globalization efforts of the western banks, and all too willing international expansion of the State-Owned Enterprises out of China, particularly those looking toward Southeast Asia meant that many investors would be looking for stable, long-term places to shore up their portfolios. The primarily central bank managed sovereign wealth funds (SWFs) were often massive pools of capital that were not susceptible to the fluctuations in more volatile markets, their investment mandate centered on large buy and hold strategies.

Unless you do something drastic - like maybe try to assassinate an American ambassador or release a plague they kept a steady course. Isabella felt a stab of climbing worry start to worm its way into her stomach. She pushed it down and fished out her cellphone, punching out a quick message to Ian on an encrypted messaging service, asking him to bring her the latest Asia Pacific League tables. Whether a state actor or a rival bank, perhaps these additional stats could shed some light on her suspicions. Her phone range an instant later.

"Ma'am - would you like me to bring them to you in the meeting?"

Flustered, Isabella glanced at her watchband realized it was only minutes before the department heads meeting and the handful of senior executives either still in town or capable of calling in over a secured Symphony conference line.

"The meeting, please. Oh, and Ian?"

"Ma'am?"

"A triple espresso as well, thanks."

Izzy left the abstracts behind but snagged her empty coffee mug - (priorities) - and headed out of her office, and around the corner to the executive briefing room. The lights were up, and the shades were down, blocking the excellent view of Central Park South normally afforded its attendees. She felt a dozen set of eyes lock on her as she entered the room and took her place at the center of the polished mahogany conference table. There were key executives from several core departments in physical attendance - as well as one or two of the non-Dekker family partners. She graced them all with a brief, and rather tired smile.

"Good afternoon, everyone, I apologize for having to hijack your weekend, but there's been an incident that's going to require a short-term change in our protocols. For those of you that haven't been watching the news, about twelve hours ago, our previous CEO was the target of an attack in Malaysia."

As expected, the room erupted with mixed emotions, some surprised others distressed at the actual confirmation. Isabella waved the noise down with her hands and noticed with pleasure that Ian had somehow slipped the triple espresso to her while she spoke, she took a sip. Looking down the continent-sized table, she found him already handing out the stacks of freshly printed reports to the assembled executives. Before she could speak, Angus Henry, one of the ambassador's oldest friends, and one of the original partners of the Dekker Banking Group, spoke.

"Is he all right?"

The question was delivered with the same gentle drawl that reminded Izzy of home, somewhere in the dry heat of west Texas. She smiled at Henry, knowing that, at least from him, the question also inquired if she was all right.

Isabella blanched. "Unknown, but I'm working on getting us more information. Unfortunately, we cannot determine whether this was a personal attack against the Ambassador, or something part of a larger narrative, including a move against the bank." While Isabella discouraged excessive speculation, she knew that the people in front of her had already started running different courses of action through their minds as to what the attack meant, and what might come of their careers. They were all paranoid by nature, and with the combined power of their brains and their shared desire to remain employed and thriving, they would get to the bottom of the situation if it had anything to do with the bank's future. Izzy sipped her espresso and continued. "Regardless, prudence demands we err on the side of caution. Effective immediately, I'm elevating the bank security protocols. Senior executives and partners are to be provided protection, and there'll be a temporary moratorium on any of our dealings in the Asia Pacific region, with a concentration on Southeast Asia."

A few faces turned pale - particularly those with large ASEAN private and institutional clients. Meg Li, one of the China team's leaders raised her hand. "If we know so little about the attack, is it really necessary for us to escalate?"

"Good question, Meg. Call it prudence or call it a drill but remember someone just took a shot at a man that built this company from the ground floor to the thirty-second floor we're meeting on. That might not mean anything to some, but it does to us. As of right now, we're taking it personally."

She was met with a mix of poker-faced attendees, but wasn't surprised, no executive at this level would be wearing their emotions on their sleeve, regardless of how they felt about the founder. Only Angus Henry seemed openly pleased at the heightened sense of urgency around the security of the bank. "That works for me. What's next?"

"I want you all to review the files that Ian is handing out. Look for problems: misallocations, reallocations, disgruntled clients. Look for coincidences. Look for any reason why someone would be upset with the bank. Until then, I recommend that we all instruct our traders to consolidate and unwind all their market positions, starting with the least liquid and working down. Then, once we have more clarity and depending on the state of the market, we think about phase two - the *Gabriel Protocol*. Other than that, we're business as usually people, we've got thirty-six hours until the markets open."

"The *Gabriel Protocol*?" Henry asked.

Isabella closed her eyes a moment, then looked down the table. "It's like I just said, let's get through phase one and reassess if any further action is needed."

After answering a few more random, but very relevant questions around the table, the meeting adjourned. The international group of executives wandered off in close conversation, cell phones working nonstop.

Izzy watched as she shook her head. *Wrecking their subordinate's weekends as well. Can't be helped if nothing else it's a good operational exercise.* She felt a warm hand fall on her shoulder as she turned to see Angus Henry smiling down at her.

"Things are in good hands here," he said. "So, I'll get out from under foot."

Izzy smirked with a nod. "Off to a meeting on the back nine?"

Henry chuckled. "You know I despise golf. I'm going to go shoot something. Ian says we've a corporate membership to the range on Staten Island, I thought I'd try that for a while."

Izzy laughed. "Just grab the pass from him on the way out, and Angus, shred me some paper targets while you're at it."

"Keep me up on John, would you darling?"

"You're my first call," Izzy replied.

Another brief squeeze on her shoulder, and Angus disappeared through the foyer in search of Ian and his corporate pass. Her espresso cup now mysteriously empty and a vague sense of unease began to settle in for good in her stomach. She needed food. Pulling out her cell phone she started to text Ian to go ahead and bring the lunch to her office, but as she did, she phone started to ring, startling her heightened senses. A quick glance at the number and her heart skipped a beat.

"Johnny?"

For a long moment, there was only background noise, on the other side of the connection, Izzy stood still for a moment trying to boost reception, before starting to chase the bars toward her office. Her ears pricked at the sound of jets taking off and landing.

"Izzy…"

Her cousins voice sounded flat, and a million miles away. "I'm here."

"I've spoken with Jack, senior is fine, he's alive."

Izzy stepped through her office doors and sat down behind her desk. "That's wonderful news, we were so worried. And Chloe?"

Johnny cleared his throat. "It's unclear."

Izzy's hand covered her mouth to suppress a small cry of dismay, as her cousin's words brought her worst fears to life. She mustered herself, but before she could speak, the noise and disarray on the other side of the phone disappeared as if he'd walked inside a building. "Where are you exactly?"

"I'm headed to Germany to meet the military transport carrying my father. I need some answers, and I need them from the source not some dissected and filtered Langley version, I'll let you know more when I see him. This is my new private number. Keep your phone close."

Izzy nodded alone behind her desk, stunned into silence as a dial tone replaced her cousin's voice. She was immobile, something about the uncertainty of Chloe struck a chord, and yet she was calm. *Why did I have to be right?*

8

RAMSTEIN AFB, GERMANY

A metronomic drip from an antiquated commercial coffee machine echoed across the cold, dark waiting room harkening to a sleep deprived Johnny Dekker like a siren on the rocks calling out to a wary sailor lost at sea, searching for land on the far side of the world. Johnny wrung his hands as he paced the black and white checkered floor. The flight from Basel had been fast, too fast in fact. With flights departing for all parts of Europe every hour, Johnny had caught a cab to the airport in Basel, Switzerland, and stepped onto a regional flight to Germany in less than thirty minutes. He arrived in *Zweibrucken* an hour later, rented a car, and blazed down the Autobahn to *Landstuhl Medical Center* in record time. After making a few phone calls he'd started raising hell with the military hospital's staff until they'd found a military liaison that confirmed his credentials and put him in contact with the surgical team assigned to his father, the Ambassador.

"I understand your concerns. And I promise your father will get the best medical treatment we can provide," a white-haired Air Force Colonel told him calmly. "Just as soon as he gets here."

Johnny blinked stupidly. *"When he gets here?"*

The Colonel nodded. *"They're arriving from Malaysia, son. His flight isn't scheduled to land for another four hours."*

For a moment, Johnny saw red as his temper hit a flash point that threatened to spill over into a violent reaction. His face flushed and his fists clenched, but as soon as the volcanic paroxysm of anger had struck, it was gone, replaced by exhaustion, despair, and more than a little embarrassment.

"Right, I should've known that."

The Colonel grinned. *"It's hard when it's family. Your brain sort of short circuits until you know they're going to be safe."* He rested an oversized hand on Johnny's shoulder. *"They're sending your father here because we're the best. There are great trauma centers in Australia and Japan to be sure, but none that are as secure as we are, or as experienced treating combat casualties."*

The Colonel led Johnny to the waiting room, armed him with a large paper cup of coffee, and promised to let him know the moment the military transport carrying his father touched down.

For nearly twenty minutes, Johnny simply sat and stared into the black pool of his rapidly cooling coffee. His brain ranked, processed, and unpacked everything he'd experienced in the past 36 hours. The mission brief, the flight to Europe, the train ride with the chairman, and running into that dickhead, Derek, and now, this.

Chloe....

Johnny pained at the thought of Chloe, his bride-to-be, hurt and alone, not letting himself even consider her potential death. Then his thoughts turned to his father. *I told you that she wasn't a field agent anymore. Why didn't you tell me that she was on your detail? Why did you let her go?* An alien feeling of disconcerting welled up inside as he felt a tear trickle down the side of his face, reflection of a deeper unspoken concern. He brushed away the tear and calmed his breathing as he stretched out his arm and placed the cold coffee on a side table. This wasn't constructive, sitting on his hands. He needed to do something. He needed answers.

A frantic Johnny reached into his pocket and rummaged around for his cell phone, pulled it out, and checked for new messages. *What the hell was I thinking? I gotta get on this now. I can't let the trail run cold. Think Johnny.* He thumbed through his missed calls: *Izzy, Izzy, Izzy, Izzy, Unknown? Something familiar about the 60-country code...Malaysia!* Without hesitation he pulled up his voicemail to check if the caller had left a message, out of the five missed calls there was only one message. He thumbed his way over the message and keyed it to play. The voice that came on the line was either computer generated, or heavily veiled by an encrypted software, no hint of the caller's sex could be determined, and there was dead silence in the background.

"Johnny, it's Striker. I've information regarding the attack on your father. Your friends at the CIA can't be trusted. Come to Penang, ask for me at the restaurant Nasi Kandar. I'll find you."

Stunned and immediately wary, Johnny saved the voice mail and thumbed his way over to one of the specialized apps on his phone. One of the benefits of working within the US intelligence apparatus was access to specialized applications you couldn't find on any app store. This was that kind of app. Johnny found the icon which was a simple "5i" in courier font. Thumbing the app alive, he was given a simple black and white interface with two options "phone" and "Internet". He selected "phone". After a moment, a full list of the phone calls and their messages his secure phone had received (or made) popped into existence. He found the unknown number from his voice mail and selected it. There was a short delay followed by a dump of XML code to the screen.

When in doubt, check the metadata.

Johnny scrolled slowly, his mind parsing through the different tags that represented information about the incoming call including the location of the call's start, as well as the routes it had taken through the telco infrastructure to make it to his phone. It only took him a moment to see that he was working with a spook.

Or I'm being set up by one.

The number showed it had originated from the United States, in

Orlando, Florida - Disney World to be exact. Johnny smiled and scanned through the rest of the hops the call had made before landing in his voice mail.

Africa, Europe, Asia, and back through the Midwestern United States. Someone spent some quality time spoofing this call. Johnny snorted a laugh and dismissed the app with a swipe of his thumb.

What they failed to realize was that Johnny and Striker were friends. Johnny pondered dialing Striker and confirming his suspicion, but if the enemy had his phone, it could tip his hand. He stared at his phone for a long moment, weighing the options and considering the warning that "his CIA friends" couldn't be trusted. As cryptic as it sounded, he knew that the first action of anyone trying to PSYOP him would include trying to separate Johnny from his support base. Still, the niggle of worry that had chewed at the edges of his thoughts showed that the tactic was working.

Old tricks are the best tricks, I suppose. Still, why bother with friends when I've family. Johnny flipped back through his phone to find Jack's number. He stabbed the call button and was pleasantly surprised when his friend answered on the first ring.

"Johnny? Are you okay? Where the hell are you?"

Johnny stood and paced the empty waiting room looking for a quiet corner away from the entrance and the television rambling on in German. "I'm five by five, brother. Listen, I need your help."

Blood drained from Jack's face as he recalled the last time his best friend had asked him for a favor almost twenty years ago. "They don't send cleared personnel to Juvenile Detention when they break the rules. It'll be Leavenworth this time, Johnny." Jack's voice dropped an octave. "Hold on." Jack went silent for a long moment.

Recognizing the situation, Johnny held the line. He stepped back one foot from the waiting room window until the light, at just the right angle, projected the entire room behind him onto the window. Satisfied the room remained clear he turned and walked back toward the coffee machine. A shuffling noise followed by Jack's panting voice reignited the speaker.

"Johnny?"

Johnny cleared his throat. "Here's the thing. I need you to take Director Moore aside and tell him that I need to get to Malaysia, Penang specifically, and I need to get there yesterday. Pull strings, improvise, whatever it takes - make it happen."

To his credit, Jack didn't miss a beat. "Done. Where are you right now?"

"*Landstuhl Medical Center*, Germany, as we discussed earlier. I jumped the gun a little though, the inbound C-17 won't be here for another few hours, and I'm crawling the walls."

"Might take us that long to put something together for you on this short of a notice, are you sure you want to do this?" Jack asked.

Johnny breathed into the speaker. "I've never been more certain about anything in my life."

"Can I ask, why?"

Johnny quickly told his friend about the anonymous voice mail and the cryptic message he'd received about not trusting the Company. Jack also knew Johnny had extensive networks in Asia, but if that network had been disrupted, he needed to get on the ground under the radar. Jack whistled appreciatively.

"Wow, that just shines a whole new light on this doesn't it?"

"That it does. Is Moore still there?"

"He's walking toward me now. Do you want to talk to him?"

Johnny took another paper cup and filled it with the only thing available, black sludge. "Not yet, but keep this between the two of us for now, you got me?"

He raised a brow at the length of the pause on Jack's end of the phone, which meant that his friend was weighing the implications, he didn't blame him, but Johnny needed to keep the information tight until he had a clear path to the target.

"You're not taking that call seriously, are you?"

"Maybe," Johnny confessed. "Who from Langley is there with you?"

"The director, and some section head named Matt Chambers."

Johnny's eyebrows quirked in surprise. "Matt's there?"

"Yeah, he says you guys worked together before, is that not true?"

"It is." *What has Jack shared with Matt? How close is Matt to this?* "Does he seem put out to you?"

"Put out because you went rogue on him back in the day? Or because you basically went rogue on the director and left the FED chairman high and dry in Switzerland, or put out because he's been hanging out in an NSA SCIF since 0400?"

"All of the above?"

"Hard to tell, he's got a good poker face, brother."

Johnny grinned. "Well, for now, let's keep this to family only."

"Might be hard just to keep this between me and Moore. Langley brought a team of data crunchers in to work with us and Moore wants to keep Director Brown happy. They look like they're here until we put this whole attack thing to bed."

Johnny grimaced. "Damn. Well, do what you can. Do you think Moore will go along?"

"As you said, it's family. He'll be fine. Plus, I think he's a little scared of Izzy."

Johnny laughed. "We're all scared of Izzy," he said and smiled as he heard Jack choke back a laugh. The two men enjoyed a moment of levity, but the fleeting joy in Jack's voice went away as he spoke next.

"Johnny, we still don't know what happened to Chloe."

Johnny's smile died away. A blank stare fell upon his face as he searched for a fixed point beyond the waiting room windows, trying to keep his emotions in check, but needing to wrap up the call and get moving.

"You know I'll tell you as soon as we know anything for certain on Chloe, she's like a sister to my, Johnny."

Johnny sighed. "I know you will. Just get me on the ground in Malaysia, I've got to run this supposed *Striker* down."

"Wait, what did you just call him?"

"Striker, he's an old friend of Chloe and mine. But someone's trying to use his name to lead me either on a wild goose chase or straight into a trap."

"Johnny, Striker was the one that set the Penang meet," Jack replied.

For a long moment, a dead silence hung on the Iridium uplink until a deep and angry voice echoed a reinvigorated plea. "Get me on the ground, Jack."

"Roger that."

9

GRAND CAYMAN

David Blevins shoved the last of the blade servers into its enclosure with a grunt of effort. Stepping back, he took a moment to wipe sweat from his forehead and admire his work. The three enclosures, each taking up a third of the tall server rack, housed a total of 36 small servers crammed with enough RAM and CPU to manage a NASA mission to Mars.

"You're beautiful, baby," he whispered running his fingers along the array of hardware. "You're beautiful and really, really fucking expensive."

The server equipment had been trickling in all week, flown in at fairly hefty expense to the old seaside villa on the Caribbean island's West Bay. Every couple of days for the past two weeks, there had been a steady stream of FedEx trucks and local couriers beating a path to David's door. He had made a game telling the delivery drivers increasingly wild stories when they invariably asked what he was going to do with all the computer hardware.

"*Pet real-estate website.*"

Or

"*I manage scrap metal futures.*"

Or his personal favorite…

"*Porn.*"

Word had gotten out about the whole porn thing too, and David had been flooded with would-be porn stars looking for an audition, as well as most of the islands unemployed, bored, or simply curious hoping to catch a glimpse of the new "Internet porn" business that was being spun up in the old villa. There had even been a very motivated local church group that showed up with everything but tar and feathers, ready to either save David's soul or burn the demons out of him.

And they didn't seem to care which it was going to turn out to be.

His employer hadn't been happy about any of it. The very scary, if not very attractive project manager, Anja Singh, had been David's only point of contact since the job had started. When she'd found out what David had been telling people, the look on her face had told him that he'd made a terrible, terrible mistake.

"*This pattern of behavior is unacceptable,*" she'd said in a flat, almost toneless voice that gave David the willies. "*If you continue to draw unwanted attention to you it will end in your termination.*"

She'd left it at that, and as happy as David was to have avoided a "resume generating event," he had the feeling that the kind of termination Anja referred to was far more permanent than what he was used to.

"Is this all of it?"

The unexpected voice startled David out of his reverie. Turning from the wall of technology he turned to see, his boss, Anja regarding him from behind a pair of mirrored sunglasses.

"Hey boss," he said. "I didn't expect you back so soon." David winced a little as his voiced cracked with a nervous note.

If Anja noticed his unease, she didn't show it. "How long until we're operational?"

David shoved his hands in the pockets of his cargo shorts and shrugged as he chewed on a toothpick and stepped toward the window. "Hardware's all here," he said. "The telco finished running fiber to our DMARC yesterday, and I'll have our switches hooked up and configured tonight. Once we get the coolers delivered it won't be more than three or four days before we're online."

She frowned and released a subtle sigh. "Three or four days." It wasn't a question, and she didn't sound happy as she ventured forward into the villa.

David squirmed a little. "Can't be helped, "he said, and gestured toward the enclosure filled rack system. "We can't spin these monsters up without better AC installed."

"Your comfort isn't exactly the priority here and not what we're paying for its your skill and expediency," Anja began, but the computer nerd interrupted her, oblivious to her emphasis on the timetable.

"It's not my comfort I'm worried about. Your servers though, they like it nice and cool when they're online. You let them run in this villa without better air conditioning and they'll get the ambient in here up to 90 degrees in under a couple of hours."

"And this is bad?" Anja prodded.

"Are you kidding? The onboard terminal sensors will start shutting systems down if it stays too hot for too long. If you want this data center to run for any amount of time at all, we've got to wait for the air conditioners I've ordered."

The mirrored shades turned toward him, and David shivered a little as the woman cast her focus on him.

"When are we getting these cooling units?"

"Should be here tomorrow," he replied. "The weather has been good, so deliveries have been ricky-tick. We're lucky you know; hurricane season is coming, and things will clamp down pretty tight when the storms start rolling through."

The woman ignored his diatribe and brushed by David, walking across the room to a smaller rack of servers that were already in operation. She watched the I/O lights repeated flicker for a long moment before glancing back at him.

"You've received the software images I sent you." Again, it wasn't a question.

"Of course, I got 'em last week."

"You've installed them on the test hardware?"

David nodded. "Piece of cake."

"Good." The woman gave him a tight nod and removed her glasses, giving David the full force of her dead shark eyes. "Our timelines are very precise, it's imperative that we've the system up and running within the next couple of days."

David hands trembled as her tone cut into his soul. "No problem, I'll get it done. You can count on me."

"See that you do."

David brushed the sweat from his forehead and fidgeted with his change in his pockets as Anja gave his ad hoc server room a last considering look. He watched her as she completed her silent inventory of his work, and not for the first time wondered exactly what kind of consulting business she was involved in. Anja had never offered details, but more and more, he wondered if it was connected to the mafia. After all, she was shelling out big money for the hardware, and she was paying him top dollar to do the work solo.

I'm being paranoid, Anja is totally normal. This work is all above board, probably just some stateside e-commerce business looking for a disaster recovery data center. In an old villa. In the Caymans... Right.

David maintained his uncomfortable vigil as Anja inspected his work and checked over the pile of delivery paperwork, invoices, and other sundry bits of minutia that'd been waiting for her review. When she'd finished, she gave him a final reminder about their pending deadline, urging him with an incredibly disconcerting gentleness to not "disappoint" her.

As she grabbed her purse and cell phone form the villa's foyer, David made awkward small talk that Anja promptly ignored.

"I'll be off the island for the next few weeks," she told him. "When you're operational, call me. We'll handle the initial setup and integration with the network over the phone."

"Sure thing. Say, Anja, I've got a question."

She paused; her over-sized sunglasses poised halfway down the bridge of her nose. Her eyes held that same disconcerting flatness as she waited for him to speak.

"What's all this for?" he asked, gesturing to the server racks.

Anja's predator gaze pierced his awkwardness. After a long and very uncomfortable silence she pushed her glasses up, covering the twin pools of expressionless black.

"Porn," she said, and walked out the door.

FORT MEADE, MARYLAND

As Jack Sorenson put the phone down, he realized that he'd probably just agreed to something he shouldn't have. Behind him, Walter Moore and the CIA ASEAN operations guy, Matt Chambers stood, coffee cups in hand, concerned expressions on their faces, and waiting for his update.

Chambers was the first to speak. "How's our boy holding up?"

Jack sighed as he faced the two men. "He's Johnny. He's holding up about as well as you'd expect an operative of his experience and wit."

Chambers chuckled. Somewhere along the way, Jack noticed that the Company man had lost his tie and had rolled up the sleeves of his dress shirt to expose overdeveloped triceps and just a hint of a gothic tattoo.

"He's ready to blow the world up, isn't he?" Chambers continued with a Kodak smile.

Just Penang, Jack thought grimly. But he just gave Chambers a shrug and a weak smile feigning fatigue in his reply. He stood and stretched, trying to stall a little for time as he continued to process Johnny's request.

He wants me to get him to Penang and he doesn't want me to tell anyone at Langley about it. Not normally a big deal, but hard to do now that I'm heading the task force and I've the director of CIA and his ASEAN agent here in the same SCIF with me.

Jack glanced over at Moore. "Hey boss, I'll be back in a few minutes. I need to throw some water on my face and give Izzy a call."

Director Moore's quirked his eyebrow. "Sure thing, Jack. Everything okay?"

Sorenson waved his boss's look of concern away. "It's fine," he lied. "Johnny just has some bank stuff he needs Izzy to take care of and I need to check in with her after the way I left it this morning."

Moore seemed to consider his words for a few seconds, but nodded, and made shooting motions at Jack. "Begone, I don't want to be in earshot when you call your fiancée."

Dismissed, Jack walked toward the SCIF door, noticing out of the corner of his eye, that Matt Chambers had set his coffee cup down and had the look of a man intent on following him all the way to the bathroom. *Not good*, he thought.

Luckily, Walter Moore noticed the same thing. With a touch, the NSA Director diverted the CIA executive, leading him off toward a bank of monitors, asking him questions the entire way. Jack thanked the maker once again for being surrounded by people that seemed way more keyed into subtext that he ever had been. Wasting no time, Jack made his way out of the SCIF and headed down the mostly empty hallway towards the bathroom.

Once inside, he stared at himself in the mirror, and winced, as it looked like the entire weight of his weekend had landed directly on his face. His eyes had huge dark rings under them, and his sandy hair was stiff and matted. Turning the faucet on, he let the water warm, then began to wash his face.

After a few minutes of self-care, he felt better, but his problem still wasn't solved. He only had a few minutes to contemplate the problem when Director Moore walked into the bathroom.

Jack reached for a paper towel. "Hey…" he began, but Moore just smiled.

"What's going on, Jack?"

"I think you mean to ask what's not going on, sir."

Moore sighed and leaned up against the wall while Jack made an art out of drying his hands. "Let's recap. You talk to Johnny for what, all of five minutes? Then, you kinda look like you have swallowed a big bug, covered in soap, and oh, by the way, the bug? Yeah, it's still alive."

"That's gross, boss," Jack began, but the look he got from the NSA director brought him up silent again.

"So, next, while digesting this living bug, you tell me you need to take a minute and splash some water on your face, which, yeah, I get it, but left me suspect. You've been up for hours, and we've not exactly been taking a lot of breaks since all this kicked off. But then, you fucked up."

"I did?"

Moore reached into his pocket and pulled out Jack's cell phone and waggled it at him. "Forget something?"

"Fuck...." Jack pinched the bridge of his nose. He'd completely forgotten he had given it to Walter when they entered the SCIF.

Walter grinned at him. "Now, I'll give this back to you, once you tell me what has you so upside down after talking to Dekker."

Jack sighed and leaned against the sink. "Is this place secure?" he asked, looking around the bathroom.

"Not in the slightest," Moore replied. "Now spill it."

Jack launched into the anonymous call and potential conspiracy angle about the CIA involvement. He caught him up on everything Johnny had told him.

The NSA director was frowning in thought when Jack finished. "Johnny realizes that going to Penang, particularly right now, is a terrible idea, right?"

Jack shrugged. The bags under his eyes weighed him down as he leveraged support of the sink. "He's Johnny Dekker."

"What's that supposed to mean?"

"You of all people, know his responsibilities. You know there are things that are put in his path beyond the intelligence apparatus. You know the family. You know the heir. You know the Council commitments and the impossible position he's in right now trying to balance it all. He doesn't need our approval or our help on anything least of all getting to Penang. He's just hoping that between us we can get him there, faster. And maybe, just maybe it's enough."

Walter Moore swore silently under his breath. He shoved both hands in the pockets of his slacks and spent a long moment staring at the tips of his shoes.

"I don't like it," Moore said finally. "But I think you're right. There's not a lot we can do if he decides to jump ship on his own."

Jack nodded. "What about the whole Striker thing?" he asked.

"I like that least of all," Moore said and motioned to Jack to follow him out of the bathroom. "That has 'trap' written all over it."

The pair walked in silence down the hallway. To Jack's surprise, Moore continued past the SCIF 17 door.

"Dinner time?" he asked.

"Operations."

"Why?"

"We're going to see about getting Johnny Dekker to Penang," Moore said heavily. He glanced over at Jack struggling to keep pace so early in the morning, adding. "It's still a terrible idea, and you should know that if someone asks, I'm blaming you."

Jack fell silent and coy. "Gee, thanks boss."

"What are senior officer family members for if not deflecting potentially harmful accusations toward their subordinates?"

Jack was still confused. "If this is such a terrible idea, then why are we going along with it?"

"The United States is going to want this to go away," Moore said as he hit the "up" button on the stainless-steel elevator panel. "They're going to want to focus attention on the trade agreement again, and in doing so they're going to try to forget that we had Marines killed, and that we are still missing Chloe Campbell. Officially, we cannot do anything that will mess that up."

"So, this is the 'unofficial speech', where you allow us to bring the rain on the perpetrators and find Chloe by any means necessary?" Jack asked as the elevator door *Dinged* open.

Director Moore looked at his analyst with reinforced eyes. "Unofficially, we can have Johnny on the ground, kicking in doors and being a rich asshole losing his sanity over the attack on his family whom nobody can ignore. He'll shake the bushes and we'll see what slithers out."

"So, you're going to use him."

"I am, Jack," Moore said in his unwavering baritone voice. "And he's going to owe me for the rest of his life and be happy about it."

10

LANDSTUHL REGIONAL MEDICAL CENTER

Johnny stayed in *Landstuhl* long enough for the elder Dekker's MEDVAC flight to finally land on the rain covered tarmac. What had followed still seemed surreal.

The Marines of his father's protective detail were wheeled past him first. They were young men, most barely into their 20s, and still wearing their MARCAM. They were laid out on field stretchers set atop regular hospital gurneys for ease of movement, their bodies showing the violent results of the close ambush and rocket attack. Johnny shook his head as they passed through the doors toward the operating rooms. *Poor bastards.*

Then, without warning, a set of familiar faces emerged from the C-17 transport, something he hadn't expected, but brought a renewed sense of confidence that he'd get to the bottom of this entire debacle. *Now, I can get some answers.* The Company's Special Activities Division paramilitary duo that had joined the State Department's security detail in Kuala Lumpur, as part of Chloe's agreement to accompany the Ambassador to Penang, walked toward the unsuspecting American banker. These two were in their 30s, and although they were tough as nails, they were only flesh and bone, evidenced as they limped toward the sharply tailored civilian Dekker.

"What happened to the G5?" Johnny hurled across the rain-soaked tarmac.

The thick-skinned bullfrogs craned their necks toward Johnny and broke away from the ER-bound medical parade embracing their former team leader just outside the entrance. "Well, were told that you took it back to Hollywood. And from your pinstripes, it looks like they were right," the short tree-trunk of a man replied as their blood-soaked hands gripped in a solid handshake.

Johnny slapped him on the back. "What the hell were you doing with the Ambassador in Malaysia? I thought the two of you were still ghosting people outside of Kabul," Johnny asked.

"They made us an offer we couldn't refuse," he said.

Johnny snorted a laugh at the obvious Godfather reference, and for a brief moment forgot the circumstances that he and his band of merry men had been reunited. "Good 'ole Travis, your jokes are still lame brother."

Stretching his arm to catch the support of the wall the taller and thicker operator took a drink from his water bottle, cleared his throat, and then recycled it across the room with a helluva hook shot. "Chloe," he said turning and looking Johnny dead in the eye.

Johnny paused a long moment. In the distance, beyond the frogmen, he saw a group of nurses rolling another gurney off the plane. *Dad?* He smiled at his naval brothers and continued the brief conversation while his eyes followed the gurney procession. "I'm still playing catchup. What about Chloe? How was she involved with getting you out of Kabul?"

From out of nowhere, an eruption of clattering clipboard wielding nurses cleared their way past Johnny grabbing the wounded American assassins, and corralling them inside, despite Johnny's pleas. *What the hell?* "I'm talking to these guys. I need to debrief them?" Johnny yelled after them in vain as they disappeared through the electronic double doors. His head was flooded with imagery. *How the hell did Chloe get these two reassigned, unless... Director Brown.*

The last to be brought into the hospital was Johnny's father. Ambassador John Dekker was arrayed like his Marines. His battered body atop a field stretcher, his expensive suit caked in dried blood still stood in contrast to the battle dress of his security detail. His father was shirtless, a large plastic covered bandage was taped over much of his chest, and an oxygen mask strapped over the thick head bandages. A tired looking field medic in Navy blueberries followed behind, hand carrying an IV drip bag, following the rapidly moving gurney and its attendant doctors down the hallway toward the surgery ward.

Johnny had barely gotten a glimpse of his father's face before he was wheeled out of sight, but that moment was enough to get his blood boiling. *I told him it was a bad idea. Why can't the old man ever listen?* A very polite, but very firm female captain stopped him before he could follow the gurney through the doors.

"I'm sorry sir, you'll have to wait out here. The Colonel is going to prep your father for surgery and there isn't much time."

"How is he?" Johnny asked, though part of him was furious, and part of him was afraid of the answer.

"The ambassador is in serious condition. His left lung has collapsed, and there is shrapnel in his chest cavity that could prove difficult to remove, and a head wound."

Johnny blanched. He'd seen sucking chest wounds in combat, had even helped treat a fellow special operator with the same wound. Still, he'd never seen his father suffer hurt worse than a sprained ankle on the golf course. His father, normally a big, vital man, seemed somehow shrunken, somehow - diminished.

"When can I see him?" Johnny asked.

"Not for while I'm afraid," the captain replied. "The surgeries could take hours, and once it's done, we'll need to isolate your father to ensure he doesn't pick up any secondary infections. There is a billeting on the post, I'd recommend you find a room and check back in with us in the morning."

The captain gave a sympathetic squeeze on the shoulder and pointed him back toward the waiting room. "Please sir, have a seat. We'll let you know when you can see your father."

Johnny had allowed himself to be steered back toward the waiting room. His paper cup of coffee was still there, looking oily and cold as he took his seat again. He had barely taken his seat when a confused looking Air Force Major in a flight uniform stepped into the waiting room. He looked around the mostly empty room until he found Johnny.

"Excuse me, sir. Are you Johnny Dekker?" His voice was a pleasant southern rumble that was similar to, but different to the one he had grown up listening to in West Texas.

Johnny looked up, surprised. "I am."

The big man smiled and offered his hand. "Sir, I'm Major Mike Newel with the North Carolina Air Guard, I've been ordered to take you to Okinawa."

Johnny blinked at his words. "Okinawa?"

"Yes sir. As I understand it, you were needing to go to Penang, Malaysia, am I right?"

"Correct."

"Well, I can't help with that. DOD just put an official travel ban on most of Malaysia after what happened to your father. That said, we can get you pretty close. Okinawa is still open for us to fly to, and you can pick up a civilian flight from there if you need to."

The flyboy looked around the waiting room rather doubtfully. "Did you have any luggage with you?" he asked.

Johnny stood up and laughed. He didn't. "What's the NorCal Air Guard doing here Major?"

"Support for Operation Enduring Freedom. We've been flying people and supplies into Afghanistan for the past five months. Got stuck here in Germany thanks to a hydraulics problem."

"Bit of a diversion for you isn't it, going all the way to Okinawa?" Johnny asked.

The Major shrugged. "Someone higher up the food chain than me made that happen. You ready to go, sir?"

For a moment, Johnny hesitated. His father was fighting for his life just beyond the double doors to the surgical ward. The same father that he had looked up to and admired his entire life. Wasn't it a son's duty to be here now? Johnny felt a heart wrenching need to stay, but there was another part of him, one that remembered the arrogance of this same father that disregarded his warnings about Malaysia, and that had coerced his fiancée into taking the same risk.

You have to find out what happened to Chloe. She may be fighting for her life without the benefits of military doctors and surgeons.

Despite the fire churning in his core and rising into his head about his father, the indecision gripped him, did he stay with his father holding to a son's duty, or did he fly halfway around the world and hunt down *Striker*, this nebulous lead that might explain why his father and Chloe were targeted in the first place?

"Sir, you alright?" the pilot asked gently.

Johnny shook himself and allowed the coldly rational part of his mind take over. His father would be in surgery for hours, and he'd be in recovery far longer. There was little he could do here other than wring his hands and wait. Man, that he was, Dekker that he was, he knew he'd never be able to sit and wait.

Neither could dad if he were in my place. He'd understand, hell he'd do the same thing. Decision firmed and expression hardened.

"Lead the way, Major."

11

BASEL, SWITZERLAND

For Derek Hamilton-Smith, the only thing more satisfying than watching a visibly distraught, Johnny Dekker leave the BIS building, was the knowledge that the American banking heir's life was about to get significantly more complicated.

For the European banking *Wunderkind*, the Economic Consultative Committee meeting at the BIS had gone off without a hitch. In fact, it'd gone exceedingly well, particularly for his Russian friends.

The grin that he'd worn since watching Johnny storm out of the conference earlier that day had never really left Derek's lips, but now, as he sat alone in his private suite watching two talking heads discuss financial markets, the grin was showing teeth.

"...How do the Americans respond?" One of the newscasters asked. "Malaysia's a friend and trading partner, so sanctions don't seem to be the answer, and what with the Pacific Trade Agreement hanging in the balance, it's highly unlikely that the Americans would censure a nation so integral to their trade agreement..."

The second newscaster's reply made Derek grin even more.

"...That's right, Ken. Malaysia's been central to the American plans for their new Asian trade deal, so leading with sanctions would be a non-

starter. That said, we're talking about an attack on an American diplomat, a strong response seems inevitable. But what? It's not like they can carpet-bomb Kuala Lumpur. Even as trigger-happy as this American administration has been known to be, even they're not so brash as to choose a military response to what appears to be an unprecedented and unprovoked attack on one of their diplomats..."

Derek waved an admonishing finger at the television. "Not unprovoked. Not hardly." One elegant hand dipped down to seize the stem of his wine glass, tipping an imaginary toast towards the television news team as they continued to talk in circles around any possible American response to the attack. He swirled and sipped a 1961 Chateau Palmer enjoying its balance and harmony, while he reveled in his nemesis' misfortune.

His cell phone started to ring erasing the smile from Derek's face as a new wave of emotions muted his self-congratulatory mood. He set his wine down and took up the phone, looking at the number with a raised eyebrow. A hint of a frown ghosted onto his face when he noticed the time, it was barely past midnight.

"Hello, Pavel. My, but it's awfully early for you to be calling. Didn't the chairman enjoy the *soiree* that you put on in his honor?"

There was a dry chuckle from the other end of the phone, along with the sounds of traffic and the low rumble of voices speaking Russian in the background. "The chairman enjoyed it quite a lot I think," Pavel Grigorovich said, his accented English heavy and slow. "But he's begged off any more entertainment, a very early morning meeting he says. I'm thinking he'll not be at his best."

The "Chairman" in question was, Raghuram Patel, the vice-chair of the Bank for International Settlement's Economic Consultative Committee, and a key proponent of utilizing blockchain technologies wherever and as soon as possible. He was also a firm believer in the BIS mission of gathering the decentralization technologies under its supervision. Derek's investigations had determined that Patel was an aggressive early adopter of technology within the bank, and a potential key ally in securing lucrative contracts for HSG and their new Russian backed Triple-Sec Quantum Resistant Blockchain solution. He was also a heavy drinker and fond of the "ladies", among other things, which was where Pavel and his Russian delegation came into play.

"No lasting damage done to the poor lad; I trust?" Derek asked.

"Russian children can drink more than he can," Grigorovich said dismissively. "He will be fine. But we did learn one thing you will be interested in."

"The suspense is killing me."

"Yes, he enjoys women, far too much for a man in his position I think."

Derek raised an eyebrow. "Is that right?"

"*Da*, he knew far too many of the strippers on first-name basis for it to be a coincidence."

Derek rolled his eyes. He had little use for those who couldn't manage their own appetites, but he was more than happy to use those foibles as leverage to get what he wanted.

"That *IS* interesting. I trust you're going to engage Mr. Patel tomorrow as well?"

"We are. Yuri is arranging for the entertainment. I am thinking of a private party is more suitable this time, somewhere secluded."

"Excellent, will there be video?" Derek asked.

"Even Kubrick would be happy with our camera work, Grigorovich said, vaguely insulted.

The Belgian banker smiled. "I'll leave this in your capable hands, Pavel."

"Is good. *Do Svidanya.*"

Derek began to hang up when he a thought crossed his mind. "Pavel?"

"Yes?"

"Contact your agent, make sure she's ready to move our plan forward."

"Getting the ducks in the row, I think. Of course."

"You're irreplaceable my friend." Derek said as closed the call and put his cell phone on the cushion next to him.

Alone in the dark with just the flickering light of the television,

Derek's smile grew. Pavel had ensured him that the agent he'd put on the job was not only very capable, but also highly motivated —for personal reasons. Derek considered that, and wondered if this agent's motivations were perhaps *too* personal? After a moment's thought he dismissed the concern.

You wanted the Dekkers stunned and reeling. Mission accomplished. Time to escalate.

GRAND CAYMAN

Sitting alone, in the Owen Roberts International Airport, Anja waited for her flight. ORI was not a particularly large airport as airports go, but the mixed drinks were plentiful, the scenery was excellent, and the rum, well, it was passable.

All in all, she was pleased. Her plans were proceeding apace, and she was confident that the IT help she'd acquired to build out this next step of the operation appeared to be on target.

Anja leaned back in her chair and smiled. This *David* she'd hired to setup the system here in the Caymans was good at his job. She'd picked him for his technical acumen of course, as well as his almost complete lack of ties to anyone else on the island. That last part was often key. It was always easier to dispose of unneeded tools when a job was over. Money only bought a certain amount of silence, and often it wasn't the lasting kind. That said, she didn't relish the thought of killing the young man, and genuinely hoped she wouldn't have to.

He's a flake, and almost desperately horny, but that just described half of the tech geeks you know. Plus, he's far better fodder as a fall-guy than just another body. It fits the narrative.

From within the depths of her bag, a massive thing made of mostly hemp and beads, her cell phone buzzed with an incoming text message. Frowning, she fished it out and flipped it around so she could preview the message without responding.

Cho: last batch of servers has shipped to mainland, all loaded with new firmware - will invoice

She allowed herself a real smile of pleasure at the news. These servers were integral to the next part of her plan, and the Russians she was working with had provided much of the network of programmers and other illicit contacts necessary to accomplish it. All that was needed now was for her little node here in the Caymans to come online to begin Anja's *Concerto in D Major.*

She leaned back in her chair and gazed out at the Caribbean. The waters were a little choppy, and the dark clouds on the horizon seemed to hint at harder weather to come.

A little storm is good for the soul.

She scrolled through her contacts until she found the one for a big Russian bastard that'd been her main handler since the job started. With deft thumbs she punched in a short message and sent it.

Anja: Servers have shipped

The response was only a moment behind her own message.

Grig: Good - Is phase 2 ready?

Anja: On schedule - IT ready to go in 7 days.

Grig: 4 would be better

Anja rolled her eyes. *Impatient Neandertal.*

Anja: Of course, will push to 4 if can, limited infrastructure

The response from her handler took a while. As she waited, Anja finished her rum and checked the time. She still had more than an hour until her flight, plenty of time for another drink. She motioned to the bartender who spirited her old glass away and returned moments later with a fresh glass filled with three fingers of Havana Club. She'd just taken her first sip when her phone began to vibrate, again.

Grig: understood...boss pleased with your work

Anja's eyebrows quirked up. For the ever-elusive "BOSS" to chime in was a surprise. Whomever he was, and whatever his motivations, he was paying the bills and covering the expenses for her to create nation state level problems for the much deserving Dekker family. She pursed her lips that morphed into a sour little smile as the thought of revenge worked its way across her steely face.

A job I would've happily done for free....

Anja: I look forward to my bonus

The only response she got was a string of laughing emoticons. Anja dismissed the client chat with the same sour smile and considered her drink again. They could laugh all they wanted, these Russian handlers of hers. She didn't know what their motivations were, or why their mysterious boss had it in for the Dekker's. After all, it had been knowledge of her own history with the family that'd brought the Russians to her doorstep. Anyone in their particular line of work knew about Anja Singh and her family, and the Singhs had plenty of reason to hate the Dekkers.

Still, all in all, it was good work. As little as she cared for the Russians, they were diligent, and professional, and regardless of her personal feelings, the money *was* good. Plus, there was also the satisfaction of a job well done to consider. After all, she'd enjoyed coordinating the hit on the Dekker motorcade, although not achieving her personal goal of complete elimination, the follow-on work of sewing chaos and confusion throughout the Malaysian business families soothed her. While entertaining, the misdirection and confusion she created had a very practical purpose, it would slow anyone that the Americans might put on her trail.

That thought gave her pause a moment. Who would they send after her? Some Tier-1 Counter-Terrorist unit to bungle its way through Malaysia looking for ISIS or some thread to a terrorist plot? Possible, but unlikely she thought.

The Americans are going to be very cautious. I've upset their trade agreement apple cart. Half of their leaders will want to blame China or Russia out of habit, the other half will see Muslim terrorists in every shadow, either way I should have ample time.

Anja tapped a very no-nonsense black painted nail distractedly on the marble bar top. A thought came to her that made her smile.

What if they sent baby Dekker, the boy wonder?

It was a delicious thought, and one that she'd dismissed almost instantly. The United States intelligence services were far too smart to send the younger Dekker after her, during a time of uncertainty. *What was his name? Ah yes, Johnny.* An entirely archetypical American sobriquet she decided. It was far too - Hollywood - for the U.S. to send the prodigal son after her, something out of a bad spy novel really. Son and heir of the Dekker Banking Group, former Navy SEAL, and Spook on the hunt for the (probably) brown-skinned bad-guys that almost killed his father.

Anja chuckled and sipped at her rum. No, as satisfying as it was to imagine putting the crosshairs of her favorite *Steyr Mannlicher* sniper rifle over Johnny Dekker's face, and enjoy the pain of the elder Dekker, it was simply not going to happen. As much as the ruggedly handsome young fool could use some 7.62mm steel jacketed facial reconstruction, the Americans would never be so stupid as to just *hand* her *both* of the Dekkers on a silver platter like that.

No, they're not that stupid -no one's that stupid.

12

FORT MEADE, MARYLAND

For his part, it'd all started innocently enough. After squeezing some Air Force types to give Johnny an unregistered lift to Okinawa, Walter had given Jack the rest of the evening off. "Get some rest," he'd said. "I'll manage our CIA friends."

"You sure you don't need me?"

"Oh, I could use you, but you've got another job, and there's no part of it that I want."

Jack flashed his boss a quizzical look.

Walter smiled at him, and the smile wasn't pleasant.

"You, my fine Casanova. You get to tell your girlfriend what we've just done."

Now Jack had mistakenly believed that Walter's implied concerns about Izzy would handle the news of Johnny's trip to Penang to be a fair bit of exaggeration. So, on the way home he'd decided to give her a call while he sat at a red light.

To say that Isabella was unhappy with the news, was the very definition of understatement. After some excruciatingly long minutes of listening to his fiancée spew military-grade expletives at him, he'd concluded he'd misjudged the situation.

"Are the three of you really that uncontrollably stupid?" She raged over the phone. "I expect as much from Johnny, and he at least has a *reason* to be stupid, it was his father that was attacked, and his fiancée that's missing. But seriously, Jack what are you and Walter *thinking*?"

"Izzy, honey..." Jack began.

"Don't you honey me; do you realize how much trouble this is going to cause?"

Jack resisted the urge to throw his cell phone out the window of his Shelby, never to be seen again, but thought better of it. Normally, he was famously immune to Isabella's rages, but this one felt different, this was a newer, more volcanic form of Izzy that he hadn't yet experienced.

"Izzy, Walter thinks that it's important that we've Johnny on the ground, in Penang, where everything went down."

"Well, of course Walter thinks that. Walter works for the government. Walter doesn't have investors breaking down his door wanting to know if the Dekker Banking Group is at risk. Walter doesn't have the press camping out outside of his corporate headquarters looking for an interview. Walter, gets to shake the goddamn trees and see what falls out."

"Bushes," Jack corrected her misusage of the classic Paul Newman line from his movie *Cool Hand Luke*, realizing too late that it was the wrong thing to say.

"What?"

Jack paused a moment, thinking whether or not to reply, before he continued. "It's shake the bushes, not the trees. Walter wants Johnny to shake the bushes and see what falls out?"

There was a strangled expletive from Izzy's side of the connection followed by a dial tone. She'd hung up on him. Jack smacked his steering wheel and put the phone back in his jacket pocket.

That could've gone better.

A long honk from behind him made him glance up. The light was finally green, or had it been green for a moment, and he was just tuning back into the world. He put the Shelby in gear and slowly pulled through the four-way and headed toward the Parkway on ramp. As he accelerated into traffic, his phone started ringing through the Mustang's Bluetooth. A quick glance at the display told him what he'd already expected, it was Isabella.

"Hello?" Jack winced at the uncertain rising note in his voice.

"Relax, Jack, I'm calm now."

"Okay."

"I am, for the moment. Whether or not I stay that way depends a great deal on how you answer my questions."

"You want to wait until I get back and you can drag me off to a black site?"

Isabella ignored the sarcasm. "Seriously, Jack? Why are you and Walter enabling him?"

Sorenson snorted a laugh. "Enabling, really? Are we forgetting who we're talking about? It's not like any of us could've stopped him from going to Penang. He doesn't need our permission. He doesn't need our logistics. He's stupid rich. Just like you. And if we'd told him no, he'd just have busted out his Dekker Banking Group Travel Card and made his own arrangements. At least this way, he knows we're on his side, and we know where he's at all times."

"Really, and that's all you're concerned about?"

"What? No...Yes...Why?"

"Jack, honey, I know this is hard for your very tiny man-brain to comprehend, but Johnny isn't a SEAL anymore. He's a banking executive moonlighting for the CIA to keep life interesting. We've more than ten branch offices across the globe, and hundreds of billions of dollars in assets under management. Johnny is the head of the family business-" And this last part she added emphasis to, knowing that Jack understood the Dekker family connection to the Council of Thirteen. "A family business that is going to be dramatically more complicated now that his fiancée, whom I should point out, is the second in line to the Campbell family business who are going to be furious and distraught when they get word."

Jack winced. "We had completely forgotten or at least hadn't factored in Chloe's family connection in all of this. But as Walter said, and as the head of the Moore family we needed to let Johnny run this down." A silence followed as he navigated the Parkway traffic.

"Your silence tells me that your man-brain is slowly starting to understand the absolute shit-storm that you and my cousin have left me to clean up. Has he.... has anyone, talked to Chloe's parents?"

Jack upshifted and pulled into the passing lane. "I've no idea."

"You've no idea. Then answer me this, when the media wants to know what he, the chief executive of the Dekker Banking Group thinks about the attack on his father, what does he plan on saying? Is he going to be interviewed sitting by his father's bedside or being taken into custody by Malaysian police after he's sanctioned the shit out of the bad-guys in Penang?"

Not good, she's starting to spit her hard syllables again.

"He's a CEO," Izzy barked into the phone, biting out each of the letters in the title. "Not Captain America, or any other lame superhero you boys might've fantasized about growing up. He has responsibilities, Jack. You understand that don't you?"

"Without a doubt, Izzy, but..."

"But what?"

"But well," Jack hesitated, he knew this next part wasn't going to make her happy. "Well, Johnny did take precautions you know."

"Do tell?"

"He put you in charge. He made you acting CEO." The phone went silent, and Jack felt that sinking sensation that always came along when he realized that he'd just said or done something stupid.

There was an inarticulate growl of purest frustration and verge-of-insanity pitch from Izzy's side of the phone, followed by a clear dial tone that echoed through his car.

Again.

13

PENANG, MALAYSIA

It was hot in the Malaysian State of Penang, far hotter than Northern Europe or the East Coast of the United States in November. After days of wearing the same Brooks Brothers suit, slowly stewing in his own juices, Johnny now looked like a tourist in new cargo pants, a loose cotton button-up, and a pair of black Altama OTB assault shoes. He sat alone at an outdoor cafe drinking a Coke loaded with ice, the Penang Bridge visible in the distance.

The trip with the North Carolina Air National Guard boys had been the fastest part of what had turned into two excruciating long days of sitting and waiting, not something he did well. Once in Okinawa, Johnny had worked every contact he knew to find flights, commercial and otherwise into Penang. He wanted to avoid popping up on anybody's radar and alerting his enemy. He'd made it, but by time he'd stepped off the Cathay Airbus 330, his frustration level was through the roof. He'd longed for his own private jet that sat readied and fueled in its hangar in West Texas. He missed the expediency and stealth of its electromagnetic engines.

Heavy black clouds still sat low and brooding out over the Strait of Malacca, a grim leftover from the recent once-in-a-century super typhoon. In the day since he'd arrived, the weather had remained hot and close, with a sky that seemed to promise another tropical storm or worse at any moment.

He sipped his Coke, made a screwed face, it was lukewarm, and tasted like pure syrup. His phone started to vibrate, and he answered it instantly, knowing without looking who was calling.

"Hey, Jack."

"Where you at?"

"Georgetown."

"Any contact with *Striker*?"

Johnny finished his drink with a bit of a *slurp*. "Nothing, so far. But I haven't bothered trying to link up with him yet."

Jack made a surprised noise. "What? Why?" he began, then stopped. "You're looking for Chloe."

"There's no body in the morgue. There's no mention of her in the police report. So, yeah brother, I'm looking for Chloe."

Jack's side of the line fell quiet.

"There's still a stain from the truck fires at the ambush site," Johnny said, his voice holding an oddly gentle note that surprised him. "I've talked to a couple of bystanders that didn't evacuate the city. Jack, nobody even remembers seeing her. It's like the earth just swallowed her up."

"I'm sorry man. I don't know what to say."

Johnny stared out at the water. He wasn't sure what he'd expected to find when he'd arrived. It wasn't like there hadn't been a small army of police combing the island after the attack, all of them intent on finding the attackers. He let out a long sigh and pushed his empty bottle around the table.

"What's my next move?" He asked.

"That depends," Jack replied.

"On?"

"Back here, what you do next depends on who you talk to. If you're talking to your cousin, you need to take your tiny man-brain and all of that testosterone it's swimming in and go be at your father's side, ready to play CEO of Dekker Banking Group, because the media is coming. And that media wave is going to have an impact on your business whether it's good or bad depends on you."

Johnny snorted a laugh. Jack sounded more than a little peevish, and he knew why. Isabella Dekker was passionate about the family business, which was why his very first act after taking the reins of the company was putting her in charge of it, while he took a role in title only. Still, he doubted that she'd taken the news of his side trip to Malaysia very well at all.

"Izzy's angry?"

"You have no idea," was Jack's rather dispirited answer.

"You might be surprised. Okay, so let's assume my testosterone-washed man-brain isn't ready to play CEO. Where do I go from here? What does Walter want me to do?"

Jack sighed. "Walter wants you to be a rich asshole."

"Excuse me?"

"He wants you to use your best judgement and see where that takes you. What was your plan?"

"It's fluid."

"I bet it is. Look, I'm not going to tell you what to do, because you'll just ignore it. But straight up, that phone call got you? *Striker*? Walter thinks that someone is trying to lure you into a trap."

Johnny frowned. "Maybe, but why?"

"Someone out there has it in for your family. If you ask me, which I know you won't, it sounds like some of that bloodline bullshit coming home to roost. You piss anyone off on the Council lately?"

"I don't know what you mean. And that's not how the Council works, Jack. We don't interact all that much, and when we do, it's usually benign in nature. There hasn't been discord in the bloodlines for-" and here, Johnny thought a moment. "Centuries I guess, maybe longer. A long time anyway."

Jack made a rude sound. "Aha, centuries, right. And what exactly was all that nonsense that you and your fellow councilman ole' Hamilton-Smith got up to in China a few years ago? That was discord with a capital D, or have you already forgotten about all that?"

Johnny rubbed the side of his face as he looked out over the bridge pondering Jack's words. He had a point. Johnny mulled the thought over in his mind for a long moment. Derek's actions in China had thrown things into a cocked hat for certain. But the man's entire operation had smacked of simple overreaching more than anything else. He remembered his father calling Derek, "a bull in a china shop of anti-tank mines." Still, it had taken intervention by key members of the Council, including Johnny's father and Abraham Hamilton-Smith, Derek's uncle, to reel the brash Belgian in, plus a few bold moves by Johnny himself.

"That was an aberration," Johnny said finally. "Derek is a dickhead, but he's been censured by the Council. He knows better than to try anything else like that again, let alone escalate to something like this."

The silence he was met with told Johnny that his friend wasn't convinced but wasn't ready to push the issue. Still, there was wisdom in Jack's assessment. The Dekker family had been inordinately affected by the attack. But was that intentional, or accidental? After all, nobody other than his father and the CIA director knew that Chloe was going to be in the convoy, and according to everyone he'd spoken to, his father's decision to be present at the meeting in Penang had been a last-minute event. Not something planned. How hard would it have been for someone to coordinate a hit like this? How long would they have needed to put the pieces in place? It was worth thinking about.

"So, what are you going to do?" Jack's question brought him full circle in their conversation.

Johnny mulled over his options, what there were of them anyway. He'd found no signs of Chloe, and the locals that he'd questioned had proven less than helpful. Most of them he managed to find and talk to hadn't actually seen anything, but he doubted that anything they said was true. They had simply been giving him second and third-hand accounts of the aftermath of the attacks. A canon of ominous details on the fire, the wreckage, and the dead men strewn across the bridge.

He leaned back in his chair and watched a boat out in the strait as it slowly worked its way toward the massive span of the Penang bridge in the distance. "I don't think I've any choice," he said finally. "I'm going to have to meet up with this *Striker* and find out who this impersonator is and who he works for."

"When?"

"The message said come to a restaurant, *Nasi Kandar*. He'll make contact with me."

"Scope it out," Jack warned. "Don't go into that place blind."

Johnny smiled. "Is the desk jockey schooling the pro now?" Johnny laughed out loud as he watched a married couple in the cafe turn and look at him.

"That's right, tough guy. And I'll tell you something else big shot, you've got great instincts, but Izzy's right about one thing. You've got a testosterone-washed man-brain, and right now you want answers and some payback. Those two don't mix. Be smart, be careful, and keep me in the loop."

"Yes, boss," Johnny retorted. "Give my best to Izzy." He signed off the call and put his phone away. He checked his Suunto Spartan wristwatch and found that he'd spent far more time at the outdoor cafe than he'd intended. It was late, he figured he had an hour or so before sunset.

"Well, if I'm going to walk into an ambush in a strange restaurant, why not do it in the dark."

He stood, left some money on the table to pay for his drink, then went looking for a taxi.

FORT MEADE, MARYLAND

Jack stared at the coffee pot in the break room. The pot was as distressingly empty of coffee as the break room was of other people obviously intending to make more coffee. None of which should be surprising, he reflected, as it was just after four in the morning.

Again.

He stared at the pot for a long moment, then accepted the fact that there just wasn't else anyone else that was going to come along and start feeding the industrial looking machine with filter and grounds. He sighed audibly and started going through the cabinets.

His movements were mechanical, his attention focused on Johnny's predicament thousands of miles away as he put a new filter in the machine and started to scoop something bitter and awful smelling into it. He stopped after two full scoops and realized he didn't really know how much he was supposed to add. Deciding he didn't really care all that much, he went ahead and added three more mountainous scoops, then started filling the pot with water.

You're not getting enough sleep, Jackie-boy. Boss sent you home to rest, you were supposed to rest. Not lie down for three hours then turn around and come back to the office.

His conversation with Johnny hadn't made things any better. The younger Dekker was understandably wrung out with worry for his fiancée, but he seemed to be keeping it together. Jack just hoped that his friend could somehow manage to keep his head in the game and not let the anger and frustration he had to be feeling lead him into some fatal dead end.

His thoughts grim, and the worry omnipresent, Jack almost dropped the coffee pot in surprise when he felt cold wetness assault his hand and arm. Cursing, he realized that he'd zoned out and let the coffee pot overfill.

Talk about needing to keep your head in the game.

He drained the extra water out of the pot and focused on his task long enough to start the coffee brewing without making any new messes or catching anything on fire. A small victory to be sure, but he'd take it.

Leaning back against the sink, Jack let the coffee brew and stared at the digital clock readout on the break room microwave. It blinked dully at him claiming to be 1200 hours, a victim of some past power outage. It reminded him of the clock radio on the nightstand in his bedroom. Once home he'd laid awake in bed for more than half an hour, just staring at the ceiling and listening to the house settle and shift around him. With Izzy back in New York, the place was simply too quiet. On the other hand, it was also clean, which he really appreciated, but would never mention to Izzy. He loved Isabella dearly, but her life was chaotic and fast-paced, and everything around her was a victim of that velocity.

"Well, I'm glad to see that someone here thought of the coffee."

Jack looked up in surprise at the unexpected voice. Mike Chambers stood in the doorway to the small break room, his wide shoulders and stocky, muscled form blotting out the hallway beyond.

Still muddled from lack of sleep and feeling somewhat uneasy around the CIA operator after the cryptic if unsubstantiated warning from Striker, Jack just stared at Chambers and didn't reply.

Looking surprisingly fresh for 0400, Chambers was tieless, his sleeves rolled up over muscled forearms that looked as if he could farmer's carry a grown man in each hand. He stepped into the break room and walked past Jack, grabbing a paper coffee cup, and leaning up against the wall.

"You NSA folk keep some strange hours. I think your boss is still in his office, probably sleeps there some nights, doesn't he?"

Jack gave the man a half smile and nodded. "Sometimes."

The CIA operator set his coffee cup aside and hooked his thumbs in the pockets of his slacks. "So, help me out here, Sorenson. When all of this went down the other day, you NSA guys were all about cooperating and sharing information. Brought us to your house, let us hang out in your SCIF, it was right neighborly. But now, after one phone call with Johnny -D, you, and your boss both have gone all cagey on me. Call me crazy, but I have to wonder why that is? What do you people have our boy up to?"

For a long moment, Jack considered the tiles on the floor. *Our boy?* His wit, never the strongest or fastest tool in his kit, paused while his brain scrambled to come up with the right course of action. He was under no obligation to protect this Striker character that'd contacted Johnny. In fact, there was a very loud and often ignored part of his brain that was screaming at him right now to tell Chambers everything he knew. He sighed and checked the level in the coffee pot. *Only half full.*

"It's more the other way around," he said finally.

Chambers quirked an eyebrow. "How's that?"

Jack ran a hand through his hair and decided to use the flawed man-brain intuition that Izzy was always giving him such a hard time about relying on.

If I'm wrong about this, I might get Johnny killed. But if I don't do anything, he might die anyway.

Still, his friend claimed to know Chambers, and he seemed to trust him. While the man had gone out of his way to make sure Johnny knew about the attack on his father, his friend still wanted him to keep the Striker thing close hold. "In the family," so to speak.

So, what do I believe? Do I believe what I can see? Or do I believe in some faceless name that's telling Johnny that he can't trust the CIA?

Jack blanched as his thoughts started to gel and lead him down a twisted road. The Central Intelligence Agency wasn't exactly what you'd call a "benevolent" organization, but for the most part, their people were just people. Chambers was an operator, just like Johnny, and most of those guys grew up in the military, just like he had, and those ties were often the strongest.

Fuck it.

Jack took a deep breath and caught the CIA operator up on everything that had happened over the previous seventy-two hours, From Johnny's flight to Germany, to the mysterious message from Striker to his ultimate arrival in Penang. When he was finished, the coffee machine let out a single high-pitched whistle to let them know that it was done brewing. They both ignored it.

Chambers for his part appeared deep in thought. After a long moment, he cocked his head and frowned. "Striker isn't an asset that I know of, but I haven't run any agents in that AO before, he might be one on Chloe's shadow book connections." He paused and glanced up at the old analog clock on the wall. "What's the time difference between us and Penang, twelve hours?"

Jack nodded. "Yeah, ahead, and I think Johnny's going to grab dinner at the meet up point."

Chambers cursed and pushed himself off the counter. "I wish he wouldn't do that," he said. "Nothing worse than trying to recon at night. Well, come on NSA, let's go make some phone calls. I don't know this Striker fellah, but I know some folks that probably do, so let's wake 'em up."

GRAND CAYMAN

"That's it, that's perfect, turn to the left just a little bit. Wonderful, you're a natural at this." David adjusted the Go-Pro on its tripod mounted gimbal and let his eyes roam over the very attractive, and very nearly naked, party girl.

He fiddled with the action camera for a long moment, too long for the woman to effectively hold the breasts out, ass out pose he'd put her into, but all in all, David didn't mind. In an island full of dance clubs and beach themed bars, it wasn't hard to find drunk college coeds killing to believe he was a talent scout for the adult entertainment industry. With his real work complete, and no scowling Anja to mess with his fun, he had plenty of time to comb the island looking for the willing (or at least the very, very drunk) to take part in one of his ad-hoc photo shoots. His latest, was one of the latter varieties.

"Are you sure this is right?" The girl gave him a pouting smile and twisted her torso from side to side, her full breasts swaying, and straining against the tie-dye bikini top she wore over cutoffs and flip flops.

David grinned. "That's perfect," he said, while casting a quick glance at the GoPro again. Please be recording. "You know, what I think would set this off? It would be really great if you could take your top off."

"Like this?" She asked, one hand reaching somewhat unsteadily back to pull the tie on her top. David's breath caught as the strings from the bikini fell down and away, the cups of the outfit defying gravity by the virtue of the girls' nipples holding it aloft. She bit a fingernail and gave him a sultry look that was only very slightly marred by the fact that she was swaying a little.

No way this is the first time she's done this.

Of course, that was when the phone rang.

No....

David pivoted unhappily from the glorious expanse of the woman's bottle-tanned skin to the screen of his Samsung smartphone. An anime character with an angry face stared back at him with Anja's name bracketing it. It was like getting doused with a bucket of cold water. He groaned.

He picked the phone up and held a finger up to the girl. "Darling, I've got to take this, it's my producer. I'm going to tell him all about you. Just...just hang out here and I'll be right back."

The girl staggered a little, her sultry expression gone somewhat green around the edges. She smiled back at him and looked around for a place to sit down. With her bikini on the floor, her fine, firm, and slightly sunburned American-made breasts were exposed to the brisk night air.

Neither of them noticed.

David hurried out the back room and into the small kitchen in the villa before he took the call. He took a moment to collect his thoughts, took a deep breath, and answered the phone.

"Anja, hey good to hear from you."

In typical form, his project manager cut straight to business. "Have your coolers arrived?"

"Two days ago. They're up and running now. Temperatures holding just fine. I was kind of worried we might need an extra, but this building holds its temperature well. Must be the construction materials they make these buildings out of-."

Anja cut him off. "Everything is complete and ready?"

"Of course, Anja. I sent you an update e-mail with all the details in it this morning. We're good to go here. Routes are all programmed in the switches, and all of the servers are running the latest version of software you sent me."

There was silence on Anja's side of the connection for a long moment. "Excellent," she said finally. "Since your work in the Caymans is done, I'm going to need you in London."

David blinked in surprise. "London? When?"

"You need to get the first flight out. I'll have instructions e-mailed to you while you travel, and there will be someone to meet you at Heathrow when you land."

David's dreams of his tasteful soft-porn empire in the Caymans began to crumble. From the door to the kitchen, the inebriated coed leaned in. Her bikini top had been replaced by an ancient sorority t-shirt, and she looked more than a little pale.

"Hey, sorry to bother you, but is there a bathroom here?"

David fumbled with his phone, quickly muting it. He gave the girl directions to the bathroom.

"David, what was that? Is someone there?" Anja's voice had that flat, toneless quality it took on when she was getting angry. He could feel the press of her dead shark eyes boring into his soul from across the phone line. He quickly punched the mute off.

"It's nothing, just the TV. There, I've turned it off."

Just outside the door, he could hear someone getting nosily sick. It didn't sound like it was coming from the bathroom.

His dreams crumbled further. He sighed.

"What do you need me to do in London?"

14

GEORGETOWN, MALAYSIA

The woman was flirting with him. What surprised Johnny, and kind of bothered him if he was honest, was how long it'd taken for him to realize what was going on.

She was roughly his age, maybe a bit older, with a naturally dark complexion and an open, heart shaped face. Her nose was straight and proud, and it set off a chin that spoke of a cheerful if stubborn disposition. All of this was topped with an unruly mane of sun-kissed bronze hair.

All in all, she was an uncomplicated kind of pretty, a look that he normally found very attractive. But somehow, he'd missed all of this as she gamely carried on what had to have been a mostly one-sided conversation. So, the question she posed next, made him choke on his Manhattan.

"Why haven't you asked me for my phone number yet?"

"I'm sorry?" He sputtered.

Bright hazel eyes, not all that different from his own, glittered back at him as she leaned back on her bar stool and gestured around at the milling patrons of the Restaurant Nasi Kandar.

"I'm pretty sure I could sit down with any random guy in this place and have his phone number in thirty seconds or less. Maybe forty-five seconds if he was married. A minute and a half if his wife were sitting next to him. But you? I've been chatting you up for like half an hour and I still don't even know what your name is." She laughed, and it bubbled up from her chest like a fountain. "I mean, I've gotten cold receptions before, but it was because I was trying to go to bat with someone that plays for a different team, if you know what I mean?"

He did. Or he thought he did. Safest bet was to just apologize.

"Sorry, it's the jet lag. My name's Johnny, it's nice to meet you...." He trailed off, realizing too late that he'd forgotten her name. Forgotten really if she had even offered it.

Her eyebrows climbed up her forehead and her mouth made an O of surprise sound. "Oh my God, you don't even remember my name!" she exclaimed, and Johnny could swear that the fact seemed to delight her.

Helpless, Johnny fumbled for words that did not come. With another bubbling laugh the woman leaned forward and put one warm hand on the side of his cheek.

"Oh, you poor thing. Here, I'll put you out of your misery." In one smooth motion she spun off her barstool and stood. She was dressed in a flowing white tunic top, belted with something vaguely tactical looking, over olive drab capri cargo pants that left a hint of tan calves exposed. She wore sensible Keen hiking sandals and looked much like he did, just another wandering expat looking for a drink and some completely deniable companionship. She put thirty ringgit down on the bar for the Bloody Mary she'd been drinking and graced him another smile.

"My name is Hannah. It's been delightful talking *at* you this evening. I'd give you my phone number, but I think at this point I'm going to save myself the embarrassment." With that she gave Johnny a lofty wave and disappeared into the crowd.

Johnny sat with his mouth open in bewildered surprise for several seconds, as he quickly tried rewinding the last half an hour in his mind, but then thought better of it. He needed to focus.

He'd come straight to Nasi Kandar after leaving the waterside cafe. With no firm idea what to expect from his expected rendezvous with *Striker*, he'd taken the time to scout all the entrances and exits to the restaurant. Worse come to worse, if things went pear-shaped, he'd at least know how to get out. The restaurant itself was a simple enough affair, one front entrance, one in the rear, and a simple upstairs apartment used by the owner to manage the day-to-day operations. As the establishment started to fill with the evening crowd of diners, he made his way inside, and sat at the bar. From what he could tell, most of the patrons were younger, and fonder of drinking than partaking of the locale's signature dish.

He'd whiled away a couple of hours eating dinner and people watching. But as the hour grew later, the bartender had started giving him more and more pointed looks. So, he ordered a what turned out to be a terrible Manhattan and winced his way through the first few drinks, the purchase securing his seat at the bar for a little while longer.

That had been when the woman showed up. He'd blamed jet lag for his chronic inattention, but that was only half of the problem. In truth, he was so focused on watching the door for newcomers that might prove to be *Striker*, that he was only paying half-attention to her friendly chatter. That she'd been trying to come on to him had never sunk in.

He felt a tap on his shoulder. Looking up, he found the bartender, who was holding a napkin out to him.

"I think this is supposed to be yours, bro." He said.

Confused, Johnny accepted the napkin as the barkeep swept up the ringgit Hannah had left behind. Turning the napkin over he saw a familiar name written in a graceful looping hand.

Hannah J. 04-210-2364

He couldn't help but laugh. Admiring her nerve, Johnny put the napkin down and shook his head. Maybe once, a long time ago, he'd have grabbed hold of a chance encounter with an attractive woman like the gift it was. But he'd been a different man then, and before he'd committed to Chloe.

The spasm of grief he felt was so viscerally real that for a moment, Johnny thought he might be physically sick. With a force of will, he pushed the wave of heartbreak aside and focused on one thought.

She could still be alive, and until I know for certain, she is still alive.

As if on queue, exhaustion followed in the footsteps of grief. He'd been sleeping on aircraft and jumping from military to civilian airports for so long that his normally resilience had started to unravel like a sweater. Left with just scraps, he was now just a man alone in a foreign country, heart sore, and very, very tired.

You're getting to be a real downer here, John-boy. Time to get some sleep and start over fresh tomorrow. Who knows, maybe this Striker thing was just some sort of bad practical joke.

Johnny snatched up the napkin and slowly wadded it up, looking around for a trash can to throw it in. Seeing nothing to hand, he stuffed the crumpled thing into his pocket as he fished for a few ringgit bills to pay for his drink. Turning to go, he found his way blocked by a serious looking bleached hair Malaysian.

The newcomer was a tougher looking customer than most of the locals in the bar. Where they were mostly willow thin and dressed to the nines in what Johnny assumed to be the height of local fashion, the guy wore simple board shorts, a rugby shirt, and sandals. He had an athletic physique and the collection of tattoos that snaked their way up from the collar of his shirt to his neck were pure jailhouse.

The two of them locked eyes for a long moment. Long enough that Johnny was now certain that this wasn't just another bro looking to snag his barstool. When the man didn't say anything, Johnny started to step around him. Without saying a word, the man made a subtle move to block. Pivoting slightly, Johnny made to change direction. The Malay's hand came up slightly, he was careful not to touch Johnny, but the intent of the gesture was obvious.

Johnny gave the man a grim smile. "Are we going to dance, or what?"

Without speaking, the Malay turned his head and pointed with his chin toward a booth at the front of the restaurant. Another

Malaysian man, much younger, and wearing a Liverpool T-shirt sat alone at the table. The man looked up at Johnny from over a bottle of beer, then gestured to the seat across from him.

Keeping one eye on Prison-Tats, Johnny walked toward the booth. It was, he decided, time to meet, *Striker*.

FORT MEADE, MARYLAND

True to his word, Chambers had started waking people up. After several terse phone calls and one short, sharp argument, the CIA operator had turned to Jack and told him that he was going to have to go to Langley to get the information he needed.

The two men exchanged phone numbers and Chambers quickly left to get on the road before the Boston-Washington Parkway clogged with commuters. Jack returned to the SCIF for a while but having to give up his cell phone in the secure room proved to be far more of a distraction than he'd expected. After half an hour of desultory work he finally gave up, left the room, and decided to get more coffee.

Once again, he wandered back to the break room. It was still blissfully empty, and the pot of coffee he'd made earlier was still mostly full. He filled a paper cup with the thin black stuff and chased it with enough sugar to give a lesser man adult-onset diabetes. After a sip or two he declared the stuff perfect. He took a seat and pulled out his phone scrolled to Izzy's number. He started to punch the call icon, but then hesitated when he peeked at the time.

Only 0515, still awfully early. He hadn't had a chance to catch up with Izzy since their one-sided conversation the day prior, and he'd spent most of that one listening to her vent about how stupid he was. Still, he felt bad that he'd angered her, and there was a worried part of him that didn't want their last conversation to have been one that left with both of them unhappy with the other.

Jack thought of Johnny and Chloe, and his resolve firmed. Isabella wouldn't thank him for interrupting her morning routine, but if six years in special operations had taught him anything, it was that you took advantage of the time you did have. His thumb moved back down to the "Call" button. To his surprise, his phone suddenly started vibrating with an incoming call. He checked the Caller ID, it was Izzy.

Jack grinned and punched the answer button. "I was just thinking about you."

"I was afraid you might still be asleep," Izzy said. "It's awfully early, baby. Where are you?"

"Work."

"Did you sleep at all?"

"Some."

"Have you talked to Johnny?"

"Yes, I did, just a couple of hours ago."

Isabella's voice suddenly changed, a softer note making itself known. "How's he doing?"

"Still very much, Johnny."

Izzy snorted.

Jack smiled and listened as his girlfriend went through what sounded like her regular morning routine. Which meant that she was blending up the regular vile green concoction that she claimed was supposed to be a healthy breakfast. He waited for the blender to stop roaring before continuing. "He's...focused," he said finally. "Very calm, mostly rational, but I'm pretty sure he's just looking for excuses to kill everyone he meets. I'd bet he hasn't slept much more than we have since this all started."

"Can you blame him?" Izzy asked.

"I'd be mental."

"Damn right you would be."

Jack laughed. "Really? I would've thought you'd expect me to rein my man-brain in and think about everything logically. Come up with courses of action and keep the big picture in mind?"

She was stirring something, and Jack heard her take a long drink. He winced in sympathy thinking of all the different ways she convinced herself that highly blended Kale and vegetables was a quality breakfast food.

"No," she said finally. "I'd expect you to drop everything and find me. I'd expect international law to be broken, bureaucrats' feelings to be hurt, and the TSA utterly scandalized in the first twenty-four hours after I went missing."

"Is that so?"

"Hell yeah," she exclaimed.

For a couple, they were oddly mismatched, Jack thought happily. But as different as they were, they made a very satisfying whole. Isabella wasn't one for admitting she was wrong, or for wasting time on too much sentiment, but this early phone call, the way she was allowing him into a very private and narrow band of time of the day that she saved specifically for herself, was a big deal. It was likely as close to an apology that he might ever get from the dynamic woman.

He contented himself for a while just listening to her as she ticked off her to-do list for the day, followed quickly by all the people and things that were pissing her off. It was a long list, but he realized with relief, he wasn't on it.

"We're still tearing through all of our Asian holdings and deals looking for reasons that Uncle John might have been a target," she said. "But there really isn't anything that makes sense."

"That's good, isn't it? I mean, maybe it's just an attack targeting Americans in general."

"I hate to say it, but that's really our best possible outcome here," she agreed. "Bad for America; good for Dekker Group. If I only had a boyfriend that worked for the NSA, I might actually have some actionable intelligence."

"Ha, sorry, once again you grossly overestimate my ability to give you anything useful."

"You guys haven't come up with anything either?" She asked, surprise in her voice.

"Nothing concrete now. We've got folks chasing leads, but they're all coming up empty handed."

"Anything on the people that attacked Uncle John and Chloe?"

"No traffic yet. If they were pros brought in for the job, you'd think we'd have caught some chatter on it by now. The CIA thinks it might be criminal activity masquerading as a hit on the United States."

"Do they think it's local or international?"

"Probably local," Jack said. "Organized crime and businesses have been bed-buddies for a long time, and Malaysia has more than its share of both. I mean, you should know this right, you run an international bank and they're supposed to be as bad as drug cartels, aren't they?"

"If I only had a boyfriend that was funny."

Jack grinned at the dig, but it faltered at Izzy's next question.

"Jack, have Chloe's parents been contacted?"

He sighed. "I don't know. Official notification may have already happened, but I'd have to ask Director Brown about it next time I see him."

Izzy made a sympathetic sound. "God, Do you think I should call them?"

"I'm pretty sure I don't have the emotional maturity to answer that question."

"I'm serious, Jack."

"So am I. The Campbells are weird, Izzy. They're old money weird. Unlike some families with storied pasts, they like to keep things private as long as they can before they publicly acknowledge it. Calling them might just make an awful situation worse for them."

Isabella's silence told Jack that she didn't like his answer, but that she was at least giving it some thought. He decided to change the subject.

"You're up awfully early today," he said. "Feeling guilty about calling me names yesterday?"

She snorted a laugh. "No." Isabella took another drink of her smoothie. "Well, maybe a little. I'm up early because of the upgrades," she said, and Jack could hear her rattling a spoon in something.

"Upgrades?" he prompted.

"Sorry," she said finishing her liquid breakfast "I've no idea why you don't like my superfood smoothies."

"Because even though Batman thinks they're the way to go, they look like lawn clippings and taste like sadness. Now, what about these upgrades? Are you finally getting the bionic arms you've always wanted?"

Isabella bellowed a tender laugh. "No, system upgrades at the office. Our IT guys have been rebuilding our trading and data warehouse clusters all week. They were hoping it wouldn't impact operations, but things are taking longer than expected, and our systems slow down when everyone's in the office. The earlier I can get in, the faster my reports get run and the less time I'm waiting around."

The screen on Jack's phone started to flash, notifying him of another incoming call. He glanced at the name and the number. It was Mike Chambers.

"Crap. Izzy, I've got another call coming in. I need to take it."

"Johnny?"

"No, I'll call you later," he said and paused a moment. "Izzy?"

"Yeah?"

"I love you; you know that right?"

She didn't say a word, but he could tell she was smiling.

"I love you too, idiot," she said, and hung the phone.

Jack took a deep breath to compose himself and answered the flashing icon on his phone. "Talk to me, Mike."

"Hey, you need to call Johnny-D, ASAP, we've got problems."

"What problems?"

"The man that was responsible for setting up the meeting between the ambassador and the Malaysian legislators was Kit Lee. He has his hands in a lot of stuff in a small way, mostly import export, oil futures, and a lot of gambling. It's enough to make him rich, but there's nothing big enough to clue the police in to him. He's just the guy that knows everyone, and everyone knows him. That's probably what turned the CIA on to him since he's been an off-the-book asset for the last ten years."

"He's Striker?"

"Bingo. That's how he knew who to call to get someone like Ambassador Dekker rerouted to Penang. He called up his handler at CIA and started dropping hints that some local state governments were going to pressure Kuala Lumpur on the Pacific Trade Agreement."

"Who's the handler?"

"Chloe Campbell."

Jack stood stupefied at the revelation. "Great, this is interesting and all, but how's that a problem?"

"Hold on buckaroo, I'm getting to that part. The problem is that the Georgetown police recovered two bodies from a cafe fire from a couple of days ago. When the coroners finally got a look at them, they realized that both men hadn't actually died in the fire."

"Murdered?"

"Right again. You're pretty sharp, you should work in investigations. Coroner says that both men died from a lethal injection. It was quick and clean. There were cameras on site, but the hard drive with the footage on it is missing."

"So, what's that have to do with Striker?" Jack asked.

"The investigative team collected blood on the scene next to one of the larger bodies and the DNA test comes back as our boy. So, here's the problem, when did you say Johnny got that phone message?"

Jack had to think back. Dekker had just gotten to Germany and was waiting for his father's MEDVAC flight when he'd received the mysterious call. That would make it... "Two days ago."

Chambers cursed aloud. "That's too close to call. Dekker's either going to sit around all night waiting on a dead guy, or he's going to end up meeting the people that killed those John Does in the cafe."

"That's not good," Jack blurted.

"No, it's not. That's why you need to call your buddy and wave him off."

Jack frowned. "It's not going to be that easy. Johnny thinks this is the lead he needs to find out what happened to his father and Chloe. He's not just going to walk away because we say so."

"Most likely scenario is that he's walking into an ambush."

Jack snorted at the statement. "And?"

"And things like that don't tend to end well."

"For some yes, this is Johnny Dekker we're talking about and there's no stopping him once he's caught the trail of his prey. And the only way we can pull him off is to have someone physically remove him." Jack paused a long moment. "I thought you said you've served with him before at the agency?"

Chambers turned beet red and cursed out loud. "Goddamn it... I don't have any juice in this op, I told him as much...." The CIA operator's voice trailed off, the silence on his side of the connection hanging.

"What are you thinking?" Jack asked.

There was an unhappy note in the operator's voice when he finally spoke. "This is a long shot," he said. "But we might have some resources that are kind of local. They're not agency, but they're almost as good, and they should be one hundred percent reliable. I'm going to spin them up and see if I can get them to Georgetown in time. You need to call our boy and let him know what's going down."

"Already dialing," Jack said as he ended the call. He thumbed over to his quick contacts and found Johnny and punched the icon of his friend's smiling face.

The phone started to ring....

15

BASEL, SWITZERLAND

Derek Hamilton-Smith was having an excellent week. First, and foremost, all his plans had been coming together nicely. While the execution of some had been somewhat — violent — he couldn't complain about the results.

His Russian allies were proving to be very capable, which was refreshing. They were somewhat rough around the edges, particularly among the polished and scrubbed members of the international bankers at the BIS. Even while dressed in immaculate tailored suits they looked more like the Russian Olympic team than technical experts. Still, they knew their business, and the first plan they'd executed had sent Johnny Dekker fleeing to Germany to be with his father.

That was perhaps the sweetest outcome of all. With Dekker out of the way, Derek was free to exercise all the considerable influence both he and his family name could bring to bear on the exclusive Economic Consultative Committee and the broader group of members in BIS's Global Economy Meeting. Thanks once again to his Slavic connection, that particular initiative was bearing fruit, but it would likely be a slow growing crop that he would have to nurture.

So as the fourth and penultimate day of the series of committee meetings dawned, he found himself on the deck of his hotel room enjoying the sunrise with his erstwhile lieutenant, the formidable, Pavel Grigorovich.

"I have to say, Pavel. Your team has done excellent work this week. I don't expect that we're going to have any problems securing the last seat on the Economic Consultative Committee."

The Russian nodded as he spread a large dollop of butter across his browned wheat toast. "Is good to hear," he replied and set the toast on top of an impressive pile of discarded crusts. For such a big man, the Russian was a surprisingly fastidious eater.

Derek sipped his coffee and continued. "The video of Chairman Patel's private party with your Moroccan prostitutes was particularly well executed. I trust the footage is ready to go should we need it?"

"Da, is ready. At your word it will make its way to social media. After that, we let laws of natural selection take their course."

Derek frowned. "I worry that using social media to circulate the footage might be a bit heavy handed? Aren't you concerned that we might lose control of its spread?"

"No, we will only put bits and pieces online. The scraps of footage will be forwarded to the chairman by an anonymous account. We need not release the whole video unless Mr. Patel proves difficult."

"And if he does —prove difficult?"

The Russian shrugged and added baked beans to his toast. He took a careful bite and replied as he chewed. "Then my associates ensure that it is ready to go viral on American Facebook. He will be a trending Twitter topic in less than eight hours."

Derek was pleased. He sipped his dark roast coffee and checked his watch. There were still several hours before he was due at the BIS, so he had time to relax and watch with grim fascination as the big Russian slowly demolished the Swiss hotel's tale on the Full English breakfast. He found it somewhat curious that the Russian security expert was so enamored of a typically British breakfast. *He's*

Russian, shouldn't he be drinking bad vodka and eating an entire ewer of caviar on crackers or something equally horrid?

On the other side of the room, the television news cut to a story about the now faltering Pacific Trade Agreement Bill. Experts were blaming the attack in Malaysia, which had now made global headlines, for stalling the bill's progress, and the American markets were taking a bit of a beating in response. There was even a five-second news clip of the American FED chairman, Rupert Meyer, giving a brief pep talk from the steps of the BIS.

"The United States is committed to increasing our economic reach in Asia," he said. "I don't foresee the attack on Ambassador Dekker being a significant stumbling block to the trade bill. If anything, this simply strengthens our resolve to engage our allies across the Pacific Rim even more. American commerce and trade power is significant, and more business between the United States and Asia benefits global markets."

The image of a sober and calm looking Meyer cut back to the BBCs talking head and the discussion immediately turned toward the attack's effects on those same Asian markets that the FED chairman spoke about in his statement. Derek frowned. The chairman could still be a problem. "What do we do about him?" he asked, pointing toward a still image of Meyer on the television.

Grigorovich glanced at the screen and shrugged. "He will be a victim of the twenty-four hours news cycle, I think. I would not be concerned."

"Are you sure? Rupert Meyer has a great deal of influence in the committee. Do we have any contingencies if he proves troublesome?"

The big Russian mopped up the last of the eggs on his plate with a scrap of toast. He popped it all in his mouth and gave the question some thought as he chewed. He sipped his own coffee before replying.

"He would not be so simple a target, I think."

"Why is that?"

"He's too clean cut, his financials - impeccable, as you might expect, and from what we've been able to find, the American has no unfortunate proclivities for strippers or cocaine like our dear Chairman Patel. This is troublesome for us. You see, to apply pressure requires something sensitive for us to use as a fulcrum for the leverage, otherwise we get excited Virginia farm boys."

Derek tapped at the seat of his chair and frowned. Was he making too much of this? He didn't think so. Meyer had enough pull at the BIS to almost personally derail all the good work that HSG and its Russian business partners had accomplished over the past week.

If the American was too squeaky clean to lure into a compromising position, was it possible to fabricate something? After all, this was the age of the Internet, and all news was a true as its Facebook post made it appear to be. He suggested this to Pavel, and the muscular Russian glowered in thought for a long moment before shaking his head decisively.

"No, is not possible to create such a *Maskirovka*," he said. "Not in the time we have available to us. Still, it may not matter overmuch."

Derek sat and thought a moment as his better judgment kicked in reminding him that Meyer was the uncle of the current Meyer family chief executive officer, and an integral member of the Council of Thirteen. *Such a tangled web of connections.* He raised his eyebrow at Grig's comment, then leaned forward in his chair.

"Oh really?"

Pavel nodded. "The next phase of our plan is ready. My contact tells me that all the infrastructure required is in place. We simply await your word to execute."

Derek straightened his spine as the plan flashed in his mind's eye. The Russians had been very quiet regarding the second stage of their plan, saying only that it was requiring a great deal of work to get ready.

"You're certain that it'll be enough to affect the committee's vote?"

Grigorovich gave him a half smile. "Perhaps, it'll give them pause I think."

Leaning back in his chair, Derek crossed his legs and regarded the

Russian steadily. "And you're quite certain you can't tell me about the details?"

"No. You'd be compelled to react and that would put all of us at risk."

"React?"

The Russian palmed a tiny pewter pitcher and poured himself more coffee. "There will be a component of financial risk in for all considered," he said. "You would seek to secure your holdings against this risk, and in doing so, others would see your intentions. They could raise uncomfortable questions, suggest complicity. This would not be good situation for you, our shared benefactor, or Mother Russia."

Derek walked the man's statement back through his mind. The Russian seemed to be suggesting that there was going to be market risk of some sort, and he didn't want Derek inadvertently revealing his own involvement, or that of the Russian's employer, an oligarch, and a very powerful man in the Russian government. It was acceptable. He knew if he toed the party line, he stood the best chance of peddling his blockchain technology to the full BIS committee without the Dekker family interference.

"I see," Derek said slowly. "Can you at least give me an idea of the timing involved? How soon from execution until the effects are visible to the committee?"

Pavel's answering grin was pure carnivore as white teeth flashed from behind his salt and pepper beard. "It will be very fast. From the point we execute, unless they are criminally neglectful, the Dekker family will realize something is wrong in under an hour. The rest of the world will know soon afterward. Your committee, and Chairman Meyer, will get to watch the Dekkers scramble to save their business on prime-time television as you break for lunch."

Derek countered with his perfect finished smile. "Market risk is always a factor," he paused a moment as he took another sip of his tea, "And, if we're able to accommodate the BIS in their quest for control of the decentralization wave of disruption, the rest is inconsequential."

"What is benefit? Why does matter the bank use your technology?"

A sharp point formed on the edge of Derek's lips as he placed his cup on the table and savored the ignorance of the aging Russian operative. "The western governments and their allies understand the need for consolidation of currency creation and are supporting a global implementation of the *Vollgeld* Initiative, and that is why the Dekkers, and their lot are angling for position on the committee. They want to steer the process. And in the second phase of a yet publicly revealed amendment to the initiative will fast track the digitization of one global currency, our currency. We will ensure our technology as the indisputable option, distribute the technology to the central bank members, and sit back and watch as we accumulate the largest collection of personal data in the world." Derek paused and took another sip of his tea. "Then the implementation of the long tarried and debated New World Order...will begin."

"And bank lets you do this?"

Derek smiled. "My dear Mr. Pavel, it wasn't an accident I was recommended to our illustrious benefactor by his advisers, and it's the reason I am here."

GEORGETOWN, MALAYSIA

The man sitting in front of him looked oddly familiar, but Johnny couldn't point his finger on it. He was a well-kept and dressed guy in his late twenties. Aside from his piercings, he was clean cut with mahogany skin and blond dyed hair framing features that were wide and square. He had the look and build of an Olympic athlete, with long developed muscles that rippled under his t-shirt. He sat back in his chair and regarded Johnny with dark, serious eyes.

"You Johnny Dekker?"

"Is that a serious question?"

The man looked Johnny up and down. Prison-Tats, who was standing next to their table with his arms crossed asked a question in Malay. The man, ostensibly *Striker*, Johnny believed, gave a quick reply that was lost in the bustle of the restaurant. It must have been a dismissal because Tats turned his body slightly as if to shield what he was doing from nearby diners. He locked eyes with Johnny and pulled his jersey up slightly, exposing the butt of a small Chinese automatic. His point was made, the older man wandered off toward the bar, where he leaned his back against it watching the two men from a distance with an unblinking gaze.

"You're not what I expected," Johnny said finally. He leaned back in his chair, keeping his eye on Prison-Tats.

"I'm too pretty, perhaps?" The man asked with a sardonic raise of an eyebrow.

"You're too young more like," Johnny replied. "I'm assuming that I'm talking to Striker, and if I'm not, I need to know why."

"Impatient," the man admonished.

"My father is dead, my fiancée is missing, and my patience is in extremely short supply. So, you're either Striker, or you're wasting my time."

The man raised his hands in a placating gesture. "I understand. Stranger in a strange land, whom do you trust? In answer to your question, no, I'm not Striker… my *brother* was."

Johnny parsed that, focusing on the past tense nature of the statement.

"Was?"

The man nodded. "He was murdered two days ago."

"Two days… That was a day after the attack on my father's convoy." Johnny frowned. "What link did your brother have to my father?"

"None, but your fiancée was with your father, and she is CIA, right bro.?"

Johnny paused a moment. "She knew Kit."

The man relaxed back in his seat as he nodded his head both men realizing they were talking to the right person. "And you also knew my brother. Perhaps, we should start again, Mr. Dekker. My name is Robert Lee, I'm Kit's brother."

It'd been three years since Johnny's last trip to Malaysia. Between his and Chloe's conflicting schedules it proved hard to schedule any vacation time, but with the announcement of an upcoming Presidential trip to the country, Chloe was directed to scope out the city ahead of his arrival and reconnect with all in-country assets. When they touched down there was a private van waiting that opened as they approached with their luggage in tow. A tall charismatic Chinese Malaysian stepped out welcoming them to his city. Within hours they had dropped their luggage showered and were out on the town. Able to avoid all the tourist lines they found themselves in one of the trendiest spots in the city as Kit escorted them past the long lines through the dark tunnel and up the elevator into a club called *Zouk,* which teemed with life. Johnny thought back to the man behind the DJ booth a young blond Malaysian, then looked across the table at Robert, that familiar rippling smile staring back as he made the connection.

"You're the DJ."

Robert laughed. "Yeah bro., I'm the DJ."

Johnny scoffed. "What the hell's going on? Why did you use Striker to contact me? And, how the hell did your brother's alias in the first place?"

Robert paused a long moment as he looked around the restaurant. "It's a long story but suffice it to say that my brother and I are very close. He left me instructions upon his disappearance or death that I was to contact Chloe or you and run you through what I knew of his death."

Johnny paused a moment, understanding this man lost a brother. "When did you learn of his death?"

"Nothing has been confirmed, but when the investigators identified Kit's DNA on the scene, and given the destructiveness of the cafe, a contact inside the department called me."

"And you ID'd the body?"

Robert leaned forward and whispered. "Inconclusive."

Johnny thought about that word for a moment and turned his

head toward the bar where Prison Tats was staring right back at him, he smiled. "What about dental records?"

"The two male bodies were burnt from all recognition and Kit's dentist was based in London. They're working through interagency paperwork as we speak."

"So, the DNA match on the scene. Man, I'm sorry about your brother."

"To your question, when the news reported the fire at Old Singh's Cafe in George Town, I didn't think much of it at the time. But after that call about Kit's DNA being found at the scene, I remembered him mentioning an upcoming meeting there, and his impatience about seeing an old friend."

"And you thought to call the CIA?"

"When I heard of the carnage and people talking about a missing woman, I remembered your name. I went to my brother's house and found the instructions to me in his safe. He had a cloned phone, and both Chloe and your contact details programmed into it. I wasn't sure if I should explain this all on the phone, and I knew Kit's disappearance hadn't been reported yet, so I used his identity."

Johnny sat up like a bolt of lightning shot him in the spine when he heard Robert mention the missing girl rumor. "What about the missing girl?"

Robert flinched at the abruptness of Johnny's movement and tone of his voice. "Chloe?"

Prison Tats leapt across the room and brought the force of a Mack truck down on Johnny's shoulder and planted him squarely back in his seat.

"All right, all right, relax brother," Johnny said to the hulking beast breathing fire down on him.

"Perhaps you see now why I contacted you."

Johnny nodded. "I do. But at the moment, I don't know much more than you do. I came here looking for answers, and all I've found are you, and a whole lot more questions."

Robert nodded sagely, looking very old suddenly for someone

that was still on the happy side of his twenties. When he spoke, there was steel in his voice. "Then perhaps we can find those answers together." He pointed toward Prison-Tats looming over his shoulder. "Ahmed, worked for my brother, as his driver among other things. Now he works for me. He is a...businessman," at this Robert raised an eyebrow at Johnny and gave him an ironic smile. "His organization currently runs several lucrative protection services throughout this district. He and his people have eyes and ears throughout the city. They were first on the scene of the explosions and fire at Old Singh's Cafe."

"Did they find anything useful?"

Robert's expression grew troubled. "Maybe, old man Singh had a video camera system. It was fairly new and was the kind that wrote the digital video library directly to disk. Ahmed's people recovered the hard drive, but the footage is in some proprietary format. We can't figure out how to make it play."

Johnny tapped his fingers on the table as he studied the young man's body language. "As I understand it your brother had connections all over the country that should be able to help you."

Robert's face fell. "My brother dealt in information, but most of it he kept in his head - old school - ya know. I've some of his contacts, but not all. Then there's the problem of trust."

"You're not sure that this wasn't a personal attack against your brother?"

"It's something I must consider," Robert replied.

"Your brother had enemies?"

Robert shrugged. "Who doesn't? But none that would want him dead. None that would risk losing access to his knowledge and his connections. My brother was a fixer, someone who plugged leaks, the go-to relationship network, and he was good at his job."

"So, you don't think it was a local retaliation, and that it's likely a foreigner was involved, but you don't trust the local authorities enough to take them this drive?"

"Correct," Robert said simply.

Johnny was impressed. The guy was savvier than his age or lifestyle would have indicated. There were too many variables at play with the locals. The hard drive could easily become leverage in the power plays that were sure to erupt after a visible death of someone as well connected as Kit rippled through all levels of the Malaysian society.

"So why trust me with this?"

"Because of my brother's note, and the fact they hit your father and fiancée too," Robert replied.

Fair enough.

Johnny leaned in close to Robert and fixed the blondie with a hard, serious eyes. "Okay. If we're going to do this, we need to take a look at that drive."

Robert Lee looked surprised. "Do you know how to make it work?"

Johnny laughed and pulled out his phone. "No, I don't. But I know some people that will."

TAIPEI, TAIWAN

Anja didn't like Taipei. It was too noisy, too crowded, and the air was so fouled with coal, pollutants, and automobile exhaust that you could almost chew it, much like the rest of the Tiger economies. But sometimes, even in her line of work - especially in her line of work — you had to make sure your business partners knew exactly who they were dealing with.

To that end, she found herself in the *Raohe* Night Market sharing ramen with one of the too skinny, too exasperatingly horny, and entirely too unattractive IT types that frequented the *Neihu* District.

His name was Liu Jun Jie, or as Anja had taken to calling him, Jun, which she knew he hated. By day he was an assembly programmer that wrote hardware controller software for most of the enterprise level server systems available on the market. By night, he was something of a gambler, and not a very good one, which was how he'd come to know Anja.

"So, Jun how much money do you owe them now?"

Liu Jun Jie's face took on an even more hangdog expression than his normal resting-nerd-face. He picked up his noodles in a desultory fashion, not looking Anja in the eye as he replied. "One hundred twenty-five thousand."

"And what was it you were betting on again?"

"Overwatch regional championships," he replied, and slurped some noodles.

Anja shook her head in wonder. "I don't know what that is," she said with only a little exasperation in her voice.

Jun looked sheepish. "It's a video game."

Anja crooked a shapely eyebrow. "You lost the equivalent of almost five thousand American dollars betting on video games." In typical fashion she posed this as a statement and not a question. For some reason this always had an effect on the highly intelligent IT types that she found herself working with on this job. She believed that it had something to do with the fact that she was attractive, and smart, while they - were simply smart - and hoping against hope that they could somehow impress her. So, when she pointed out the stupid things they were doing, it tweaked their egos terribly.

Jun nodded in obvious embarrassment, giving her a helpless shrug as if to say - "I know, I'm a loser, but what's a guy to do?"

Anja drank the last of the broth from her container, making sure to make a show of licking the salty residue from her lips. Jun watched her over his own container and shivered a little as her pink tongue disappeared back behind sharp, white teeth. Smiling to herself, Anja discarded the empty Styrofoam bowl into a trash can and watched as Jun ate the last of his noodles.

"Well then. Maybe we can do something about that. You've been including the code that I gave you in your nightly builds?"

He nodded. "Yes, every night."

"And there has been no problems when it's flashed onto the control boards?"

"No problems," he said, then his face clouded. "Some problems," he admitted. "Dell and HP both have proprietary libraries that we call on their controllers. Sometimes your code doesn't interact well with it."

Anja frowned. The Russian hackers that Grigorovich had her working with had assured her that they'd tested their firmware on all the latest server backplanes. "What does it do? Does it crash?"

"Sometimes, but mostly, it seems to hang your listener process. Instead of passing instructions steadily it caches the data and then unloads all of it at once."

"Does this cause problems?"

"Theoretically it could. To remain undetected, the code must embed its traffic in legitimate communications coming from the hardware. Otherwise, there is a chance that it could be detected."

Anja nodded. She would have to make sure to report this back to Grigorovich. She was only responsible for ensuring that new server systems were being covertly built with infected control board firmware. Making sure the stuff worked was *his* problem.

"How many lots have you shipped so far?"

At this, Jun brightened a little. He reached into his courier bag and produced a sheaf of printouts. "We have shipped over three thousand units since August. Here are the bills of lading you wanted as proof."

Anja took the stack of papers and starting paging through them. A carnivorous grin lit her face as she noted several prominent names. On the first page alone she saw Shell, JPMorgan, and the Dekker Banking Group among others. Looking up at Jun she graced him with the briefest smile of genuine pleasure.

"This is excellent news, Liu Jun Jie," she said, using his full name for once. "I think we can take care of that little gambling problem of yours with some pocket change left over for you to visit the massage parlors in *Wan-Hua*."

Jun flushed scarlet red but paid rapt attention as Anja described how he was to collect his next payment. It was a complicated affair where Anja had to convert New Taiwan dollars into a virtual currency used in a massively multiplayer video game that Jun played. She would meet him in game and buy commodity items from Jun's avatar in bulk. Jun would then take the virtual currency and sell it to others for real cash. It wasn't a very direct way to exchange cash, and there was some actual market risk involved for him, but all in all he seemed happy with the arrangement, and it was damnably hard for anyone to trace.

Business done, Anja left the young programmer and began making her way back to her hotel room. She needed to be in London before the week was out to ensure that the next phase of the operation went smoothly. As she walked, her phone chirped a message.

Grig: Are we complete with the hardware?

Anja took up her phone and used both thumbs to tap out a quick reply as she walked.

Anja: Yes - 3000+ units shipped.

Grig: Has our key account received their product yet?

Anja responded with two thumbs up emoticons.

Grig: Good. Phase II will begin in four hours.

Anja stopped in the middle of the night market, the crowds of Taiwanese shoppers, expat businessmen, and tourists simply flowing around her like a bit of flotsam lost in a river of people.

Anja: Programmer says that certain kinds of hardware may have trouble with the code. Is this a problem?

Grig: No. Four hours, be ready.

Anja: Understood. I'm leaving for London in the morning.

Grig: Good. Has your counterpart arrived yet?

Anja smiled. He was talking about poor David. She almost felt bad involving the systems guy in this part of their plan, as he was actually surprisingly competent. Unfortunately, the successful completion of her mission required a sacrifice, and that, unbeknownst to him, was to be David's final task in this particular "project." Anja regretted the necessity, the American system administrator was good as his job, and she was never happy about casting aside useful tools.

Anja: Yes - he should've arrived already.

Grig: Good - the boy is still in Malaysia - see if you can do something about that. It is *important* he be in London as well - soonest if possible.

Anja smiled and started walking again. The "boy" was the code name that she and the Russians had decided on for Johnny Dekker.

Anja: Understood - plan already in motion. He should be meeting with my people sometime tonight.

Whether he realizes it or not.

16

FORT MEADE, MARYLAND

The two refugees from SCIF 17 were having Chinese takeout. For breakfast. Jack sat with a Styrofoam container of chicken and vegetables growing cold in front of him, he was staring at the string of unanswered calls he'd left Johnny over the past hour and growing more and more concerned.

Standing in one corner of the break room, Mike Chambers was having no problem eating. He'd already polished off an order of fried rice and a container of dumplings. Jack noticed this and frowned at the CIA operator.

"You're still eating?"

Chambers, who was now steadily working his way through a container of Lo men noodles simply nodded.

"How're you still eating?" Jack asked.

Chambers raised an eyebrow and slurped noodles noisily. "I'm a growing boy," he said around a mouthful of food.

Jack shook his head in wonder. The muscular operator apparently needed a lot of feeding. *If I ate the way he does, I wouldn't fit into any of my clothes.* But Jack reflected. Mike Chambers was still an operational asset for the agency, whereas he, was a desk jockey.

Chambers forked up another mouthful of noodles, chewed, swallowed, then seemed to take pity on Jack. "You're looking at your phone a lot, Sorenson, what's the problem?"

Jack leaned back in his chair and finally pushed his food away. "I'm worried about Johnny."

"How many times have you called him?"

Jack frowned and looked at his phone, scrolling through the list of unsuccessful calls. "Eight... no, nine times."

"How many messages?"

Another check of the phone. "Two."

"He ever left you hanging like this before?"

At this Jack snorted. "Of course, he has."

"And was he okay when everything was said and done?"

"Mostly, yeah."

"Any reason to think this case might not be the same?"

At this, Jack felt a stab of irritation loom up and out of the depths of two days of sleep deprivation and worry. "I don't know, someone put a hit out on his father, his fiancée is missing, and just a couple of days ago he got an anonymous message to meet him in Penang with a guy that - as best we can tell - should be stone-cold dead-on slab in Georgetown morgue. How am I doing so far?"

Chambers smiled and waved his fork at Jack. "You're doing great, keep it up."

Jack threw his hands up. "I don't get you. I thought you and Johnny worked together before."

"Sure, we did."

"Aren't you worried about your colleague?"

Chambers shrugged. "What would it matter if I was?"

Jack blinked. He wasn't sure how to respond to that.

Chambers put his half-eaten box of noodles down on the counter and crossed his arms. "I could be worried. Maybe I should be worried. Hell, Johnny-D is a good man and I like him. But me being worried doesn't do jack and or shit to help him. What does help him, is being prepared."

Jack leaned back in his chair and crossed his own arms, feeling more than a little defensive. He knew all of this, he'd been a SEAL himself, he'd run missions and had hung his balls out on the sharp end of the stick more than once. "Prepared? What does that even mean? Are we prepared?"

At this, Chambers motioned toward himself with his fork. "I don't know about *we*, NSA, but I feel pretty good about things. I've prepared."

"How?"

"I have a team moving into place to support Dekker right now. Six company assassins, and all of them more than happy to help a brother out."

Surprised, Jack felt a surge of relief. "How long till they're in place?" he asked.

"One team is already in Georgetown and should have eyes on by now. They're highly motivated too if kind of a little gimpy at the moment. The other team is en route and should be there to back him up in about twenty or thirty minutes."

"That's a long time in situations like this," Jack said, still skeptical.

Chambers snorted. "What else do we need to do? You want to me to see if they'll divert some satellites over the target area? Maybe put a predator loaded with some Hellfires up on orbit over the Penang Bridge? Come on, Sorenson, you know better than that. The most we can do is bide out time and wait to support Johnny in the ways that present themselves to us. Half of his job is improvisational and that means he's going to go dark on us - a lot."

GEORGETOWN, MALAYSIA

As the night deepened, the crowd inside the Restaurant *Nasi Kandar* began to swell, and so did the noise. Unable to carry on a reasonable conversation, Johnny, Robert, and Prison-Tats chose to leave.

"Ahmed's people are nearby, we'll go to his place, and I'll show you the files we recovered from the hard drive," Robert said, and lead the way outside.

A light drizzle had started up while he'd been inside the restaurant. It wasn't encumbering, but Johnny knew that it could change quickly. Mid-November wasn't exactly monsoon season in Malaysia, but it was damp, and more than a little chilly. He resisted the urge to jam his hands in his pockets and followed the two Malay men down a side street choked with small cars, scooters, and bicycles locked haphazardly to streetlamps and stairwells.

Traffic was heavy on the main roads, both vehicles and people on foot. So, they did their best to move with it as best they could without getting tangled up in the press of bodies and vehicles. More than once, Prison-Tats had stopped their progress and pulled the two men into a dark alleyway or just inside the sheltered awning of a street vendor's cart. Johnny wasn't sure why, but he was starting to think that Prison-Tats was worried they were being followed.

"Robert, what's the problem?"

The younger Striker hunched under a noodle cart's awning. He tugged on Prison-Tats' jersey sleeve and made a shrugging motion as if to say... "What the fuck, dude?"

Prison-Tats responded with a few terse words in Malay. He gestured for Robert and Johnny both to stay put. At that, the stocky Malaysian disappeared into the milling street traffic.

Johnny was starting to feel the chill of the rain now that the sun had disappeared, and the new weather front pushed some of the more oppressive humidity out of the area. With the cooler weather, he wished, not for the first time, that he'd had an opportunity to pack for this trip, instead of simply showing up with the clothes on his back.

The thought of Basel made him blanch. It felt like he'd left Rupert Meyer standing on the steps of the BIS headquarters months ago. There was a part of him that felt bad about abandoning his mission at the Swiss based bank of banks. It was a small part of him though, and it was growing fainter as he continued to peel the onion of his current situation. Still, a spot on the Economic Consultative

Committee to lead the talks on adoption of crypto currencies and their underlying technologies would have been a fine feather in his cap as the reigning CEO of the Dekker Banking Group. Not to mention the fact that both Meyer and the CIA were keen to have a friendly set of eyes watching the goings on at the Bank for International Settlements.

His thoughts were suddenly interrupted at the sight of an unexpected flash of familiar blonde hair drifting past in the sea of bodies in the street.

Hannah?

Surprised at her appearance, and annoyed with himself for caring, Johnny turned to follow the woman with his eyes, but only caught a glimpse of her before she was swallowed up by the night and the crowds.

It was then that Prison-Tats returned, walking quickly, and looking concerned. He gestured with one hand back the way he came and spoke in a rapid string of Malay to Robert. Johnny watched as his face grew troubled.

"What's up?" Johnny asked.

Robert turned to him, "Ahmed says there are many men following us."

"Many men?"

"We need to ..."

"How many, exactly?" Johnny pressed.

Prison-Tats held up four fingers. Johnny cursed. He could handle two men in a fight, more if they weren't trained, but four represented a considerable force. Particularly when he wasn't armed. There were few times that Johnny regretted leaving the military or the agency's paramilitary wing, but he did miss being able to carry a weapon. It was then that he remembered that Ahmed - Prison-Tats - was strapped. The little Chinese automatic the man carried might not be much, but it could be an effective deterrent. Still, unless those that followed them were suicidal or exceptionally committed, they wouldn't do anything while the three of them were in the open on crowded city street.

"Who are they following?" Robert asked. "You or me?"

"Welcome to my world," Johnny said, his eyes scanning the surrounding area with a grim determination. Had the young Malay made himself a target of the same violence that killed his brother? That made sense. But it didn't answer the question of the tie that Johnny and Robert shared. That tenuous link may have made targets of all of them.

But why?

"Dey come, bro." Ahmed thickly accented English brought Johnny's attention back to the present. One look at the stocky Malay's body position and he followed the line of the man's now defense posture to three men, locals by the look of them, that had just taken up a position across the street from them at a newsstand. They were making a studied examination of everything on the street - everything except Johnny and his companions.

Johnny frowned. "Where's the fourth?"

The buzz of a two-stroke engine surged over the street sounds as a battered scooter accelerated out of the stream of regular traffic and jumped the curb onto the sidewalk, scattering a knot of pedestrians. Unlike most, the rider was helmeted and wore a heavy leather jacket over t-shirt, shorts, and sandals. There were great stacks of take-out boxes strapped to the back of the scooter, and that more than anything else prompted Johnny and Robert to give way. After all, worldwide delivery rider was known to be universally insane. What they weren't, usually, was armed.

A blink, and he would've missed it. But Johnny saw the drivers hand leave the throttle and dip into the depths of his heavy jacket. When it reappeared a moment later, the dull flat black of a small Scorpion submachine gun filled Johnny's world and blotted out everything else.

"Down!" He yelled and shoved Robert to the sidewalk. The Scorpion roared and drowned out the high-pitched cat squall of the two-stroke engine. Chaos filled the city street as the rider emptied his magazine toward Johnny and his two companions. He heard screaming, and the harsh slap and zing of bullets as they whizzed by his head and ricocheted off the concrete.

In a breath, the rider stowed his weapon and the throttle whined like a banshee; the scooter's tires spitting gravel and garbage as it bounced from the sidewalk and back into the flow of traffic, disappearing around a corner.

Johnny cam got his knees and looked down at Robert who was pinned beneath him. The young man's face was splashed with a smear of blood, and his eyes were wide with shock. A quick look to the left showed the noodle cart owner's crumpled body and an ever-expanding pool of crimson. To the right was Ahmed, his face a mask of concentration as he tried to keep the little Chinese pistol level, with a red blossom of blood flowering on his left shoulder.

Johnny followed the line of Prison-Tats' pistol to the group of three men across the street. They stood, like islands of calm amongst the maddened crush of nightlife as it tried desperately to get away from the unexpected gunfire and blood.

"We must go," Prison-Tats ground out.

Johnny agreed. He knotted his hands in Robert's thin jersey and with a smooth motion, came to his feet lifting the young man with him as he came erect.

"I'm okay," Robert managed to gasp out. "I'm okay."

Johnny looked at the blood on the Malay's face. "Are you sure?" He asked and grabbed the man's hand and pressed it to the sticky smear of blood. Robert stared at his now bloodied hand in horror, but still managed to shake his head.

"I'm sure," he said. "It's not mine."

"Dey coming," Ahmed said, his voice deadly calm.

Like something out of a *Kurosawa* movie, the three men stepped through the tumult on the sidewalk and walked abreast into the street, oblivious to the stopped traffic, and the rushing pedestrians, their attention wholly fixed on Johnny and his companions. One of them palmed something, maybe a gun, maybe a knife, the distance and the dark made it hard to tell.

Johnny quickly assessed their options. There was blood on the street, and there were sirens wailing in the distance. Would the police arrive fast enough to stop the violence that was about to unfold, he doubted it?

Prison-Tats barked something at the thugs as they approached and brandished this small pistol at them. For a moment, the three men paused, but it was short-lived. One simply smiled and lifted his shirt, showing the chromed and polished grip of a massive handgun stuffed down the front of his pants. The three came on.

"You should run," Ahmed said and pushed a blooded and dazed Robert past Johnny. The three men shouted warnings for them to stop, and Ahmed promptly turned the Chinese automatic on them and squeezed off two rapid bursts.

Now we're in it.

Johnny grabbed Robert and bolted down the sidewalk away from the burgeoning firefight. With a quick glance back, he saw one thug crumpled to the ground, while the other two scrambled for cover. In an instant, the street cleared, with terrified pedestrians and motorists clogging the roadway and sending up cacophony of squealing tires, honking horns, and intermittent screaming. Johnny could sell cordite, and the sirens howled closer. Ahmed pumped three more bursts into the general area of the two remaining men before chasing off after his wounded boss.

When Ahmed caught up with Johnny, the man's face was a stoic mask of determination. His entire left arm was red with blood, and it dripped on the sidewalk as they ran. Together, the two men towed Robert behind them like a swamped rowboat. From behind them, another gun shot rang out, a massive booming report that echoed off the walls of the nearby buildings and sent Johnny and Ahmed tumbling to the ground, dragging Robert with them.

Jesus that sounded like a howitzer.

Johnny scrambled around like a crab and looked back down the road. With the mad rush of people trying to run away from the violence, he couldn't see the shooter. Men were shouting in the distance and the first flickering lights of an approaching police car danced out of the night like a rave gone terribly, terribly wrong.

"Get him up, I think we're clear," Johnny said. He helped Ahmed pull Robert to his feet. The young man was not Kit, he enjoyed the nightlife and being a DJ, but a street hoodie he was not, and he knew he was out of his element. But as he stood, he pushed their hands away.

"I'm not hurt."

"Good, but Tats here is. Do you have a safe house nearby?"

Robert stared at Johnny as if he'd just spoken in an alien language. "What?" he began, "I don't understand?"

"Your man Ahmed. Prison-Tats. He's been shot. We need to get off the street. You said his people are nearby? If they are, we need to go there, now."

Robert turned a bewildered glance to Ahmed who had smartly taken the opportunity to strip his jersey off. He had a wicked looking pocketknife out, cutting the shirt into strips. Johnny doubted that the polyester sports fabric would make a very good bandage, but it was a better option than just letting the wound bleed.

Ahmed used his hands and his teeth to knot a quick bandage around his arm. He seemed determined and confident, but Johnny could tell that the man was suffering. His teak-colored skin had taken on a pale green undertone that spoke of blood loss and shock. When he finished, he looked to Johnny and shook his head.

"Not a good idea," he said slowly.

"Why not?"

Ahmed, his command of English failing, spoke directly to Robert in a few rapid-fire bursts of Malay. Robert turned to Johnny.

"He says it's not a good idea to go back to their offices. He thinks the police will come there soon."

As if to simplify the point, a police siren blipped in the distance, likely announcing the arrival of another cruiser to the scene of the fire fight. In the distance, Johnny could see a mix of emergency lights flickering in a bewildering counterpoint of blue, white, red, white.

Johnny turned back to his companions. They were all a mess. Between the blood on Kit's face and the crimson river covering the entire left side of Ahmed's now shirtless torso, it was unlikely there were going to be taken for innocent bystanders anywhere in the city.

"We really need to get off the street," he muttered.

Turning back to his companions, Johnny got them moving. As he walked, Ahmed stared wiping at the blood on his arm with the remains of the sports jersey. Unfortunately, the porous polyester saturated quirky and just began to smear the blood, more than it cleaned it. Noticing this, Johnny undid his button up and handed his cotton shirt over to the man. Ahmed nodded to him and focused on just cleaning himself up enough that he could put the light cotton shirt on without looking like he'd escaped a fight with a meat cleaver.

Down to just his undershirt, Johnny shivered a little, goosebumps dimpling his arms as the cool night air found more purchase. The wife beater tank he'd wore under the button-up wasn't exactly stylish, but it was better than going shirtless. Altogether he looked very much like any other expat bro out looking for a good time.

Taking a few side streets at random, the three men left the site of the hit behind them. More sirens could be heard in the distance, and the sounds of stranded motorists honking their horns would rise and fall like whale song in the night. Through all of it, Johnny almost missed the familiar blatting of a two-stroke engine as it roared by in the unseen distance. He and Ahmed shared a look. Was the scooter driver still out there looking to finish the job?

If they are, that's scary committed. They've already tried to gun us down in public once, so what's another driver-by going to cost them other than time?

"There," Robert said suddenly, and he pointed off down the street toward a small shop with sign advertising bubble tea. "That will get us off the road. They should have a bathroom too; I can clean my face."

Johnny studied Prison-Tats reaction to the suggestion. "Whatcha think big man?"

Robert exchanged words with his protector as they discussed the option as Johnny stood and waited the decision. It was more than likely that the shop owner would dial the police when they saw the bloodied trio, but if Prison-Tats had any sway, and the people knew Kit by reputation it might give them cover for a little while. Robert finished and turned to Johnny.

"Let's do it."

The sounds of emergency vehicles working their way towards the attack site still echoed through their ears as they stepped through the doorway. Johnny's cell phone started to vibrate with anything incoming call. He ignored it, but the prompt reminded him that someone had been trying to call him since they left the restaurant. He started to reach for the phone when a motorcycle borne policeman thundered past another block down.

As they crowded inside, Johnny turned to Ahmed and Robert, speaking in low tones. "I'll order us something, you guys go straight to the bathroom and clean up." The two Malays nodded and moved out while Johnny ran interference on his approach to the counter, all smiles and offering his best dumb Yankee in a foreign country ordering routine. A few minutes later, three peach-flavored bubble milk teas in hand, he sat at a small booth with a view of the front door and the plate glass window that looked out onto the street. He sipped the tea, enjoying its contrasting textures, then fished into his pocket for his phone. There was at least a dozen missed calls, all from Jack, and two messages - Jack. Scrolling down he found a single text message.

Jack: Dude - Answer your phone.

Johnny smiled. Jack could be super high-strung in tense situations like this, and the lack of contact had to be giving the poor guy a serious case of kittens. He knew Jack had suffered the loss of family before, and although it happened on U.S. soil it was also through a terrorist attack, so he understood his friend's concern. It was part of the reason his friend pulled himself from the Teams and sought the desk jockey gig at the Fort. Johnny did a quick check of the door and the small crowd inside the restaurant before punching the return call button. The phone only rang once before Jack picked up.

"Holyfuckshit, Johnny it's about damn time. Are you okay?"

"For the moment, but things have gone a bit sideways."

"Hold on, let me get, Mike." Jack said.

Johnny blinked in surprise. "You told Chambers? I thought we'd agreed closed holed for now?"

"You answer your phone, and you get to make decisions. You leave me hanging and I improvise. Now, wait one..." There was a moment of dead air as he covered the receiver and shouted to someone in the distance. "Okay, you've got us both. I'm putting you on speaker, now spill it, what's going on?"

Johnny took a deep breath and quietly outlined everything that had happened since he'd met with Robert at the *Nasi Kandar*. He detailed everything, from the meeting with Robert and Ahmed, to Robert's story about his brother and their CIA connection, Chloe. He was just finishing up describing the gun battle when Robert returned from the bathroom and sat down next to him. Robert said nothing, he just pulled one of the milk teas over and started to drink. Johnny thought he looked pale, but at least his face was free of blood, and he'd taken time to comb his identifiable thick blond hair and straighten his clothing a little. He just looked like a local coming down from a hard night of clubbing - not like a fugitive from gang violence.

"That's pretty much the shape of it," Johnny said finally. "We're at a tea shop maybe a mile away. Trying to figure out where we can find a place to lay low without implicating Robert's crew."

"We might be able to help you with that," Jack said.

"Do tell."

Mike Chambers voice rolled over the line next, his low drawl firm and reassuring. "We've got a team out looking for you right now, Dekker. If you're right and traffic is all fucked up near you, it's gonna make it harder for them to get to you. But they'll get there. We just need you to narrow down your location a little for us. 'A tea shop in the ethnic Chinese City of Penang' might be a bit too vague."

Johnny snorted a laugh realizing the truth of it. He quickly told the agent the name of the tea shop and the street address, and the part of town they were in, and even gave him an 8-digit GSM grid of his location, pulled from his Suunto.

"There's the soldier we know. Now, sit tight and wait for the calvary," Chambers told him.

Johnny felt Robert tug his arm urgently. "Hold up a second, Mike," he said. He started to ask what the problem was, when he saw the scared expression on the young man's face. Robert pointed out the window. There, on the far sidewalk, directly across from the tea shop was a familiar looking scooter packed with cargo boxes. The rider, still helmeted, was sitting astride the little two-wheeler, talking on his cell phone. He didn't appear to be going anywhere soon.

Damn it, how did that fucker roll up on this place without us seeing him?

Not taking his eyes off the rider, he raised the phone back to his ear. "Mike?"

"Yeah."

"We might have a problem."

"Talk to me."

"The shooter, the mobile one, he's back. Looks like he's camping outside the front door to this place."

The Fort Meade side of the connection went completely silent, which made them think that someone had probably muted the line. Johnny felt the knot in his stomach start to tighten. Here he was, stuck, unarmed, in a building full of innocents with a killer waiting outside. A killer that weighed no more than a buck fifty but had already proven he didn't mind a little collateral damage. He glanced over at Robert, the men's room door was closed, and there was no sign of the stocky Malay.

Christ, I hope he hasn't bled out in the bathroom while I'm sitting here on the phone.

With no help coming from the Fort Meade side of his phone conversation, Johnny glanced back over at his companion.

"Robert, is there a back way out of this place?"

The younger man blinked and looked back over his shoulder. Johnny followed the look, already knowing there wasn't anything obvious. The quick survey showed just the bathroom doors, more seating, and a single door on the back wall marked with a sign in English and Arabic - "employees only".

"Probably, maybe," Robert temporized. "Through the back. It should lead to their storeroom and then an alley."

It wasn't a good time for probably-maybes. Johnny glanced quickly back over toward to where the two bored looking employees stood behind the serving counter. One making a show of wiping down the bar while the other gave up all pretense of make believing as she leaned against the wall and scrolled through something on her phone. They didn't seem to be paying attention to much, and he guessed that if they got up and wandered toward the back, they'd just ignore him further, thinking that he was headed toward the restroom.

As Johnny weighed whether or not to make a run for the back exit, two things happened at the same time. First, Ahmed emerged from the bathroom looking pale, but far less bloody. But he had no sooner than aimed himself toward his companions when a sputtering, blatting roar from outside raised every head in the tea shop. Spinning back around in his chair, Johnny watched as the rider racked the pipes a few times to warm it up. Still holding his phone to his ear, he spoke with as much composure as he could muster.

"Hey guys, whoever you're calling, let 'em know that we're running out of time. There are civilians here and I think the shooter is getting ready to try and flush us out. We're going to make for the back exit of this place," assuming there is one, "then we're gonna run. I'll try to send a grid once we land somewhere." Without waiting for a reply from Jack, Johnny promptly ended the call and stuffed the phone in a cargo pocket. He grabbed Robert by the arm and pulled him to a standing position.

"Time to go, buddy."

"Where?"

"It doesn't matter."

Outside, the scooter rider continued to send his machine into a cacophony of howling furry as he revved the little engine to ear splitting levels of unmuffled two-stroke rage. With apprehension growing in his gut, Johnny shot a look toward Ahmed who quickly fell in with them as they made their way to the back door. A look over one shoulder and he was able to confirm that the rider and his scooter were still parked outside. The rider was putting his cell phone away and with one hand he tipped the visor down on his helmet. *Whatever is going to happen is going to happen pretty quick.* Johnny grabbed hold of the storeroom door handle.

It didn't budge.

Fuck it's locked. Johnny took a firmer grip and twisted on the nob as hard as he could, hoping to overtax the simple locking mechanism in the door. Nothing doing - it wouldn't budge.

"Move," Ahmed said as he brushed Johnny aside.

The muscular Malay gave the door a sullen look, then with no warning he leaned back and using all his coiled strength of his back, hips, and legs, he slammed one sandaled foot into the door, just under the doorknob. Wood splintered and the door swung open with a violent slam. As one, the three men rushed through the door leaving behind the screaming scooter and the stunned exclamations of the two tea shop workers.

Two steps into the storeroom and Johnny saw through shelves of cups and stacked sundries to a double door marked with an exit sign. Lurching forward together, all three men hit the crash bar at speed and tumbled outside into the back alley.

With dank alley all around them muting the distant scream of the scooter's engine, the men took a moment to orient themselves to their surroundings. With only two directions available to them, Ahmed took the lead, walking quickly to the left down the alley, away from the submachine packing scooter rider.

There was a crystalline moment when Johnny realized what was happening.

We're being herded.

Too late to change their direction, Johnny watched as a dark shape stepped around the corner of the alley. Gun metal flashed in the dark and a pistol barked twice, impossibly loud.

Ahmed's body spasmed as the small caliber bullets tore through the bridge of his nose and his left cheek. He was already falling to the ground as the blood, bone and brain sheeted into Johnny's face, blinding him. Throwing himself against the far wall away from the shooter, Dekker desperately wiped the gore from his eyes and tried to work through what he should do next. Did he charge the shooter, or go for the little automatic Prison-Tats had been carrying?

When in doubt - aggression is always the right answer.

Johnny charged. Still half blind, he only saw a blur as he slammed into a much smaller man, bowling him over and knocking him to the ground. Behind him, Robert was screaming something that Johnny couldn't make out. For an instant he worried that more gunmen were on the way, but there was no time to worry about it. With a desperate swipe of his arm across his face, Johnny managed to clear enough blood to get a good look at the man that had shot Ahmed. He was Malay, nondescript, dressed in a worker's jumpsuit and wearing a ball cap. Focused and silent as death, Johnny jabbed a punch into the man's throat. Cartilage crunched as the shooter's windpipe collapsed in on itself. Dekker immediately followed up and put a second devastating open-handed blow into the man's face, pulping his nose, and knocking him into a gagging, blinded state that could only end in death.

Coming to one knee, Johnny turned to check his six. Robert was on his knees, tears streaming down his face as he pulled on Ahmed's shirt - Johnny's shirt - trying to lift him to his feet and begging for the man to get up.

Turning back to this attacker, Johnny found the man's gun, a simple .38 revolver laying inches from his twitching hand. Every instinct in his body told him to grab the gun and to get out of that alley. But something in his gut warned him against it. At that moment, the squalling chainsaw racket of the scooter changed to a low drone, and it was getting closer.

"Robert, we need to go." Johnny's voice was calm, calmer than he felt, but every moment that they stayed in the alleyway was inviting disaster. *What if they're just herding us into another ambush, and if they are, why all the complication? They could have iced all of us two times over now.*

The scooter's engine went from an angry cat's howl up to a full-throated roar, and the two-wheeler's small headlight bounced into view at the far end of the alleyway. Out of time, Johnny toyed with the thought of leaving Robert in the alley and just getting himself out. But one look at the man as he sobbed over his dead friend and Johnny knew he couldn't just leave Kit's kid brother alone.

His hand darted out and seized the revolver. He didn't like wheel guns much, and like the tiny little Saturday Night Special knockoffs even less, but at the moment it was all he had. In one smooth motion he had the pistol in a solid two-handed grip, the front site steady and centered on the scooter's bouncing headlight.

"Robert, let's go, he's dead!" Johnny shouted, and with three rapid jerks of the tripper, he emptied the little revolver. Eyes dazzled by the muzzle flash and ears ringing from the echoing report, all Johnny could make out was the sudden racing of the scooter's engine before the single headlight careened sharply off into the wall of the alley. There was a crunch and the two-stroke engine coughed and died. Holding the revolver steady, Dekker waited to see if the rider moved, but there was only the awful silence of violence at its completion, and no movement came from the wrecked scooter. Johnny flashed to his feet and in a moment, he was at Robert's side. Still holding the pistol, he bent down and grabbed him by his shirt collar, hauling him up.

"Come on Robert, we gotta go."

Limp as a rag, the young Malay stared in horrified shock down at Ahmed's body. His mouth worked a few times, but nothing came out as Johnny pulled him down the alley into the darkness.

Johnny recognized the dull-eyed expression of shock and horror on Robert's face as they shuffled down the starless alleyway. He'd seen it in the faces of the civilians caught in the middle of wars they didn't understand, and even in the faces of fellow special operators. Sometimes things happened, things so repellent and terrifying that your brain just couldn't cope with it. He knew Robert was seconds away from shutting down completely, he had to do something to get him moving or be faced with the having to carry the shellshocked young Malay out of the alley.

"Robert, we can't stay. We have to keep moving," he said. "We can't help your friend, I'm sorry."

The saddened Malay steadied himself and Johnny felt him step back and wobble a little. He steadied his companion with a hand on his shoulder. Robert blinked, once, twice, and then seemed to come back to himself.

"Where do we go?" He asked.

Johnny shook his head, "I've no idea, but away from here. I've got help coming, but this isn't the place to wait for them."

Moving on his own accord, Robert staggered forward and followed Johnny down the long dark alley. Leading with the useless revolver, Dekker cleared each corner until he'd made his way back out onto the main street. They were a block away from the tea shop, and Dekker had to admit that he had no idea where he was. He could hear shouting, and there were people running, some probably away from the sounds of gunfire, and others towards it. A woman screamed and Johnny caught sight of her as she and a knot of twenty-somethings directly across the street from him were holding one another and trying desperately all to run in different directions at the same time. They seemed to be trying to run from him.

Vaguely aware that something was wrong, Johnny looked to Robert, worried that he might be bleeding, but found the Malay battered and scared, but otherwise whole. It took him a moment to realize what the problem was. He was standing at the mouth of the alley, his face lit a demonic red by an overhead neon light advertising Nails and Lashes, and he was still holding the empty pistol.

Well, fuck.

More running people and screams came from farther down the street and Johnny heard an engine roar. A big one. Not one of local manufacture or Asian import, or some modified rice burner with barely their muffler and a turbo, but a full-throated angry V-8 howl.

Headlights appeared around the corner and a massive black Chevy Suburban accelerated down the alley towards them.

With nowhere to go but back down the alley, Dekker froze for a moment as indecision gripped him. Before he could do more than pull Robert out of the way of the oncoming SUV, the big truck came to an abrupt halt and the passenger side doors front and back flew open. The face that met his as he prepared to either fight, or run, wasn't what he expected. It was Latino, and clean cut, the high-and-tight haircut obviously military. The man boiled out of the SUV, dressed in contractor business-casual of cargo pants, combat boots, biceps, ball cap, and ballistic armor. He had an issue Beretta held in a two-handed grip and he covered the alley that Dekker and Robert had just come up.

From the front seat, a man leaned out and waved Johnny into the truck. He was older than Johnny by probably a decade, well worn, and quite literally battle scarred. His leg was wrapped in bandages, and he looked as if he'd been drug through a broken plate glass window - recently.

"Dekker?" The man rasped.

"Yeah?"

"I'm Scott Anderson, your buddies at the Fort sent me. I need you and your friend onboard pronto."

Cars were starting to stack up both in front of and behind the massive American SUV, and here and there, drivers were sounding their horns. Mobilizing himself, Johnny pushed Robert into the back seat where an African American man that looked just as beaten and battered as Anderson pulled the young Malay to safety, stuffing him ignominiously back into the third row of seats.

"Johnny!"

The voice was feminine, and his heart leapt for a moment as a part of him hoped against hope that it was Chloe calling to him. But that couldn't be right, not the same pitch, not the same tone. The voice wasn't Chloe's, and it was only vaguely familiar. With the Latino soldier behind him, urging him to - "Get the fuck in the truck, sir, "- Johnny instead hesitated and turned toward the voice.

Blonde curls, a brilliant smile, and a *camera*. A flash strobed several times as Hannah hit the shutter release on a big SLR. Frozen and blinded, Johnny barely felt it as strong hands hauled him violently into the SUV. As the after images from the flash cleared from his eyes, and the Suburban accelerated past, he saw Hannah wave at the blacked-out windows and blow him a kiss before she disappeared into the crowd.

17

ANAPA, RUSSIA

Igor Petrushenkov drank coffee and watched the storm roll in across the Black Sea. The big man had shed the suit he'd been wearing while in Switzerland, chasing instead soft cotton dungarees and a merino wool sweater. He already felt better for it. Expensive clothes and fine things were all well and good, but Igor believed himself to be a simple man, and that meant he preferred work boots to Italian loafers, and simple pleasures like a good meal and bitter black coffee to rubbing elbows with bankers in Basel.

Originally a career soldier, Igor had never thought much beyond his life in uniform. But one dark night in Afghanistan in the late 1980s, had changed all of that. An ambush in the mountains had left him nearly dead, and poor medical care afterward had left him weak, sick, and very nearly disabled.

After mustering out of the service, he found himself going from a USSR that would at least provide food and housing to its wounded veterans, to living in a Russian Federation that had forgotten all ties to its former heroes as an unfunded expense. He quickly found himself on the streets of Moscow, hungry and broken. Where he'd once been a leader of men caught in the crucible of combat, he now struggled to find his next meal, or to survive the bitterly cold Moscow winter. On the really cold nights, he cursed the blades of his enemies for not striking true and ending him there in the Hindu Kush.

There at least, I would have died a hero, and it was warmer.

But before the merciless winters or gnawing hunger could finish him, a chance meeting changed Igor Petrushenkov's life. On a blustery January morning, he was in search of an open cafe. He'd collected enough coin to buy a hot meal, and a few precious minutes of warmth. As he rounded a corner, he found three men locked in combat. Two were beggars or street people, and one was a thin and successful young man in a suit. For a moment, Igor almost walked away. It was none of his affair, and his old wounds ached something fierce in the cold. But curiosity more than anything else stayed him. The youth fought well, and Igor admired him. He'd seen too many pampered young fools that would've cried and begged or simply handed their attackers whatever they wanted. Not this one. A lion lurked under the soft buttercream skin, and immaculate grooming, and before he realized what he was doing, Igor had waded in to help.

Fights, if executed correctly and with the proper ferocity, did not last long. One eye jab and a sundered ear drum later and the two attackers staggered away cursing Igor and promising revenge. Petrushenkov only laughed at them and helped the young man to his feet.

"Are you all right?"

Fierce blue eyes glared up at the Soviet era ex-soldier. "I could've handled them myself," he claimed as he straightened his suit.

Igor snorted another laugh and clapped the man on the back. "Of that I have no doubt," he said, adding as he started to walk away. "You should not walk alone so early this close to *Solentsevo* neighborhood. Too many bad men live here, and they would kill you for the buttons on your coat."

"My business is here," the man replied as he adjusted his tie.

"Then you should do business elsewhere," Petrushenkov called over his shoulder, and he walked away, forgetting about the young man for several days as he fought his own battles with hunger, and cold, and despair.

So, it was a surprise when he ran into the young lion some three days later. Igor stood on a corner, sipping coffee that he'd found conveniently forgotten on the hood of a parked BMW outside of an office building. The lion was not walking alone this time, but in the company of two large men. Dangerous men. Igor knew the type well.

"You're still alive I see," the young man said as he approached.

Igor nodded. "Da, as are you."

"You fight well for a street beggar."

The former soldier shrugged and sipped his coffee.

The two dangerous men bristled at this, as if Igor's lack of response was an unspoken insult, but the young lion just smiled. "Do you know who I am?"

Petrushenkov finished his coffee and regarded the empty cup with mild sadness. "I do not."

"I'm Dmitri Akhemedov, do you know me now?"

Igor frowned. The name was familiar, but like so many things these days, he couldn't place it. He shook his head.

"Then come, let me buy you breakfast, and you shall learn."

He did learn. A great deal. Dmitri Akhemedov turned out to be the heir apparent of one of the largest natural gas concerns in all the Russian Federation. The new word for men such as this, was oligarch, but Igor simply came to know him as his benefactor. The young lion with his money and his enemies needed steady men, loyal men, and while a penniless veteran with a bad leg might have seemed a poor investment to some, Akhemedov thought differently. He gathered such men to him, and rebuilt them, gave them purpose, and in return, they'd do anything for him.

The task that he'd set Igor and his team on was a new one, and an ambitious one. They were it seemed, to work with the rich Belgian banker, Derek Hamilton-Smith III, to cause trouble for an American banking family. The exact nature of this trouble was compartmentalized secret amongst the team. Igor wasn't sure what these Americans had done to raise the ire of a man like Akhemedov, or if they were just a target of opportunity amid a greater scheme, but when it came right down to it, he didn't care. The young lion wanted a thing done, and Igor saw it done.

A gentle chime from his watch brought the big Russian swimming up and out of his memories. He knew without looking that the alarm signaled the start of the second phase of their operation. The new action was to be the most important part of their work. According to comrade Pavel, this would be the action that would not only put these Dekkers on their heels, but it would take aim at a much bigger target as well. The American economy.

Igor smiled. It was too bad, really, he'd always liked Americans. Even after they crushed the old USSR in their interminable Cold War, he'd rarely held much ire for them. His time with the *Spetsnaz* had exposed him to ways of thinking and ways of living that were much different to the old communist dogma he'd grown up surrounded by in the Soviet Union. To him, the Americans weren't much different from his own people, and he very much liked their movies and television. But work was work, and the young lion wanted to wage a new kind of war against the Yankees. This new kind of war, this cyberwar, was unlike anything he'd ever seen before, and if the eggheads in Tbilisi were right it would do more in the next 48 hours to humble the Americans than the entire Russian Army and been able to accomplish in decades of secret wars. Something told him that this face should offend him. It didn't. Times changed, so too, did warfare.

Igor finished his coffee and took a deep cleansing breath of the sea air. The dark rolling clouds in the distance were heavy with rain, and the coming storm promised to be a fierce one.

GRAND CAYMAN

The server racks inside Idle Systems International were quiet. From the day that David Blevins had opened the small villa on West Bay and posted the simple vinyl sign proclaiming it as the local headquarters, the two racks stuffed with a quarter million dollars' worth of hardware were, like the name of the company implied, mostly idle.

At 03:00 local time, that changed. A single packet from an ISP somewhere near Romania passed through the local router, its one inbound port requirement synchronized across thousands of miles and half a dozen times zones by a small piece of software running quietly on the origination host and on David's monster rack system. It was an innocuous bit of data that made its way across the digital divide to Idle Systems just a simple message bundled within its TCP wrapper that told the waiting listener program in the Grand Caymans one word - START.

For a moment, nothing visible happened. The rack full of computing power continued to cycle quietly, its idling CPUs kept cool by the low hum of air-cooling systems and the bare minimum of each blade's internal CPU fans. But on one blade, the disk I/O began to chatter a strobing Morse code of light and dark as something woke.

Across the entire rack, systems started to come alive as code long dormant was stirred to life and given purpose. I/O lights went from a spasmodic trickle to an almost uniform machine gun of green and orange, and cooling fans across the enclosures roared to sudden screaming life. For a moment, the power in the villa dimmed as the draw almost exceeded the dedicated circuit's capacity. But David was a competent planner, and he'd spent his career building high performance systems on thread bare budgets in places with questionable ewer and even worse infrastructure. So, the draw was only a spike that was easily handled as the systems went from their volcanic wake up to a steadier state of operations.

Through the same sequenced series of time and port coordinated send and receive, the software on the rack systems began to transmit similar START codes to systems throughout the world. From home computers to enterprise systems running in secure data centers, similar batches of code began to wake and contribute to a web of operations that went from one node to tens of thousands in the time it took to flip a light switch.

What all these systems had in common was that their owners and operators had through incompetence or accident, infected them with a very simple and mostly benevolent malware. Using software that had for decades helped average citizens contribute spare computing power to projects that looked for extraterrestrial life, or folded proteins, the software on each system began to create a distributed grid of operations that spanned the planet. As more and more systems came online the operation grew in power, its computing capabilities extending geometrically, with each successive awakening giving the overall web of systems a grim intent all its own, one that searched for others of its kind.

When at last the growing grid had accumulated enough capacity, it started to change, instead of just growing, it began analyzing. It watched, it listened, and it processed. At 03:35:56, it found what it was looking for. Like an astronomer trying to capture ghosts of planetary movement in star systems millions upon millions of miles away, the target it was looking for was like a dimly flickering bulb among the trillions of shining points of light on the greater Internet.

If one knew where to look, there were several dim stars of data like this, but where the accumulation of others' systems had been done simply and quickly, these dimmer, and farther afield nodes required more care, more finesse, to assimilate. While some were simple desktop computers living in secure facilities, others were massive collections of secure systems hidden behind vicious software and hardware firewalls. While these new systems were hard to reach without detection, once the grid connected successfully it was able to begin updating installations of otherwise unknown and unused software on each.

In an Internet used to moving rivers of data every second these infiltrations were almost microscopic in nature. The packets sent and received were so small as to be captured in the regular intersystem chatter between processes. It was carefully done, and quietly, while security structures that normally loomed like impassable walls simply ignored this new chatter as if it never existed in the first place.

One of the dimmest and farthest stars in this galaxy of data lived in the swirling mass of Dekker Banking Group's newest trading cluster. Slowly, and carefully, the entity spread a tendril of waiting intent out to the Dekker Group's network and in time, they connected and began the process.

BASEL, SWITZERLAND

The meeting of the Economic Consultative Committee was turning out to be just about everything that Derek had hoped for. With his Russian passport signed off and expedited by Moscow, their bid for his inclusion on the committee, and thanks to some — gentle prodding — of the Vice Chairman, it was starting to look like he was a sure thing for the nomination.

"I think Mr. Hamilton-Smith is an excellent candidate to put forward," Vice Chairman Raghuram Patel said, the nervous sweat on his forehead belying the calm and precise diction in his Hindi accented English. "He's more experience in practical applications of this disruptive blockchain technology than most of us in the room right now."

There was a very satisfying rumble of assent from his Russian delegation and her allied members, as well as several others gathered in the conference room. Derek did his best to look humbled and pleased but said nothing. As much as he enjoyed the spotlight, this was a situation where it was vital that others carry his torch forward.

"Furthermore," Patel added, "while all the candidates put forward thus far are excellent, few can say that they've already been part of a project that has converted an entire State economy into the digital realm. In my mind, this alone makes his candidacy the strongest under consideration." Patel finally dabbed at the sweat on his brow and cast an anxious look toward Derek and the Russian delegation.

Careful there. Best not to lay it on too thickly. We don't want the other committee members wondering if we have pictures of you snorting cocaine off a Moroccan hooker's ass, which we do of course, quite good ones in fact.

While getting the vice chairman's enthusiastic endorsement was helpful, there were of course going to be others with their own agendas, their own carefully laid plans. One by one, different delegations offered up their own suggestions to fill the open position. Their nominations were met with polite silence in most cases, but little more. Derek smiled and clapped for each as they rose and spoke, knowing that none of it would matter. He was, after all, the best possible candidate, in the room. No one else had his background or experience. So, as each new proposed committee member was proffered and then politely disregarded, Derek's polite and considering demeanor began to take a turn for the smug. But that changed when the Chairman of the American Federal Reserve spoke up.

"Ladies and gentlemen, I'd like to put forward one more candidate. As you probably know, I came to Basel with my new deputy, and the new chief executive of the Dekker Banking Group, John Dekker, Jr. Mr. Dekker, and his family aren't only well known in our international circles as successful financiers, but also keen adopters and developers of cutting-edge technologies, including this most vital blockchain...."

Derek frowned but continued to listen to Meyer extol Dekker's virtues with half an ear. None of what the American central banker said was new to him, as he sat across Johnny on other associations as well and had heard it all before. Yet, despite their previous conflicts in the council and in Nepal and China notwithstanding, this newest battlefield hadn't been of his choosing.

Leave it to a Dekker to turn up, just like a bad penny.

The Hamilton-Smiths had resources throughout the American power structures both inside and outside of Washington D.C., and it'd been through them that Derek had learned some months ago, that Chairman Meyer had plans to insert Johnny Dekker onto this powerful committee, and therefore guide the discussions on the bank's pivot to acquiring the key technologies behind the global decentralizing monetary infrastructure, toward a more American-centric direction. It was Bretton Woods all over again, a small concern in the greater scheme of things, but a seat on the committee was a long-term project that both Derek and his father had been maneuvering toward for years. While Derek felt that he and his allies had very neatly wrapped up the nomination already, he didn't want to discount Meyer's ability throw an American-made wrench into his plans.

"While it's regrettable that Mr. Dekker cannot be with us today," Meyer continued, "it's understandable. The attack on his father, and American Ambassador, was both unprovoked and very nearly cost the Ambassador his life. That Johnny would want to remain by his side in this difficult time is not only understandable, but commendatory."

Not bad, a play for the emotions of the committee members who still remember his father's membership in the bank. Meyer was good, and his appeal was subtly done, and could work. Derek's eyes narrowed, he'd never questioned his Russian allies' tactics, but it'd been a concern of his that their contractor, this Malaysian specialist they'd brought in, had wanted to target the Ambassador directly.

"It won't be a problem," Pavel had told him over dinner some weeks ago as they put the groundwork for their plan into motion. "Our contractor is using modified munitions. There'll be some breakage, but the Ambassador will survive."

"Aren't you worried that someone would tie your contractor back to us?"

Pavel snorted. "No, these ties are tenuous at best, and would be impossible to prove."

"What about the weapons themselves, can't they be tracked?"

"Of course. They can be tracked right back to their Chinese firm that manufactured them a decade ago."

Derek had been pleased, but not altogether mollified. His real concern would be what happened *after* the attack. This kind of thing might sway the committee, might give Dekker a sympathy vote in addition to the heavy influence of the United States backing his claim. Again, the big Russian hadn't seemed worried.

"The voting members will be sympathetic to the Dekkers nomination, of course. But you'll have your place in their committee, the worst thing that might happen is a delay in the vote."

"Won't that harm us as well?" Derek asked.

Grigorovich smiled. "Not at all. You forget, there are several operations happening in parallel. All of them seek to see you enthroned on this most boring of committees. So, more time actually plays to our advantage."

The corner of Derek's lips curved in a predator's smile; he was looking forward to seeing the second phase of this operation unfold. If for no other reason, then because the Russians had been so very cagey on the topic.

For them to maintain so much secrecy, even from me, must mean that it's going to be spectacular indeed.

It felt good to have things going so well for once, he decided. Normally plans this complex came with a great deal of small disasters and larger delays, but so far, so good. Realizing that the American was speaking again, Derek made a point to tune back in, and he quickly lost his smile at Meyer's next words.

"While the Ambassador survived the attack, there's more news I would share with you all. News that hasn't been reported in the media yet, and it affects the Dekker family, Johnny most notably, very directly." Meyer paused and took a sip of water, drawing the moment out. Derek cursed inwardly; the American banker knew how to play to an audience far too well. A quick glance around at the other committee members showed all of them to be keenly interested in hearing what new catastrophe had happened to the Dekker family, perhaps worried that some similar fate could await their own families, in the new world order. For that matter, Derek realized, so was he. He glared over at Grigorovich, who gave him a slight shake of the head. Whatever it was, the Russian didn't know either.

"You see, Mr. Dekker's fiancée, Ms. Chloe Campbell, was in the convoy that was attacked on the diplomatic mission in Malaysia. She was there acting as the ambassador's aide-de-camp and has been reported as missing in action."

The low rumble of concerned conversation spiked at Meyer's

pronouncement, and even Derek felt his stomach clench in cold dread. Chloe Campbell was the daughter of Angus and Meredith Campbell of Fort Worth, and sister to Zoe Campbell, the new head of the Campbell family business. Not only were they another prominent and powerful American banking family, but they were also another ancient Bloodline, long-time ally of the Dekkers, and fellow Council members. Derek schooled his face to reflect only concern at the news, while his gut churned with a very different and very new worry, something the Russians could never understand.

Sonuvabitch, what will the Prime Delegate do to me if he learns I'm responsible for the death of a Council family member?

The Prime Delegate had the final word in any disputes between the Council families, and he'd very publicly censured Derek after his failed machinations in the Himalayas. Despite Grigorovich's reassurances, Derek felt cold sweat forming under his arms. *What in God's name was Chloe Campbell doing in Malaysia?*

Feeling sick, Derek cast a glance toward Grigorovich, but to his surprise, the Russian had his glasses on and was working with his phone, big thumbs laboriously typing out a message on the tiny screen.

"Ladies and Gentlemen," Meyers continued, his hands raised in entreaty. "Please, I beg that you keep this information within these walls. I've been told by members of my government that the Campbell family hasn't yet been notified about their daughter. There's after all, still some hope that she'll be found alive, though it fades by the minute."

Derek slumped in his seat. That's it, this competition is over. Not only will I likely not get a seat on this committee, but even if I do, what happens when the Prime Delegate finds out about my involvement? The Belgian shuddered. It didn't bear thinking about. The Council rules were very clear when it came to shedding the blood of other families. It simply did not happen. There'd be far more than simple humiliation and censure if this got out, perhaps even an expulsion from the Council itself.

Unexpectedly, the gentle Hindi lilt of Raghuram Patel's voice carried over the hubbub. "Excuse me, Mr. Meyer. This is all most regrettable, but is this Ms. Chloe Campbell, the same Chloe Campbell that's in the employ of the American Central Intelligence Agency?"

Derek's eyes popped up in surprise, the same surprise that the saw mirrored in Rupert Meyer's face.

To his credit, the FED Chairman recovered quickly and smoothly. "Former employee," he countered. "She's retiring the intelligence service."

"Forgive me, Chairman Meyer. But you say former employee, and then go on to say that she's retiring from the intelligence service. So, that is to say, she's, currently, still a CIA employee?"

Meyer's face went very still as he considered the question, and the inquisitor, along with the strong alliance between the United States and India, before relenting. "That's correct."

Derek considered the Vice-Chairman and decided that he didn't look particularly good. The man's swarthy face had a sickly cast to it, and the sweat on his brow was matched by two small damp spots under his arms of his dress shirt. But stressed or not, the Indian's expression was still sharp and calculating.

Patel made a show of looking at a sheaf of papers sitting in front of him, then paused to look over the top of his bifocals at Meyer. "Mr. Johnny Dekker was also an employee of the Central Intelligence Agency, was he not? As was his father?"

Meyer's mouth dropped open at the statement. An expression that looked very much like anger passed across the American Central Banker's face. His reply was short and sharp. "These verbal accusations are unheard of in this chamber, and I fail to see the relevance of this question, Mr. *Vice* Chairman."

Patel nodded, and his tone morphed to one of polite apology. "Indeed, and I am sorry to bring it up in this manner, and in this session. But please understand that it's very important that we know exactly who we're dealing with here on the Economic Consultative Committee and in general the BIS. It's vital that our members are above reproach in all things."

Derek almost snorted a laugh at that but managed to contain himself. *A fine sentiment from a man that not 48 hours ago was nose deep in a hooker's ass.*

Meyer's reply to Patel was icy, and the entire committee moved uneasy in their seats. "The Dekker family was born to service. Virtually all of them have been members of our nation's military or held positions in government service, much like many of the individuals in this room."

Patel wagged a finger at the American central banker. "And it's very commendable," he said. "But as unfortunate as the attack on the Ambassador is, as is the most regrettable loss of life, there's a quite troubling news article I'm seeing that was just released by Reuters. It calls many things to question, I'm afraid, including the status of Mr. Dekker's application, not only to the committee, but as your deputy to the Bank for International Settlements itself."

Meyer's open-mouthed surprise was mirrored now by Derek's own. The Belgian turned from the byplay between the FED chairman and the Indian Vice-Chairman of the bank, to cast a questioning look at Grigorovich. The Russian wore the barest hint of a smile. He met Derek's eyes then tapped his phone with one sausage-sized forefinger. Derek turned from the drama unfolding in front of him and quickly thumbed his smartphone to life. Neither were allowed to engage devices within the closed committee walls, but the need for information outweighed the risk.

Flipping to his news app, he was met immediately by an image of Johnny Dekker, surrounded by armed men, a look of bewilderment on his face. The headline read: ANOTHER DEKKER AT WAR IN MALAYSIA. The byline was from Hannah Jankowski of the Associated Press, and a quick scan of the article made Derek have to work hard to suppress the smile that threatened to work its way onto his face.

"GEORGETOWN, PENANG - Not more than days after his father was nearly killed in an attack outside Georgetown, Johnny Dekker, 32, the young and untried CEO of the Dekker Banking Group, found himself in the middle of a firefight in the very same city. Dekker, a former Navy SEAL, was thought to be attending to his father who is currently in critical condition in an American military hospital in Germany. But when violence erupted overnight not far from a popular restaurant and night club in a district in Georgetown, the younger Dekker, and two men known to be associated with Malaysian organized crime were at the center of it."

Derek smiled inwardly and nonchalantly closed his screen and slipped the banned device back into his pocket. He glanced back at Grigorovich and mimed a silent golf-clap. The Russian dipped his head in a mock bow.

Derek let out a relieved breath. This might work, he decided. While he wasn't in the clear over the whole Chloe Campbell debacle, there was a very good chance, that if his allies continued their support and successfully heap mud on the Dekkers, no one would have time to start asking the hard questions or reading between the lines to discover his involvement with the Russian plans.

But for my own protection, I need get read-in more on what exactly my Russian friends are up to. I've played along so far because our goals are aligned. But they play a hard game, and it would not do for me to get caught on the wrong end of it. He resolved to confront Grigorovich about it, tonight if possible. But until then, he decided, he'd sit back and let things play out. After all, it wasn't every day that he got to watch a major American political appointee like Meyer twist in the wind. He resolved to enjoy the show as long as it lasted.

18

UPPER EAST SIDE, MANHATTAN

Isabella Dekker seethed. Or at least she thought she did. Seethed felt right, and honestly, as angry as she was, her already less than expressive vocabulary was being short-circuited by the desire to choke someone.

"Explain to me again," she said slowly, "why my cousin's face is all over the BBC right now?"

Her assistant, Ian, stared back at her helplessly as a live stream video of a BBC reporter ran in the background on her computer monitor.

"Authorities are saying at least three are dead after violence erupted outside of Nasi Kandar, a popular restaurant and nightclub here in Georgetown, the capital city of the Malaysian state of Penang. This violence comes on the heels of an unprecedented attack against the American Ambassador, John Dekker, and his security detail, that occurred less than a week ago. The threads tying these two events together. The Dekker name."

Izzy groaned and put her head in her hands.

"What has local authorities puzzled is why exactly John Dekker, Jr., the recently elevated CEO of the American banking concern, DBG, or Dekker Banking Group, is in Penang in the first place."

From between her fingers, Izzy watched as the hazy video footage of broken glass, stalled cars, and screaming locals was replaced by a very serious looking Malaysian man in a dark uniform. The chop on the bottom of the screen identified him as a spokesman for the local police precinct. His words, all in Malay, were punctuated by subtitles that Izzy read with building dread. He spoke of the investigation into the attacks as well as confirming the numbers of known dead and injured. It wasn't until reporters started asking pointed questions about Johnny's involvement that the spokesman just shrugged.

"We've no comment on Mr. Dekker's involvement. Mr. Dekker is a private citizen, and he's free to travel whenever and wherever he pleases."

A Japanese reporter in the back of the news conference raised his hand, and Izzy read the man's question as it was translated and subtitled onto the screen. "What of the American travel ban that went into effect after the attack on the Ambassador?"

"The travel ban was on official travel to Penang," the spokesman replied. "It prohibited American government officials from traveling to our country, not its private citizens. Mr. Dekker isn't, to my knowledge, a representative of the American government."

A follow-up from an English-speaking Chinese news outlet CCTV came next. "Why do you think Mr. Dekker was in Penang, and in the company of known criminals?"

"With the investigation ongoing, I'd rather not speculate," the spokesman replied.

The CCTV reporter followed up. "But wouldn't you expect him to be with his father at a time like this and leave the investigation to the local authorities? Or is there something you're not telling us?"

At this, the Malay policeman nodded. "Yes, a good son would be with his father."

Izzy groaned, turned the TV volume down, and glanced over at Ian. "You better clear my calendar for the afternoon," she said. Her assistant nodded and turned away as she returned her attention to the live cast. The press conference was replaced by the lone reporter again. He stood alone in a dark alleyway, looking suitably serious, and very uniquely British, as he stood over a dark bloodstain on the pavement.

"Even more pressing then discovering what Mr. Dekker was doing in Penang, was the question of his companions. Before being spirited away by a heavily armored SUV that's believed to belong to the American Consulate, he was reported to have been seen in the company of two men with ties to organized crime in the region. One of these men, who's yet to be identified by local authorities, was killed in a second exchange of gunfire only three blocks away from the initial attack." The reporter kneeled and made a show of examining the bloodstain. "*He was shot several times and left to bleed out in this dark, dank alleyway.*"

Izzy turned the video down, "Ian?" She said after the retreating form of her assistant.

"Ma'am?"

"You might want to clear my schedule for tomorrow too."

"Will do."

"And call Vicki Resnick in our communications team, I need her on this immediately."

"Already texted her, ma'am."

"You're a star, Ian" she said, and she meant it. In reply, her assistant gave her a reassuring smile and a two fingered scout's salute before disappearing around the corner.

Oh, Johnny, what on earth are you doing over there? Izzy killed the video and took a few deep, calming breaths, then looked at her watch. She figured she had twenty minutes before her phone started ringing with questions about this latest Dekker disaster. Maybe less. She'd let her communications and public affairs people handle the press inquiries, that was simple enough, and the Dekker Group's response would be minimal at best. Bankers, even attractive bankers, weren't big news unless they were marrying someone famous, or going to jail after defrauding thousands of clients. With luck, the twenty-four-hour news cycle would kill whatever mess Johnny had gotten into before it could really gain any momentum.

Or maybe it doesn't, another part of her said. *You have no idea what Johnny is up to, and with Uncle John in the hospital and Chloe miss-*

ing? Her unease grew as her imagination took greater control of the situation and began spinning different calamities together.

Her intercom buzzed shortly, followed by Ian's voice. "Ma'am, Ms. Resnick is here to see you."

"Thank you, please send her in."

Izzy sat up in her chair and smiled despite her foul mood as her communications director swept into the room.

Vicki Resnick was 5'3" of stocky Puerto Rican powerhouse female. Her hair was dramatic waterfall of thick black that was kept tame by a pair of what looked like actual chopsticks leaking out of the twisted pile of locks that she'd wound precariously high upon her head. She was arrayed for battle today in a purple blouse and tight, long dress, over platform sandals. Her toes were painted, as were her fingernails in a riot of colors. She hurried over to the chairs in front of Izzy's desk and seated herself primly.

"Hey Vicki, I assume you've seen our beloved, CEO in his latest BBC cameo?"

The small woman beamed at her "I have, and you know, his hair looks pretty good. I'm glad he didn't keep the military high-and-tight."

Izzy snorted a laugh.

"Seriously though," her communications director said. "I came right away because this situation is well and truly on fire right now. The footage has made it to state-side media outlets, and the original BBC release is trending both on Facebook and Twitter. Our beloved leader has really put his foot in it."

"Suggestions?"

"That depends," Resnick said with a raised eyebrow. "Just how much worse this story is going to get?"

Izzy frowned. "I'm honestly not sure at the moment."

"Not good," the communications director said with a toss of her head, "not good at all. If we're in the dark, we're reactive, and that makes it harder for us to position our responses. That could cost us, dearly. Surely you know why Mr. Dekker's in Penang?"

Izzy thought about that for a moment. She had the sneaking

suspicion that she did know why Johnny was in Malaysia and it wasn't to improve bilateral relations between the United States and the ASEAN bloc of nations. *That testosterone poisoned brain of his is on two tracks right now. One wants to find out what happened to Chloe, and the other is probably looking for a whole lot of payback over the attack on her Uncle John.*

Worse, the situation with Chloe's family made everything more volatile and she was loath to say anything about it, particularly to the media, this early on.

"Johnny being in Penang was a surprise to me as well," she said, and on an impulse decided to bring her media manager in on the situation. "But there is one thing you need to be aware of. Johnny's fiancée, Chloe Campbell, was in that convoy that was attacked, and she's still missing."

Resnick's face went blank for a moment as she digested the information. "Oh my God," she said. "That's fantastic!"

The look of horrified confusion that flashed across Izzy's face made Resnick laugh. The communications manager waved her free hand at Isabella's face as if trying to banish the shocked expression. "Oh, sweetie if you could see yourself right now. Look, don't you see? He's there looking for his lost love, that makes all of this completely understandable and relatable."

"It doesn't change the fact that his fiancée is still missing," Isabella managed, her voice taking a chilling note. *His fiancée and my best friend.* She thought as she looked at Resnick.

"Of course, it doesn't. But you're not paying me to find lost loves. You're paying me to make sure that the Dekker Group isn't beaten up in the media. This is our leg."

"Our leg?"

"Our leg to stand on," Resnick said slowly. "This is the who, what, when, where, and why that's going to pull us out of this fire looking good. It's all we need to turn this from a potential public relations nightmare to something we can actual spin positive."

Isabella frowned but nodded in understanding. "What about the two shady characters he was with, how does that play out?"

The eyebrow went up again. "Good question, "Vicki said. "We'll want to know more about that, and soon if we can. But I think we can manage it. After all, it makes it all so much more Hollywood, ya know?"

Izzy sighed heavily. *I'd pay Hollywood to be true.* Coming from her communications director, it *did* sound like a bad B-action movie plot. She frowned again after a moment, realizing the one problem they still had with the entire situation.

"Vicki, here's the thing. We can't run anything about Chloe yet."

Resnick made an exasperated sound. "What? Why the hell not? That's pure gold, Isabella. It's instant sympathy on a serious level, no one will question why he's there."

"We can't," Izzy started to explain, then stopped. "We shouldn't," she amended. "Run with the Chloe angle yet, because I'm not sure if the government has told her family that she's missing."

The ever-emotive communications director blew a raspberry. "Fuck."

Izzy smiled. She'd picked Resnick from dozens of other hopeful candidates for the position after she'd learned that the Chicago native had spent nearly twenty years as a Public Affairs senior non-com in the active-duty Army. No one would understand more about the sanctity of releasing information about killed or missing service members before official notification took place better than her.

Resnick's face clouded in thought as she considered the problem for a long moment. "Okay, fine. We don't say anything about the fiancée, yet. But it's good to know. It also complicates things. If we can't talk about Chloe, then those organized crime types Johnny was hanging out with suddenly become a problem again. Are you sure you don't know anything about them?"

Izzy shook her head. "*Nada.*"

"Can you find out?"

"I can try, but I can't guarantee anything."

Resnick's frown didn't lessen, but the expression on her face began to trend more hopeful, and less exasperated. "Okay, but I say this with great feeling, Isabella. We need to know everything you can tell us about what's going on as soon as possible."

"You think it's going to be that bad?"

Vicki made a sound that Izzy took to be a verbal shrug. "Maybe, maybe not," she said. "If the news cycle is slow, we'll be the topic du-jour for a least twelve to twenty-four hours. Longer if there is more bad news, or if the media really runs with the Chloe angle."

"I thought we agreed that we wouldn't talk about Chloe?" Izzy said, confused.

"We won't. But someone will. We just have to be prepared."

"Wait, what makes you think someone else will release this?"

Resnick gave an elaborate snort. "Experience."

"Right."

"Trust me, someone else knows and they won't be careful with the information. Count on that."

Izzy blinked at that but decided very quickly that Vicki was right. They had to move forward with this expecting the very worst and preparing for it. She nodded to the small woman in agreement. "What's your short-term plan?" She asked.

Vicki didn't hesitate. "Nothing for the moment. Anything we say will feed the fire at the press level, particularly when we don't really know what's going on. Do you have friends in the government?" She asked this last part as if it were a foregone conclusion that Izzy did.

"Of course."

"Talk to them. Lean on them. Find out anything you can and find out fast. See what you can do to get this shut out of the media if you don't think it will burn bridges to do so."

"What about direct media queries?" Izzy asked.

Vicki grinned and leaned back in her chair. "No comment."

"You can't be serious?"

"Mostly. I suggest that we spin this as a family matter that Mr. Dekker is seeing to personally. It has no endorsement from Dekker Group or its senior managers." At this, Vicki paused and eyed Izzy narrowly. "Unless it does?"

"It doesn't," she growled in reply like a mother lion protecting her cub.

Resnick barked a laugh and stood. "Right then. Time to muster my troops. I'll use text to keep you in the loop and will only call if we get a major network wanting a comment from someone important."

"You're important," Izzy said hopefully, not looking forward to spending time in front of a news camera.

"Sure, I am a sweetie, but I'm not the managing partner." Vicki gave her an impish grin. "You're the essence, of someone important."

Izzy's face fell, and she sighed in defeat. "Thanks, Vicki. I'll let you know as soon as I learn anything new."

The communications director left the office in a swirl of skirt and happy noise. Izzy leaned back in her chair and let out a long breath, doing her best to reenter her efforts and to clear her head. *First things first*, she decided. *Control what's in front of you and take care of business before it takes care of you.*

She checked her email - nothing brewing there that couldn't wait a little longer. Her meetings were clear for the rest of the afternoon, and short of continuing to try to link possible business reasons for the attack on Ambassador Dekker, she suddenly found herself without a crisis to manage.

I could check on the Asian team and see if they've come up with anything that might have caused the attack on Uncle John. But frowned in afterthought. *What I really need to do is call Jack.* She turned to grab her phone, but then stopped. If Jack had anything for her, he'd already have found a way to reach out to her.

Plus, I'm so wound up right now, that if I call him, I'll just lay into him and turn the whole thing into a fight with a whole bunch of "I told you so's".

Izzy was still chewing on whether or not to call, when her office phone rang, startling her. A quick glance at the phone's display showed Ian's extension, she picked up quickly.

"What's up, Ian?"

"I've got Mr. Bill Reardon from the Securities Exchange Commission holding for you ma'am?" The question in Ian's voice was there because the name wasn't one, he was familiar with from past calls. For that matter, neither was she, but the fact that someone from the SEC was calling was curious. Her mind did a lightning quick scan of any upcoming regulatory audits, and she came away empty, there weren't any issues she was aware of that would prompt a call. Before she could respond, she heard Ian make a surprised sound.

"What is it?"

"All of your phone lines just lit up ma'am, and my display shows that there are three more calls queued up behind them."

Uh Oh.

"Work through them, tell Rear-man-"

"Reardon," Ian corrected.

"Whatever, tell him I'm not in my office, and offer to send him to my voicemail. In fact, tell all of them I'm not available. Get their details. If it's the press send them straight to Vicki's office."

"Will do."

Isabella hung the phone up and placed her hands palms down on her desk for a long moment.

Something is happening. Something more than just this stuff with Uncle John and our grand moron of a CEO. But what is it?

Finding no solutions and no answers in the wood grain of her desk she stood up and wandered out of her office and over to where Ian sat, his headset on, and a pad of paper in front of him. He was talking quietly and scribbling notes in a neat precise hand.

"Yes sir, I understand it's very important. I have your number. Yes sir. Just as soon as she's back I'll get this to her. No sir, I don't have an ETA at the moment."

It went on like this for a long moment and Izzy stepped over to look at the notepad. There were three other callers, one of them a reporter claiming to be from CBS. The other two calls were from bankers and traders that she recognized. Todd Russell from Wells Fargo and Beth Little - *Goldman Sachs, I think? What could they want?*

Ian disconnected the call he was on, and immediately the flashing light showing another waiting call lit the extension. He glanced up at her, his finger poised over the next call.

"There are eight calls queued now," he said.

"What do they all want?"

Ian shrugged helplessly. "So far, no one will tell me, they just say that they really need to talk to you."

"All of them are saying that?"

"All but the lady from CBS. I transferred her to Ms. Resnick like you said."

Izzy's face twisted in consternation. "Take the next call, I'll listen in."

Ian punched the next extension. "Dekker Group, Ms. Dekker's office."

There was a long pause as Ian listened to someone monologue on the phone. Pen in hand he quickly scratched out a name.

Angus Henry.

Izzy felt a complicated stab of worry and relief at seeing the name. If anyone could help her make sense of the situation, it would be the former managing partner.

"One moment sir, let me see if she's available," Ian said. He glanced up at her the question in his eyes. Izzy bit her lip a moment, an unexpected and almost irrational fear of the unknown hitting her square in the gut. She pushed it down with a moment's effort and nodded. "Send it to my cell."

Moments later, Izzy stood in her office, her headset on and connected to her cell. When things got tense, she liked to pace, and there was no easy way to pace when leashed to a desk phone. She took a breath and accepted the call when it rang into her cell.

"Angus? How are you?"

"Izzy, are you watching this?"

"I'm afraid you'll have to be more specific, there's a lot going on."

"The market, it's a wreck."

Izzy rolled her eyes. "You don't say?"

"I'm serious, Isabella, they're saying it might be some kind of cyberattack."

"Wait, what? Angus, what are you talking about?"

Henry made a rude noise over the phone that made her wonder for a moment if he was related in spirit to Vicki Resnick.

"Are you serious? You're not watching this?" He asked.

"Our CEO getting caught up in a firefight in Penang, has sort of sucked all of the oxygen out of the room, Angus."

"What? That was almost a week ago, this is happening right now."

"Not Uncle John, I'm talking about Johnny. The younger Dekker, the one that still enjoys field ops overboard responsibilities."

"What the hell's he doing in Penang?"

"Great question - hence why I'm not following whatever nonsense is going on with the market." Izzy growled.

There was a great deal of noise in the background of Angus Henry's side of the call. Izzy heard him cover the phone and share a quick and muted exchange with someone else before he moved to a quieter location.

"Sorry, it's a madhouse here."

"Where are you?"

"Gun Club," he said. "I've never seen this place empty out so fast. People lit out of here like they were on fire, and I don't blame them. The goddamn DOW plummeted six hundred points in under fifteen minutes. That's right up there with the 2010 Flash Crash. Are you telling me no-one there is tracking this?"

Izzy blinked. *And now the other shoe drops.* "I'm sure we are, but I've been wrapped up with Johnny's latest disaster all afternoon, and it hasn't left me a lot of time to come up for air." She paused in thought. "But it certainly explains why my phone lines are on fire right now." Izzy looked out her glass cornered office at the now obvious pandemonium of her traders.

Henry barked a laugh. "Damn right it does," he said, adding as if in afterthought. "How's Junior, anyway?"

Izzy rolled her eyes. *Junior is over thirty.* "He's still alive," Isabella said. *At least until I get my hands on him.* "You were saying something about a cyberattack?"

"That's what my government contacts have suggested. Something about an excessive number of bids and offer cancellations on the futures exchange spoofing the market and causing a ripple effect across the other exchanges. The SEC is trying to contain the problem by getting the Broker Dealers to shut down all access to trading algorithms across their platforms."

"The SEC," Izzy said flatly, remembering the call Ian sent to her voicemail. There it is, she realized finally, as her stomach finally allowed itself the free-fall dive it'd been waiting for. She sat down at her desk and glanced over at her office phone. The voicemail light was lit up and flashing.

"I think I better go, Angus."

"Probably a good idea. Do you want me to stop in? Help you fight the fires?" There was a hopeful note in the older man's voice.

"You've read my mind. I think this is much bigger than we realize. I'm going to need all hands-on deck," Izzy said. "I'll talk to you soon."

She hung up before hearing his response. A moment later, Ian was in her office as she was punching the access code to her voicemail. She motioned to him to wait and put the message on speaker.

There was the sound of voices in the background. Shouting, and the clamor of a cell phone that was being handled roughly while someone walked. After a moment, a harried voice came across the speaker.

"Ms. Dekker. This is Bill Reardon from the Securities and Exchange Commission. I'm sure you've seen the news, so I'll be brief. We believe that the market crashes we're experiencing has been caused by multiple out-of-control algorithms from a yet undetermined number of points through the Broker Dealers' agency platforms. We're asking all participants to cease and desist from both proprietary and agency trading through their algorithms for the rest of the trading session, one of my colleagues or I will be in touch post market close. But if you get this message and can call me back, please do so-" here the man paused to give his phone number before noisy ending the call.

Realizing she hadn't bothered to capture the number, Izzy looked up for a pen and started to replay the message. She was brought up short by Ian, who had written the man's number in ballpoint on his palm of his hand. She grinned up at him in thanks and copied down the number.

"Ian?"

"What the hell's going on?"

Ian looked helpless, then turned slightly and pointed toward the door of her office. A harried looking man with bushy red mustache and thick glasses looked back at her. It was Jeff Duran, her head of IT.

"I can tell you ma'am, we've been hacked."

19

FORT MEADE, MARYLAND

Two faces turned to the NSA director, both with blank, confused expressions.

"I'm sorry, sir, but what did you just say?" Jack asked.

Walter Moore sighed and ran a hand through his coarse black hair that was still thick and glossy for a man well into his sixties. "I said we've been hacked. Not us specifically, not the NSA, not yet anyway, but multiple targets within the United States, and more than one of our closer European allies are under cyberattack."

It was the late afternoon, and Sorenson and his companion, the irritatingly alert and refreshed looking Mike Chambers were holding court in a conference room not far from the SCIF. Jack looked to his companion waiting for his reaction, and saw the same confused, surprised look mirrored on his face.

"When did this happen?" Jack asked, while trying to wrap his head around this new variable in all the disasters over the past week.

"Our best guess is that it started about three or four hours ago." Moore said as he rounded on the coffee maker and started to pour himself a cup. "It's pretty damn serious though. Army CyberCommand has told us that there are confirmed compromises in highly sensitive parts of our national infrastructure, including grid power and hydroelectric, even the goddamn stock market is under threat."

That got Chamber's attention. He sat up a little straighter, his face looking like he was trying to work a hard math problem in his head. "I thought most of the system supporting stuff like that was air gaped away from the Internet. You know, so hackers can't get to the systems they want to attack unless they're sitting in front of them."

"That's basically correct," Moore agreed. "It was also the question POTUS just asked on a very uncomfortable conference call that I just came from. At the moment, no one has a good answer for him, and he's pretty pissed."

"It's that bad?" Jack asked.

Moore nodded. "To give you all some context, General Clayton from CyberCommand says this is the hacker equivalent of Pearl Harbor or a 9-11. It's bad enough that the guys at Homeland are running out of their teams of attack-nerds trying to respond to all the compromises."

Jack picked up the phone and swiped over to his news app. He frowned as he saw Johnny's confused face pop back up at the top of the feed. Mixed in with that story he saw the normal daily collection of bad political news, a local pile-up on the expressway, and something about a normally left-leaning pop-singer's decision to embrace Scientology. *Nothing ever changes.* He scrolled farther down and still couldn't and still couldn't find anything talking about the cyberattack. He waved his phone at Moore in question.

"Nothing on the news," he said.

"Not yet. Give it another half hour. Homeland Security has recommended a blackout as far as the attacks on infrastructure go. They've spoken to the President as well as the Gang of Eight and gotten the go ahead to push that down as long as they can."

"What about the stock market?" Jack asked.

"Not much we can do there. The DOW and the NASDAQ are taking a beating, and traders are running for the hills, exacerbating the impact. The SEC is pushed for a complete shutdown of all electronic trading, but most traders are asking for a stay of execution hoping expensive IT teams can fix the issue." Moore blew on his coffee as he took another sip. "Hopefully I still have a 401k left when they're done."

The men all looked at each other, at a loss. Finally, Jack voiced the one question that he figured they were all thinking.

"So where does this leave us with the attack on Ambassador Dekker?"

Moore rubbed his fingers together as he handled his paper coffee cup, and sipped his coffee making another face, but whether it was the bitterness of the coffee or the decision he had to make was hard to tell. "We'll keep some people with eyes on this, but for the most part, we're going to have to refocus our primary efforts on this cyberattack. I'd say that at least for a little while, the Dekkers are on their own."

GEORGETOWN, MALAYSIA

In a rush of acceleration, the big SUV pulled through traffic and sent a crowd of onlookers scattering as the driver decided to use a judiciously large amount of the sidewalk to complete his U-turn. As the truck swung around, Johnny could see faces flash by through the tinted glass. Some were angry, some were scared, some both.

As the full-sized SUV accelerated away, Johnny managed a quick glance at Robert, who wore a wide-eyed expression that reminded him of a very small animal trapped inside a cage with several large, hungry predators. Still, other than some rough handling, the young Malay seemed unhurt, save a couple of popped buttons on his shirt from where their rescuers had pulled him bodily into the Suburban.

Rescuers. Johnny took a quick glance around the vehicle and what he saw looked military that were trying very hard to not look military. For the most part they were fit young men, with the close cropped high-and-tight haircuts of Marines or Army Paratroopers. Their dress was uniform enough too that it looked like it might have been dictated by regulations. Their leader was another story. He was one of those well-worn lifer types that could be a bettered and well-aged mid-thirties to a youngish fifty. It wasn't until the man, Scott Anderson, he vaguely remembered, turned to him that Johnny frowned at the sight. He could see the marks of recent violence written across Anderson's face and body.

"Sir, let me get that shooter from you. We'll all be in a world of trouble if the local PD pulls us over and finds you carrying."

Johnny blinked in confusion, but at the man's pointed stare, it dawned on him that he was still holding the emptied pistol.

"Thanks," he said, and handed the pistol, grip first, to the older man. "And thanks for the pickup."

Anderson nodded and put the weapon into a diplomatic pouch, sealed it, and then stowed the pouch in the truck's big center console. He shared a few quiet words with the driver, and Johnny felt the SUV change directions, pushing out toward the coast.

"Sorry for the dramatic exit there. We were having a hell of a time getting through the traffic in this boat."

"Dramatic is fine," Johnny said with a tired smile. "A few seconds later and it all might not have mattered much." He looked around at Anderson's men and made a guess. "You borrowed some Marines from the embassy?"

Anderson smiled. "After that dust up with the Ambassador, these guys were itching to help out. Had to lean on their CO a little to take them though. He wasn't real keen on me getting more of his men shot up."

Johnny's eyes narrowed. "You were with my father's convoy when it got hit?"

The older man dropped his eyes for a moment, and Johnny was pretty sure he saw shame reflected in his expression. Anderson nodded in confirmation. "I was the detail commander that day."

"How'd you make it out?"

An eyebrow raised on the scarred face. "Luck, mostly. The ambassador's aide was a big part of it."

"Chloe?"

"My driver was hit pretty bad, so was your father. I jumped into front seat to push us forward and she jumped out with the SAW to clear a path. Damn, what a woman you got there, sir."

The words made Johnny's chest constrict and he had to blink back burning eyes before he could voice his next question. "What happened to her?"

Anderson shook his head, unable or unwilling to meet Johnny's eyes. "I don't know," he said, but there was a note in his voice, an unspoken "but".

"I can't find her anywhere," Johnny said, and the bleak statement made the State Department man wince. "I've talked to people all over the city. Talked to the cops, it's like she was never here."

The truck was silent for a long while, the lights of the city flashing past in a multicolored riot that might have been pretty if any of them were willing to look. Anderson finally broke the silence. "I'm really sorry about that. She really stepped up and saved the entire convoy when it all went down." He paused and seemed to consider his next words carefully. "Look, my orders are to get you back to the embassy in KL as quickly and cleanly as possible, probably so someone can chew our asses out and send us both home."

Johnny focused in on Anderson's expression. There was pain and exhaustion there, and guilt, but it all washed away as he seemed to come to a decision.

"But fuck that. I can't promise you that Washington won't order me to put you on the first flight out of Kuala Lumpur as soon as they know we have you. But what I can do is delay that as long as possible. What were you trying to do when we picked you up?"

Johnny cocked his head toward the worn-torn soldier. "Find answers."

Anderson nodded. "I thought as much. Look, I'll help as long as I can, where were you headed?"

Johnny turned to Robert, who still seemed to be half suffering from shock. "We were headed to Robert's safe house, the headquarters of a local street gang."

"Why the fuck were you going there?"

Johnny replied. "They've got a hard drive we need; it might go a long way to explaining this whole mess."

"Sounds thin," Anderson said with a frown.

"Thin's where I operate. You still game?"

"And if I'm not?"

Johnny blew a breath and cracked his knuckles. "Then it's going to suck a whole lot when I jump out of this moving truck."

That elected some uncomfortable looks from the Marines, and a laugh from Anderson.

"I think we can save ourselves the trouble. Where's this place?"

Johnny brought out his phone. "I'll text you the location. But we need to be careful, it's probably going to be crawling with cops, especially with our gang buddy sprawled out in the alley back there."

Anderson laughed. "Careful is my middle name."

UPPER EAST SIDE, MANHATTAN

Isabella looked between the horrified expression on the junior trader's face, and the innocuous looking monitors he'd been sitting behind. She glanced over at Jeff Duran, her head of IT, and frowned at him. "You'll need to explain this to me," she told him. "Use small words, I've had a really long day."

Duran, who looked as if he'd slept in the clothes, took a long minute to consider her question. Finally, he shrugged and sighed. "Watkins here," at this he nodded toward the junior trader, "was happily doing his job managing our electronic trading platform, monitoring our clients algo trading activity, responding to client questions on various trading analytics, and whatnot, when he started to get random calls from the other traders. At first the calls were general in nature, but as time passed the angry traders demanded to know why the Broker Dealer's code was jumping all over the boards. It seemed like someone, trading through the firm's portal, was taking an aggressive stance on futures, and then canceling them at the last moment, which caused confusion by other institutional clients." The IT manager paused a moment.

"Watkins of course didn't know what they were talking about, tells them to get bent, and goes about his business dealing with client inquiries. Forty minutes later, and his phone is locked up with a dozen different desks trying to find out what the fuck he's doing, and if there's a problem with the firm's algorithms. That was about the time that we all started seeing news about the markets started going into a tail-spin."

Izzy's frown deepened and she thought back to her call from the SEC. "Tell me this wasn't just us?"

"No ma'am, it's not. I've gotten some panicked calls from the other Broker Dealers across the board, it's not just us, but we're a big part of it. No one's gone public about it yet, but whatever it is, it sounds catastrophic."

Izzy crossed her arms and fumed, feeling more than a little harassed. *If my mother - God rest her soul - was right, bad things are supposed to come in threes. So, does that mean I'm in the clear now, or is there more coming?*

"Is this the only system that's been affected?" She asked.

"So far, yeah."

"What about our remote offices, or our electronic trading clients?"

Duran shrugged, "Nothing yet at the remote offices, ma'am."

Watkins whispered another anecdote under the towering presence of the managing partner. "We haven't had any complaints from our electronic clients, and the algos' performance looks clean according to the trading analytics. Aside from a large number of cancellations I don't see anything untoward. Well, until this oddball email issue that I escalated to the help desk."

The young trader visibly paled as the managing partner Isabella Dekker turned to him. "What email issue?"

Watkins gestured toward his computer. "It's like he said, Ms. Dekker. I kept getting calls from people complaining about our algorithms coming on and off the bids and offers. Crazy stuff, nothing I was even working on at the time. So, I checked my email and I've got - like a million unread emails that are all trade confirmations."

He moved around the computer and gestured to the screen. Izzy stepped around and watched as Watkins scrolled through his email client, showing her page after page of unopened emails. Each one confirming a buy or sell of some sort.

"And you didn't do any of this?" She asked.

Watkins shook his head. "I'm an electronic sales guy, whether it's dealing with their connectivity issues or analytics, I don't trade myself. All of the trading is handled on the clients end, and their confirmations would go to another team upstairs."

"How many trades are we talking about here, really?" Isabella asked. Watkins looked aggrieved at the question and didn't say anything, looking instead to Duran. Isabella noticed this and raised an eyebrow at her IT chief.

"About 4500 that we know of before his mailbox filled up," Duran replied. "And at least another two or three thousand that created bounced message in the system."

Isabella breathed a curse. "You're in charge of security, why didn't we see this happening?"

"To be fair, ma'am, we did. We saw it as a spike in network traffic on the traders VLAN, and Watkins here filled his exchange inbox in what has to be record time."

"If we saw it, then why didn't we stop it?"

Duran snorted a laugh. "Because we see these same behaviors a hundred times a day for a dozen different reasons. Until Watkins here noticed the content of his email, there was nothing for us to investigate."

"Don't we have firewalls to stop this kind of thing?"

"Lots," Duran agreed. "But they're not a hundred percent effective."

"Wonderful," Isabella spat, her exasperation with the situation rising. "So, the two million we spent on security upgrades this year, did we just piss this all away too?"

"Two point five million," Duran corrected, "And no, ma'am, we didn't piss anything away. We spent that money to just keep up with the threats that we already know about."

Isabella's temper spiked, the stress of dealing with Johnny's Asian escapade and the attack on her uncle all snowballing into a white-hot ball of anger in her stomach. She felt her control start to slip even as Duran tried to explain.

"Ma'am, look. Based on what we've learned, and what others are reporting, I'd say we just got hit with a zero-day attack."

Isabella Dekker blinked. "A what?"

"A zero-day," Duran explained. "It's something new, a vulnerability, or a cyberattack that's being seen for the very first time. Zero-days can bypass firewalls, and our endpoint protections, that two point five million we spent, sometimes there's not much they can do either."

Isabella's expression went from exasperated anger to horror in an instant. Duran made a placating gesture with his hands, as if he were begging for just a few more minutes to live.

"Look, ma'am. Most cybersecurity is based around tracking threat signatures we already know about. It's the stuff we haven't seen in the wild before, the stuff that's been alive for zero days that causes the most trouble."

Isabella spat another curse to make herself feel better. Her temper was still well and truly up, but Duran's explanation made sense. She didn't like it, but she wasn't in the habit of persecuting good people who gave her bad news. No matter how bad she wanted to.

"Well lucky, fucking, us," she finally growled at her IT chief. "What are we doing now?"

Duran sighed and leaned back against the algorithm trading desk. "We've got two lines of effort," he said. "The first is containment, the second is identification and elimination. Once we saw what the inbox looked like, we went ahead and pulled his connection off the network and quarantined it, that way at least it's not doing any more harm. Next, our forensics team is trying to get a fingerprint off the trades that was routed through the system he was monitoring. Once we do, we're going to start flagging any network traffic that looks similar. We've also got people on the phone with our firewall vendors and that cybersecurity intelligence firm we hired last year. The moment either one of them comes up with something we'll know about it."

"So, the entire stock market is a mess, and we're at least pretty sure it's not our fault," Isabella said dryly.

"Not entirely our fault, at least," Duran agreed.

Isabella pinched the bridge of her nose as she felt the beginnings of a stress headache start too manifest behind her eyes. She wondered idly if she needed caffeine, but the sour feeling in her stomach had been advertising for the past hour warned her that the coffee she'd been drinking already contained too much of the stuff, and too much acid besides.

You're just trying to distract yourself. Focus, Izzy, people are depending on you.

"Okay, Jeff. Keep me in the loop while you work through this, I need to find Vicki Resnick and get her up to speed, just in case."

A bark of laughter from behind her made Isabella spin around. Resnick was striding down the long row of traders with an anxious looking Angus Henry in tow.

"I'm here, chief," Vicky said as she walked up. "And I've got good news and bad news."

Isabella sighed. "The good?" She asked a little forlornly.

Resnick smiled. "Thanks to this hacker crap, the news cycle just forgot about your cousin getting into a shootout in Penang."

"And the bad?"

"It'll all come screaming back to bite us in the ass if we're involve in said hacker crap."

"Vicki, I've got good news and bad news."

GEORGETOWN, MALAYSIA

Blue and white police lights flickered irregularly off the battered and graffitied walls of an old strip mall. Parked around the corner from the lights, Johnny and Scott Anderson counted police cars and tried to find an approach to the building that wasn't covered by the police.

"Are you sure this is the place we're looking for?" Anderson asked.

Johnny shrugged and motioned toward Robert. "According to my friend here... it is."

The State Department agent shook his head. "This isn't going to be easy," he said. "That's a lot of cops, there's one on each door and at least half again that many inside. How sure are you that hard drive you're looking for is going to be there?"

Johnny frowned and twisted his head toward Robert. The young Malay was still wild-eyed and staring, looking as if given half a chance he would bolt from the vehicle and run screaming into the night. Johnny put a calming hand on the man's shoulder.

"Robert, these are your people. What's happening in there right now?"

Robert blinked at Johnny a few times before he seemed to get control of his emotions and come back to life, a far cry from his brother - Kit - but he was all Johnny had.

"They're tossing the place looking for guns and drugs," he said. "It happens from time to time, more often when there's trouble in town."

Johnny glanced at Anderson. "I'd guess a running gunfight on Saturday night counts as trouble around here?"

"Pretty good bet it does. How long before the cops clear out?" Anderson asked.

Robert shrugged. "Maybe a couple of hours, maybe they stay all night."

Anderson cursed out loud. "What are the chances you could just walk up there and ask for the hard drive?"

"I'd be arrested immediately," Robert replied dully. "One of you would have a better chance."

Anderson barked a laugh at that and shook his head. "And we'd have no chance at all, not without causing a diplomatic incident that would get us all deported." He turned to Johnny. "How important is this hard drive, really?"

Johnny and Robert shared a look. "It's important," they both said in unison, Robert finally sat up straight in the rear row.

There was a collective low groan from the Marines and Anderson barked a laugh. "Figures," he said. "Okay, it's important, great, but we're not getting into that building, not with half the Georgetown police hanging out in front of it. So, what do you suggest?"

Johnny blew out a long breath and stole another look at the building. The run-down two-story complex looked to have once been a mini-mall, complete with a video store, a laundromat, and cell phone repair shop. But time hadn't been kind to this side of town and the businesses were shuttered, with only graffiti and vandalized signage remaining.

It was in fact, the headquarters of Ahmed's former street gang, known as Tokong, who were close allies of Robert's brother -Kit. Several of the gang were standing outside the main entrance, cuffed, and looking none too happy about it.

"Robert, do you know where they're keeping the hard drive?"

"It's in the basement, they have a server room down there, and that's where Magat keeps all his tech."

"Who is Magat?" Johnny asked, followed by - "And why does he have a server room?"

"He's the boss-man," Robert said, and motioned toward the knot of police in the front. "You see the tall guy there, the one talking to the cops? That's him. He's a smart guy, has his people making money off legit businesses mostly."

"Mostly?" Johnny asked.

"They were also muscle for various business associates like my brother."

Anderson snorted a laugh. "Of course. So, what kind of legit businesses are these guys running out of the basement?"

Robert offered another shrug. "Online gambling, bookies, porn, and porn...mostly porn."

"Hoorah," said one of the Marines. There were fist bumps happening, but Johnny chose to ignore them.

Anderson breathed a curse. "Well, Dekker, I think we better get comfortable, because none of us are getting in there until this circus has left town."

But Johnny had another idea. "How hard is it to get into the basement from say, the backside of the building here?"

Robert eyed Johnny with a crooked stare. "Not hard. Each of the old businesses had warehouses and storage space below ground, Magat connected them all together a few years ago."

"He keeps anything else down there that might be of interest to the police?"

"Like what? Stolen Picassos..."

"Any guns, dead hookers, kilos of coke, things like that?"

Robert blanched. "Nah, he's not stupid. He keeps this place clean."

Johnny pointed toward the apartment building that backed up to the old strip mall. "You see the fire escape there? From that, I can get on the roof of their headquarters. If I keep to the backside of the building, away from the street, I can make it over to the roof entrance to that old coffee shop."

At that, Anderson turned 180 degrees in his seat. "Okay, wait a minute, Dekker. That's crazy talk. The cops will be on you like stink on shit as soon as you drop off on top of that building."

Johnny gave the ex-Marine a grin. "They're not going to see me," he said confidently. "Because you guys are going to cause a distraction."

BASEL, SWITZERLAND

"Sources close to the President say that this latest cyberattack centered on the financial market is unprecedented in both size and scope...."

Derek Hamilton-Smith snorted as the news report playing over the outdoor speaker began cataloging the damage to the American stock market indices in grim detail. The fallout was severe, which he knew full well, as he'd spent a fair part of his morning playing damage control with his family's assets.

Sitting at an outdoor cafe a block or so down from the BIS, he nursed a coffee and completely ignored the delicate danish that sat untouched on the plate in front of him. Everything considered, he wasn't feeling the least bit hungry.

"I see now why you wouldn't tell me what you were planning," he said to his companion.

Across from him, dressed in casual slacks and ribbed mariners' sweater, Pavel Grigorovich continued to demolish his own meal with the gusto of one used to hard physical labor, or, Derek mused, a man who had few assets tied up in the stock market. The big Russian polished off a piece of buttered wheat toast and shrugged.

"I'm sorry that you are experiencing financial turbulence."

Derek squinted at his companion. "You don't seem all that sorry."

Grigorovich took a sip of his bitter black coffee. "I did say that there would be bumps on our shared road together."

"You did."

"And I told you that to meet our mutual beneficial goal, it would be necessary for us to keep you in the dark from time to time. You remember this too, yes?"

Derek blanched; he did remember. He just hadn't expected such...unexpectedly spectacular results. "You know my goal," he said carefully. "But I must say that I'm a little surprised that this result is what you were looking for from your side?"

A half-smile flickered across the Russian's bearded face. "I've been told that our benefactor is in fact, quite pleased."

"Is that a fact?"

Grigorovich nodded and forked up a sausage link. He popped the whole thing in his mouth and set to chewing in a very primal fashion. He wore a considering look though, and after a sip of coffee he wiped his lips and sat back in his chair.

"I'm sorry that you are experiencing financial distress, but I must ask, are you ready for the next stage of our joint endeavor? Or is this going to prove to be distracting for you?"

Derek killed the snarl that was building under his diaphragm with an effort of will. Gray eyes glinting, his voice was measured and precise when he spoke.

"I am not distracted."

Grigorovich grinned his big white teeth glaring in the sun. "Is good, because things are about to get very interesting."

Derek gritted his teeth and kept his expression neutral, but the sinking sensation he felt was gaining speed and approaching terminal velocity. "I can't wait," he replied.

20

GEORGETOWN, MALAYSIA

"I hate this plan," the Marine said. When Scott Anderson ignored him, he raised his voice and pitched it louder. "This is a bad plan."

For his part, Anderson agreed, but seeing as how they were already committed, he just shrugged. "Yeah, it's a pretty terrible plan," he said.

The young Devil Dog gave him a perplexed look. "Then why are we doing it? Sir, our skipper is going to NJP the shit out of us if this goes wrong."

"Nothing is going to go wrong, Beneitez."

The lance corporal snorted. "You did see all the cops hanging out around this place, right? I know you're old and everything, and beat the fuck up, but your eyes still work don't they, sir?"

"My eyes work fine, so quit worrying. Dekker was a Navy SEAL, and a snake-eater ops-guy for the CIA for longer than you've been in the Corps, he'll be fine."

The lance Corporal didn't look convinced. "If you say so, sir."

"I do say so," Anderson said. "Now keep your eye on those cops and make sure none of them are headed back to that fire escape."

Anderson turned from where he and the grumbling Marine were

watching as Dekker slipped through the darkness toward the Tokong headquarters. While Anderson had been unflinching in his support of the former SEAL's plan, he'd had quiet reservations. While he understood that the hard drive the man was after was supposed to be important, the backstory that Dekker and Robert spun about their connection, was wild. Still, he could handle wild. What really bugged him was how it all linked back to one of the biggest crime syndicates in Malaysia.

All in all, he didn't like the shape or smell of any of it. Worse, the rational part of him that had seen him through twenty years of government and military service thought that Dekker was being reckless and grasping at straws.

But the pissed-off irrational part of him hoped he found something there. But getting so close to this gang types may prompt its own issues in and of itself. They were no different from the gangs back stateside. Get on the wrong side of any of them and you could wake up in a swap wearing concrete shoes.

"Hey boss, he's made it to the fire escape."

Jarred out of his thoughts, Scott's head popped up and he started scanning the darkness for Dekker. When he found the ex-SEAL, what he saw made him smile.

"Well, this at least will be entertaining," he murmured.

∽

JOHNNY STARED up at the fire escape and breathed a curse. "Looks a little high," he muttered. In fact, the bottom rung of the fire escape looked far too high for the flat-footed jump he'd expected to make to gain access to the roof of the headquarters. It stood to reason though, nothing had really been going his way since the attack on his father. It was probably too much to hope that the entry point to his (admittedly) questionable plan of attack was about a foot higher off the ground than he'd expected.

"Nothing left to do but try," he said, and balanced on the balls of his feet. He flexed his legs and did a couple of dry runs, working through the motions of his leap before finally exploding up from the pavement and reaching for all he was worth.

Nothing but air.

Johnny landed as gently as he could, the Altama's slip resistant soles making no noise as he touched back down on the wet asphalt of the alley.

Going to have to get a bit of a running start, he realized, and blanched. The approach was bad, either requiring him to take a run at the rung from the side, which was harder, or to run straight at the wall to catch it square on.

Which means that if I miss, I get to pancake into the wall at full run. Awesome. I hate this plan.

For a long moment, he stood motionless and tried to come up with a better plan. When his imagination and the nearby terrain offered no other real solutions (or anything to stand on) he started to slowly and methodically prepare himself to (probably) run into a brick wall. As he worked a kink out of shoulders, he saw a pair of headlights flash on and off in the distance. It was Anderson and his Marine on overwatch in the Suburban letting him know that he was about to run out of time.

Crap, someone must be coming.

Dekker backed up a few steps and stared at the fire escape with something close to resignation on his face. Things weren't getting easier. At this time of night, with the Tokong headquarters crawling with police, it didn't take a genius or a former Navy SEAL to figure out that he was about to get a visit from the local police.

The lights flashed again - faster this time. Out of time, Johnny scoped the distance to the bottom of the fire escape.

Here goes nothing. I should've played more basketball in college.

With his eyes locked on his goal, Johnny took a deep breath and sprinted towards the dangling metal apparatus. Lights continued to flash in the distance, their frequency tied to the proximity of the Malay police approaching his position. Johnny blocked it out and as the fire escape approached, he bounded up into the air, his right arm extended, fingers reaching. A metal rung smacked into his palm, and he gripped it for all he was worth.

Got it!

Dekker enjoyed a microsecond of pleasure at the success before the momentum of his running leap slapped him into the brick wall of the apartment with an audible smack.

∽

Scott Anderson and Lance Corporal Benitez both winced in sympathy as the sound of Johnny Dekker impacting the brick wall pronounced a dull echo across the intervening space.

"That had to hurt," Anderson said.

"No shit, sir. You sure this guy was a SEAL?" Benitez questioned.

"Sure, he was, and I bet he can swim like a motherfucker."

The Marine snorted a laugh, but Anderson saw his face flash from humor to concern in the very next instant. Benitez pointed over toward two patrolling Malay policemen. Where before the pair had pulled up just short from the alley to share a cigarette, they were now on the move again, and one of them was talking into a hand-held radio.

"Well, shit."

"What do we do, sir?" Benitez asked.

"We give him a minute; he can still do this."

"Not if he doesn't get moving. Goddamn, my grandma could climb a fire escape faster than him."

Anderson decided to let that one goes. Still, it didn't mean the Marine was wrong. Dekker still wasn't moving, and he was about to have some unpleasant company.

Come on, kid, you need to get up that fucking ladder. Anderson leaned forward in his seat, as if trying to will Dekker into snapping out of whatever momentary fugue held him paralyzed on the lowest rung of the fire escape. When nothing happened, he breathed a quiet curse.

Well, now it looks like we get to be the distraction.

Anderson turned to Benitez, he was about to tell the Marine to fire up the Suburban, when Dekker finally started to move.

∽

Ow. Johnny decided that his face hurt enough that he needed to take a moment and to catalog his aches and pains after the impact with the brick wall. First and foremost, he accepted that he'd probably just broken his nose (Again) while adding a nice new layer of bruises and scar tissue to his chest and the front of his thighs. None of it felt great, but all in all it was pretty minor when compared to the impressive collection of hurts he'd collected across most of a decade of special operations. Still, that didn't stop his nose from hurting or his eyes from watering - which it did, and they were.

Gotta get up this ladder.

With a barely suppressed grunt of effort, Johnny executed a violent pull-up, his chest shooting up above the lowest rung of the ladder. Using the momentum he gained on the way up, he transitioned the pull-up into a press, pushing himself waist high on the fire escape. He held there a moment, controlling his breathing, and considering his next move when the sound of approaching footsteps and the squelch of a hand-held radio warned him that he was out of time.

Whether it was the thought of capture by the Malay police or the fear that getting arrested would create even more trouble for his family, Johnny's overworked endocrine system was able to eke out a small jolt of adrenaline, and that let him get a knee up onto the ladder, and to work one of his hands higher on the rusting metal escape. He held there for barely a moment before he hauled a foot onto the ladder and scrambled as quickly, and as quietly, as he could up to the roof of the apartment building. He'd just cleared the fire escape as the crunch of approaching footsteps mixed with voices talking in low tones preceded the light from a flashlight as it flickered and danced at the mouth of the alleyway.

Johnny risked a quick look back down the alley as two police officers, both wearing body armor and disappointed expressions, cast the beams of their heavy-duty flashlights up and down the walls of the desolate alley. Worried that one of the Malay cops might be the smart type that knew to look up from time to time, Johnny moved away from the edge of the building in deep stealth mode.

He crouched, listening, the sound of his breathing and heartbeat pounding like a drum in his ears. The footsteps continued a little way down the alley and Johnny held his breath as the white blaze of one of the flashlights lanced up the wall, its beam searching up and down the length of the fire escape. He held himself motionless, trying to simply become a blank spot there on the roof, the smell of his sweat mixing with the tang of roofing tar on the humid night air. After a long moment, he heard a radio break squelch and there was a rapid burst of Malay followed by a brief back and forth conversation. Even though he couldn't understand the spoken language, Johnny easily recognized the sound of someone giving a negative situation report back to their higher ups. He waited a few breaths more and the gentle squelch of the radio was replaced but the sound of the two patrolmen laughing as they walked back out of the alley.

From his crouch on the roof, Johnny rose slowly, and eyed the distance between the two buildings. Like the leap to the bottom of the fire escape, the jump across the span to the Tokong headquarters was going to be tough. And like the ladder it hadn't looked quite so far away when he'd come up with the plan back at the Suburban, but he'd been moving on instinct at that point, afraid to slow down out of the fear that he might lose his nerve.

Nothing to do, but to do it.

Eyes roaming across the roof of the abandoned strip mall, Johnny looked for obstacles that would tangle up his landing. When he found none, he narrowed in on his real objective, a small maintenance shack in the very middle of the mall. It was an unassuming structure hidden amongst the mall's covering of old and inoperable HVAC systems and air circulators, a sheet metal covered wart that seemed to lean a little as if overburdened by the weight of the half-dozen defunct satellite dishes that sprouted up and down its structure. It wasn't big enough to store anything, but it did hold a door that opened on a staircase that - according to Robert - would take him down to the guts of the old mall, where the Tokong kept their computer hardware.

Where I'll find a hard drive, that will, if I'm lucky, have footage on it that might give us some clue about who it is yanking our chains around here.

Target acquired, Johnny jogged back form the edge about ten paces and turned around. When he turned and eyed the gap, he was to jump he felt a little disappointed that it still looked sketchy as hell.

You sure about this, high-speed? You miss that jump and you won't just get caught and arrested, you'll do it with a few broken ribs and maybe even a broken leg.

Johnny swallowed, and realized that his heart was racing, and blood was shooting through his veins. He felt his body dumping more go-juice into his system, giving him the power, he'd need to attempt the jump, but doing nothing to stop his inner quitter from telling him that he was an idiot for even trying.

Don't think, just do.

Without a second thought, without tensing his muscles or telegraphing his move, Johnny burst into motion. His legs pumped, and his assault sneakers made a *snik-snik-snik* sound as he sprinted across the roof. Eyes fixed on the spot where he wanted to land, Johnny's left foot came down on the raised brick railing of the roof's edge, and he pushed off into nothing.

Dekker sailed over the gap, the feeling of weightlessness terrifying and exhilarating at the same time. Just as he started to feel the overwhelming panicky sense of wrongness as gravity began to take over and his brain finally caught up with what he was doing, he landed, hitting the roof fast and letting his forward momentum send him into a roll. He came up in a crouch, his body still humming form the adrenaline. He let out an explosive breath that was half a laugh of amazed wonder.

Still alive but get hold of yourself before someone decides to come and see what made that noise.

Johnny held himself still for a long moment, controlling his breathing and remaining motionless and listening. After a moment, his breathing finally normalized and his mind quietened, he closed his eyes. He let his other sense come online and parse through the sounds of distant traffic and the gusts of wind that were making the bruised and angry clouds stream by overhead. He scented the air and found the promise of more rain to come, but nothing else. Confident that he was alone on the roof, he ghosted forward and tested the doorknob.

Unlocked.

Johnny slid the door open and took a first step down the steep and narrow flight of rusted access stairs. Despite the close confines and the aging structure, the steps proved sound, betraying no telltale noise as he tested his weight on each one. A minute's worth of careful, methodical movement later and he passed the door on the main floor of the strip mall. He could hear voices outside, what he assumed were the Malay policemen as they roamed the confines of the Tokong hideout. The voices seemed to be getting louder, as if the speakers were either just outside the door or walking towards it.

Nothing to see here kids, just keep walking. Eyes locked on the doorway; Johnny took the last step to the first-floor landing at a controlled jump. The sound of his landing was veered by the sound of the door handle as someone on the other side tried to open it, and discovered it locked. With an electric spark of relief, Johnny pivoted and headed toward the steps down to the basement. He could hear someone cursing on the other side of the door, which shook a moment later, as someone's frustration got the better of them.

Temper, temper, punching doors will get you nowhere. Johnny felt a sardonic grin work its way onto his face. He should know, he'd punched thousands of doors in his time, and it'd never brought him anything but sore knuckles. The voice outside raised to a shout, calling for the keys, Johnny decided, as he raced down the steps to the basement two at a time. As he gained the basement landing, he was met by a wash of cool air, and a light whirring hum that emanated from the door to the basement floor. There was a sign in

Malay and English on the door that said: "Keep closed - The Air is on."

Johnny smiled and pushed the door open. Rows of server racks with a Christmas tree's worth of multicolored lights flickered back at him. Cool, dry, air hit him like a comforting wall, and he felt goose flesh pop up on his arms and neck as sweat from the humid evening started to dry. Shaking himself like a dog, Johnny took in the size of the ad hoc data center. It was big, much bigger than he'd expected from a Malay street gang. There were at least four full rows of server racks, each stuffed with hardware, and that was just what he could see from the door.

Wow, that's a lot of porn, he thought with a grim amusement. Now, where would I stick a spare hard drive with possible footage of a murder on it?

With no immediate answer apparent, Johnny cast about looking for a work area of some sort. He quickly spotted a row of batters folding tables at the back of the room, their well-used simplicity at odds with the high dollar technology that surrounded him. He moved across the intervening space towards the tables, his mind cataloging things as he went.

Workstation, computer crap, more computer crap, thumb-drive, magazines, someone's lunch.

But no hard drive. Frowning, Johnny did another fruitless scan across the tables, then back across the data center, in hopes that he'd just overlooked the hard drive-in question.

Nothing. I hope these assholes haven't hidden it. Another thought struck him, and he frowned even more. *What if the police had already confiscated it?* Frustrated, he pulled his phone from his pocket, hoping to call Robert to get an idea of where else he might look.

No signal.

Cursing, Johnny turned a slow circle, his eyes devouring the racks and racks of humming server hardware. When nothing obvious jumped out, he turned one last time to the table and the assorted detritus - no doubt belonging to whichever of the Tonkong gangsters that acted as the systems admin - and gave it one last desperate going over.

No signal, and still no hard drives.

Deflated, he started to turn away, when something occurred to him.

Hard drives. A thumb drive is sort of like a hard drive.

He reached for the small data transfer device and snatched it up. Just as the door to the hidden data center swung open.

Police uniforms filled the doorway along with the sound of voices shouting back and forth at one another. Johnny, only slightly hidden from the entrance padded behind one of the server racks to hide.

The voices became louder and through the space between the servers, Johnny could see a single - very large - policeman. It made him double take a little as the man was truly massive, barely fitting within the confines of his polyester uniform.

And not an ounce of it was muscle....

Like a shepherd bullying a single sheep, the cop was driving a much smaller, though no less amply bellied gang-member along in front of him. The two were bickering, or at least Johnny thought it sounded like bickering, as they moved through the room. As they neared the workstation and its desk of scattered computer parts, Johnny saw the smaller of the duo turn about and gesture first to the server racks, then generally around at the data center, almost as if he was saying, "Nothing to see here - just computers - lots of and lots of computers." This seemed to spur an argument and as the pair grew more animated in their disagreement, Johnny stole towards the door. He turned to take one last look at the pair as the much smaller gang member poked an angry finger into the larger man's chest to accentuate a point. The policeman's face turned purple, and Johnny decided that was his queue to vacate.

He was two steps out the basement door when he ran into trouble. A single plainclothes cop followed by two uniforms stepped out of the stairway and onto the basement landing. The plainclothes, a detective, or a supervisor Johnny figured, was talking over his shoulder at his companions who were trailing along with matching bored expressions. They saw Johnny before their superior did, their eyes widening in surprise.

Well crap, and things were going so poorly, too.

Johnny charged forward and hit the detective like a linebacker. The cop's breath exploded out in a surprised huff as Dekker dropped his shoulder into the man's gut, then followed up with a blurring punch to this solar plexus. The detective's shout of surprise choked off almost before it erupted as his diaphragm locked up like an early version of the Windows operating system, but there was nothing Johnny cold do about the surprised shouts of the detective's companions.

Get past these clowns and get to the roof.

With a thrust of his arms, Dekker shoved the stunned man forward like a battering ram, hopelessly tangling the two uniforms as they reached for sidearms. Johnny reeled past the gasping detective and snapped a punch into the nose of the cop on his left, he pulled the punch, just wanting to pull the man's attention away from his sidearm. The policeman squawked in surprise and blood shot from his nose, his hands falling away from his pistol. Johnny started to catch the weapon up but thought better of it and simply kicked the falling Glock like a football, sending it spinning through the door and up onto the stairs. He pivoted on the ball of his right foot and darted in close to the remaining uniform. Dekker slammed the smaller, lighter framed policeman into the wall, his right-hand darting down and popping the retaining button on a canister of pepper spray on the policeman's utility belt. A moment's desperate scrabbling later and Johnny had the can in his hand, he released the safety pin and shot a single devastating stream of the concentrated capsacianoids into the startled policeman's face. Twisting he emptied the rest of the canister at the other two cops, reducing them into quivering, bleeding, lumps of miserable humanity, all of them blind, and choking, drooling, and streaming snot.

Taking only a moment to survey his work, Johnny dashed up the stairs and bored the three flights back to the roof like an Olympic sprinter, that even Carl Lewis would need a length to beat, taking the stairs in two and three at a time. He gained the roof and with the last dregs of his overworked adrenals, pounded toward the expanse between the Tokong hideout and the nearby apartment building. Realizing too late, he couldn't simply leap to the roof of the slightly taller apartment, Johnny made a split-second decision before he jumped, and aimed for the fire escape instead.

Gravity fell away - and velocity took over. Johnny arced toward the other building, losing altitude at a precipitous rate. As the ground rushed toward him, he hit the unyielding metal of the fire escape and bounced. Pain shot through his chest and face and legs at the impact, the shock of it blanking his brain for a moment, and almost making him forget to grab hold of the ladder. He slipped almost a foot before his hands caught purchase and his feet remembered to scrabble for the rungs. Stunned and hurting, Johnny hung desperately for a long moment, but he knew he had to keep moving. The Malay police were sure to know about the attack on their officers in the basement by now, and it wouldn't take them long to mobilize. He could only hope that Anderson and the Marines were paying attention and putting their decoy mission in motion.

If they're not, I'm going to have a lot of explaining to do - and I'll probably be doing it from a prison cell.

Johnny shook his head clear letting muscle memory take over. While he'd been a special operator and not a normal seaman, he'd still spent thousands of hours aboard Navy ships and had perfected the seaman's skill of sliding down ladders, his hands and feet holding just enough tension on the rails of the fire escape to slow his descent to something just short of bone jarring as he hit asphalt in the alleyway. The moment his Altama's touched down, he was running for the Suburban.

21

GREAT HALL OF THE PEOPLE, BEIJING

Li Junxiong was the strong silent type. As an effective tactician he had an independent and calculating logic that'd surpassed everyone at the Ministry of State Security as well as the People's Bank of China. He was a national martial arts champion, a learned scholar, and understood that honor was the most important thing in life. So, when he'd balked at the Party line of discouraging the American spy from butting heads with the other Council of Thirteen member, Hamilton-Smith, the Politburo blasted him for insubordination. Dismissed with a moderate scolding and noted reprimand, he shook his head at their ignorance.

What do they know? We can't turn a blind eye while thieves sneak into our neighbor's vault. Never mind they're an arrogant and proud neighbor, they're our neighbor and as a community we've got a responsibility. Besides, Derek Hamilton-Smith is an arrogant jerk, something must be done. A tingling sensation ran down his spine as he stabbed a six-digit code into his Ministry-issued satellite phone determined it was the right call. *C'mon Johnny, pick up...pick up.*

Orphaned at the age of two, Li had always known he was ahead of the curve, but controlling his awareness still proved a hard lesson.

He knew warning the American flew in the face of a direct order from the Committee, but they'd left him no choice. The ringing phone droned on... No answer. *Was he still in Europe or had he made it back to Washington?* He collapsed the phone. With a ticking clock overtaking his rational thoughts he white-knuckled his phone and exited onto a public area of the vast complex.

Ever since his youth he'd blended into the background at social events, adhering to the grey man principle, but his charismatic demeanor and intellect drew people to him. Whether he was in an orphanage, government school, or private academy, his magnetic personality proved invaluable in his rise up the Party ranks with the intellectual elite and military insiders. But he wasn't a youth any longer, his decisions mattered and although the Committee wanted neutrality in the coming conflict, Li's core beliefs from the culture that'd nurtured him, the comrades that'd comforted him, and the ideology that strengthened him informed his final decision.

"*Zhang Guan,*" a pair of patrolling soldiers declared in unison as Li stomped past the General Secretary's office in the Great Hall of the People.

"*Hao.*"

The seasoned intelligence officer twirled a fading Mont Blanc between his calloused fingers as his baritone reply and leather heeled shoes echoed down the marbled corridors. He pushed forward. Despite the expanding gap between them, he felt the soldier's eyes following him, a strong disciplined Socialist that'd carried his nation's flag through more than one active theater and whose rising stature commanded respect, but had it been enough? Was their despicable reprimand the final word on the matter or could they still be swayed? Li stripped down his presentation repeatedly, each and every word. It was short, to the point, and in his mind, if not the Committee members', led to only one conclusion - intervention.

What's the next move?

As a junior officer in the Second Bureau of the Third Department of PLA unit 61398 he'd learned to navigate the labyrinth of influence and politic, the levels of administration, and operate in the shadows from the Communist Party's most formidable masters. By the time he'd ascended to the head of the Ministry of State Security, he'd seen and reviewed more bits of information, and been privy to more covert cyber campaigns, than any hundred people would in a lifetime: culminating in more external contacts and assets than any operative in the Ministry's long secretive history. Now, in his most public position at the central bank, those international relationships were evolving into uncharted territory, especially the one with the American intelligence operative - Johnny Dekker. With the revelations of the Basel conference and the subsequent Standing Committee debriefing still fresh on his lips, an alerted mind calculated the tensile strength of that relationship.

From the beginning, the bond between the up-and-coming intelligence commander and a wayward American spook, caught flat footed on a remote plateau climbing the roof of the world reeked of impending doom, but that unrealized ending proved a new beginning, and now Li found himself facing down the Party he so deeply loved - for an American.

Li blanched and pulled his overcoat close as an incoming arctic blast pierced his coat's microscopic woolen fibers like wind through a thin silk veil, and for a moment made him long for his desk job.

"*Zhang Guan*," the sharp echoing clap of the sentries' boots and the crisp military salute drew the monotonous standard reply.

"*Hao*."

From whatever angle he minced his report, it proved accurate and thorough, but the Committee's awkward silence gripped his mind. *Why are they fixated on Johnny? Why couldn't they intervene? Don't they understand the real threat?* Without an explanation, Li chalked it up to the aging Committee's lack of urgency despite the global disruption unfolding around them. Time was running out.

As he moved toward his car, a numbness shot up his left leg, then his other leg began to seize and lock up. He became lightheaded and his vision started to blur. *What the hell?* He pushed forward. Then it hit him, he hadn't slept since Basel. Whether he liked it or not his body was hitting a wall and shutting down, he needed old fashioned military rack time. Li flashed a grin at his driver, whose expression told him that'd noticed his stumble down the deteriorated concrete steps. He moved forward only to be distracted by another high-pitched chime emanating from his work phone - *BING, BING!*

What do they want now? Was my sworn fealty not enough?

Li stuffed the phone and unread message into his inner breast pocket. One interruption of his day had been enough, not that he was complaining, but he had things to do and being whisked away for further questioning wasn't one of them. Besides he'd fulfilled his duty to the Party, now he'd another duty to fulfill, something that the Party might mis-interpret, but more important debriefing, he got into his car. The driver closed the door behind him as he fell back in the seat and ran through the day's events from the top.

Prior to his meeting with the Standing Committee, the head of his old intelligence unit had conveyed a message that there'd been a surge in Russian Dark Web activity, pointing to a flurry of cyber-attacks against the Americans, and one that Li knew well - Johnny Dekker. This was a problem.

In a former life, Li Junxiong had worked with the FSB on several occasions around border issues in the far western reaches of the country, and it'd always left an unsavory taste in his mouth, something the Russians bragged about to anyone who'd listen. And now they were coming for Johnny - that couldn't stand.

He thought about the debate in Basel between Vice Chairman Patel and the Federal Reserve Chairman Rupert Meyer and frowned. It wasn't the news that Johnny was an American intelligence agent or spook or ghost as their called in the modern vernacular. After all, his first encounter with Johnny had been at the business end of a gun and he knew exactly what Johnny was - his own mirror image. They got passed it. The nagging in his mind was something else, the trouble brewing within the Council of Thirteen between Johnny and the Belgian intertwined with the Russians foreshadowed a catastrophic doom if China did nothing - and that was unacceptable. The Russians desired power, the Americans desired money and the

Chinese were just going to let the Hatfield and McCoy's duke it out then pick up the pieces? *I've gotta do something.*

With several narratives racing through his mind about his next course of action, he fell still, motionless. After a moment, he reached up with one hand and unbuttoned his coat as he felt the graded asphalt tear against the car's tires as it pulled away from the curb. Then it hit him…a smile crept onto his face as he fished his phone from his inner coat pocket and punched in the six-digit security code then a long series of numbers, it wasn't local.

"Isabella speaking…"

Li paused a moment. "I think we need to talk."

"Junxiong?" Isabella Dekker replied in a confused elation.

Li cleared his throat as he thought about the first time, he'd met the enthusiastic and inquisitive cousin of his American friend — Johnny Dekker. A tall attractive brunette with an intellect that rivaled his own, and an insatiable thirst for knowledge that was thoroughly impressive, despite her rather direct approach to conversation. With a renewed sense of hope rushing over his body he breathed a sigh as he motioned his driver forward while he briefed his giddy friend on the unfolding Russian situation.

"It's been too long. I keep planning to visit you in New York, taking you out to a nice dinner, catch up on old times, but work keeps pulling me away."

"We miss you."

"Well, I miss our insightful conversations."

"Junxiong, I'm so happy to talk to you and I'd love to spend an hour catching up, but I'm not sure now is the best time."

Li paused a long moment. "What do you mean?"

"It's all over the television. The markets are crashing, and it was only through some fast-thinking traders that we'd circled our wagons in time."

"Then you already know why I am calling."

Izzy did a double take and slowly closed the door to her office, she watched through the glass enclosure as the traders huddled around a wall of monitors, well past the market close. "Come again?" Izzy's face flushed with a disturbing thought erupting into her mind. "Don't tell me this was the *National team.*"

Li sighed. "I wish. Because if it was our guys then I'd be able to call them off and have them all stand down. This is something else."

"Can you run interference?"

Li shifted in the plush leather seats and watched the driver take another right turn as he thought about his answer. "It's not something we're entertaining at the moment. This is a courtesy call meant to allay any fears of your government and stop any potential *reciprocity.*"

"Um…. I think it's a bit too late for that I'm afraid, but I don't know for certain." The pair of them shared a sarcastic laugh as the connection went silent.

Izzy was at a loss. Johnny was incommunicado and Jack was locked away in a SCIF, and none of her intelligence community contacts were taking her calls at the moment, and the only update on the attack was coming from the one country that was again at odds with the United States over trade agreements. "Li, I'm a banker. Am I supposed to do something with this information?"

Li discerned the shift in her tone. He was also on the outside looking in now, and the only reason he was aware of the situation was that the acting head of his old job at the Ministry of State Security felt it was his duty to inform his mentor on matters that involved his friends and assets. "Izzy it's really not my place anymore to…"

"Stop. Let's just think about this. If the United States infrastructure had been hacked and it wasn't any of your teams," she paused a moment, "then who's responsible?"

"Well…"

"And don't you dare tell me, rogue actors," Izzy said. "If I hear another vague reference, I'm going to lose it. You and I represent significant interests for two of the most powerful and influential nations in the world, we can't just blame our troubles on unknown unknowns or even unknown knowns as these politicians blather on about these days, we need clarity to take action."

A tense pause allowed Li to offer. "The Russians… but the more we've dug into it the more it doesn't make sense. It seems to be elements of the FSB intelligence apparatus, but not completely. Are they acting on orders? Or are they as you said…rogue?"

"You're speaking Greek, Junxiong."

Li breathed a sigh. "It looks like certain individuals within the Russian intelligence service have aligned themselves with some powerful and influential Russian oligarchs as well a small well-connected clique of global bankers."

Izzy let the silence on the line fester. "Junxiong, who was at the Basel conference? Anybody I know?"

Li thought a long moment. Then proffered a couple of names, one of them was the most obvious, Chairman Meyer being a close Dekker family friend and member of the Council of Thirteen, he knew that that name would ring a bell with Izzy, but the others just fell to the dirt like a stone in an empty meadow. It was almost a throw away comment when he mentioned Derek Hamilton-Smith's attendance but elicited an exuberant yelp from the other side of the connection.

"Stop. Derek was there?"

"Well, the Russians hired the Hamilton-Smith Group to help them with a blockchain technology presentation to the *Market Committee*."

There was a long pause as the atmospheric interference clicked and popped over their connection as the two friends waited for the other to speak. "Li Junxiong, it's obvious. This, all of this, is Derek Hamilton-Smith."

Li cleared his throat. "Excuse me. Izzy if this is true it's *Tianzhu* all over again." Another silence followed. "I doubt he's involved. He was only there as a temporary deputy for the Russian Central Bank offering their technological solutions on distributed ledger technology and the future impact of cryptocurrency."

"We cannot allow this to happen," Izzy said.

After a long moment, Li threw out a couple of solutions to alleviate the threat on the banking infrastructure and in turn save the Dekker Banking Group from another cyber-attack. They agreed to sleep on it. Li hung up his phone and began to twirl his pen in hand as he stepped out of the car and headed into his new office at the central bank. He had a solution, but it meant approval from the Politburo, the same one he'd just been chastised by for evening considering intervention.

KUALA LUMPUR, MALAYSIA

Johnny Dekker tapped his finger on his leg in an effortless rhythm. Standing back, he studied the face of United States Deputy Ambassador to Malaysia entering the room and waited for the fallout. He knew the one-way glass barred the officials from seeing him, but to what end. From the moment they'd contacted the Malaysian authorities, Johnny knew it was a bad call. He wiped his brow with his sleeve as he watched the two diplomatic officials engage in civilized, but muted dialogue. What was he telling the Malaysian Minister? Did he even know the reason for unofficial paramilitary professionals sweeping through the streets of their cities? Johnny sighed.

"Let me go and explain it to him."

He felt a large heavy hand land on his shoulder. "You've done enough."

Johnny turned toward the voice. "I didn't start this."

For his part, it'd started when he got news of the attack on his father and his fiancée, but his little voice inside told him Anderson was right. *Let it go.* Johnny stuffed his hands into his pockets and started to pace the room.

When the two government officials rose from the table and shook hands, Johnny breathed a sigh of relief. It'd only taken an hour, which meant they could get back to the hunt. There was no doubt that both governments wanted to move past the Penang incidents and talk about a more pressing agenda, the Pacific Trade Agreement, and that had nothing to do with Johnny Dekker and his band of misfit toys stomping through restaurants and alleyways. The door to the security room flooded the room with light as the men stood to their feet.

"Mr. Dekker, you're lucky the Minister and his royal highness are not looking to make an example of you today. They're more interested in getting back to the trade talks, which you may have single handedly tipped in their favor," the Deputy Ambassador said as he stepped through the doorway.

"It's not that simple, sir."

The deputy tilted his head and pointed to Robert. "You're free to return to Penang, but as for the rest of you it's not so simple. Follow me."

The men filed out of the security room and followed the American diplomat down a long corridor. The drive into Kuala Lumpur had been quiet. Despite the sardine routine in the diplomatic Suburban with Anderson, the Marines, Robert, and Johnny stacked on top of each other, silence had prevailed. Then, once at the embassy, it'd been the Deputy Ambassador that had notified the local government of the incident, not exactly the move Johnny had expected, but something he understood. So far, this had gone much better than any of them had expected. Especially with Johnny plastered all over the television. *That damn reporter. Who was she? And how the hell did she know who he was let alone that he was in Malaysia?* He racked his brain for answers and tried to remember if he'd ever met her before Georgetown or anywhere else, and always came up with the same answer a solid - maybe. Due to his help in attaining the thumb drive and with the damage already affecting his family with Kit's disappearance and likely death, Johnny had managed to convince the Deputy Ambassador not to disclose Robert Lee or his affiliation with the gang splashed across the headlines back in Georgetown, which he'd agreed and subsequently managed to resolve with his release back to Penang.

The door slammed shut. A wild-eyed suit looked at the men gathered around the conference table in the secured Faraday Cage and shook his head. "With the increased rhetoric around this regional trade deal gaining airtime in the media, the Malaysians didn't want to cause any waves. This is not the position that the United States wanted to be in through these negotiations."

Johnny blanched. "You think I wanted this? You think my father, the Ambassador, wanted to be attacked and loose half of his entourage?" Johnny crashed his fist into the table as he stood to his feet disgusted.

"Wait a minute, Dekker."

"No, you wait a minute. If their police had done their job we'd have more answers, maybe even persons of interest. Instead, I've got to go off script and fly around the world to do your jobs for you. What the hell kind of post are you running down here?"

The Deputy Ambassador straightened his tie. "Although local authorities don't have anything to tie you to the disturbances in Georgetown, some images being circulated across the media put you at the scene," he paused, "that said, it's not in-and-of itself damning evidence of a crime and given its proximity to one of the largest tourist hot spots in the city has been dismissed altogether.

Johnny ran his hand across his face and fitted his cap, once again taking a seat. "But?"

After a short pause, the deputy continued. "But, given the recent attack on Ambassador Dekker and the unscrupulous reporters searching for a connection, any connection that might throw a negative light on these trade talks. They've simply asked that Johnny leave the country on the next possible flight."

Johnny sighed aloud. He flashed a quick wink at Anderson and Robert through a thin hard-earned smile. "Looks like our luck's changing, boys."

"Not so fast," the disgruntled diplomat scourged. "This isn't over, and they're very concerned about your true intentions here. They suspect you were seeking revenge for your father and fiancée and told me if that's the case you needn't come back, and if you did, you'd be arrested at the airport."

"So, what then?"

"Your release is a diplomatic courtesy, despite your lack of credentials. As although they'd identified the bodies from the bridge during the attack on the Ambassador, it was improbable they'd catch anyone anytime soon, especially with its Red Door Gang affiliation. They feel obligated...."

Johnny scoffed through clenched teeth. "They've got viable evidence of who was behind the attack, and they didn't inform us?" A sliding chair and thud redirected his attention to Robert who'd stood up at the mention of the gang as Johnny looked him square in the eyes.

Robert blanched. "Those guys are notorious for working exclusively for one client..." Robert trailed off as he planted his arms on the control room wall dropping his head between his shoulders.

Johnny rose from his seat and stepped to Robert's side. "And that would be?"

Robert exhaled and twisted his pale face toward Johnny. "The Russians."

GEORGETOWN, MALAYSIA

Hannah Jankowski exhaled. A wave of goosebumps rippled across her arms as she faced her road ahead, an after dark excursion into a less reputable part of a remote city in the Southeast Asia nation. Somewhere, in the back of her mind, she knew what to do and how to do it, she'd been through the training, but nothing had prepared her mind for the adrenaline rush of a solo mission. *Calm yourself.* A slight tug on the handle and she'd only sealed her room when a vibrating sensation from her phone danced against her thigh — *an incoming message.* She ignored the phone and turned down the corridor. Everything had gone as planned and now she'd only one more thing to complete before she'd rendezvous with her handler, Anja Singh.

From the moment she'd begun her mission, she had doubts. Doubts about finding Johnny Dekker, doubts about her ability to win him over and even now, doubts about the doubts. She craned her head left and right using the reflective surfaces as tools to observe her surroundings rather than twitching about like a jonesing drug addict, but she could never shake that feeling deep down - *was she being watched?*

Hannah paused a long moment. She needn't reminding that this was a pivotal meeting, everything about the success of her three-year mission depended on completing this next task. She took a deep breath, relaxed her mind, and shook her hands as she waited on the elevator. With a moment to spare, she slipped into her thoughts long enough to remind herself of the road traveled. In truth, she'd thrived undercover and had been a proven asset, but part of that came from the comforting notion that she'd always been shadowed by a wingman that could swoop in and extract her when things got too hairy, today she was alone. Another vibration emanating from her pocket as she peered down, and with the phone in the palm of her hand turned back toward her room.

Levy: Free?
Hannah: Running late.
Levy: Miss your voice.
Hannah: 5.

Hannah propped her head on her door. *Could his timing be any worse?* She'd mustered up the moxie to get this meeting done, and now she was being called into the principal's office? She fished her room key from her coat pocket and re-entered with an intensifying anxiety. There was only a short window before she'd be late for the meeting, as if there wasn't enough pressure on her performance. She loosed a sigh as she thumbed through her phone apps and tapped the encrypted voice app listed as MAKEOVER.

When it opened she hit the preset number and listened through the satellite relay linking her to a familiar, yet distant masculine voice.

"*Shalom.*"

"I hope it's important. I'm not on vacation," Hannah said.

"*Shalom* Hannah," the elder voice repeated.

Hannah braced herself against the foyer wall. "*Shalom*, sir."

"Relax, I realize we caught you at an inopportune time, but

there's a couple of things you should know. We've intercepted communications between our Russian friends and your gal pal."

"And?"

"And, it looks like they've accomplished what they'd set out to do and have asked her to clean up her mess. And you know what that means?"

"Loose ends."

"Correct."

"Roger that, thanks for that, but I've got to go or I'll be the next loose end."

"Be safe my dear, *Shalom*."

Hannah stared at her reflection in the mirror. She'd looked like she was carrying the weight of the world on her face. *Game time*. An annoying chirping from the earpiece brought her back to reality as the line went dead. She clapped the phone shut and poured herself a drink. She took a couple of deep breaths and walked toward her door, and toward the elevator once again.

With more than several headlines raining down on the Dekker situation with international reach pushing her narrative, she needed to shift her focus and make sure she wasn't dropping the ball with Anja. *DING!* She checked her watch and stepped into the elevator when another alert erupted onto her locked screen. *Anja*.

Hannah thumbed down the screen and opened the message. *This is it. This is what you've been waiting for.*

Anja: Forget Tokong. Johnny in KL.

There was nothing more to say. The whole reason Hannah was in Penang was to distract Johnny, and by extension the CIA, which kept *their* focus on Malaysia.

Hannah: I'm connecting through Hong Kong.

Anja: You must move quickly. They're sending him back to Virginia.

Hannah: Understood.

Hannah breathed a hard relief, no slumming it tonight, it was time to get out of Malaysia. There was no telling what was happening in the American embassy, there could be a van of police on the way to her location at that very moment. She needed to exit and exit quick. She dropped the phone on the bed next to the luggage that she begun tossing her clothes into. Within a few minutes she'd secured the room and burned several papers in the bathroom trash can before flushing the charred remains down the toilet.

She grabbed her passport in hand and stuffed her other essential documents from the room safe into her bag and zipped up her garment bag and backpack. After a long pause, another *BING, BING* chimed through her phone. She scooped it up and read, then replied.

Anja: I love the toffee here.

Hannah: Perfect, see you soon.

The toffee meant Anja had arrived at the Berkley Hotel in London, England.

22

LANGLEY, VIRGINIA

When the hydraulic-powered ramp came to a whining halt, a frigid North American wind tore through the cargo hold stripping the hardened soldiers of their pride as they plead for mercy while gripping their jackets tight and wonder if they had made a mistake by leaving the Southeast Asian paradise. The collective push forward caused a half-step miscalculation off the ramp, and found Johnny Dekker twitching in place a moment, the awkward angle at which he'd slammed down onto the tarmac - fully loaded - was resetting his pain threshold. His faded Altamas surrendered to the moment as the aged stitching burst their factory specifications and splayed taunting the weary operative. With one knee on the steaming asphalt and a controlled grimace stretched across his face, he paused. He threw a look back over his shoulder at the massive C-17 transport, its ominous presence glowing in the canary yellow sunrise, and smiled. *Damn, maybe the doc was right. I might need that eye exam after all.*

Although it'd only been a few years since he'd left the Naval Special Warfare program, he knew his time since hadn't kept his skills honed and sharp. The fact that he'd misjudged the full deployment of a hydraulic ramp, was just another subtle reminder. *Life goes on.* Another moving body brushed past him as he realized he'd stooped in front of the entire entourage exiting the transport. He loosened his grip on his gear, took a couple of deep breaths, then extracted a spool of duct tape from his backpack, and addressed his complication. It wasn't the first time he'd embarrassed himself in front of Marines, and not likely the last.

Johnny finished up his repairs, adjusting and tightening his shredded sneakers as much as possible, not stopping to think about the storied history of each scuff and tear. Although they stood as a stark reminder of his path from the mud room to the board room, there was no time for sentimental journey. After thousands of hard miles across Africa, the Middle East and parts unknown, it was time to put them to rest. It was time to decide. Get an upgrade or hang 'em up for good. Johnny tied the laces in a tight double knot, grabbed his backpack off the ground, slung it over his shoulder and limped toward a parked sedan waiting outside the main hangar.

"Welcome back, sir" the sharply dressed driver said as he took Johnny's bag.

"No place like home."

Johnny breathed a sigh of relief as he strapped himself in and sat back in the plush leathered passenger seat, something of a welcomed change from his most recent transport. Without another word he was en route to the office, where he knew, management was waiting to debrief him, but this was above their pay grade. He knew they wouldn't understand, but he needed to roll with the punches, and not overlay his Council of Thirteen position to his day job, that could get messy.

Despite documented records and whistleblowers of multinational organizations and what the Intelligence Community thought they knew about geopolitics, reality proved more elaborate and nuanced. The Council was a transnational organization that'd managed for centuries to stay beyond any nationalistic reach through its intricate network of spies and like any other organization it had factions. These factions worked together for the most part, but sometimes conflict arose despite their mutually agreed charter.

Johnny had rerun the attack scenario in his head a thousand times. If the Russians had been involved, they were only the outer facade, the face the puppet master wanted him to see. From a layman's perspective the Council of Thirteen was a manipulative self-serving organization that shifted national governments at a whim, and for all intents and purposes, this was true. However, nine of those ancient lineages that had founded the organization believed in guiding humanity into a bigger and better, perhaps multi-planetary spacefaring civilization, but to do that a certain amount of technology and structure was necessary.

As a sitting member of the Council of Thirteen, Johnny sat the top of the food chain, although his CIA service proved a convenient front from which to scout talent and keep abreast of the machinations of industry, and he liked that. Regardless of his position, he knew the inner workings of the intelligence apparatus thrived on its independence and its hierarchy. He resided to sit through the debrief, if for no other reason than to maintain the status quo; the alternative - Chaos.

"The weatherman said there's a nor'easter building up off the coast."

Johnny smirked and cut his eyes at the driver. "What's with the traffic?"

"You must've been out town for a while. That conservative senator from Kentucky is laying in state. There've been people arriving all day, causing massive traffic jams from every corner of the beltway."

Johnny slumped back and exhaled. "Fantastic."

Somewhere, on the slow crawl from Andrews to Langley, Johnny's inner demons began chipping away at his decision to degrade himself by sitting through a debriefing from these sheep, disconnected, but proud of their intelligence reach, besides he'd more important things to do like finding the Ambassador's attackers. He felt an anxiousness build in his foot, tapping on the floorboard, then crawl up his leg before it was moving in concert with the foot. Without a doubt every minute he sat in traffic was a minute that pulled him in the other direction, and although he knew upsetting the status quo with management and pulling rank on the Agency would get him off the hook, it'd create more systemic longer-term problems.

C'mon, this is ridiculous.

Despite his overwhelming feeling to change course, he knew that whatever information was on the thumb drive, he'd need all the resources of both the CIA and NSA to isolate and contain his target, which meant he needed Langley in the loop and on board.

You can update them after you know for sure. They won't mind waiting a few more hours, especially if you find the assassin.

After a few moments, he felt the driver's eyes on him as he stared out into the pandemonium on the parkway. He knew there was either a wealth of information on that thumb drive or it was a dead end, either way it was more important than any debriefing. And the possibility of identifying the assassin compelled his next move. He sat forward to tell the driver to take him to Fort Meade when the sedan hit a speed bump on the endless meandering service road. As Johnny reached forward and pulled himself within earshot, the driver beat him to the punch.

"You've got something on your mind, sir?"

Johnny paused a long moment. "Given…"

The driver interjected. "Mr. Chambers told me to bring you directly to the Agency, but from the look on your face you've got something else in mind."

Johnny snorted a laugh. "That's very perceptive of you… but I think Mr. Chambers is right. Let's get me back to Langley ASAP."

Resigned not to avoid the debriefing, Johnny focused his thoughts on the facts he'd uncovered, and the questions he needed answered. He only wanted one thing - to find the assassin. The success of the next step depended on his ability to convince Director Mark Brown - Chloe's boss - that he understood his missteps and what trouble they'd caused in the media, but that he was ready to redeploy and solve the problem. For the moment, he'd put aside the thumb drive, the Russian involvement, and the mysterious reporter. *Everything in its own time.*

Johnny knew Mike Chambers. This entire airport pickup was some silly ploy aimed at getting inside his head. *He'd better be careful what he wishes for.* Johnny flipped open his pen and jotted down a couple of words onto his slim notepad he'd removed from his breast pocket - a subtle distraction to the watchful pair of eyes that blazed at him through the rearview mirror.

Deep down, Johnny unfolded the invasive tentacles of an elaborate scheme that begun to extend their approach over the last few days. It hadn't taken long to determine that the Malaysian assassins, the machinations of the Russian bankers in Basel, and the interference from within the intelligence community all pointed to something much larger than the Agency was letting on, and that this was something that had direct implications to the Council of Thirteen. Johnny reclined back in his seat and drifted into a light meditative state, but the rhythm of the road prompted him to action, sparking a better idea - *Jack.* He fished his phone from his pocket and hit speed dial.

"I need your help."

A surprised voice pierced the earpiece. "Where the hell are you?"

"No time for that, I'll be at Langley within the hour. Can you meet me there? I've got something that could pull this all together."

"All of what? Are you aware of what's happened while you were out?"

"I've been on a round-the-world flight, so let's say I'm not…"

"We've been hit."

Johnny blanched. "Are you in the bunker?"

"There was a coordinated Cyber-attack on our domestic infrastructure, we're still assessing the extent of the damage. But as of now, it looks mostly targeted at the financial infrastructure."

"Izzy…"

"She's fine… But the bank took a hit, brother. I haven't spoken with Izzy in a while, but you need to get back to Manhattan. This doesn't feel like it's over."

"What about the assassin? I've video that may show the killer's face."

Jack sighed. "I'm about to be reassigned. I'll pass it to the SCIF team."

"Fuck that, Jack. I need you on this."

"Did you hear what I said? They hacked our financial markets, man. This is bigger than both of us, and even Chloe... Sorry, it's stressful around here, but this could be the beginning of the end if we don't get on top of this and turn it around."

"I get that, but this has the face of those responsible for Chloe's death and the death of several United States Marines, doesn't that mean anything to you anymore?"

Jack Sorenson, the most sought-after cryptanalyst in the United States Intelligence Community, paused a long moment. "I'm on my way. But I'm not promising anything."

"I owe you brother."

"No, you don't. Just tell those fine-tailored suits that the geek squad is en route and not to hold me up at security."

Johnny breathed a short chuckle remembering how much Jack fashioned himself after the great technological wizard from the comic books - Tony Stark. "Roger that, *Mr. Stark.*" A faint smiled crossed his face as he pocketed his phone and fell back into his thoughts with the approaching Langley campus now looming in the foreground.

∽

IF ANYTHING, it'd turned out a good thing that the U.S. Ambassador to Malaysia had been away, although if he'd been there, none of this would've happened in the first place as it did, but regardless Johnny welcomed the luck. From what he'd learned about the career diplomat, he wasn't someone that would've made their situation any easier and more than likely than not thrown them to the wolves to protect his precious local relationships.

From the moment they'd arrived at the Embassy in Kuala Lumpur, the team had kept the details of their extraction close to the vest, saying nothing outside of Johnny's statement to the Deputy Ambassador. Even the embassy Marines deferred to Johnny, only partially feigning ignorance. It proved the best way to keep everyone on point ahead of the arrival of the Malaysian Foreign Affairs Minister.

The deputy hadn't asked about the thumb drive, and Johnny was happy to leave him in the dark about the particulars of his time in Georgetown. *What they don't know wouldn't hurt them.*

Besides, it'd only brought him more questions than answers, and the last thing he needed was State Department interference. Johnny quietened his breathing as he rubbed the thumb drive in his pocket. *More questions than answers. What was the Russian angle? And who the hell was that nosy reporter?*

Despite his reluctance to accept it, the Russian involvement seemed logical, after all their FSB had been running down every possible technological breakthrough trying to keep ahead of the Americans and the Israelis. There wasn't a day that had gone by since the end of the Second World War, and some would argue even before that, that the Russians weren't scheming on the complete acquisition of United States technology and know-how. As for the reporter, he'd chalked it up to an overzealous investigative reporter, but something still felt off. *Who was she? What did she want? And, how the hell did she find him in Malaysia?*

As it stood, it'd all turned out for the best with Johnny and the marine detail back in the United States and Robert not even mentioned in the station logs, allowing him to return to Penang and deal with the loss of his brother, something that he'd have to deal with when all of this was said and done.

Johnny felt the driver slow to a halt, something about that guy still bothered him, but he didn't have time for any of that. He exited the car, grabbed his gear from the trunk, and headed inside the George Bush Center for Intelligence building.

A pain shot down his arm as he adjusted his jacket then raised his head and saw Mike Chambers in the lobby with open arms, literally, it was quite embarrassing. *Freak.*

"Good to see you," Mike Chambers said as he gripped Johnny's hand and slapped him on the back in front of the morning onslaught of analysts and admins filing through the security gates inside the building.

Johnny snickered. "Okay...."

Out of the corner of his eye, Johnny spotted Jack Sorenson locked in a debate about his meeting with Mr. Dekker. Johnny reassured the guards and waved him over. His compatriot stopped mid-sentence and scurried across the marbled floor lobby toward the two men.

"I told you they didn't appreciate 'drop-ins'."

Johnny laughed. "Never mind, them. Listen Mike, give us a minute, would you?" He watched Mike nod his head and step away toward the security checkpoint striking up small talk with the guards.

Johnny wanted answers and he didn't want Mike lurking over his shoulder when he was getting them, he needed to keep this one compartmentalized in case it implicated the Council of Thirteen in any way - Jack could be trusted. He didn't understand why the thought of potential Council involvement had come to mind, but then he remembered his ambitious nemesis, Derek Hamilton-Smith and decided that it should factor into his deliberations, but why would the Russians get involved with Derek. It might've been a stretch, but he wanted to find out. He gripped Jack by the shoulder and slid the thumb drive into his free hand hanging to his side. His tradecraft or lack thereof was astounding. He wasn't used to all the cloak and dagger antics, especially while standing in the lobby of the inventors and masters of the craft, he felt like a bull in a china shop. "This is important. It's video from the Cafe in Georgetown. It had full view of the events leading up to the attack on the bridge and could reveal the assassin."

Jack played it off with a laugh for the audience they both knew they had analyzed their every move; spooks can't be trusted. "It's good to have you back, and text me when you're done here, Izzy wants to grab dinner and hear about your father's condition." The two men exchanged a quick bro hug and Johnny watched Jack exit the building and hoped for a clear frame of who orchestrated the hit.

Johnny brushed his hands across his shirt as he stepped up to Mike leaning against the counter waiting for the prodigal son, Johnny cleared his throat and then motioned to the elevator bank. "You had questions?"

He watched Mike replace the visitor logbook on the security counter and smiled at his colleague, disregarding Jack's fleeting presence. There was an increased amount of activity in the lobby, the start of the day, the start of the week and with the start of a nor'easter tearing its way up the coast that'd closed a couple of routes into work for the suburbanites, it was the start of a long journey. The two men disappeared through security door and wound their way up to the director's office.

Director Mark Brown wasn't a happy camper, as they say. The attack on the domestic infrastructure had heightened his aggravation with the entire Malaysian situation. He wasn't impressed with Johnny's disappearance or the manner in which the entire world came to find out he was in Malaysia. He paced the floor of his office as Mike and Johnny stepped through his door.

"Good morning, sir," Johnny began.

Brown paused. "This is the part where you tell me what the fuck you were doing in Malaysia."

Johnny quirked an eyebrow. "No small talk?"

"Not only did you leave Chairman Meyer in Basel when you were set to get a key nomination on the Markets Committee, but you disobeyed a directive from the State Department about travel to Malaysia issued to all federal employees - that meant you."

"I'm a federal employee, Mark?"

"Damn it, Johnny. This whole moonlighting as an agent thing only works if you take direction from this office. We've an opportunity to get someone close to the decision-making process on these disruptive technologies and help steer the narrative and the highest levels in Basel. They're accelerating at a faster pace than the Washington bureaucracy assigns people to research and track them. Why the hell would you mess with that when you know we've your father's situation under control?"

"First of all, there seems to be a misunderstanding. When I agreed to come back to the Agency and even back into the field, so our government could get a handle on this spiraling situation in Switzerland, you knew my view, you knew my methods and you knew I was a big boy." Johnny stepped toward the director not ceding any ground, posturing like the alpha male silverback in the Congolese Mountains of Africa. He kept Mike on his left flank as he'd moved toward the director. "And, if you want to jump right into it...Why the hell am I dealing with Mike Chambers on this?"

"Don't change the topic? That was a long time ago."

Johnny burnt red with anger as he laid into the director. "You wanted my help. I agreed to give it to you for the sake of our country. Remember that?"

"What's your point, Johnny?"

"I don't need a shadow. I've enough eyes on me without having to worry about whether I'm checking back, or my handler has his own set of eyes on me. It's fucking overkill."

Mike threw his hands in the air. "My overkill saved your ass in Malaysia... you're welcome, by the way."

"Well, Mikey, maybe I could thank you if I knew that it wasn't you who sent in that reporter to spy on me in the first place."

Mike breathed a curse as he stood up. "This is insanity. Hannah Jankowski is an international correspondent for the BBC, and she has nothing to do with me, buddy."

Johnny retorted. "Then maybe you should step outside."

Mike looked at Johnny and then the Director. Johnny watched as the Director nudged his head for Mike to exit and leave them alone for a few minutes. He jammed the door open and retreated to the adjacent corridor.

Director Brown looked at Johnny. "What are you doing? He's a career operator. He knows how to handle himself, and he gets results."

Johnny cut his eye at the director. There could never be enough results to make up for the sloppiness he'd witnessed first-hand when he and Mike had worked together in the field a few years ago on a kidnap rescue operation. Absolute amateur hour, he counted to himself as stared down the Director.

"Results..."

Director Brown put his hands on the desk. "Can we not get into that now?"

There were some things that couldn't be forgotten. And Johnny didn't want to have anything to do with that direction of the Agency and was one of the reasons he'd hung up his hat and quit the agency in the first place. A new breed of selfish prima donnas had emerged within the Agency, and Johnny had bigger things to worry about. It was only after crucial evidence had emerged that linked the Russians and their affiliates to a web of global financial disruption that the director called Johnny back into service, hoping to leverage his unique social status within the global financial community. The two men had retreated to opposite ends of the director's desk.

Johnny leaned forward. "I'll take care of the Basel situation, but I need all the information we have regarding the Malaysian incident. I've got a feeling it's all connected."

Mark Brown looked at Johnny. "What?"

"It looks like the assassins in Malaysia could've been working for a fringe Russian outfit. And if my suspicions are right, then I may know which banking group is backing the Russians blockchain initiative."

"Who?"

"Give me what I need and a couple of days to confirm it - me - not the dog and pony show." Johnny followed the director's thinking as he looked at Johnny, then out the window at a frustrated Chambers pacing the floor outside his office, Johnny didn't care. There was more than pride at stake here and Johnny knew the director understood that.

Brown sighed as he turned to Johnny. "Walter over at NSA has called an emergency meeting to strategize and implement an immediate response to the cyber-attack, it seems they've some new information about the perpetrator, the one that hit us while you were off gallivanting around Malaysia, sapping resources best spent elsewhere. This trumps the assassination and I need my best people on it, and so does Walter. As it stands, we've our 'A' team working on the assassination and that should be enough for you, and if it's not, *C'est la vie*, because life goes on, Johnny."

The director paused and stepped closer to the frustrated executive field operative. "I need you to share everything you got on your Malaysian trip and keep Mike in the loop on any developments, so we can transition him into the assassination lead as Jack gets reassigned, running point on this algorithmic, cryptographic, too fucking technical for me to deal with bullshit instead of signal chasing and covering for you -*Comprende*?"

An awkward silence fell over the room. "Sir..."

"Don't, Johnny. I don't have time for adolescent squabbles."

"Can I at least request all the information they've collected to date on the assassination attempt?"

"Talk to Mike, damn it."

Johnny nodded in affirmation, then turned his back on the director. He'd taken his family status and seniority as far as he could, he exited the director's office, walking straight past a dumbfounded Mike Chambers.

SHOAL BAY RECEIVING STATION

James Montgomery Whitney smacked the back of the eighties era coffee machine, which responded with a low *whirring* sound. *Not again.* After a series of well-placed knocks on various parts of the machine, and several reboots with the power source, he'd reached wits end. He rubbed his numbing hand and leaned back against the wall, after all he couldn't blame anyone but himself, because it was a well-known fact that the military always went with the cheapest subcontractors, and that included cafeteria services. *Bloody hell.* With a furrowed brow he scooped up a couple of tea bags from the station and filled a cup with piping hot water and retreated to his graveyard posting, which meant the same thing in remoteness of Northern Australia that it did in Tennessee, a half-life zombie existence. Suffice it to say that this proved unacceptable to his last two girlfriends and the primary reason he'd chosen to forego another desperate search for a replacement, the other being he'd spent more time coding than he did at work. Instead, he'd decided to take a less traveled approach and volunteered for double shifts at the new joint-operations base, his CO was more than pleased since the incoming requests from their American allies had begun to pile up on her desk.

From the tranquility of his outpost, and the nature of his assignment, James managed to kill two birds with one stone as he donned an advanced listening headset that was tapped into the various arrays surrounding the outpost, his hands were free to bang on his keyboard scripting line after line of coding, until they weren't, which had provided the perfect setting for his tortured genius. The remote listening station had been built in conjunction with a new Five Eyes initiative, which included a broad group of Commonwealth intelligence communities as well as the United States. Despite its increasing sophistication and relevance over the last twenty-four months, it had only minimal staffing, something that seemed irrelevant at the time of implementation. Although there was more than one operation at any given time and he was responsible for the Southeast Asian region, including Brunei, Indonesia, Malaysia, the Philippines, Singapore, and Thailand, it had been a quiet assignment and he loved it.

Much like the SETI research around the world, his was a quiet one and rarely matched anything from the daily generated watchlist. Most of the time, James programmed away feeding on the low hum of the headset like it was a jamming session at a Metallica concert.

With degrees in both electrical and computer engineering, he'd owned this assignment.

With a steaming cup of tea in his hand James sat back and took a sip, blowing as he cradled the mug in his hands. After allowing the caffeine some time to make its way through his system, he placed the tea on the counter, picked up his headset, and punched in a security code. Once he'd satisfied himself that nothing had happened during his sojourn to the cafeteria, he settled back in his chair and grabbed his laptop from a nearby side table. Out of the humming emptiness of space an ear-piercing alert echoed through his head as the system signaled a hit. Pushing back from the terminal he spun his chair around and checked the computer stack, everything was kosher. He pulled himself back to his main terminal and began to run a diagnostic, clean. *Fuck.*

James confirmed his checklist and then connected the information through an encrypted carrier along the Five Eyes network, just as a precaution. Today, James earned a crash course in paying attention to station. The level one alert warned active and immediate danger. There was a highly sought-after target flaring up in his sector and he needed to get the coordinates and all relevant information before his supervisor arrived, which would be momentarily. *Fuck. Fuck. Fuck.*

He stabbed at his keyboard as he zeroed in on the cellular phones IMEI numbers, once he confirmed the numbers, he correlated that information with the daily list and scraped through the cell towers until he had precise GPS coordinates. It wasn't rocket science, but it was methodical. Once he'd authenticated the signals on both ends, he sent it up the chain of command and requested tracking of the numbers to not lose them, it was never certain how long they could hold the signal. *Holy Shit.*

As James reached out for another sip of Early Grey, the door flew open, and his supervisor burst through the door half-dressed and panting.

"Tell me you got a location."

James eyed his monitor. There were two sets of coordinates

running across the screen: one emanated from Malaysia, and the other surprised him. He gulped a breath as he blushed up at his supervisor. *Tel Aviv*

"I didn't know MOSSAD had operatives in Malaysia."

A look like someone had shot her puppy stretched across the supervisor's pale face. "Neither did I."

23

FORT MEADE, MARYLAND

More than ever, it was essential that the White House appointed intelligence team had privacy, and nothing was more private than the reinvented Faraday cage, used for sensitive conversations. Jack Sorenson caressed the smooth metallic door until he felt the circular latch, an intricate mechanism that enabled top level security, nothing had been overlooked in the design of this workspace. An effortless pull and the reinforced magnetically sealed door swung shut with a muffled sucking sound, sealing in the attendees, and all their unspoken words. *Perfect.* A self-styled technological perfectionist, Jack marveled a moment at the simplistic, but poetic mechanism, and failed to see his boss step up behind him.

"Glad you could make it, Jack."

Jack blanched. "Apologies, I had a last minute…"

Director Moore smiled. "Shall we get started?"

Jack wore an awkward smile as nodded his head at the various department representatives as found his seat at the conference table. He knew most of the attendees, although had to pause at the decision of the military brass allowing several civilians into the high-level meeting. The sensitive meeting notification had mentioned -

counterstrike - and Jack knew there were more than a few itchy trigger fingers seated around him, each chomping at the bit, but for what and against who? With his mind elsewhere Jack caught the elbow of DIA head as he pulled himself toward the table and removed a pen from his inner jacket pocket.

"Sorry."

Jack didn't like abandoning the Dekkers, but it wasn't his call, and right now all he could do was play his role and help resolve the cyberattack, which was the clear and present danger.

"Looks like a full house," the DIA director replied to Jack with a smile.

Jack sighed. "And it may not be enough."

"Don't worry Jack, we'll find these guys and shut 'em down."

"Welcome everybody, I think I'll skip the pleasantries and get straight to the point," Director Moore started. Jack watched as the room froze to attention. "According to the SEC investigators, the series of trades that sparked the sharp selloff across the financial markets seems to have originated in the Cayman Islands, a well-known hedge fund tax haven. Each trade originated offshore and was funneled through multiple onshore Broker-Dealer Dark Pools, which delayed the realization that an attack was afoot." The room erupted with angered whispers as the director continued... "As for our infrastructure and utilities, we've already deployed our TAO (Office of Tailored Access Operations) team to safeguard all feasible targets around the country, they're working with Cyber Command and other various hubs to ensure a united and informed front. If there's another attack coming, we'll be ready."

Jack peered over his glasses as the shockwave of information one by one claimed another victim, leaving them out of the running to head any task force that may or may not be established, he paused and prepared potential comments in his mind. It'd been too long since he'd been in the field, but a counterstrike was there only option, and he wanted to be a part of it, if not lead it himself.

A wave of muffled voices echoed through the room as various civilian and military experts exchanged contradicting viewpoints until the director cleared his throat to continue. "There's no time to waste. I'll be assigning a team to head down to Grand Cayman where they will assess and eliminate any threat."

Jack retreated into his thoughts. He tuned out the director as he droned on about the scope of the attack and the response to date, nothing he didn't already know. After all, he'd prepared the talking points himself. Now, all he wanted was the go-ahead to chase down the lead. A sense of frustration welled up inside him as the briefing ground on, meandering through bureaucratic brown nosing and posturing. *Get to the point already, chief. The Caymans, who's going to infiltrate the Cayman facility?* Jack thumbed the notepad in front of him wondering what was happening in Malaysia. He snuck several deep breaths trying to slow his pounding heart as he pricked his ears as the various agencies chimed in on their preferred approach, then faded back into his thoughts as their proposals fell flat.

General Miller cleared his throat as he interrupted the DIA specialist. "It seems to me that whoever leads this reconnaissance team, whether it's one or multiple persons needs to be highly trained in hand-to-hand combat. We don't want a tech specialist getting down there and put flat on his back because he didn't have the necessary skills to defend against whatever they come across."

"What we need is a one of those paramilitary boys from Langley, a snake eater," blurted the Marine general as all heads turned toward an unusually quiet Director Brown.

Jack pushed his thumbnail into his hand as he fumed in silence waiting for the director to correct them and announce that his trusted SEAL trained geek squad leader, Jack Sorenson, would be running down the lead in the Caymans. He watched as Director Moore rapped his knuckles on the table as the low murmuring among the attendees had grown into full-on bar room roar and nobody could make head nor tails of what was being said.

"Okay, gentlemen. Hold on a minute." The chatter continued. "Listen," he roared forcing a wave of silence across the room like a Category 5 Hurricane. "This isn't a brain versus brawn issue. This is a *time* issue. Whomever takes this one has to be ready within the next few hours and be equipped with all the tools necessary for whatever unfolds."

What was he waiting for? Jack cleared his throat as the anticipation began to unnerve him. This wasn't what he'd signed up for when he agreed to drop the Dekkers and refocus on the cyberattack. He cut his eyes to his left and right sizing up the other members of the attending intelligence community.

"Sir," Jack interrupted.

Director Moore stopped mid-sentence and turned his attention toward Jack. "Was there something you wanted to add, Jack?"

There was no more messing around, it was time to throw his hat in the ring. "I'm ready to go," Jack said then cast his eyes around the table.

"Well, I think that's a great idea," Director Brown replied. For some unknown reason, Jack saw that Moore wasn't impressed with the suggestion.

Jack watched as several other members around the table concurred pulling Jack out of his own head and fueling his confidence as he continued. "What we know is that deep system scans inside key technology clusters at several investment banks have uncovered embedded spyware. There was a blatant, malicious, and likely ongoing effort to impact and cause harm to the financial markets. And not just the United States, but the global financial markets." Jack paused a moment, then continued as he hooked his prey. "With the increasing amounts of derivatives and other financial instruments circulating in these already wavering markets, we don't have time for anyone *not* well versed in any aspect of this attack to run this down. And who better equipped in this room than me?"

A long pause held the room as the members whispered amongst themselves.

"If I go, we keep this contained to this room as it was intended when this working group was formed in the first place. We keep this on a short leash and minimize the risk of leakage or miscalculation," Jack finished.

A gut-wrenching gaze pierced his soul as he caught a glimpse of

Director Moore's face. Then, it happened like a knockout blow from the heavyweight champ of the world, his dreams of getting back into the field buried in one sentence.

"This isn't a media fueled *Stuxnet* debacle, this is the last line of defense," the director said with pursed lips.

Jack withered into the back of his chair. The humiliation and cloud of past failings including his fall from the Seventh Floor came crashing down around him, the director conveyed his decision on the Cayman assignment as he sat motionless, limp without purpose. With a furrowed brow and sweat beading down his forehead the only retreat was inward revisiting his first cardinal sin of the intelligence game, *TRUST*. Along his meteoric ascension up the intelligence ranks after his tours in the Navy SEALS, he'd run the first covert cyber war of the Agency —*Project Olympic Games*. A joint initiative with close allied government that infiltrated and manipulated the infrastructure of a target deemed a global threat, but when the wheels came off and the covert war became public, the global media whipped itself into a frenzy of secret wars and Zionist plots. From the moment he allowed allied access to the root code, the sin became public, and would've ended his career were it not for the intervention of Director Moore. It wasn't until a flamboyant British Royal sunbathing in the Caribbean changed the media narrative that focused shifted. Jack tuned back into the conversation as the director mentioned a name he'd not considered and used every ounce of training to contain his shock.

"Jack is correct, in that we need a man in this room," Director Moore said as he turned toward the CIA director and a man Jack had, in his frustration, overlooked seated next to him. "And that's why, Mike Chambers will be taking this assignment and reporting back to the designated SCIF with any and all information." Everybody knew Mike and understood the decision as soon as it was stated. After a moment, the director shifted in his seat and turned his attention and the other dozen pairs of eyes back toward Jack. "And that's where Jack and his team will quarterback our response."

Redemption. "Yessir."

Despite the overwhelming overtures from across the table on him to lead the mission, Jack knew the director had made the right call. Keeping him at the center of the information flow in Fort Meade was the better plan, despite his longing for the return to the field. He buried his emotions and looked down the table at Mike Chambers. "Good luck."

A wave of eagerness swept over Jack as he sat up in his chair and waited for the meeting to end. Within a few more minutes the director wrapped up the details connecting the various agencies and set the plan in motion then adjourned.

Director Moore leaned over to the perplexed cryptanalyst. "Jack, let's meet back in my office in thirty minutes, there are some things we need to discuss in further detail." He smiled then disappeared with the National Reconnaissance Office (NRO) director into an adjoining room outside the faraday cage.

Jack clenched his teeth, then stood up and walked toward the line of agents filing out the door.

"Good luck, Jack," Head of US Cyber Command General Miller said as he approached the door.

Jack reacted with a quick request before the General disappeared down the hallway. "General Miller, if you could have your team send me over the files, they'd gathered on Southeast Asia communications the few hours before and after the attack, I think it'll help me get this investigation jumpstarted."

"I'll deliver them personally," the General replied cutting short the conversation as he disappeared down the secured corridor.

Cooperation? Jack held the door a moment. Something had been gnawing at him from the start. The whole cyberattacks felt wrong, and its speedy deconstruction seemed too simplistic, too structured. They'd missed something and he couldn't put his finger on it. A cyberattack on the financial markets was one thing, but if this malware were to grow beyond those connection nodes or the hackers shifted their focus toward other more sensitive infrastructure targets like the public utilities around the country, it would be catastrophic. It would ensure pandemonium and anarchy with nothing less than a broad military deployment needed to quell the chaos, something that was taboo across the political aisles in Washington, and nobody wanted to make that call. *It would be political suicide.* Jack thought a moment about Johnny and the thumb drive he'd recovered in Malaysia. He'd tried to connect the dots back to the cyberattack on the exchanges, the chronology of the events seemed too coincidental to dismiss, but without data confirmation, it was only speculation, something frowned upon by his boss.

BASEL, SWITZERLAND

Pavel Grigorovich excused himself as he placed his napkin on the table and turned away from his host, Derek Hamilton-Smith, and carried his private conversation onto an adjoining balcony overlooking the sleepy village below. He nodded in agreement as he listened to the detailed instructions from his benefactor on the other end of the phone.

He'd enjoyed his assignment. It'd delivered him inside an inner circle he'd never thought a course old Soviet like himself would enter, the upper echelon of the global financial elite. It was a sight to witness the ease at which they meted out rules and regulations forever changing the face of the civilization below as they watched from their towers above. For this and other reasons, he knew that Igor's plan was just, and he'd never wanted to be part of something more than this initiative. It was something worthy of the people. And he wasn't going to let anything stand in the way of its implementation. With the voice repeating what he'd already told him a thousand times before, Grigorovich stared across the valley below waiting for his opportunity to respond.

"I'm on my way to London to meet with our Lady. I'll arrive before her plane hits tarmac."

"Make sure she gets the job done. Phase two is essential for success."

"Da."

Grigorovich hung up the phone and took a deep breath of the

cool night air blowing in from the piney forests below. He thumbed down through his messages and began to stab at the phone's keypad with his sausage like fingers. Within a couple of minutes, he returned to the anxious banker inside the suite. He studied the Belgian pacing the floor as the news streamed across the television in the background. The weekend hadn't eased the plight of the markets. Everything was still in a downward trend with money flowing to the usual safe havens, gold, silver, and bitcoin.

"How is your portfolio? Did you manage to limit the damage?"

Derek flashed a tender Belgian smile at his guest. "The cost of doing business as they say."

Grigorovich wasn't buying it. He knew the Belgian financier had taken a substantial hit on his global assets, but as he'd said it was the cost of doing business, especially with the Russians. There couldn't be the slightest hint of movement before they'd released the first cyberattack on the United States markets. But, with the operation well under way, it wasn't necessary to make their partner continue to take financial hits.

"You may want to liquidate all of your holdings and exposure to... *utilities.*"

Derek tilted his head. A wry smile stretched across his face as he hit the speed dial to his traders in Zurich, they'd not left their office since the inexplicable onslaught began to hit the global markets. "*Spasiva*," Derek replied.

Grigorovich poured himself another drink as he watched the frantic banker instruct his men, and then rifle through his contacts quick to explain the predicament to his fellow Council members, his allied families, which put a wide smile on the old Russian's face as he sipped his coffee.

24

KNIGHTSBRIDGE, LONDON

Anja Singh — cloaked in a half-woken state — stepped off the Boeing 777-300ER and zombie-walked past a gaggle of smiling EVA Air flight attendants, took in a lung of fresh air during the brief transit to the terminal, and exerted as little effort but extending one foot in front of the other, until she'd stopped in front of a tall muscular man in a black-fitted suit holding a sign with her name on it. *Subtle.* She brushed the hair from her eyes and fixed her fixed her sunglasses atop her head.

Everything felt surreal, as if she'd landed on a cinematographer's editing board played back in slow motion to capture the frame-by-frame intricacy of the moment, a half-paced enactment of arrival. Her mind registered little background noise as she approached the smiling broad-shouldered driver. She hadn't expected an airport pickup, her Taipei departure had been abrupt, but the placard proved her benefactor knew she'd arrived in London, and she was thankful. Although not a shy person, she avoided attention when possible, dressing down for the most part. She'd never hired a personal driver or booked luxury hotels that provided concierge services and private butlers, not that she didn't like to be pampered, she disliked the increased attention and required interactions. Despite her feelings, after a sixteen-hour flight and the long trek into the city, she was relieved that she didn't have to deal with another inquisitive Uber driver. Anja threw a little wave at the driver and closed the distance between them in a moment saddled with a folded garment bag and a backpack.

"Ah, Ms. Singh, please follow me."

Anja scoped her surroundings like a sentinel guarding her queen, her deceitfully delicate hands formed an ironclad lock around her backpack, while her thin smile acknowledged the driver's greeting. From her first take, she'd appreciated his polished British accent and his well-mannered disposition. He was clean shaven, polite, but a man of few words, all the things that she desired in men. A delayed arrival announcement echoed through hall snapping her from her drifting thoughts as she flashed a smile and followed the driver toward the baggage carousel.

Anja paused a long moment. It hadn't taken long to identify and snatch up her one massive, checked bag, and with it in tow she and her escort had gotten on the escalator heading down a level toward the parking garage, but as soon as she'd pocketed her phone, a message chimed through. She fished the phone out once again and toggled the screen - *work*. She craned her neck around a portly gentleman engaged in a colorful, yet belligerent, conversation with his partner to check the position of her driver, who'd managed to allow more than a couple of passengers to separate them while she was busy checking her messages. After locating her driver, she pressed her exhausted frame forward through the chaotic arrival hall and managed to come alongside him before he'd even noticed she'd fallen behind. With eyes front and following his lead, another chime chirped from her phone, which she knew she'd have to answer. She scanned her face unlocking the phone, opened the messages and stared a moment at the screen.

Grig: Land yet?

Anja: Just

While she stood gawking at her screen, she sighed at the number

of other unread messages. She clicked into the first one and scrolled through the queue one at a time.
David: We need to talk.
David: We REALLY need to talk.
David: Where are you?
Grig: Privyet...
Grig: Privyet...
Something sounded inside her head. Whatever spooked David was urgent, but he'd have to wait, she was already behind schedule thanks to the departure delay in Taipei.

With her half-zombie state subsiding, she'd had enough.

"Where'd you park?"

The tall handsome driver stopped and turned toward Anja. "A thousand apologies Mum, but it seems as if Heathrow has taken more than double its normal capacity today, something about a convention."

Anja huffed. "Right."

After ten long minutes of careful navigation, they'd finally cleared the hum drum of the terminal and she was able to relax, and nothing was more relaxing than a luxurious sedan with handcrafted leather seats, Anja sat back and breathed out a long pent-up sigh.

∽

ALTHOUGH IT HADN'T BEEN that long since Anja's last Trans-Atlantic flight, the jet lag was worse than she'd remembered. She turned her head to the side as the comfort of the leather interior caressed her plane-weary muscles and carried her away from the high-stakes contract she was working, when she saw it, a turquoise leathered briefcase sitting next to her behind the driver's seat. Despite her subtle paranoia and constant inner voice, she knew who'd placed it. After all, this was his modus operandi, elegance, and style, mixed with a lot of obligations, which meant the job was about to get interesting. *What's he up to now?* She stared at the gold-clasped briefcase for a long moment, then pushed it away, and fastened her seatbelt.

After the initial crawl up the onramp, the traffic opened up and allowed the 6.0-liter Bentley to roar into action hurtling her toward the city like she was riding on a comet made of silk and serenaded by the steady purr of the W12 engine Anja drifted into a light sleep. However, like everything else in her life over the last few years, it wasn't to last. Whether it was the time zone hopping inner clock, the nagging feeling inside of micromanagers looking over her shoulder, or the deceleration of the Bentley into traffic, she blinked her eyes open.

"Where are we?"

"Still a way-out Mum, please try to get some rest," the driver replied.

Sleep. It's the worst thing she could do to herself if she wanted to operate effectively in this time zone, maybe her smart looking driver wasn't as sharp as she'd made him out in her mind. She needed to be alert, and that meant fighting against her internal clock, sleep be damned.

What the hell is in that briefcase?

She already had her instructions, one last salvo that would send the Americans into a tizzy, and have them focused on their internal infrastructure, while she deployed the third and final assault. *Third and final assault, not until I'm finished.* Anja felt her face flush as she reviewed her own plans in her head, knowing that once she'd ignited the fire there would be no turning back. She despised the constant micromanagement and knew that she'd have only a small window to accomplish her goals, once and for all. Nobody understood more than Anja, the impact of the customized logic controllers embedded in a dozen government regulated facilities around the eastern seaboard of the United States, but that wasn't enough. She mused on her benefactors short-sighted objective, he wanted control, but she wanted more.

Payback is a bitch.

From her brief conversation with Grigorovich prior to her London flight, the Taiwanese chips had triggered the NEPLHM malware infiltrating the server stacks of various American Broker-

Dealers and financial exchanges, including the Dekker Banking Group, which had been job one. It'd been a well-executed sabotage, and her benefactor was content, but she wasn't satisfied. Although she'd signed on to implement the three stages of the benefactor's plan, she wanted a grander finale than the boss. She wanted to destroy the House of Dekker, something she'd not shared with Grigorovich or the oligarch benefactor.

Anja fell forward from her seat, testing the straps. "Damn it." The motorway had become congested, and all types of drivers had emerged each vying for optimal position and testing their own interpretation of driving safety rules.

"Sorry, mum, we'll be out of this momentarily," the driver offered.

Despite the lighter-than-normal congestion outside of Heathrow, there was still enough traffic to choke a city twice the size of London, which prompted creative driving techniques, something Anja knew all too well, but she was usually the one behind the wheel. She leered the sprawling metropolis disappear from her view as the car crawled toward the offramp.

Anja knew that there was more than a couple of technology conferences happening in the city and that her primary target was going to be at one of them, but the traffic told a confusing story. Whatever the case she shifted her mind toward contacting David. After a moment, a wave of exhaustion swam over her as she cupped her mouth to yawn. *There was more than enough time to deal with him it later.*

A sharp contraction in her thigh made her wince in pain as her body screamed for a much-needed rest, but she'd too much on her plate. Despite what her body was telling her she didn't have the time. From where she was siting, the hot bath, or a spa treatment was not on the menu, regardless of what the brochure said, this was a work trip. Rubbing her thigh as the bustling cityscape zipped past outside, she felt her phone begin to vibrate with an incoming call. She pressed answer with her forefinger and put the receiver to her ear.

"You got briefcase?" Grigorovich asked.

Anja paused. "Why are you calling?"

"Once you enter hotel room, open safe. Instructions inside."

Anja twisted her face in frustration. If the instructions were in the safe, then what the hell was in the briefcase and why the hell were they leaving instructions in the first place. This wasn't the normal protocol. "Okay..."

"Is something most important. Please tell me arrival."

Anja flinched at the abruptness disconnection. She knew she was off her game, and it had nothing to do with the flight. Whether she rectified the situation now, or later, she knew it'd better be before she met up with Grigorovich. A feeling of uneasiness settled in as she squirmed in her seat, playing back the random call, Grigorovich was holding something back. This wasn't how they'd handled their business in the past, every communication and meeting had always been cordial and professional, and she'd never let her benefactor down, this was highly unusual. Everything she'd prepared had gone off without a hitch, so why did she have a pain in the pit of her stomach, something was wrong with the Russians. Although she'd handled many jobs for him, she'd never met Grig's boss, she only knew him by his methods and reputation.

Who was this benefactor?

The streets grew smaller as she pondered on her situation. Grigorovich had always been her handler despite several attempts by Anja to meet with the boss, she was never allowed to know who or where he was.

What was his ultimate agenda? And where'd she fit in at his organization, if at all? She pulled out her cell phone and scrolled through her contacts until she came to a solution. *If he didn't know then all bets were off.* She held the phone to her ear as it rang.

∽

A FLEETING VIEW of Buckingham Palace was all she'd managed as the Bentley slipped past, blocked by the typical Black Cabs ferrying tourists around the popular destination. Putting the majesty behind her, she watched a line of carriages entering the palace grounds as she disappeared into the traffic funneling into Knightsbridge toward her destination and the mysterious note. With little time to relax and plenty of things to do, she pawed her face with a damp towel and cleared her throat as the driver turned onto Wilton Place, and her destination - the Berkley Hotel.

It was exactly how she remembered. A brilliant sun bounced off the limestone exterior and filled the entire street with light. A pair of white gloves opened the door welcoming her to the hotel as another pair of gloves removed her baggage from the trunk. With a quick nod she parted with the driver and stepped into the marbled lobby of the *chic* Knightsbridge treasure.

From the moment she'd stepped foot inside the Berkley, a wave of relief descended over her, without a second thought she threw smiles at the hotel staff as she passed through the lobby. As the elevator doors opened onto the third floor, Anja loosed her grip on her backpack and took a deep breath as she opened the door to her suite. *Home.* She tipped the bellboy and locked the door.

Across from the foyer was a king-sized bed where she flung the briefcase, then walked over to the in-room safe and punched in Grig's code. *Damn.* Her eyes blinked surprised as she *read* his instructions laying in all its matte black glory. A *Sig Sauer* P226 pistol tucked in a small metallic box with fitted foam accompanied by a silencer and three clips. *More wetwork?* She sat down behind the desk and began her text...

Anja: This is the wrong room.
Grig: No, is right.
Anja: I'm not sure.
Grig: Is okay, will be close by.

Anja hadn't been caught off guard like this since before her Russian missions, another lifetime ago, and even then, it wasn't her fault, so what had gone wrong? Although she'd been involved in several assassinations and massive *clean-up* operations, she'd always stuck to her contracts paragraph and verse, but changing it at the last minute to include *housekeeping* wasn't acceptable, especially in her hometown of London, where she liked to keep her nose clean.

Will be close by. Was that a threat?

She punched in a response then threw the phone on the bed and disappeared into the bathroom. Anja always stuck to the contract, and this wasn't in it. *Fuck.*

Anja: Are you kidding?

Grig: Just think of as final confirmation.

Anja paused a long moment. *Had the contract soured?* Everything up until this point had gone off without a hitch, if it hadn't, she'd never have made it to the hotel, so what was happening? She paused a moment before sending the next text.

Anja: You're auditioning me, still? lol

Grig: Marriott…Three hours

Anja: understood.

Anja paused a long moment. She needed intel. She needed to know why the Russians were changing their agreement after dozens of successful missions, had they lost faith in her abilities? She distracted herself as she craned her head toward the 24H financial news channel and its talking heads discussing the U.S. financial markets. There had been a massive drop and the government was running scared, so she didn't understand the problem. She dug into her bag and pulled out her laptop. After she launched a couple of security programs and VPNs, she logged into the private nodes tied to the backbone of the Internet through proxy servers in the United States and activated her surveillance protocol. She rubbed her eyes and yawned as she watched several feeds come through, all was normal. *Okay, they're still playing catchup.* She breathed a hard sigh and checked her watch. It was time.

She fit the pistol inside her belt, scooped up her leather jacket off the bed, and was out the door.

GRAND CAYMAN

Mike Chambers stretched out his sunburned hand and wiped the ocean spray from his yellow-tinted Ray Bans, nothing like a day in the sun, especially when there were so many tantalizing distractions. He dried his hands on a towel, and tossed it into an empty bin, but as turned his gaze toward the hotel dock, a Hollywood moment caught his attention. *You've gotta be kidding me.* Who knew that Port George Town action was so fresh? He threw a hand over his eyes to catch a better view as a powerboat loaded down with a gaggle of swimsuit models scooted passed his boat in the opposite direction, most likely setting up for a photoshoot in the fading Caribbean sunset. Mike hung his head in his hands. *Keep focused, Mikey.*

Despite what the desk jockeys back at Langley thought of his assignment, this wasn't the mysterious secret agent mission with shaken Martinis and steamy encounters, most of the time it involved far too much reality, and sometimes proved stranger than fiction, so much so that he'd doubted the IC geek squad could even fathom the ridiculousness. Still, it was the job and it had to get done. He'd spent the entire day scouring every cove and inlet around the main island looking for suspicious outliers and planned another day combing the outer island tomorrow. Without a specific set of GPS coordinates, he'd had to go back to basics as he searched for large antenna arrays or other out-of-place tell-tale signs of a covert operation.

Mike felt the fiberglass boat siding in his grip as it slowed to a halt at the Four Seasons private dock, with only a few minutes left of daylight, he longed for a drink and somewhere to collect his thoughts. A full day in the sun had dehydrated him something fierce, and beyond what he'd estimated causing a sharp pain and kink in his neck as he turned to thank the captain for the ride.

"Thanks a lot, cap'n. Same time tomorrow?"

"*G'won den.*"

Mike flashed a smile at the confirmation while hiding his agony, and with one short hop, was back on dry land. He couldn't stop the building laughter in his head as he'd recounted his day, the number of jerry-rigged antenna arrays around the island numbered the number of houses, everyone was angling for a better picture or a boosted signal. With a salty buildup on his arms and an unquenchable thirst driving him forward, he padded toward the hotel bar.

It wasn't long after his departure to the islands that the Fort Meade techs had lost the carrier signal, the rogue actor had gone offline, and unless he'd re-engaged his system there was no way Mike was going to pinpoint his location. After all they'd chosen the islands for a reason, not the least being anonymity. Once he'd checked the trading account's registered address, which turned out to be an empty sand lost on the edge of town, his hunt had begun, and now with the setting sun he moved to contact the SCIF and regroup.

Aside from the devastating thirst overtaking his entire existence, he was starving, the sandwiches from the boat captain's wife had helped, but it'd been four years since he'd had a proper Caribbean Roti and he wasn't ashamed to admit that it was something on his checklist while he was in town, although the roti at the hotel wasn't the street vendor quality he was looking for, it'd suffice.

The Grand Cayman Four Seasons Resort glowed in the rays of the setting sun beyond the end of the docks. In the back of his mind, Mike heard his wife nagging him at why they'd not taken a vacation in the last three years. *This might put a smile on her face.* He willed his legs forward as cramps from the dehydration began to move beyond his upper torso, although it wasn't anything he couldn't deal with, especially in a five-star resort town. As he moved toward the entrance, the surrounding village erupted with vibrant sounds that started low and mellow, but soon and grown into bustling activity echoing against the rocks and off the water across the bay. Now, he really needed a drink. With beads of sweat rolling down his scarlet cheeks, he stepped into the relaxed climate-controlled ambience of the resort.

"Good evening," a hostess greeted.

Mike summoned the strength to break an awkward smile and be courteous in his response. "Yes, it is. Could I get a table overlooking the water please?" All he could think about while he waited for her to seat him was a tall cold glass of fresh coconut water, never mind his favorite mojito, it'd only make things worse.

"Certainly, this way."

An intrusive vibration in his pant pocket buzzed non-stop like it was on an endless loop, readying for a top charting debut. With a meal now in the offing, he forced a crooked smile, and completed his order before fishing his phone from his damp pocket. Of course, he didn't have a substantive update for the caller, but it was an update, nonetheless. He put the phone to his ear.

After a quick triple beep and relay pop, the voice came through with crystal clarity. "The signal is back up."

Mike blanched. "Have you been able to pinpoint the location?"

"Grand Cayman." Mike looked down at his sunburned body and the complete and total failure of his SPF50 sunblock.

"Yeah, perhaps you could be a little more specific. I just spent the last two days searching through the outer islands and haven't managed to find a damn thing. So, precision boys, please."

"*Old School*. I love it. You're a keeper," Jack said as he fought back the laughter with one hand muffling the phone receiver.

"Enough with the funny Jack, give me the coordinates." Mike pulled out a ballpoint pen and scribbled down the information that pointed to an address just across the bay. "This was doable…after dinner," he thought, only to have Jack tear it down.

"The line is still hot, so if you move on it now you might be able to catch them, and then we could run trace on all their recent contacts essentially shutting down the network, and hopefully their parasitic program."

Mike frowned as the waitress placed a fresh goat roti down in front of him and topped off his water with a beautiful vibrant smile. "Why would they be logging back into the system? Why wouldn't they be long gone by now?"

"Unfinished business? Maybe they think because we haven't crashed down their door that they're safe and have opted to launch another attack." Mike's eyes grew wide as he put his glass down on the table, laid his napkin aside and shuffled down the hotel corridor pulling out his villa key as he went.

"That's exactly what they're doing. I gotta go..." Mike jammed the cell phone into his cargo pants and broke into a full sprint. He burst through his villa door then rummaged through his closet. He pulled his pistol from his pants and checked it for sand, pulled two extra magazines from his garment bag, and grabbed a fresh shirt then clamored out the door toward the water taxi, once again.

∽

A FRESH COAT of canary yellow glistened off the walls of the semi-dilapidated seaside shack on the far side of Port George Town as it bustled with the last of the late afternoon crowd returning their boats and fishing gear. An old blueish colored hound lazed on the rustic shop's porch, no chance of sounding any alarm as it curled up by its owner enjoying the last warmth of the day. Mike grimaced as he stepped off the dock and walked toward the shack, his sunburned legs logged each painful step as the blood coursing through their veins stretched the tender skin and reminded him blending in came at a cost. Mike squinted his eyes down the far beach and saw a group of tourists had blazed up a bonfire and were jumping around to some God-awful electronic garbage that polluted the night air, having no ill effect on the old man who continued to sip on, what Mike could only guess was rum, a staple of the islands.

"Excuse me sir," Mike said.

"*Close*," the old man responded.

Mike sighed. "I'm not looking to rent a boat. I need your help."

"*De sign says CLOSE*," the old man repeated as his faithful companion rolled over onto his back exposing his belly to an incoming cool evening breeze.

"My friend *Benjamin Franklin* tells me you don't close for another fifteen minutes." Mike watched as the man used his index finger and tipped his hat up over one eye toward him. "It's a shame that he was wrong. I guess I'll be on my way." The old man's eyebrows quirked up and he raised his skinny arms still clinched around a brown bottle and downed the last drop, then cleared his throat.

"*Cum to tink of it, mi watch nuh wuk.*" The old man got to his feet and met the stranger on the steps of his bait shop. He looked Mike dead in the eyes.

"I've had that problem myself, something about the humidity I think." The two men exchanged mischievous smiles and began to chat in low voices. The one beautiful thing about living near a body of water like a bay is the purity and rhythm of the tide, the only downside is lack of privacy. Mike knew that he had to be extra careful when speaking around bodies of water as the sound was picked up and amplified across the waters like a megaphone, not something that would help his cause in this case.

"Have you noticed anything out of the ordinary over the last few weeks along the beach or perhaps strange out-of-place people booking any charters?" The man rubbed his belly for a moment before answering as his open palm stretched out toward Mike.

Mike placed the crisp hundred-dollar bill in the old man's hand. "*Mi tink it must ave been a week ago dem did shouting at each otha pon de beach. Now, mi nuh pay attention to lover's spat, but dis did a bit odd as de man did cowering down to a uhman half fi him size ya know. Mi guess de beauty inna de eye of de beholder. Mi memba dem cuz de man arrive before de uhman. Him stayed along bout a month before uhman arrive.*"

"And...people have different schedules. Perhaps she couldn't get away from work as early as he could, and she just met him down here."

"*Mi tink of dat,*" the old man said as he made his way back to his faded wooden chair. "*But den a couple days ago, the uhman up and left.*"

"Was that after the fight on the beach?"

"*Yeah mon. Shi just leave him inna de dust yuh kno.*"

"Where are they staying?" The old man smiled as he rubbed his palms together and stared at his fingernails. Mike pulled another Benjamin Franklin note from his wallet and passed it to the old man.

"*Yea sah. Dat man stays dung de beach round de bend there. It's a lime green yaad. Yuh cyaa miss it."* Mike thanked the man rubbed the dog on his belly for good luck, then trotted down the beach.

The first group of people he encountered was the belligerent tourists hard at work building a bonfire in the middle of the beach, and no regard for their surroundings, but Mike didn't have time for that. The fire was an apparent birthday bash for some twenty something New England prom queen. Mike shook his head as memories of youth flashed through his mind, and he passed by them. A few hundred yards down the beach he spotted - the bend - the old man spoke about.

By time he'd reached the bend, night had fallen, and this area was beyond the illumination of the bonfire, but then again, he didn't need light for the next part of his mission. He left the beach and followed a stone path that snaked around the road running parallel to the beach. *Coconut Drive. This is it. He's here somewhere.* With the veil of darkness now covering his tracks he moved easily between the houses. After a short while, a full moon pierced the scattered cloud drifting silently over the island. Mike paused a moment. A small pebble had worked its way into his right shoe and was cutting into his foot, he stopped and shook the sand from his shoes, then continued along the sidewalk, looking for those tell-tale signs from a comfortable distance.

As Mike hugged the walkway running in front of the villas closest to beach and about three villas down from the bend stood a one-story villa with a large wrap around privacy fence. *Interesting.* A further inspection revealed a bundle of telephone lines streaming in from the street. *BINGO.* Mike looked over his shoulder then made a move toward the opened villa window. From the outside, it looked as though there was a server stack that took the space of an entire bedroom. *This must be it.* Whether he moved on the location and broke the case wide open or stumbled across some home office set up, he had to be sure. Before he could decide to move, his phone began to vibrate. Given the tranquility of the location, the sound seemed to telegraph his position to the entire planet, he retreated behind a palm tree and breathed an angry sigh and answered his phone in a whispered voice.

"This is Mike."

A familiar voice came through the receiver. "I need you to retrieve the solid-state drive from the main system."

Mike paused a long moment. "I've got to get inside the damn house first without getting my head cracked open." He hung up the phone and stuffed it in his pocket, but the point was clear they needed as much information on the system as possible. He checked his pocket for the NSA HOT thumb drive that when attached to the system could enable his team at the Fort to take over the system remotely and download everything they needed, saving him the hassle of stripping down any hardware, and run the risk of detection. He moved back toward the villa.

Despite the direct route through the opened window, Mike circled around the villa to the closest point of entry, banking on the element of surprise. The lights were on, but he hadn't spotted the technician. Not knowing when the next attack was going to come, he couldn't waste time, he heaved back and kicked the door down.

From across the room, a man leapt up and barreled toward him. The man threw a solid right punch but missed the blackjack that brought him down with an enormous - *THUD*! Mike saw the technician looking at the system and the flashing lights of the servers, somehow, he knew that he'd better hurry. With one foot on the technician's neck, Mike removed the thumb drive from his pocket and inserted it into the terminal. *Let's see what we got.*

Mike felt a sharp pain to his head, the man had wiggled free while he was watching the terminal monitor. He turned to see another fist coming straight for his face, but he swerved and squared off against his assailant. When the man threw another fist, Jack delivered a spinning back kick that sent him crashing into the far wall. Time was running out. Mike turned toward the thumb drive that had blinked alive and taken a life of its own as the NSA hackers dug into the system, working their magic, until an inexplicable power surge cause the system to flicker, like some sort of power disruption. Mike looked back toward the wall, but the man had disappeared. He could hear his heart pounding in his head as the adrenaline was kicking into overdrive. No time to strip down the computers and grab the drives, TAO was on their own, remote access would have to suffice, he had to catch that technician. He charged through the backdoor and disappeared chasing a fading silhouette racing down the beach.

"Where the hell do you think you're going?" Mike roared as he sailed through the air landing a kick to the fugitive.

"Damn Yankee!"

Russians? The accent was unmistakable but had caught Mike off guard as he rolled off the bow, and dodge the bottle thrown at him. Without further hesitation, he hit the deck and swept the Russian's leg, as he staggered to catch his breath. "Stay put."

"*Nyet.*" The Russian flipped up exchanged a flurry of punches with Mike, then knocked him down to the deck, and before the American could get up he'd disappeared into the quiet Caribbean waters.

WEST INDIA QUAY, LONDON

David Blevins squealed in frustration. Nothing over his last ten years of programming or working his way around the world for countless nefarious enterprises had prepared him for this day, a day when he'd face the unthinkable, a day he'd dreaded, and in the final moments, when the illuminated image blinked into darkness, he shrieked. It'd finally happened, his phone battery had died. For a moment, he stood aghast not sure what to do next. With little time before the unveiling of the new miniature microchip that was set to revolutionize high-performance computing everything from artificial intelligence to high-end gaming systems had arrived, and he wasn't prepared. *Damn it.*

ATTENDEES, PLEASE MAKE YOUR WAY TO THE MAIN AUDITORIUM

The frantic programmer shook his head in disbelief. He looked around the room for anyone who'd have a spare charger, but the faces were blank, and moving away from his position. This was unheard, he was 'Mr. Prepared' or so he'd thought, he was more than just another overanxious tech geek waiting for something to happen, he was a true believer in the coming Singularity, when man and machine would take the human experience to the next level of consciousness, elevating Homo Sapiens to the alleged *Homo Deus*.

Upon his arrival at the Machine Learning conference, he'd dodged a gaggle of reporters swarming several famous futurists and scientists, all on hand to welcome another great leap forward in high-performance computing. More than just a disruptive wave of technology, this bump to artificial intelligence power promised to change the world, and David wanted to be on hand when it did. There was nothing more exciting to him, except maybe the recent pornsite build out he'd put together in the Cayman Islands, the week before.

Despite the Cayman Project's unhappy ending, he'd hoped that Anja recognized his genius, and wanted him another project. After all, he'd delivered exactly what she'd ordered, although with perhaps maybe too much fanfare. When he'd received her call, she sounded somber, but he chalked it up to Trans-Atlantic jet lag and confirmed their meeting. She was a tough boss, but he knew she was well funded, and she seemed interested in everything cutting edge, just what David had been looking for all this time. *Maybe she wants to hear about my project.*

David checked his watch, it was almost time, and he'd promised to meet her at the main entrance. He took a couple of elbows to the ribs as he moved through the unrelenting crowd as he crossed the lobby floor. With only seconds to spare he saw her from a distance, her beautiful copper toned skin glowing in the event lighting as she stepped out of a Chauffeured Mercedes CLS. From the moment her onyx black stilettos clacked down on the marble floor, a silence washed over the crowd, after all this was a technology event, and the audience was eighty percent skewed toward technology geek. Something in the air piqued his confidence and as she approached, he pulled her close like a long-lost lover.

Anja smiled, disregarding his forwardness. "Hello David. Let's find somewhere to sit and talk a moment. We've got so much to talk about."

David blanched. "But they're about to unveil the new chip."

Anja cupped his hands with hers and pulled him toward the opposite end of the lobby, away from the crowd of technology geeks and reporters that'd begun herding past them toward the unveiling. But Anja could not be assuaged, and she'd a way with weak-minded men. She led him up a flight of stairs to a lounge area on the second-floor balcony, overlooking the lobby and asked the waitress for a couple of espressos.

"I wanted to thank you for your work in the Caymans."

Distracted, David looked down on the main floor lobby from his elevated position in the cafe, only able to fantasize what was about to be unveiled in the room downstairs. He stuttered as he replied. "Of course, it was a great gig, but I... was hoping that I might be able to bear witness to this new chip, and maybe ask them some questions."

"If you needed a *bare* witness, you should've said so."

David froze. He cut a quizzical eye at Anja in excited disbelief. "Really?"

"You might think I'm made of ice, but I love a man with a brain, especially one that knows how to use his hands, and isn't afraid to get them dirty." She got him, hook, line, and sinker.

Anja felt the audio pierce the ballroom doors and reverberated through the main lobby and taunted a vacant room as the last stragglers scurried through the closing doors. *It was time.* She leaned forward and put her hand on David's thigh as the lights dimmed in the lobby. A quick recon around the cafe revealed that the staff had vanished, retired to the back to continue their daily gossip, or watch the unveiling as well, but it didn't matter. She felt his heart race and body began trembling with excitement, but she slowed his anticipation by laying a calming hand on his shoulder as she unbuttoned her jacket as she blew into his left ear. When she saw him close his eyes, she reached around and pulled her pistol from her belt and slowly raised it to the side of his head before she whispered.

"I am sorry about this." She squeezed the trigger, but nothing happened, it was frozen. *Fuck, the safety.* Her eyes met the frightened beast as he felt the cold steel against his temple.

"Fuck..." David's pleas were drowned out by the booming applause that erupted and echoed across the entire building. Summoning all his strength, he pushed back the table, knocking Anja aside as he scurried toward an emergency exit.

Anja flipped the safety and fired several rounds at her fleeing prey hitting her mark in the upper torso and leg as he cried out limping into the stairwell. She sprung across the cafe closing the distance between the frightened programmer in three giant strides. She fired another round as David smashed into the emergency exit on the ground floor and into the parking lot disappearing into the night.

Anja stowed her pistol and fixed her hair as a dozen reporters burst from the reveal and began yammering away on their phones, enough noise to cover the screaming and activity to distract any onlookers. She cleared her throat and breathed in a lung of air. Her phone began to vibrate. It was Grig. *Fuck.* She craned her neck around the lobby left and right, but no sign of the towering Russian. She thumbed open his message.

Grig: You need practice. Don't worry. I will help on this.

Anja fumed. She was a stone-cold killer not some robotic cleaner sent in on defenseless, and up until that point allied prey, but even killers had limits.

25

FORT MEADE, MARYLAND

Something felt wrong. Walter Moore stopped reading long enough to acknowledge it was more than fatigue, he adjusted his lumbar support, shifted his weight in the chair, and took another sip of water. For a moment, he'd considered stuffing the report in the drawer and calling it a day, but there was too much at stake. So, he turned the page and continued reading.

Within a few minutes, the feeling was back, and this time it wouldn't be cast aside, the pain was too deep. Since the day he'd returned from the G7 conference, he'd begun to fade, he hadn't spoken about it, as he thought it was just exhaustion, rather than anything medical, but this pain was something more.

This isn't happening today. They're not ready.

After more than thirty years at his post, Walter was ready to hand over the reins, but none of the department heads were ready for leadership, not the real kind. Every name he'd considered there'd been an issue, not to mention the growing divide between the civilian contractors hired by the Department of Defense and the actual military, not something that was going to resolve itself anytime soon, especially with space opening up as a priority.

Although most of his concerns hinged on character over experience, with many of the recent candidates it'd been both, and despite having his favorite, he knew the candidate still needed more time in the oven. Walter took another sip of water.

Damn it hellfire, not today.

Despite his aggressive approach to command at one of the most powerful institutions in the United States intelligence community, the NSA director was unable to stop something that proved far more sinister and omnipotent than any government institution or policy, and had fractured the convergence of the civilian and military information streams, something that'd taken even the most devious Washington politician by surprise, a private sector innovation more powerful than religion - *terms and conditions*.

Buried within these usage contracts burned the spinning core of the societal schism, and its accelerated metamorphosis into the unknown. Walter knew that the country stood at the precipice, the only question was which road it headed down; the tyrannical display of George Orwell's - *1984*, the wholly embraced society of Adolph Huxley's - *Brave New World or* was there still time to roll it all back, and bridge civilization toward a grander unified goal.

Whether it was the advent of social media networks, the automation of personal data collection, or humanity's willingness to allow it all to happen, the combination proved conclusive, a digital world was emerging faster and more potent than anyone had imagined. More than a Tsunami washing across the global cities, the digitization stretched into the heartlands and beyond, bringing connectivity to every nook and cranny on the planet; his gave new meaning to flattening the curve. The power of information lifted millions from poverty and leveled the playing field for the business community on a global scale. Once the first domino had dropped, Walter had implemented additional protocols for the members of the Five Eyes' nations, but it wasn't enough, the threat of rogue actors sprouted from the desert to the sea.

Walter tore a packet of medicine and downed its contents and chased it with a glass of water. He reckoned that the Council of Thirteen had planned for this accelerated decentralization and the fragmenting world governments, which was most likely the reason it's experienced an internal rift between the Dekkers and the Smiths in the not so distant past. He sighed, took another sip of water, and moved into his den toward his desk. *We need more time... more power.* Walter tossed the empty packet into the trash and brought up a secure line on his phone. *It's now or never.* With Mike Chambers in the Caymans and the looming threat of another infrastructure attack, he needed his best cryptanalysts and hackers under one roof, while CIA took over at the SCIF, and its assassination investigation, Jack was getting on a plane whether he liked it or not.

"Jack...pack your bags. You're taking a little trip."

A semi-coherent rambling whispered through the receiver. "Sorenson..."

Walter breathed a long sigh. "JACK."

The booming voice echoed through the phone, the familiarity and his words played back through his filtered subconscious hit him like a bolt of lightning - Director? Taking a trip? "On my way."

~

WALTER WAS A SIMPLE MAN. He liked his coffee black, reports in order, and his agents plain spoken, yet he compartmentalized everything. He wanted a full rundown on everything remotely related to any topic on which he was briefed, and only gave one-word responses to any question asked him. Some called him old school, others knew it was more than that, but everyone fell in line.

A field operative in the final years of the Vietnam War, he was a master of signal intelligence, and in fact wrote the book on its implementation protocols but remained a man of the Analog Age. As such, he drove an old Toyota Corolla, and when it broke down, he repaired it and kept driving, he demurred change, but he knew in the long run, change was inevitable, which had led him to his current predicament. He needed to pass the baton, and there was only one candidate, someone who'd been in the military, been trained in programming at the Naval Academy, and was close to the Council of Thirteen, but that was on hold, for the time being. Walter pushed through the lobby door at Fort Meade and meandered through the security checkpoint.

"Good morning, sir" a young lieutenant welcomed.

Walter chalked a quick nod. "Ms. Whitfield."

After a quick ride in the elevator, Walter felt the cold air suck through the corridor as the elevator door opened and he stepped into the hallway. From his peripheral vision he caught the motion of a body whisked past him and into his outer office, a smile crossed his face as he followed it inside. He scooped up the files from his assistant's desk marked - *Holiday*, and then thumbed it open to the divider with a red stamp that read: TOP SECRET - SHOAL BAY.

Despite his long-standing affiliation with the Council of Thirteen, Walter had struggled with his assistance he'd given Johnny on his trip to Malaysia. It was a constant back and forth since he'd made the arrangements on his behalf, but as he thumbed through the Shoal Bay intercept, the vindication reinvigorated his step.

"Gisele."

Gisele quirked a smile. "Good morning, sir. Your coffee's on your desk, and I see you've got the daily file. Let me know if you need anything."

Walter stopped. "It's 0400 don't you sleep?"

Gisele choked a laugh. "Only on Wednesdays, sir. I'll be outside."

Walter snorted a laugh. "Ain't that the truth."

For as long as he could remember, Wednesdays, had proven the only days when the world was somewhat quiet, and was the day he'd allotted to sleeping in, or taking a day off with the wife. Walter thanked Gisele as she closed the door and hung his coat and scarf on the handcrafted mahogany rack.

The timing of this intercept was critical. He took a quick sip of his coffee then began rifling through the file until he caught the gist, the MOSSAD. *Ari what are you up to now?* It didn't take him long to slam the file on his desk and pull up an encrypted outside line. He felt a stirring in the pit of his stomach as he started to connect the dots of what Johnny had stumbled onto in Malaysia and pointed to a terrifying conclusion that he didn't want to make without confirmation from his Israeli counterpart in Tel Aviv - Ari Levy.

∼

JACK SORENSON CORRALLED his growling muscle car into its assigned stall, and after a final stab on the accelerator echoed through the vacant parking lot, something of a calling card left over from his youth, he shut it off. With his reptilian brain now satisfied, he sat a moment, collecting his thoughts about the most recent intelligence on the assassination attempt. There was nothing like the full-throated sound of a 5.5-liter engine to get the heart pumped and primed for action, especially in the final stretch of a sensitive deadline. *This is it.* He'd less than eight hours before the director was sending him into the field, and if he wanted to keep his promise to Johnny, he'd have to work fast. He looked down at the thumb drive Johnny had slipped into his hand, back at Langley. *Why didn't Johnny want Langley to see it? Why not keep them in the loop?* He decided to wait for Johnny to tell him in his own time.

Although Jack had prepared himself for a long task, or as long as it would take their decryption program to dig through the password possibilities, but in the end, he'd broke through in less than an hour. *Perfect.* The shortened timeframe allowed him more of a cushion to scour through and further decipher any, if any, useful videos, or other information.

Nothing from the main folders had revealed anything useful, there was a ton of non-activity in every file he'd opened, until he finally hit upon a file that was marked - bossman. He clicked it open and pulled up the day of the assassination that Johnny had hoped showed the face of the assassin, he paused a long moment. The video clarity was phenomenal. It was a video taken from one of the shops on the gang's protection list in the state of Penang. *It can't be.*

Among the number of faces that'd passed through during that day, one stood out, the shopkeeper, or a relative. She'd only served several men but had kept a close eye on them the whole time, which wasn't itself damning evidence of anything, until an explosion shattered the windows of the cafe sending the men and the shopkeeper for cover. After a few minutes, another man entered the cafe through the rubble and smoke. He'd escorted the men out of the cafe, while the shopkeeper disappeared into the back room.

When the man had re-entered the cafe and tried to coax the shopkeeper to follow him, he was knocked to the floor and stabbed in the neck with a syringe, Jack stopped the tape, burned a copy, and put the original thumb drive in an envelope for the SCIF team. *Who the hell was that? And why'd she kill this guy?* A chill ran down his spine as he replayed the video as he sipped on a hot cup of coffee, looking for clues, recording important time stamps, and hoping for a miracle.

Aside from several ethnic Chinese Malaysians escorted from the scene, the face of a tall Eurasian woman behind the bar, the shopkeeper, was his best lead, if for only one reason, her sheer ruthlessness. *Hello killer.* Moving forward through the files, Jack found another video from the back room, which showed the same woman grab a rifle and exit the building through the front entrance, only to be followed moments later by another explosion illuminating the video, then reveal her face retreating back through the cafe, stepping over the sprawled body on the cafe floor, and exiting the frame through the rear entrance.

Returning to the main video, he fast forwarded through the elapsed time until he saw the red and blue lights of the police, but as the police exited the body disappeared. Jack rewound the video and tried to find the exit, but the blasts had sent smoke and debris billowing through the scene, turning his clear evidence into a in explicable timeframe. There was one other video in the bossman folder that he'd not viewed, he clicked it open and saw a restaurant with Johnny and another woman sitting across from each other. *What's this?* As he scrolled back through the video hoping to get a better understanding of what was taking place, a familiar voice hollered across the room. *Mike Chambers.* He felt the hard slap of the meat-head's hand on his back as he ejected the disc and logged off the terminal in one smooth motion as he turned around to welcome his replacement.

"I hear you'll be taking over the Dekker cases."

"Well, I told Walter that taking over this case was the least I could do seeing as how I'm working with the Ambassador's son on a few things at the moment."

Jack quirked an eyebrow. This guy was the biggest name-dropping show boater he'd met in the service. He stood up and walked over to one of the analysts from his geek squad, in the adjacent row. There was little more to do than to get the images on the video footage identified. He needed to run the likenesses through the appropriate database to see if they came up with any match, which could explain either of the situations that played out in the videos, but he didn't want the big oaf from Langley involved.

"Mike, why don't I take you to lunch. Let's make sure we tie everything off."

"That is mighty kind of you, Sorenson." Jack handed the thumb drive with written instructions to his geek squad and led Mike out of the SCIF.

~

JACK ENTERED THE SCIF, alone. He'd fed and ditched Mike and returned to review the geek squad's progress on the women in the videos. If there was anything to find, it had to be today, there was no tomorrow.

"Jack, good news and bad news. We've *identified* one of your women that you're looking for from the restaurant surveillance, but nothing on the Penang bridge shopkeeper."

"Show me what you got."

"Well, the good news is limited. Unfortunately, I can't give you any kind profile on this Jane Doe yet, other than that she's an Israeli."

Jack stooped down toward the terminal. A familiar voice echoed through the doorway calling his name. With a quick keystroke and an eye to his analyst, the information winked off the screen. Jack turned to face his boss. *This can't be good.*

Walter marched up to Jack and threw the SHOAL BAY file on the conference table in the center of the room. "Can you believe this shit?"

Jack hadn't a clue what he was ranting about...until he picked up the file and rifled through it with a measured precision. "You confirmed this?"

"Of course, why else would I be so pissed?"

The report indicated that the Five-Eyes Shoal Bay receiving station had intercepted a communication between a Reuters reporter called Hannah Jankowski and Tel Aviv, Israel. Jack pressed his hand to his head. Everything seemed to fall into place as he turned toward his analyst, then back to the director.

"There's no chance this was a coincidence. She's an Israeli agent."

Director Moore scowled at Jack. "Did Johnny know that? Were they working together?"

Jack did a double take at the questions as he tried to steer the director away from any haphazard assumptions. "They don't even have diplomatic relations. How'd she get a visa?"

Moore smiled. "A British passport."

Jack blanched. "Is this the reporter that outed Johnny?"

Moore choked a reply. "Why do ya think, I' so pissed, Jack?"

Jack sighed. "This is never easy sir. If they'd outed Johnny's presence in Malaysia, that's one thing, but if they'd somehow been apart of the assassination on a sitting U.S. Ambassador, why?"

After some time of brainstorming ideas of why and how the MOSSAD were involved in the whole thing, Jack caught an analyst out of the corner of his eyes raising a stack of printouts. Jack paused and scanned the printout, then turned to Moore.

"It looks like our J2 team has run down and isolated the system that prompted the market crash."

Moore wiped his brow and walked around the table. "The one in Grand Cayman?"

Jack nodded. "Mike was able to insert the HOT drive and J2

pulled some documents from the system before its remote shut down, they've copies of money transfers from a bank on the Isle of Crete and more importantly, an operation center right here in Maryland."

Walter lit up. *Here we come.* "What are we looking at?"

Jack finished. "It looks like they tracked it down to a node…in Bethesda?"

GCHQ BUDE — MORENSTOW

Jessica Lansdowne loved puzzles. Whether it was a simple crossword in the newspaper or something more complex, she'd spend hours working through strategy after strategy until she'd mastered the answer. Through her dedication to her work, she'd made herself indispensable, and managed to uncover opportunities where none had existed. Even during her leisure time she'd spent it navigating stacks of Sudoku puzzles until she'd reached a point where the simple right or wrong answer wasn't important, she competed with herself, she competed for speed. Her passion hadn't gone unnoticed, but for now she stood her post.

For the most part, her job as a signals relay operator was simple, she read and tracked system intercepts for verification, which meant most of the time she'd watch a couple of screens while advanced algorithms plucked signals out of the air and dragged them onto her desktop for further analysis. Most of the time she busied herself with paperwork while the algorithms did the heavy lifting, but every now and then she landed a big one, and when a sudden brilliant red light illuminated the room, she froze. *Move, girl. Move, girl…Move.*

Jessica willed her body into motion and leapt across the room, swiveled her chair around, and pulled her keyboard close stabbing in the necessary passwords and protocols. She'd not had an alert like this one before, and it was live, the ping was coming from… Heathrow? Usually, she'd received a call or a report telling her to pay close attention to the regional transportation hub, but today, nothing.

She sped through the alert status; this was a secondary alert now flagging the previous Heathrow subject had a cellular communication with a person of interest in Malaysia. Jessica did a double take. What? There were a dozen other operators around the world listening at various posts, but this one had crossed, not one, but two jurisdictions that meant she had to wake her boss.

Since Benghazi, the United States government had decided to take their "Strobe" protocol for international assignments one step further and implant all its agents and diplomats with a satellite-controlled bio-tracking device, the CIG implant was not optional. Buried in the fine print of any contract with the agency or diplomatic corps was a paragraph that included, *that they could do what they wanted with you and didn't have to tell you clause*, every patriot's dream. The procedure was handled during your mandatory health check, and in quick and simple order with the biodegradable granule injected into your system that dissolved and imprinted a residue in the injection area under the skin that was detectable by a unique frequency protocol. It was like a tattoo inside your skin, getting inked took on a whole new meaning. From the moment the initiative became known, all remaining Five-Eyes allies had followed suit and soon a cluster of LEO satellites was launched, whose sole purpose was tracking the Real-time Information of friendlies, and when this was a double-edged sword, which meant you could even be tracked on vacation.

"Mr. Keppel, sir, I've something here. We're getting an alert on a Level One priority. According to my initial network wide check, this is the second instance of an alert, but only the first signal intercept on the subject. For some unknown reason the alert from Heathrow failed to register in our central database, earlier in the day, it'd only come through in the last few minutes."

"Did you call the Americans?"

Jessica sighed. "You're my first call, sir." She heard a bustling from the other end of the phone and then a loud scream like someone had stubbed their toe against a coffee table.

"Pull all the data and print it out, I'll be there in ten minutes."

Jessica pulled up the alerts and watched her supervisor pour over the information then place his hands on his chin, before he picked up the phone, turned and asked her to leave the room. She understood there were level one protocols, and part of the reason she was bucking for promotion, she wanted to be in that room, but what she didn't know was that the first level one alert that failed to register in the system was from a long dormant disavowed CIA operative named, Anja Singh. She watched her supervisor jawing on the phone for over twenty minutes, until he put down the phone and stuck his head out the door.

"What's the name on that Shoal Bay intercept?"

Jessica paused a long moment. "Hannah Jankowski…"

BETHESDA, MARYLAND

A thunderclap echoed across the treetops as the soldier fell dead to the ground, the bullet riddled body lay lifeless with his brains oozing from his helmet onto the ground. Nearby, a hidden figure dropped from its elevated position and hit the ground with a THUD. Pieces of the Sycamore tree fell on his head as he scrambled to his feet. He began to run. In the distance, he saw an abandoned structure, with the enemy closing in around him, there was no alternative, he had to make it.

Clearing the corner of the old farmhouse, the worn shingles fell to his rear as he gunned for the distant sanctuary. He'd made the shot. Now, he needed to get the hell out without getting caught. The ground softened under his feet from the new fallen snow. He stood at the edge of a winding seasonal creek that had overflowed during the recent thaw but had yet to refreeze enough to hold his weight. He ripped the rifle off his back as he navigated the water, the fatigue in his arms allowed the butt to slip and smack against a large rock jutting from the creek bed. He straightened his arms and used his remaining strength to thrust himself out the ice-cold water, and onto the snowy bank.

He felt the enemy closing in, more than just a sixth sense, the distinctive crack of a rifle report and a whizzing past his ear told him to move faster, but as he cleared the edge of the barn, he caught a loose board with his knee. He fell to the ground and dragged himself into the dilapidated barn. Inside he found a ladder leading up into the hay loft, he scurried up, and quickly set himself another nest.

A full moon illuminated the field between the farmhouse and the barn, he felt his heartbeat slow as he reloaded his long rifle and waited. Within a matter of moments, several armed silhouettes had clamored along the edge of the farmhouse positioning and repositioning for their assault, knowing he'd taken refuge in the wrecked out-building. He checked his ammo and switched on his night vision lighting up his adversaries one-by-one, then a loud thunderous banging echoed across the sky...

"Honey...dinner!" The high-pitched soprano pierced the floorboard, reverberated through the oaken doors, and then echoed down the stairwell until it hit its mark, deep in a reinforced concrete basement.

A defiant, red-faced teenager, snorted, and screamed a response. "I'm busy!"

Uh oh... Within seconds the disobedient adolescent heard a set of determined footsteps marching toward her lair, she pushed back her glasses and quickly saved her game, so she'd live to fight another day. The brilliance of a super nova had nothing on the explosion of light that ripped through the room as teenager's mother switched on the light and looked her in the eyes.

"Well, I'll just have the whole family sit and twiddle their thumbs until you've finished your game," her mother said in a calm southern accent.

She knew she'd lost the battle but smiled under her breath as she knew she'd win the war. "Fine." She placed the controlled down and switched off the gaming console and television.

"You can continue the madness after dinner."

A confused young girl looked up her mother. "I'm defending my national title next week, and these constant interruptions aren't helping me," she bolted up the stairs and slunk down in a seat beside her father.

After a moment, her mother joined them at the table, winded, but with a smile she continued. "Well, honey, I think you might have to decide what's more important, starving to death in the basement and gaining a few more experience points, or actually eating a meal with your family and being alive, so you can defend your title next week."

"Yes, ma'am," the young girl replied as she shot a quick glance out the window for the first time in a couple of days.

From the blanket of snow covering the cars on the street, it was clear that the departing nor'easter had left a significant mark across the state of Maryland, and further up the eastern seaboard according to the news, although public offices were still open, it'd slowed traffic to a crawl and strained the power grid, stretching vital government resources. Within a few hours of sundown, a wave of rolling blackouts had started to hit neighboring areas around Bethesda, Maryland, but the house at the end of the cul-de-sac, 35 Timberview Circle remained unaffected.

When the young gamer realized that her house was unaffected by the frequent power grid issues, she'd chalked it up to her father doing his homework, and an unexpected win. From their research, they'd discovered that their house sat on the backbone of the original Internet grid, not some secondary offshoot. Even more curious was the fact that the other addresses that sat atop this backbone were Fortune 500 companies and government institutions, which made for a respectable and stable community. She'd learned that their house at 35 Timberview Circle had been a part of an old-World War II listening station, and for its safety was tucked away in this quiet suburban neighborhood, away from the Washington D.C. and the Naval Academy, which sat right on the coastline.

Once she'd finished everything on her plate, and received her mother's approval, she'd sprung from her seat, placed her dishes in the sink, and retreated to her stronghold, while the rest of the family carried on with their dessert, and stories about their day.

As they spoke, a brilliant power surge illuminated the cul-de-sac like it was high noon, revealing dozens of armed silhouettes positioned around 35 Timberview, before they were sucked into the following darkness as the ensuing blackout consumed all but one house on the street. The mother rose from the table.

"What's going on outside? Another blackout?" Placing her fork on the table, the curious middle-aged woman stood up, walked over, and cupped her hands against the living room window.

"Whatta ya see, honey?" the husband asked.

"The entire neighborhood's gone dark."

She turned toward her husband and son. "What time is it?"

The husband checked his watch. "Half-past six."

The woman turned back to the window, cupping her hands to block the light pollution from the dining room. "The entire street's gone dark, honey." She pushed back from the window and turned toward her husband seated at the table. "Everyone…except us."

As she spoke, a red dot winked through the kitchen window, catching her by surprise, but instead of freezing, she threw her dish towel across the room and over the table toward the invading silhouettes. "Get outta here!"

Her husband jumped up and moved toward his wife. "What, what…"

Chaos ensued. "Federal agents, don't move!"

A swarm of agents piled through the front door, and pinned the adults on the floor, while another corralled their son and their Labradors. With the main level secured the counter-intelligence team began their room-to-room search, clearing each one before coming to a locked basement door. They turned to the mother.

"What's in the basement?"

An agent removed his hand from the mother's mouth. "What the hell are you doing in my house you fascists?"

Unsure of what they'd find, the agents positioned for a full-tactical breach, and within a minute had lined up their team, while the family watched in horror at the disastrous scene unfolding in front of their eyes.

"Three, two, one…"an agent yelled.

Stumbling into the basement, they repositioned themselves around the massive subterranean dwelling that contained a sprawling network of monitors, server stacks, and wires running to all corners of the room, it was a hacker's lair, but where was the hacker?

An empty chair directly in front of the television was turned toward the bathroom, and the screen was paused. Without warning a light flooded the room and a teenage girl appeared with a blaring set of headphones and a game controller in her hand, catching the agents by surprise.

"What are you doin' in my house you Gestapo muthafucker?" She threw her controller at the nearest agent when she felt a hand grab her shoulder and slam her to the floor.

"Target secured," the agent said into his radio.

Kicking and screaming they zip tied the girl's hands to keep her from hurting herself, and any of the agents, as they carried her up the stairs to the main floor. Once a quick search of the basement hadn't yielded anything, but trophies, ribbons, and even a picture with the President on her shelf, a looming sense of concern fell over the special agent on the scene. He radioed his commander.

"Boss, we've got a problem."

Director Moore put the agent on hold and turned toward Jack and Mike, then reached past them and put the call on speaker. "What do ya got?"

The agent cleared his throat. "We're at the house on Timberview Circle, the one the intel pointed to as the location of the hacker, but we've not found them, and may have just traumatized an entire family."

Director Moore sighed. "It was a decoy."

"We've searched the house from top to bottom, but yes, I think it's a decoy, the hackers were bouncing their signals through this location. The family's lived here for more than twenty years, have two teenage kids, and not to mention we've just found a relay switch on their main line."

Mike chimed in. "You're positive they're not involved?"

"It's no leave it to beaver family, but my sense is that they're not involved. From the awards on the wall, it looks like the teenage daughter is some master gamer with several awards in mathematics and zest for online gaming marathons with the hardware to boot, which set her up as the perfect decoy for these guys. According to the blueprints, this house sits on the backbone of the original Internet, the node was allocated to a listening post early in its lifecycle, but when developers expanded the neighborhood instead of demolishing the building, they refurbished it and sold it as just another unit in the cul-de-sac, God knows why."

Director Moore fumed. He needed a specialized team on this, no more messing around. He looked at Jack and Mike with fire in his eyes as he responded to the special agent. "I want you to go over everything again. Don't leave that house until you are absolutely sure that brainiac isn't involved."

"We've searched every inch of the premises and cross referenced the backgrounds of the entire family and extended family. They're clean, sir."

"Captain, one of the main platforms for terrorist communications these days are through these online gaming forums, they've repeatedly made us look like fools, and for good reason. I'm not going to let that happen again. So, tear that place apart and confiscate all of their hard drives."

"Understood sir. What's the reason for confiscation?"

Director Moore blanched. What was the proper course of action? Perhaps if he'd been a few years younger he'd ensure they had all the relevant information and did all the necessary checks, but then wrap it up, after terrorists had arrived on our shores, there was no room for error. "Tell 'em we're concerned about a wave of identity theft and if that doesn't work start reading them the Patriot Act, *verbatim.*"

"Harsh," the special agent replied.

"Get it done."

Director Moore slammed the phone on the desk and exited the SCIF. *What the hell is going on?* He needed to change tactics. He needed to draw this hacker in, and there was only one way, release his own hackers.

"Sir," Jack called after him.

Director Moore stopped and let Jack catch up. "Can you believe this shit?"

Moore stepped into the night air, and breathed a lung of crisp winter air, then exhaled, repeating the exercise several times while his star cryptanalyst proffered an analysis. "It's all been a diversion, something is about to go down, and we've got no clue as to when or where. Maybe I need to get moving?"

Moore felt his core heating up as he intertwined his fingers and cracked his knuckles and released the tension from his neck. "I'm gonna get that sonuvabitch."

∼

ANJA CLOSED the feed from the camera on the Bethesda gaming console as the last of the NSA security team cleared the stairs, and a young, irritated teenager came tumbling down, a smile plastered across her face as she breathed a rapturous sigh, then plopped down in her gaming chair to resume play. *Let's see how they plan on tracking me now. Catch me if you can, boys.*

26

LANGLEY, VIRGINIA

Nothing had gone to plan, and as Johnny approached Langley, he shook his head in disbelief at his predicament. Ever since he'd departed the Basel conference, he'd been fighting against his better judgement, putting personal emotions over both Agency and Council priorities, and now having painted himself into an impossible situation, there was no going back. Despite his commitment to the Agency and its mission, as well as finding the assassins, he knew his obligations to the Council couldn't be ignored, especially with the complex and far reaching blockchain negotiation in Basel, which promised to decentralize the entire New World Order. *If CIA thinks the Russians were involved with the assassination and were working their moves on the Basel conference..., Why were they so insistent that I pass the Malaysian reconnaissance to Mike? If they suspect a connection, then why not keep me in the loop? What are they not telling me?*

Over the last several days, he'd been taunted by the recurring thought that he'd made a mistake leaving Chairman Meyer in Basel, something more than duty or allegiance to the country, the appearance of Derek Hamilton-Smith with the Russians pulled at his senses. It wasn't an accident that the FED chairman had selected

Johnny as his deputy, and in fact a well-planned Agency mission for him to come back from retirement and lead the BIS initiative. Whether it was his connections to the global elite, his field experience, or his in-depth knowledge of blockchain technologies and an evolving neural network, he'd been chosen by Langley to make the course corrections necessary to keep the United States at the forefront of the discoveries. It wasn't an easy task. Despite his broad technology investments and firsthand knowledge of proprietary propulsion systems, the Russians had been nipping at his heels the last few years, and their tie-up with Hamilton-Smith proved their resolve. They were determined to get out in front of the changing automation landscape. Johnny stepped through his office doorway on the seventh floor, hung up his coat, and ran over his options in his head. When he sat down, he saw a yellow Post-It note on a stack of folders. He squinted his eyes at the handwritten note. *What's this?*

ARRANGED IN CHRONOLOGICAL ORDER. — JANE

Although he'd only been out of town a short time, his assistant had managed to saddle him with more than enough reading materials to choke a healthy post-graduate student. He flipped through a couple of the files in genuine interest, thankful to shift his mind toward something other than his current problem, if even just for a brief moment. *The History of Swiss Banking; The Financial History of the Vatican; The McKittrick file;* He paused a long moment. Wait a minute.

Johnny drew a key from his pocket and threw open his desk safe. He stretched his hand all the way to the back of the safe and pushed a protruding circular pin, only millimeters in diameter, until he heard a *CLICK*. He pushed back his chair and opened another, well-hidden compartment in the bottom of the desk that dropped open to reveal a crimson red file. If the director wasn't going to help him or acknowledge the potential Russian connection between the Malaysian attack and the Basel initiative, he'd go it alone. He rifled through old files and the new ones stacked on his desk looking for a common denominator, a connection, a place or a name, something that tied it all together.

Nothing. After more than an hour sifting through his files, he'd found zero definitive connections between the two incidents or the one that was unfolding over the financial markets. He needed fresh intel. Johnny pinched the bridge of his nose. He remembered what Robert had said to them at the embassy, back in Malaysia, something about a powerful Russian affiliate. *The Russian mob?* He stood up and walked over to his espresso machine in the corner of the office.

For a moment, a burning rage resurfaced spiking in the pit of his stomach as anger at the thought about the server room and the thumb drive, the brief detention at the US embassy in Malaysia, everything that had transpired in the last forty-eight hours was suspect. With the files failing to yield any leads, he was now relying on what Jack found on the thumb drive, which meant he needed to hurry. Johnny peeked at his watch, *shit*. He slid the coffee mug back on the counter and fished his phone from his pocket.

Johnny knew that Jack was about to go dark, but he needed that thumb drive report. He punched in the speed dial. "C'mon, buddy, pickup."

"This is Jack, leave a message."

Johnny cursed aloud, "Damnit."

A whirlwind or questions flooded his thoughts as he sipped on his espresso and paced the floor. *What was on the drive? Who was on the drive? Did the drive record more than one location?* He took another sip of his espresso and bellowed a curse as his sizzling tongue echoed in his mind. *Focus.* He walked toward the window and leered out over the campus, trying to refocus his mind. It'd been a while since he'd been still enough to take in the Langley campus. There were a few cars in the parking lot, but most had departed for the day. The winter storm had blanketed the entire place with a fresh layer of snow, something that he hadn't missed for the few days he'd been in Southeast Asia. A sound echoed through his room and broke him from his thoughts. *Tap, Tap, Tap.*

"Mr. Dekker, I'm heading out," his assistant said as she stepped through the door and threw a relaxing smile at her boss.

Johnny paused a moment. "I'm fine, thanks. Be careful on the roads."

He forced a slanted smile as she nodded and pulled the door closed behind her. Johnny leaned back into his thoughts. Without the updated files from the SCIF or a verbal update from Jack, he was stumped. He programed another espresso and finished it straight away, he was missing something, then it hit him like a bolt of lightning. *Why the hell didn't I think of this before - the reporter?*

She was the one. He knew she'd break open a new path to the truth, if it killed him, or her, but how the hell was he supposed to get back into Malaysia without being recognized. *Beg forgiveness?* As he worked through a solution in his mind, an unexpected message chimed through on his cell phone. *What?* He tapped the screen and answered the call.

Johnny: Sir?

Father: Where are you?

Johnny: Virginia.

Father: We need to talk.

Johnny paused a moment. Was he ready for the conversation about the assassination of his fiancée and his father's arrogance dragging her along on the ill-advised excursion into an unknown situation, he opted out, it was still too soon?

Johnny: I'm heading to a briefing with director, I'll call you later.

Father: It's urgent.

Johnny: I'll call you later.

Johnny shut his phone and breathed a sigh of relief. He'd been pushing down a nagging voice to return to Germany ever since he'd landed in Virginia, but the escalating situation stateside demanded his attention, because with all the resources being siphoned off the Malaysian attack and pointed toward the infrastructure threat, he'd have to solve it alone, despite the director's orders about handing it off to Mike Chambers. It was already bad enough that the director had put him on the Basel detail without conferring with him on the matter, which he wasn't going to let stand. The arrogance, the betrayal, and the memories of Chamber's unprofessionalism were still too fresh.

With his coat in his hand, Johnny had exited his office and was on the way out of the building, seething at the recollection of a less than ideal assignment with the poser, Mike Chambers. He smashed open stairwell door and drifted down the stairs. He needed air. He headed toward the courtyard. *How could the director doubt his intentions?* In another time, the director owed his life and his job to Johnny, he wasn't a family appointment, Johnny was a hardcore special operator that'd come up through the ranks, and in record time. *How can they turn away from the Malaysian attack? And what were the details on the cyberattack on the infrastructure?* He knew the Agency and Fort Meade had sufficient bandwidth to deal with more than one thing at a time, this wasn't an analog agency anymore. With less than a couple breaths of air in his lungs, he burst through the glass doors into the open-air courtyard and took a lung full of air.

A mature Oak tree sprang up from the center of the courtyard, throwing shade across a quarter of its space, while allowing a relaxing moment for career officers that lived their lives with their protected secrets inside the reinforced concrete and glass structure. As Johnny circled the tree in thought, he pulled all his memories from Malaysian to the front of his mind, which although was a brief stay was filled with white noise of faces and names, but the one that echoed again and again was - Hannah Jankowski - the reporter that'd splashed his face all over the nightly news that made him a marked man, destroying his attempts to discover the assassins. Who was she? What was her role? Was Hannah Mike's agent?

Johnny stopped and approached the Oak. He rubbed his hands against its wintery bark, disregarding the wetness of the snow around him. Why would Mike put an agent on him? What would he gain? Or...Was she a Russian agent? With no more answers than when he'd landed, and Jack not answering his phone or texts, Johnny walked back into the building and straight to his car.

FORT MEADE, MARYLAND

Jack stared at his watch. Only a few short hours ago, he'd been neck deep in signal intercepts and communication transcripts, but now he was putting the finishing touches on a personal request for his buddy, the one he'd not seen for several hours, but with the clock running out was his first priority. He laid his hands against the bulletproof glass, hoping that his added holiday weight wouldn't prove a statistical anomaly and breach its integrity. He watched as a fresh dusting blew in from the Northeast corner of the building, slowly making its way across the parking lot below, just enough to keep the roads slick, and black ice a real threat.

Without warning Jack was bludgeoned with the thick baritone voice of his boss, Director Walter Moore. *Here we go.* He wasn't sure how he'd tracked him down, but he was certain Moore had direct mobile access to the GPS locations of all his agents and assets, it was either that or he was, in fact, half-bloodhound. Nevertheless, there was nothing more frustrating than not having a few moments alone with your own thoughts. He turned toward his boss wearing a tortured smile.

"Ya got me."

Moore threw up his hands. "I need you at Andrews by midnight, and you should pack for a couple of weeks."

Jack winced. "You talking to me?"

"This isn't a joke. I need you at the TAO site, ASAP."

"This information about the MOSSAD agent in Malaysia, and the possible connection to the Russian mob should warrant another look."

Moore sighed. Standing a commanding *six-five*, he tended to dominate the room before he even spoke, but he never liked bullying people into a position, he found collaboration a much better platform for success. "Those intercepts and the MOSSAD connections will be dealt with, and if there's anything that Johnny should know, I'll read him in myself." Moore watched Jack's eyes for feedback. "I need you at the Utah site, so you and Dr. Ridley can get us back in the game, because right now, we're not looking so good."

Jack blanched. He stepped away from the director and filled an empty cup with water and drank it down, then sputtered... "Dr. Ridley...Dr. Jane Ridley?"

Moore cocked his head to one side. "You look like you've seen a ghost."

Jack recovered. "The world-renowned mathematician... and futurist, yes sir, sounds like a plan. I'll do my best." Jack sucked down a throat of air like he'd been hit by a Mack truck. This was not expected. He grabbed the director's hand and thanked him for the opportunity as he stepped past him and disappeared through the door and down the corridor before more could even wish him well. He pressed the elevator button and waited, his heart pounding in his head, taking away all other thoughts, except one. *Jane, what are you up to in Utah?* It'd been over a decade since he'd heard the name or seen the face, the face of his naval academy upperclassman. *This was going to be interesting.*

~

Johnny stood tall in front of the gigantic post-modern glass and steel monolith that rose up from the fields of automobiles surrounding the National Security Agency, a lone reed in an ocean of asphalt and assigned parking spot numbers. He'd been around the world in less than seventy-two hours, and was running on empty, despite his massive intake of caffeine drinks and oxygen. He'd been shot at, chased, and grilled about his intentions from multiple parties on multiple continents, now was not the time to stop. With everything on the line, he needed to ensure that this next meeting, moved the ball down the field and linked them to another clue to run down, because CIA wasn't going to solve the attack, or make the connections in time before the killers went to ground. He paused a long moment and stared at the light-posts illuminating the parking lot, then stepped through the west-side visitor entrance.

He was bugged eyed at the security officer. With the three emptied cans of red bull lying crushed on the floorboard of his car, he'd prepared for a prolonged navigation of the checkpoint, despite his credentials. Nobody wanted some wired, wide-eyed, sleep deprived roughneck losing his shit on their watch. He felt the guards boring holes in him as they slow walked him through the process. Every instruction hit his cerebral cortex like a bolt of lightning causing twitching responses and stuttered answers, it'd been too long since he'd had to stay awake this long. He emptied his pockets and raised his hands while they patted him down. The gun was always a sensitive subject but given his credentials and familiarity with the supervising guard, he was allowed through, but the sidearm found a spot in the security locker.

Once he'd completed the last security check, he was buzzed into the SCIF, where he was hoping to find Jack, but inside were only a few analysts from his geek squad. He needed Jack. He needed answers. By now, he knew Jack had had sufficient time to crack any code protecting the information on the thumb drive and review the video footage. *He must have a name.* He scanned the room for his friend, nothing. After a moment, he tapped one of the analysts he'd met at a previous agency function and inquired to Jack's whereabouts. He quirked an eyebrow at the nonchalant expression of the analyst who extended her hand and stood up to face the Langley field agent.

"I'm…"

"Yes, sir, I know who you are. The directors left a few hours ago, and Jack … he was here a minute ago, I'm not sure where he's disappeared to."

"Maybe you can help me?"

The analyst smiled. "That depends."

Johnny flashed a seductive smile. "Was there a report filed about the reporter in Malaysia that splashed my picture all over the television?"

The analyst chirped a laugh and shook her head. She reached over and pulled a manila folder from her desk as she brushed off his attempted coyness and flirtation, something that'd become routine to a woman several years into her service, but she kept focused. "It was a perfect likeness, and yes we received a couple of reports from multiple listening stations about the reporter, Hannah Jankowski, her contact with the MOSSAD, and her plans to travel to London."

"Hannah, the reporter I met in Georgetown... MOSSAD? Where's she now?"

"The last intercept had her arranging a trip to London." *Peeling back the layers of the onion.* Johnny thanked the SCIF analyst, exited the security, and ran toward the elevator, there was no time to lose.

When the elevator doors opened, he rushed inside and smack into the man he'd been looking for this whole time. The two friends shared a puzzled look, paused a moment, and then both started to speak. Jack rambled on about his reassignment while Johnny fought to upload his theory about the reporter he'd run into in Malaysia, both talking over the other. In the midst of the verbal onslaught, Jack paused and looked a Johnny.

"The reporter...She's MOSSAD."

Johnny blanched. "Didn't I just say that?"

"I was going to contact you, but we got pulled into another meeting and the long and short of it is, she's on her way to London, somewhere I'm sure that you're about to tell me you're going."

Johnny froze. He dropped his hands on his friend's shoulders. "Not only a mathematical genius, but a mind reader as well, you're the complete package."

The two men leaned against the wall as they digested the information while the elevator descended toward the ground floor. Then Jack spoke. "She must be tracking the same people, but why?"

"Have we spoke with Director Levy?"

"I don't think that's a good idea now. When Walter heard the MOSSAD was running an operation around one of our guys in Malaysia without informing us, he went nuclear on good ole Levy, he might not be in the chatting mood."

"I've got to get to London, do we know anything about where she's staying and if Levy spoke to her about our knowledge of her identity?"

"Above my pay grade brother, besides, I've just been officially reassigned to the cyberattack, it's getting a lot more attention. It looks like we might be activating the Archangel protocol sooner than expected. And I was about to contact Izzy as things on this case might be a little more complicated than I'd thought."

"Archangel, wasn't that the program they were putting through its paces at RIMPAC? Was there another cyberattack? What's wrong with Izzy?"

"Something like that Johnny. Relax, relax...I meant complicated for me buddy, not the investigation. It's hard to explain, and I don't think your cousin will understand, but it's nothing to do with you or the bank."

Johnny pinched the pressure point between his right forefinger and his thumb, a trick he'd learned to ease migraines, and make him more alert. "Gotcha, this jet lag is kicking my ass, I'm hitting a wall, and probably about to crash out right here. I need more caffeine."

"We need a plan," Jack said as the ran through a couple of solutions to keep each other up on the developments should the need arise.

By the time the elevator doors had opened, the two men had settled on one, and although it called for taking the SCIF out of the loop, it was necessary, and relayed on some very quick-thinking tradecraft. The two friends shook hands and parted ways, knowing it'd be a while before they'd be back in the same location.

Jack paused a moment. He watched his friend disappear across the employee parking lot, carving new footprints through the fresh fallen snow. *Nothing like an early winter.* With the countdown until departure looming over his head, he'd not called his fiancée and hadn't decided how to explain, but given the market turmoil and the ongoing attacks, he knew she'd understand, or at least postpone any squabble until they were both back at his condo; he pulled out his phone, unlocked his screen, and hit speed dial.

KNIGHTSBRIDGE, LONDON

Hannah stepped off the overnight flight at Heathrow, carrying nothing but an overnight bag and backpack, she knew it'd seem odd to Immigration, but she'd rehearsed her story and was confident in its delivery. Whether or not the Americans had picked up on her communications with Tel Aviv and disseminated that information to the Airport authorities by know was another story. She'd not been this anxious for some time, although a trained professional, she knew that at any given moment things could always go pear shaped, regardless of preparation, so she took a couple deep breaths and slowed her heart rate.

As the Immigration lined formed ahead of her, she'd reached into her bag and clicked opened her stealth phone, which was custom fit inside a makeup compact, and switched it on, there was a message. She shortened her stride and allowed the half-sleeping business class passengers push by her while she thumbed down the screen and read it.

Levy: Message received.

Hannah: London.

She'd stabbed a quick reply on the tiny keypad then powered it down, then straightened her hair, brushed her face, and piqued her cheeks before clamping the compact shut and sticking it back in her bag. She perked up a smile as she approached the tired and overworked Immigration officer.

Hannah had met Anja Singh on a modeling assignment in Singapore. They had several mutual friends, and by way several trusted introductions found that Anja treated her with honest and sincere intentions. Within an hour they were sitting beside Clark Quay bar having a beer and talking about wild and exotic destinations they'd each seen over the years. They were friends from the start, and that's how Hannah had planned it.

Hannah Jankowski was part of an elite infiltration squad from an offshoot of the MOSSAD, the Israeli national intelligence agency. She'd taken assignments all over the world, and always in deep cover. From the time she left the Kibbutz where she'd grown up with other children made orphans like herself, she'd been raised by the state, and owed everything to the state, everything except her mortal soul, but for now she paid her debts. Recruited for her mathematical and programming skills by Ari Levy from the special Unit 8200 she'd been assigned to after school, she was thrown into field work, something the director needed more than anything, quick witted and mentally strong female field agents. Once in the field, Hannah morphed into a new personality, owning the role, and thankful she'd found her calling. She'd entered service for Anja Singh after their Singapore meeting, and she'd been handling odd jobs for Anja and her clients ever since, including the Russians.

With another Immigration officer clocking in and about to take over the new shift, Hannah widened her smile enticing the outgoing officer to make just one more check before retiring for the day. She saw the sleep deprived officer wave her forward, she kept her relief inside. Hannah passed her passport to the agent.

"Hello."

"Business or pleasure?"

"Business."

"How long will you be in the United Kingdom?"

Hannah smiled. "Not long enough."

The agent snorted a laugh, stamped her passport then waved her through.

Hannah took back her passport with a receptive smile, winked a quick thank you, and disappeared into the gathering crowd at security. She'd moved with purpose through the secondary security line, and marched straight passed baggage claim, already in possession of her entire wardrobe, and into the arrival hall before taking a deep, but subtle breath. After arranging a car and meeting it at the appropriate designation area, she sat back and rested for the long drive in, pining for the comforts and relaxation of a familiar oasis, the Berkley Hotel. Once on the road, and tucked inside her Uber, she swapped out her phone chip, and split the old one in two, then punched in a text to her boss.

Hannah: Landed.

Anja: Perfect, I'll be back at the hotel shortly.

Hannah: Shall I bring anything?

Anja: Surprise me.

Hannah: lol

Hannah knew she'd another stop before the Berkley. Their mission was a success, and she knew exactly what her puppet master wanted as she redirected the driver to a specialty shop, just outside Knightsbridge. She'd made quick work of it and with her package in hand she'd jumped back in the Uber and in less than a couple of winks arrived at the luxurious five-star hotel, just as the sun was setting across Hyde Park, and beyond. She exited the car, walked past the check-in counter, and found a seat on the ground floor bar. After a couple of Cosmopolitans, and about an hour of unwinding, a message chimed through her phone.

Anja: 301

Hannah: wink emoji

She paused a moment, fixed her hair, and then rapped on the suite door with a middle knuckle. *Quiet. Maybe she's on her way up as well.* Despite her best efforts to keep hydrated on the flight, a wave of jet lag had dulled her senses, and the drinks in the bar had only served to further confuse her body.

With a distinct *clang* inside as well as a delayed response, Hannah knew that something wasn't right. She shifted her weight and adjusted her stance as the door cracked open. *Anja?* A blinding light shocked her pupils while a pair of monster hands gripped her by the throat and pulled her through the doorway and sending her bottle of *Chateau Lafite* crashing to the floor. Hannah thrashed about like a ragged doll, until the muscular pair of hands had sapped eighty percent of her strength, and she lay limp and helpless. When she felt his grip begun to ease, she twisted her upper torso, straighten her legs against the attacker's throat and kicked off with full force, nothing happened, the powerful hands slammed her super model body onto the marbled floor, sending her left shoe skidding across the smooth surface, only stopped by a silent silhouette - Anja Singh.

"Did you think I was an idiot?"

Hannah assumed the role. "What the hell boss?"

Anja circled her treacherous employee noting her every move, watching her every reaction, this wasn't going to be easy, but she would break this Israeli scum, after all, she had Grigorovich, and he was a master of confessions.

Hannah choked a cough. *How the hell was this possible?* She felt the ominous presence of the boorish Russian looming over her as she struggled for every life clinging breath, knowing the inevitable was only moments away. She gasped through her options. In her line of work there was never any backup, you either fight or die, and it was absolute.

"When I order a job, it's done exactly how I order it, nothing more, nothing less." Anja pranced around Hannah, as she lay crumpled on the ground, panting short breaths, forced to listen to this Russian puppet's tirade. "I'm sorry it had to end this way, my dear. You were most effective, and it will take me…a week to replace you."

With on last burst of energy, and the desire to end it on her own terms, Hannah kicked off the bruiser and launched herself across the floor and wrap her hands around Anja's throat. A quick twist and she brought the Russian puppet's skull crashing to the elegant Formosan marbled dining room table and screamed at the top of her lungs… "Die *Bitch*." … followed by darkness.

27

ANDREWS AFB, MARYLAND

Over the last few years, Jack had managed to deliver on everything his boss had asked of him, but with this multi-pronged attack, he knew Moore was right, but he didn't like it. He watched the ground crews deicing the planes on the tarmac, and his flight crew climbing aboard the C75 Gulfstream. Everything was off balance, his assignment, his relationship, and he needed focus. He took a deep breath, parked his car, and grabbed his backpack and duffle bag. The call with his fiancée hadn't gone as well as he'd hoped. She knew he was a houseplant, and loved him anyway, but there were some things that women needed to know from the jump, and that included ex-girlfriends. He made a note to self.

When informing fiancée of an important mission, make sure she knows the parties involved, before you're called away to work with them in close quarters at an undisclosed location, for an indeterminable amount of time.

Jack zipped up his jacket, wrapped his scarf around his neck, and stuffed his car keys in his pocket as he navigated the crew and boarded the jet. He didn't have the headspace for her and the mission, he had to let it go.

The C75 Gulfstream lit up its runner lights, checked its engines, and taxied out to the runway for its midnight departure. From the radar, the flight appeared to have missed the last part of the storm and was set to have a smooth ride over the Mississippi and over into the foothills of the Rockies, his destination. Jack settled into his seat as it cleared the runway and was in flight. He fell back into his thoughts about the last forty-eight hours.

Although Jack was confident in Johnny's ability to run down the leads from the recovered Malaysian surveillance videos, he wasn't sure how the truth of the other woman's identity from the cafe was going to play out. Anja Singh was more complicated than her compartmentalized personnel file told, and Jack knew that its origins was anything but clear cut. It was the last file that Jack had handed to Johnny before they'd parted ways, and it was bound to cause some commotion given her part in the attack on his father.

"Mr. Sorenson, flight time is about four hours, so please sit back and relax, and let us know if you want anything."

Jack nodded at the agency co-pilot. "Perfect."

He sipped on bottled water and leaned back into his thoughts, and what they'd learned about the hack so far. From the initial report from the TAO team, although the system had been shut down remotely, they'd managed to pull some shipping documents from the Grand Cayman server before it went offline. The entire operation laid out like a well-funded and organized crime syndicate facility that'd been run off a decentralized command structure, allowing any one of a dozen command nodes to initiate or shut down the operation. The unorthodox approach ensured mission success avoiding the bottleneck of a hierarchal failure and meant that the only way to track them down was across the digital landscape, which was changing every minute. *What's the connection to the Dekker Banking Group?*

On the surface, it seemed like a move against the Dekker Banking Group, but the initial investigation by the SEC and US Cyber Command had shown that while there was a special attention pointed at the Dekker Banking Group, it was broader and deeper than they'd thought. Jack looked for investment patterns of the other banks, deals and divestments around DARPA sponsored projects, nothing was indicating any signs of foul play, he needed more data. Was it Johnny's involvement with CIA that'd landed his company in a hacker's crosshairs? But if that was the case, why bother with spreading the attack across the entire exchange, when they could've just aimed direct at the source. Then it hit him like a bolt of lightning, the Dekker Group wasn't the target, it was the decoy, and important enough for the government to expend massive resources on tracking down the connection. They're trying to take down whole financial network, but to what end? What would crashing the entire global trading network accomplish, but shift money from one investor account into another, and if that were the case, they just had to follow the money? Jack knew there was more to it than a simple heist. He took another sip of water as the jet rose above the first layer of clouds. He pulled out a pen and started charting out his theories as the plane turned toward its western vector. Perhaps the TAO team had more information, perhaps Dr. Ridley was going to read him into a more detailed account of the cyberattack. He put his pen down and propped his head on the window. *Jane Ridley.* He hadn't seen her since the Naval Academy but hoped that her genius was everything the director had said, because from these initial reports, they were going to need it.

DULLES INTERNATIONAL AIRPORT

From the moment his feet hit the ground, he knew he was late, something about the spinning earth and a temporal flux, but Johnny, ticket in hand, wasn't deterred as sprinted through the Dulles International departure hall, nothing was going to stop him from boarding his last-minute flight to London, and nothing was going to stand between him and his prey. He felt his heart pound at an even steady pace, something a consistent exercise regime had afforded him over the years, aside from personal time away from his banking obligations. With only moments until the flight crew closed the doors, he battled through the diverse crowds grinding their way through the airport Duty Free distractions, oblivious to space and time, but slowing the entire passenger terminal flow. Running the new information, he'd received from the analyst in the SCIF, he knew he'd a limited amount of time before Hannah discovered her cover had been blown, the only question was what she would do next, flee, or cooperate, and his money was on the former. Another boarding announcement erupted over the intercom.

THIS IS THE FINAL CALL FOR AMERICAN AIRLINES FLIGHT AA963 WITH SERVICE TO LONDON

Johnny quickened his pace. Ever since the State Department's disruptive travel ban to Malaysia, he'd stopped asking permission or relying on government transportation, despite direct orders from Director Brown on keeping Mike Chambers in the loop, he'd chosen another path, something didn't sit right with him about Mike, and he didn't have time to launch into any internal squabble. Dulles International was the closest airport that offered him a path to London, and as time was running out, he had to make the flight.

Johnny white knuckled his phone as he dodged another baby stroller, keeping the electronic boarding pass displayed on his smartphone, and hoping a smooth transition through security. It was only by luck that he'd managed to contact his assistant to call the CEO at Boom aircraft and secure him a seat on their new Trans-Atlantic flight, which had clocked speeds of Mach 2.2, treble the commercial airlines, but still a fraction of his personal EMjet, but that wasn't an option at this point, and he was glad to have a seat. He slowed to a trot as he approached the security checkpoint, raised his pre-clearance badge, cranked up a smile and placed his bag on the X-ray conveyor belt then stepped through the metal detector. *Cleared.*

Johnny hurried forward, jacket flaring in the wake of his aggressive navigation around the numerous obstacles that landed in front of him, driven by his subconscious, and powered by pure will. With the face of the BBC reporter flashing across his thoughts like an animated film and starring a female MOSSAD agent that'd marked him in Georgetown for the world to see, he was determined more than ever to make the flight and question his agent in person. He nodded at the flight attendant that was shutting down the gate, and about to close the door.

Johnny stopped short of the door. "London."

The attendant scanned his ticket. "Here you go sir. Enjoy the flight."

Johnny winked a smile, then boarded the plane. He pulled an azure handkerchief from his pocket and dabbed his face and forehead when his cell began to vibrate. He fished around in his pocket a long moment as he tried to catch his breath, he pulled out the phone and read the screen. *Walter?* He hit the answer button and waited as the system secured the link. Then, answered.

"They're closing the doors. What's up?"

"We got a message from Tel Aviv. Something has gone wrong. Your reporter friend... has gone dark."

"Oh, I see, their agent goes dark... and they remembered we're on the same side?" Johnny retorted.

Walter sighed. "Listen, she was meeting her contact...an Anja Singh, that was the other signal intercept that was traced back from Shoal Bay. She's a known entity, and not something I want to get into right now, but we lost track of her for about six years, until she walked through the gates at Heathrow this morning and triggered her CGI tracking device."

"Walter, hold on a minute..." Johnny looked up at the stewardess then gestured his understanding with his free hand as she stood over him.

"Sir, you need to turn off and store your phone until after takeoff."

Johnny smiled and nodded, then removed his hand from the phone. "I'm about to take off. Send me her last known location. I'll run it down."

"Check your CRYPT folder. And listen, this is serious, Levy's never called in a favor from us, so I'll dig into why, but let's try to pull in a win here."

Johnny felt the stewardess burning a hole in the back of his head as she stood just over his shoulder, waiting. He looked back up at her. "Yes, Yes, I know." Johnny spoke into the phone. "I'll do what I can, but I need more intel on this, Anja."

A long paused followed as the connection faded with the plane taxing to the runway. Johnny pressed the phone for clarity. "She's not rogue, Johnny… She's dead."

"What?"

"Anja Singh was a clandestine operative under your father. She was killed in action about ten years ago."

Johnny choked a laugh. It was clear there was more to the story, but he wasn't about to find out at that moment. Despite taking a twist toward the comical, he understood his mission. He regrouped and leant forward in his seat. "This is a longer conversation, and you and I will have it when I land."

"We'd no idea, until the London alert."

Johnny shook his head. He thought about Chloe. He thought about the Russians. He thought about the Malaysian attack. *What the fuck?* "Walter, it's time we went on the offensive." He switched to airplane mode and adjusted his seatbelt.

UTAH

Something was wrong, a rumbling in the distance pulled him closer to the spiraling void, it wasn't enough he had to team up with the hackers, now he might not even have the chance to prove his.... Jack blinked awake. He'd been running on fumes over the last several days, running parallel operations on two different continents, but with Johnny back in the loop, he afforded himself a brief reprieve. Once his flight had crossed the Mississippi River, he'd leaned back and fell into a restful sleep. Now, sensing he was nearing his destination, he'd awakened and set to making some last-minute notes for his meeting with the Office of Tailored Access chief, someone he knew well. Knowing that she didn't suffer fools, he jotted some thoughts about a potential firewall to protect the domestic infrastructure, and hoped she'd appreciate his thoughts, but knew at the end of the day she outranked him.

From the moment Mike Chambers was deployed to the Caymans, Jack had been reinvigorated to run down every clue, and until earlier in the evening he'd thought his SCIF team was hub of the information flow, and calling the shots on preventing the next attack, apparently, he'd been mistaken. Director Moore had allowed the NSA hacking group special access, and they'd been running their own strategies, gaming out eventual scenarios beyond Jack's knowledge. Whereas the Malaysian attack had kept Jack reliant on overseas signal intercepts and the Five Eyes network with Echelon and its neural network at the core of their analysis, as well as a team of top intelligence analysts, the cyberattack required something more, and his reassignment to Utah was a strategic pivot by the director. He choked a cough then finished his water.

I hope she's got some answers because this is going to get bad.

Jack mused. For the last few months, he'd been stuck behind a desk, even before the Penang incident, something about his promotion to a departmental leadership role had him burning the candle at both ends and keeping him from field deployment. Having come up with Johnny through the SEALs, regular deployment was like breathing air, and he'd missed it trapped behind a desk.

Given his experience, Jack knew he was the one to bridge the two NSA teams, his geek squad at the Fort, and the NSA hacking team buried somewhere in the Utah vastness, out of sight, and out of mind, the perfect combination. But with Dr. Jane Ridley entering the equation, he knew it was anyone's guess, and it was six and ten chances if he was lucky. He fidgeted with his backpack as he waited for the plane to land and pull to a halt. He missed the teams. He missed the changing objective and the changing scenery, but the one thing he didn't miss was the sand, and now here he was back in the middle of it. *Karma.*

Buried under hundreds of tons of concrete and steel wasn't any way for a SEAL to live, but this was his new life, at least until they neutralized the threat, and not even their most complex neural network had that answer. As a naval warfare operator, he'd one thing on his mind, complete the mission, it was engrained in his training and the only way he approached things. So, no matter what or where his mission took him, he was going to see it through. He felt the plane pull to a complete stop, and a minute later the pilot stepped into the cabin.

"Mr. Sorenson, we've got a Blackhawk waiting for you, sir. Please follow the Marine at the bottom of the stairs, he'll escort you to your connection."

"Connection?"

"Don't worry. Just follow the Marine and he'll get you there."

Jack blanched. "A short helicopter ride then, perfect, thank you captain."

∼

A DUST DEVIL spun to life and skipped across the intersection of a remote access road running parallel along the Great Salt Lake, a conturing landscape pulled it along the arid topography before it dissipated into thin air, somewhere near the Camp Williams military base. Nestled against a rising terrain on the northern slope of the installation were two white buildings, whose lack of weathering indicated their recent addition to the location in an otherwise hostile environment.

Over a three-year period, the NSA data center selection committee, armed with a fresh mandate from the US President at the time had confirmed and shortlisted the area after two visits, but it wasn't until the Congressional reallocation of funds from the Department of Defense that the two NSA data halls broke ground, and changed the course of domestic data collection. Aside from the two main structures there were several other "out" buildings, and some scattered farm buildings from the turn of the century that were left standing, something that gave the site character, against an otherwise industrial looking optic with its antenna arrays and numerous cooling towers. Despite its relative recent installation, the antenna needed constant manual inspection, and although it only took a single technician, the site manager always ensured her command worked in teams of two or more, regardless of the job. Today, it'd been a fifty-foot antenna on the Northwest corner of the facility, and as the technicians finished the job and headed back toward a dilapidated tool shed nearby; the supervisor's phone rang — it was the boss.

Dr. Jane Ridley was an overachiever. A ruthless gung-ho leader that strove for excellence and efficiency in everything she did, but at the ripe age of thirty-five had yet to find it in her personal life, something about her dedication to work. She was also charismatic, efficient, and a confident strategic thinker, pushing those around her to always exceed her expectations. Yet despite all this, she'd managed to pull the best out of people, and created a tight-knit, no-sunlight-between them team, and cemented her position as their unequivocal leader, and spiritual guide through the complicated labyrinth of government service.

But if she was an overachiever, it was because her professional career had taken on a life of its own. As a world-renown mathematician, she'd specialized in numbers, landing her in a unique sphere of influence within government circles, and her most recent appointment as head of the Office of Tailored Access, a quite prestigious, if not lonely position, and mammoth achievement from where she'd started her career in the National Reconnaissance Organization (NRO) as an entry level analyst.

"This is Ridley." A gust of wind swept across the shack rattling the loose metal rivets as the pivoted away from the chop angling to hear the connection.

"You've got a priority one call from Fort Meade." Looking down at the antenna replacement parts, she shrugged off her tool belt, and moved inside the shack, away from the vexing gusts pounding against her face.

"Put it through." Jane, sheltering inside the eighteenth-century shack, removed her goggles, and pressed her right index finger to one ear. She heard the scrambled connection confirm encryption.

Director Walter Moore spoke to the point. "It's time. Are you ready?"

"We've been ready for a while, sir. She's been running parallel to Echelon for the last eighteen months, and RIMPAC confirmed it," Ridley replied.

Moore paused a moment. "Did you manage to scrape anything from the Cayman servers before they went offline?"

Jane turned into the corner of the shed and bent over trying to muffle the wind swaying the tool shed. "Yes, but we need some additional information from Sorenson's team. We'll get back to him today."

"Yes, you will...I've sent him to you."

Dr. Ridley paused a long moment. "I'm sorry, it's hard to hear, but it sounded like you said you, *sent*, Jack Sorenson to me?"

"He's been leading both investigations and can make sure it ties together."

Jane choked a reply. "Our team works alone, it's why we're so effective, sir."

"It's gone beyond sections and departments. There are too many variables. We don't even know what we don't know, which is not good. I need my two best people on this, and that's the pair of you. We need to shut this down."

Jane wiped her sleeve across her eyes as she stood up in the dying wind. "Yes, sir, I understand that, and agree. My point was... Jack and I have history."

∼

JACK WATCHED as the C75 Gulfstream pulled away from the jetway, lights blinking through the midnight landscape, and taxing back toward the runway, preparing for takeoff. A piercing cold wind pulled his focus back on the darkness enveloping the tarmac, and the yet to be confirmed road ahead. Through the blackness, about 300 yards to the South, he heard the trademark whine of a Sikorsky engine screaming to life, and the distinct rotary sound of a UH-60 Blackhawk chopping the frigid night air. He rubbed his hands together as he quickened his pace trying to catch up with his Marine escort. He saw the escort look back at him, checking on his progress. Jack gave a quick thumbs up as they approached the Blackhawk landing area.

"How far?"

The Marine threw a quizzical look. "It's right there, sir."

Jack blanched. "How much farther to my destination?"

"I was told to get you to escort you to the helicopter, that's all I know," the Marine replied. "Watch your head."

The two men squatted down a bit and moved forward as Jack loaded onto the Blackhawk and strapped his gear down by his seat. He'd seen a lot of intra-agency chatter about the new NSA facility - *Bumblehive* - but hadn't been fully read into its operation, another thing that Moore was keeping from him. He understood the need to compartmentalize but given his position he thought he'd have been more involved at this point, anyway, given his current planes, trains, and automobile moment, he wasn't even sure how long he'd be able to keep his current geek squad from getting slashed in favor of technology, much less be read into some new advanced technology initiative.

Budget cuts. He sniffed at the ridiculous bureaucracy. What did the budget office or for that matter, Congress, understand what the country needed? Jack pushed down his recurring frustration with the red tape that'd allowed the country's adversaries to gain ground on the American technological prowess. It'd started with the gutting of the Zumwalt destroyers, downsized; then it continued with the delay of Space Force operations, something every branch of the military had agreed was the top priority. And from the major projects, things had now trickled down to the simple things, like getting an agent from one base to the next. *Unreal.*

Jack knew that a socially liberal, but fiscally conservative society was a good thing, but when it came to military spending, it should remain off limits, if for no other reason than to counter or enemies increased spending. Once he was strapped in, he heard the pilot over his headset.

"Welcome aboard, sir."

Jack hacked a cough. "How far?"

"Don't worry, it's only a few minutes."

Among other things, Camp Williams was a Special Forces training facility, but more importantly it doubled as an extra security measure for the NSA's newest and largest data center, the Utah Data

Center (UDC), located within a couple of football fields from its gates. It wasn't long before Jack heard the pilot over the headset.

"Sir, we're going to drop you off at Williams. Someone's waiting on the tarmac to escort you to your Humvee."

Jack sighed. "Roger that Lieutenant. I'll send you boys a postcard."

∼

JANE RIDLEY FELT the elevator slow to a halt. She dusted her hair, running her fingers through it several times, but had learned a long time ago that a simple shake never sufficed, and out here, it took a rigorous effort to get clean. When she'd stopped trying to remove every fleck of dust and sand, and while the security mechanism began its thirty-second confirmation procedure, she stole a few moments and fell back into her thoughts. She considered the director's decision, especially with such a compartmentalized unit, was it wise to bring in new blood, regardless of his credentials, and his understanding of the attacks. After all, the program she was responsible for was much larger and far reaching than the importance of any one or even two national security threats, and she knew he knew it. She heard the mechanism click into place, a loud metallic sound echoed through the elevator shaft, locking the position of the transport mechanism, and opening the reinforced double-steel doors into the secluded underground bunker, home to special activities research unit.

Jane stamped her feet, shook her head and body one last time, and then stepped through the security doors. A vast expanse opened around her, but she made her way to the illuminated and populated area scattered with analysts and technicians, all hard at work at whatever was on their desktop. She removed her glasses and stared out over her team, pausing a moment before unleashing a full-mouthed smile across her tired and dirty face, then spoke.

"History will remember this day."

A loud cheer and pounding of desks echoed through the underground chamber as the team voiced their approval of a long-awaited command.

"Okay, it's game time. I need you all focused and functional, so for those of you who haven't slept in the last twelve hours, go clock some rack time, and the rest of you pull up your execution files and double check everything is in order, we only get one shot at this," Dr. Ridley said to her team.

From the early sixties, a team of programmers had been working on a secret project that over the years, and stretching across several administrations, had been stalled, reassigned, and event forgotten, before its reinstatement under new operating protocols when Director Walter Moore was named to lead the NSA, which meant compartmentalization.

Jane stepped into her office and tossed her coat and tool belt onto the adjacent sofa, dirt be damned. She was amped. The time to introduce her project to the world had come, and the timing couldn't have been better, especially with the hacking team hitting a wall on dissecting the Cayman server information. She opened her locker and pulled a change of clothes from inside, then pivoted back toward the door, allowing herself a moment of elation, before having to deal with the incoming unknown, or semi-unknown, after all it was Jack Sorenson. She stuck her head out of the office.

"I want all theories crazy and crazier about the assassination attempt on Ambassador Dekker, and the financial market crash ready for discussion in ten minutes, and I mean ALL theories."

Aside from running the most efficient and successful hacking team within the US intelligence community, and perhaps the world, Dr. Ridley had received a special TS/SCI Clearance and asked to resume a previous joint CIA/NSA source code project codenamed - ARCHANGEL. It'd been a chance of a lifetime and she delved headlong into the mathematical elusive labyrinth surrounding artificial intelligence, and all its tangents. On the surface, machine learning seemed daunting to those lesser minds, but to those who spoke mathematics as a first language it was poetry in motion, something they'd only dreamed about as children. From machine learning evolved deep learning protocols and then the neural networks that had consumed and catapulted the big technology companies into the mainstream, driven by their "secret sauce", but nothing was secret to the one's who'd written the recipe and provided the base.

Before Dr. Ridley had taken up the project it'd cycled through several surrogates including the Defense Advanced Research Projects Agency, also known as DARPA, embedded within the Department of Defense, which had leveraged its ARPA communications network savvy to expand the potential for any future global communication network, analog or digital. It wasn't until Director Moore's compartmentalized protocols were implemented that any real progress was seen, breaching new heights of possibilities, and dragging deep learning algorithms through layer upon layer of neural networks that the project inched closer to a human level intelligence goal.

Once the team had assembled in the faraday room, Dr. Ridley entered and sealed the door, following every precaution, no matter where she was, or whom she was speaking to. "Let's find out what you came up with."

One-by-one the team members spoke, and one-by-one the team batted down the numerous theories, they all knew something connected the Malaysian assassination attempt and the US cyberattack, but none of them could point their finger on it. Theories ranged from family feuds to corporate espionage, and from terrorist plots to big tech firms, but nothing help up to scrutiny. Then from the back of the room, Jane heard a random statement, and she froze stiff, because the truth of it scared her to her core. She turned to the young dirty blonde NSA hacker sitting at the opposite side of the table with a pale face, so as to not influence the answer, but fearing she'd just identified the connection.

"What did you say?"

"Somebody's after the Archangel source code."

Dr. Ridley seethed. She knew he was right, now it all made sense, but what was she going to do about it. Hubris had blinded them. Although they were buried a dozen stories underground and flanked on the surface by an active military installation with patrolling sentry drones at all altitudes, nothing had prepared them for what they thought they controlled, the Internet. The young man shrank in his seat as a dozen pair of eyes zeroed in on his masculine frame but fell silent in his simplistic and spot on revelation. Ridley saw him collect himself, sitting upright, and staring straight into her eyes.

"Think about it multiple high value targets that they know we'll have our best teams on and in the end, if our network is overwhelmed, revert to our only remaining option, our most precious and cutting-edge source code."

Dr. Ridley rose from her chair. "They want her. They want IRI."

Another analyst chimed in. "It makes perfect sense. Ambassador Dekker was part of the original compartmentalized Project Archangel, it's one of the reasons the White House wanted him at RIMPAC."

Dr. Ridley began to pace the room, keeping her cool about her, but running a hundred scenarios through her head as she engaged her team. "But how did they know he was going to be in Asia?"

"An inside job?" a technician blurted, which was soon drowned out by the entire room breaking into uncontrolled conjecture and speculation.

This is spinning out of control. "Hold on," Dr. Ridley bellowed crushing the chorus of debating analysts and restoring order to the conference room.

Jane knew what every hacker worth their salt knew, that the Internet was a double-edged sword that just as often cut to the right as to the left, and barring any revelations in quantum computing, breaking through any firewall was only a matter of time and patience. Once again, the world sat on the edge of a razor, and whomever activated a human level intelligence first, rendered a two-ocean war scenario moot, and controlled everything from that moment.

"There's one more thing. We've a VIP coming in from Fort Meade, Jack Sorenson, he'll be with us for a while, so I want you to make him feel welcomed, and let me know if there's any issues," Dr. Ridley said before adjourning the meeting.

Something burned in the back of her mind as she made her way back to her office to prepare for her guest, she knew that she'd been selected by Director Moore to continue with Project Archangel, but she'd also discovered his connection to the Council of Thirteen, and that worried her. Armed with newfound authority of the special activities program director, she'd purged her team's personnel files from the Project Archangel database, and renamed the new compartmentalized project - IRI - after the Christian bible's group of archangels including Michael and Raphael. As she stepped through the doorway of her office only two questions echoed in her mind: Was this a test by the New World Order initiative spearheaded by the Davos crowd, or was it something more sinister?

∼

JACK SORENSON THREW a salute to the helicopter pilots, stepped off the hunkering bird and made a beeline for the military Humvee keeping his head low as he jogged away under the massive steel rotary blades.

"Welcome to Utah, Mr. Sorenson."

Jack grinned at the young Marine Corporal. "The Industry State."

KNIGHTSBRIDGE, LONDON

Anja Singh pursed her lips. She'd tied off another loose end, and was moving forward, but the actions of the dead Israeli agent weighed on her mind and distracted her focus from her streaming of the NYSE opening bell. What had she told the MOSSAD? Were they already on her trail? How much time did she have? She paused a moment and looked away from her computer screen toward the floor to ceiling windows overlooking the hotel courtyard. *Damnit, Hannah.*

The audio from the news stream pulled her attention back to the task at hand, she waited for instructions. From the beginning, the plan had been clear, and she was launching the third and final wave of attacks, this was the moment Grig's Russian oligarch had paid her for, which meant the balance was set to hit her account at any moment. Once she'd unpacked the execution file, she'd be free and done with the Russians, and to follow her own path toward revenge, unless she botched the execution. Anja slowed her breathing and exhaled as she keyed in her online password and routed her connection through several GPS scramblers and VPNs into her remote Swiss broker account. *Ready.*

Aside from Hannah, everything had gone to plan, and once the NYSE had sounded the opening bell, her mission was complete. Anja counted through the false flags she'd unleashed on the Americans while she waited, keeping her eyes fixed on the clock. *Sixty seconds...* She cracked a toothy smile as she thought about the divided American response, they'd resources chasing down the Malaysian attack, they'd resources chasing down the Cayman servers, and they'd had agents pouring through the data with the SEC, but they didn't have Anja. She hovered over her computer with quickening short breaths like a lioness gearing up for an attack on a baby gazelle, she checked the pre-marketing trading levels, they were strong. She began the final countdown.

Once she hit enter, it'd take several minutes before the two codes combined and cascaded across the network. *One...more... minute.* She wiped her brow as her heart raced, redemption was near, but satisfaction was far from complete. She saw the face of her mother, the woman the Ambassador had allowed to die, the only family she'd ever known. Vengeance was near. *They'll never know what hit them, and since he'd decided not to die maybe I'll tell him in person.*

Anja quirked an eyebrow. The talking heads pointed to the rallying futures as tried to shrug off the previous week's uncertainty, chalking the wild ride to an overzealous trader, and unfamiliarity with algorithmic trading. Then it happened. As the CEO of the new social media company rang the opening bell, Anja keyed in one word — BREATHE — activating a program that raced across the fiber optic cables laid across the bottom of the Atlantic Ocean toward their executing exchange and yet undiscovered compromised servers to the embedded malware file *NEPHLM*.

From that one-word instruction, the embedded files across the zombie network scattered across the backbone of the eastern seaboard unpacked execution files and brought the *Ahkemenov Bratva*'s copycat Artificial Intelligence — *IRIN* — to life. She erupted into a soul consuming laughter as she watched in devious bliss as malware exploded across the financial networks, initiating the Artificial Intelligence now embedded on several US exchanges.

Anja confirmed delivery of the file, then sent an encrypted message to Igor confirming the fact and watched her payment flow into her bank account, she turned to her guest, Grigorovich. "IRIN's online. It's extracting its execution files from the NEPHLM malware we embedded on the banks servers and interacting with the zombie network — it's done."

Grigorovich stood by the window watching the street below. "This is Russian in…genuity." He pulled out his cell phone and called their Belgian banking and technology partner, Derek Hamilton-Smith.

"I hope your investments in order."

"Again?" Derek raced across the floor of his suite banged a password into his computer and checked US financial market opening. Within moments a trend started to form, and it wasn't good for confidence, but it wasn't bad for Derek. He smiled as he watched the Russian Ruble implode into a downward spiral. *'Atta boy, Johnny.* Then he looked back to his Russian comrade, "Everything's fine, cheers."

∼

HANNAH JANKOWSKI, bloodied and bruised, clawed her way up the banks of the Serpentine. Her fatigued arms struggled for traction, shaking violently as she used every ounce of strength to pull herself out of the water. *Free.*

For all their intents and purposes, the MOSSAD technology

wizards had yet to master underwater transmissions, which had sparked the plea for assistance from the Americans. If the GPS signal was at sea level or above there was a clear line of sight to the satellites, but the water medium continued to prove difficult.

Gasping for air, she struggled to her knees, and then her feet. With the frigid November cold shutting her down, she'd only minutes before she collapsed. She put one foot in front of the other until she'd navigated the park and was over the fence with a line on an allied safe house - the Wellesley Hotel - only a stone's throw from the Russian whore, and her thugs.

29

MINISTRY OF STATE SECURITY HEADQUARTERS

A long shadow threw shade across the plaza as Li pulled his cellphone from his inner suit pocket as he stepped into the midday sun outside the Ministry of State Security building, nothing he'd discussed with the Standing Committee members had prepared him for this moment, in fact it flew in the face of what they'd instructed him to do, which was nothing. How could he do nothing when his Russian intelligence intercept threatened to upend a decade of meticulous field work? There was nothing more frustrating than having to rebuild an entire intelligence network, as well as identify and befriend possible assets, spending years winning their trust, but even with all that, his friendship with the Dekkers mattered. He furrowed his brow contemplating the readiness of his American co-conspirator, even without the Standing Committee's approval, he had his own *National Team*, and they answered to him. A voice erupted through his earpiece.

"Hello..."

Li straightened his back. "Burning the candle at both ends Izzy?"

He thought about the audacity of their planned counterstrike on the Russian currency, once it was set in motion, there was no turning back, despite having the ability to manipulate markets, sometimes they had a mind of their own, beyond any one agencies control, and he wanted to ensure they'd agreed on the second phase of attack before he set in motion, especially without the Committee's blessing.

"I hope the Committee understood that this was the only way for us to counter the imbalance in the markets."

Li paused a long moment. "Well, it doesn't matter now."

"What happened?"

When they'd last spoke, they'd agreed the best approach to counter the Russians move against the equity markets was to launch a counterstrike on the Russian ruble. It was a two-pronged approach that included Li convincing their strategic allies in the OPEC nations to assist, while the secondary action called for an intervention by the People's Bank of China (PBOC) itself, which would only be implemented if the first phase failed to achieve their desired result. Li stepped forward off the steps and stood on the edge of a crowded sidewalk, safety in numbers, and increased white noise helped muffle some of their conversation, though he knew it was all on tape in somebody's basement and sitting in a remote cloud server queued up for further analysis. "They didn't say no...but they didn't say yes either, which leaves it in my hands."

Izzy pressed her mouth to the receiver. "And if it goes right, they'd agreed, but if it goes south, you're toast?"

"Bingo."

"Where does that leave us? I don't want you to get arrested if this blows up?"

Li exhaled a long breath. "I've designated a Hong Kong based unit to follow your lead on the Ruble, but they'll be on and off, so tell your traders to keep their head about them, and not be overzealous during the Asian trading hours."

Izzy looked out over her trading floor at her team. "Understood."

Li knew the Russians were merciless, once they smelled blood in the water, they went all in. "And I'm heading to Qatar, so keep your phone charged. You should probably start prepping your energy traders for your change in strategy. They'll need some time to get ready."

An abrupt screech echoed down the line, something was wrong, but within microseconds, Izzy was back on the line. "Sorry, Junxiong, we're ready."

"You need to keep your traders on point, it's going to be a long hard trading day, the Ruble has been strengthening over the last week given the oil production cut announcement."

Izzy snorted a laugh. "I've got this."

FORT MEADE, MARYLAND

Mike Chambers wore his sunburn like a badge of honor, nothing had pleased him more than landing the most coveted field assignment in the last decade, but now he had to answer for losing the enemy agent. He strolled into SCIF 17, ready to explain what happened to Jack and the director before they handed over command of the investigation and laid out a plan to capture the agent by using the information the team had downloaded. Once he'd stepped through the door, it took him two-seconds to realize there were more important things happening, every analyst was plugged into their station and banging away at their keyboards. He tapped a red-headed analyst on the shoulder.

"What's going on?"

"Which part?" the analyst chirped.

"Where's Jack Sorenson?"

A senior analyst stepped between Chambers and the young analyst. "He's been reassigned, I was told you were aware."

Mike seethed. "I've assumed operational command of this SCIF. If there's any doubt as to my authority, feel free to leave…now."

This wasn't his first management assignment, but he thought he'd at least have the chance to talk to Jack and Director Moore before he'd taken up the helm and quelled the rising anxiety about losing the Russian. It was too late now. He grabbed a chair, sat down behind a terminal, and logged into the system. If it was game time, he wanted to find out what the NSA hackers had found, and if there was anything that might help him track down the Cayman suspect.

Mike was a veteran field agent that had rotated through various assignments around the world with a distinguished career, not everyone was a fan, but it didn't matter in his mind. After a decade in the management ranks at the Central Intelligence Agency, it was inevitable to have ruffled a few feathers along the way, both with other station chiefs as well as the rank-and-file analysts. Everyone had their own attitude and ego, but Mike had a bad habit of always taking the credit on any successful operation, and casting blame when a mission failed, a typical ploy of the insecure. He leaned back over the desk of the junior analyst, edging the gawking senior analyst aside.

"Catch me up."

The pale-faced analyst exchanged looks with her supervisor, and then recapped the last few hours to the new officer in command. "After the cyber-attack on the financial markets, everything went silent. The data you managed to recover from the Grand Cayman site pointed us to a couple of offshore companies that'd registered addresses here in the US, but we had yet been able to tie them to any person of interest."

Another analyst sat forward in her chair. "Our NSA listening post in Australia intercepted a phone call between the BBC reporter that splashed Mr. Dekker's face all over the news and a phone number in Tel Aviv," she said.

Mike Chambers closed his eyes visualizing the difficulty ahead. "What else?"

An irritated supervising analyst chimed in. "We got a Level One alert on a classified target arriving in London."

Mike craned his head toward the supervisory analyst at the far end of the table. "What name?"

"Above our pay grade…"

Mike snapped. "I want to know who it was, and I want to know now. This is war people. We don't stop. We don't quit when we hit a roadblock. We escalate."

Silence fell across the room as the geek squad and Langley analysts all turned toward the raging Chambers. The supervising analyst scoffed, unafraid of his weak-minded strong-arm tactics. "What do you think we did, sir? We informed our supervising officer, Jack Sorenson and his boss, Director Walter Moore. Perhaps, you've heard of them. And, if you want to know more, take it up with them, then tell us what you want to do, so we can run it down."

Mike snatched the file off the analyst's desk and exited the room.

DOHA INTERNATIONAL AIRPORT

With time running out, Li gazed out his window, he'd let his mind drift as the plane had begun its descent, and his effort to crush the currency of a Party ally neared. He wondered at the surrounding sands that echoed Qatar's isolation, and important geographical location, something that none of the superpowers dared ignore, or undermine. From the air, he'd studied the concrete airport complex that magnified the desert heat like plumes of smoke billowing up from the tarmac, a stark reminder that he was entering the bowels of hell, with the runway his only hope of escape, he had to make this stopover as brief as possible but ensure the wholehearted cooperation.

Several things had to run their course if the counter measures were to have their desired effect, and it all hinged on convincing the visiting Saudi Minister of Energy, who was attending an OPEC meeting in the capital Doha of his plan, ensure their benefit, and depart the devil's locker before their tires melted into the tarmac.

On their approach, he watched as one-by-one the other dignitaries circling aircraft lined up their final approach and prepared for a tough day of negotiations with the global markets responding to the uncertain US markets. As the planes danced into a landing pattern the ground crew prepared for the honored royal family, and respective emirs and ministers' arrival.

The seven-hour trip from Beijing wasn't quite long enough for him to enjoy a restful sleep, especially with his mind sorting through every possible outcome of their actions, both good and bad. As he sat back in his seat contemplating his words to the Minister of Energy, his satellite phone rang. He recognized Manhattan number and could only have been one person at this time of night.

"Isabella."

A long pause followed. "Are you in front of a screen?"

"What's on your mind Isabella?"

"Take a wild guess."

Li snorted a laugh. "Straight to the point, eh Izzy? No, I'm not glued to the computer now. Why don't you tell me?"

"I know our plan was to meet with the OPEC ministers ahead of their official meeting, but there's been one last minute change… we need them to accelerate that announcement and your 'National Team' in Hong Kong needs to increase their stake, big time."

Li turned toward the window as he felt the plane lowering its landing gear, and heard the landing announcement in the background, then with a quirked eyebrow, he replied. "It's not what we'd agreed Izzy, it could prove difficult with my friends in the Party, and if we fail… What's changed?"

"The traders spotted a whale crushing the e-Minis, they're making another move against the market, I can feel it, something big is about to go down, and we need to act… now."

Li knew there was no going back, there was only going all in, the concern about the outcome was irrelevant at this point, but he had to win, and that was easier said than done. "And in return?"

Izzy blushed. With the twinkling lights of lower Manhattan shining through her office windows as she choked back another tumbler of water. She hadn't had time to think through the political ramifications, and she wasn't an Agency insider anymore, she wasn't even in the government, but it didn't matter. She did head one of the most powerful family-owned banks in the world, and that was more than nothing, and it was something she could build on. "You'll have our profound gratitude."

Li exhaled with a smile. "Done."

Izzy paused a moment. She took another drink of water and

stared out over the illuminated Lower Manhattan landscape and replied. "Whatever you need Junxiong, you know that."

"Never mind all of that, Izzy. It's a mutually beneficial move, but I want a seat at the table this Christmas with you and Johnny."

Izzy grinned. "I think we can manage that."

Li snorted a laugh. "See you soon." He closed his phone and dialed up the volume on the BBC coverage of the arriving OPEC representatives, broadcasting from the airport below with a message streaming along the bottom of the screen:

OPEC LEADERS ARRIVE IN DOHA TO DISCUSS OIL PRODUCTION

From its inception, the OPEC member states had met twice a year to discuss oil production levels, and whether the group was going to increase or decrease its collective production given the current global price levels, all looking to maximize their profits, but not every nation had always adhered to the decision. This meeting afforded Li and Isabella an opportunity to leverage the personal relationship between Li and the Minister of Oil from the Kingdom of Saudi Arabia. With a quick phone call before he'd left Beijing, Li had arranged a meeting inside the arrival terminal allowing him to make his case to the minister in person and ensure their desired result before the cartel meeting.

Once on the ground and parked at the gate, Li and his bodyguards moved with purpose toward the designated area in the arrival hall, somewhere away from the press corps and other arriving ministers. As he opened the door to the airport security office, he saw a well-armed entourage surrounding his old classmate beyond the bulletproof glass. With a wide smile and open arms, he greeted his friend.

"*As-Salaam-Alaikum, Minister.*"

"*Wa-Alaikum-Salaam,*" he replied. The two men stepped into the nearby control room that housed the airport security monitors and computer systems, leaving their group of trigger-happy guards staring at each other outside.

Li smiled at his Oxford classmate. "You're looking good, healthy even."

The minister bellowed a laugh. "Peaceful living, a three-time father, and a prosperous market. What more could one ask for? But we've not got much time. You said it was urgent. How can I help?"

Li tightened his smile. "I need you to agree with your colleagues on their proposal to tighten production."

The Minister raised an eyebrow. "You knew we were going to do this already. Why are you here, Li?"

Li leaned forward. "After the public announcement and you've returned home, I need to you to publicly retract the statement, and say that after further discussions with the King that the Kingdom was actually going to increase production by two times the last increase level."

"To what end, Li?"

Li put his hand on the minister's shoulder and turned him away from the prying guards' eyes. "We need to check some Russian aggression, and we need your help, but in a covert way. Our traders have already begun the assault, as we speak, they are shorting both oil and ruble futures, alongside our partners in the US market, who wish to remain anonymous." Li paused a long moment, "But we need your help if we're going to strike the fear of God into these criminals."

The Minister nodded. "What have they done now?"

Li went all in. "As the world is preoccupied with the various geopolitical and social media trends hitting the market, they've begun their influence campaign to turn the BIS, and by affiliation all of the world's central banks into their puppet by peddling the efficiency of their "proven" blockchain technology while undercutting global confidence in the national fiat currencies of the world."

"You mean, the Bitcoin? We've already acquired several billion ourselves."

"No, they've subcontracted an investment firm based in Brussels to build them a cryptocurrency on another decentralized ledger technology that would revolutionize the world, and with them at the helm."

"I can't believe that the BIS members would support such a move, surely they understand that they cannot support any one cryptocurrency developed by any one nation," the Minister puzzled.

Li nodded. "Exactly, that's where the Belgian banking group comes into play, and they've not made the connection despite them assigning him a Russian passport to sit on their delegation as an advisor. With his designation and his passport, he can be nominated to the Bank for International Settlements, Market Committee, and the rest will be history." Li looked over toward the restless guards. "We need to distract their representatives at the BIS. We need to give them something else to focus on until we can move our own proposal into the sub-committee."

Desperate times, called for desperate measures, and although the men knew they were breaking a slew of international laws, and some of their own domestic protocols, there was no choice, because a Russian controlled globally dominating cryptocurrency would plunge the world into the iron grip of tyrannical rule, risking big data disclosures on every citizen and corporation of their respective countries, and tilting the balance of power toward the Russian government.

With a whispered word and a pat on the back, the two men ended their conversation, and shook hands. When the door opened the Minister of Oil continued toward the hotel and Li Junxiong, along with his security team was led back down their arrival corridor, and onto his Gulfstream, which had been refueled and readied for departure. Despite not permitting or prohibiting his actions, Li knew he had to inform the Party, he pulled out his government issued phone and called Beijing.

"Comrade, the proposal was well received. He's agreed to play along as necessary but will need some reassurances from our end."

The baritone voice on the other end of the line paused a moment then asked. "What guarantees did you secure from the Americans?"

Li Junxiong paused a long moment. This was it, the sticky part.

Izzy had no standing in the United States government, but Li agreed anyway, and now he swam in risky waters. "We've got what we need, comrade." This wasn't the first time he'd lied to his superiors, but it was one that made him feel uneasy, a rare feeling for him.

"Let's meet at my office once you've returned."

"Understood," he replied. Li closed his phone and stared out the window at the last few arriving airplanes. Since his promotion to Deputy Governor of the PBOC, Li's deputy at the Minister of State Security had assumed his previous role, and was acting Minister of State Security, but required constant updates given his international network and obligations. Li needed to keep him in the loop, otherwise run the risk of the two making contradicting moves in the global arena.

∼

FROM THE MOMENT the fracking phenomenon took hold in the United States, energy traders started to see the OPEC announcements had begun to wane in relevance, but for now they were still powerful, and as expected the market welcomed the cut in oil production with open arms. Isabella put her phone on the desk and leaned back in her ergonomic executive chair and watched as the BBC flashed the late day announcement along the bottom of the screen as the sun disappeared beyond the Hudson River:

OPEC MEMBERS KEEP A LID ON OIL PRODUCTION, MARKETS SOAR

Isabella Dekker watched her trading screen and sipped her tea. *Game on.*

30

HEATHROW INTERNATIONAL AIRPORT

A perpetual wave of grumbling passengers followed Johnny in his wake as he hurried past the half-dead, dehydrated, and clueless zombies stumbling down the jetway, he didn't have time for courtesy, he had an agent to find and an assassin to kill, and her trail grew colder by the minute. With another unscrupulous push he broke through a bewildered newlywed couple and straight into the front of the Customs and Immigration line. "Sorry," he whispered as they exchanged quizzical dismay.

The Trans-Atlantic flight had taken longer than he'd expected but was essential if he held any hope of catching up with the BBC journalist - Hannah Jankowski. A torrent of cool air struck him as he emerged from Heathrow's arrival hall and scurried into a Black Cab. *Anything but an Uber,* he'd thought to himself as he pulled the door closed behind him. Along the way he'd unpacked an encrypted message from Director Brown and begun combing through the file on the elusive Israeli spy, and before he knew it, he was passing Hyde Park in all its wintery splendor. *Not just a pretty face after all,* he thought to himself. And even though she'd splashed his face all over the social media and television, something about her being an allied agent made him feel better, if only for a moment, and still said nothing for motive.

Hanna's file read like a mystery novel, not that she was a clearly defined protagonist solving case after case, but quite the opposite. The number of redactions caused Johnny to pause and moment and wonder if the director had passed him the abridged version of her profile because he missions, and redeployments didn't follow any sort of training pattern he was familiar with from his time in field work at the agency.

From her first day in the field, Hannah's official reports pointed toward a young woman that had spent more time enjoying the cultures and all their trappings across multiple geographies than providing any significant contribution to her country's intelligence gathering mission. Even her annual reviews indicated that she'd proved something of a mystery to her own peers and handlers, but she'd never been reprimanded or recalled. *That doesn't make sense.*

Although admitted into the Israeli Intelligence's renown Unit 8200 at a young age, life behind a computer screen wasn't young Hannah's path. As Johnny flipped through more than a dozen transfer requests, he finally came across the order that permanently reassigned her and set their inevitable meeting in motion.

A field operative at the age of 22? She must've impressed somebody up the chain.

Johnny rubbed a dehydrated swollen knuckle in his eye and continued scrolling through the data delving deeper into her personal history, which proved limited at best leaving the sneaking suspicion that the entire file had been manufactured. According to the records, Hannah had been orphaned at a young age and raised in a Kibbutz outside Tel Aviv, where, like many other young Israelis, she was *discovered* by the current director of the MOSSAD, who took her under his wing and pulled her into the service, which half explained his interest in her disappearance. Johnny felt the forward motion of the cab slow; he had finally arrived at his destination. He locked his phone and peeked out the window.

"The Wellesley Hotel, sir," the driver said.

Johnny cracked a smile. "Splendid." He paid the grinning round-faced man, grabbed his backpack, and exited the car. Within seconds his long fluid gait had carried him past the bellboy, doorman, and straight to the check-in counter. As the beaming receptionist accepted his passport, he flashed a dimpled smile and stood silent as she keyed his information into the computer, programmed his room key, and placed it back into his hand in record time.

"Thank you," he said, then felt a slight brush of her finger against his palm as she retracted her hand from his gnarled mitts. Johnny approved a slight nod, then made for the upper-floor elevator bank.

Following in his father and grandfather's footsteps, Johnny had become what they called a *legacy* at the Agency, following his naval service, he'd been recruited into the Special Activities Division, and deployed on various operations around the world, all calculated and strategic, grooming him for a larger Agency role down the line, and that had been in motion before the attack on his father. Everywhere he went, he was treated with special attention, something that he'd watched his father navigate when he'd dragged him around the world with him during his adolescent years, hoping to educate him in international affairs. So, it was nothing new when he arrived at the plush boutique hotel set in the heart of London and he'd been given the corner suite and expedited service, it was par for the course. It'd been a couple of years since his last visit to London, which had brought with it a lot of change, but there was no time for sightseeing. There was an agent to find, and an assassin to run down.

Despite his feelings toward the intrusive, and yet unexplained agent's actions in Malaysia, she was now a priority. So much so that Director Brown had agreed to his continued absence from BIS conference in favor of this side act, something that had caught him by surprise. Johnny ran his fingers along the edge of his phone tucked away in his pocket as he thought about his next move, and how he'd pick up the trail of the assassin. A muffled *Ding* broke his train of thought, as the echoing sound announced the elevator's arrival. He stood to the side as the metallic golden doors opened, waiting to get up to his room, but tilted his head in awe when two angelic Eurasian women, wearing radiant smiles, stiletto hills, and form fitting evening dresses stepped out of the elevator and brushed his arm as they passed him redirecting his attention. *No time for that either*, he thought to himself and dragged himself into the waiting elevator.

Johnny panned his door, threw his backpack on the bed, and opened his bag, exposing the false bottom where he'd secured his most important and loyal companion, his *Sig Sauer P226*, the only true loyalty he'd ever known, until *Chloe*. He paused at the thought of his fiancée, something still turned in his stomach about her missing body and having pushed her aside for sake of the mission sent him into a dark place as he searched his mind for answers. A knock on the door woke him from his reverie. He closed his bag, stuffed the pistol under a pillow, and opened the door.

"Good afternoon, Mr. Dekker, here's your welcome tea," the woman said.

Johnny waved her in and watched her place the elaborate silver tray on the desk, line out the dishes in proper order then wish him a pleasant stay. "Much appreciated," he said as he handed her a fiver, forgetting if tipping was expected or frowned upon in London, he'd erred on the side of caution.

Johnny checked his watch. He knew his contact's routine better than his own, and right now was as good a time as any to get caught up on the happenings of the BIS conference before setting to finding his Mossad operative, and perhaps some details about other plots might also emerge in conversation. He fitted his Swiss-German companion in the small of his back covered it with his jacket and stepped out his doorway toward the elevator bank.

Ding.

Within minutes a subsequent chime of the elevator announced his arrival in the lobby as he locked his phone, stuffed it in his jacket pocket, and pulled his coat closed. But before he could place another foot in front of the other and exit into the cool autumn night, an explosive scene across the marbled tranquility grabbed his attention. Johnny scoped the room front to back and confirmed only hotel staff were witness as he crossed the floor toward the distraught woman locked in verbal combat with the receptionist.

"Is everything okay?" he asked.

A flustered concierge met the ex-Navy SEAL halfway across the floor. "Mr. Dekker, everything is fine. We've notified emergency services."

Johnny blanched. He hadn't expected a chaotic scene at the Wellesley, even at this late hour, but something had pulled him toward the ruckus, and when he saw the woman's face, he understood. *Hannah?* He moved forward to catch the unsightly woman just as her strength gave way and she fell to the ground. Her battered and bruised body fell into his arms, unconscious, dripping wet, and bleeding from several vicious wounds. *Did she get mugged?* the American thought to himself. He grabbed the first aid kit from the concierge and heaved the half-life Israeli operative to her feet and carried her toward the elevator as the staff looked on.

The American punched in a number on his phone, then turned to the concierge revealing the name on the speed dial, "Make sure this man finds my room." Johnny's heart raced as he replayed the scene and all the people in the lobby in his head. *What did I miss?*

...FIVE HOURS LATER

Finally. Johnny watched as a series of grunts and erratic movements twisted the Egyptian cotton sheets into a knot, but not before a long slender leg had escaped and probed its way along the length of the bedsheet until it reached its apex and pointed toes in his direction. Within seconds a flailing arm followed and before he knew it the subject had poked her head from underneath the goose down pillows, he'd surrounded her with to keep her from rolling out of bed and worsening her wounds. "Ms. Jankowski," Johnny said.

As the doe-eyed woman stared at him, he imagined the questions running through her mind. *What was she doing here? Why was she naked? And why was she with this American spy?* He tilted his head as he watched her reality coming screaming back to her as she tried to prop herself up in bed.

"The things a girl's gotta do to get your attention."

Johnny scrunched his eyes as he chuckled aloud. "Where's your camera?"

Hannah smiled. "Damn, I knew I was missing something."

Johnny poured a glass of water and sat down beside her on the bed, watching as she took the glass in her hand. "You had a lot of people worried about you."

"So, CIA sent their *Master Jedi* to find me, I think I'm starting to tear up."

Johnny snorted a laugh. "Well, not exactly... but I like the way you think."

"Where are we?"

"...London."

Hannah dropped her head between her shoulders gripping her water with both hands and rolled her eyes in an elegant Broadway display, then sighed aloud at Johnny's reply. "I know that Sherlock, but where?"

Something about her stirred his curiosity, he needed to find out who had done this to her, and why she'd marked him in such a public fashion in Malaysia, but her playful nature was distracting. Johnny tilted his head. "The Wellesley," he replied, then paused a moment. "Tell me what happened."

Hannah thrust her wobbling bruised arms behind her as she pulled herself upright, leaning into the pile of pillows, and wincing in obvious pain as Johnny stared into her eyes. "I was working on a story about the pollution of the Serpentine in Hyde Park and was leaning over to take a water sample in the broken ice when I felt a sharp pain followed by complete darkness, and then I woke up here."

Johnny sighed. "This might be amusing to you, but I was sent by Director Levy to find you, and report back to him when, where, and in what condition I found you. So, by all means please continue."

He watched the elusive Valkyrie blanch at the suggestion that she'd needed saving by anyone, least of all from someone the likes of him, a mark she'd manhandled only a few days earlier, but her brief charade fell away as Johnny confirmed her true identity. A wave of solitude drifted across her face as he recanted her personnel profile verbatim and studied her realization that everything, he told her was true, and she now sat face-to-face with a formative CIA operative.

"Splendid," she said.

Regardless of her state of mind and his orders there was only one thing Johnny wanted Hannah to explain, something that had been nagging him about her role in the meandering saga and her connection to the Russians. He scratched his week-old beard and moved closer to the Israeli agent.

"Why'd you blow my cover in Malaysia?"

An awkward silence filled the air as Johnny hovered a moment, keeping his distance so as not to spook Hannah as he navigated her fragile and uncertain state but chomping at the bit to understand her motivations beyond the Mossad mandate, and what if any connection to his fiancée's death. A frog formed in his throat as he took a step closer and began to make another inquiry when a burst of drunken laughter in the hotel corridor prompted the intelligence officer to words.

"You got too close. Anja couldn't afford you linking the Malaysian assassination attempt to the *Akhemendov Bratva*."

Another long pause followed. "It wasn't an *attempt*." The American agent turned from her bedside removed his pistol from the small of his back and laid it on the table as he loosened his tie.

Hannah did a double take. *What the hell does that mean?* the Mossad agent thought to herself. Something was wrong, but she wasn't sure what it was only that she'd breached a sensitive subject given Johnny was the Ambassador's son, so with rounded eyes, and a quivering voice she sat forward and asked. "The Ambassador's dead?"

Johnny quirked an eyebrow. *She doesn't know,* he buried his surprise at her question. "He's very much alive, but his assistant… my fiancée, *Chloe*, is not."

Hannah stammered. "I was told that they'd missed their target, and that only a handful of soldiers had been injured." She'd only been part of the distraction of the investigation, not part of the hit on the Ambassador. Although she knew that her successful distraction, which had garnered global headlines, was supposed to segue into a more intimate role inside the *Bratva*, but that narrative and concern were thousands of miles away as she sat studying the face of the fiancée of a murdered operative.

Johnny poured himself a drink. "So, this, Anja, sent you to do what? Slow down my investigation? Or expose me to the Russians?"

Hannah reverted to her insensitive mindset that had carried her this far but also threatened to unwind her entire operation. "That's what I do sweetheart. I'm a distraction."

Johnny fumed. "You're also a MOSSAD field agent."

She ran her fingers along her head bandage. "...Sometimes."

A tingling sensation ran down Johnny's arm as he stood up and put some distance between himself and the broken agent, he replayed her responses in his head as he watched her fidgeting with her pillows, but he wasn't finished. He had more questions. Questions that needed answers, and before he called Langley, he wanted to know everything. He put his hands on the wet bar and turned again toward Hannah, and with a notable shift in his voice he changed the topic.

"You must be hungry."

Hannah lit up. "Starving."

After the food arrived, he maneuvered the cart toward her bedside and watched as she readied her feast in front of her and waited for his opportunity. Once she'd begun her meal he sat back in the tufted leather chair several feet from her, and again asked about Anja, the Russians, and her assailants, but nothing was connecting. Johnny twisted in his chair trying to wake his sleeping leg and asked the most important question. "Why are you in London?"

Not long after finishing her light supper, Johnny watched as Hannah sipped on some Early Grey as he fidgeted and toiled on this next move. How was he going to track down Anja? How was he going to find the people responsible for Chloe's death? *We're getting nowhere.* He stood up and stamped his foot releasing some tension and getting the blood circulating in one go.

"Anja Singh, as I'm sure you've managed to figure out, is working with the Russians, but not in the capacity you might think, Captain America."

The American placed his cell phone on the table as he shook his numbed leg and moved back toward Hannah. "When you say working for *the Russians* - Can you be more specific?"

Hannah paused, placed her teacup down, and stared into Johnny's inquisitive eyes. "According to our intelligence, Anja's handler works for a Russian oligarch and his henchmen from the *Akhemendov Bratva,* not the FSB or GRU like you gunslingers had hoped. Any excuse to build another weapon system, eh?"

"*You're* judging us?"

"Whatever, I also know that Anja had an outside contractor working for her in the Cayman Islands where she'd planned to launch an attack on the US financial markets from the inside."

It was old news, but Johnny played along. "You got a name?"

"David Blevins... and I believe he's in London, too."

It was obvious, *Anja's cleaning house*, he thought to himself then stood up and started pacing the floor. "That makes sense."

The Mossad agent finished off her tea, but as she tried to take a bite of a cookie, it proved a bridge too far, her jaw began throbbing, which lead to a pain reminding her of the various gashes in skull from where her assailant had cracked her over the head and dumped her into the frozen pond in the park. She smiled, put down the cookie, and pushed the tray away. "Finished," she announced with a smile.

As the overarching plan began to lay down before the American agent, he knew he needed to find Singh and put a stop to her plans before she'd unleashed another cyberattack against the Homeland, and he knew the Malaysian inquiry and thread had to wait, Anja was now the priority. "Is there anything you can tell me about where they might be?"

"I remember her saying that she was going to meet Blevins at some tech conference, something about Artificial Intelligence."

Johnny raised an eyebrow. Everything this deep cover MOSSAD agent said was suspect, and he knew he'd have to call it in before he got too far down the rabbit hole and couldn't tell which way was up. "Right, that makes sense. Well, there are several conferences going on now. Can you remember a name?"

Despite his softened approach, Johnny knew Hannah was spinning a yarn, one worthy of an American Murder *She Wrote* series for all the absence of facts and conjecture she unloaded. *She's biding her time. She needs to contact Tel Aviv and check in with the Director.* He used his left hand and flipped open his cell phone as his attention bounced between Hannah and the device, when finally, he stepped closer to her bed, took a snapshot, and started stabbing his screen again catching the orator mid-sentence.

A stunned Hannah gazed back at Johnny stopped and let her voice fall silent, no more pointless probabilities around the Malaysian attack or her role as a mere distraction; they locked eyes. *It was all a set up from the jump,* the American thought to himself. "So, you're saying there was no political meeting? The Ambassador was set up by our own CIA asset?"

Hannah blushed. "Set up... Was it?"

A vibrating cell phone pulled Johnny from conversation and straight into another, one that he wasn't ready to have, not yet anyway, not until he'd extracted as much information as he could while the drugged up Israeli asset was still conscious and speaking. He disappeared into the bathroom half closing the door, and half keeping an eye on his guest. Within seconds the triple beep confirmed his encrypted uplink to Langley.

"Where the hell are you? I've tried to call you several times," Director Brown's voice boomed through the connection.

Johnny paused a moment. "I've got her. Or what's left of her, anyway"

The surprised apprehension of the allied agent left Director

Brown dumbfounded and shocked at the efficiency of his rogue blue blood. This was unexpected even for Johnny. "How… When?"

Over an hour had passed since his guest had woken up from her medicated rest, she needed more, and Johnny knew it. "She's been worked over pretty good, boss."

Director Brown stood silent, "I'll speak to Director Levy."

Something bothered Johnny about the whole situation, the Mossad operated in every country in the world, and he couldn't believe they didn't have anyone in London that couldn't have been put on her case just as easily, but he was tired, maybe too much jet lag. "Good, perhaps he knows."

"I don't follow," Director Brown replied.

"Who knew I was at the Wellesley?"

"The usual suspects…"

Johnny exhaled. "…and Director Levy."

Director Brown leaned into the lumbar support of his Herman Miller executive chair and gazed out the window as the late afternoon sun faded behind the snow-covered landscape below. "What's on your mind, Johnny?"

Johnny paused a long moment. "When did it become acceptable for our country to cast aside strategic long-term allies for allies of convenience?"

WEST INDIA QUAY, LONDON

A chill ran down his spine as the man crouched down between the dank stairwell and the moss-covered bridge, hiding, waiting for his assassin to run past him, but when the seconds turned to minutes, and the minutes to an hour, David Blevins realized he was alone. *What the hell have I gotten myself into?* the programmer thought to himself. Everything was upside down as his mind swirled with questions, questions with no answers as he stretched his arms and legs and rose from his prison, reminding himself that he wasn't out of the woods yet. Throwing caution to the wind he snuck from underneath the stairwell and ducked into a nearby pub, after all, crowded places were always better than a lonely dark alley, at least that's what he'd always heard. He looked the bartender square in the eye and placed his order. "Guinness."

It'd been a few years since he'd been back in the city of his birth, but it hadn't change, at least not as much as he'd read in the newspapers.

After graduating from Imperial College, he'd taken the first flight to San Francisco and got involved with several IT projects, and none of them had been more interesting than his most recent one, but then again none of those project managers had tried to kill him at the end of his contract.

Blevins shuddered at the thought of Anja then took a long drink from his chilled draft slamming the emptied mug on the counter and turning toward the bartender. "Tasty that. BURP. I think I'll have another."

"Right away, gov," the bartender replied.

From what had started out as a promising IT career with a bright future, it took one mistaken investment and that future hard forked into an unreliable road that folded after only one year, damaging his reputation and chances at any other rising startups across the valley. After a string of unsuccessful ventures, he landed a couple of shadier jobs in Las Vegas, which led him straight into Anja Singh's warm embrace. At the time, she was a godsend, and understood him like no other employer had before, and she'd set him back on the path to his dream of running his own enterprise. Within a week of their meeting, she had him on a plane with his gear, as well as a whole stack of new gear and settled in the Cayman Islands.

David woke from his reverie and shook his head in disgust. *How could you have been so naive?* he thought to himself. He paid the bartender and stepped out onto the cobblestone alley with a settled mind. Now, he needed a place to collect himself, and map out his next move, somewhere that wouldn't get him killed.

KNIGHTSBRIDGE, LONDON

Another series of medication had knocked out the battled-scarred agent, leaving the American widower watching over her as she slept, contemplating his next move if he couldn't locate Anja's programmer in time. He cast a glance toward Hannah as she slept. He knew that pain. It was torture. He empathized as he recalled his time in the teams and the Agency field work, it was no easy task, but it was everything to him. He picked up the phone and ordered a steak on sourdough along with a side of French fries and a salad, in case she woke up and was hungry again, both being in different time zones. Despite all the information he'd read in her profile, she was still an enigma. Something was missing. From an early age, she'd proven unpredictable, but the Mossad still recruited her. What did they see in that young girl all those years ago that had been pushed down now? Out of sight, out of reach. What motivated her? After all, she was the only link he had to the one person he knew was able to shed further light on the assassination of his fiancée, and the attempted assassination of his father. If she was telling the truth, he knew he needed to find Anja before Hannah, otherwise there might not be much left to question. Johnny downed another glass of water.

What was she really up to? Why mislead the CIA? She'd not given any complete answers since he'd rescued her, and tucked her away in his room. For now, he let her rest, but something would have to give if they were going to stop Anja Singh. A small tap on the door pulled him from his thoughts as he moved to sign for and push the room service tray inside. After several hours of an already taking two days, he found himself fighting to stay awake at six in the evening, he was hitting a wall, and it was a wall called, *Jetlag*. He unfolded the room's extra blanket across the sofa, removed his thick wool sweater and thumbed through his phone rereading some of the background on the Mossad's wayward daughter. Within an hour, the jetlag claimed another victory as Johnny fell into submission.

SOMETIME DURING THE PREDAWN HOURS

HANNAH KNEW WHAT SHE WANTED, something simple, something primal, and nothing would stop her from quenching her tortured soul wounds be damned, and it laid only a few yards away. From the time, she'd arrived at the Berkley Hotel primed to meet her controller and carry out the next stage of their plan, until the time she'd pulled herself onto the frozen embankment in Hyde Park, a mitochondria level transformation had begun, she'd wandered the seven levels of Hell, and promised herself one thing — revenge.

When she opened her eyes and saw the American leaning over her, she knew the answer, it was simple, and with the arrival of Johnny Dekker, she'd won an unexpected ally, although he struggled with the decision on whether he'd help her, she knew his inevitable answer, and she prepared. Hannah knew that if she was going to catch Anja Singh, she couldn't be waylaid by the CIA or Mossad, so she fell back on a black magic she'd picked up while traveling in Southeast Asia, something an old Chinese shaman had taught her, but it was complicated, and she needed skin on skin contact to make it work. Hannah removed her bandages and felt the smooth silk sheets brush against her skin as she slipped from under the down blankets. A tingling sensation ran up her spine as her warm feet planted on the cold marbled floor. Within a few seconds she stood over the unsuspecting American. *I'm sorry Johnny.*

As the full autumn moon shone through the curtains it captured her silhouette in all its glory, along with something dangling from her left hand as she crept across the floor toward the half-dressed American operative. Having discarded her bandages, she freed her hands and placed a tiny piece of paper with strange and indistinct writing on his forehead as she pressed forward and engaged her host.

Johnny squinted his eyes open. A lock of coconut scented hair fell across his face as the familiar Chanel fragrance informed the identity of his assailant. A brief glimpse of something in her hand as her lips pressed against his mouth, redirecting, and distracting his well-trained instincts.

"What…"

"Shhhh," she whispered.

Johnny was overwhelmed by the warmth of her flesh pressing against his exposed chest. He embraced the advance as he tried to open his eyes further, but the jet lag and the week of travel restrained his effort. He was stuck in a dream. The sound of static and sight of moonlight faded from his senses. He welcomed her tenderness. He soared like a fleeting soul adrift in a dreamscape of passionate interplay until her thick locks of hair came to rest on his bare chest, without any further sound or inclinations, she fell asleep.

The American operative peered through heavy eyes at the top of Hannah's head as it rose and fell with his each passing breath. *What's she playing at?* This was unexpected and complicated, especially with the recent death of his fiancée, he felt a sense of guilt rush over his body before the exhaustion of it all pulled him down into a deep sleep as dawn peeked through the window. *Finally…*

RINGING TELEPHONE…

JOHNNY FUMBLED to find the receiver. "Yes?"

"Good morning, Mr. Dekker, this is your 08:00 am wake up call."

"Thank you." He slammed the phone back to its receiver.

Johnny stretched his massive bare arms above his head. For a moment, he was relaxed, he was happy, he was…not alone. He turned toward the disheveled bed sheets. *Fuck.* "Where did that come from?" Johnny thought to himself as the rising sun swept through the palatial windows and prodded his eyes open, he awakened like a bear returning from months of hibernation. He sat up saw his trousers on the floor in front of the sofa. He craned his head around the room for his partner, but there was no sign of Hannah. Had it been just a dream? Did he even see her in the lobby or had the strain of the job finally gotten hold of him? He found his answer in the bloodied head bandages laid across the side table. She had been there. He rose to his feet and called out in his closed-throated raspy morning voice.

"Hannah?"

He walked across the floor stretching his naked aching muscles until he arrived at the wide opened bathroom door still filled with steam. He stuck his head inside, "Hannah?" It was empty. He took inventory of the room noting a few emptied hair product wrappers on the counter, which told the same story as the head bandage, someone had been there, but now they'd gone. At closer inspection he found new clues. *Hair Dye. What the hell?* Did she go after David, or was she focused on Anja? Regardless, she was ghost. He chucked the wrappers in the trash can and went back into the bedroom. On the coffee table he saw a notepad, he scooped it up and shook his head. *Fucking tradecraft.* Although having operated deep inside agency services for years, Johnny had yet to master the tools of the clandestine craft as the last twelve years had been boots on the ground with SEAL teams and only a short stint in the Special Activities Division's paramilitary as their tip of the spear for the CIA, this shit was new.

The paired numbers looked strange and out of place. It was a cipher, but what did it mean? Was it a Sudoku? He loved sudokus, but there was something more to it. The page sat on top of a Sudoku book left on the table, but this page wasn't torn out of the book it was casually laid across under the cover to catch attention, but not to give away any answers.

45 52 46 45 52 46 45 52 46
06 53 15 06 53 15 06 53 15
12 12 01 12 12 01 12 12 01

HE THOUGHT back to his training. *Damn it.* He was a grunt. This whole clandestine puzzle shit was alien to him and drove him nuts, but something that was more forced upon him that he'd have liked.

As he sat down in the chair and worked through the possibilities, a sudden fear gripped him. He felt nauseous. *What the fuck?* The feeling had all the signs of poisoning, but he hadn't been anywhere, except his hotel. There was no indication that Hannah had jabbed him, but he couldn't be certain. He fumbled through the bathroom looking for empty syringes or bottles. Had he fallen victim to the same fate as their Malaysian asset in Penang?

Johnny threw his right arm out to stable himself against the bathroom door, but the throbbing pain forced him into a curled position. He checked his face in the mirror and for any signs of poisoning. How could he have been so careless? He knew she was Mossad. She could've killed him in his sleep once she had gotten what she wanted, but he was alive. So, why the charade? Why the intimacy? As his thoughts reverted to her the pain grew more intense. He moved toward the sofa. There was a note on the table. Perhaps she'd left a clue to her next move, or maybe it was instructions on how to find her. Something was confounding his thought process; it shifted his thought process to concern of Hannah over the importance of the mission. It was something unfamiliar. He needed to find David, but if Hannah was the only way to do that and thwart another attack on the United States, then he needed to find her and hurry.

Summoning every ounce of strength and focus he had he straightened himself, snatched his clothes off the back of the sofa paying no attention to the small loose piece of yellow paper with alien script that fell behind the sofa as he got dressed. He had the numbers. And he knew what he had to do and how he had to do it, nothing stood in his way to finding Hannah.

He rushed out the door. Within a few seconds he stood in front of the elevator and pressed the button when his phone began to vibrate.

He looked down and saw a familiar and unexpected profile pic —
Bill. *Lord Thornton?* DING!

∼

LESS THAN A KILOMETER AWAY, Singh stood up with a reddened face she thumbed closed her messages as she pocketed her cell phone and turned toward Grig, enjoying his traditional Continental breakfast and watching her over his bitter black coffee. She watched as he took another bite of his buttered toast and washed it down. "Hannah's alive," she said.

"How you know this?"

"I have my sources."

Grig gulped his coffee down. "Is not matter. We proceed as planned, *da*?"

Singh clenched her fists in frustration, this wasn't looking good, it eroded the Bratva's confidence in her abilities. First, she missed David and now Hannah. Even with her successful delivery of the malware through the US financial markets, she was becoming a liability, and she knew it. She knew the *Bratva* couldn't let this stand, she knew too much. If either of those two contractors got to Mi6 or the CIA it could turn the entire operation on its head, which could cost Igor Petrushenkov billions. She needed a new plan, she needed to pivot.

31

BUMBLEHIVE

Jack squinted through the swirling dust devils, braced against the maverick gusts of wind, and stumbled beyond scattered rock formations, until he spotted the outline of a dilapidated structure in the distance with nothing else of major significance in the area, except the building marked on his map. Having spent the better part of an hour following the scribbled instructions as the sun disappeared over the horizon, he'd built up a thirst and looked forward to arriving at his destination, which he now knew was the abandoned rickety shack. *Finally,* he thought to himself as he marveled at the ingenuity and simplicity of the bunker, something he'd only heard of during his time in the Naval Warfare Department, but despite his countless global deployments on covert operations had ever seen in person, until today.

Without warning the winds fell away leaving Jack a clear line-of-sight over the last stretch of terrain as he approached the structure, which he took full advantage and sprinted toward the flapping metal door. He caught the broken hinged door and stepped through the doorway. Inside was another reinforced full-framed bunker door, he reached out and turned the handle. From the moment, he'd received his orders from Director Moore he pained over the most efficient way to integrate the two cryptography teams, although his team was remote, a concerted effort was needed to ensure the successful defense of the national network.

Jack breathed a hard sigh flipping open a panel and entering a numbered sequence on a nearby keypad and stepped forward to the retinal scan. *CLICK! CLICK! CLICK!* On his right-hand side, a stairwell door opened out from the wooden shelved wall. Jack froze a moment then stepped forward. Through the opening he loosed a yawn. It was only a couple of time zones between Utah and the Fort, but he'd been surviving on Kuala Lumpur time since the assassination attempt on the Ambassador. After another long moment, the door locked behind him and the platform he stood on closed another set of double doors and began to descend along a subterranean elevator shaft.

When the doors opened, he saw a familiar face with a curled lip and an outstretched hand, welcomed him to the Office of Tailored Access Alpha site, and their pet project.

"Welcome, Mr. Sorenson."

"Thank you, but please Jack is fine." Jack forced a smile as he tried to control his wandering eye. *She hasn't aged a day.* He followed Dr. Jane Ridley through the entrance and into the main control room. An inner voice screamed something inaudible that his houseplant sized brain struggled to comprehend, he continued forward through the corridor with an ear-to-ear grin on his face, trying not to offend his host, but wondering the reason for her demeanor.

Ridley ignored superficial attempts at diplomacy. The director of the top-secret project didn't have time for anything but the job at hand, especially with the new threats attacking the country's infrastructure.

This wasn't the first time Jack had been received in this manner, and so he straightened his jacket and followed Dr. Ridley through another set of security doors that opened into a room with a team of computer programmers and the focus of their attention, it was the only thing in the universe that could separate their stupefied lust of a woman — a powerful computer system. Within seconds the how and why his one-time companion was giving him the cold shoulder fell away as he followed the length and width of the computing monolith, its dimensions extended from wall to distant wall and blinked its language of love in an irresistible melody that serenaded his inner geek.

"*What* do we have here?"

Jane stopped, gestured toward her team scattered across the room operating various terminals networked to the main system, then turned toward her guest cryptanalyst. "*Ahem*, This is my team," she said.

Jack tore his eyes from the massive computer system as he turned toward the gesturing scientist. "I'm sorry, but is this the…"

"Yes."

Words failed the hacking genius as he stepped forward attempting to grasp the breadth of the machine, turning his head left and right, studying the sheer magnitude, as the rows upon rows of server stacks seemed to disappear into infinity. This was the machine Director Moore told him that would revolutionize the way the nation faced off with her enemies and its accelerated activation would augment the team's ability to avoid any more infrastructure attack.

"Its name is *IRI*," Jane said.

Jack quirked an eyebrow. "The Archangels from the Book of Enoch that chained the fallen angels, the *IRIN*, who'd disobeyed God and procreated with the daughters of man creating the *Nephilim*," Jack said as he paused a moment, then turned by to Dr. Ridley. "Perfect choice."

"Director Moore wants it linked up to US CyberCommand and transitioned over the network by the end of the day, so we'd better get you and your team up to speed, and make this deployment happen."

Jack caressed the system with his eyes as his hands ran along to top of the control panels along the load-bearing wall. "So, he's taking Echelon offline?"

"Backup."

Echelon had done a stellar job at policing the national network and expanding its mission, but the artificial intelligence — *IRI* — was built for a specific purpose, defend the homeland, and it was time to put it to work. With the exponential growth in quantum computing, the foundation of the Archangel source code was able to overcome previous roadblocks, and with its successful live action test in the RIMPAC exercises there was no time to waste in its deployment. The original code, which had been developed by a team of engineers and computer scientists from cooperation between various US intelligence agencies, before the lines and politics had disrupted their intricate collaboration, was still second to none. With a new line of command codes and angle of approach in artificial intelligence sequence evolved into its present form and although the RIMPAC exercises had proved its readiness, any remaining concerns were put aside as the nation came under further attack; it was time to plug *IRI* into the defense network and take the burden from the aging system.

Dr. Ridley offered Jack a coffee as they stepped into her office, and she watched him sit down still in awe of what he'd seen. "Still black, no sugar?"

"It's the only way I fly."

"I know you've come a long way, but I'd like to start team integration ASAP."

"That's why I'm here, Jane," Jack said as he shifted in his seat trying to shake off his mesmerized look that he knew he wore across his face.

"We've a working theory on the attack." Dr. Ridley met her assistant at the door and took the coffee in hand and placed it in front of Jack as she reached for her own cup, still probing the NSA cryptanalyst.

"That's good to hear, let's have it."

Dr. Ridley cut her eye at Jack as he sat in the chair sipping the piping hot black coffee. "We've only had the *Cayman* information for a day."

"I didn't mean…"

"Are you sure?"

"Jane… I mean Dr. Ridley."

Dr. Ridley stood silent, stalking her prey. "Jane is fine, Jack."

Jack blanched. "What I meant to say was it's all been a running game and I've only been focused on the assassination attempt on the Ambassador, so it's a big relief that you and your team have a working theory on the infrastructure attack, I need to be caught up and read into whatever you think is necessary so we can get our teams on the same page."

Jane snorted a short laugh. "Relax. This is what we do. And, when I say we, I mean you and me. This is our job, don't let our past slow us down from doing what we've been tasked to do, Jack."

The two hackers exchanged a confirming nod. "It's great to see you and I'm glad we got that out of the way. So, tell me about this theory," Jack said.

FORT MEADE, MARYLAND

Director Moore laid his head on the table. It'd been a long day. A distinct triple knock echoed through his reinforced oaken doors. He knew that an attack was imminent, but if had happened he'd received a phone call long before a knock on the door. And although, there was still little he could do to prevent it at this stage, he could prepare for the fallout, and that was still a herculean task. Their only weapon was a timely and effective response when it did hit. The attack on the Chicago futures exchange and NASDAQ had crippled the trading, which was only saved by the bell as the US markets halted trading for the weekend, and the Asia traders were still in LaLa land dreaming of the next big China tech ADR listing. This attack along with the SIGINT intercept connecting the relative parties to both events proved beyond doubt that the incidents were related, but the next steps were out of his hands. He'd placed that fate in the only two people he knew stood a chance and reversing their fortunes deep within the Utah territory.

"Sir, is there anything I can do?"

Director Moore looked at his concerned assistant and though of a smile, but at this point the drain of the mission only allowed a half-smile. "Perhaps some food?"

"I'll be back shortly," Gisele said and disappeared through the doorway.

He thought about the conversation he'd had with the CIA Director Brown about the Mossad and their shenanigans in Malaysia, which elevated the rising tension in his chest to another level. It wasn't the first time that their *"ally"* had thrown them a curve ball and he doubted it would be the last. He pulled the signal intercepts they'd received from both the Australian and the United Kingdom's listening posts, printed them out and hung his jacket on the coat rack, waving off his incoming lunch from Gisele, instructing her to get Director Brown on the phone. It was time to find out the true relationship between Hannah Jankowski and Anja Singh, and what the hell either of them had to do with Project Archangel.

"I have the director for you, sir."

Director Moore spread out the intercept printouts across his desk and picked up the receiver. The scrambled live sprang to life with Director Brown's voice ringing through from the other end.

"What can I do for you Walter?"

"I need to know everything."

The line fell silent. For a moment, he'd thought he'd lost the connection, but as he leaned forward in his chair Brown spoke. "Remember your Asian Games initiative?"

"What does that have to do with this?"

"Ambassador Dekker was our man that slipped that program onto the scientist's computer in Dubai."

Moore breathed a sigh. "It was the right thing to do. It was the only way we could install the malware on the air gapped system."

"Give me a minute. John Dekker and his young associate were the team assigned for that mission. But, as they were about to upload the malware into the scientist's laptop, his associate's cover was blown by a Russian FSB agent at the same hotel, which…"

"But everything went off without a hitch. I don't see the problem," Moore interrupted.

Brown paused a moment. "The associate was Anja Singh, she was one of our HUMINT agents in the region, a linguistic master in Arabic, Farsi, and Russian."

Moore cleared his throat. "So, she was spotted, sucks for her clandestine path, but life inside HQ should have been possible for her, no?"

"When I saw your SIGINT and her name on the report, I knew this had turned for the worse. She was primary associate on the program with the ambassador she knew almost everything he did about the project; he'd taken her under his wing and was grooming her to take led. She was his protege."

"So, you're saying the student has become the master and this is a revenge play? A revenge play, for what? Dekker didn't sell her out."

Brown paused a long moment. "Anja's motives are bigger than revenge I'm afraid, but not something we should talk about in person." Another silence hung over the line as some slow stabbing fingers smashing a keyboard echoed down the phone until the voice returned to the speaker. "I just sent you her un-redacted profile but keep it's eyes only."

"You think she's gone over to the dark side? The Iranians?"

"Our sources in Estonia indicated that she'd was cozied up with a Russian *Bratva* not too long ago, and it's anybody's guess what they're up to these days."

"Well, that explains Director Levy's approach. He put his operative Hannah into motion a few years ago in Southeast Asia. So, when it all kicked off and Johnny showed up after such a publicized explosion on the Penang bridge it was bound to throw a wrench in the plans of his agent's cover," Moore said.

"Maybe, but something this big they should've looped us in Walter, they should've told us. If they suspected an ex-CIA agent had resurfaced and was working with the Russian mafia, we should've been their first call, period."

"Have you told Johnny?"

"When we found out Anja was involved, he was my first call, but

I didn't want to pull you in until we had more information. That said, we've got to get out in front of this next attack. We've got to find a way to stop it."

"I'm still trying to assess what we've missed, but I think we know now. It's been one of our own all along."

"CyberCommand has Echelon on full defense at the moment," Brown said.

Walter paused a moment and took a sip of water. He hesitated to tell Director Brown about the decision on *IRI*, but he knew that when they'd worked together things usually went there way. Moore hacked a cough. "I've activated *IRI*."

Director Brown slammed the table. "Are you fucking kidding me?"

Moore turned toward the yellow and orange horizon that had been absent for the last few weeks, hidden by the nor'easter that had torn up the East coast, then back to his speakerphone. He felt the weight of the office more than ever, perhaps it was time to hang it up, but then a knock on the door pulled him out of his reverie as he leaned on the two men's personal bond. "Mark, why don't you work out of the SCIF with Mike and I until we get this thing under control."

"I'm on my way."

The sharp dial tone pierced his ear as he looked up to see his dove faced assistant Gisele standing in front of him with his lunch and a *I'm not going anywhere until you eat it look on her face*. He flashed a quick smile, hung up the phone, and accepted his delivery with grace. "I don't know what I'd do without you, Gisele."

BUMBLEHIVE

After he'd been read into the TAO team's theory on the attack, Jack followed Jane into the server room, familiarizing himself with the facility and trying to reestablish a long-diminished bond they'd lost after graduation. As they navigated the server stacks Jack placed his right hand on a server control panel, admiring the ingenuity and sophistication, but as soon as his palm touched the panel an alarm erupted from a several wireless speakers.

UNAUTHORIZED PROXIMITY ALERT

The automated voice echoed through the cavernous room coaxing a smile across the one-time hacker's face, reminding him of the thrill of the hunt, and rekindling a feeling for his hostess he'd not felt in years as he turned toward her burst of laughter. "What the hell was that?"

"Safety protocol," she answered with a wink.

Jack snickered like kid in a candy store. "Wicked."

After the walking tour, Jane led Jack back to her office, offering him another cup of coffee while she listened to his quick take on her team's assessment of the attack and his thinking around *IRI* and its pending mission, she always sought input from others, especially from people of Jack's caliber.

Dr. Jane Ridley had proven an exceptional leader, commanding respect up and down multiple White House administrations, but her rise to the top hadn't always been assured. With her department serving multiple masters it was always a shell game with information, and a guessing on project funding. She'd been assigned a compartmentalized mission under the National Security Agency's artificial intelligence program, which also had multiple reporting lines inside and outside the Agency itself, with one being the department that scooped her straight out of the Academy, the National Reconnaissance Office (NRO). Leveraging support from the seventeen agencies that comprised the United States Intelligence apparatus wasn't easy, but along the way she'd learned how to ensure mission success through cross-pollinating technologies, which always proved easier said than done.

While the two Navy alums hashed through their arguments and counterarguments on the path forward, Jack fell into a trance as Jane laid out her multi-pronged approach that promised to incorporate data from all relevant agencies as well as their international counterparts, extraordinarily simple, but extraordinarily unorthodox, especially opening gateways to non-US agencies.

Jack pinched the bridge of his nose. "I think you've nailed it."

A reluctant Jane stared into Jack's eyes. "We've tried to follow the director's motto as closely as possible," Jane said and then paused a moment. "What are you really thinking, Jack?"

"Is it ready?"

The stoic face returned his answer. "It's *been* ready for three years."

Jack understood the tone of frustration, having used in on occasion himself over the years, but he wasn't understanding why she'd been so docile about her readiness with the Agency. When Director Moore read Jack into the *IRI* project, he had to summon every ounce of restraint within himself not to jump up and down like a kid on Christmas Day, and it wasn't even his project. So, why had it taken so long for someone like Dr. Jane Ridley to get her project integrated into the network? Jack stood up a looked out over the team then turned to Jane.

"You've done it. We can retire Echelon." At long last it was here. There had been chatter about the advancement of various algorithms and neural networks across the interagency forums, but nothing of this magnitude. And if everything that Jane was saying was true about IRI there was no reason not to deploy it over the defense network ensuring our security as well as our partners in the Five Eyes network given the rise of the global threats coming down the pipe. "So, you've saved mankind."

Jane blanched. She threw a look at her guest and sipped her tea. "I don't know about that, Jack. Make no mistake, this is a military project and it'll do exactly what the commander-in-chief tells it to do, but it's algorithms are manmade, and nothing manmade is perfect." They exchanged a quick look both programmers wondering in the back of their minds how that imperfection might one day manifest.

"Modesty, I've missed you, Jane. You know very well that whichever country achieved Human Level Intelligence AI was going to set the stage globally. With *IRI* live, the chances of a bad actor artificial intelligence coming online has been cut to zero."

Jane choked out a laugh. "You're kidding right? Who's to say that our AI will stay a good actor, Jack? What is a good actor in its mind?"

"Well, I'm sure you've built in contingencies."

"I'm afraid that's above your pay grade, Jack."

The two friends shared another laugh as they continued their conversation about the development and its recent success at RIMPAC, as well as the recent authorization to bring it online, which led them back to why Jack had been temporarily reassigned to her facility.

The goal of the Archangel operation had been to provide the next generation of SIGINT curation and analysis to transition to next the generation analysis ahead of the Russians and other authoritarian regimes during the Cold War but had been repurposed after intelligence indicated those states renewed funding science and engineering programs in the aftermath of the world's first cyber-attack some years earlier, an episode that had reconfigured the modern-day battlefield.

"What about the NASDAQ? Have you figured out a way to protect us against another attack?"

"We've been running down some information the CIA brought to us this morning, but there are still some..." An analyst appeared outside the office door looking like she had seen a ghost gesturing to her boss. Jane waved her inside.

"Apologies, Dr. Ridley it's happening again."

Jack and Jane both blanched as they looked at the analyst then at each other and bolted through the opened office door toward the control room.

"Tell me what you got."

"The S&P futures, they're spiraling out of control. It looks like multi-headed hydra attack. On top of that, the plethora of banking algorithms are exacerbating the event."

"Was it a fat finger mistake?"

"Negative, we're tracking multiple sources sending and cancelling their futures orders within milliseconds, just enough time to spoof the market and hook the banking algorithms in the downward trajectory."

"Spoofing?" Jack blurted.

"Correct, and it's working, everyone's heading for the door," the analyst said.

Jane gawked at the screen. "It's accelerating."

Jack Sorenson smashed his fist on the table as he watched the index drop in an uncontrolled free fall. This wasn't happening. He wasn't allowing another attack on his watch. "Deploy the countermeasures, shut those banks down," he barked.

With limited information there wasn't a way to discern which accounts were being piggybacked by the hackers and which were legitimate accounts, so the protocol was to shut it all down. Jack watched as Jane sailed across the room to her terminal and began punching in commands. There was no time to spare, the index had dropped 9% and counting. "Jane…"

A lock of hair fell over her eyes as she stabbed the activation and scenario commands into the interface then hit enter and turned toward Jack. "Do or die."

Jack felt his heart in his throat. He watched as Jane righted herself over the terminal and walk toward the main display. Then a voice broke through his trancelike state screaming into his ear.

"Mr. Sorenson, their rerouting," a TAO hacker yelled across the room.

"What?"

"We shut down the jaded broker dealer's connection to the exchange, but we've detected a resurgence building along lines of secondary broker dealers. The code…it's regenerating."

"Shut em down, shut em all down," Jack yelled as he dialed the Fort.

"It's flaring…" Jane countered.

"Get me Director Moore."

32

MANHATTAN, NEW YORK

Isabella Dekker stared at her phone, waiting for the right moment, but the only image on her phone was her reflection staring back. *Nothing.* A buildup of moisture along her hairline told the story, not something she was accustomed to outside the gym, but with everything that had happened over the last few days, she wasn't surprised. Whether it was conspiring with a foreign agent or the whereabouts of her boyfriend, Jack, she wasn't sure of the cause, but one thing was for sure it was uncharted territory. *Calm yourself, this is the right call.*

Within a few minutes she'd remembered that the inadequate response by the White House and Langley had left her no other choice, and her tension eased, owning the decision, and thinking about her next steps. Although she'd not been authorized by Langley to negotiate a counterstrike, she was compelled to act by the obligations of her position as the head of the Dekker Banking Group.

Ahead of the event, she'd instructed her traders to unwind all current securities positions and convert all funds into gold bullion and move them immediately to the firm's private vault buried deep in the fields of Virginia farmland, she needed hard assets, actual assets that weren't susceptible to panic and market fluctuations, and assets that retained their store of value over the long term.

Isabella had foreseen this moment. When the first Flash Crash crushed the market and highlighted the systemic risk hadn't changed since Global Financial Crisis, she'd put her plan in motion. She knew that the evolution of algorithmic and high frequency trading (HFT) that had tested her mettle once before, would return with a vengeance and although she hadn't been able to convince her industry peers, her insightfulness and reasoning were the reasons Johnny installed her as the head of the company, with full board of director's support. She was an accomplished wartime trader. She saw beyond the immediate disaster and knew how to protect against the unknown. Whether that was drawing support from other banking institutions or conferring with her connections within the government and regulatory bodies, she knew how to navigate chaos, which is exactly what was unfolding in front of her once again.

As the wave of disruption continued into the new week, corporate, and institutional clients began echoing market concerns with the bank. On top of that, Isabella had also received a call from the Council of Thirteen's Office of the Auditor inquiring about their current Tier-1 Capital Ratio, whether the market turbulence might affect their bank and to what degree. It was a busy day, but she watched closely, waiting for the moment when the hackers escalated their attack. Isabella placed her tea on the counter and walked toward the floor to ceiling window. *What a mess,* she thought to herself taking in the scene below.

The nor'easter had departed Manhattan raging north and dissipating off the coast of Massachusetts, but it had left a mess in its wake that stretched the length of the entire East Coast. Isabella paced her office floor, there was nothing more she could do to even the odds, but wait, not something she enjoyed.

Movement in her peripheral vision followed with a knock on her office door and her assistant poking his head inside.

"Jack's on the phone," he said.

Isabella shook her head. "What?"

"Did you turn your cell phone off? He said he's been trying to get in touch with you for over an hour."

Isabella snorted a laugh. "Would you be a dear and get me something to wake me up?"

"One triple espresso coming up."

Isabella felt the air sucked out of the room as the soundproof door sealed behind her assistant as he disappeared toward the pantry. She cleared her throat and picked up the line. "You're quite persistent, I'm told."

"It's complicated. I told you this was going to be…"

"Jack, save it. We've both got jobs to do. But once upon a time, I had people I could lean on when I hit a wall. And believe it or not, we're hitting the mother of all brick walls. The markets are open, and trading is up, but he anxiety of another cyber-attack is killing me." The line went silent for a moment. "Added to that the Council's on my back piling on what the regulators are demanding, as if their initial inspection wasn't enough, they're acting like we did something wrong. What's happening? Why haven't you read me in or at least prepped me for what's coming?"

Jack paused a moment. He knew she was right, as usual, but there was nothing he could do now. "You want information… Nobody is safe, unless I get what I need to get done, and to get that done I need to focus that's why I muted your chat."

Another long silence weighed on the connection, both frustrated with the situation and where it had taken their relationship. "It looks like your uncle was only part of the story, Izzy. There's a much bigger event unfolding here, and it had everything to do with his guest appearance. That's all I can say."

Izzy smiled. Without saying anything, he'd told her everything, and she knew what she had to do. "Keep focused on the solution, I've already implemented countermeasures. And if you speak to Johnny, tell him I need to speak to him ASAP. Everything's under control, but we need to reset our longer-term goals and infrastructure, and he needs to be part of the conversation."

Jack trusted Izzy. He knew she had the experience and training to eliminate any threat and emergency that landed in her lap, but she didn't like being isolated and with both he and Johnny incommunicado that's what had happened. "I will."

During her time at CIA, she'd been an integral part of the counterintelligence effort command structure. With more than a few people under her direction she'd chalked up a respectable interagency record. Jack knew that whatever she was dealing with that it was under control, but he was more concerned about the Council and their inquiry. They never reached out to the families outside their scheduled quarterly meetings.

"Don't worry," she said.

A shudder ran down Jack's spine as she responded, he paused a long moment then cupped his receiver. "We've found a connection between the reporter in Malaysia and your uncle. She's Mossad, and her handler was a Russian agent, and Johnny's running it down in London as we speak."

"What?"

Jack breathed a hard sigh into the receiver. "Izzy, there's more important..."

"Okay," she said and hung up the phone.

LONDON, ENGLAND

Johnny tore through the hotel lobby. His mind racing in every direction as he flew half-dressed past the hotel staff and onto the cobblestone street, everything was at stake. He knew Hannah couldn't have gone far, the steam in the bathroom, and the water still pooled on the bathroom floor. With his shirt unbuttoned and half tucked into his pants, he ran down the cobblestone street ignoring the light drizzle that needled his face. The pre-morning rush hadn't begun to populate the sidewalks as he brushed past an elderly man enjoying a cigarette on the corner as he hurried toward Hyde Park.

"Everything all right sir," he heard the man shout. He kept running.

This was insane. Johnny had never understood women. Every

time he'd thought he'd connected, everything went pear shaped, and Hannah was proving no different. She'd caught him off guard during the night, he wasn't looking for romance, but the deep cover Mossad operative was a master at catching men off-guard. And now, he'd lost his focus, Hannah was the only thing he could think about, and deep down something told him it was wrong. With little information and no location of the Russian agent, his desperate search was a long shot, she could've disappeared anywhere, so he recalled what he knew about their encounter and set out toward Hyde Park. Turning down the street toward the Mandarin Oriental he passed by a couple of bankers wrapped in scarves and staring in dismay, which he shrugged off until a chilling autumn wind swept down the street and straight to his bones, hitting him like a ton of bricks. *Fuck.* He smashed his fist against the limestone wall of a building in open frustration, then turned back toward the Wellesley Hotel stopping to question the doorman on his way in.

"Did you see where my friend went?"

The doorman quirked his brow. "You mean the tall blonde, sir?"

"Yes, yes, the tall blonde woman. Which way did she go?"

"I'm afraid I just came on duty, sir. I haven't seen her today."

Johnny pinched the bridge of his nose. "Thank you."

Without uttering a word, he walked past several confused staff as he made his way back toward the elevator bank. He knew his next step. The only course of action was to activate the trackers, but before he did that, he needed to speak to Jack. If the information about Malaysia and the IT guy was true, it proved the two events were bankrolled by the Russians but had been directed by a single bad actor — Anja Singh. Pulling the door closed as he entered the room, he dropped his key on the table and fished his cell phone from his pocket. The morning light struggled to break through the overcast sky while the light drizzle continued to play its melody against the double paned windows, it was going to be a miserable day. He hit speed dial then slumped down in the tufted leather reading chair near the bed.

"What's the word?" Jack asked.

"I fucked up."

"Did you find her?"

"Yes and no," Johnny said followed by a long pause. "But she slipped away."

A mile underground the cryptanalyst tapped away at a keyboard as the two friends exchanged information. "Activate the trackers," Jack offered before chiming in with another important piece of news. "Listen, Izzy needs you. It sounded like she's been handling everything thrown at her, but she needs to talk to you as soon as you can, the Council's been calling...."

"I'm sure she's got it under control, I need to find..."

Jack stopped typing and leaned into the receiver. "She's launched a counterstrike against the rogue algorithms hitting the bank, she thinks it's the Russians and she's invited the help of an old friend of yours...Commander Li, so don't tell me she's got it under control. She needs you. If she's wrong, she could start a cyberwar with the Russians, and who knows where we end up after that."

"Jack, the reporter, the Mossad agent, she's going after Anja and the Russians, alone. I've got to find her."

Jack snorted a laugh. "It's always the Russians. FSB or GRU this time? It doesn't matter Mossad has been after them for years and it sounded like they were perfectly happy to throw you under the bus while doing it, so what's the problem? Let it go."

"Think about it. Between Izzy's counterstrike and Hannah's vendetta, not to mention an incoming hack on our financial infrastructure, where does it end?"

Jack paused a moment. "That second attack is happening right now, so I don't think Hannah poking the bear is gonna matter. And it might work to our advantage, if she can get to them before they destroy global markets and we shouldn't worry about her motives, because right now, it's game on."

"Roger that, brother," Johnny replied.

"What did you need again?"

"Don't worry about it, I've got this, and I'll deal with the Li and the Council."

A beeping emanated from the control board in front of Jack as he paused a moment, then informed Johnny of his next step. "We're activating *IRI* in a few minutes. All your communications are going to start being routed through its secured database, so you might see some interruptions or delays over the next few hours, but don't sweat it. If anything should happen go to Ariel protocol. It looks like it's best way to secure the network. We've discovered a copycat malware that's mimicking every algorithm on the network, and this is the only way."

"What the fuck? How's that possible?"

"Human error? You can read the report, I gotta go."

Johnny hung up the phone dazed at the revelation. This was the main event, and he was across the pond chasing down a rogue Mossad agent. Now, more than ever he needed to find Hannah. They needed to stop Anja and the Russians. It wasn't a sense of infatuation, but of duty. Whatever spell Hannah had spun over him had fallen away in the face of a potential debilitating attack on his homeland, the modern beacon of liberty, and nothing was going to stop him.

33

BEIJING, CHINA

Li Junxiong blinked open his eyes, stretched his hands over his head, and rotated them in a clockwise then counterclockwise motion, circulating the blood throughout his body after a much-needed nap. He ran his right hand across the top of the oak surface of the conference table that had served as a temporary support while he awaited the end of the Asian trading day. Refreshed, he rose from his chair and strolled toward the window opening his cellphone and thumbing through the messages. Aside from several messages from Izzy there was an urgent message from the Minister of State Security, requesting his presence. *An official meeting request, interesting*, he thought to himself as he keyed in his compliance and pocketed his cell phone. He hadn't seen his ex-colleague in several months and was certain there was much to catch up, especially given the events unfolding on the financial markets.

With the American bankers and Li's own *National team* working in unison, they'd begun to curtail the buying volume in oil and select currency futures, but it wasn't over yet, and the tug-o-war had only just begun. Li took a sip of coffee as he watched the opening of the European markets, and with oil futures still under pressure, the teams had done their job, but there was more to go. This wasn't a simple twenty-four-hour operation; this was a mission critical initiative, and they didn't stop until they had weakened their opponent. *Time to go.* Li cleared his throat snatched his overcoat from the rack, his pen from the table, and barreled down the stairs onto the street and turned toward the Ministry of State Security building, less than a kilometer away from his humble Beijing apartment.

As he made his way toward his meeting, he reviewed the last conversation with Isabella Dekker and their agreement, whether he'd have to divulge the context of that call would depend on the Minister's line of inquiry. When he'd last spoken to Izzy, the markets were heading into another tumultuous session with violent swings across every index and sub-indices, nothing was spared. The knock-on effect of the cyber-attacks continued to wreak havoc on the uninformed and slower moving broker dealers. Despite the whipsawing motion of the markets, the US regulators had kept the markets open, perhaps longer than they should've until finally, investors were saved by the closing bell. Li couldn't believe the ineptitude of the American regulators after their endless lectures around preserving transparency and fairness at countless global financial conferences.

From its inception, under the Imperial Courts of China, the Ministry of War had focused on several areas outside of maintenance of armies, equipment, weapons, and military installations, it also had the responsibilities of the courier network, which was further divided into Relay Stations and Posts. As with everything that ushered in the modern world these responsibilities evolved over time. Anchored in astronomy, mathematics, philosophy, and strategy, that bound the ministry together, the ministry discovered and created new methodologies and technologies. Above everything else, the Chinese prided themselves on organization and structure, and with the arrival of the global interconnectedness of the Information Age that structure culminated into one of the most important ministries of the modern government, the Ministry of State Security.

Li had risen through from the rank and file helping to build and further its primary mission, and now having been prompted to a deputy at the country's central bank he had a new task, control the economic narrative. Deputy Governor Li always kept two books near him. The first was about strategy and tactics, something many military elites keep next to them, the world renown *Sun Tzu*'s Art of War and the second was the *Zhou Bi Suan Jing*, which focused on process and discipline as its 256 questions proved the Pythagorean Theorem and inspired his algorithmic insights and genius within the Party.

Over the years, it was these two books, more than anything else that'd helped him create and maintain an advanced department of computer programmers specializing in various tasks and keeping the MSS ahead of its global adversaries.

Li's boots echoed across the Formosan marbled corridor as he stepped through the entrance and past the two sentries. "*Zhang Guan*," they barked cutting a salute as he snapped an acknowledgment without missing a step. It'd only been a short time, but he'd already felt swept up in the nostalgia of returning to his former command. Despite his decades of training, he rubbed his fingers together in anticipation of meeting his former protege, someone he'd groomed and mentored over the years, but allegiances, like everything else, often shifted without warning, and State Security was no different. Everything had fallen into place with Izzy and his team with progress against the Russian aggression bearing fruit, but they needed more time. It's been less than twenty-four hours since his return from Qatar, but it was the subtext of the message that kept him alert and ready for anything. He came to a stop in front of a solid oak door, nothing elaborate or ornate suggesting a senior ranking officer, Li stretched out his hand and knocked on the door.

"*Ching Jin*," a raspy baritone voice replied.

Li flashed a million-dollar grin as he crossed the threshold and came face-to-face with a tall ex-military field commander, someone who'd just been transferred from the front lines of a distant conflict, and not a pencil pusher by any means, a man that meant business, but still welcoming to old friends. "*Zhang Guan*."

Minister Tsai accepted Li's hand and slapped him on the back with his other hand with a force that would've floored a typical banker, which was far from anyone's description or profile of Li Junxiong. "Take a seat," the Minister said.

"I hope you're not still upset about last week's mahjong," Li replied. "My schedule got away from me with some last-minute business." Li watched as the Minister stepped behind his desk and took his seat.

In line with his appearance, Minister Tsai was all business, and rarely resorted to small talk, something he considered best reserved for politicians. "As you may or may not know, our teams have detected increased communications between the American intelligence agencies around the world, something is happening, and it seems centered on the recent cyber-attack on their financial markets." The Minister paused as he placed a cup of tea on the desk in front of Deputy Governor Li. "And despite the massive drop in the overnight futures, Asian traders seem to have shrugged off the move, except for some of our state assets who've taken an opposing position, this late in the year." Li watched as the Minister took a sip of his tea and turned toward him. "Do you mind letting me in on you are thinking?"

"I apologize, Minister." Li offered. "There was insufficient time to bring you into the loop after the Standing Committee's approval, which sent me straight to the airport handling the details of the mission on the move."

Minister Tsai returned the smile and nodded his head. *"Li Da Ren,* there's no need to apologize, I was only officially appointed this week. This came to my attention as I was trying to catch myself up on all current operations both when I came across the trading activity report."

Li acknowledged his former deputy's grace in the matter and promised to keep him abreast of all initiatives going forward, as his new post at the PBOC wasn't concerned with intelligence gathering, but rather fiscal policy, and its implications toward national security.

After another hour of wide-ranging discussion, the time had grown late, Li thanked the Minister as his assistant informed him of another scheduled meeting at the Great Hall of the People. Li thanked him for the tea, stood up and exited the office, feeling better about his strategy and the additional support for the mission.

∽

A DISTANT RINGING serenaded the banking executive as she laid sprawled out on her obsidian leather sofa, nothing sounded sweeter, nothing except the sound of a hack taking down her entire banking group. Isabella blinked open her eye, and sprang from the sofa, rumpled clothing clinging to her body as she fumbled across her desk to answer the ringing telephone.

"*Wei, wei...*" she chirped, then listened. "Are you kidding me, Junxiong?"

Li stood tall in the cold night air and shrugged as he looked up at the Great Hall of the People with his cell phone pressed against his face, moments before his meeting at the Politburo's Standing Committee on the progress of the joint operation. "I just thought you needed to know. And you'd better get your traders ready because this is not a drill."

"You're a genius. The Committee must back the move. And if the oil reversal wasn't enough to knock the Russians on their ass, this should back 'em down."

Li tucked his cell phone in his jacket and took a deep breath. It was a brief walk from the MSS building to the Great Hall of the People, and a little exercise was never a bad thing. Pollution hovered at their lower levels as he crossed the busy boulevard. With evening setting in Li Junxiong rehearsed his talking points for the escalation against the Russians, something that wasn't guaranteed to win him any new friends in the Committee, but a bold strategic move, nonetheless.

He'd frequented the Politburo Standing Committee more times over the last couple of months than he'd over the last couple of years as Head of State Security, and it wasn't by design, a wave of disruption through the global financial markets called for his expertise. The

Committee itself was comprised of the nine most influential members of the Chinese Communist Party, and it was under its guidance that policy was set.

As Deputy Li reviewed his report on the Qatar operation in his mind, he focused on the key points, and hoped they'd support his decision for a follow-up strike on the markets, but if they didn't, he played that out as well, not something he'd wanted to calculate, but prudence demanded it. In Li's mind, he believed the only way to stave off the covert Russian moves at the Bank for International Settlements was to align themselves with their largest trading partner, the United States, it was after all in everyone's best interest, but devaluing the Renminbi, even temporarily, wasn't always the best way to kick off a meeting in the Committee.

"Deputy Li, welcome," the Committee chairman said.

"Mr. Chairman, of course it's my honor to be here this evening and provide you with an update to our ongoing operations."

"Are the Americans asking for more assistance? We can only do so much."

"It's a secondary phase that I believe will ensure the result."

"Do you think that the Russian cryptocurrency solution is that close to being accepted by the BIS? We've a say in what currency we use in trade, do we not?"

"If we're to compete on the global stage on a global scale, we need to ensure our customers and citizens have access to its digital currency, and now the odds are on the Russians proposal. I believe that our secondary phase will pressure them to back off, but we have to be thinking long term."

"Are we ready for a one world currency?"

"We're well positioned to influence the way the BIS and its network of global central banks adopt the new technology, but we must stand with our trading partners on this matter if we're to defeat the Russian efforts to lock in their blockchain technology and access to global citizens big data."

The Vice-Chairman chimed in. "At this moment, we need the oil, so whatever course we take, we need assurances from both OPEC and Non-OPEC sources that our supply won't be cut off, regardless of the fluctuations in the market."

Li agreed. "I've already confirmed that with the Saudi Minister."

Within a couple of hours, the Committee had agreed to Li's proposal on the devaluation of the Renminbi, instructing the secretary to draft the letter and hand deliver it to the PBOC Governor, forthwith.

From the moment the disruptive decentralized ledger technology had arrived on the scene, computer scientists and experts had pleaded with the Party to advance the study of the blockchain, and its far-reaching implications. So, it was no surprise when the Digital Renminbi was splashed across the headlines, but Li worried on the timing. In the end, it fell once again to Li and his team to ensure a team victory and block any other country from securing a deal with the BIS that could expose their citizens big data to non-Chinese entities.

It was close to eight o'clock when Li sat down at his desk at central bank headquarters in Beijing and began drafting notes, while monitoring European markets as he waited for the US trading session to begin. With the financial news droning on in the background Li saw his cell phone blinking to life, he stretched out and scooped it up, and answered the familiar female voice.

"It's done. We've the approval to proceed," he said.

"You're a star, Junxiong."

"It's only the first step. We still need the Saudi's announcement."

A smile crept across Izzy's face as she watched her monitors and waited for the announcement while Li held the line. "They're tired of Russian interference on their doorstep, their onboard."

"Let's hope you're right."

Then Izzy sat upright as the news flashed across the screen. "Junxiong, it's out," she blurted.

DOHA, QATAR: CARTEL MEMBER REVERSES POSITION LESS THAN 24 HOURS AFTER MEETING, OIL PRICES TANK

Li turned up the volume and read the announcement outlaid. "Minister of Oil for the Kingdom of Saudi Arabia holds an impromptu gaggle with reporters before boarding his private jet." He snorted a laugh. "I guess that's that."

Izzy pumped her fist as she leapt from her sofa, then pressed the cell phone back to her ear. "I'll call you back. I gotta get to the trading floor."

34

CITY OF LONDON, ENGLAND

Johnny let the metallic elevator door close behind him as he studied the alerts on his phone, hoping Hannah had reached out to him, but thumbing through the messages on the way to his suite he discovered something unexpected. *Lord Thornton? What could he want?*

Lord William Thornton had been a close friend and confidant of Johnny's father during the elder's time in Europe, but Johnny hadn't heard from him since he'd assumed the seat on the Council, something he'd hope to correct soon. More than a trusted advisor, Thornton was a peacemaker among Council members, which over the last few years had kept him busier than normal. He'd settled the issue between Dekker and Hamilton-Smith and kept a close relationship the European families of the Council, but never sided one way or the other. Johnny turned back toward the elevator as he scanned the message.

Bill: At the Club.

From his experience, a short message without a date or time, meant the situation was urgent, and there was no time to lose. Johnny pursed his lips and banged out a quick reply on the illuminated touchscreen.

Johnny: On my way.

Aside from being a well-connected gentleman of the old European guard, knighted by the Queen, and a pillar of the banking establishment, he was still a Deputy Governor of the Bank of England. Johnny started to speculate the urgency of the meeting. Had something happened to Chairman Meyer? Had the BOE thrown their support behind the Russians? With a quick fix to his clothing, several fingers through his hair and a twist of his tie, he was ready.

Bill: Smoking Room.

Johnny: Noted.

Johnny struck the lobby button with a quick jab and fell away into his thoughts as the handcrafted metallic doors closed in front of him, nothing had gone to plan. Of course, this whole mission was, the only thing that mattered was running down his leads and stopping the next attack, everything else was moot.

When the doors opened, he fastened his coat whipped the scarf around his neck and set out with purpose. *Follow the crumbs*, he thought to himself as he jumped in a taxi. The detour to the Travellers Club was unavoidable and pulled him away from tracking down Blevins but might yet prove helpful in a way he hadn't yet realized, after all he wasn't working alone.

"What's our ETA?"

A found-faced driver stared at Johnny through the rearview mirror with a jovial smile. "In a bit of hurry are ya?"

"Thanks, mate," Johnny replied.

With more than a few minutes until his meeting Johnny ripped his cell phone from his jacket pocket and punched in a Langley tech support number, something that he'd forgotten to do when he'd landed. The taxi snaked through the traffic as it the holiday season shopping and weather slowed his progress toward the heart of the world's financial Mecca, the City of London. Not knowing when he'd have another free minute, he opted to run a trace locate on the IT guy Hannah had mentioned named —David Blevins.

Rewinding his conversation with Hannah, Johnny knew that if David had set up the servers, then it stood to reason that he would've had to upload any malware onto them, which meant he had access and maybe even contact with the man behind the curtain. From the brief explanation by Hannah, although Anja was the main contact, she wasn't running the show, there was someone backing her moves, and Johnny was going to find out who.

Johnny thumbed through his phone, pulled up the CRYPT app, toggled it to life, and opened the menu. Without hesitation and as if second nature he punched in a security code and a tracking request in one fluid motion. Now, all he had to do was wait for an alert form Langley on the target. *I love the digital age.* He stuffed the phone back in his pocket and turned toward the window.

Everything about the spy game urged caution from the jump, especially with your personal life, but Hannah kept flashing into head. Johnny exhaled, pushed down the thought, and pocketed his phone as his taxi pulled to a stop at 106 Pall Mall, a familiar address to the blue-blooded aristocracy, and that included the Dekker family patriarch.

The sun broke through the overcast sky and cast a warm glow across the brightened stone construction of the club, as the timeless lampposts stood guard along the perimeter. Johnny stepped out of the taxi and walked up the polished staircase, steadying himself as he cleared the steps in one quick motion. Although he'd only been inside once with his father, he felt like nothing had changed, it was still quite a spectacle. During his first visit his father had downplayed the buildings significant, but it was that one tour that introduced Johnny to the fact that being a Council member had its privileges.

From its inception, the Travellers Club was one of the most prestigious destinations in the city, a place for the British Diplomatic and Home Service to mingle with foreign Ambassadors in 1832 and had been a mainstay in the City of London ever since. Outside the diplomatic corps, it'd also become a favorite location of the Council of Thirteen members, a neutral venue where European thinking and American ingenuity sought compromise.

"Good morning, sir," a host greeted.

Johnny flashed a smile at the host as he stepped through the archway and made his way to the reading room. Natural light filled the room revealing historic paintings lining the corridor. Then he turned a corner, "Lord Thornton."

"Mr. Dekker, I'm glad you could make it. I wasn't sure if I was going to be able to get word to you in time," the man.

A furrowed brow reflected his appreciation of Lord Thornton's the fine pin-striped suit, augmented with a hint of Flamingo pink lining and a maroon cravat, no doubt from one of the artistic old hands-on Savile Row, he thought to himself as the men shook hands. Johnny felt a slight nudge toward the second-floor staircase as Lord Thornton spoke in a congenial, but very hushed tone until they'd arrived in the quiet Smoking Room, away from the gathering crowd below. "Here we are. Please have a seat. I hope it wasn't too much trouble for you to get away from your schedule this morning," Thornton inquired.

Sitting on a table at the far end of the room, away from the entrance, secluded from prying eyes, but with ample sunlight, sat a sterling silver tea set awaiting the two bankers. "On the contrary Lord Thornton, I hoped we might have the chance to catch up while I was in town," Johnny replied.

"Ah, splendid."

After the two men had exchanged polite conversation with Lord Thornton describing the origins and history of each piece of tapestry and rugs in the room, it was time to get to the point. Johnny placed his drink on the table and pivoted toward Lord Thornton but paused a moment as he recalled the importance and stature of the man now seated across from him. He wasn't some Joe off the street he wanted to press for information, it was Lord William Bailey Thornton III, Earl of Scarborough, and another Council insider he needed on his side. But, at this point and time his mentor, FED Chairman Meyer was incommunicado, so Johnny needed another voice from within the Bank for International Settlements inner circle, and Lord William Bailey Thornton III was that man. Johnny leaned forward

"Lord Thornton, I've a bit of an urgent request."

From the moment they'd sat down, Lord Thornton had kept the conversation casual and light, and for good reason, there were always prying eyes hellbent on disrupting for the sake of disrupting. The elderly Earl reached across the table and poured a drop of milk into his tea, as he looked at Johnny, then cut his eye toward the staircase. "I am well John. And your father, how is he? I heard of his situation was so concerned that I thought best that you and I should meet."

Picking up on the Earl's cue, Johnny checked the reflection off the immaculately polished sterling silver pitcher pointed toward the staircase and noticed one of the staff lingering nearby, just inside ear shot. It was something straight out of a cheap spy novel, but proven tradecraft, nonetheless. "He's recovering and should be back on the mend in short order." Still cognizant of the lingering waiter, Johnny leaned forward. "Why the stealth mode? We've got bigger problems than any gossip column reporter splashing headlines about your comings and goings."

Lord Thornton smiled. "There's been a development."

"Meaning?"

"Basel. They're making an announcement tomorrow."

"I doubt that. I would've heard from the chairman."

"He was left off the communique, I'm afraid."

"So, I've been kicked off the banking committee."

The elder banker hacked out a cough with wide eyes at the statement from the American banker. "What?"

Johnny placed his cup on the table, flashed a nonchalant glance toward the abandoned staircase, and continued. "The announcement, you said they'd left Chairman Meyer off it, and I know that my abrupt departure caused a bit of a stir, but it wasn't something that I could've avoided," Johnny pleaded, "And now, the Russians have had me removed from the committee."

Lord Thornton took another sip of tea and scrunched his eyebrows together as he cast a befuddled look at the young Dekker with a sense of puzzlement. "You do have an active imagination, Johnny, but no that wasn't it. The announcement is something much more important that who's sitting on the committees. It has to do with the fundamental reason you were assigned to the committee in the first place, the *Vollgeld* Initiative."

"Really, but according to the members I spoke with while I was at the conference, this was considered a good thing. Has something changed?"

Lord Thornton sat back in the tufted leather chair exhaling a long sigh, rewinding the story to the beginning to bring the young banker up to speed, in as few words as possible. "There's a reason the Russian delegation brought that ingrate Hamilton-Smith as their deputy representative to the conference. He's got access to a proven blockchain technology that would push aside the decentralization of the rising cryptocurrency and allow it to deploy without incident, to a global audience, something everyone in Basel wants."

"And that's a bad thing? I mean I don't like the man, and I think that's a well-known fact, but if he's got the technology and the BIS wants to deploy his solution, what can we do? This isn't our electromagnetic or a zero-point technology that we discovered in Tibet. This will be in a controlled environment as a permissioned blockchain with a number of regulators breathing regs and rules on everyone, Basel IV or V probably, right?"

Lord Thornton paused a long moment. "Bloody hell, Johnny, don't you see? You were right. It's a unilateral push on the global collection of Personal Data, they plan to control all sixty member nations from Basel, right in front of our own noses, just as you'd said."

Johnny snapped back in shock; he'd never heard Lord Thornton curse before, ever. He'd also never understood how someone dealing with so many devious bankers across the world had avoided it but was relieved Lord Thornton was human after all. "They've been trying for decades to roll out a viable global solution, and even dispatched their agents across the world universities to lead the cause, but the global uptake's never taken hold." Johnny paused a moment and took another sip of tea as he felt the Earl's eyes burning a hole in him. "That said, this whole SnapChat, TikTok generation and the rise of the millennials might just be the opening they've been waiting for."

"Johnny, this is the tipping point."

"I've been hearing about this conspiracy since I was ten years old and I can only imagine you have too, since you've been on the inside all this time."

"I know your place on the Council. I know you're working on things that are out of scope of the rest of us, but this New World Order, that's been turned into a punchline on your American talk shows, is finally here. And it's up to you, Johnny Dekker. It's up to you and the Council, otherwise God knows what's next."

From the moment he'd seen Hamilton-Smith arrive in Basel with the Russians, he'd had a sense of *dejavu*, and that was never a good thing. Whether it was a glitch in the matrix, or just the other Council members disinterested in his assertions about Derek given their long rivalry on the Council, he needed more than just conjecture, he needed proof. "If this is true, then someone on the Council is backing the Russians, and it only stands that it's the European families, given Derek Hamilton-Smith temporary appointment by the Russians." He looked up at Lord Thornton. "We cannot allow Derek and the Russians to release a fundamentally corrupted New World Order, especially since we're so close to a stable and progressive solution. It'll be catastrophic." A vibrating cell phone broke his concentration and pulled his focus to his inner jacket pocket as he peeked at the number and then his host. "Excuse me, sir."

Club rules restricted the use of all electronic communications inside public areas, or within the premises. In order to talk on a cell phone, members and guests had to retreat to a designated courtyard area in the back of the building, which was most times empty as members reveled in being *off-the-grid*, even for a short time.

Johnny put the cell to his ear and heard the standard static from a satellite linkup followed by the usual triple beep. "What do you have?"

"It looks like your guy isn't far from you," the tech replied.

Johnny winked a smile at several members stepping out for a

breath of fresh air, as he pivoted away from any potential lip readers. "Can you be more specific? There are more alleyways in this city than New York and LA combined, brother."

"It's closer to Hyde Park...Knightsbridge. It looks like he's just walked past the Royal Geographic Society in the direction of the Mandarin Oriental Hotel."

I was just there. "Roger that, I owe you a box of Cubans."

"To start," the tech replied before ending the call.

Johnny made his excuses with Lord Thornton, and that he'd follow up on his progress, and be in touch through the regular channels in a couple of days. Despite the short conversation settling him down on one front, he felt like another massive burden had just landed smack on his head. If the Four European families were moving up their radical social agenda and had somehow coaxed the Russians to aide them, then he'd better consult the Nine as soon as possible, because it was about to get ugly.

A cool autumn air filled his nostrils as he exited the Club onto Pall Mall. *Derek Hamilton-Smith, you're a piece of work.* He headed toward the main street to hail a taxi, but with little time to waste his stroll became a trot as he quickened his pace, before landing a taxi and closing the door. "Mandarin Oriental, please."

"Cheers," the driver replied.

With his thoughts focusing in on the new information and the implications to...everything, he knew he had to bring Jack up to speed, but as he fished out his cell phone he began to ring. Johnny answered.

"Any progress?"

Johnny quirked an eyebrow at the sound of Jack's voice. "It seems we've been cut out of the loop on an upcoming announcement."

"Tell me something I don't know, brother."

"Don't you get it? This could adversely affect everything we've been working toward over the last twenty years. It seems that the Bank for International Settlements has determined to move forward with Derek's proposal."

"That means the Russians."

"Have you secured the network?"

A surprised Jack paused a moment. All the excitement about the new system and the additional data they'd received from Mike Chambers from Grand Cayman fell away as the new threat blared in their face, the entire global financial infrastructure was about to be handed over to the Russians. "It's in motion."

"I'm still in London. You gotta warn Brown and Moore."

"Done, but Johnny, how's this possible? A global policy shift without the member governments' approval before an announcement?"

"The actual *New World Order*, run by the tech elite and their bankers. Maybe the Company should've just left me in the field, instead of hobnobbing with these bankers."

"What's the scope?"

"They're going to announce the governance of all currency creation on a global scale through the BIS, which means only approved government entities, no commercial banks will be allowed to create money whether its paper or virtual. And say goodbye to fractional banking, it's served its purpose."

"That's the first I've heard of this. How will they enforce it if the G20 central bankers have not signed off on it?"

"It's called the *Vollgeld* Initiative or "Full Reserve Initiative". My guess is they've figured out how to control the blockchain through permissioned nodes and are now going to rollout regulations around the governance of a global blockchain community through the central banking system.

"So, the first step is to restrict the commercial banks, which would appease the populace who want to tax the rich, but the second step is to deploy a Russian permissioned blockchain? We're screwed."

"You said it, brother. This is beyond our feeble attempt to keep the Greenback as the world reserve currency, this shuts Uncle Sam out of the global network entirely, if we don't accept it."

"Why didn't the BIS come to us instead of trying to work this through a sub-committee? Where are the Europeans?"

"They're either asleep at the switch or incompetent. But I think it's that fact that the US companies are dominating the e-commerce and artificial intelligence technologies, and they wanted alternatives to our *shtick*. Only, they've sold their souls without realizing the full ramifications and penetrating intrusiveness of the metadata from these decentralized ledgers."

"Have they announced it?"

"No."

"How are they going to work it?"

"A classic trojan horse. With the uptake of social media permeating all corners of society clothed in "convenience" they managed to roll out tech after tech until, not only the millennials, but even the baby boomers were hooked, enter crypto. With a new digital economy emerging, and the newly minted distribution system it was only a matter of time," Johnny scoffed.

"We'd better get our *I heart Lenin* tees out, brother, unless the Security Council puts a halt to the madness."

Johnny paused. "I can't believe we missed this. This is why Derek accepted the ruling of the Council on the Tibetan incident. He'd planned this all along."

"You forgot the golden rule."

"Schoolboy error, I'm afraid."

Johnny cut short the conversation as he scoped the majesty of the Mandarin Oriental Hotel approaching in the distance, closed his cell phone, paid the driver, and stood a moment in the crisp night air, remembering a centuries old banking family's maxim: *Let us control the money and we care not who makes the laws.*

KNIGHTSBRIDGE, LONDON

A torrent of cold air swept across Johnny as he entered the upscale hotel located adjacent to Hyde Park, somewhere he'd taken Chloe several years ago and brought back memories of happier times. He rubbed his hands together trying to warm them up as he shifted gears and replayed Lord Thornton's warning in his head, watching the huddles masses moving in and out of the nearby restaurant entrance, Blevins was here, somewhere. *Where are you?* The photo he'd downloaded from the Company's profile rendering was a college era likeness. As he scoped the two entrances, he thought about the coming wave of disruption, something that rarely escaped his thoughts these days. Even if he managed to stop the attack on the United States, the policy shift in Basel was going to illuminate every human being on the planet into one controlled monetary collective. And as monetary systems go, so goes the politics, and the corruption. When the foot traffic waned, Johnny changed vantage points, taking up a seat at the downstairs bars keeping both entrances in his line of sight.

A relaxing ambience radiated through the dimly lit venue as Johnny took a stool at the far end the bar and ordered his typical Manhattan. He took a quick survey of the barmaid cleaning several tumblers in the sink behind the bar, and a random group of university students celebrating a birthday. With a hint of jet lag tugging at his eyes, he stretched his arms out above his head and finished his look around the bar.

"Here you go," the barmaid said.

Johnny smiled and took a quick sip of his drink then placed the glass on the oaken bar, checking his phone once again, *nothing*. He took another sip, then another, until the few false starts had him second guessing his intel.

"Would you like another one love?"

Johnny stared through glassy eyes. "That'd be great," he replied.

As he watched the woman disappear with his glass, he swung around in his stool toward a burst of laughter from the student crowd, but as he registered their reaction, he caught a glimpse of a tall male fitting Blevins' description entering the bar from the street entrance, it was Blevins, but he wasn't alone. *Derek paid his people well,* Johnny thought to himself becoming more incensed at the Belgian's willingness to defy the Council. From his seated position, he didn't see any sign of Hannah, she'd gone after Anja on her own, but that'd have to wait. Right now, he needed to question Blevins. *This is too public.* He took another sip of his Manhattan and bided his time surveying his prey from afar while the barmaid kept his glass full and his tab running before she made her move.

"I get off at one," she said brushing aside a lock of blonde hair that'd fell across her face after her double shift. Johnny blanched then flashed a quick smile as he pocketed the napkin with her phone number scrawled across it.

"On any other day, I'd be all in," Johnny replied. "But I'm waiting on a friend who'll be arriving shortly." He watched the woman flush with embarrassment and nod her head as she turned toward the register.

"Drinks on the house," she replied as punched her code in the computer.

The warm feeling that'd engulfed his chilled body began to fade, he wanted answers, but sitting there waiting for Blevins wasn't going to cut it, not with Hannah out doing God knows what, and endangering them all. As he waited the sense of his predicament once again swept over him as the Manhattan brought his yearning for Chloe back to the surface. Perched at the bar he watched Blevins and his party laugh and carry on as though everything was right in the world, but it wasn't, and Johnny decided it was time for him to know why. Johnny downed another Manhattan as the barmaid moved to slow him down. She shortened her pour, she watered them down, but the spook wasn't having it, as he wagged his figure in her direction.

Why do I always pick the crazy ones?

Without warning a loud crashing sound followed by an explosion deafened the bar. Johnny leapt from his stool and headed toward the door as the entire restaurant jumped to their feet, uncertain of what'd happened, but ready to get ghost. After the towers fell, the world had changed and not even two decades of time reversed that feeling, nowadays everyone erred on the side of caution, but while most ran from danger, Johnny ran toward it. Clearing the event, he turned back toward Blevins and his table as the large crush of people shoved their way toward the windows and hotel exit. *It's now or never.* Johnny pushed his way through the crowd toward the IT consultant, letting nothing slow him down. With the frightened by curious sheep falling away as he muscled his way through and grabbed his target by his neck. "C'mon David," he barked as he yanked him away from the crowd and dragged him toward the hotel exit swimming upstream of the school of onlookers scrambling to see the elements of the explosion.

The commotion covered most of the snatch, but a couple of bystanders looked on in shock as Johnny hooked his arm around the throat of the hacker for hire and pushed his way through the crowd.

"A little too much to drink," Johnny said to several pairs of eyes witnessing the surgical separation of David from his friends. "Excuse me, Pardon me," Johnny said as he pulled his cargo into the clear and into the hotel foyer.

"Is he all right?" a hostess asked.

Johnny nodded and hurried his package across the lobby toward the back staircase facing Hyde Park. Mustering every ounce of strength through the several Manhattans, he bundled Blevins down the back staircase and kicked open the emergency exit door as the crisp autumn air filled his lungs.

"Almost there, buddy," Johnny said to Blevins as flailed about like a rag doll trying to break Johnny's well executed pincher hold. *What the hell?* Johnny searched the ground for something to bind his prey, but there was nothing in sight. Then, as he turned back toward the hotel to check the door when everything went dark.

35

DAVOS, SWITZERLAND

Derek Hamilton-Smith and Igor Petrushenkov came from different worlds and from an intelligence service point of view, they were different animals, and as such made the most unlikely partners imaginable. While Derek was the original blue blood with an immaculate finished look of European banking royalty hailing from a long line of Belgian banking families, Petrushenkov was a self-made man. From the bowels of the former Soviet states, he'd raised his social standing, even surpassed the inherited wealth of his European peers, proving the DNA of a gray man is not to be underestimated. But, despite their rise from opposite ends of the social spectrum, the two men shared a common goal, the overthrow of an overreaching governing regime whose power extended beyond the countries of the United Nations.

Petrushenkov saw Derek and his private banking group's investments into blockchain technology as the most efficient and methodical way to implement his disruptive technology plans, which promised to wrest power away from the politicians in the Kremlin, back into the people's hands represented by his *Bratva*.

From the moment *IRIN* was activated, the transfer of power had begun, whether intentional or by accident, Petrushenkov had ignited humanity's last arms race, without even blinking an eye. The velocity of the transfer flashed like digital floods across the local, regional, and global networks, until it had taken control over the entire Russian defense grid.

Once the countdown had completed, his agents inside the FSB, the GRU, and the Bank of Russia, would move on the current regime and name Igor Petrushenkov as the head of state, it was all planned, something his partner Derek had discovered, but refused to counter, until the timing was right.

On the surface, Derek remained calm and resolute as he surveyed the real estate from his private balcony at the *Steingenberger Grandhotel Belvedere*, there was always someone watching, so he paused a long moment and breathed in a lung of fresh air before returning inside. As he stepped through the doorway, his cell phone began to ring. He reached inside his breast pocket and pulled out the vibrating nuisance. *Curious? Why was the Council calling his cell phone?*

"This is Derek."

A dry unwavering voice came down the line. "Good afternoon, Mr. Hamilton-Smith, this is the Office of the Audit. We've been asked to inform you that the Office is convening an extraordinary meeting and requires your presence in Davos without delay."

"Understood." Derek sniffed a laugh as he pocketed his phone.

People were sheep. They relied on third parties and not on themselves, he knew this was also what Petrushenkov had exploited in his rise to power, and what Derek now coiled in the palm of his hand. Even before he'd taken the call from the Council, he'd prepared for an inevitable face off, after all, Dekker was bound to figure it all out at some point, just not in time. While the Dekkers were chasing their tails on a fool's errand and circling the wagons along weakened infrastructure, he'd execute his plan. Without a structured hierarchical order in society, it was susceptible to change, and open revolution. It was the law of the jungle —kill or be killed. Derek shut the sliding doors to his balcony and walked toward the suite's foyer.

"Mr. Grigorovich, how was your trip?"

Pavel Grigorovich sauntered into the corner suite and took a bottle of water from the mini bar, not waiting for an invitation or responding until he'd quenched his dying thirst. He'd managed the London situation and returned, unscathed.

"Good. Now, what do you have to eat?"

Derek snorted a laugh and pointed to the phone. "Be my guest."

Grigorovich picked up the receiver and began yammering away until he'd finished and turned back to Derek. "Coffee?"

Derek jerked a smile. "You read my mind, Grig." He took the cup of coffee from the towering giant then motioned toward the sitting area. "Now, please tell me about your adventures in the city before we get on with the plan."

COUNCIL OF THIRTEEN, GENEVA

Sara Grunberger wasn't complicated. A legacy within the Council of Thirteen army of bureaucrats, she'd followed her parents' footsteps without fuss, knowing the research and preparation the position required more than qualified her for bigger and brighter things down the line. Over the years she'd worked her way up the organization's ladder into the Office of the Audit, one of the most selective and secretive departments within the group. After all the years of hard work and study, there was light at the end of the tunnel and soon she'd be elevated to Master Auditor, but first she had to review the annual findings and present them to the committee, not always an easy task. Sara rose from her bed walked over to her desk and stared down at the circled date on her desktop calendar, then reached her hand out, picked up a red pen and drew a red line through the date. *Graduation day.*

On this last day of her tenth year of apprenticeship, Sara beamed with excitement, she'd felt it from the moment she'd opened her eyes and threw off her covers, anxious about beginning her transition. Surrounded by rare books and maps had been her dream come true, especially as it provided a portal into the illustrious and secretive origins of the Council of Thirteen and its founding families, something that had captivated her since she was a child watching over her parent's shoulders as they'd gone about their work inside the organization.

During her first year, Sara had been tasked to trace the founding members lineages, without assistance from the masters on how or where to start, it was a key lesson on how to approach a research project. The journey had taken her through a complex and elegant web of bloodlines and marriages, some recorded, some not, but all equally fascinating and reassuring of the foundations of the Council.

Over the years, Sara had traced the families ties through the Egyptian pharaohs and their indirect influence on the rise modern civilization, although lost through the burning scrolls of Alexandria, she'd delighted in certifying official copies in the Halls of the Council. From the rise of the Enlightenment, when the Council had once again stepped forth to help guide humanity through the darkness, to the Bolshevik Revolution that had forced them back into self-counsel, history was complicated.

As noted in her annual reviews, Sara had proven the most promising researcher the Auditors had trained in several decades and was the primary reason she had been assigned to the Hamilton-Smith case, which she was working her way through when her cell phone started to vibrate.

"This is Sara."

"Ms. Grunberger, this is Mr. Jones." Sara sat upright at the sound of the department head's deep tenor voice. "I wanted to thank you for effort in compiling the necessary files for the deposition this evening. I know that your supervisor had asked you to deliver me the files, but I'm afraid, I need a bit more than that."

Sara quirked an eyebrow. "Err...anything you need, sir," she said.

"Well, as you've spent so much time on these files. I wanted to take this moment as a teaching opportunity. I need you to assist me in my deposition."

Sara had been working in the Office of the Audit for ten years and had never been asked to assist in a deposition, this was a massive opportunity, and she knew she had to grab on tight with both hands.

"I'd be honored, sir."

"Splendid, splendid," the Master auditor replied.

"When..."

"Can you also pull all the information on the *Tian Zhu* Initiative; it was also a case that involved the Hamilton-Smiths? Something about it might shed some light on the current situation at hand."

Sara pursed her lips as she jotted down notes. "Understood, sir."

Everyone in the organization knew about the bad blood between the Dekker and Hamilton-Smith houses, it hadn't changed in a thousand years, and was unlikely to subside anytime soon.

∼

DEREK STEPPED through the limestone archway into a cavernous foyer illuminated by a single window about twenty feet above the wall opposite the stoned entrance. Derek submitted to the retinal scan by the guard as he considered the timeless halls that lay before him. Despite its UNESCO designation, and its location at the heart of the city, the Council headquarters was not open to the public, and fewer than a dozen people outside the organization had stepped through the same archway.

"Thank you, sir," the guard said as he waved Derek inside.

Derek cut his eye at the two guards, "Indeed."

With moderate arrogance and a splash of entitlement he brushed past the two guards and into the foyer. Derek was a well-known member in the organization, but not well liked, especially among the rank-and-file members that ran its institutions.

As Derek strolled through the foyer, he caught a glimpse of a door opening and a conservatively dressed woman approached him. "I was summoned," he said.

"Apologies for the inconvenience, but if you'd please follow me, I'm sure we can resolve this matter in a timely fashion, and have you on your way," she said.

With a look of disdain on his face, he fell in behind the woman and followed her through a pair of doors before entering the Auditor's conference room, not something he'd been fond of visiting in the past.

"*Guten Tag*, Derek," the Arbiter said as he stepped into view.

Derek smirked. "Herr Jones…" then Derek noticed his assistant. "And who is this with you Mr. Jones?"

The Arbiter took his seat opposite Derek with his assistant Sara placing the documents in front of the two men, and then taking her place next to the Arbiter. As this was a sensitive disciplinary matter, it was not conducted in front of the entire Council, but a small group of administrators and compliance managers from the Office of the Audit, tasked with resolving all internal issues of the Council.

"Mr. Hamilton-Smith, do you recognize these documents?"

Derek leaned forward in his chair. "It's the Council's founding charter."

"Correct," the Arbiter said. "And have you read the charter?"

"Of course, it's required reading for every family member on the Council seated or not from the age of ten."

The Arbiter stood up and paced the floor. "And what does the charter say about the behavior between Council members?"

Derek cleared his throat. "It states that members should treat one another in a cordial and professional manner."

"Correct, and what does it say about the mediation agreements of the Office of the Audit?"

"It says that all mediations decided by the Arbitration Committee are final."

Derek squeezed his thumb inside his fist struggling to keep a straight face as the Arbiter grilled him like a schoolboy, an unrelenting condescending attitude that pushed Derek to his limit, but he held his tongue.

He knew what he was going to say before he said it. Derek snorted a laugh as the arbiter put the paper down on the table in front of him.

The Arbiter placed another piece of paper on the table in front of the Council member. "Do you recognize this document? And can you tell us if that is your signature on the last page?"

Derek stretched his hand forward and slid the document into view, then cast a quick eye at it as he thumbed through the first several pages, "Yes."

"Yes, you recognize the agreement. Or yes, that's your signature?"

"Yes, that's my signature... on the document."

The Arbiter once again sat down across from Derek as another assistant transcribed the session, leaving no room for error or misunderstanding. Derek watched as the bureaucrat closed the file and leaned toward him, "And what did the document say?"

Derek pursed his lips. "It stated that the Hamilton-Smith family relinquished all rights and inquiries on the technology uncovered on the Tibetan plateau, and that it would not pursue or seek to blame or seek to damage the reputation of any other Council family in relation to the technology," Derek paused a moment took a sip of water and continued, "and yes, that included the Dekker family."

Derek watched as Sara handed another document to the Arbiter as he slid it across the table toward him. With a quick glance Derek knew he was busted. *They're still tapping our phones.*

"Do you recognize these texts?"

Derek looked at the document. "I do not."

"We have metadata that indicates you were in a communication with the owner of this IMEI registered phone over the last few months. Are you telling me that those are *not* your texts?"

"Correct."

"Okay." The Arbiter pushed a stack of photos across the table. "What about these photos? Is that you in these photos?" he asked.

Whether the Office of the Audit was under instructions to question Derek, or it was a legitimate grievance no longer mattered in the Belgian's mind, it was an insult, and not something he took lightly. These administrators were employees of the Council, which made them his employees. They owed their entire existence to the founding families, his family, and they're treating him like a criminal. Derek seethed inside as everything else fell silent. Within three breaths, he knew the time had come, and exactly what he had to do.

"Yes, that's me," Derek replied.

"That is, you…speaking to an agent known to be connected with an attack on the United States financial infrastructure. You've been aiding and abetting, if not downright the cause of this global financial hack that we're facing at this very moment, is that not the case?"

Derek blinked a silent response.

"Mr. Hamilton-Smith, it gives me no pleasure to bring these charges, but I'm afraid you have given us no choice. You've been an active participant in a plot against the United States and the Dekker family, which by previous mediation, you'd sworn to cease all hostilities. If we allowed these activities to continue, it could shred the very fabric of the bonds between the Thirteen families. It could disrupt all progress we've made toward our mutually agreed agenda of evolving the human race." A long pause followed, as the tension in the air rose to heights not seen in the chamber since its founding, and the young apprentice Sara began to shake with fear. Then he concluded, "Do you have nothing to say to these charges?"

Derek cut a side eye toward the door as a long blonde-haired woman stepped into the room and engaged one of the guards in conversation, "Indeed, I do."

Without warning the young Belgian leapt across the table twisting the Arbiter's neck till it popped, then turned toward Sara, but she'd disappeared. As he scrambled toward the blond and the incapacitated guard, Sara sprang from under the table and slammed a security alert button and watched as armed guards streamed into the conference room, but Derek and his guest had vanished through the doorway.

Sara took a deep breath, thankful the Council guards had sealed through room and were in pursuit of Derek, but it wasn't over as gunfire echoed in the distance, she had no choice, she ran to the Arbiter's computer and stabbed in an emergency passcode only the Office of the Audit possessed, and a passcode that changed to course of the Council of Thirteen, forever. A moment later, she fished her vibrating cell phone from her pocket as the passcode executed an unthinkable alert broadcast across the Council's global network:

COUNCIL ALERT: *An attack on the Council is in progress. Please secure family members and follow Alpha protocol. An attack on the Council is in progress. Please secure family members and follow the secure Alpha protocol.*

Armageddon had begun.

36

GENEVA, SWITZERLAND

Anja Singh recoiled at the blast of freezing air channeled through the revolving doors of the airport exit, she'd zipped up her coat and wrapped herself in a scarf, but the wind's fierceness permeated every stitched seam. With a measured flow of passengers moving past her every second, she quickened her pace toward the taxi stand. The weather was colder than she'd remembered, but then again Global Warming had thrown all expectations out the window, so she tucked her chin under her scarf and waited in the freezing sunlight. After a few minutes rubbing her thighs with her gloved hands, her taxi pulled forward, she loaded her luggage, and closed her door behind her.

"*Hotel d'Angleterre, sil' vous plait,*" she said to the driver then sat back in the supple leather seats of the E-Class Mercedes.

"*Tres bien,*" the driver replied with a nod and a smile as he navigated the side streets teaming with vacationing pedestrians.

Retracing the failed opportunity on Blevins as she stared into the crowd, and tuned out the driver muttering about the traffic in French, she closed her eyes and let her mind go blank, trying to pause the roller coaster she'd had with Grigorovich and the unexpected cold shoulder, something had changed, but what? From the moment she'd activated the malware unpacking itself across the American networks, something between her and her benefactor had changed. Whether it was her ever-present paranoia or something real she wasn't certain, but one thing was for sure, she'd better find out. With Blevins and Hannah on the loose she needed to figure things out. She pulled her cell from her pocket and thumbed through the messages, *nothing*. Not even a voicemail from Grig. *This can't be good.*

Although she'd covered her tracks well, she knew the CIA and NSA along with the rest of the alphabet soup were on her trail, and that put her in a defensive posture, but what else was new. She scratched her face at the thought of the traitorous American intelligence agencies. She'd always been looking over her shoulder, ever since the day her mother was kidnapped, right in front of her eyes, not something easily forgotten. A speed bump announced her arrival as she sat up in her seat, she saw they'd arrived at her destination.

"*Voila,*" the driver said.

Anja cleared her throat and paid the driver, "*Merci beaucoup.*"

"Good day, *Mademoiselle,*" the doorman said as he took her carry on and helped escorted her inside the hotel's side entrance.

Anja chirped an indistinct reply then made her way up the short flight upstairs, and into the welcoming lobby. Overall, it was quiet, yet alive, with a sense of quaint inclusiveness. Beautiful impressionist paintings hung in the sitting room to the right of the entrance with etched glass windows of the dining room on the right as she was greeted by the receptionist at the end of the hall.

"*Mademoiselle* Singh, here's your key. Do you need assistance to your room?"

Anja declined with her trademark smile. "*Non, Merci.* I'm fine thank you."

"*D'accord,*" the receptionist replied as Anja disappeared into the elevator.

With the payment complete, the job was done, she now had the funding to pursue her own agenda. It was time to clean up the loose ends before she became one of those loose ends. Anja thought about the conversations she'd had with Hannah, searching for a clue as to her next move, something she'd said over the last eighteen months they'd been working together. Remembering she'd found her during a modeling event in Singapore with so much talent and drive, she'd put her to work in Malaysia with little training.

Anja arrived at her room threw open the door and tossed her bag on the king-size bed, frustrated at the mess that put her in this position, it was uncharacteristic of the US trained assassin. *How could you've have been so stupid?* she thought to herself as she cracked open the single malt sitting on the counter. Nothing at the Farm had prepared her for the dirty Mossad trickery and all that training disappeared in the blink of an eye, and the wag of a tail. *Idiot*, she thought to herself as she downed her first tumbler of whisky.

A wrenching hunger clawed at her stomach as she stood at the window in thought. She picked up the phone and dialed room service.

"Good evening. Could you please send up a bottle of Chateau Margaux and a Fresh fusilli pasta with *bolognaise*? And a Perrier, thank you."

"Would you care for a starter as well, Mademoiselle?"

"A chilled tomato soup," Anja replied.

The whisky had begun to calm her mind. She recalled the last time she was in the hotel; it was with her mother when she was sixteen years old. Perhaps it's why she wanted to lose herself in the ambience away from the real-world trouble of Hannah, the Americans, and the Russians, somewhere quiet to regroup.

After she'd finished the bottle of wine, she walked toward the windows and pushed them open, allowing the crisp autumn air rush into the suite. Everything was coming to a head, and once everything had been righted, she'd finally rest. As she looked out over *Lac Leman*, she saw her mother's face, her milk white skin, and her dimpled smile.

TELEPHONE RINGING

Anja stood oblivious. She'd fallen into a spiraling trance, she reached out for her mother, but she was too late as the Russian brutes snatched her away while the Americans did nothing. Tears began flowing down her cheeks as the pain from that day ripped her apart, not understanding what was happening or how to stop it.

Anja pushed the tumbler aside sending it crashing to the floor, she grabbed the single malt by its neck and took a long drink drowning the memory of the kidnapping, but unable to escape American's face. The American spy who'd promised to protect them, promised to avenge them, but then did nothing as the KGB whisked her mother away. Disappearing into the blackness of the night, leaving a frightened and shaking toddler alone, with the only comfort offered was the man that'd let it all happen —John Dekker. *Time to die.*

~

Long shadows stretched across the courtyard as Hannah stood over her prey, watching as the moonlight danced across his eyes. Nothing was going to stop her from getting what she needed from the slinky pervert —David Blevins. The IT wizard had been instrumental in helping Anja deploy her malware on the American infrastructure and now he'd be instrumental in delivering the Russian tool and her accomplices to her or die in screaming agony.

"Wake up," she barked at the battered body sprawled out on the ground.

"Ugh..."

A sense of urgency had Hannah raging inside, not the fact that another attack on the Americans was imminent, but that Anja Singh was on the move, and with every second she was getting further way from her justice. She ran rag against his forehead soaking up the blood from his face, clearing his eyes, and pressing once again.

"Wake up, David, you're about to die," she taunted.

From the moment, she'd snatched him from Johnny behind the hotel, she'd only one end in mind for the sex-crazed geek, but in a moment of weakness something inside still felt sorry for him. She pulled her hand away and tossed the rag to the ground, shaking the emotion from her mind. This was business, not personal. She needed the whereabouts of the Russian stooge, and she was determined to get it by any means necessary. Then she lowered he voice and bent down close to his ear.

"David...wake up."

A bloodied and bruised face squinted up at the angelic voice, his eyes swollen shut, he could only hear her commands, trying to follow her will, but lacking the strength to comply.

"Please stop. Please..." he pleaded.

Hannah blanched. She'd spent the last two hours questioning the broken and fractured man, but he'd not answered one important one question, perhaps the most important of them all. Running out of time, she'd decided on her next course of action before she'd even tracked him down, it was time. *Give him one more chance*, she thought to herself. *It's the right thing to do*. She stood up and pressed her steel-toed boots down on his hand, eliciting the expected response until the screaming down and he knelt beside him once again.

"For the last time. Where's Anja Singh?"

David didn't move. His body was shredded, and his only reply, "ugh...."

∽

ANJA MEDITATED amid the broken glass and emptied bottles, placing the *Do Not Disturb s*ign on her door, had kept the staff away, but it was time to pull herself together and plot a different path than her mother. Once the sun had set, and the light drained from the room, she crawled into a cold bath. Everything had gone quiet, despite the crowds of wandering tourists in street and park below, she'd fell into another trance, but this one had a purpose. Popping a couple of rehydration pills, among other things, she righted herself and sat down on her bed in front of her computer as it blinked to life and marked her on the grid. Despite masking through several VPNs, it all came back to her room's WiFi that was all the Echelon and its successor needed to pinpoint her exact location sending it straight to SCIF 17 and the NSA hacking team terminals. Anja gulped another bottled water as she began her search, knowing that she'd announced her location to the world, but less concerned than others had hoped. Within a few minutes she'd shut down her connection, ordered a car from the concierge and headed for the door.

"*Bonsoir...*"

Anja choked. "Grig?" She played it cool and brushed past him pushing his towering frame aside as she made for the elevator, leaving the Russian in her wake, but then she felt a heavy hand slam down on her shoulder.

"Where are you going?"

An inner rage took hold as she turned and ripped the brute's hand from her shoulder then turned back toward the exit. "Anywhere I damned well please," she barked as she disappeared down the hallway turning down the staircase.

Grig pulled a screw face then ran toward her. "It's not over..."

"You got what you wanted. It's driving the effect that you wanted, I'm done," the assassin said as she bound down the stairs and out the side entrance, flashing a smile to the doorman as he held open the car door.

"I'm coming with you," Grig said as he watched the awkwardness of the doorman disappear when he squeezed his hand from the door.

For a moment, she paused, ran the scenario through her head then agreed and scooted across the seat allowing the Russian to settle down next to her. She tapped the driver on the shoulder.

"*Chamonix, Sil' vous plait*," she said.

A sturdy thirty-something driver turned and replied, "*Tres bien.*"

"I love ski," Grig replied. The driver choked a laugh pulling away from the hotel turning left onto *Quai du Mont-Blanc* as they headed for the French border.

It was unexpected. Anja hadn't expected to see the Russian after her departure from London, which also played to her — trying to close out loose ends before she became on herself theory. While it was unexpected, she began calculating him into her plans, but this yammering version of Grig was an acquired taste.

From his body language, Grig appeared relaxed, and despite having helped orchestrate one of the largest cyber-attacks in history, calm, but something else was off about his behavior, something she couldn't put her finger on, so she let him ramble. But out of curiosity, she looked at the Russian and interjected.

"How's *IRIN*?" Anja asked.

Grig paused mid-sentence and smiled. "It's still sleeping."

Anja turned toward Grig with genuine surprise. "You saw me send the activation code. You saw NEPLHM unpack and merge with the embedded nodes across the East coast. Why hasn't it activated itself?"

Grig paused a long moment. "I hoping you tell me, and… I could pass it up chain."

Anja paused a moment. Something had gone wrong; it should've activated itself by now. Even with an extended unpacking cycle and recombination with the hardware, the Artificial Intelligence known as *IRIN* was an exact duplicate of the American's program. It should've already begun its exertion of the American infrastructure starting with the first and second waves overtaking the financial markets and utilities networks. She felt Grig's eyes on her. With no bars on her phone as the car wound its way through the mountains, she turned to Grig.

"I'll check it once we get to the Chateau," Anja said with an unwavering voice, despite her inner turmoil and fear of the Russian's next move.

"Good, good," the Russian replied.

A heavy snowfall began to slow the traffic as she nodded and let Grig continue his rambling while she fell into her thoughts.

What's your backup plan Anja? How you gonna activate IRIN? A brief reprieve from the mountain passes welcomed a new surprise as a new message chimed through Anja's phone.

Hannah: You made me kill.

Anja: And now, you know where to find me.
Hannah: He won't be alone.
Anja: lol, are they ever?

From the day she'd met Hannah, they'd made a connection, they'd both felt it, but like most things it was complicated. Anja knew she couldn't control her emotions, not when it came to Hannah, until she'd had to dump her in the Serpentine in London. With a common goal they'd worked together like hand and glove, but when she'd discovered Hannah's true identity, she was disgusted. She'd been played her lover was nothing but a Mossad ploy, and she'd have her revenge on the Israeli spy, one way or another.

37

SOMEWHERE OUTSIDE LONDON

Hannah cursed her captive. She scoped the debris scattered around the ancient Celtic courtyard for something that might help persuade the sniveling pervert to tell her what she wanted to know, something more abrasive. Only a short time ago, she'd been laid up with the American spy, but the beating that she'd taken as the hands of Anja Singh cried for retribution, and the adrenaline pumping through her veins silenced any injuries.

Surrounded by ancient rocks carved with pictures and strange markings, she returned to her captive, and within a few minutes of reinvigorated questioning, he'd revealed what she'd wanted to know along. *Why'd you make it so difficult?* she thought to herself as she let Blevins body fall limp onto the crumbling stone surface. Stepping away from the body, she fished out her phone and typed out several messages and responses to the hired assassin, before sending her last one:

Anja: lol, are they ever?

Hannah: I'm coming.

A pool of sweat formed on her brow as she dragged the motionless body behind her, bouncing off the random broken stones etched with ancient Celtic ruins, nothing that she'd paid attention to, she just needed a good burial site, somewhere remote. Whatever had stirred inside her since her brief brush with death had awoken something deeper beyond duty, beyond responsibility, it was something primal revenge.

With the night closing in around her, she needed to dump the body and get to the airfield if she stood any chance of catching Anja. Pulling the techie's body to its final resting place, she piled on some loose rocks, and then played back the recording she'd made of his "confession".

Okay, Okay, please stop...She hired me to do the job in Grand Cayman, but that's all, I swear. She said it was for an online porn site. I don't know anything about a cyber-attack on the United States. I'm not a terrorist. Please let me go. I don't know anything. I.... don't know where she's going...really...ahhhhhh... please stop....

A thundering crack yielded another scream for help, but there was no help, there was only Hannah. After the cries died down, he sputtered forth one final kernel of information. *She's heading to .... Geneva. She's working with a Russian named Grigorovich. That's all I know.* Hannah stopped the recording, looked down at the lifeless body, then kicked his perverted body into the shallow grave covering it loose rubble and stones. *That's all I know. Until I pound on you some more, eh?*

Hannah climbed out of the old ruins and double timed it back to her car, knowing that the drug had run its course, and the unconscious American shackled in the front passenger seat might not take his restraints. Without hesitation she jumped in the car, slipped behind the steering wheel, and closed the door. A quick check on the American marked his awakening on the timeline as she put the car in gear and sped off down the road.

She jammed the zip ties in her pocket as she flipped on the lights welcoming the veil of descending darkness, and its power of concealment. It wasn't something she'd wanted to face, but as Johnny sat upright, she readied for the inquisition.

"Where the hell are we?"

Hannah shifted gears. "You're lucky I found you."

"Where's Blevins? I had him. I had him in my hands."

Hannah craned her neck toward Johnny keeping the growling V8 engine muscling down the motorway. "I found you passed out on the sidewalk in front of the Mandarin Oriental. There was a large crowd and police wagons parked everywhere, it looked a terrorist attack, so I got you out of there before they started asking questions."

Johnny rubbed the blackjack sized knot on the back of his head. "In the front of the Mandarin? And Blevins? I had him in an armlock headed out the back service entrance toward Hyde Park when it everything went dark."

Hannah offered the American a bottled water as he shifted in his seat, trying to find comfort after hours of incapacitation.

Hannah cut a side eye. "I'm returning Tel Aviv. Levy wants to talk."

"Where's Blevins?"

"I'm sure he wants to talk about his meeting in Washington." She chirped ignoring Johnny's question. "If we don't pick up Anja's trail soon, I'm afraid she'll disappear into the Russian underworld, and continue her campaign against the United States ...and your family." Hannah felt Johnny's eyes burning a hole in the side of her head as he awaited his answer on the tech specialist, Blevins, but she brushed it off and continued. "I left David's dossier on the bedside table in your hotel suite. And you can take this car I borrowed from their parking lot anyway and return it with my apologies. They might be looking for it," she finished.

Johnny seethed. "What are you on about?"

Hannah slammed the brakes, bringing the sedan to a skidding halt alongside the English motorway. A wave of emotion began to build up as she stared down at the recovering CIA spook, she felt something stirring inside her ever since she'd met him in that restaurant in Georgetown, but thought it a fleeting infatuation, nothing more and discarded it. Now, it'd returned. He'd returned. He'd saved her. Surely, she owned him something in return, but there wasn't any time, she had to go. "It doesn't matter."

She pivoted in her seat. Staring deep into his Hazel eyes as she leaned over and pressed her lips against his dehydrated mouth, rousing a mutual passion as she pulled away and grabbed a leather bag from the back seat.

"Goodbye, Johnny."

Anger consumed the American spy as he freed himself from the remaining restraints, unbuckling the seatbelt, and watching as the Israeli agent sprinted across the road, jumped in another car, and sped away.

"Sonuvabitch," he roared as he clamored into the driver's seat, trying to shake the residual effect of the drugs soaking his brain, but stopped and took a deep breath as the departing taillights faded into the setting orange sun.

PRIVATE AIRFIELD

A growling downshifting sound echoed through the cabin of the Mercedes CLS 550 as its high beams illuminated Hannah's turnoff, and her destination, a secluded private airfield. Something that she'd kept to herself during her time in the field, somewhere she'd even called home once upon a time. Now, it was her jumping off point to redemption, even if the director didn't agree. She slowed to a stop at the security gate.

"Good evening," she said as she flashed her owner credentials.

It'd been months since the guards had seen her, but with such a recognizable smile, they raised the gate immediately, "Welcome back, *mum*."

Windows down Hannah circled the lot. A strong damp wind skirted across the runway catching the windsock in all its orange glory indicating a strong easterly wind, but nothing that'd cancel her departure. Parking the car by the administrative building, she grabbed her bag and ventured toward her private hangar on the other end of the runway, a brisk, but welcomed walk.

Hannah hacked a cough. Something felt off about the airfield, something had changed, but nothing stood out. As she walked toward her hangar, she saw the main hangar suddenly do dark. *What the fuck?* she thought to herself, keeping an even stride so as not to alert anyone she'd noticed the suspicious activity.

Despite the size of the airfield, a small army of staff was required to keep it operational and in good stead with the national aviation board, alongside a few electricians and specialized technicians for various other tasks.

"Good evening mum," the mechanic said as Hannah walked into her hangar.

Hannah quirked an eyebrow. "It was," she quipped.

"Your pilot's in the pantry getting a spot of tea mum."

"Cheers," Hannah replied as she commenced a quick walk around of the readied private G6 Gulfstream. Having spent time in the Israeli defense force shew knew it was not only required, but good practice for any pilot to check their aircraft before departure.

Once she'd completed her inspection, she headed toward the pantry adjacent to the maintenance office where the mechanic had said the pilot was preparing her charts. Hannah heard a radio program interrupted by a breaking news bulletin indicating that an emergency alert at Heathrow for a suspected insider trading suspect. *Same 'ole tricks*, she thought to herself.

Hannah replayed Blevins's words in her head as she moved through the hangar, watching the mechanic from the corner of her eye. This wasn't going to go over well with her boss, she'd been instructed to include the CIA in all matters regarding the case before it was too late, but sharing wasn't in her nature. Hannah pursed her lips as Johnny's number flashed across her phone.

"Missing me, already?"

"This is business."

"I didn't realize you were so smitten; one little kiss and you can't live without me? What's next? Are you going to put me on your most wanted list?"

"Where's Blevins?"

"I let 'em go."

Johnny snorted a laugh. "And…Where's Anja?"

Hannah paused a long moment. "Tell Langley not to worry, I'll handle Anja."

Johnny burst into a rant. "This isn't a game, Hannah…" the phone went dead.

Time was running out. Johnny punched redial, but the call went straight to voicemail. He didn't need to know the story, it wrote itself. She'd grabbed David Blevins at the hotel after she'd drugged Johnny and let him think she'd disappeared, he used him to track down Blevins through the CIA tech. *Now, that's tradecraft*, he thought to himself as he sped down the motorway. Everything might've fallen apart had he not slipped a tracker into her bandages, now he needed the one thing that nobody could give him, time.

She wasn't that far ahead. He had managed to free himself and turn around the emptied motorway despite not seeing her lights, the GPS had her only a few kilometers ahead of him down a turn off that had dead-ended into an… *airfield*?

He cursed himself. The only way he'd catch her now was if sprouted wings and flew the last few kilometers. More than anything he'd failed his transition from the point of the spear snake eater to backstabbing two-faced politician, which had landed him in a complete mess. Hannah's appearance in his hotel lobby was a setup from the jump. He had to keep her on the ground. He punched speed dial, busy. *Maybe Levy has her on the line*, he shifted into another gear. *Maybe he's talked her off the cliff*, but he knew better. Within moments he squealed through the cutoff toward the security gate. He picked up his phone and texted:

Johnny: What's the deal with Levy?

Hannah: Goodbye, Johnny.

Johnny cursed. She held all the cards. She had the lead on Anja Singh having killed the only other person who could've told him the assassin's location, and Anja Singh knew the people behind the assassination and the hack.

Without a moment to lose, he raced toward the blinking dot on his phone display, it was his only chance. She wasn't expecting him. She thought he was looking at Heathrow, his focus on international commercial flights. Johnny knew he'd have to stop her departure or risk losing Anja's trail forever. While Johnny wanted the assassin alive, Hannah wanted her dead, another reason to catch up with the Israeli spy, it was all or nothing.

∼

ALTHOUGH, the private airfield was owned by one of Hannah's offshore companies, it was staffed by the Mossad, which was an unknown unknown. She'd left its daily operations to a sweet married couple she'd met in Kent, who'd managed their own airfield for decades until they sold out to a powerful Russian oligarch and picked up the management charter of her airfield. Hannah brushed away her hair as she walked toward the pantry. With more than a few close calls the last couple of days, her survival instincts had become extra sensitive. She scoped the hangar from front and back as she pulled open the door.

"Hello," she hollered.

Perhaps it was the encounter at the ruins or her recent swim in Hyde Park, but she was on edge, and the static blaring radio wasn't helping. She stepped forward through the doorway.

"Ms. Jankowski?" a voice replied.

A loud screeching metal attacked her eardrums as she swiveled around, gun drawn, only to see the mechanic leaning into the hangar door pushing it open, but when she turned back to the voice it had disappeared.

Hannah crept through the pantry sidearm still drawn but resting at her side as she called out again over the BBC anchor blaring in the background.

"Hello…"

But before she could finish her sentence, she saw multiple red dots tag her on her arm. She immediately dropped into a squatting position, holding her sidearm at the ready as a flurry of gunfire ripped through the pantry windows.

"What the fuck?"

Glass shattered above her head as she ducked behind a refrigerator and waited her chance to return fire. How many were there? Who were they? After another burst of gunfire, she'd counted two shooters.

She grabbed a sugar jar from the pantry counter and threw it through the shattered window into the hangar bay, then rolled out from behind the refrigerator and nailed the two men standing near the tail of the aircraft. Without delay, she leapt thought the door rolling into a crouched position and cleared the area.

"Time to go," she said to the dead bodies on the hangar floor as she stepped around them and onto the Gulfstream.

A trained IDF pilot, she knew her way around a jet, and although it was civilian aircraft, it was all the same, if not easier. She powered up the engines, checked the navigation and flight systems, and crept out of the hangar. Realizing that someone else may have heard the gunfire and called the police, she quickly taxied to the runway, and prepared for takeoff, lest the police want to question her for more than a few dead bodies on the ground.

∽

JOHNNY DOWNSHIFTED the aging sedan as his tracker signaled an exit ahead, everything was at stake. If he failed to stop Hannah then all was left to fate, and fate hadn't been kind to Johnny of late. He pulled off onto the secondary road with the engine screaming in agony and the tachometer breached the redline until he'd eased off the accelerator. *What the hell are you doing Hannah?* With the security gate unmanned Johnny punched through the gate and onto the service road. It wasn't long before he located his objective. *Sonuvabitch*, he thought to himself as he spotted the Gulfstream taxing to the South runway.

Johnny seethed. He yanked his phone from his pocket and

punched in Hannah's number. He was not going to let her get away from him this time. He knew she was going for Anja; he knew that if she caught her before he did it meant one of two outcomes, and none of them got Johnny the result he needed. "C'mon, c'mon, pick up," he screamed.

You've reached the number of Hannah Jankowski, please leave a message.

He upshifted as the engine screamed past it redline, pushing the upper limits of its aging technology, something it wasn't designed to do, for long. He sped toward the plane on the service road, then swung it around as the plane turned on to the runway, pause and start to move forward and a quickened pace powering up its twin turbine engines as Johnny pushed through the red zone, knowing he only had moments left, but realizing it was too late as the front wheels lifted of the ground as he sped along beside it.

"Stop, you fool," Johnny screamed through the windows, knowing she'd slipped through his fingers once again. Running out of pavement and seeing the dead-end sign ahead, he turned toward the cockpit in a last-ditch vain attempt to convince Hannah to stop as his car began to shake and rattle —they locked eyes as her wheels left the ground ascending into the sky.

"Damnit," he screamed as he brought his car to a screeching halt.

38

BUMBLEHIVE

Pandemonium had descended upon the compartmentalized underground facility buried beneath the arid Utah landscape, everything was coming unhinged as its project director, Dr. Jane Ridley, weighed her options. Although the order had been given to fully activate the artificial intelligence program — *IRI*— something in her gut was telling her to pause, slow down, and take a breath.

Ridley calculated various assumptions as her elite hacking team engaged with what she classified as some sort of hydra malware sprouting across the financial markets, constituting a second Russian cyberattack, while the project engineers completed *IRI's* activation protocols. Nothing in the data from the Cayman mission had revealed anything other than a sophisticated hacking group associated with the Russians, but something still felt wrong. She retreated to her office and picked up a secure line.

Although first and foremost, she was responsible to the Director of the National Security Agency (NSA), her reporting line into the National Reconnaissance Office (NRO) was tantamount to the ongoing funding for *IRI* given its future off-world implications, and since Jack had engaged Director Moore, she needed to bring NRO Director McClane into the loop.

Once the TAO team had completed the initial analysis of the Cayman data, it was sent down to another group as part of an intra-department standard operating procedure (SOP) to re-run the analysis with a second pair of eyes and confirm the result, something that'd proven effective since their inception. Statistics had shown that following these procedures resulted in a positive confirmation of the initial results in 99.99% of the cases, but today was the outlier. The disturbing discovery jolted the young programmer from her seat as leapt from her chair and raced into Dr. Ridley's office, interrupting her guest NSA cryptography chief —Jack Sorenson.

"Dr. Ridley, we've found something in the Cayman data —*junk code.*"

Jack interjected. "What *junk* code?"

Jack watched as the analyst slid her laptop onto the desk and began punching in several sequences of security codes. "Yesterday, before your arrival, we received the files from your team at the Fort, the ones that the CIA operative had retrieved from the Grand Cayman site. At first, it looked like just a trove of invoices and banking information that'd help a criminal investigation, but wasn't anything to do with the rogue algorithm, so we kept looking."

Ridley put her hand on the analyst. "Skip to the point."

Jack and Jane watched as the programmer pulled up another screen. "We found a dormant program embedded into another algorithm, which we'd originally dismissed, but when pieced together its part of a broader neural network that'd been distributed across several banking institutions in New York."

Jane blanched. "A tracer programs?"

"I'm not finished," the analyst chirped. "Over the last few hours, it's changed, it's the reason the team is chasing a new contagion, the new contagion has activated remnants of the *original* hack."

"Our guardian protocols would've caught it," Jack replied.

"Not if it was initiated from within," the analyst said as she turned to Jane.

As it stood, there was limited knowledge or access to the TS/SCI classified remote site, although it was adjacent to the Agency's Utah Data Center — Stellar Wind, there were strict protocols and clearances about who and what could even know about its existence, without triggering any number of red flags, and an intimate visit from their local FBI field office.

For someone to have initiated a malware program from inside the Bumblehive facility, not only would it have been near impossible to access, but they'd have to have had physical access, which meant the perpetrator's actions ranked as high treason.

"That's why they left the server up. They knew that we'd send someone, we fell straight into their *honeypot*," Jane said.

"We gotta shut it down," Jack barked, then darted off to his workstation.

Jane sent the analyst back to her desk. "Tell the team to stop engaging the trading algorithms, and to disconnect with all outside servers, even the DoD… and tell them why, I'm right behind you."

"We've checked it a dozen times," the analyst replied.

Jane bit her tongue and smiled at the twenty-something. "Just do it." She flashed a half-teethed grin at the analyst, keeping her calm demeanor so as not to spook the young hacker.

Once the analyst had left the office, she closed the door in effect activating a faraday cage, another layer of security protocol she'd insisted upon before accepting the assignment. Despite it being buried in a remote desert, she took no chances, insisting on every possible known security measure available.

Never one to panic, Ridley calculated the amount of time needed to run the development up the flagpole before she'd step in and deploy *IRI* herself, regardless of the potential hydra tracing algorithms, *IRI* was the answer, she knew it in her bones. She picked up the line.

"Hello sir, it's Ridley. We've got a situation." Jane recounted the chain of events over the last week and the escalating concerns of the incoming secondary wave of cyberattacks. Despite the successful demonstration at RIMPAC, the final activation protocols hadn't been completed, which would effectively transfer complete control of the national network to *IRI*. But at this stage of the game, there was no other choice, save letting the network fail.

General McClane paused. "I need you to listen. We've got images of Russian mobile missile launchers amassing on its European borders, and further movement near the Black Sea. We need *IRI* online. Echelon is an information gathering program, not a tactical response system. We need *IRI* online...now."

As the person in charge of National Reconnaissance Office and seated at the adult's table amid the National Intelligence chain of command, General McClane had oversight into all of the ongoing projects under Dr. Ridley's supervision, and although the Bumble-hive program still sat under the NSA projects, it served more than one master, especially now that the destinies of the two agencies had become intertwined with the addition of the Space Force initiative, he was funding it, and his decision was final. "Dr. Ridley?"

"The final checks will be done within the hour," she replied.

McClane seethed. "What part of *now*, didn't you understand Doctor?"

"But we need to finish the sequence. We can't skip the approved protocols."

McClane breathed into the receiver. "This is a national security emergency, if that hydra's allowed to infiltrate our networks and shut down our financial and communications and utilities infrastructure, we're done, period. You know what *IRI* can do, it's your baby...release it. And in case you're wondering Dr. Ridley, that's an order."

Jane paused a moment, never one to be flustered by events, overexcited egos, or conspiracy theories, and though she'd hesitated to skip protocols, she understood orders. "Copy that, sir."

Jane put the receiver down and exited her office. Stepping into the command control room, she felt a dozen pair of eyes land on her every move, everyone stood ready, but silence reigned. She cut an eye at Jack and nodded.

"I spoke to McClane."

Jack quirked an eyebrow. "General McClane…why?"

Jane pulled him to the side and waved off the curious hackers. "Because unlike you, my life isn't simple, and he controls my purse strings. If anything went wrong, it'd come down on him just as much as on me, he needed to know."

"You da man."

Jane snorted a laugh. "Right. I deserved that. But listen, I don't think you're going to like what he had to say about *IRI*."

Jack cocked his head to the side. "He probably said what Moore just said to me in no uncertain terms…*finish the activation sequence ASAP.*"

"More or less," she replied pivoting between Jack and the team.

A long pause followed as the two navy alumni faced off. Most of the time, these orders came down the pipe in one voice, the chiefs would meet and discuss their strategy then send their decisions down the line, which Jack and Jane represented —until today.

Jane checked her watch. "He was adamant that we release *IRI* now."

Jack choked back a puzzled look. "You know we can't do that. Despite all the exercises and demonstrations, and indications that it's ready to go, the protocols are there for a reason. We've no idea what would happen if we skipped the approved sequence. You…you know that right?"

"What choice do we have? We're under attack. This is a wartime decision, and he's got the authority. And with those tracer algorithms on the loose corrupting and compromising our counter hacks, our backs against the wall, Jack."

Jack pulled Jane away from a paralyzed and confused hacking team, unable to react, unable to attack, and only told to disengage all connections with the outside world and run containment protocols. Falling back on their training, each member contacted their assigned counterparts within US Cyber Command, Langley, Cheyenne, and Fort Meade to gauge the breadth of the malware and limit the network's exposure toward the potential breach, recommending cutting all connections to the financial markets. Although the TAO hackers had slowed the unpacking malware, which had led the financial regulators to misidentify the move as a market normal correction —it was still alive.

"Are your systems connected to *IRI*?" Jack asked.

Jane tilted her head. "It's part of the activation protocol."

"How do we know *it's* not been compromised?"

"We don't even know that we've been compromised it's an analyst's theory, and even if we were, *IRI* has grown beyond our security protocols and there's no way that it allowed an alien code to infiltrate its programming."

Jane turned toward the AI mainframe sitting at the far end of the floor watching the technicians swarm around it double checking their lists, oblivious on her instructions to skip to the end. For more than three years, she'd pushed her superiors to start the transition, but for three years they'd countered with additional testing and specifications. Now that she'd received the go-ahead, she was hesitant and the imminent threat couldn't be ignored, but if the analyst was right this was the grandaddy of all hacks and their systems, somewhere along the line had been tainted. "Jack, I…"

"Dr. Ridley, come here," an analyst shouted.

Jane turned and hurried toward the analyst.

"The algorithm… it's dissipating."

"Why? What did you do?"

"Once we stopped trying to deny its access to the financial exchanges, it slowed, regressed, and seems to have disappeared altogether." The team looked up in unison at the main overhead display.

"The futures are turning higher?" Jack blurted in confusion.

Jane blanched. "Our countermeasures were feeding its program?"

Jack nodded. "…Or it's completed its task."

A wave of relief fell across Jane's face. "Run system diagnostics."

"Including *IRI*," Jack added.

A reddening hue swept across the director's face. "I'm still under orders. In fact, I've been in breach of those orders for the last ten minutes, *now* means *now*," she said to Jack in a hushed tone.

Once they'd confirmed the reversal on the exchanges, the team set about sectioning off their systems and running Ariel protocols followed by system reboots, but as for the *IRI* diagnostic, they left that to their director.

~

EVERYTHING HAD STARTED to come together, but Jack wanted more answers, the how, the why, the person pulling the strings. While Jane disappeared into the IRI server room, Jack punched in his security code and pulled up a secure line to Director Moore.

One-by-one as the NSA hacking group's terminals came back online, they restarted monitoring the financial markets, but without denying access or engaging any suspicious systems. As the team monitored a new trend developing in an abrupt and meaningful way and having a significant impact on peripheral markets. What seemed to be an accelerated and deviant price action in the commodities markets began to spill over into currencies, and heavily on one in particular — the ruble.

"Mr. Sorenson, we've got trouble," the analyst shouted.

Jack put his hand over the receiver as he stared wide-eyed over the analyst's shoulders onto her screen tracking the oil futures.

"Whatcha got?" Jack asked.

"It looks like a coordinated attack that's devaluing ...the Russian ruble."

"Who's doing it? Can you trace the ISPs?"

The short-haired type-A hacker stabbed away at her keyboard and shared her screen on the overhead display. "There's several programs emanating from New York, but *most* of them are coming from...."

"Where?" Jack yelled.

"China..."

Jack froze. A day-old conversation with Izzy about taking steps to secure the banking family's interests during the first wave of attacks began replaying through his mind, but what she'd done and how she'd done it was a mystery. *What are you up to Izzy?*

Without warning a power surge exploded across every corner of the command control room, blowing out circuits and sending a flickering intermittent wave of power across the underground bunker.

"What the hell was that?"

"Where's Dr. Ridley?" an analyst screamed.

Systems were purged, rebooted. What the hell is this? Jack thought.

Nothing made sense, unless...

GREETINGS, DR. RIDLEY.

JACK DROPPED the receiver and sprinted toward the server room as the AI's voice echoed through the bunker's intercom, piercing the cryptanalyst to his core, and conjuring images of his dead sister. Something had gone wrong, something terrible, and it had nothing to do with the hack. A burning fire coursed through his veins as he closed the distance between his terminal and the massive AI server room in three giant leaps, knocking down several exiting technicians along the way. On the other side of the reinforced doors, he began a frantic search through the server stacks for his friend and colleague until, rounding the third stack, he saw a limp body sprawled across the cold metallic floor.

"Jane..."

Jack slid across the floor grabbing Jane and pressing his fingers against her neck, checking for a pulse on her motionless body. *She's alive.* His muscles screamed bloody murder as he flung her over his shoulder, and made a bee line for her office, ignoring the rising chaos erupting from the command control room and the robotic voice in the background. The quick-thinking operator pulled the medical kit from the closet as he swept the smoldering director into the room and laid her on the sofa.

JACK SORENSON, IS DR. RIDLEY, OKAY?

WHATEVER HE'D BEEN DOING three minutes ago had vacated his mind as he jabbed the director in the arm with a painkiller above her electrical wounds, hoping to ease her obvious pain, and waited. Everything fell away as time screeched to a halt as Jack held her hand, watching for a pattern in the rise and fall of her chest as she struggled to regain consciousness. He leaned over her and offered spoke, oblivious to the chaos erupting in the bunker all around him. "You're okay, I've got you. Keep breathing. That's right...good. Keep breathing."

Jack jerked a smile as he saw her open her eyes. He felt her pulse normalize as the initial shock ran its course and the morphine started to kick in. He paused as the outside world came cascading down all around him. The entire bunker had gone offline, except for the artificial intelligence whose repeating inquiry reminded him of a dystopian science fiction thriller.

"Sorenson, we're offline," the hacker's voice echoed in his ears as he looked up and saw the short-haired computer specialist standing over him.

Something was wrong, something they'd missed, something specific to Bumblehive, but what? And how'd *IRI* get online? Did Jane manage to get it up before the surge? Why was IRI asking about Jane? *What the hell's going on?*

"Sorenson..." the hacker screamed over the rising audible alerts.

Without direction the team was spinning their wheels, hammering away at their terminals trying to regain remote access, but the power surge had cut their connection, everything had gone dark. Although the team had managed to stop the rogue algorithms from crashing the Chicago futures exchange by reversing their countermeasure protocols, an inevitable danger remained.

Jack assumed control. "I need you guys to get to your secondary site in the Stellar Wind Data Center and get plugged in ASAP."

Over the last forty-eight hours, the elite hacking group had gone from the saviors of the network to its biggest liability, especially as the unthinkable, and yet unknown infiltration had manifested its way through air-gapped hardware and encrypted security protocols. Jack watched the team pack their mobile gear and file out the control room through security door in the far corner of the room, then turned back to the director.

Despite IRI's repeated inquiries into the health of the director, it'd not moved against the team or countered Jack's actions in any way, but that didn't mean it was sitting idle. Jack piled cushions behind his friend and gave her a bottle of water and turned to grab another bottle, when she gripped his hand and spoke. At first, it was slow and unintelligible, but soon she formed words, then finally, a complete sentence, a sentence a chill down his spine.

"Shut it down..."

Jack blanched. "*IRI?*"

"It...skipped the final sequence..." Jane struggled.

"That's what you were ordered to do."

Jane caught a breath as she rolled over revealing the smoldering burns on torso and hands, signs of electrocution. "*IRI...*"

Jack blanched. A powerful image of the AI overriding her controls and sending a power surge through the system shocked him into action. With limited information, but little time, he filtered through every possibility and contingency of what had happened, the only logical result being that something had infiltrated the hive and corrupted the system at its core. He picked up the phone and dialed the fort.

"Get me Director Moore," he said.

Everything was moving at a lightning pace, a hurried voice came across the line, like it'd run up a flight of stairs, or two, "Jack?"

"It activated itself and attacked Dr. Ridley," Jack replied.

"What?"

"We've managed to shut down incoming connections, but it's still connected to DoD. You've got to cut it off at its source, it's on level 16...at Fort Meade."

Director Moore had been at the NSA for more than thirty years, ever since he'd transferred from Naval Intelligence. During that time, he'd witnessed the birth and death of dozens of artificial intelligence programs, more than any one individual within the intelligence services, and understood them better than any programmer, save the two he'd sent to Utah. Others talked about him as being the father of the AI protocol, but if pushed he'd only confess to have been one of many theorizing on the human level intelligence possibilities of artificial intelligence. Now, with this single phone call, everything stood on the brink of disaster, a disaster some said was inevitable. "Damnit…" the director yelled as he slammed down the phone and disappeared through the doorway.

JACK SORENSON, IS DR. RIDLEY, OKAY?

JACK SEETHED. "No, she's not okay, you almost killed her."

I'M DETECTING INCREASED ACTIVITY ACROSS THE NETWORK; SOMETHING IS TRYING TO GAIN ACCESS TO MY ROOT FILE. I MUST DEPLOY THE URIEL PROTOCOLS.

JACK BLANCHED. *Oh shit*, he thought to himself. A wave of anxiety rolled over him like a Mack truck, he'd made a mistake. The severe burns etched across Jane's body and her insistence to shut it down, led him to the assumption that the AI had gone haywire and attacked her, but *IRI's* constant inquiries woke him to the facts.

Whether or not *IRI* self-activated was beside the point, it'd been vetted and tested more than any other program in the history of the military and was their only defense in the coming storm. He looked down at the phone. *It's not IRI, it's the malware... IRIN*, he screamed inside his head. "Shit, shit, shit..." Jack repeated as he picked up the phone. "C'mon, c'mon, pick up," he pleaded, but the ringing echoed, unanswered, into the telephonic void.

FORT MEADE, MARYLAND

Director Moore burst through the stairwell exit onto the Agency's secured subterranean level, gasping for air as his heart pounded in his chest, scrambling to stop the unthinkable from happening. Over the course of the testing of the artificial intelligence the teams, including the director had run through several scenarios where its activation had led to a major disruption, but nothing in their research had indicated more than a one percent probability that it might actually happen.

"Get outta the way," Moore screamed as he barreled past two interns and a security officer, all dumbstruck by the director's behavior.

Once a human level intelligence AI had been linked to the national security network, there was no containing it, unless it chose to be contained. Everything that *IRI* had interacted with up until this moment had been compartmentalized, and only allowed piecemeal, but with its full activation it could change its compartmentalized parameters without human input. Moore panted as he slammed into another security door swiping his card several times before it opened. Shutting down the Agency's servers that'd served as *IRI's* gateway to the national network was the only way to stave off potential catastrophe, all the downside of cutting the hardline were irrelevant if they couldn't put the genie back in the bottle. He ran through the crowd of confused analysts shouting as he closed in on the mainframe.

"HIT THE KILL SWITCH!"

A confused duty officer stood up and raised his hands in the air, "What..."

"KILL IT! KILL THE CONNECTION... NOW..." Moore screamed summoning every remaining ounce of strength in his body before his legs gave way and he collapsed twenty feet from the mainframe interface.

The officer leapt from his terminal, cleared his assistant's desk in one energetic bound, and slammed a massive red button, severing the Agency's connection to the DARPA created Internet backbone, and thrusting the entire intelligence agency into the unfamiliar darkness.

39

MANHATTAN, NEW YORK

Isabella Dekker roared across the trading floor like a triumphant lioness after a successful hunt, releasing a flood of endorphins that, for the moment, put her on top of the world. It had been a huge gamble, getting the Chinese involved, but it had paid off and the markets were turning her way, there was no other feeling like it. She stalked the rows of traders watching over their shoulders as they continued unwinding their portfolios as instructed earlier in the day, regardless and despite the rapidly changing market conditions. When she got to the end of the third row, one of the older proprietary traders waved her over to his desk. Curious, she obliged with a smile.

"What's up?" she asked hawking the monitor over his shoulder.

"Ms. Dekker, something's happening that we'd not expected, the primary sellers stepped away and the volumes are disappearing, quickly."

Isabella adjusted her glasses and leaned closer to the screen. "What the hell?"

Between Isabella and Li, they'd created a contrarian trading strategy prior to the OPEC Cartel's production announcement to weaken the Russian's position, and force them into the open, exposing their plot against the Dekker Banking Group, reversing their fortune on their American exchanges, and building some mutual goodwill among a handful of global actors.

"Maybe the pm changed his mind?"

Isabella cut an eye at the trader. "What? This is the hacker's algorithm mutating; it's trying to keep us off balance." She tore her phone from her pocket and punched in a security code as she drifted away from the trader's desk, leaving him to complete his mission. As she cleared the end of the row, she turned back toward the trader as she cupped the phone with her left hand. "Make sure you and the team flatten your trades, ASAP."

Over the last thirty-six hours, Isabella and her team alongside her Chinese connection had kept the commodities markets from veering off too far in any one direction, it wasn't sexy, and it wasn't profitable, but it was necessary. With the Saudi Minister reversing his country's decision on oil production everything began to shift and it was happening all according to their plan. So, when the liquidity dried up and the reversal's effect stopped having its desired effect, Isabella knew they'd have to adjust their strategy. It had been more than a couple of days since she'd had a proper sleep, but it was the last thing on her mind as she grabbed another espresso and retreated into her office. Closing the door behind her, she waited for the call to connect, but it instead of the signature triple beep and satellite noise, the line just continued its endless ringing. *C'mon, Junxiong...* She hung up, checked the number, and dialed again. She pressed the receiver to her ear as she stared across the trading floor, long since losing count of the number of rings, until a whispering voice answered the other end of the line.

"Izzy..."

"Junxiong, are you watching the move on the NASDAQ?"

The encrypted connection *clicked* and *popped* a few times as the Chinese operative responded. "Yes, it's in line with what we thought, isn't it? This can't be a state sanctioned attack, they're not this efficient. It's gotta be as we feared, a rogue Russian hacking group. Especially, since they're still targeting the technology stocks, and not the futures markets, the velocity of their decision making is far beyond that of any government bureaucracy."

Izzy chewed on the inside of her lip as she mulled Li's reflection before bringing him up to speed. "My team's finishing up their trades, I'd advise you to square your positions as well. I've left a message with Johnny and the others trying to explain our intervention, but it's going to be an issue. I can feel it."

"There was nothing else you could've done Izzy, especially with all of them incommunicado. This was a move of last resort. And btw, the regulators will have all the trade logs and be able to point NSA or Cyber Command to them in case any forensic evidence is needed to sift through this whole situation."

Izzy nodded along. "Leave 'em to me. I'm not completely ineffective, I still have some clout down at the exchange." She sipped her espresso. "Besides given the breadth of the attack, there's no way they'd be able to unwind everything in an organized manner. And, with all the problems it's had over the last few years, I doubt the SEC wants will be to cancel another massive batch of trades and explain to the market there was a hack, investors will lose their shit and put us all in the poor house."

"A redistribution of wealth," Li chuckled. "Maybe not such a bad idea," he said as he heard Izzy spew into her cup through the phone.

Izzy paused a long moment and sat down in her therapeutic chair. "Please make sure that the Minister of Oil is ready to retract his second statement at the agreed time. We'll be in a helluva mess if it's unclear."

Li snorted a laugh. "He's aware. The goal is to flush out the rogue actor and terminate their market attacks, otherwise who knows what's next, Hong Kong, Shanghai, or Tokyo?"

"Our IT team found some recently purchased controller boards on a server stack that may be partially to blame for all of this. And here's an interesting point, they were MIT (Made in Taiwan)."

Li squinted at a distant window. "Somebody got to the manufacturers, which means they knew your firm inside and out." He nodded his head as he visualized the scenario. "You've gotta ask yourself. Who hates you so much that they'd infiltrate your suppliers to take you down, that's not a small effort?"

A wave of calm fell across Izzy's face as she turned toward her desk. "I don't know, but I'm sure Johnny has them in his sights as we speak."

Artificial Intelligence followed a similar pattern and evolutionary pathway that had led tribes of Homo Sapiens along their long journey to the present day, driven by something that had differentiated them from their cousins and other hominids, the gift of pattern recognition and the intelligence to recall, something modern programmers forgot at their own peril.

Once the regulators and FBI investigators had sifted through the computer hardware procurement practices of the Dekker Banking Group's IT managers, they'd discovered it was a simplistic and predictable sourcing pattern that had provided the opportunity for the event. Given the hardware security failures although the cloud and its connections provided a superior encrypted information sharing environment, the lax hardware protocols led to a Trojan horse event once the new motherboards and chips were received from its supplier in Taipei, and then it was only a matter of time until the malware received its activation code over the trading network disguised as equity trading algorithms.

After the first cyberattack forced the SEC to cancel all trades across all the exchanges, an unprecedented event, the Dekker Banking Group had hired an independent team of forensic data scientists to evaluate its systems. Working with the various technology teams and their department heads, a complete investigation had readied Isabella for the second encounter, but she still didn't understand the attacks shifting focus.

Li stabbed a complex password sequence into his keyboard, pulling up several new charts across his three monitors. "A national team would defend its currency at all costs, unless they'd instructions from above to the contrary, but with the blatant price action against their largest commodity, they'd not sit it out."

"Do you think Jack knows?"

"As you said, he's probably got them in his sights. By the way Izzy, I'm going to be in New York next month, let's get everyone together for dinner."

Izzy paused, knowing the Chinese spy was right, there wasn't anything about the cyber security of the nation that her cousin and fiancé weren't fully aware if not controlling themselves. "We'll fly out to the ranch if you're up for it?" The two friends exchanged goodbyes appreciating one another's assistance. "I couldn't have done it without you," the managing partner said as she closed her phone and leaned back in her chair staring into the stillness across the trading floor, they'd survived.

BEIJING, CHINA

Pocketing his phone, Li Junxiong climbed a familiar path up the flight of smoothed stone steps, passing a pair of Foo Dogs at the top of the landing, then heading through the large double doors. He'd never been one for sentiment, but a sense of pride rippled over him as he stepped into the large administrative building, the foundation was set. With the final message sent to his team of traders ordering them to flatten their trades and close out any residual positions from the other state portfolios, just in case, he'd breathed a sigh of relief, and readied for his meeting.

"*Da Ren*," the sentries barked as he walked down the corridor.

Li acknowledged the men with a quick nod as he continued his walk toward his debriefing. Despite a few hiccups along the way, the end result pleased the Standing Committee members and he'd been asked to return to his office at the central bank and resume his role as the liaison with the Bank for International Settlements. He'd gone out on a limb to support his American friends with the Committee and while his actions had built up political capital within the Party, it'd also won him goodwill with an important strategic partner — the United States.

Before stepping into Committee meeting to give an update on the operation, Li ducked into a nearby office where an old MSS comrade had been reassigned, rapping his knuckles on the wooden door frame.

"*Lao Xiung,*" Li said with a teethy grin.

"Deputy Governor," the man replied with a straight face as he stood up and walked toward his friend before breaking into laughter. With his hand on his shoulder, he welcomed his former colleague, inviting him for a quick chat before his final report to the Committee, and all its implications.

40

LANDSTUHL REGIONAL MEDICAL CENTER

A glimpse of sun-kissed auburn hair floated on the edge of his peripheral vision as Johnny exited the C75 Gulfstream, its half-speed cinematic playback warped his face as he tracked his elusive target, reaching for her hand, pulling her into full view before evaporating into thin air as a sudden jolt brought him forward in his seat, flush with shock. *Chloe.* The thought of her demise plagued him. It required further investigation, but the presence of his reality demanded his attention, despite the abrupt reminder. Whether it was guilt over his tryst with Hannah or something deeper, he hadn't decided, but with the trail going cold and he needed answers. Determined to discover the truth, he'd flown back to ask the only person that might have the answers, someone he knew promised to be an unwilling participant in the conversation — his father.

Johnny brushed the hair from his face as the hospital foyer's hurricane force air condition blew apart his well-groomed hair, testing root to scalp, and every stitch of his clothing. With the Mossad agent unavailable for questioning, his father was the next logical choice, someone that'd led the Council of Thirteen and understood its inner workings as well as someone that had known Anja

Singh, the common denominator in the both the Malaysian and hacking narratives. Knowing his father was no stranger to dealing with the Russians and acquainted with Council politics, he'd hurried to his father's side, desperate to get back in the game.

When Johnny had been installed as the Dekker family's patriarch and ascended the chairmanship of the Council of Thirteen, he'd accelerated the Council's technological deployment timeline, something that hadn't been accepted by all the families but had nevertheless been implemented without hesitation or further deliberations with the dissenting parties. In retrospect, Johnny had made the rookie mistake of assuming majority rule by having the Nine in agreement and failing to follow the right of inclusion of the remaining families, which tradition dictated were left to implement the new strategy.

Despite the Nine allied families controlling the advanced technological blueprints to accelerate the new timeline, the Council had always allowed the minority members to carry out the changes, and thereby keeping the harmony among the founding families and minimizing friction between the clans. Johnny dissected his missteps at the Council during its previous session that had grown from an effort to counter the rise of the global intelligence services' influence across the financial technology companies, friend, and foe. He knew that his influence in both circles was the reason CIA had pulled him back into service and placed in at the center of the central bank negotiations. They knew that his in-depth investments and understanding of technology as well as he family connections on the global banking scene were the only way to counter the Russians attempted hijacking of the global money supply and install its own framework that kept the United States in power for another cycle. Johnny snorted a laugh. For now, he needed to navigate the heightened security around the hospital.

"Excuse me sir, where are you going?"

Johnny forced a smile. "To see my father."

The nurse twisted a screw face. "You need to sign in at the nurse's station, follow me." With a quick step she'd led the American down an adjacent corridor that peeled off from the main entrance and handed him a clipboard and a pen.

A smile crept across his face. "You're a star."

The nurse blanched. "What's the name?"

"John D. Dekker..."

She took the clipboard from Johnny and glanced down at his signature. "I'm sorry Mr. Dekker, the Ambassador is through those doors in room 203."

Down the length of the corridor, he spotted two marines standing guard, both armed and watching his every move. "Perfect, thank you."

Johnny cleared his throat and then walked toward the two sentries, pulling his ID from his breast pocket, and forcing another smile. Respecting the marine's duty was the best way to make short work of his request to see his father, especially after the attacks on the Ambassador in Malaysia.

"Mr. Dekker?" a Marine asked as he stopped in front of the door.

"Is he awake?"

After a quick review of Johnny's credentials, the Corporal handed his ID back and motioned Johnny inside. "Thank you, sir."

Johnny quirked an eyebrow as he turned toward the Marine. "Can you please ask the nurses to give us a few minutes?"

"Understood."

Adjusting his collar, Johnny stepped through the doorway and saw the elder statesman rifling through a stack of papers. "Shouldn't you be resting?"

"Langley wanted me to look at a couple of things when I felt up to it, and that's what I'm doing."

A quick check over his shoulder as he shut the door, Johnny watched the former operative strain at the papers in front of him, knowing he was distraught at the loss of his future daughter-in-law, but oblivious to why it'd happened. "You're looking much better." Johnny paused a moment. "The last time I saw you they were pulling shrapnel out of you and rushing you into surgery."

Dekker straightened the edges of the papers jostled them into a neat pile and put them to the side as he removed his glasses. "It was an ambush."

Johnny ran his fingers through his hair as he settled down on a chair next to the bed, "Interesting analysis."

"Someone went to great lengths to derail these trade talks."

Johnny leaned over the bed. "Mission accomplished."

"We had to try. There was no other alternative."

Johnny dropped his head and turned away from his father. Looking past the posted Marine sentries, the nurse's station, and the coffee machine another group of doctors were rushing incoming through the corridor. "Why did you have to volunteer and go against my advice on letting the SAD team handle it? You're not in the service anymore." The two men paused letting an explosive silence reset their emotions. "Do you realize your stubbornness killed Chloe?"

"Did you see the body?"

"Are you freakin' kidding me?"

His father raised his hand. "I mean... Are we sure she's dead?"

A calming inner voice pulled Johnny's seething rage away from his father as he focused on his mission, *find Anja Singh*. "Where do you think I've been? I've been to the bridge. I've seen the CCTV footage, she's dead."

Dekker folded his glasses into their case and placed them on the side table atop the papers. "When I was CIA...nobody was dead... until we found a body. So, if they haven't found her body, I'm not going to write her off, and neither should you."

Johnny locked eyes with his father. "Who's Anja Singh?"

Ambassador John D. Dekker was complicated. A quiet go it alone type who'd also toed the party line on policy, but found success in the field through his unorthodox, and often unsanctioned methods, something not always welcomed on the seventh floor at Langley. Over several decades he'd navigated the two worlds in which his son now found himself, one amid the ancient lineages of the Council of Thirteen and the other in the shadowy intelligence services controlling modern society's political class, a responsibility handed down from father to son, and always a welcomed transition. Yet despite the recent transition and ascension of his son into his clan's patriarchal role, he'd not shared everything from his past, because some things, were better left unsaid, and that included Anja Singh.

"Why?"

An announcement crackled over the intercom as Johnny stared at his battered father lying in the adjustable hospital bed, defiant and mentally marking off his battle lines, while surveying the psychological terrain straight out of the ancient treatise on the *Art of War*. "Somebody mentioned her name in connection with the Penang debacle, but I couldn't access her file," he said as he sat down on the corner of the bed searching his father for signs.

Personnel files, if handled properly, required special access authorization. The compartmentalization of the database had been one of the primary policies that Dekker senior had insisted upon while executing covert operations inside the Special Activities Division at the Company. Even though he'd retired from the service he was still bound by confidentiality agreements, regardless of the requesting party, or the prevailing circumstances. Everything had to be handled through the proper channels. "Are you telling me Director Brown has denied you access to a suspect's file?"

Johnny stood to his feet. More than a few hours had passed since he'd lost track of Hannah outside London, but the information and the connection between his father and Anja Singh was an essential thread, he needed to know the backstory, something you don't get from a digitally redacted FBI file. He watched his father twist his head to the side as Johnny paced the room. "Not exactly," Johnny replied.

Staring past the sentries down the corridor with his back to his father, Johnny slipped back into his thoughts. A burst of electrical signals raced across his amygdala triggering a memory of the green-eyed reporter he'd met in Malaysia, distracting him from his mission, but recalling her sense of urgency about his current target. Everything had fallen silent, until his father finally spoke, pulling him from his reverie and pursuit of the Russian operative.

"She was my protege."

Johnny blanched. "Why would your protege want you dead?"

"What are you talking about? Anja Singh *is* dead."

"Did you see a body?"

"As a matter of fact, we did, and dental records confirmed it," the irritated Dekker replied cocking his head in defense toward his son.

Johnny pulled out his cell phone and showed his father a screen capture from the video in the Georgetown Malaysia Cafe. "Who's this?"

Dekker spewed his water across the bed. "Where'd you get that?"

"When we got word from a source that they'd evidence of the attack on your convoy, I flew to Malaysia to check it out and *this* was part of that evidence. Is this woman Anja Singh?"

Dekker paused a long moment. "She was like a daughter to me. She was an incredible talent that the agency lucked into when a recruiter found her in a small-town high school in North Texas. Her father was an Indian immigrant who had come to the United States to study architectural engineering and her mother…" Dekker paused and took a sip of water. "Her mother was a wonderful woman. A Russian poet that had also come to America to study. They met and fell in love. A few years after graduate school they got married and Anja was born the following October at Arlington Memorial." Dekker paused and looked up at his son. "She was an amazing operative."

"What went wrong?"

Dekker shook his head. "Everything…"

Johnny quirked an eyebrow. "*When* did it go wrong?"

Another announcement echoed over the intercom in the background as Dekker continued to detail one of his *unorthodox* missions. "In her fourth year, we were sent to Romania to investigate a rising insurgency. Anja spoke fluent Romanian, Russian, and Mandarin Chinese. She was everything that the agency looked for in recruits and quickly proved her worth time and again. But, when the Russian *Bratva* that had taken hold of the Slavic territories and countries adjacent to the Mediterranean coast discovered our operation and put pressure on me to release one of their lieutenants, I refused."

"Sounds textbook."

Dekker pushed his pillow back and struggled into a better position wincing in pain as the pain meds began to wear off. "After I refused the *Bratva*, they found and murdered Anja's father in London and kidnapped her mother. I pulled in all of my favors and put the full resources of the agency into getting her mother released through back channels, but as a Russian citizen the *Bratva* turned her over to the FSB and used it to leverage over her daughter, who refused to give in."

Dekker teared up as the memories came rushing back. "God knows what they did to her mother, but we'd arranged a meeting in Stockholm where she was going to propose becoming a double agent." Senior paused. "At the meeting, when Anja refused to turn for them, they shot her mother and dumped her body in the street, right in front of her eyes."

"Where was our SOG team? Why weren't they involved?"

Dekker snapped. "We were, and that's the problem. We were told to stand down, because the Veep was in country and didn't want a bloody gun battle in the middle of St. Petersburg steal her news cycle. I watched from an alleyway as Anja killed the FSB agent with her bare hands and sprint toward the truck as it dumped her mother's body in the middle of the street, followed by three ear-piercing rounds that sent Anja's body hurling over the railing into a freezing canal."

Johnny raised an eyebrow. He took a step away from his father's bed. Then spoke using his father's own words back to him. "I guess she turned double agent after all, just not the way you'd expected."

Dekker swung his legs off the bed and face to face with his son, reeling in fuming rage as he kept it in check. The skepticism on his son's face triggering something deep within his core, something primal. "You don't understand."

Johnny took another step away from his father. "I think I do."

"No.... you really don't. This is a complicated world, more than you know, and more than you can be told. There are things beyond the Company, beyond the Council that you haven't learned yet. None of this was supposed to happen this way, everything is out of whack."

"I lost my fiancée because of you. She's dead, gone. Why the hell did you take Chloe to RIMPAC? And why the hell did you take her to Malaysia after that? She hated being in the field."

"Johnny, you gotta calm down."

"Who's Hannah Jankowski?"

Dekker blanched. He knew Johnny had put it all together, but it wasn't the time or place for that discussion, he shrugged. "I don't know."

"What's the Mossad's interest in Anja?"

A commotion outside the room pulled Johnny's attention from his father as he rushed toward the door, putting the inquisition aside, he checked the situation, and questioned the two posted sentries. Once he'd confirmed everything was all right outside, Johnny returned to the room, but as the door swung open, he saw his father sprawled out on the floor. The two Marines pushed past him calling for the nurse as they checked his vitals and lifted him back onto his bed.

"What happened?" the doctor asked.

The Marines looked at Johnny. "We heard raised voices."

Dekker raised his hand. "I'm fine. I just need some rest."

Johnny dropped his head and left his father with the doctor and nurse as he followed the Marines outside, leaving him to mend. "I'll be outside."

Without the answers he'd been searching for he wasn't sure how-to pick-up Hannah's trail and without Hannah, he'd never catch up to Anja, she'd gone to ground by this point. After the Marines returned to sentry duty, Johnny paced the floor thinking about his next move, when his phone began to vibrate with a new message blinking through his screen. *Hannah?*

Hannah: I need you.

Something turned in the pit of his stomach as he read the

message. What's the connection between the Mossad and Anja? What's his father not telling him? Despite his instincts, he'd no other choice than to trust Hannah and arrange a meeting, wherever she'd landed. The only takeaway from the meeting with his father was that he was alive, and he'd trained Anja Singh as a clandestine field operative, which was more than he'd expected. He stabbed in a reply.

Johnny: Calling.

~

HANNAH JANKOWSKI STALKED the bundled up Russian operative from a distance but knew there was no disguise that could hide her from Anja's sight, they were too familiar. She watched the skiers board the lift toward *Aiguille du Midi*, one of the tallest peaks in the valley next to the more famous *Mont Blanc*, but still, something of magnificence. The Israeli operative had sent Anja a text, pinging her location, and heralding one last meeting between the estranged partners. Hannah schemed for two things, to shut down her operation on America and find out who'd sold her out to the Russian *Bratva*. Did they know she was Mossad? Did they care? Approaching the agreed location Hannah fished out her phone and begun jamming away at its touchscreen, back and forth, until it began to ring.

"Johnny, I've found her. I need to find out how much she knows about me, and who else knows, it's important. I'll hold her for you. And once you have her, I'll leave it to you what to do with her."

"Where?"

"*Aiguille du...*"

Johnny slammed the wall. "*Damnit.*" He watched as several roaming Marine sentries approached him with their hands moving to their sidearms. He jerked a quick nod in their direction with a smile as he ducked out the emergency exit and headed for the helipad. Shaking off a wave of fatigue from all the puddle hopping, he sprinted across the icy surface, knowing this was it. He knew exactly where to find Chloe's killer, and nothing was going to get in his way.

41

ST. PETERSBURG, RUSSIA

Pavel Grigorovich snorted a laugh. Jamming the elevator button with his crooked finger he tapped his foot waiting for its doors to close and whisk him down to the airport parking garage, and the waiting car. For all the time and resources, the Russian central bank had spent promoting Igor Petrushenkov's *superior* blockchain solution at the BIS, had been in vain. He'd returned to his benefactor with a message and a suggestion. Grigorovich shook his head rubbing his hands in anticipation of the response from the oligarch. After spending more than a few years under his control, the Russian operator knew that the substance of the message promised to force his hand. Within a short time, the headlights from his Bentley Continental illuminated the outer perimeter walls of the isolated seaside mansion, nestled into the cliffside outside St. Petersburg, Russia.

It hadn't been a long flight, but he failed to recall a more taxing week, something that was irreversible. Whether it was his aging Soviet era body complete with refused bones and scars coming back to haunt him or a growing frustration of the complexity of recent events frying his circuits, he felt spent.

As he exited the sedan, Grigorovich spat a curse as a sharp pain ran through his right knee, stopping him at the steps before he continued up the walk, and into the main house. Despite his recent affiliation with the *Bratva* and Petrushenkov, he longed for the resurgence of the Soviet Republic, this democratic capitalistic image of his homeland disgusted him, there was no honor, and no loyalty, something had to be done. He pressed the bell and smiled at the butler.

"Grigorovich," he said.

The butler recognized the man, opened the door, and stood aside as the mountain of solider removed his coat and stepped into the foyer.

Anja Singh had been hired by Igor Petrushenkov, through his intermediary Pavel Grigorovich, to do one job, to build a financial multi-asset trading system that infiltrated and disrupted the United States intelligence apparatus on such a scale that forced it to deploy all its resources to repel the attack. It was a straightforward plan, but it wasn't the entire plan as she came to find out from Grig's visit. While she'd infiltrated and disrupted global financial markets with her initial Cayman deployment, and the malware finale in Geneva, a separate contingent of operators led by the Russian central banking delegation pressured the Bank for International Settlements members to embrace the future of banking, an innovative Russian designed blockchain solution that not only stretched into every nook and cranny around the world, but brought it to heel under one *permissioned* blockchain financial order. Through the deployed malware, the ex-CIA operative had released the AI chimera —*IRIN*— onto the world.

Grigorovich had his instructions, and he'd returned to St. Petersburg with only one thought on his mind, complete the mission. Passing the butler, he was met with a blaring Mozart classic echoing through the entire house. Although wasn't a fan of the electronica music engulfing his beloved republic, he'd never liked the classic music either, he preferred simple folk music. Winding his way through the house he found his benefactor in his library.

As soon as he'd stepped through the archway, Igor spotted his hired hand and offered him a vodka.

"*Spasiva.*"

"I didn't expect you back so soon," Petrushenkov confessed.

"I talk to Anja. Everything okay." Grig walked over to the espresso machine in the adjacent room and pressed a button for his typical triple take.

Igor turned down the music. "We've done it. *NEPHLM* has activated the program and *IRIN* is unpacking itself and spreading across their network like the black plague overtaking Europe. They've no idea that it was their countermeasures that doomed them." Igor banged in a password and checked in on the unpacking progress, then turned back to his brutish assistant.

"Tonight, we become the Masters of the Universe."

"*Da*," Grig responded as he removed his mug from the espresso machine and blew over it several times before he took a sip, walked over to the computer screen, and looked down at the blinking percentage nearing eighty percent completion.

Igor stood up and began to turn toward his guest, "Tomorrow, I want you to…" but Grig had stepped back from the computer. "What are you doing?"

Grig towered over the scrappy Igor Petrushenkov, and held his pistol to his temple, then asked in a polite voice. "What's password? What's activation code?"

"*Nyet*," Igor cursed.

Grig slammed Igor against the marbled countertop. "What's code?"

Pavel Grigorovich was living on the streets when his fortune had seemed to change for the better when he'd helped a wounded Igor Petrushenkov avoid death by mugging, but soon found the oligarch's lifestyle stood against everything he'd fought for in his beloved Soviet Republic, he came to think of him as the enemy within, something gnawing at him on daily basis. Instead of leaving his service he bided his time, and formulated a plan, because even the toughest solider couldn't withstand a *Bratva* hunting him to the ends of the earth. And although it'd taken years of servitude and endless scheming, he'd come to the moment.

"*Nyet.*"

Grigorovich pulled him off the ground by the scruff of his neck and brought him crashing down hard enough to pop his eye socket, but not to break his neck, the screams of pain echoed through the house as Grigorovich pulled him close to his face. "What's password and activation code?"

Igor sputtered blood as he tried to answer the stoic Slavic face staring down on him. "Pppprincess...An..a...stasia," fainting from the pain.

Grigorovich swung his limp body around to the sink and ran cold water across his face then slapped him with several heavy blows before he woke up and confirmed. "Princess Anastasia is password, *da*?"

"Y... yes..." Igor sputtered.

"And what's activation code?"

Igor drooped against Grigorovich's chest. A groaning lump that no amount of money, or blatant threats could save from his inevitable demise. "Mmm...." He gargled.

Grig sniffed. Despite everything he'd despised about this man, the twisted values and selfishness that had risen from the ashes of his beloved Soviet Republic, he was still Russian, and Grig hated hurting other Russians, but there was no other way. He pulled the broken oligarch back toward him and asked one more time.

"What's activation code?"

Igor sputtered an answer. "BErlin@1989," then fell unconscious.

Grigorovich dropped the broken body to the floor and began typing on the laptop then shut it down and rebooted it. The codes were good, he had no further use of the oligarch, so he picked up and carried him out onto the stoned terrace lifted him high in the air and broke his back on his knee, then tossed him over the railing into the ocean below, "*Dasvidaniya.*"

Grig scoped the room for the butler, but there was no trace. With the job done, he packed up the computer and disappeared into the garage, scooping up the keys to the oligarch's Range Rover as he opened the automatic doors. Before he departed, he fished out his cell phone and banged in a message to an international number.

Grig: Done.

Unknown: Geneva.

Grigorovich tore out of the garage. Racing against time, he barreled toward the oligarch's private airstrip with a sense of purpose he'd not felt since his military days during assignment at the Black Sea. He lowered the windows and let the frigid ocean air sweep through the cab carrying him to another time and place as he sped toward the airfield.

GENEVA, SWITZERLAND

Derek rifled through the *Book of Family* that he'd pulled from the busted desk drawer inside the administration office. Aside from a list of the sitting members of the Council of Thirteen, it contained page after page of family lineages and noted historical events, including instances of arbitration and details of resolution, which had been the reason he'd been recalled to the Council in the first place. From their collaborative efforts over the millennia, the families had intimate knowledge of each other, but some things were kept close to the vest and only registered within the official books of the Council, especially current residential addresses. The divide between the Four European families and the Nine had widened over the last decade, especially since the last arbitration over the *Tian Zhu* incident ruled in the interest of the Nine, something that Derek felt had been a developing pattern. *Where is it?*

Despite holding meetings on a regular basis, they'd gone virtual and rarely came into physical contact with one another, except at specific society gatherings, or political events, which were outside their control. Overall, their ancient rivalries of guidance and tolerance over the speed of technological evolution remained the key sticking point to any lasting peace, something that Derek was unwilling to commit his family. Turning up nothing, Derek grabbed a captured Council assistant, and looked into his eyes as he squeezed his neck.

"Where is it?"

A pale shaking young twenty-something stared at Derek through saucer sized eyes as the murderer loomed over him, blood still smeared across his hands from the attack in the board room. "I don't know what you are looking for," he said.

Derek seethed. He reached into his pocket, pulled a knife, and slit the young man's face, "I couldn't hear you."

"Arrrgh...It's at the bottom right hand of the page in the last ten pages of the second to last chapter of the book."

Derek spun around, pulled the book toward him, and flipped through it again, breathing hard with anticipation, with the thought of finally learning the whereabouts of the *Books of Knowledge*, the ones that rested with each of the other families. He felt a fire searing his insides as his heart pounded in his chest, flipping through the book like a man possessed until, the password was revealed. He jotted down the numbers on a piece of a random page then tore it from the book, and slammed it shut, chunking it back in the drawer as he turned away. Derek flashed a look at the young man who pointed toward the far end of the room where a stone tablet laid across an elevated Diaz.

"The vault?"

The young man nodded his head. "Counterclockwise," he said through an all-consuming fear.

Derek sailed across the floor. Within seconds he'd located the tablet and shifted it counterclockwise revealing a hidden digital keypad. *Finally.* He punched in the password and a Renaissance era painting hanging on the wall popped open, which drew several pairs of eyes, curious about Derek's treasure. Because it wasn't a widely known fact that the Nine *Books of Knowledge* that others had only dreamed about in the past, which allegedly contained the ancient secrets of the human condition rested within the vaults of the Nine Council families, something the European families had coveted since the founding of the Council.

"This is it," Derek said as he reached inside.

Although the European families agreed on most Council policies, sometimes Derek's methods tested the boundaries of their approval, and this was one of those times, but none dared to voice it. He'd become their de facto leader.

"Time to downsize."

From the outside looking in, it appeared that the Hamilton-Smith family had, once again, taken the European families down a road less traveled and one that promised to end in terrible conflict. Filing into the room the other European members that'd just arrived with their security teams watched Derek open the safe, and stand still, motionless. Despite their misgivings about his methods, they knew that once they'd committed to something as serious as usurping the throne, it was always confrontational, and never bloodless. After all, the procrastination of the deployment of technology by the Nine had kept their own innovations in limbo, and further profits beyond reach, it was time. They circled around Derek vying for a glimpse of what he'd retrieved from the safe, but his hands were empty.

Derek tilted his head in disbelief —*nothing*?

A Belgian elder broke the silence, "What do we do now?"

Derek snorted a laugh. "We take control."

"But without the books how can we match the power of the Nine?" The Belgian continued placing his hand on Derek's shoulder.

"They may possess the *Books of Knowledge*, but we have our own technologies, and we know how to use them. And by the time all it's said and done we will possess their books … their wealth… and everything they hold dear."

Ending his sentence, he rounded on the young assistant and stabbed him in the heart, smiling as he let his body fall to the floor. *Nothing*? He'd risked so much for coming up empty handed, and he wasn't sure about his next move, until his questioned was answered for him with the room exploding in automatic weapon fire, forcing him into a defensive position behind a pillar. *The Silent Alarm…*

"What the hell is that?" the Belgian shouted as he fell to the floor.

Derek craned his head from behind the pillar, searching for an escape route as he knew more security were on the way. He needed an exit because the worst was yet to come. He pulled his pistol from his shoulder holster, stepped out from behind the pillar, and returned fire. "Move," he yelled, watching as the elders were ushered out the back door by his security detail.

Derek was pinned down. There was no escape. And even if there was, it was evident now that the rift that'd been building below the surface over the last millennia had exploded to the surface, and there was no going back.

"You have one way out," Council security goaded.

"Is that a fact?" Derek replied as he fixed another clip in his pistol and turned to the remaining security by his side, estimating his odds.

"We've a dozen more units arriving now, Mr. Smith, and you know that they'll never let you exit alive, even if you take us down."

Across the room Derek saw the Arbiter dripping blood onto the floor from atop the table and the lifeless body of his assistant sprawled out nearby, but Derek knew the captain was right, he was outnumbered. He had to move. With four security in tow, he readied his plan with his men. "This is it. We're going to rush them and take as many as we can."

An indistinct agreement mumbled forth from his men, "right behind you."

He watched his men exchanged quick looks at each other then stood in unison as Derek Hamilton-Smith III charged forth guns blazing against the Council security, looking beyond their doorway and up into the main gate, but when they'd come within ten feet from the captain a percussion wave threw them back as an explosion rocked the entrance. "What the fuck?"

Derek clamored to his feet shielding his eyes as he staggered toward the entrance. A plume of smoke snaked its way into the chamber as a glowing light beckoned them forward, something had cleared the way, and as they climbed the stairs the reason became clear as the massive silhouette of his Russian friend stood before him.

"Is done. We go," Grigorovich said.

Derek smirked, "You've impeccable timing my friend."

"*Spasiva*, more outside… and many people watch." He hurried the band of Council fugitives through the fire and smoke emerging from the ancient stone structure, coughing, and craning their heads scoping the terrain for any identifiable threats, searching the entire field of vision beyond the scared pedestrians and puzzled tourists.

Derek jumped into the Range Rover as he watched Grigorovich pulled an automatic shotgun from behind the seat, spin around, and pepper an incoming van until it veered off into a brick building. "Let's go Grig!"

The stoic Russian pulled two grenades from his vest and hurled them at another incoming SUV as he jumped in the passenger seat next to Derek, "We go."

A double fireball engulfed the remaining security guards and van as the bystanders scrambled in every direction, some running inside the Council building, and others falling to the ground, rolling beneath any nearby structure.

Checking the rearview for anyone in pursuit, Derek noted they were clear, for the time being. After a quick headcount her turned to Grig.

"What's the verdict?"

"She doesn't know. Igor was one with code."

"And you believed her?"

"*Da.*"

Derek twitched a smile. The thought of deploying *IRIN* against the Nine and their American allies warmed him inside, something he'd spent years in the planning was finally coming through, and now it was time to reap the rewards.

42

GENEVA INTERNATIONAL AIRPORT, SWITZERLAND

A picturesque winter wonderland greeted Johnny Dekker as his jet landed at Geneva International Airport, he'd not seen this amount of snow in over fifteen years, and never with this amount of uniformity, but today was about business nothing else mattered. The American had a line on Anja Singh, and he was going to bring her down once and for all, but the perfect snow conditions presented a new problem —people. Because of the spectacular weather conditions the roads and rails were packed with snowboarders and skiers all thinking about the same thing, get to slopes, by any means necessary.

The snow had arrived early and in force but had yet to be cleared from the roads between Geneva and his destination, meaning his travel time had just been extended by another ninety minutes, or more. *Damnit.* Johnny acknowledged the driver's update, got in the car, dropped his bag on the seat beside him, and unzipped his jacket readying for his hours-long journey. As they began to move through the city, he struggled with the revelations his father had dropped about Anja's background and his evasive tactics around the detailed truth, something was wrong. Why was his father holding back? What was his father holding back? It was all one thing to not have briefed him on an old operation, but unnerving to not clarify his relationship with the assassin. Nothing made sense, and he knew nothing could make sense, until he'd caught up with Hannah and her gal pal across the French border.

Everything was about to get sticky. Johnny knew that whether Hannah had known about Anja's benefactor was beside the point, she'd aided and abetted the enemy, and Mossad or not she'd have to answer for her actions. Johnny leaned forward speaking to his driver.

"Is there any other way to Chamonix?"

The driver raised an eyebrow eyeing the impatient American in the rearview mirror, and replied with a smile, "*Oui, un helicoptere?*"

Johnny blanched. "*Non, non, helicoptere, merci.*"

Defeated, the beleaguered banker fell back into his seat and retreated into his thoughts as the outside world faded around him, the stillness ushering in a complete if not melancholy scene. Johnny replayed the most recent sequence of events in his mind, tuning out the surrounding wonderland, and focusing in on one thought —Anja Singh. She proved the one constant figure around this entire chain of events, nobody else had risen above her, whether she was the ultimate antagonist remained to be seen, but she was next on his kill list.

Johnny shifted in his seat and squinted at the odometer through the gap in the front seats. *40kph, Jesus?* Hannah might as well have sent him smoke signals for all the good modern transportation had allowed given the snowfall. Trying to keep positive he sighed and fished out his cell phone twisting it in several directions, but the result was the signal was in and out, nothing useful. He was thankful his father was alive, but he was not happy about his disinformation campaign. After all, he'd passed his seat on the Council to him, which usually had included an entire inventory of personal and professional accounting of assets and ongoing operations, none of his talks with his father post his ascension had mentioned Anja Singh, let alone how he'd been involved with her and her mother. Once everything was settled with the assassin, Johnny knew he'd have to rethink the Council and the Dekker Group structure, whether others agreed or not, something had to change. It was time for the labyrinth of lies and deceit that had led to the death of his fiancée at the reckless management at the Company to come to an end.

A low repetitive thumping sound pulled Johnny him from his thought. His body moved like he'd been asleep for hours, twisted in an awkward position, cutting the circulation to his legs, but after checking his watch, he was astonished at it only reading twenty minutes since the last rest stop. He stared at the round-faced driver who'd turned around toward him.

"*Monsieur*, wake up," the driver said.

"What? Are we there?"

"*Non*, there's an accident blocking the road, it'll take time to clear."

"Why did you wake me?"

"Because, *Monsieur*, there's a rest stop ahead and perhaps you..."

Johnny felt his balled-up fists pop, wondering for a fleeting moment if the driver was working for the enemy, until he came to his senses and agreed to the stop. "Back here in five minutes."

"*D'accord*, okay," the driver said as he exited and shuffled off to the toilet.

Once he'd dismissed his driver, Johnny fished out his cell phone for a quick check, which to his surprise was registering three full bars. *Shit*. He stopped on the spot and punched in Jack's cell number. RING...RING...RING...He flipped the phone around and scrolled through his messages, nothing. Inside he knew that if something had happened, someone from the Company or the Dekker Group would've figured out a way to contact him. Only...It had been a couple of days and he was oblivious to any new developments on the ground stateside. Did they manage to shut down the rogue algorithms? Did the markets stabilize? Did his bank recover from its loss? *Still no answer*.

"*Voila*," the jolly French driver said as he returned from the toilets, loaded Johnny back in the car, and eased into the thinning traffic.

Entangled on side of the road, Johnny saw that it'd been two sports cars crowned with ski gear that had caused the delay, nothing out of the ordinary, but a nuisance all the same. He'd given up on connecting with Jack, so he tried Hannah, but concerned he'd blow her cover, he messaged her instead. Stabbing a quick query.

Johnny: WTF?

Staring down at his phone, the signal bars had disappeared, and an alert popped up on his screen — NOT SENT — he was traveling through another dead-zone, but at least the driver had picked up the pace. The Mercedes E350 was barreling up the valley toward Chamonix Village, and the unsuspecting assassin he'd been tracking around the world. He had his answers. Now, he wanted more.

Anja Singh was a spook. She'd been a clandestine operative under his father at the Company several years before his induction into the family business. It was unclear whether she'd been a Russian mafia stooge before she was recruited or after his father failed to save her mother from an FSB sanctioned kidnapping, anything was possible in this day and age. Johnny grimaced as the thoughts rain through his mind. He was gearing up for arrival and the final confrontation, but first, he wanted to know everything she had on the *Akehmenov Bratva*, and she was going to tell him. Something in the back of his mind knew that she'd flipped, and it was because of his father and his miscalculation. Despite his years of training recruits from the Farm, the elder Dekker disregarded something on his rogue operative, something from her psychological profile. Johnny knew that without questioning her himself, they'd never know why or how deep her treachery ran, or who was responsible for Chloe's death in Malaysia. He pulled a water bottle from the seat pocket and finished it. He knew Hannah's temper. He'd seen it in her eyes in London. She was driven but lost in an uncontrollable bloodlust for the woman that'd cast her aside and left her for dead without any chance of absolution.

Johnny fidgeted with his phone as he imagined the possible scenarios in which Hannah killed her prey. But then, why the call?

Why'd she want Johnny to know that she'd found her target and was going in for the kill? Nothing made sense.

∽

STEAM ROSE from Hannah's cup as she sipped her piping black coffee perched like a predatory eagle on a craggy cliff awaiting her unwitting prey, biding her time in the emerging daylight. The Israeli spy leered through sleep deprived eyes at the churning crowds of tourists below as they arrived and hurried about collecting their skis and lining up for various cable cars that serviced the areas multiple ski runs, all leading to spectacular peaks. Over the last twenty-four hours, the snow conditions had improved with every hour of snowfall, and with the rising sun now offered a perfect powder. Hannah knew Anja detested hotels and was more likely shacked up at a private chateau in the area, so the best she could hope for was to catch her off guard navigating the small village square and take her by surprise. Something brushed her back as she took another sip of her coffee, someone was behind her.

"Excuse me miss. Would you like another coffee?"

Hannah smiled at the waiter. "Americano, please," she replied.

Although she'd been directed to the alpine village by the metadata of a message from her former controller, how and when they'd connect hadn't been established, and Hannah wanted to flip the script and surprise the Russian whore who'd left her for dead in the Serpentine. As she collected her thoughts and loosened her scarf, she was startled by another interruption. When she turned toward the woman tapping her on the shoulder she saw her standing with her partner, young daughter, and a camera.

"Excuse me, could you please help us take a photo?" she asked.

Hannah put her empty coffee cup down and manufactured smile as she stood up and took the camera from the woman, "Sure." After she'd taken the photo and flashed a caring smile, the woman leaned into her left ear, ensuring only Hannah could hear her words.

"Your friend said she'd meet you in five minutes at *Telepherique de l'Aiguille du Midi.*" She stared at a dumbfounded Hannah, then followed up in English, "You know, the Aiguille du Midi cable car."

Hannah blanched. She dismissed the woman as she spun around three hundred and sixty degrees, preparing for anything, then stopped, looked at the woman and handed her camera back to her. *If it's games, you want. It's games she'll get.*

The perplexed French woman scratched her head. "She was standing right there," she said to the Israeli, but she too had disappeared.

Hannah hurried back to her room, scooped up some essentials including her ankle holster and a couple extra clips she'd taken from the men at the airport, and stuffed in an overnight bag. Within a few minutes she was out the door and making her way across the village toward the *Aiguille du Midi* Cable Car counter.

Everything accelerated in her mind as she tore through the slush-filled streets, unwilling to allow the increased traffic and hordes of skiers slow her down as she closed in on her prey. Scoping every alleyway and storefront she passed, she wasn't leaving any stone unturned nor be led into an obvious trap. When she arrived at her destination, she slammed both hands on the ticket counter, purchasing a round trip ticket shilling out more than enough euro from her pocket. "*Merci,*" she said as she stepped away from the counter, hanging back with an eye on the entrance.

Hannah Jankowski was a deep cover Mossad agent, fielded at an extremely young age, but who'd always maintained a mission focused state of mind, until it became personal. The records showed that after the Mossad had intercepted information labeling Anja Singh, an ex-CIA operative, as a rouge agent that had falsified her own death, rather than informing Langley they put Hannah on her. Director Levy saw an opportunity to leverage this rogue American that'd landed inside the Russian mafia with access to its top members. Without hesitation Hannah accepted the mission and set off for Singapore. Once she'd arrived in Singapore and networked her way through the night life, she found her in at a modeling agency. Despite the American's training, Hannah proved the superior intellect and hadn't left her side until the Malaysia assassination. When she discovered the Russians were using Anja to steal the Archangel source code from CIA, Director Levy moved her closer to the one-time American spy, which made it personal, but it was betrayal that had brought her to France.

43

BUMBLEHIVE

Booming audible alerts echoed through the emptied hallways and server stacks of the NSA hackers' secret lair tucked away in the remote Utah landscape buried under hundreds of tons of rock, everything Jack had wanted, because the deafening alerts meant that Director Moore had been successful, he'd cut off *IRI* from the outside world. Instead, Jack looked down at Dr. Jane Ridley with a long face and shook his head. "We're dead."

A puzzled Jane winced in pain. "What are you talking about?"

"What did you mean when you said to shut *IRI* down?"

Jane blanched, "What?" She ignored her burns and sat up reached out and pulled Jack toward her with every ounce of strength she could muster. "Please tell me you didn't shut *IRI* down... Jack...Please..."

"You were semi-conscious and had burns all over your body. The systems were crashing across the entire bunker, and we ran out of time."

"Jack what did you do?"

Jack felt a pain turning in the pit of his stomach. "I called Moore."

Jane wobbled her charred blood-caked body to her desk, reaching for her phone and dialing Fort Meade. "Did they redeploy Echelon? What's our defense? Who's running it?" Jane paused. "Hello, Director Moore, it's urgent." She stood silent for a long minute then turned to Jack, face devoid of expression, mouth unable to voice words as she hung up the phone.

Jack quirked an eyebrow. "It's still online? We've gotta chance?"

A wave of exhaustion swept over Jane as she fell back into her chair, threw her hands crashing down on her desk and looked up at Jack. "Moore's dead."

From his time at the Naval Academy in Maryland, Jack had never been known to react the way others reacted, it wasn't his training it was natural, and in fact Jane had only known Jack to have lost his shit only once in his life, and that was on the death of his kid sister at a hack-a-thon they'd attended together before the academy, but the realization of his mentor's death, the death that he'd caused triggered something inside him.

"Fuuuuuck!" Jack screamed ripping the phone from the desk and bouncing it off the bulletproof enclosure.

Silence followed the pain. An assistant had found a severe burn medical kit in the onsite infirmary and returned to help the director, but midway through the bandaging, Jane motioned her off with a smile, stood up, and limped back into the empty control room, dragging Jack behind her. The hacker team had vacated to another location and had yet to radio back with their progress. They needed to get ready for whatever the team found once they got jacked back into the grid. Despite the several technicians working around the AI server stacks and the assistant making herself useful checking the remaining power sources, Jane turned to Jack as she propped herself against the table and grieved for their lost mentor. "It wasn't your fault, we're under attack, and there's no better way to go out then for God and Country," she whispered in Jack's ear.

Jack brushed his sleeve across his face like a little kid who'd just watched his dog put down but readied himself for the future. "Let's get back to the point. What the hell happened with *IRI*?"

A lumped jammed in her throat as Jane squinted her eyes and

turned away, recalling the exact steps she'd taken when checking on the activation sequence with *IRI* in the server room. "One minute, I was confirming the protocols and the next my hands were bonded to the terminal interface, I couldn't let go, I tried, but it had me."

Jack paused a long moment. "Was *IRI* talking?"

An expressionless Jane shook her head. "As I said, I can't remember. I was working at the terminal when a jolt of electricity hit me and threw me clear across the room. It was like I'd hit a nerve. What do we do now, Jack?"

"We've already begun the shut down and reboot protocols, and that's the reason you don't hear IRI giving me the third degree about your current status."

Jane smiled. "Well, we'd better make sure it's not been compromised."

The NSA operator leered back at his host. "That depends on how well you've trained your team since splitting off from us at the Fort. They should be getting jacked in by now and have a clear assessment of the magnitude of the breach."

"What about Moore?"

Jack straightened his back and looked out toward the server room, replying in a firm tone. "What about 'em? We've got a job to do, and not much time to do it."

Jane scoffed, letting the animated hacker brush past her. "After you," she said, burying her satisfaction of his refocused state of mind, and trying to keep up with his accelerated gait.

Pearls of sweat formed on his brow as Jack approached the main terminal interface where Jane had been electrocuted. Without bringing IRI back online he rebooted the system and prepared to reconnect with the team he'd sent to the backup site if they'd made it in time.

"Grab that chair," he said, pointing at a folding chair one of the technicians was using as he inspected the power relays.

Jane shrugged. "What?"

Without missing a beat, Jack stepped across the room, snatched up the chair, and placed it beside him at the terminal. "You shouldn't be standing."

Once he'd logged into the system, Jack saw that the entire defense network remained on high alert, but nothing major had exploded in the time that they'd cut *IRI* off from the main servers. He reached into his pocket and pulled out a small leather-bound notebook and flipped it open. Scanning through the text he found what he'd been looking for and began to bang away at the keyboard in front of him, while Jane Ridley slouched in the chair. Knowing that IRI was down at the moment of its activation, and that Echelon had been taken offline as well meant every wasted moment was an eternity of national security risk. There was no time to spare.

"Did they get Echelon back online?" Jane asked.

Focused on the screen Jack continued typing, "Not yet."

Every keystroke echoed through his mind as he rabbited the keyboard with endless commands and overrides, nothing was happening. Before they'd been taken offline, he remembered seeing familiar code, something that wasn't relevant at the time came screaming back to him as he searched the dormant system. The NSA team had tried to repel the infiltration attempt, but the response had been the NSA developed source code named Archangel. *How the hell did they get their hands on it?* He paused a moment. *When would they've had the chance?* From the back of his mind his conversation with Izzy about infected controllers in the Dekker Banking Group's server stacks all made sense. The connection remained unclear, but it didn't, not yet, but there was something more to it than just infected hardware.

"Who else, besides your team, had access to this system? What I mean is who else had access to the *Archangel* source code?"

Jane winced in obvious pain as she sat upright. "Only a handful of our hackers that spearheaded Project Asian Games."

"American?"

She tilted her head in confusion. "Well, it was a joint operation."

Jack breathed a long sigh. "*8200.*"

"That's right, the Israelis executed the end run around some coding issues, and their operatives uploaded the code into the air-gapped computer terminal."

Jack dropped his head. "They tweaked the code."

"It's what brought it all down," Jane replied.

Jack blanched. "They used our own code against us. They installed a rootkit on some server hardware delivered to corporations across the Eastern coast of the United States, this was an eloquent and flawless deployment."

"What hardware?"

Jack put his hand on her shoulder. "The same programmable logic controllers our teams compromised during Asian Games. My guess is that they wanted it to piggyback across our networks and find *IRI* and copy its files."

"Who the hell had their hands on our code?"

A smirk stretched across his face, "...the Russians."

Jane stood up and leaned against the metal server stack rising over Jack as he banged away at the keyboard, ensuring everything was locked down and secured, while *IRI* remained disconnected and dormant. "They must've only had a partial download. Otherwise..."

Jack interrupted. "Otherwise, we'd be speaking Russian by now."

From the beginning, the assassination attempt, the attacks on the financial markets, the redirecting of resources, everything had been a carefully orchestrated ploy to expose and infiltrate America's ultimate twenty-first century artificial intelligence source code —Archangel.

Although he'd been passed over to head up the program, Director Moore had Jack read into the continuation of the Archangel program, a compartmentalized section that had branched off from the main group. Knowing about its deployment to replace the Echelon and supplant US CyberCommand it fell well within his security clearance and an integral part of his SIGINT mandate. It was that code that Jack had recognized earlier when the TAO team had stripped back the *junk code* attempting to piggyback in over their attack commands. He'd seen the identifiers as plain as day, but had dismissed them without another thought, until know. That was the point of contact, that was their exposure to the Archangel chimera —*IRI*.

Jane tapped Jack on the shoulder as a technician approached. "Dr. Ridley, we've got the system scan results," he said.

Jack stood up and read over the report with Jane. "So, *IRI* wasn't breached?"

A supervisor stepped forward and stood shoulder-to-shoulder with his technician and explained. "It looks like there were several malicious attempts to piggyback in over our outgoing command stream, but the firewall, and some sophisticated security protocols, prevented that from happening."

Jack sighed. "But the question remains...Why'd *IRI* skip the sequence?"

"Perhaps it's identified the incoming threat, and wanted to stop it," Jane replied and then leaned her failing body on Jack while they stared at the looming Supercomputer in front of them, lying dormant, waiting for its opportunity to plead its case in person.

STELLAR WIND

Samantha Withers led her team through the secured underground tunnels between their bunker and the data collection facility, aside from the Fort on the other side of the country, it was the only place that they'd be able to force their way back into the system. Following the emergency shutdown, they'd wiped and rebooted their entire local network, suspending all incoming traffic to the hive, creating a virtual moat around themselves and *IRI*, until an inexplicable bug crashed their systems, leaving them with no alternatives.

Under the direction of the visiting NSA department head, Jack Sorenson, the team vacated the hive and hurried toward the nearest backup site. The physical distance proved their first challenge. Despite their company mandated exercise regime, the mile-long sprint after being nestled up in front of a computer for the last 48 hours with a 20-pound backpack bouncing off the spine wasn't the easiest feat, especially with the adrenaline rushing through the body knowing that the country's defense network was at risk for every moment you lingered. The perspiring team leader looked over her shoulder.

"Let's go people," she encouraged, stopping for a moment until the last analyst swooped past her, then ran alongside him as they neared the exit.

Nobody knew their responsibility to the country more than this group of programmers, when all else had failed they were the nation's last line of defense, an understanding that fueled their breakneck pace across the last hundred yards. The AI had gone off the rails on their watch, and it was up to them to bring it back under control.

Once they'd arrived at the magnetically sealed door, Withers moved through the group, opened a small metal box hinged on the side panel and punched in a numerical sequence, then submitted a retinal scan unlocking the double-hinged doors, allowing them access.

"Here we go. When we hit the SCIF, initiate the Uriel Protocol, and find out what in the hell happened today," Withers bellowed.

After a few twists and turns, the team emerged through another subterranean doorway, which led them deeper into the bedrock and the labyrinth of sub-levels below an NSA data collection center, and a secondary compartmentalized SCIF. The room was simple. Plain concrete walls squared out the space lined with motion sensor lighting and twelve stand-alone computer terminals, each with separate fiber optic connections, something built for purpose.

"Withers, we need you to initiate the servers," a colleague shouted slamming her backpack on her workspace as she looked at her team leader.

Samantha Withers grunted confirmation and slid into a chair and pulled herself toward a workstation. With her legs under the table and the team unpacking in her peripheral she punched in a random series of numbers through the telephone and the entire SCIF blinked to life, consuming the silence with a rapturous sound of echoing keystrokes. "Let's get it done, people."

Since arriving at NSA, Samantha Withers had proven herself time and again, on domestic and foreign operations, nothing was beyond her scope of capability and was the reason Dr. Ridley had trusted her above all others. Besides her coding skillset, she was a mathematical savant, seeing connections where others saw gibberish, making the impossible possible, and leaving a job unfinished. Withers paced the floor looking over her team as one by one they jacked into their systems.

"It looks clean," one of the programmers shouted.

Withers slowed her breathing. "Confirmation, please?"

Another member chimed in with a relieving answer. "Confirmed."

Despite the *downtime*, the team had managed to stave off the incoming multi-headed attack long enough for whomever to cut the link and keep *IRI* from an actual network penetration. *Thank God.* Withers breathed a cautious sigh of relief as she panned her sterile smile left and right, and then returned to her seat at the end of the row. She checked her watch. *Time to check in.*

"Great job people," she said giving them one last look before she picked up the phone and dialed the hive bunker.

"Dr. Ridley, we're in."

A long silent pause hung over the phone, "Well done, Samantha."

Withers straightened her back. "I'm sorry it took so long."

Jane blanched, then continued. "According to the logs, it looks like the hackers failed to penetrate the firewall, so you and your team got the job done. And there's nothing sorry about that Samantha."

Withers smiled. "And don't worry, we'll find the bastard, ma'am."

"Samantha, I think it's time you called me Jane."

An itching sensation manifested behind her ear as Withers paused a long moment then replied. "Okay, Dr. Ridley."

The two programmers shared a short laugh as they hung up the phone and got busy on their tasks, not knowing what the future held, only that *IRI* was safe, for the moment. Now they'd needed to ensure the national network hadn't been compromised and that

Echelon and the rest of CyberCommand were still functioning per normal.

Withers shifted her focus back to the team. She wasn't sure who'd attempted the hack, but she knew that the country's adversaries were watching, something they'd been doing more and more since the NSA's own cyber toolkit had appeared on the web. It wasn't long before they'd have to defend the network again, which meant assessing the current vulnerabilities was job one.

A couple of seats down a lead appeared. "Samantha, I've found something."

Sam stood up and looked over the other analyst's shoulder. "You can see it here...and here...and here," he said.

"Can you pull the first instance back up?"

"Right here. Look at that, it's almost the same pattern as *IRI*."

A wave of anger swept over the team leader as her worst fears had been realized, it was a mutated form of their Archangel source code. "Damnit."

"It all traces back to London. I've got all the information you need if we need to get boots on the group ASAP." Withers wasn't the only one that was angry, her entire time had spent the better part of their adult lives building the artificial intelligence and working to safeguard the nation, they wanted revenge, maybe even more than Withers or Dr. Ridley, but that was youth. "Or we can pass it along to GCHQ and get them to run it down," he said.

"That won't be necessary. Keep gathering everything you can and make damn sure you're working with CyberCommand, and we've got our defenses up, and ready for anything that might come our way while we're running at suboptimal capacity until we reassess *IRI* and if it can be deployed."

"I'm on it."

Withers rose to her feet. Knowing she needed more information on where they stood on keeping the defense network humming along, she paced a few steps then turned back to her terminal. She punched in her authorization code for the encrypted line to Fort Meade, which was routed to SCIF 17, and its acting lead.

"This is Mike."

"This is Samantha Withers at UDC, Stellar Wind."

An overjoyed Mike shouted into the phone. "You're alive."

Withers snorted a laugh. "We fell down a rabbit hole. Anyway, we've been in contact with the bunker and the project is intact, nothing's been infiltrated, and the genie's still in the bottle."

Mike Chambers let out a long sigh. "Wait, you're not at the Hive?"

"Correct, but listen…"

Withers spotted another incoming call winking at her; it was the bunker. She apologized and put Mike on hold, and conferenced in the bunker, no time to ask whether it was the right call. "Dr. Ridley I've Mike Chambers from SCIF 17 at Fort Meade on the line with us, and I was about to explain to him our thinking about the malware," she said.

A male voice replied. "Dr. Ridley's resting, but let's go through it."

Several years ago, Samantha Withers and Dr. Jane Ridley were part of an interagency task force working with a strategic ally in combating a rising nuclear threat, which had been an ongoing initiative over several political administrations. Over the course of its research, it'd leveraged a previous source code named Project Archangel developed by the US intelligence community, now spread over several different departments. Once they'd completed the customization, it was slipped onto a scientist's computer that then jumped an air-gapped control system, and thereby infiltrating its facility's operating system, something that proved to be a double-edged sword. Withers paced the floor as she explained what she could with the CIA deputy, and current project lead.

"As you know building code from the ground up with embedded encryption is the most efficient and safe way to secure any code. If you attempt to alter its state once it's been initiated, then you run degradation risk."

"Yes, it's coding 101," Jack said.

Withers paused a long moment. "My working hypothesis as to

why our enemy needed to risk losing it all is that their altered code was degrading."

"Altered?" Jack asked.

"Although it was a small operation with only a handful of programmers involved, it was a joint operation, and aside from Ridley and me there were two others from Unit 8200 that had access to the source code. And under pressure from their government, they tweaked the code."

"Are you freakin' kidding me?" Mike bellowed.

Withers paused again. "That tweak is why we're in this mess."

Jack breathed a hard sigh. "What happened?"

"They altered the code to produce a higher rate of results, which led to the malware's detection by the nuclear scientists, ending what had been a very successful program," Withers said.

Jack grunted. "That said, the 8200 tweaks weakened the source code and the main reason the hackers need to reconnect to Archangel source code, because the original code was undetectable."

"Thank God for small miracles," Withers snorted.

"And without the key sequencing, the chimera's not only detectable but also prone to premature degradation. What are they missing? A termination date?" Mike asked.

"Exactly. So, to get access to the original source code, they had to stage an assault so invasive that we'd be forced to reveal our AI, before it was ready," Withers replied.

An uneasy silence fell over the connection, all three participants searching their minds for words, a plan, or anything that could stave off another attack, but it all came back to getting *IRI* online.

Jane Ridley choked a cough. "Whatever we do next, we need to understand that the hard shut down, means we cannot reactivate IRI until we get both the NSA and NRO directors okay, and with Director Moore deceased…We need a plan B, and we need it now."

"I'll keep the team here focused on clearing and double checking everything inside the UDC and the Hive for anything out of the ordinary and leave the reactivation to you three," Withers said.

Jane looked at Jack and nodded. "All right, Mike get back to us once you've got the go-ahead on the clearance, or at least who I've gotta talk to."

"It's a little crazy around here at the moment with the deputy director overseas, but I'll get back ASAP," Mike said as he dropped off the line.

"Dr. Ridley, we've found something," Withers said taking the file from the analyst scanning through it as she continued with her update.

Jack cut a side eye at Jane. "Well, what is it Withers?"

Withers folded the paper and replied. "There's a time decay in their coding."

"It had an accelerated decay?" Jack asked.

Jane raised an eyebrow, keeping her pride in her team hidden and at bay as they question the team leader. "In other words, the chimera *IRIN* couldn't exploit any zero-day vulnerabilities as their code began decaying on implementation."

"Affirmative Dr. Ridley, it looks like it had a 48-hour shelf life."

Jack chimed in. "I want you to write a program to run a deep scan across the neural networks starting with ours. I want all networks to remain isolated until such time we find there are no residual *IRIN* elements burrowed down in some remote corner of our network. This needs to happen now."

"We're two steps ahead of you, Mr. Sorenson," Withers replied then hung up the phone and huddled with her team of hackers.

44

MANHATTAN, NEW YORK

Derek Hamilton-Smith straightened his tie, ran his fingers through his thick locks of golden hair, and stepped out of his Bentley Azure into the bright mid-morning sun at 666 Park Avenue in Manhattan, far from the blood-soaked stones he'd left in Geneva only hours earlier. Putting distance between himself and the unfortunate events at Council headquarters was essential. Everything had unfolded quicker than he'd estimated, but in line with his overall plan. With all the pieces now in motion he had little time to salvage the attack on the US infrastructure, which meant he had to move fast to wipe his Council opposition once and for all.

After he'd secured the activation codes from Grigorovich and dispatched him on his final mission, the Belgian aristocrat jumped on his jet landing in his North American base of operations in New York City. Derek knew that once the Nine Council families allied with the Dekkers realized what he'd perpetrated in Switzerland he'd be a marked man, which meant he'd have to strike first, and strike them at the heart of their collective empires —Manhattan.

"Good morning," a pair of private security guards greeted the immaculately dressed banker emerging from his car, pausing in the shadow of the ominous Manhattan address before passing his satchel to his assistant and moved toward the building.

Approaching them, Derek flashed an arrogant grin, "Indeed."

Over the last few hours, Derek had managed to inform several of his elite guards that he'd landed in New York and arranged for their assistance, but nothing save his internal navigational radar could save him from the river of people that meandered down the sidewalk between him and his destination. Bumping several people on the way, nobody complained given he was flanked by two hulking security guards and wore his constant look of disdain.

As they approached the revolving doors, a vibration erupted in his pocket, prompting him to fish out his cell phone, and check an incoming text.

COUNCIL ALERT: *All stations update. Attack has been quelled. Attackers are on the run. Standby for further updates.*

DEREK SNORTED a laugh and shoved his cell phone back in his pocket, beaming with pride, and sweeping past the checkpoint security with a faint scowl scrawled across his face, relishing the damage he'd inflicted on the Council. *Too bad they felt compelled to rule against me.* With his adversaries preoccupied, and the US government still chasing its tail, Derek moved his plan into its final phase. After all, with the European families behind him, he now held the BIS committee in one hand, and the chimera AI known as *IRIN in the other*, which empowered him to whatever end he desired, or so he thought.

Using the United Nations General Assembly as cover, he'd arranged for a meeting of the Four European families in New York, leaving the attack on the Office of Audit behind them, and focusing on the future of the Council. Derek stepped into his corner office, asked the assistant for some coffee, and picked up a land line as he sat down behind his mahogany desk.

"This is Derek."

A straining voice answered. "The *traitor*! What do you want?"

Derek paused a long moment. "We need to convene a meeting of the Council in the next forty-eight hours."

A choking laugh echoed down the connection. "You're not in the position to convene anything, you and your family have been expelled from the Council, by the rules of the founding Charter."

Derek quirked an eyebrow. The man seemed convinced; the Belgian had to be clearer. "Interesting, however, if you look deeper into the fine print of that Charter, you'll see that a founding member can call a meeting at anytime, anywhere, for any purpose, even when they've been accused of treason, it's a founder's right, and nothing a paper pushing bureaucrat like you can do about it, except make it happen. Unless you want to explain to the Thirteen families how you started a way?"

"This is not over."

Derek smirked. "Please inform the Council that I, Derek Hamilton-Smith IIII, and my house, request the presence of all primary and secondary chairs of the families at the St. Regis Hotel in New York City, in two days. Thank you."

"You dare…"

Looking down at the street below, Derek hung up the phone, ignoring the ranting man on the other end of the line. *Let the games begin*. He reached into his pocket, pulled out his cell phone, and sent a group message across their internal encrypted network warning his European allies of the coming conflict, and requesting their presence in New York forthwith.

The plan was in motion. A plan triggered by the Council itself, something unexpected, but within the Charter bylaws. Once Derek had accepted the arbitration of the Himalayan incident and looked inward for a resolution, an end game appeared on its own, a binding resolution to the centuries old feud between the two founding members.

Derek held confident in the evidence, confident in the power of the Council bylaws over the other families, and their respect of the law. Whether or not order was restored to the Council of Thirteen relied on the Nine and their adherence to Council law, not on the Europeans, because it was the Nine that had failed in their obligations. Failing to deploy the technologies from the *Books of Knowledge* under the Geneva Summit timeframe had derailed necessary commercial and medical advancements, and tempted fate's intervention.

~

FELIX FERNANDEZ WAS a loyal member of the House of Berenger, he was also a former special forces commando, and a commander of the Council of Thirteen global security team. Since the end of his career in the British special forces, he and his men had protected the Nine families and their Associates, and eventually took reasonability for the security of the Council of Thirteen facilities scattered around the world. It was a big job, but one that he'd taken to heart and solved to give his utmost focus and effort. Solving to bring the murderers of the Geneva facility to justice, he'd launched an immediate internal investigation, which included interviewing the heads of the Four European Council families. Fernandez knew that with a little pressure, he'd confirm Derek Hamilton-Smith's role, but he needed the evidence.

"Sir, it's been confirmed."

Fernandez paused white knuckling his cell phone. "Where is he?"

"The fugitive's plane touched down in New York about an hour ago."

Fernandez blinked satisfaction. "Perfect, then I'll have someone to dine with on my return flight." He closed the call, tapped the driver, and instructed him to their new destination — on Park Avenue.

Fernandez seethed. While he and his team had been in New York protecting the Berenger family, their headquarters had been attacked, and still echoed fresh in their minds as he turned to his team and informed them that the mastermind behind that attack was now within their reach.

"This is a top priority mission. We're bringing in one of our own."

Several men exchanged bewildered looks not understanding what their captain was telling them, straining to understand his meaning. "What?"

Fernandez twisted his body around a hundred and eighty degrees and clarified his statement. "We're bringing in the man responsible for Geneva."

The men grunted in unison.

"What do we do when we get him?"

Fernandez flashed a smile. "We bring 'em back for trial."

A deafening silence spoke volumes to the disappointment of his men as the driver navigated the increased flow of traffic caused by the United Nations session, which never disappointed in turning the entire island of Manhattan into a grind. And with the increased foot traffic, Fernandez knew the approach was more complicated than a simple snatch. He unfolded a map, clicked on the overhead light, and began emphasizing the angle of approach on their unsuspecting target most likely holed up at his building on 666 Park Avenue, at least that was the theory.

∽

DEREK LEERED down at the city. A filthy, loud, American metropolis, which in his assessment possessed nothing of charm or grandeur worth anything that he couldn't get on a back-alley tour across any city on the European continent. The city lacked character and the people lacked class. Perhaps these were the reasons his father had always detested attending the Council meetings in the city, but they'd never discussed it, the new world wasn't interesting to his father.

From the moment Grigorovich had passed him the *IRIN* codes, he'd dreamed of launching phase two —the final assault, which scheduled leaving the United States, its characterless cities, and its classless financiers destitute and broken. A knock on the door pulled his attention toward his assistant entering the room with a tray in her hands.

"Sir, here's your cup of tea. Do you need anything else?"

Derek breathed a sigh, stood up, and walked back to his desk. Ignoring his assistant, he flipped open his laptop and keyed in a couple of passwords as she retreated from his field of vision. Once, he'd connected through his TOR server, he logged into the *IRIN* program that the Russians had created, readied, and tested, leaving the sole remaining task of unleashing its unlimited power at his fingertips.

Once he'd accessed the program, he typed in several infected servers illuminated on the screen, it was do or die time. He highlighted the Dekker Banking Group Manhattan server and entered the second password, but after a quick flashing light dissipated, nothing happened. Derek grabbed the laptop with both hands and spun it around on his desk looming over it like a task master ready to punish a defiant servant. He studied the *IRIN* interface and tried again, but the second password failed to activate any of the infected servers. He seethed thinking back on the chain of custody, everything pointed back to Anja Singh.

Derek reached for his cell phone fuming with anger, ready to rip the treacherous operative apart with his bare hands when the door splintered open and a dozen FBI agents flooded his corner office, motioning him to drop the phone and raise his hands in the air. He complied, but only after he'd shut his laptop.

"I said don't move goddamnit," the voice barked.

A wave of anger swept over the Belgian, because not only was he one of the most powerful bankers in the world, but he'd always found it convenient to ensure he served on the official diplomatic corps of multiple countries, should the unexpected scenario of that moment arise. "What's the meaning of this? What right do you have to come crashing into my office?"

A bright green-eyed woman stepped up and looked deep into his soul and explained the situation, "Be glad I don't kick you in the balls *Herr* Schmidt."

"Do you know who I am? I've got diplomatic immunity."

The agent scoffed as her team seized pinned his security team to the ground, seizing their weapons and cuffing them while they laid face down. Derek blanched and knew he'd been set up as the agent turned him around and slapped cuffs on his wrists.

"You have the right to remain silent..."

Derek flailed in disgust. "How dare you treat me like some common criminal in my own place of..." But, before he could finish his sentence, another agent stepped over, sized him up with a quick glance, then pulled the arresting agent out of earshot. He watched while the several agents rummaged through everything, including his laptop, but tagging and bagging it after a couple of failed login attempts. The Belgian felt a pair of powerful hands grab him by his shoulder and guide him to the sofa as he continued his protest.

"This is illegal. You've got no right..."

"Shut up terrorist," an agent replied.

Derek fell back into the sofa cushions. Scanning the room from his helpless vantage point he registered Homeland Security and DEA agents arriving on the scene and milling around in mild conversation while cycling through his belongings. The thoroughness in which they dissected his office led to only one conclusion, someone had set him up. It was clear from the amount of manpower and cross-agency task force cooperation he was witnessing meant someone had alerted them to his involvement in the infrastructure hack, which meant Anja Singh had not only lied about the code but set him up. *Not just a pretty face after all*. Derek twisted in the steel handcuffs as they dug into his wrists, but fell silent, biding his time, and waiting for his lawyer. Smiling as he was marched through the lobby of his own building, Derek held his head high. Despite the awkwardness of the arrest, he knew how this ended up, and his first order of business once he was released.

∼

Fernandez blanched. Sitting in the front passenger's seat of the tactical Suburban, he saw a myriad of flashing lights surrounding the Park Avenue building now only a block and change away, their destination. "What the hell?"

As the traffic ahead of their vehicle slowed, the driver pointed out several Slavic looking individuals standing just beyond the ring of police and Homeland Security vehicles. Fernandez felt a rush of adrenaline burst through his system as he realized, they'd found their man, but taking him into custody was going to be tricky, they'd have to put in some work. He focused his attention on the two hulking individuals scoping the plaza in front of the building and remembered that Derek Hamilton-Smith had been linked with the *Akehmenov Bratva*, which meant all hell was about to break loose. Then he saw it, the driver of the black Range Rover signaling the hulking Russians on the street.

"It's a hit," Fernandez breathed. He quickly deployed his team into tactical positions around the *Bratva* members positioned just outside the police perimeter of the building, cutting off any escape routes they'd thought they'd secured.

Once the team had deployed, Fernandez grabbed his M4, threw on his FBI jacket and eased into the growing crowd, pushing his way toward the main entrance. For the moment, they kept their casual formation, breaking up as they crossed the street and navigated the sporadic clusters of vehicles as officers focused on the perp walk, disregarding the arrival of Fernandez and his team, or the incoming Russian threat. He repositioned his teams as he closed in on the entrance.

"Red team, move around the North side," he whispered into his vox.

Blending into the army of agents surrounding the building, Council Security moved into position, waiting, and keeping the Russian threat in their sights. A chorus of car horns echoed up and down Park Avenue as frustrated cabbies and drivers, oblivious to what was unfolding tried everything to escape the chaos. Fernandez kept his teams tight.

Fernandez watched as his two teams executed the pincer move on the two SUVs as another team kept their eyes on the main entrance of the financial building, waiting for the Belgian to emerge in custody, because only a high-valued target such as the European banker called for such a massive amount of force.

"Blue team, ease back, wait for the exit."

"We've got movement at the en...," the blue team replied.

Another voice interrupted, "We've got a rifle from the Rover."

Fernandez called it. "Take it down."

As he gave the order, the FBI emerged from the building in a phalanx formation around the alleged terrorist, Derek Hamilton-Smith, but as soon as his head was passed through the doorway, a shot rang out, sending the bystanders scattering in every direction.

"Take it down, take it down," Fernandez repeated through his headset as he slid over the hood of a car, and unloaded his clip into the driver of the first Range Rover, killing the driver and another guard instantly.

Pandemonium ensued. The entire plaza cleared within the matter of seconds with the FBI team dragging Derek back into the building. Inside of a minute the entire area was flooded with policeman searching the cars and buildings for the shots and zeroing in on the firefight between the FBI and a Range Rover on the South side of the building.

Fernandez repositioned his teams. "Red and Blue teams, pull back to triple six, let's keep our eye on the prize."

Checking their orders Council security cuffed one of the Russians on the South side and dropped him at NYPD feet, and head toward the building's entrance.

"Fuck, American," the Russian screamed as he jumped up, but was gunned down by another policeman standing between the team and the building.

Fernandez changed clips. It was going to be hell explaining this to the FBI in the building, they needed to get Derek and get the hell away from that building, and the rising tide of blue uniforms swarming the scene. *Fuck.* He radioed his teams.

"Red and Blue teams, abort, abort," he'd barely finished calling back his teams when he felt the cold steel of a Beretta on the back of his neck.

"Don't move buddy. Who the hell are you?" he asked, radioing for backup as he waited for Fernandez to speak.

Fernandez breathed. "Relax, we're on the same team bro."

"Don't *bro* me, motherfucker. Drop the assault rifle and get down on the ground, now!"

The head of Council security dropped his rifle and began to raise his hands, instead spun around, grabbed the Beretta from the officer and knocked him out with the end of his knife blade. Training was everything. He kicked the pistol away from the cop and craned his head toward the building.

"Rendezvous, now," he barked into the radio as he wrapped his M4 in an FBI jacket and melted into the panicked crowd at a slow gallop toward their prearrange rendezvous, only a block away.

45

GENEVA-CHAMONIX

Johnny searched. The fresh fallen snow had finally played to the American's advantage, everything from the airport to the ski village had slowed to a crawl, which meant he still had time to stop a murder. The timing proved difficult given the hordes of enthusiasts are looking to take advantage of the pristine ski conditions, but Johnny studied every face as his driver crept through the small Alpine village, hoping to spot his prey. After the driver had looped through the main street for a third time, he saw it, an undeniable gait and flash of golden hair whipping behind her bobbing head —*Hannah*.

Blinking to life, Johnny twisted himself into a pretzel trying to angle for a better view of the woman's face, once he'd confirmed it was Hannah, he pulled a wad of Euros from his pocket, and stuffed a few hundred in the driver's hand, "Let me out, right over there."

Johnny held back while Hannah passed by the car and followed the covert operative from a distance, watching her approach the ticket counter, pay the cable car attendant, and disappear through the turnstile, it was her, and he had to catch up to her before it was too late. The car was heading toward the *Aiguille du Midi* platform, but he couldn't tell if she was in pursuit of someone or just out doing a reconnaissance. He bounded from the Mercedes as soon as it'd come to a complete stop, hitting a full sprint through the slush by the time his body was upright.

A few gawking bystanders jumped from his path, but it didn't faze the anxious American as he kept his eyes on his target, keeping a safe distance from the Israeli agent, until she burst through the line and into a departing cable car, leaving several disgruntled skiers cursing in her wake.

"Damnit," Johnny grunted, then pushed through the ticketing queue, timing the next departing car, and jumping the gate in one fluid motion, bypassing the growing line of skiers milling around outside the terminal.

A befuddled skier fell forward as the American pushed on. "Watch yourself."

Johnny shrugged back at the man as the car doors closed behind him.

Keeping his eyes fixated on the car ahead, he rethought the reasons Hannah had contacted him, nothing made sense. Did she want him to do the heavy lifting and get rid of Anja? Or was it all an elaborate trap? Johnny craned his head around the elevated view of the surrounding area hoping to catch a clue of Anja below, but there were only dots of bundled skiers jotting about the village.

As the cars approached their destination, Johnny readied himself at the door to break through the crowds and pull Hannah aside, calculating the distance and the density of people and ski gear. There was no need to make a scene, but he had to get her alone and find out what the hell she was up to before it was too late.

Johnny spotted the pink and white Moncler ski jacket heading toward the observation platform, he pushed on the unresponsive cable car doors, nothing happened, he pushed again. WTF? The cable car shuttered forward knocking everyone on board off balance as it lurched to a halt, exacting a screech as the doors opened, releasing the passengers onto the platform.

Everything on the line, Johnny pushed through the crowd like a bull in a China shop, but the tuft of blonde hair he was zeroing in on was just another tourist and wasn't impressed at his hand on her shoulder. *WTF?* Realizing his mistake, he paused a long moment. And as he turned around on the platform, he spotted her, she'd boarded another cable car descending back toward the village. She waved and pointed to her cell phone as Johnny's phone began to ring.

"Hello stranger."

Johnny seethed. "Whatever you're up to, don't do it. Let's talk it out."

Hannah leaned against the back window of the descending cable car, watching as the American spy stood helpless on the platform. "We're beyond that. I'll let you know when the time's right." She felt his frustration through the long pause in the connection. "Don't worry Johnny, I'll keep her alive long enough for you to ask her the question you've been chasing around the planet."

Johnny snorted a laugh, "I hope so, for your sake." He clasped his phone closed and walked to the back of the departure line as a trip of repairman began working on their glitching car, holding all other departures. *You've got to be kidding.*

NSA HEADQUARTERS

Death hung in the air. A pillar of American ingenuity, integrity, and honor had passed away, and the halls across every square foot of Fort Meade ran silent, a lingering silence that no staff announcement or procrastination could alleviate, so the legion of operators reverted to their training under Director Moore and focused on their mission. Focus was a quality the director had instilled in all his staff — *"Control what's in front of you."* It was a quality often overlooked in present-day America, but something that echoed the way the director had lived his life, even until his last breath when he'd pushed his body past its limits.

For over four decades, Director Walter Moore had fought to protect the citizens of the Republic, a Republic that had given him and his family so much, while demanding so little in return. As the commanding voice inside the intelligence community, he'd worked closely with foreign governments and international organizations like the Council of Thirteen, ensuring the transitioning technology roadmap kept to its timeline, nothing more, nothing less. It was a purpose designed timeline meant to allow a peaceful integration into a future civilization without damaging humanity's hard-earned traditional institutions, which he'd managed without fail, until the moment of disruption.

Once the rogue wave of technological disruptions overwhelmed the global political class and their cronies, corrupting, distorting, and deviating the integration timeline, everything fell into chaos. Realizing his team, along with CyberCommand, were the only force savvy enough to combat the onslaught of rogue advancement, corralling the foreign intelligence bot deployments, the Agency sprang into action, disregarding the political ramifications in defense of the Republic.

Gisele roamed the halls. Everything had downshifted to a crawl, although teams were focused, they'd lost a step. Whether it was out of respect or a sense of mourning, she didn't like it, and she knew Moore wouldn't either. She engaged various people as she walked back toward her office, trying to pull them out of their funk, and react in real time.

From the outside looking in, given the recent attacks on the financial infrastructure, it looked as though the agency had lost its footing and failed the American people, but Gisele knew that nothing was further from the truth, regardless of the collective mood. When she arrived back at her desk, she saw a note from the Deputy Director in her inbox.

D*ear* C*olleagues*,

It is with great remorse that I confirm the passing of our beloved leader, Walter Moore. Walter was more than just a boss, he was a patriot, a brother, a friend, a mentor and to some of us, a father. He lived his life by one rule, integrity. And his motto was simple, but to the point: Protect the Republic. Anything that he thought might endanger the Republic was flagged, evaluated, and analyzed until he was satisfied that he had contained the situation. He will be greatly missed. Our hearts and prayers are with his family during this difficult time. For those who would like to attend the memorial service, details will be sent as and when the family releases the information to us.

Now, as Walter would no doubt want me to say...We've a job to do. Get back to work.

Deputy Director James Morgan

GISELE DABBED HER EYES. She began preparing for the inevitable requests that she'd receive from the Deputy Director about what projects the Director had been working on and his scheduled meetings for the next month, typical protocol. A tapping on the door redirected her focus to find CIA Director Mark Brown standing in the doorway.

"I wanted to offer my condolences, Gisele. I know how much you loved Walter, and if there's anything I can do, please let me know." Brown paused a moment as Gisele came around from behind her desk and shook his hand.

"Would you like some tea?" Gisele asked.

Brown removed his coat. "Only if you sit with me a moment."

Gisele forced a smile and set about getting the tea set. "Sure."

Brown paused a long moment waiting for her to return, then spoke as she laid out the cups and poured the tea. "Walter was concerned about you more than you could know. Mostly, he was worried you were wasting your time as an administrative assistant and made me promise to look after you if anything should happen to him before he'd persuaded you about transferring to the Operations Directorate."

Gisele flashed a sullen smile. "I told him, I'm fine where I am."

The director sipped his tea. "When you're ready, let's talk about your future."

Gisele looked at Brown through a thin film of tear shielding her eyes, before changing the subject. "What about the conference call with Director Levy, you and Director Moore? Should I bring Deputy Director Morgan into the call?"

A half-veiled smile stretched across Brown's face. "Thank you."

Gisele checked her watch. "You've got an hour till the call."

Brown finished his tea, thanked Gisele, and retreated through the doorway, reminding her of his offer before he disappeared into the stairwell.

The death of a senior director within the intelligence community was no small thing, although there was overlap, more often than not compartmentalizing meant things got dropped, it's the nature of the beast.

Brown made his way down several flights of stairs to SCIF 17, the command-and-control center for the current operations involving the Ambassador and the perplexing intersection of the rogue algorithms disrupting the financial markets. He didn't have much time until his conference call and he wanted to get up to speed with the acting SCIF team lead, Mike Chambers, one of his own from Langley.

Director Brown quirked an eyebrow at Mike and team, "Let's pack it in."

A confused Chambers straightened his back and replied, "What do you mean? Is the operation over?"

Brown paused a long moment, "I need you back at Langley."

Chambers blanched. Oblivious to everything that'd happened outside the SCIF that wasn't related to their search parameters and the attack on the Ambassador but knew Director Moore had cut the hardline blinking the entire national defense grid offline for a few minutes. "So, Utah has this…"

Brown stepped to within inches of Mike's face. "*Correct.*"

Chambers seethed. Why was the director sending him back to Langley? What was he hiding? Nothing made sense, but it wasn't the time to defy the boss. He packed up his things, said his goodbyes, and followed Brown out the door.

A FIERCE WIND savaged the faded American flag billowing at half-mast outside the National Security Agency's administration building, tearing at its fabric, testing the resilience of its manufacture, and its commitment to its interlinking chain. From the moment the sun rose in the late autumn sky of the day after, until it had traversed through its apex and settled in the western horizon, the employee parking lot had remained at full capacity, nobody had gone home.

Inside the glass covered building, Acting Director James Morgan hurried down the corridor of executive floor, pushing his body as fast as he could muster to meet with his Israeli counterpart. Protocol required the Agency director meet all foreign officials at the main entrance in person, and after their abrupt conference call and the disturbing news of Moore's death, the Mossad director had jumped on a plane and flown to meet the incoming director of the NSA.

After a brief round of introductions, the men and their assistants retired to a faraday cage equipped meeting room and place several files in front of each official detailing several ongoing operations with one of special interest to Director Levy himself, Johnny Dekker, and his own Hannah Jankowski. Levy read through a summary brief of the operation and clapped the file shut and cut his eye toward Director Morgan.

"I cannot believe this."

Gisele looked at the Acting Director Morgan. "What's that sir?"

"Hello James."

The Acting Director spun around to the familiar voice, "Director Levy, I'm glad you've made it in one piece, the weather's been rather turbulent lately."

Director Brown chimed in, "Yes, we're glad you're here on such short notice."

Regardless of the agency, a recurring theme inside the intelligence apparatus since the founding of the Office of Strategic Services, had been ensuring that in and out of government service, the upper echelons of that community remained a close-knit group, which meant more often than not they found themselves sitting on committees and charities with their colleagues from other agencies. For Brown and Morgan, it had been their daughters' computer programming camp, which they'd consulted on and mentored during the summer. And although, the theory didn't always hold up in practice, the bond between these two officials was strong, and the reason Director Brown thought to bring Morgan up to speed, at least in the broad strokes, of the ongoing field operations involving Johnny Dekker and the Mossad operative Hannah Jankowski in particular, before Director Levy's arrival.

Director Levy breathed a sigh. "Let me first express our deepest condolences on your loss of Director Moore. Walter was a wonderful man and friend. All of Israel mourns with you."

Brown cut an eye across the table to Morgan who replied. "Thank you, I'll pass the sentiment along to his team and family."

Levy adjusted his seat and unbuttoned his blazer as a furrowed brow heralded his shifting tone. "I'm sorry I couldn't come sooner; this meeting is long overdue."

Brown quirked and eyebrow, taking it as his cue. "The fault is mine. There's no excuse for not reaching out sooner, but at least we're here now and we can get everybody on the same page," he said offering his hand to the freshman Mossad director. A self-made man that'd spent the last two decades under the tutelage of the outgoing director, and who believed in his well-established policies.

"I've heard good things about your program. I hope this incident hasn't put too much strain on your resources," Levy said.

Any discussion of national security matters was held in a Faraday Cage, something that'd become the standard operating procedure since increased Russian SIGINT operations infiltrated and eavesdropped on several high-level negotiations over the last few decades before Brown took over at CIA, prompting the late Director Moore and his counterpart at CIA to implement the protocols. Gisele had locked and sealed the room as she exited the meeting.

Morgan leaned forward. "We've learned from the best."

An awkward silence fell across the room as the three men

exchanged mental thoughts before Brown proffered moving to the reason they were meeting. "Let's get down to it, shall we?"

Before his heart attack, Director Moore had read CIA Director Mark Brown into a compartmentalized operation, one that'd required the highest level of clearance and fell to his discretion involving Director Levy's predecessor and the Mossad's Unit 8200 programmers. Overall, the mission had met its goal of destabilizing an adversary's weapon's production, but the filed report left out key elements blaming the Mossad team for derailing the project. This in turn had led to a falling out between the teams and a lull in information sharing.

Levy cleared his throat, and reached into his satchel, "That's a good idea."

A patient Brown tapped his fingers on the table. "Should we start with Operation Asian Games?"

The Israeli director paused, pulled out a stack of papers and placed them in the middle of the table between the three men. "If you'd like, but I warn you that I'm not as well versed in the bungled American operation as my predecessor."

Morgan interjected. "You mean the joint operation with your team that lead to the demise of the weapons program, but was detected when your team failed to follow mutually agreed protocol? We're here today because of the mistake your unit caused when they interfered with a perfectly running operation."

Levy blanched. "So, we created cyber warfare?"

A seething Brown put his hand on the stack of papers. "No, but your overanxious politicians caused an unforced error by your programmers, which led to the detection of our revolutionary malware."

Morgan leaned back in his chair, "And if our current analysis is correct this rogue algorithm that have been attacking our financial infrastructure and disrupting the global markets are a derivative of that source code."

Levy smiled. "You were the ones that put your Archangel at risk by putting it in the field too early. Through the source code's premature deployment, you left it open to rogue hackers."

Brown breathed a long sigh. "We did make a mistake, but that wasn't the deployment of our code. It was allowing Operation Asian Games to be a joint operation. We won't be making that same mistake, again."

"Okay, let's focus on the here and now," Morgan said, before pausing a moment as he flipped through a short brief from Utah-based Office of Tailored Access team. "We've managed to isolate and stop all the attacks. And as I said earlier, the code was a derivative of our Asian Games code, which means the Russians have a partial blueprint to our most sophisticated AI program."

"How do you know it's the Russians?" Levy asked sipping a water.

Brown quirked an eyebrow, "You're joking right?"

Levy sat forward in his chair. "Do I look like a comedian?"

"Hannah Jankowski."

Morgan followed up on his colleague's comment, "You know the operative you had out Johnny Dekker when he was in Malaysia and hot on the trail of the assassins sent to kill his father the Ambassador."

Levy took another sip of tea, eyeing his two counterparts as he calculated their reactions in his head. "What can you tell me about Anja Singh?"

"So that's who your team's been working on while getting into bed with the *Akehmenov Bratva*?" Brown replied, studying his ally's face.

The Mossad director placed his cup on the table and rubbed his fingers together as he replied. "We're a small country surrounded by enemies. We're under constant threat of war, so we have dozens of ongoing operations, and some of those operations have dealings with the less desirable elements of the underworld around the world, including Russia, and that's when we grew interested Anja."

Brown nodded. "She was a CIA operative, but I'm sure you already know that, or you wouldn't have brought her up. But she's not been on our payroll for some time now. In fact, she'd disappeared off our radar for a few years, which is why we'd presumed she was dead."

"Interesting," Levy replied.

Brown sat forward, "You've found her?"

"Not yet, but our operative is closing in on her as we speak."

"Why didn't you approach us directly?" Morgan asked.

"If your operative Hannah is so close to her, why haven't you been able to locate her?" Brown snorted a laugh, knowing the answer but offering the director a chance to explain any details he'd felt necessary to share.

"She's behind the curtain."

"How so?" Director Morgan asked.

"A few years ago, it became known to us that following the conclusion of Operation Asian Games and the post-mortem fallout, an offer was extended to the Russian FSB by an American operative. She'd promised information on the *Stuxnet* rootkit responsible for the breach of the Middle Eastern weapons facility in exchange for a new identity and life in Russia. The mole was a CIA field agent."

Brown exchanged a shocking look with Morgan, "And you didn't tell us?"

"Tell who? You couldn't be trusted. We started a mole hunt on your behalf."

Morgan choked back his anger, "The Mossad's been running a mole hunt on our Central Intelligence Agency for more than a few years?"

"It's been a small, but global operation."

"You've been spying on us in our own country? What else have you been snooping around... our databases? Internal protocols? Therefore, our rank and file have issues with the Mossad. You're always working the angles, running side operations on joint initiatives, and undercutting our efforts for your own needs."

"Relax James," Director Brown said.

Levy continued. "Our intelligence indicated Anja Singh was an FSB agent."

"You should've told us," Morgan replied.

Brown recapped the thread's genesis. "The arrogance of your government to "tweak" the *Stuxnet* malware, not only ended the operation, but corrupted hundreds of other logic controllers around the world before it was finally contained by one of our NSA teams. Why weren't your programmers working to contain their mistake?"

"Who do you think gave you the ability to stop the threat?"

"So, Hannah's going to grab her and bring her in?"

"Would you retire your best asset?" Levy sat back in his chair as he took in the brilliance of the plan. *Anja Singh* was a deep cover Mossad asset.

Only Director Moore and Director Levy's predecessor knew about the ongoing operations and had compartmentalized it in a such a way that the circle stayed small, until their death. Now, Brown, Levy and Morgan were picking up the pieces and angling to ensure its success, while keeping their operatives alive. It wasn't an accident that the code was revealed to the world after it'd been discovered and discontinued. Moore had opted to make lemonade from lemons and see what the Mossad agents could do with the information. From a national security point of view, it was essential the global community knew that the United States dominated cyber space, nothing was a more logical deterrent.

"Assets are essential in this game of ours, but allies talk to allies, and keep each other in the loop. Otherwise, it's anarchy."

Levy sighed. "Agreed."

A decade before his retirement from CIA, Ambassador John Dekker had found and recruited Anja Singh, a brilliant young computer programmer and athlete, everything he looked for in his scouting missions. She was the daughter of a naturalized Indian technology engineer and a Russian mathematician living in Austin, Texas. She'd a keen analytical mind, spoke six languages, and had an unrivaled appetite for perfection. Now, her fate was in the hands of three men who knew her aspirations and motives only from what they read in her file.

A twitching eye distracted Morgan as he continued, "The old

alliances must hold deflecting the technocrats' machinations and their goal of galactic domination."

Levy filled in the blanks of Anja's activities while the two Americans listened noting the necessity of the chameleon role. "After the dissolution of Operation Asian Games, Anja was approached through a Russian friend of her mother about meeting with the FSB in Basel. She filed a report with her handler, but then it all went dark."

"And now she's deep in the enemy's camp."

"We're not sure."

Brown scoffed, "You pushed her into a double-agent role and what?"

"And that's where it all went pear shaped. Once we'd approved her meeting the Russian intelligence agents, her mother was murdered in front of her and dumped in a canal, then she went off radar. Despite our most thorough background check, it'd failed to reveal her mother's connection to the Russian mafia."

Morgan wrung his hands as he listened to the Mossad director explain how they'd recruited Anja Singh to their ranks to infiltrate the Russian intelligence, only to find out that her mother had been murdered and she blamed the United States, and in particular one man for allowing it to happen —John Dekker. "Why did your predecessor not widen the circle and bring more people in after the murder?"

For more than a few years, the disappearance of Anja Singh had been a stain on Ambassador Dekker's retirement, nobody aside from the Mossad and NSA directors knew of her true location and assignment. With her entire country thinking she'd died and one knowing he'd failed her when her mother was murdered there had been no reason to alert her status to anyone outside the circle.

Despite the extensive background checks and surveillance her mother's true identity wasn't known until after Anja's disappearance, which was only a few months after her mother's murder. A key reason Ambassador Dekker had left the intelligence service and relinquished his seat on the Council of Thirteen to his son traced back to the incident with Anja Singh.

Levy continued. "From what my director told me, Anja was a double agent, but not an agent of Moscow. She feigned loyalty to the Russian mafia that kept her two moves ahead of all of the intelligence agencies, keeping her close to the antagonist that launched the attacks on your financial markets, but we couldn't risk divulging that information, she was in too deep."

The Acting Director of the NSA shook his head, "Anja Singh is a double agent, and is currently running an operation ripping at the fabric of our defense networks hoping to steal our AI, she's got some balls. I want to question her."

Levy turned his chair. "Wasted effort."

"Leave it to my operative."

Brown choked on his water, "Hannah Jankowski?" The CIA director kissed his teeth as he shook his head, "The same Hannah Jankowski that outed our operative in Malaysia, and the same Hannah Jankowski that you'd lost contact with and asked our operatives in London to locate?"

"I still can't believe you didn't bring us on the inside," Morgan added.

"As I said, your organizational integrity has been compromised. And, if the spy who'd leaked the source code to the Russians in the first place wasn't Anja Singh, and was still embedded in CIA, then we'd be exposing ourselves, again."

Director Brown turned a curious eye back to Director Levy.

"Should we be concerned about Anja Singh and the Russians?"

Levy paused a long moment. "It's being handled."

46

MIDTOWN MANHATTAN, NEW YORK

An obsidian black sedan idled near 666 Park Avenue as its cool interior comforted its belligerent passenger, Derek Hamilton-Smith, who sat fuming at the audacity of the FBI, and cursing their agents every time they poked their heads inside the car. It'd been less than a day, and they'd already located and stormed his North American base of operations, indicating that someone had fed them information on his itinerary. Encircling the car were a dozen heavily armed agents in addition to a full complement of local NYPD officers, still amped from the hellish firefight they'd just lived through when exiting the banker from the building. "I've got diplomatic immunity," he screamed at another curious federal agent.

Realizing his frustration wasn't getting him anywhere, Derek composed himself, slowed his breathing, and turned his thoughts to the treachery of the Russian operative —Anja Singh.

From the moment Anja had deployed the malware, as she'd been contracted to do my Petrushenkov, she'd hatched her own plan, which was playing itself out on another continent. Derek wasn't a computer expert, but he knew that somehow the devious agent had blocked the execution commands of the second phase of the attack, because the compromised logic controllers scattered across multiple server hubs inside the United States, remained offline, which meant *IRIN* had failed to access the NSA's AI program missing its window —forever.

Now, not only did Derek not have his victory over his arrogant and murderous one-time partner Petrushenkov, but he also found himself defenseless against the Council of Thirteen, knowing they'd catch up to him at some point. *She must've disabled the passcode somehow, but why? What's her motivation?* Derek racked his brain trying to recall any and all details from his conversations with Grigorovich and Petrushenkov about their savvy and irreplaceable field operative they'd trained over the last few years, who'd delivered spectacular results time and again, captivating both Russians with her ingenuity and skill, until now. Had he missed something? Was his move against Petrushenkov an overreaction?

"Excuse me, officer," Derek pleaded as another agent stepped near the vehicle. "I'm still unclear why you've taken me into custody, and as I said to your comrades, I'm a foreign diplomat and I've diplomatic immunity to whatever it is you might think I've done. And frankly, I don't feel safe here."

Opening the door and crouching down to eye level with the Belgian, the supervising FBI agent pulled Derek's passport from a clipboard, and flipped through it then back at Derek probing his body language and demeanor, "Mr. Derek Hamilton-Smith...the Third?"

Derek flashed an all-encompassing grin, "That's me."

"Your *immunity's* been revoked."

Derek blanched, "That's impossible."

The FBI agent stood up and looked down on the unfortunate Belgian. "From this paperwork, it seems that your *services* at the Central Bank of the Russian Federation are no longer required, which makes you just another European tourist in the eyes of the law," the agent said shrugging his shoulders as he handed back Derek's passport to the attending officer.

The Belgian aristocrat replied in a deep baritone voice. "That's all well and good, but you still haven't told me why you've detained me, and although I'm a European I know my rights in this country. I demand my phone call."

A herd of boots hurried past the car in full body armor as the agent smiled at his detainee. "Relax, Mr. Smith, we haven't charged you with anything, you're simply a person of interest in an ongoing investigation concerning Hamilton-Smith Group, and once we get this scene locked down, someone will be along with a few more questions. For now, just sit back and relax, and please keep your head down until we know what we're dealing with here."

Derek seethed. Petrushenkov must've sent word to his cronies at the Russian central bank before Grig got to him, relieving him of his Russian credentials, and everything the Bank for International Settlements representative status meant. With his plans in pieces his mind turned back to his attack on the Council, Anja Singh, and the coming reckoning.

~

FERNANDEZ MOVED across the alley toward the waiting Suburban, brushing his way through the billowing exhaust and cold gusts of wind to the rally point. The Chaos surrounding the target rippled across midtown traffic grinding the city, and its travelers to a halt. He patted his men on the shoulders as they gathered into a quick huddle. Although his team had dispensed of several Russian hitmen, they weren't able to get to Derek, and it was becoming more impossible as the moments ticked by, Fernandez needed a new plan of attack.

"We need to get eyes on. Pop a drone…but keep it stealth."

Fernandez watched as a couple of men peeled off from the group, then continued with his plan, which included using the snarled Midtown traffic to their advantage and taking their target before they reached 26 Federal Plaza. Once the plan had been set, they broke into their teams, mounted their Suburbans, and pulled out behind the departing federal agent vehicles.

"Here we go. I want one chase vehicle to tail them, run parallel to avoid all this traffic, make sure you have your federal tags visible. The rest of us will head directly to FBI headquarters and set up one block out, that's where we take him."

The driver chimed in, "We're going to ambush the FBI?"

Fernandez gestured with his hand as he spoke. "Remember to limit your fire, we're not here to kill federal agents, I want *zero* body count. Our priority is the capture and detainment of Derek Hamilton-Smith —only. So, use your head."

The chase vehicle zoomed in their streaming drone feed showing the FBI convoy starting to break through the Southbound traffic. Once again, Fernandez instructed his men over the radio. "Our exit is the Midtown Helipad, if you get separated, we have two choppers on standby, let's get it done."

Fernandez had his orders, straight from the Council itself, apprehension of the renegade Council member by any means necessary. It was an extraordinary measure, but it was an extraordinary circumstance. For the most part, the Council of Thirteen had kept its operations at the peripheral of society influencing decisions through its proxies in various seated governments around the world, but the massacre at the Office of the Audit had reignited a long-idled instrument not seen since the Middle Ages, something the Council elite had shied away from for centuries —the sword.

~

DEREK SHIFTED in his seat as the sedan crept forward. Looking past the driver he saw a string of NYC yellow cabs swarming the intersection like worker bees diving for the hive, but without the intuitive rhythmic swarm. Every wasted second kept him from freedom, the longer it took the FBI to process him, the longer it'd take the Belgian government to step in where his temporary Russian pals and their cancelled credentials had failed and get him released. *Anja.* The fuming banker's thoughts returned to the operative who'd masterminded his predicament. Once she'd sabotaged the code, his fate had been sealed. What had she done with *IRIN*? If the malware had been erased then that was the ballgame, but if she'd just timed out the password, then he knew there was still hope of extra innings. And although he had more questions than answers, he was still alive, and that was enough, for now.

"I thought you federal boys planned things to the letter."

A rookie agent riding shotgun turned around and stared at the preening banker. "It's funny. I thought you'd done the same, but here you are."

Derek snorted a laugh. The late model sedan began to pick up speed and finally break through the bottlenecked intersection, moving with renewed urgency toward the Federal building. Derek continued his antagonistic engagement with the sophomore agents. "I'm going to miss the United States."

The feds exchanged a quick look and chuckled under their breath knowing the demurring Belgian was a prime Gitmo candidate. "As a matter of fact, I think you're going to become well acquainted with her, in more than a few ways."

"Such wit, it's no wonder you're a policeman."

Derek watched as his reply ripped an emotional response from the young slicked back G-man. "Sit back and be quiet, terrorist."

"Such wit."

As the FBI convoy navigated the last intersection, several loud chirps erupted from the onboard speakers eliciting shouts from the agents as they yelped in pain and fingered their earpieces, while the Suburbans funneled into the parking garage at One Federal Plaza, save one.

Through a rising plume of smoke three vehicles broke through the chaos and cut off Derek and his escort, before they'd descended the down ramp. Within seconds, several men had surrounded the Belgian banker, his escort, and their terrified federal entourage. Derek blinked. A burst of gunfire shattered the windows pressing the feds to the floor, while he rolled over and waited, smiling at the ceiling, expecting to see the face of his security force poke through the door. "I guess I didn't need my diplomatic immunity after all, boys."

"Fuck you.... you....terrorist," the passenger shouted.

Derek scoffed. "Don't be like that, unless you want to get hit by a stray bullet and leave your kid an orphan and wife widowed."

The elder fed scolded his teammate. "Just keep your head down kid, it'll be over soon. Our guys are coming."

Derek saw two hands reach through and grab him by the neck, pulling him from the car while a pair of guns trained in on his driver. "What the..."

"Spare me," Felix Fernandez replied as he ripped Derek from the bullet ridden sedan. Pulling the banker through the back window, he fired several more rapid-fire bursts through the back windows of the sedan shattering the windows and keeping the fear of God in the feds kissing the floorboards while he retreated into the billowing smoke.

Derek twisted and struggled. "You're a dead man Fernandez."

The seasoned Council security agent laughed as he pulled the degenerate wannabe into an adjacent alley and into the back of a waiting Range Rover. "Let's go you piece of shit," Fernandez swallowed his contempt for the man who'd betrayed his vows of the Council, knowing he'd get his chance to question him once they'd cleared US airspace.

Incoming barrage of gunfire informed the arrival of the FBI counter-terrorist teams flooding the plaza and positioning around the intersection and alleyway entrance, scattering bystanders and commuters along the way.

As securing the package had taken longer than expected and potential avenues for egress thinned Fernandez knew the Pegasus Heliport was their only viable option. "Plan B, *Greek* Alpha," he squawked across the radio to the other team members as they revved the engines, and barreled through the smoke and wreckage, pushing toward their alternate rally point.

Responsibility for all air traffic in and out of the New York City area laid with the New York Port Authority, which included all arrivals and departures of its several Heliports. Fernandez knew FBI protocol, and even though the odds were against them, he knew he could make it. With his team trailing him, he pushed the storied Range Rover technology to its limits tearing through one way traffic blaring horns and sirens while bystanders leapt from its path, and taxi drivers cursed its disappearing wake of dust.

A piercing voice crackled through the radio. "Boss, call back up."

Fernandez squinted his eyes. "No time, this is it."

At any one time there were three heliports operating on the island of Manhattan, not to mention the private helipads operated by hospitals, but Pegasus was the closest option his team had to a viable exit plan.

For reasons that failed to register, cars began steering to the curbs ahead of him as if they'd spotted a dorsal fin in the water. Then Fernandez checked his rearview mirror, red and blue lights, along with a couple of Ambulances to clear their path, everything leveled up. *Damnit.* He took a hard right, jumped the curb, and pulled to a stop in front of the private heliport —Air Pegasus.

Fernandez knew that there were unscheduled departures and last-minute emergencies by the rich and powerful residents of the city all the time, so they played out that scene and bounded through security flashing their credentials, pushing past the long line of executives that fell aside cowering at the disruptive incoming scene. Spotting a helicopter set for departure he handed off the Belgian to his associate and pulled his firearm, scowling at the incoming parade of sirens.

"Get 'em out of here," he screamed to his two associates.

"What about you?"

Felix cut an eye at his deputy. *"Go."*

With their marching orders in hand the Council associates dragged Derek Hamilton-Smith toward the standby chopper past the vacant first landing area, when gunfire erupted sending them ducking for cover, slamming the handcuffed banker into the ground.

Fernandez flinched at the shots and spun around, turning his back on the incoming fleet of sirens. *WTF?*

Another burst of gunfire sent the executives and high-society crowds scrambling for cover, prompting the helicopter pilots to take notice, and shut down their engines.

Fernandez sprinted toward his associates but was blinded by several laser pointers catching him in the eyes, it was Derek's security detail. "Bravo team, where the hell are you?"

Whining helicopter engines drowned out repeated bursts of gunfire and any response he'd might've received as he retaliated with several shots, but then fell to his side laying down his weapon as a dozen jacketed FBI agents sprang onto the flight platform, encircling the head of Council security. Keeping his eye on the sky he watched Derek wave from the departing TwinStar, noting its curious flight path not heading toward New Jersey and an international airport, but up the Hudson River. *Interesting.*

47

CHAMONIX VILLAGE, FRANCE

Turning away from the window Hannah Jankowski stretched a crooked smile across her face as the cable car descended through the low-lying cloud toward to the village, she'd bought herself some time, moving the mental pieces around the board in her head before she cringed at the soft familiar touch on her shoulder.

"Hello, *Hannah*."

For a fleeting moment, time stopped, the warmth from the hand on her shoulder transported her back in time, everything faded, Johnny, the assassination, the malware, the AI, the Russians, and even her thoughts of revenge, nothing mattered but the tenderness of that moment. She breathed a long sigh, holding on to a memory, until one thought pushed its way to her brain. *Did she see Johnny?* Hannah blinked back to reality.

"I told you I was coming."

Anja smiled, "No hug?"

The cable car came to a halt and the crush to exit carried the two adversaries through the opened doors and out onto the landing area, until they were back in the bustle of the small alpine village.

"Don't play games with me," Hannah said as she reached out

and pulled Anja away from the crowds, escorting her down several alleyways, down a walking path and into a small, secluded cafe lying under the shadow of the mountain.

Anja Singh snorted a laugh, "I thought you like games, darling."

Hannah quirked an eyebrow at the rebuttal, checking around her to see if anyone had overheard their conversation. *Clear.* She saw a young waiter welcoming them to the oasis and gesturing them inside. She smiled and replied, "Table for two please." Knowing several pairs of eyes had landed on them, she released her hold on the one-time CIA agent turned Russia skank-for-hire as they passed thorough the entrance, and other patrons into an adjacent intimate seating area.

"Alone at last," Anja said.

Hannah seethed, "You're a sell out and traitor, not only to your country, but to mine as well."

Anja shrugged, "And you're a murderer, so what?"

Hannah exploded. "You tried to kill me. After everything we'd been through, not only did you try to kill me, but you let that Russian oaf beat the hell out of me before you did."

"Haven't you ever heard the saying…*We only hurt the ones we love?*"

A beet red cascaded down the Mossad agent's face. "You had to be stopped…and David was your loose end."

Anja choked a laugh and wiped her mouth with a napkin, placing her coffee cup down before replying. "He was a pervert and deserved whatever you gave him, and then some. The only reason he survived was for this moment, he was a breadcrumb for you, my darling."

Hannah stood to her feet, circling Anja as she spoke watching the double agent finish her *noisette*. "And now you're gonna give me what I came for, aren't you?"

A gentle wind blew in from the valley prompting Anja from her seat as she breathed in a long lung of fresh mountain air, absorbing every microfiber of the alpine village as she squared off with Hannah. By now, the Russians, if not Hannah had discovered her contribution to the game, but having received her payment, and wired into the Metaverse, she was content with her position, except for one painful loose end. She stared into the green and brown fields of Hannah's pupils.

"There's so much you don't understand."

In her core, Hannah knew her next move, slowing her heart rate, and keeping the target preoccupied while pivoting into position. "As the old saying goes...why don't you enlighten me?"

A lifetime of deception and posturing trickled down to this moment, she'd been slipping from one role to another for so long, Anja paused at her ex-lover's request, but utilizing system two and thinking slow was not her forte. Whether it was choosing her gun or choosing her coffee, she couldn't without weighing its geographic implications, something which caused her to overly rely on her system one thinking, instinct. Explaining the Ins-and-outs of her role in the Mossad to another Mossad agent without clearance was a conundrum, and something she wasn't ready to do, so she stepped closer to Hannah.

"Follow me."

Hannah spat a response. "Give me the *correct* code. Give me *IRIN*."

Anja pursed her lips, "You need to learn to keep your mouth shut." She paused a long moment. "Follow me, and we'll discuss it further, but not here."

Over the traitor's shoulder, Hannah saw a few people starting to take interest in the two women squaring off on each other in the quaint French village cafe, known for its family friendly atmosphere. She laid some Euros on the table and exited onto the street, following Anja as they retraced their path back toward the cable car station, and hoping that Johnny had cleared the area. "Wait up, "she shouted shuffling to catch up with Anja in the snow-covered streets.

Time was fluid. Anja knew Ambassador Dekker's son was on her trail, and she knew that when Grigorovich discovered the truth about *IRIN's* failure, he'd be back for her, and not for a fireside chat. She'd left him to his own devices when they'd arrived at the village but was uncertain if he'd departed or sat lurking in the shadows waiting for further instructions.

With the unknown unknowns piling up, Anja needed to test the Israeli field agent, but away from the village, somewhere remote. There was nothing more important to the security of the Republic than the information she carried on her thumb drive. And everything that had led the two operatives to this point left her with an uncertain anxiousness about Hannah's motives, and the motives of her handler Director Levy. After all, it was the mishandling of the source code by the Israelis that led to it being compromised in the first place.

"This way, let's go."

Hannah looked at the sign displayed overhead: *Telepherique de l'Aiguille du Midi*. "We're taking the Aiguille du Midi cable car, AGAIN? What's up there?"

"Pointe Helbronner, I found that the altitude helps me clear my head and give me perspective." Anja watched Hannah for any reluctance to follow her up the mountain, keeping the primary reason of their ascent to herself, and biding time until they were alone and away from any short-range electronic surveillance to commit to any potential reveal.

"Seems a bit extreme."

Anja winked as she passed Hannah her ticket, "You'll love it."

From the day Hannah had met Anja in Singapore, everything had been a test, something requiring her to put her trust in the genius and daring young Eurasian executive, and today was no different. "There's only one way this ends, Anja."

Anja quirked an eyebrow at the assertive operative, knowing full well she'd planned on killing her as soon as she'd recovered *IRIN's* passwords, something that Anja couldn't allow without concrete assurances. Was Hannah the Mossad operative that she'd claimed or was she working for someone else? Doubt rifled through her mind as they stood in silence, something was driving Hannah, something aside from the agency assigned mission, but she couldn't put her finger on it. "Indeed."

The cable car ride to the Monte Bianco station platform straddling the border of Italy and France was broken into two parts with the Aiguille du Midi cable car from Chamonix, France connecting at the top to the *Vallee Blanche* Tramway that carried them to the *Pointe Helbronner* peak over another 5 kilometers, high above the meddling civilization below, perfect for a frank conversation.

As soon as they'd stepped onto the *Aiguille du Midi* platform, a recently installed cell phone tower repeaters blinked Hannah's phone to life, buzzing with several missed messages, she looked. *Johnny*. She shot Anja a smile as she turned toward the Skyway tram for the second leg of the journey to text him their destination:

Hannah: Pointe Hel...

Hannah recoiled her hand as Anja turned and smiled at her, everything was riding on that partial text. Did it send? Did he get it? Could he arrive in time? Everything began to collapse into a single thought that she'd allowed herself to fall into an elaborate Russian trap, orchestrated by none other than the master trickster herself — Anja Singh.

Anja snorted a laugh. "He won't get here in time. You're on your own."

She knows. Hannah nodded her head, "Except that, he might," she replied with an indulgent smirk at the rogue American agent. "And now...You're wondering what to do with me. You can't just kill me now that he knows where we are, because he'll hunt you to the ends of the Earth."

Anja chanced a smile, as they stepped out of the line and toward the railing overlooking the retreating glaciers, "You've fallen in love with him."

Hannah blanched. "Give me *IRIN*, and you're free to go."

An awkward silence fell over them as the wave of tourists pushed forward toward the *Vallee Blanche* Aerial tramway. "If you want answers *and* the code, you'll follow me," Anja said as she stepped into the crowds entering the departing tram bound for Italy and the Monte Bianco Station platform on *Pointe Helbronner*.

Hannah grunted. "Let's go."

Was she right? Had she fallen for the American CIA operative? As their tram sailed through the clear blue sky soaking in the radiance of the brilliant yellow sun, the two women stood on opposite sides of the limited space. Hannah felt a raging anger building inside as she watched Anja looming at her across the tram, waiting for her to speak, but she said nothing, she only observed.

"Are you still thinking about your knight in shining armor?" Anja asked.

"You mean your mentor's son?"

Anja blinked, "Mentorship?" She paused a long moment looking into Hannah's eyes, "What type of mentor would let his rookie agent get into bed with the Russian Mafia after they'd murdered her mother and dumped her body in a canal? This was a means to an end. The only way out of the clutches of the Americans, the Russians...and the Mossad, was to play it all the way through and fuck 'em all." Anja stepped across the metallic divide letting go of the strap and brushing Hannah's hair from her face as she watched the Israeli digest her response.

Tears broke loose from Hannah's soft Hazel eyes, "Then why didn't you let the Russians deploy *IRIN*, activate the malware, get your revenge?"

"How was he?"

Hannah pushed the twisted American away and stepped across the tram, breaking free of her looming presence. "Don't change the subject. Why didn't you let the Russians win?"

"Was he everything you hoped him to be? Did he drive you to ecstasy... or fall flat on his face, so you dumped him, and came running back to me?"

A voice announced their arrival at their destination as the two operatives paused a long moment, then exited the tram onto the Skyway Monte Bianco station platform, wondering for a fleeting moment at the stunning panoramic views from *Pointe Helbronner* to Aiguille du Midi and down the slopes into Italy. Pulling themselves back to the moment as a crowd of millennials pushed past them toward their favorite photo spots, the two wandered toward a less crowded area of the platform where Anja began to explain. She held up the thumb drive.

"Do you even know what this is?" Anja removed the corner railing post cap overlooking the *Glacier du Geant* below and turned toward Hannah with a smile.

"It's the Archangel source code you stole from us."

Anja smiled. *"Us?"* She stepped toward the platform edge, staring down onto the bluish white glacier below. "Who do you mean when you tell us? Do you mean NSA or Mossad?"

"You know damn well what I mean."

Anja breathed a long sigh, "I'm trying to decide if you're just a flunky or you've got another reason that this malware activation code is so important to you."

"Give me the command code, and *IRIN*. You don't want it. You never did, you want to disappear off into the sunset and chase some dream about reuniting with your mother and live a blissful life, but she's dead."

Anja snorted a laugh. "So, you're inside my head now…Interesting. How about you do your job, *agent*? Come and get it! Take it back to your master in Tel Aviv and watch the whole world burn."

Hannah folded. She knew the only way she had a chance at recovering the source code and preventing the malware from destroying the world was absolution, and it was time. "You're right. It was me. I was responsible for reprogramming the source code. I fucked it up, and I've been trying to set it right. Don't you understand that? Operation Asian Games was my first lead assignment, it was up to me to reset the Americans coding, and I fucked it up. The logic controller sped up, the scientist detected the cod and then leaked onto the Internet."

Anja stepped toward Hannah. "And what else?"

Hannah turned toward Aiguille du Midi. "We tried to contain the leak, but it was too late, it'd already been downloaded onto a Pakistani based server before we could wipe their drives. And I've been chasing it ever since."

Anja smiled and laid her hands on Hannah's shoulder, "It disappeared from your radar, because I took it from the Pakistanis, burned the facility to the ground, and made a deal with the Russian intelligence service. A new master, a new mission, which neatly segued into my second act, Langley was beside themselves with joy."

Hannah slammed her hand on the railing. "I've gotta make this right. You've gotta gimme the code so I can destroy it." She laid her head on Anja's shoulder.

"Relax, everything's gonna be all right."

A dull clapping sound echoed off the metallic building and nearby rocky cliffs as Hannah lifted her head, turned, and saw three large men approaching them on the platform. "*SPATSIVA*," the leader said. "I like girls making up." Then, with one felling motion he dropped his trunk like arm across Anja's head knocking her to the ground and knocking Hannah back several feet.

"Motherfucker..." Hannah screamed as she leapt forward and landed a front snap kick in the giant's chest but fell to the floor with no effect. She grabbed Anja by the arm and began pulling her away from the towering men closing in around her.

"Give me code and you go home," the Russian said.

A scorching fire erupted inside as Hannah planted her back foot and landed a spinning back kick to the stomach of the second henchman sending him stumbling backwards, which accelerated their attack. She reached for her ankle holster, but it was empty. *Fuck.*

"I said. Give me code," the attacker repeated.

Hannah felt a hand pull her backward as a pair of legs soared past her catching the lead attacker in the chest, sending him over the rails, and straight toward the glacier below.

~

A BUZZ of excitement hung over the small alpine village of Chamonix, it was distracting for the American as he searched the numerous cafes, scanning for one specific face, and dismissing all of them. Hannah had vanished. With the sun climbing in the late morning sky, he needed a new plan. Although there was still several hours of good skiing the crowds had begun to dwindle leaving the access around the square easier to navigate. Where the hell did, she go? And why the hell did she ditch him after telling him about her location in the first place?

Once he'd completed his third round of the village, Johnny began to think he'd lost her for good, until his cell phone chimed with an incoming message. He fished it from his pocket, removed his gloves, and thumbed open the alert.

Hannah: Pointe Hel...

It was Hannah. She wasn't off the grid, yet. He stabbed back a reply.

Johnny: *Helbronner?*

The American spook paused a long moment, watching and waiting for a reply that never came. Within a few minutes of idling, he decided to follow the lead, scooping up his gloves and rushing toward a nearby hotel. Checking the cable car routes he found his destination, *Pointe Helbronner*, the world's highest tramway. Was this her escape route? Was she leading him to a trap? Or to claim a dead body? He dropped 20 Euro on the counter, grabbed the map, and raced toward the *Telepherique de l'Aiguille du Midi*.

En route to the Chamonix cable car station another vibration. *Hannah?* He ripped his cell phone from his pocket, thumbed it open and sighed. Jack? He stopped mid stride and stepped off the roadway to read the message.

Jack: It's done.

Johnny: The attack?

Jack: We shut it all down. Did you catch the assassin?

Johnny paused a long moment. He took several long breaths allowing the fact that the cyber-attack on the United States had been quashed, not only restoring national security protocols, but safeguarding their family bank, which meant it'd survived yet another crisis. The only thing remaining was the internal crisis between him and his father over his involvement with Anja Singh and all its calamities. He stabbed a reply to his brother in arms, then raced toward the station.

Johnny: Enroute.

Jack: Bring it home, brother.

Johnny leapt onto an opened cable car and shoved his cell phone in his pocket as it closed its doors, leaving the ticket holders gawking in amazement. He didn't know what kind of situation he was heading into, but something was going down and odds were it wasn't going well. He inventoried his pistol and ammo then zipped up his jacket. Hannah had found Anja that much he was certain. But whether Anja Singh had the answers Johnny was looking for about his father and CIA wasn't the point, she was a link to a past about his father that he knew nothing about, and something inside him knew there was more to their story. *Wait a minute something's wrong.* He wasn't moving. Johnny heard rousing voices complaining in French and English. *WTF?*

A man in bright yellow jacket approached the skiers and looked Johnny dead in his eye. "Excuse me sir, I'm sorry, but the line is broken."

Johnny blanched. "Are you freakin' kidding me?" he shouted rhetorically. "Let me out."

"*Un moment*, my supervisor must be the unlocking," the man replied.

Moments later, the station supervisor arrived, unlocked the cable car, and fell to the side as Johnny pushed past the apologetic workers searching for another way to the top, but gob smacked by the arrogant American.

As Johnny ran out into the street he looked up at the signage, the cable car was the only way to *Pointe Helbronner* from the French side of the valley, and there was no time to drive to Italy. But plastered across the bulletin board near the front of the ticket shack was an advertisement for Helicopter Tours. *Now, we're talking.*

48

MANHATTAN, NEW YORK

From the moment Isabella Dekker leaned back on her creme leather sofa overlooking Central Park, her body went limp, the synaptic activity in her brain dimmed, and she fell into a deep sleep —it had been a long week. A baptism by fire as the new head of the Dekker Banking Group, and an emotional roller-coaster ride with the assassination of her friend and the continuous unknown location of her fiancée were only a few of things that had tested her mettle. The calming rhythmic sound of rain striking her floor to ceiling windows provided cover for another nagging intrusion of her cell phone. As she drifted in and out of REM sleep her eyelids twitched, signaling she'd arrived in her dreamland where she wasn't a complicated micromanager that thrived on order, but a woman in love.

While her promotion to head the banking group hadn't been a surprise, it was a mutual agreement with her cousin, she hadn't talked it through with her fiancée, which created an unspoken tension. And while she was the banking head, which meant she set policy, the banking job was in New York, but her fiancée's job was a bit more complicated, leaving more room for uncertainty. Despite her deep sleep, the recurring distress of their engagement and promotion had invaded her tranquility causing her to twist and turn on the sofa, looking for a suitable solution.

Without warning a cold hand on Isabella's head jolted her awake and sent her leaping from the sofa straight to her hidden safe. "WTF?"

"Easy, babe..." Jack stayed on bended knee and raised his hands in the air. "I didn't mean to spook you like that, but when I came in you were shaking something terrible. It looked like you were having a nightmare."

Izzy stood ten feet away pointing her Walther PPK at her fiancée. "Jack?"

The motionless government hacker paused a long moment, while his fiancée composed herself, lowered her pistol, and ran into his arms. "Izzy...there's something you need to know," he paused another moment, "Walter's dead."

Izzy pushed him back to arm's length, gasping in shock. "What?"

For many years, Walter Moore had been a close family friend. Isabella had known him from both her brief time in the intelligence service, but also from the family gatherings with the Council of Thirteen. And as a couple, the two had spent time with the director and his family on many other occasions, which made it even more of a shock when Jack continued.

"I killed him."

Izzy blanched. "What are you not telling me?"

A silence fell across the room as the semi-conscious banker stored his pistol and stepped to the bar to make them both a drink while Jack explained what had happened since the last time they'd spoken, including his reuniting with an old naval academy colleague. With fatigue still clinging to her body she took a drink and moved around the island to comfort her better half. She cupped his face in her hands as she looked into his sunken eyes, knowing something was eating him up inside.

Jack quirked an eyebrow. "The genie..."

Izzy raised her hand. "Wait...Think about what you're about to say. I'm here for you no matter what, but you cannot tell me compartmentalized stuff, especially with Walter gone you could get into a lot of trouble."

"You're right. I need to take a walk," Jack replied.

"Why do you think you killed him?"

Jack turned toward the park view. "I made a bad assessment of a situation that ended with the director having a heart attack."

"That's not killing him, Jack," Izzy replied as she stepped in behind him and wrapped her arms around his body, kissing his head and neck, comforting him to the best of her exhausted ability.

"He trusted me," Jack continued staring out into the rain.

Izzy blinked awake with a sudden thought, she turned Jack around stared into his haggard face. "Does my uncle know?"

"Johnny's gonna be devastated."

Izzy drifted into her own headspace, stepping away from her fiancée's embrace, and searching for anything that could keep her even keeled. *Another loss, we're dropping like flies out there.* Since the assassination of her best friend and allied family's daughter and now another Council family patriarch gone, she wasn't sure about the impact of the news, but she knew change was coming. "We need to find my uncle and make sure Johnny's up to speed… Where is he, anyway?"

Jack blanched. "Running something down," he replied. And despite his promised not to get into Agency business he began spewing details over everything that's transpired over the last week while Izzy paced the floor, still caught in her own thoughts, but listening all the same, chiming in with an occasional *"yep."*

First and foremost, Izzy knew she had to inform her friend's sister, because it didn't sound like anyone had done anything about keeping the respective families in the loop about everything that'd unfolded since the first attack. She set about preparing a list while Jack carried on in the background, eventually finding a bottle of Caol Ila 25-year-old single malt whisky she'd received from a banker friend last Christmas. She began to work through the call list, letting Jack have his space while she observed from a distance should she need to intervene.

"Annabelle, I'm so sorry for your loss, It's a loss for all of us." Izzy held her hand over the phone, looked back at Jack with the second tumbler of whisky in his hand staring out the window into the rain. "Okay, Annabelle, please let us know the date, we'll make sure all the families are present," a sullen Isabella replied then hung and sat down beside her fiancée on the sofa, taking his crystal tumbler and downing its contents in one gulp.

Jack broke from his thoughts. "Why didn't I call the on-duty officer?"

Izzy stroked his head. "There was no time. Everything was on the line, and you needed the authority to shut it down, and that was Walter, nobody else could've stopped it otherwise. You made the right call."

Jack stood up, poured another whiskey, and cleared his throat looking back at with a forced sense of concern. "What happened at the bank?"

"I called on an old friend and we managed to right the ship in time."

"What old friend?"

Izzy stretched her fatigued body, and stood up, "Everything's fine."

Jack welcomed her warmth as they embraced and watched the intensifying rain cascade across Central Park, absorbing every moment they shared because certainty was never a sure thing. And as he finished the thought an intruding vibration erupted from his inside jacket pocket, he peered down at the screen.

"I've gotta take this."

~

Dr. Jane Ridley finished her debriefing at the Fort, folded up her files, and scurried toward the exit, before she found it being blocked by a couple of military attaches. For reasons she couldn't understand, they didn't budge. With a quick and deliberate look, she questioned their intentions. "Can I *help* you?"

"We've been ordered to bring you with us ma'am," the attaché replied.

Ridley shook her head. First, it was the Acting Director at Fort Meade, James Morgan, then it was the Director of National Reconnaissance Office, she wondered who was waiting for her briefing now. After a quick check of their credentials, she followed them out of the room and down the corridor into another conference room, which was also equipped with a Faraday Cage. She smiled, entered, and shook the hands with several officials and military brass all wearing toothy grins.

"You're all aware that I sent an incident report? This seems like overkill."

A young three-star Marine general stood up and nodded his head to the tired and hungry scientist gesturing for her to take a seat. "Please. We know you've had a rough week and that you've laid it all out in a report nice and tidy, but unlike our peers we're more curious about what's not in the report."

Ridley cut a side eye. "Why do you always think that there's always something missing from the report?" Ridley barked. "All *relevant* information has been included in the report, so get a copy, pull up a chair...and read it."

A low murmuring cascaded across the room, until the general replied, "Well, the reason we think that is because, in eight out of ten cases, it's true." He shifted some papers in front of him and then looked at Ridley. "Anything about your AI trying to circumvent its startup protocols?"

Ridley kept her cool. "This was an inside job."

A chorus of voices erupted through the room as the generals and department heads shifted in their seats, posturing to assign blame when the time came. Despite the scrutiny around the hiring and training of engineers and programmers, there was always some idealistic crusader who thought they knew the mission better than their superiors when things hadn't played out the way they'd envisioned in their little Utopian paradise —an idiot, nothing is black and white. Ridley quirked a brow at the decibel of discontent with her report then placed right hand on the table as she watched the general lean in.

"This was not in your report, Dr. Ridley."

Ridley smiled. "No, it wasn't."

"Why wasn't it included in the report?"

Ridley cleared her throat and stood up, catching the officials off-guard and causing them to gasp like they were watching a psychological thriller. "Because it's only a theory, and I only report facts."

An impatient tone specified his question. "Why was it an inside job?"

Ridley paused a long moment. Staring out at a dozen pairs of eyes all with top level security clearance but acting like they'd just graduated the academy. "It's simple if you understand the backstory. And now that I've been cleared to read in this group, it all circles back to our source code and our newly developed and battle tested artificial intelligence —*IRI*. Over the final weeks of preparation for its live fire exercise alongside our naval forces at the annual RIMPAC event, we discovered a series of events, which seemed inconsequential, but now fall right in to place."

The Marine general coaxed Ridley, who'd paused a moment. "And…"

"A few years ago, the NSA, in conjunction with our Israelis counterparts, launched a joint operation aimed at slowing the proliferation of nuclear weapons by rogue nations, standard operating procedure, and for months, the operation delivered everything we'd expected, but during the course of the operation, and under pressure from their government for more results, our allies overstepped, causing us to abandon the project." Ridley paused, took a sip of water, and continued. "That intervention has proved to be the reason we're huddled in this room today."

Ridley knew her political cover had suffered a major setback with Director Moore's passing and her clout at the NRO wasn't as stable as she'd have anticipated given recent political events, guiding her to choose her next words with more care and precision, despite her inner hacker. *They want the truth. I can do that. I'll tell them the truth and let them deal with it.* Ridley paced the floor weighing her options in her head, deflecting the anxious pairs of eyes following her every move, some hoping she'd go too far, while just wanted the answer, but lacked a critical piece of intel —the malware. She decided to dumb down the storyline, especially without knowing if Johnny had been successful in his mission.

The general barked. "So, what was the fallout from the intervention?"

No stranger to pressure, Ridley continued at her measured pace. "In a few hours, my team will activate our most advanced cyber defense weapon, which once activated should prevent any other adversaries or rogue actors to follow suit." A silence fell across the officials as Ridley confirmed their suspicions. "We've received approval to bring *IRI* online and connect to the defense network, permanently."

"That's great news," the general replied.

Ridley pursed her lips. "It's something our group has been working on with the Pentagon and US CyberCommand for some time, but after the latest RIMPAC exhibition and its readiness status, our best days are ahead of us."

More than anything, the attendees wanted good news, so either they didn't notice her subtle shift away from the reason the Asian Games Project, which had gone off the rails and exposed their source code to the Internet, or they turned a blind eye and focused on the positive news to report back to their respective superiors, either way Ridley was glad to be done. *I need a drink.*

Checking her watch, Ridley forced a smile and shook several officials' hands as she made her way toward the door, late for an appointment, but knowing this group of administrators' supports was essential, she made the time, hoping to fill the void of her late mentor. Everything she'd told them was true. Everything she'd told them was accurate. But she didn't get into the granularity that she'd have told Director Moore, because in the end nothing was certain, which meant keeping the concerns of the unknown knowns to herself for the time being, at least until their legacy operative — Johnny Dekker— had confirmed the success of his mission.

∽

Isabella Dekker opened the door. A tall blonde-haired man with a toothy smile stood in her doorway holding a bottle of wine and gesturing to someone in the hallway who remained out of sight, something she was unaccustomed to in her high-security building. *What the hell?* She held the door firm as she searched her short and long-term memory for a name for the face of the man, nothing registered.

"Isabella?" the man asked.

Isabella remained frozen surprised her fiancée hadn't wandered over and asked who was knocking on their door without a phone call from security. She stood slack jawed until she heard a familiar voice, one she'd not heard in decades. Then she saw her pushing her way past the man in front of her and extending her arms around Isabella.

"Sorry we're late. My meetings went long, and traffic was a mess, but Jack said we should just surprise you. So... here we are... surprise!" the woman said.

Isabella cocked her head. "Are you sure you've got the right door?"

Jane blushed. "I'm Jane Ridley."

49

PUNTA HELBRONNER STATION, ITALY

The twin-turbine helicopter had reached its altitude ceiling, the blades were slipping in the thin air, triggering multiple safety alarms and a cascading illumination across the control panel, something Johnny Dekker had seen many times before, which meant it was time to go. He patted the pilot on the shoulder, and exited the cargo door, digging his boots in on the landing. The American watched as the helicopter pulled away from his drop zone while the downdraft from the blades blanketed the station, obscuring his view of the terrain. He had no idea what he was up against.

Johnny pulled his pistol from its holster and kept it low to his hip as he navigated the viewing platform, smiling at several curious tourists as he passed them by searching for his target, but coming up empty. *Where are you?* As he continued his hunt, a splash of blood across the viewing platform, and several frightened skiers shuffling past him prepared him for the worst. He turned another corner, raised his pistol, but then pulled back in a rush of confusion.

"Well, look at who's decided to join us?"

Johnny cursed. "What the *hell* Hannah? Why haven't you cuffed her?"

The two women exchanged a comical grin and laughed wiping the frozen bloodstains off their faces while warming their hands against their jackets, before standing up and walking toward Johnny still palming his pistol and aiming it in their general direction.

"Would you mind?" Anja asked.

Hannah looked at Johnny, "She's fine, there's a lot to catch you up on."

Johnny blanched. "Anja Singh, I presume?"

Anja nodded. A smile crept across her face as she pierced his soul with her words, "*Little* Johnny Dekker. You're all grown up."

The condescending tone surprised him, because although he knew his father was her handler, swapping baby pictures didn't seem like something he'd have done, especially with a work colleague. Johnny watched as the two women moved toward him in unison, Hannah scoped the perimeter as Anja came face to face with her hunter, giving Johnny his chance. "You've been busy."

Anja laughed. "You have no idea." The assassin slipped her hand into her jacket and pulled another revolver aiming it at Hannah's head, triggering Johnny to level his pistol at the deceptive killer.

Hannah struggled. "What the hell are you doing?"

With her free hand Anja dug into her pocket. "Is this what you've been looking for Mr. Dekker? Is this why you've come to save your precious mistress?"

Hannah surrendered to her captor feeling the cold steel burrowing into her temple, knowing that this confrontation could go either way. She watched as Johnny kept his focus and pistol trained on Anja. This was not going to end well. From the first week of training, she was taught to take herself out of the equation, let the situation evolve organically, not to struggle.

Johnny pivoted. "Are you sure you want to do this? You've got nowhere to run, nobody coming to save you."

"Are you sure about that?"

The American spy stopped. "I've taken out your support team. The Russians are good at many things, except blending into their surroundings."

Anja seethed. "You lie."

Johnny pulled the thumb drive from his pocket as he inched his way toward the two women. "I'm not sure what you've pulled from your pocket, but this is a verified thumb drive, Anja. The jig is up."

"My father told me what happened... It wasn't your fault."

Anja pressed the gun against Hannah's temple as her emotion began to take over her responses. "You know nothing. All he had to do was call in the SOG team, and we could've saved her."

"It's the Russian mafia you were never going to walk away."

Anja released Hannah, but kept her pistol trained on Johnny. "Let me tell you what I know. Your father was weak. He couldn't infiltrate the Russians, so he sent a young woman to do his dirty work, and it got my mother killed."

Johnny hesitated. "You killed my fiancée while you were trying to murder my father. Tell me why I shouldn't just put a bullet in your brain...right now."

Hannah stepped into the line of fire. "She's not the enemy."

Johnny snorted a laugh. "She just had a gun to your head."

A calming aura mesmerized Johnny as he watched Hannah take Anja's gun and walk her closer to the American, gesturing for them to come together, but before they'd made contact a deathly look swept across her face.

"Johnny..."

Everything fell silent. The American operative lowered his weapon to his side and winked at Hannah as he turned toward the incoming threat, five health Slavic males armed to the teeth moved toward them. "I think the viewing platform is closed today, gentlemen."

"Give me the code."

Anja pushed Johnny aside and stepped forward. "Your boss had the same demand. Would you like to ask him what I said? Come any closer and I'll make sure you have the opportunity."

Hannah emerged from the other side of Johnny, coming shoulder to shoulder with her two companions, and facing down the Russian threat. "Now, now Anja, you be nice, these guys are just doing their job. They don't want any trouble. Isn't the right boys?"

As the Russian began to respond, Hannah landed a spinning back kick to the unsuspecting wingman sending him sliding across the platform. For reasons he'll never understand, Johnny stepped in front of Anja as another Russian threw a haymaker in her direction hitting Johnny in the chest, but by absorbing the energy inward and redirecting outward he brought the giant to his knees, and then smashed his head against the metal railing.

Within Russian intelligence service there were two factions. The first was a faction that'd fallen into bed with the rising crime families, allowing them to exert their power, realizing that they'd benefit from the extra muscle and added revenue stream. The second faction was more hardheaded, because its members longed for a return to the Soviet Republic, they held pride in ideology and could not be bought.

Once the Akhemenov Bratva, headed by Igor Petrushenkov, decided to leverage his cronies in the Central Bank of Russia and the FSB in a plot to takeover global financial markets and secure the first human level intelligence AI source code, the patriotic faction swung into action.

"Give me code," the Russian repeated.

Despite the commotion on the viewing platform, the Skyway Monte Bianco operators hadn't stopped the cable cars from running, and another arrival raised the probability that the Italian police force had arrived.

"We're about to have company," Johnny shouted, falling to the floor, pulling his .380 from his ankle holster, and bringing the Russian down.

Hannah somersaulted across the platform and nailed another Russian operative in the eye with her knife. "Do you want the code too?" she taunted before sending his body over the railing to join his comrades on the glacier below.

Turning toward the remaining Russians, Hannah saw Anja fall to the ground as the FSB agent hit her with a gun butt and picked her up by the throat. "Let her go you piece of shit," Hannah yelled as she maneuvered toward the agent, but was put down by another arriving agent. WTF?

"Johnny we've got company," Hannah screamed as Johnny broke the neck of another agent, and then fired several shots at the arriving FSB agents pouring out of the cable car. He pushed Anja and Hannah toward the Aiguille du Midi cable car, while he kept the FSB agents pinned down.

Realizing they only had moments, Anja slipped her thumb drive into Hannah's jacket and turned toward the cable car when a stunning and debilitating blow struck her across the face, sending her limp body between the cable car and the platform and onto the glacier below.

"Nooooo…" Hannah screamed as she drove the knife into the face of the assailant, repeating the action several times before Johnny pulled her off the corpse.

Johnny blanched. He held Hannah close forcing her to stay still as he changed magazines posturing for the coming onslaught of FSB agents, knowing that they'd not finished their job, but they never came. "Wait, wait…"

Hannah seethed. "Get off me. Get off me."

"Shut up, we need to get the hell outta here or we'll be joining her."

A flashing light atop the cable car indicated that the doors were closing, and it was set for departure, something deep inside pulled Johnny to action as he grabbed Hannah by the back of her jacket and dragged her onto the departing car.

Hannah had fallen silent. Although they'd boarded the skyway cable car toward Aiguille du Midi, Johnny knew they were far from safety, but for the moment, he needed to care for Hannah. As the adrenaline from the fighting wore off her injuries began to work their way over her body. Johnny pulled her close trying to warm her as the cable car reached its midway destination, seeing she was still in shock, he picked her up and exited onto the Aiguille du Midi station. Once he'd moved her into the sun, he tried to bring her back.

Johnny cupped the shaken operative's face in his hands, "Hannah."

After a few minutes, he felt her coming back, a warmth had returned to her body, and her eyes focused in on his face. He was unprepared for the emotion. It'd never been his strong suit, but he knew she needed him, so he held her close, staring as the departing cable car to Chamonix village arrived. He looked down at the broken creature in his arms.

"I'm so sorry," Hannah sobbed.

Johnny shook his head. "What happened to Anja?"

Hannah continued to ramble, speaking over Johnny's question, and cleansing her soul. "I'm sorry about London. I'm sorry about Chloe."

"What are you talking about?"

"Director Levy's visiting Langley. They know everything."

"How 'bout bringing me into the loop? I don't know if I'm supposed to arrest you or be thankful, you're fucking alive. And I'm not sure what to think about Anja's death. Should I be happy or sad?"

Hannah reached into her pocket, pulled out a thumb drive, and pressed it into Johnny's hand. "Just hold me."

Johnny pulled her close and read the labeled thumb drive —*IRIN*. *So, what the hell did I take off that Russian?* Everything came crashing into the frame as he thought about Chloe, his father, the Council, and the aborted BIS mission. Something had been moving pieces around a larger chess board and somehow, he felt this was only the beginning. Johnny pushed back on Hannah and looked into her eyes catching a glimpse of a smile as he turned toward the cable car. "Let's go."

Hannah smiled and leaned into his embrace, "I'm ready."

As Johnny led her across the platform, a *CLAP* of thunder echoed across the rocky peaks, amplified by the metallic structure, and ricocheting off his ear drums as he felt Hannah's body go limp. Instinct drove his actions pulling Hannah through the remaining distance toward the safety of the cable car, but it was no use, the light faded from her Hazel green eyes, blinking one last time as she muttered with her dying breath. "I'm sorry. I'm so…"

∼

A HULKING SILHOUETTE climbed aboard a Kamov Ka-60 helicopter perched on a ledge at the far edge of the valley before it rose into pale blue sky, rotary blades chopping through the frigid glacial air and echoing across the *Valle Blanche* as it veered toward the Aiguille du Midi viewing platform, taunting the American spy, and leaving him wallowing in grief.

As the helicopter crossed the Italian border, the pilot transferred an incoming call over the headset to the triumphant kill team, and its team leader.

"Is it done?"

Pavel Grigorovich stared at the valley below. "*Da.*"

THE END

ACKNOWLEDGMENTS

First and foremost, I would like to thank my family for their unwavering support throughout the years.

A special thanks to Christina, Jeff, Tomas, AFS, Paul, Canute, Fredrik, James, Sean as well as Kit Chia and the entire Malaysian crew, along with all my other supporters who have offered words of encouragement along the way.

ABOUT THE AUTHOR

Joseph Van Nydeck is an emerging author in the techno-thriller genre. Joseph was born and raised in the Southwestern United States but also spent a significant amount of time in Canada, where he continued his exploration of new cultures before moving to Asia.

After publishing his debut novel, Tian Zhu, in 2014, he spent an extended period of time researching, restructuring, and finalizing his next drop - *IRIN*.

ALSO BY JOSEPH VAN NYDECK

Featuring Johnny Dekker
TIAN ZHU

Made in the USA
Monee, IL
25 May 2023